P9-CBM-324

SONIC™ THE HEDGEHOG

THE IDW COLLECTION

02

SEGA®

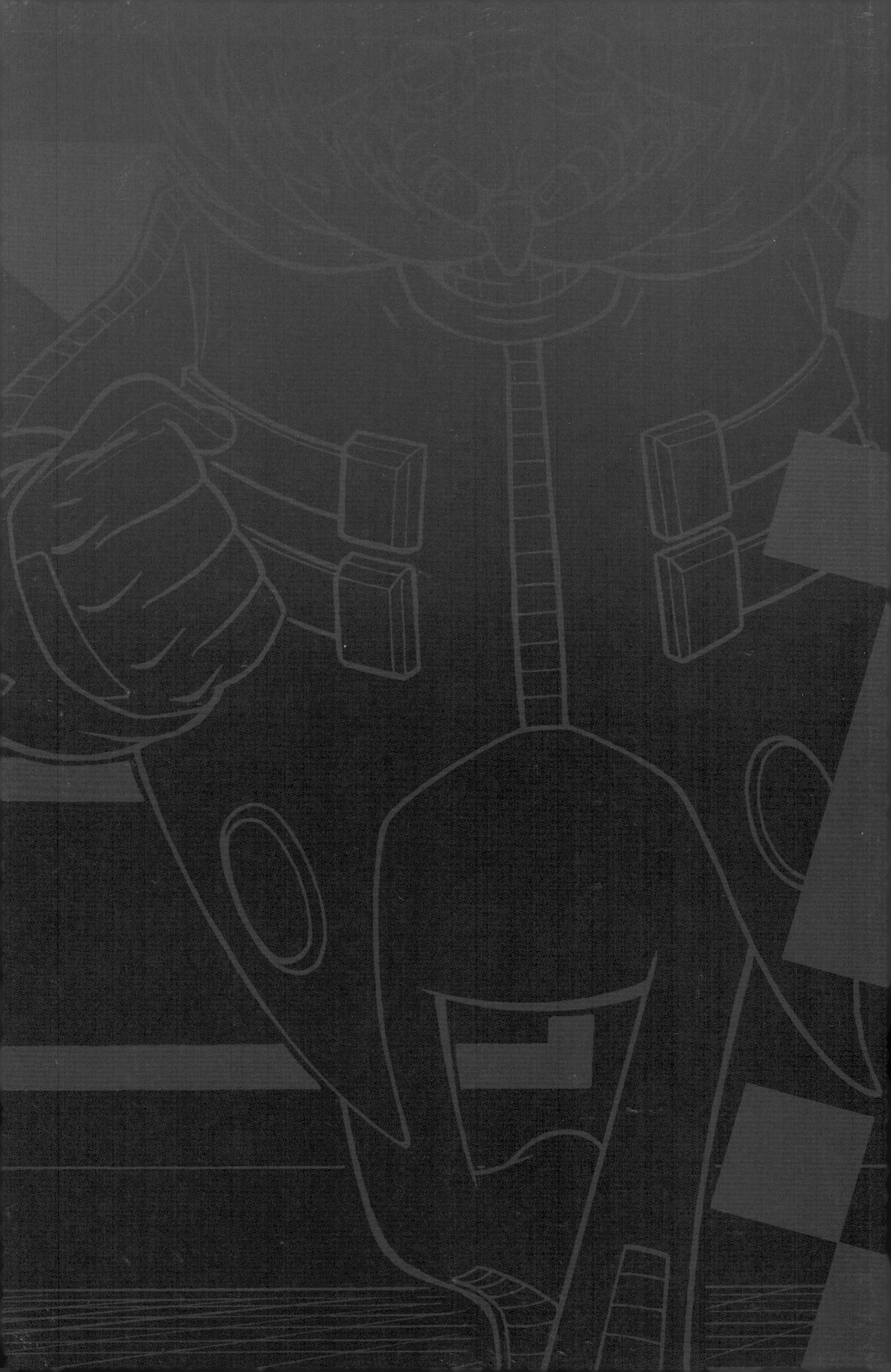

COVER ARTIST **EVAN STANLEY**
SERIES ASSISTANT EDITOR **MEGAN BROWN**
SERIES EDITOR **DAVID MARIOTTE**
COLLECTION EDITORS **ALONZO SIMON** AND **ZAC BOONE**
COLLECTION DESIGNER **SHAWN LEE**

Nachie Marsham, Publisher • Blake Kobashigawa, VP of Sales • Tara McCrillis, VP Publishing Operations • John Barber, Editor-in-Chief
Mark Doyle, Editorial Director, Originals • Erika Turner, Executive Editor • Scott Dunbier, Director, Special Projects
Lauren LePera, Managing Editor • Joe Hughes, Director, Talent Relations • Anna Morrow, Sr. Marketing Director
Alexandra Hargett, Book & Mass Market Sales Director • Keith Davidsen, Director, Marketing & PR
Topher Alford, Sr. Digital Marketing Manager • Shauna Monteforte, Sr. Director of Manufacturing Operations
Jamie Miller, Sr. Operations Manager • Nathan Widick, Sr. Art Director, Head of Design • Neil Uyetake, Sr. Art Director, Design & Production
Shawn Lee, Art Director, Design & Production • Jack Rivera, Art Director, Marketing

Ted Adams and Robbie Robbins, IDW Founders

www.idwpublishing.com

Special thanks to Mai Kiyotaki, Michael Cisneros, Sandra Jo, Sonic Team, and everyone at Sega for their invaluable assistance.

SONIC THE HEDGEHOG: THE IDW COLLECTION, VOLUME 2. MARCH 2022. FIRST PRINTING. ©SEGA. All Rights Reserved. SEGA is registered in the
U.S. Patent and Trademark Office. SEGA and SONIC THE HEDGEHOG are either registered trademarks or trademarks of SEGA CORPORATION. The
IDW logo is registered in the U.S. Patent and Trademark Office. IDW Publishing, a division of Idea and Design Works, LLC. Editorial offices: 2765
Truxtun Road, San Diego, CA 92106. Any similarities to persons living or dead are purely coincidental. With the exception of artwork used for
review purposes, none of the contents of this publication may be reprinted without the permission of Idea and Design Works, LLC. IDW Publishing
does not read or accept unsolicited submissions of ideas, stories, or artwork. Printed in Korea.

Originally published as SONIC THE HEDGEHOG issues #13–20, SONIC THE HEDGEHOG ANNUAL 2019,
and SONIC THE HEDGEHOG:TANGLE & WHISPER issues #1–4.

Facebook: facebook.com/idwpublishing • Twitter: @idwpublishing • YouTube: youtube.com/idwpublishing • Instagram: @idwpublishing

ISBN: 978-1-68405-893-8   25 24 23 22 1 2 3 4

TABLE OF CONTENTS

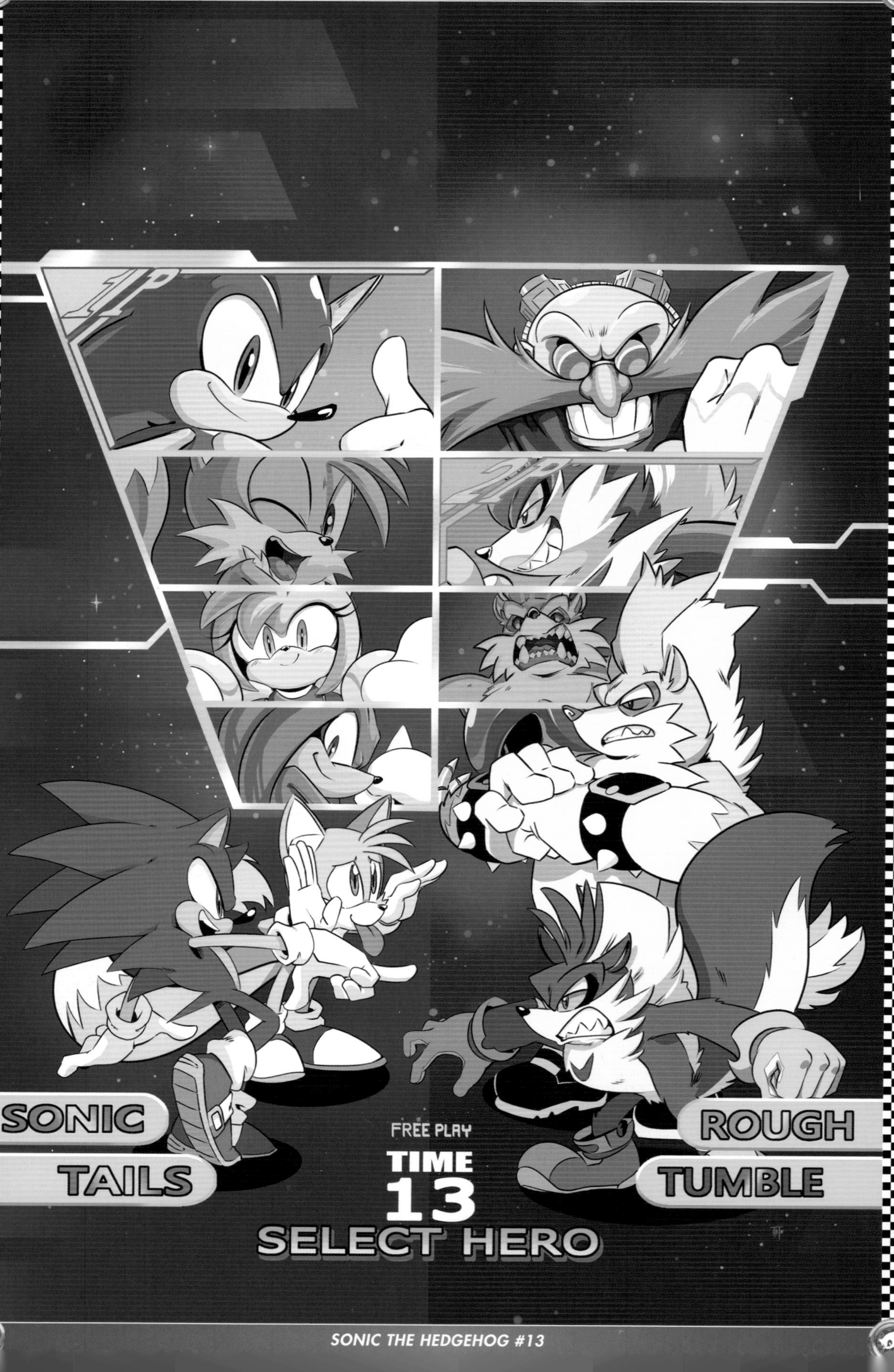
1P
2P
SONIC
TAILS
FREE PLAY
TIME
13
SELECT HERO
ROUGH
TUMBLE

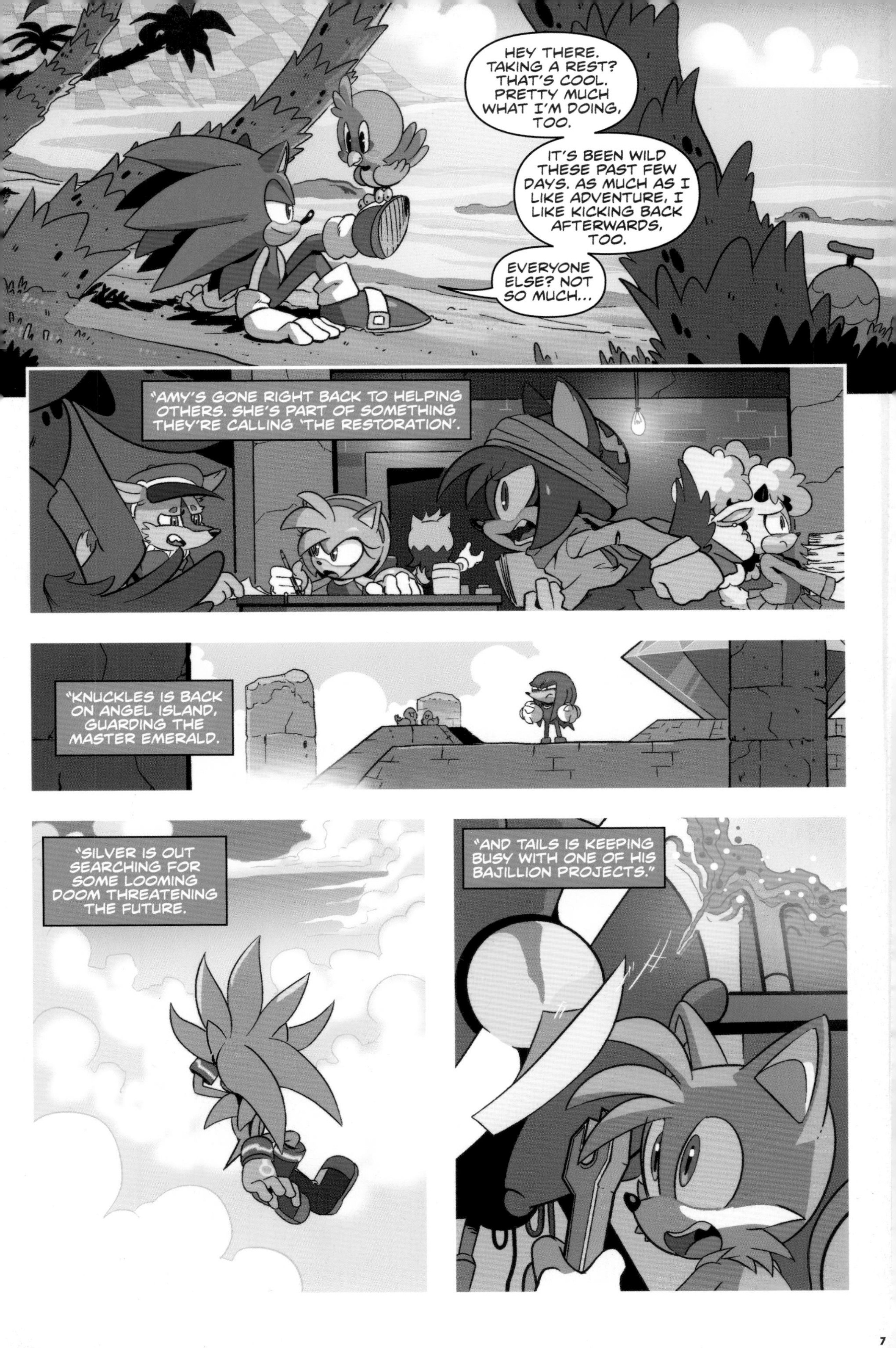
HEY THERE. TAKING A REST? THAT'S COOL. PRETTY MUCH WHAT I'M DOING, TOO.
IT'S BEEN WILD THESE PAST FEW DAYS. AS MUCH AS I LIKE ADVENTURE, I LIKE KICKING BACK AFTERWARDS, TOO.
EVERYONE ELSE? NOT SO MUCH...
"AMY'S GONE RIGHT BACK TO HELPING OTHERS. SHE'S PART OF SOMETHING THEY'RE CALLING 'THE RESTORATION'.
"KNUCKLES IS BACK ON ANGEL ISLAND, GUARDING THE MASTER EMERALD.
"SILVER IS OUT SEARCHING FOR SOME LOOMING DOOM THREATENING THE FUTURE.
"AND TAILS IS KEEPING BUSY WITH ONE OF HIS BAJILLION PROJECTS."

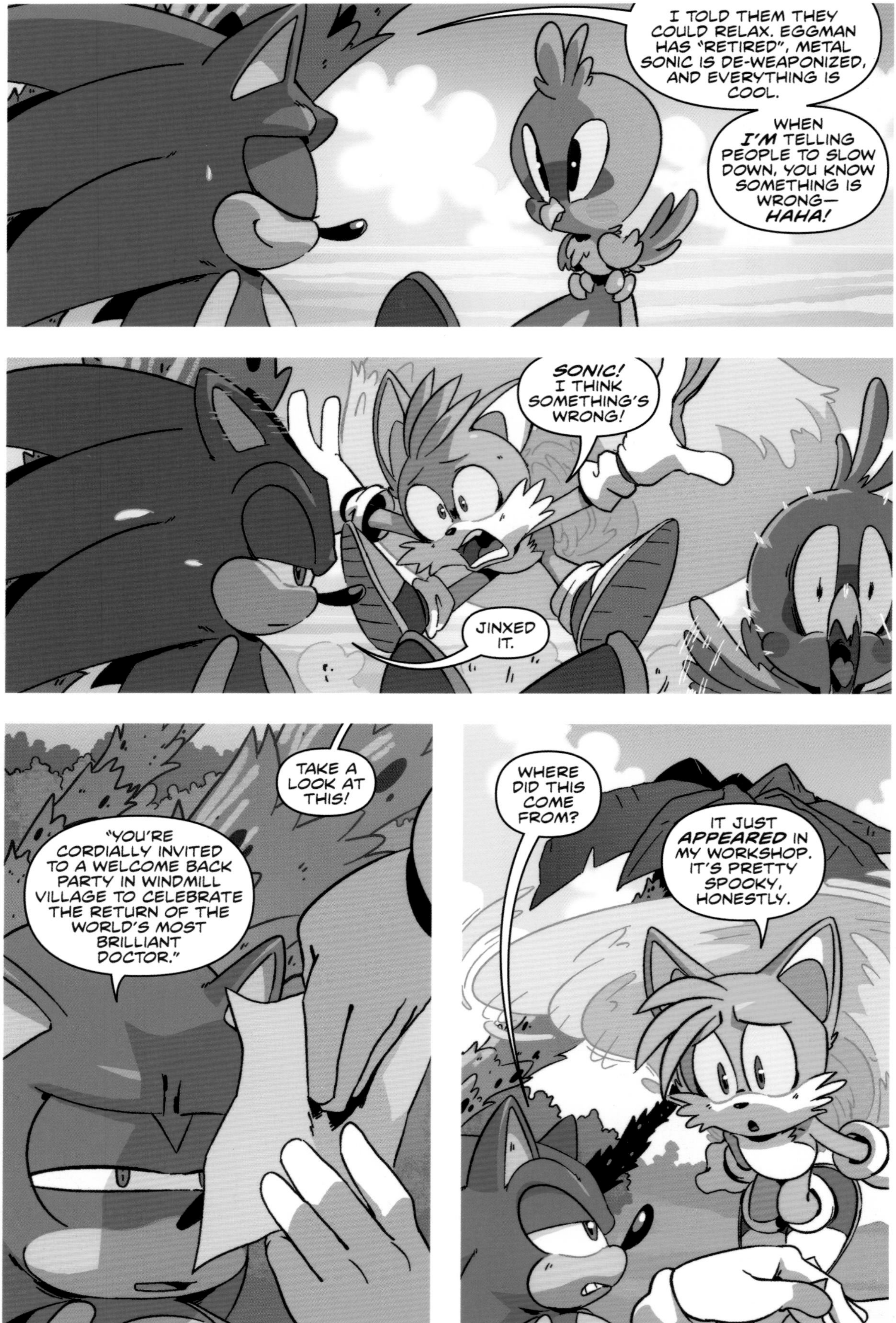
I TOLD THEM THEY COULD RELAX. EGGMAN HAS "RETIRED", METAL SONIC IS DE-WEAPONIZED, AND EVERYTHING IS COOL.
WHEN *I'M* TELLING PEOPLE TO SLOW DOWN, YOU KNOW SOMETHING IS WRONG— *HAHA!*
SONIC! I THINK SOMETHING'S WRONG!
JINXED IT.
TAKE A LOOK AT THIS!
"YOU'RE CORDIALLY INVITED TO A WELCOME BACK PARTY IN WINDMILL VILLAGE TO CELEBRATE THE RETURN OF THE WORLD'S MOST BRILLIANT DOCTOR."
WHERE DID THIS COME FROM?
IT JUST *APPEARED* IN MY WORKSHOP. IT'S PRETTY SPOOKY, HONESTLY.

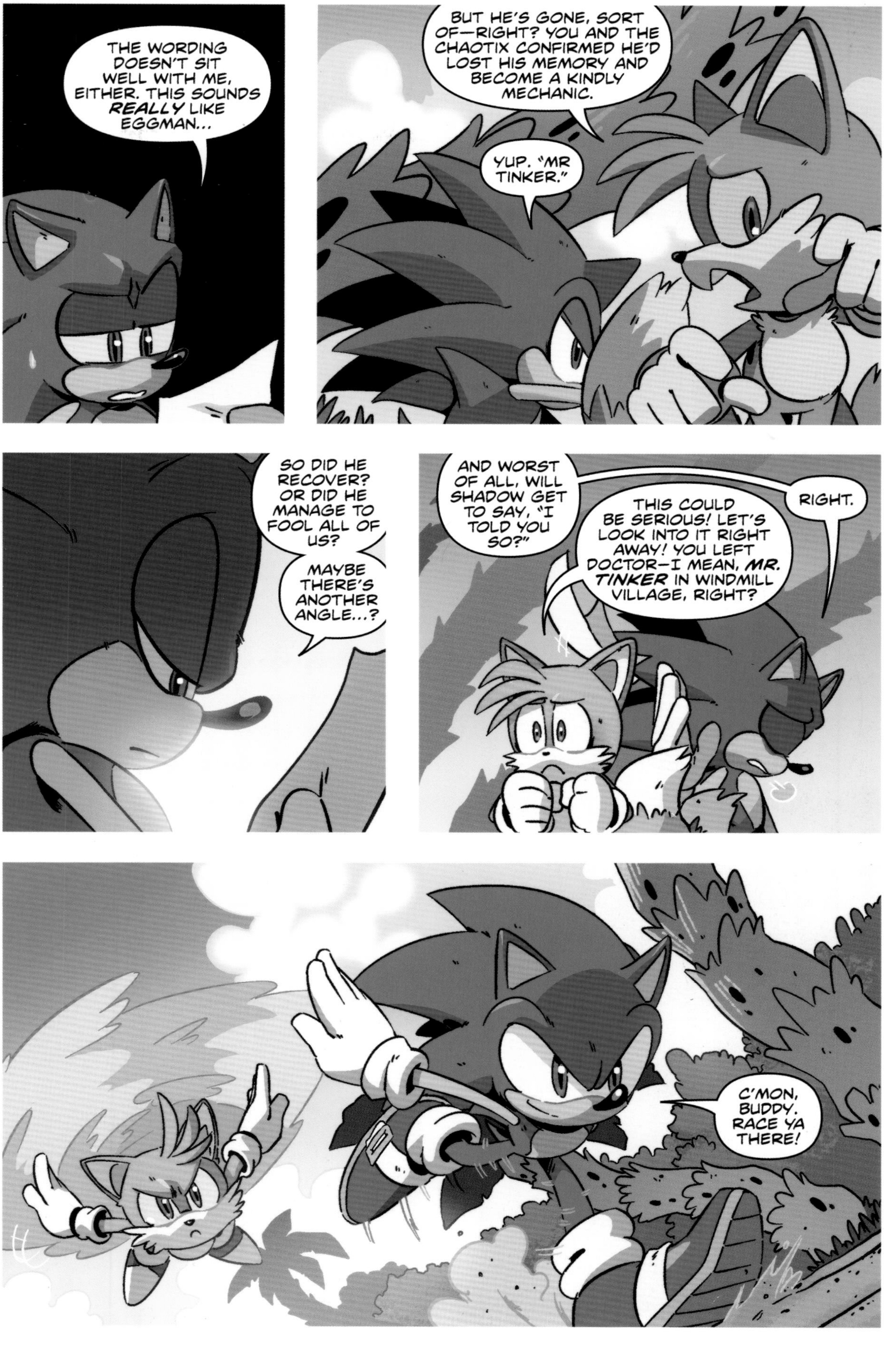
THE WORDING DOESN'T SIT WELL WITH ME, EITHER. THIS SOUNDS REALLY LIKE EGGMAN...
BUT HE'S GONE, SORT OF—RIGHT? YOU AND THE CHAOTIX CONFIRMED HE'D LOST HIS MEMORY AND BECOME A KINDLY MECHANIC.
YUP. "MR TINKER."
SO DID HE RECOVER? OR DID HE MANAGE TO FOOL ALL OF US?
MAYBE THERE'S ANOTHER ANGLE...?
AND WORST OF ALL, WILL SHADOW GET TO SAY, "I TOLD YOU SO?"
THIS COULD BE SERIOUS! LET'S LOOK INTO IT RIGHT AWAY! YOU LEFT DOCTOR—I MEAN, MR. TINKER IN WINDMILL VILLAGE, RIGHT?
RIGHT.
C'MON, BUDDY. RACE YA THERE!

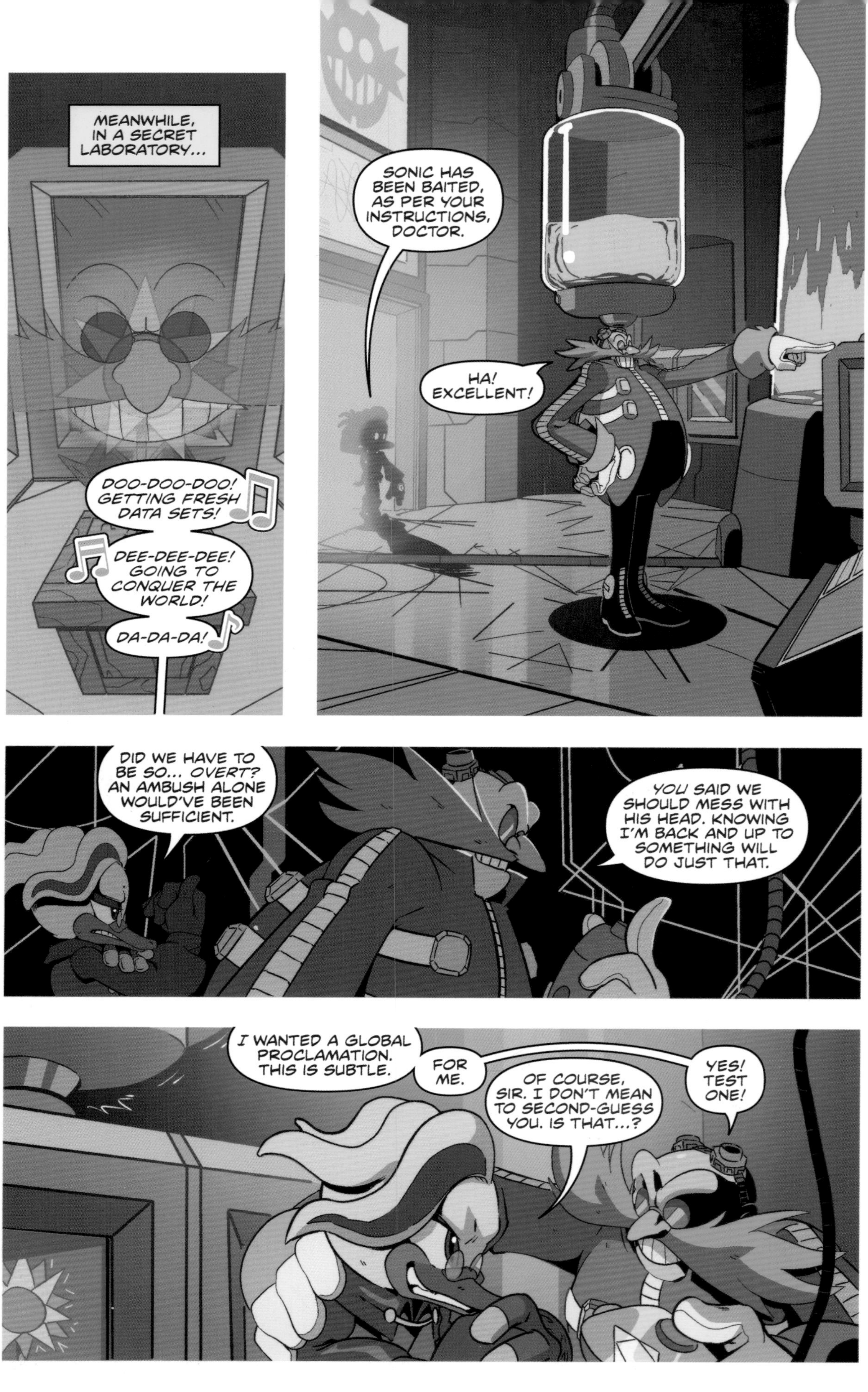
MEANWHILE, IN A SECRET LABORATORY...
DOO-DOO-DOO! GETTING FRESH DATA SETS!
DEE-DEE-DEE! GOING TO CONQUER THE WORLD!
DA-DA-DA!
SONIC HAS BEEN BAITED, AS PER YOUR INSTRUCTIONS, DOCTOR.
HA! EXCELLENT!
DID WE HAVE TO BE SO... OVERT? AN AMBUSH ALONE WOULD'VE BEEN SUFFICIENT.
YOU SAID WE SHOULD MESS WITH HIS HEAD. KNOWING I'M BACK AND UP TO SOMETHING WILL DO JUST THAT.
I WANTED A GLOBAL PROCLAMATION. THIS IS SUBTLE.
FOR ME.
OF COURSE, SIR. I DON'T MEAN TO SECOND-GUESS YOU. IS THAT...?
YES! TEST ONE!

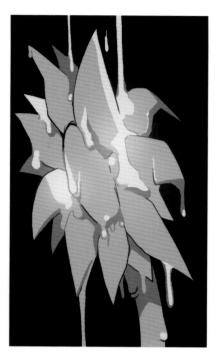

MARVELOUS! TOTAL AND INSTANTANEOUS TRANSMUTATION!

HMM... OF THE ACTIVE PLANT TISSUE, YES, BUT NOT THE PROCESSED WOOD...

I NEED MORE DATA.

BRING ME THE ANIMALS.

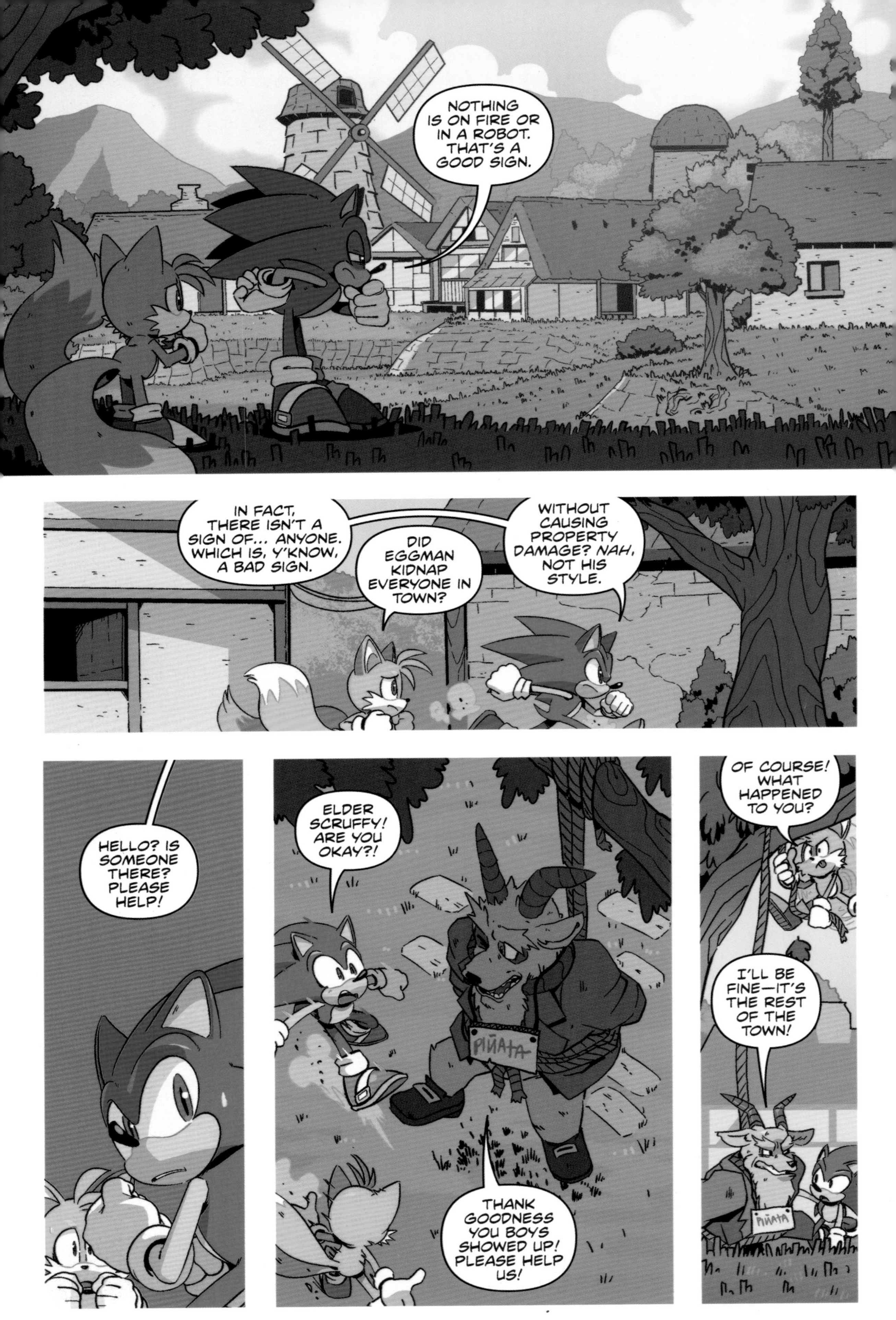
NOTHING IS ON FIRE OR IN A ROBOT. THAT'S A GOOD SIGN.
IN FACT, THERE ISN'T A SIGN OF... ANYONE. WHICH IS, Y'KNOW, A BAD SIGN.
DID EGGMAN KIDNAP EVERYONE IN TOWN?
WITHOUT CAUSING PROPERTY DAMAGE? *NAH*, NOT HIS STYLE.
HELLO? IS SOMEONE THERE? PLEASE HELP!
ELDER SCRUFFY! ARE YOU OKAY?!
PIÑATA
THANK GOODNESS YOU BOYS SHOWED UP! PLEASE HELP US!
OF COURSE! WHAT HAPPENED TO YOU?
I'LL BE FINE—IT'S THE REST OF THE TOWN!
PIÑATA

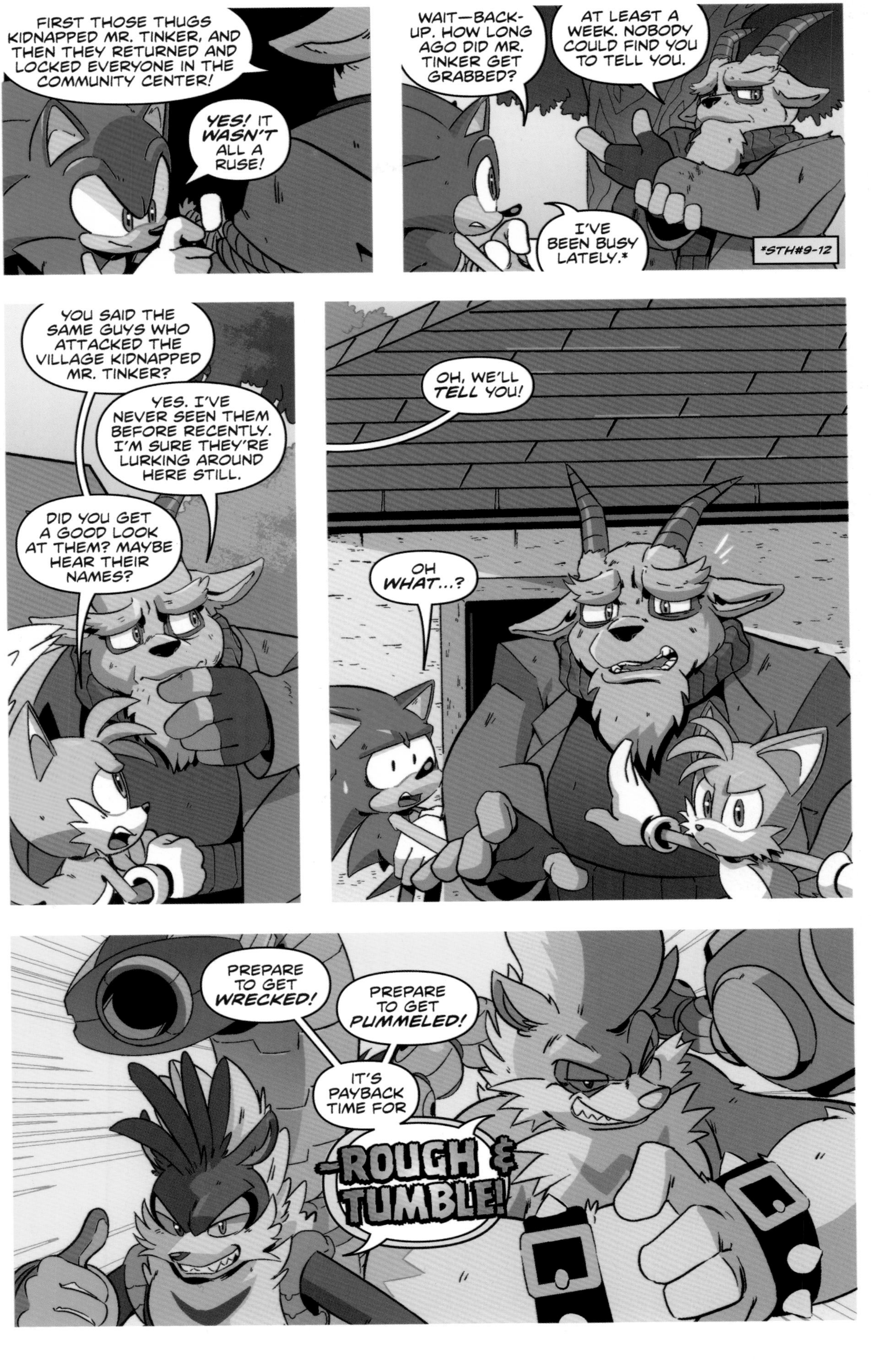
FIRST THOSE THUGS KIDNAPPED MR. TINKER, AND THEN THEY RETURNED AND LOCKED EVERYONE IN THE COMMUNITY CENTER!
YES! IT WASN'T ALL A RUSE!
WAIT—BACK-UP. HOW LONG AGO DID MR. TINKER GET GRABBED?
AT LEAST A WEEK. NOBODY COULD FIND YOU TO TELL YOU.
I'VE BEEN BUSY LATELY.*
*STH#9-12
YOU SAID THE SAME GUYS WHO ATTACKED THE VILLAGE KIDNAPPED MR. TINKER?
YES. I'VE NEVER SEEN THEM BEFORE RECENTLY. I'M SURE THEY'RE LURKING AROUND HERE STILL.
DID YOU GET A GOOD LOOK AT THEM? MAYBE HEAR THEIR NAMES?
OH, WE'LL TELL YOU!
OH WHAT...?
PREPARE TO GET WRECKED!
PREPARE TO GET PUMMELED!
IT'S PAYBACK TIME FOR
ROUGH & TUMBLE!

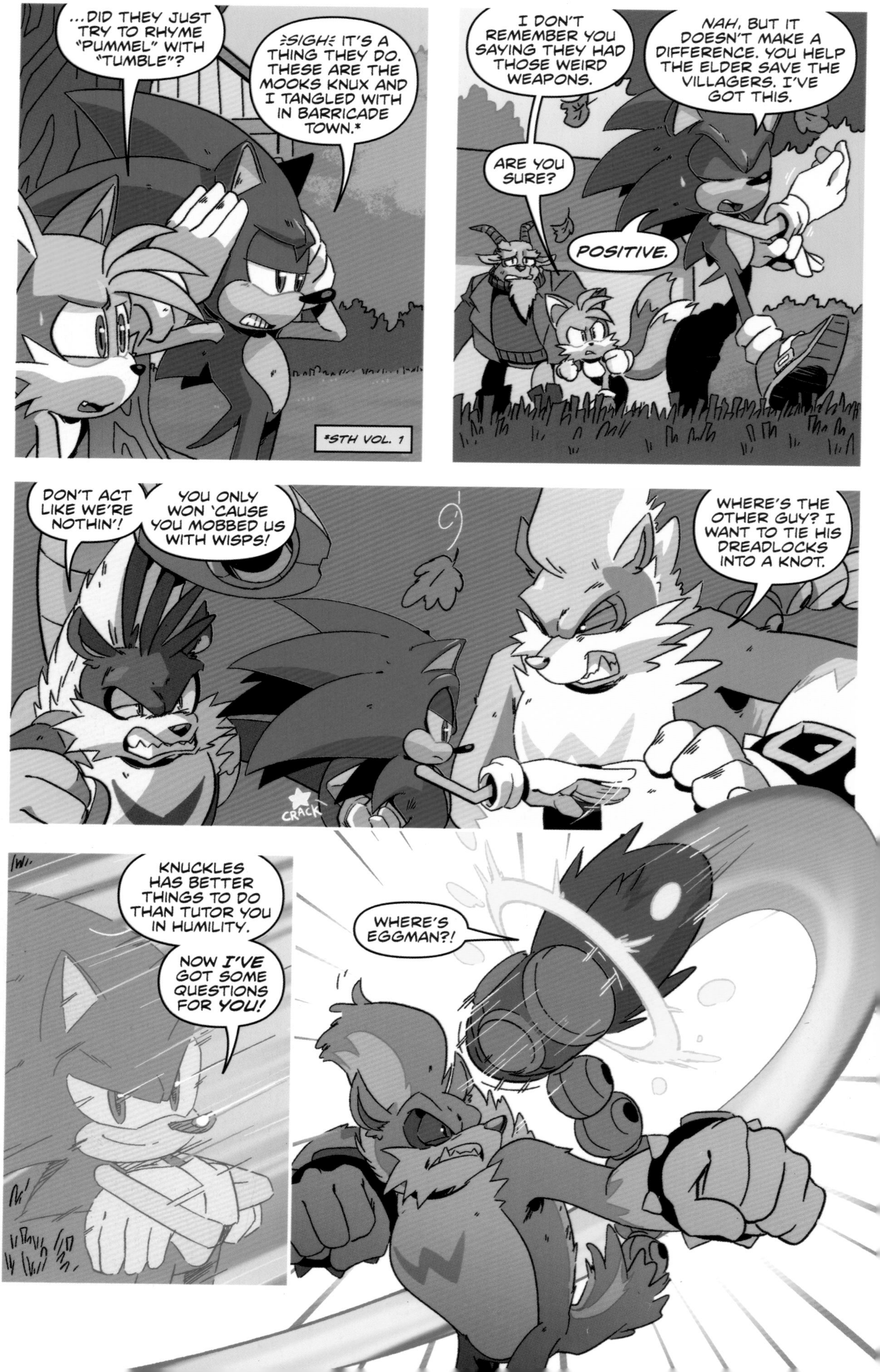
...DID THEY JUST TRY TO RHYME "PUMMEL" WITH "TUMBLE"?
≥SIGH≤ IT'S A THING THEY DO. THESE ARE THE MOOKS KNUX AND I TANGLED WITH IN BARRICADE TOWN.*
*STH VOL. 1
I DON'T REMEMBER YOU SAYING THEY HAD THOSE WEIRD WEAPONS.
NAH, BUT IT DOESN'T MAKE A DIFFERENCE. YOU HELP THE ELDER SAVE THE VILLAGERS. I'VE GOT THIS.
ARE YOU SURE?
POSITIVE.
DON'T ACT LIKE WE'RE NOTHIN'!
YOU ONLY WON 'CAUSE YOU MOBBED US WITH WISPS!
WHERE'S THE OTHER GUY? I WANT TO TIE HIS DREADLOCKS INTO A KNOT.
CRACK
KNUCKLES HAS BETTER THINGS TO DO THAN TUTOR YOU IN HUMILITY.
NOW I'VE GOT SOME QUESTIONS FOR YOU!
WHERE'S EGGMAN?!

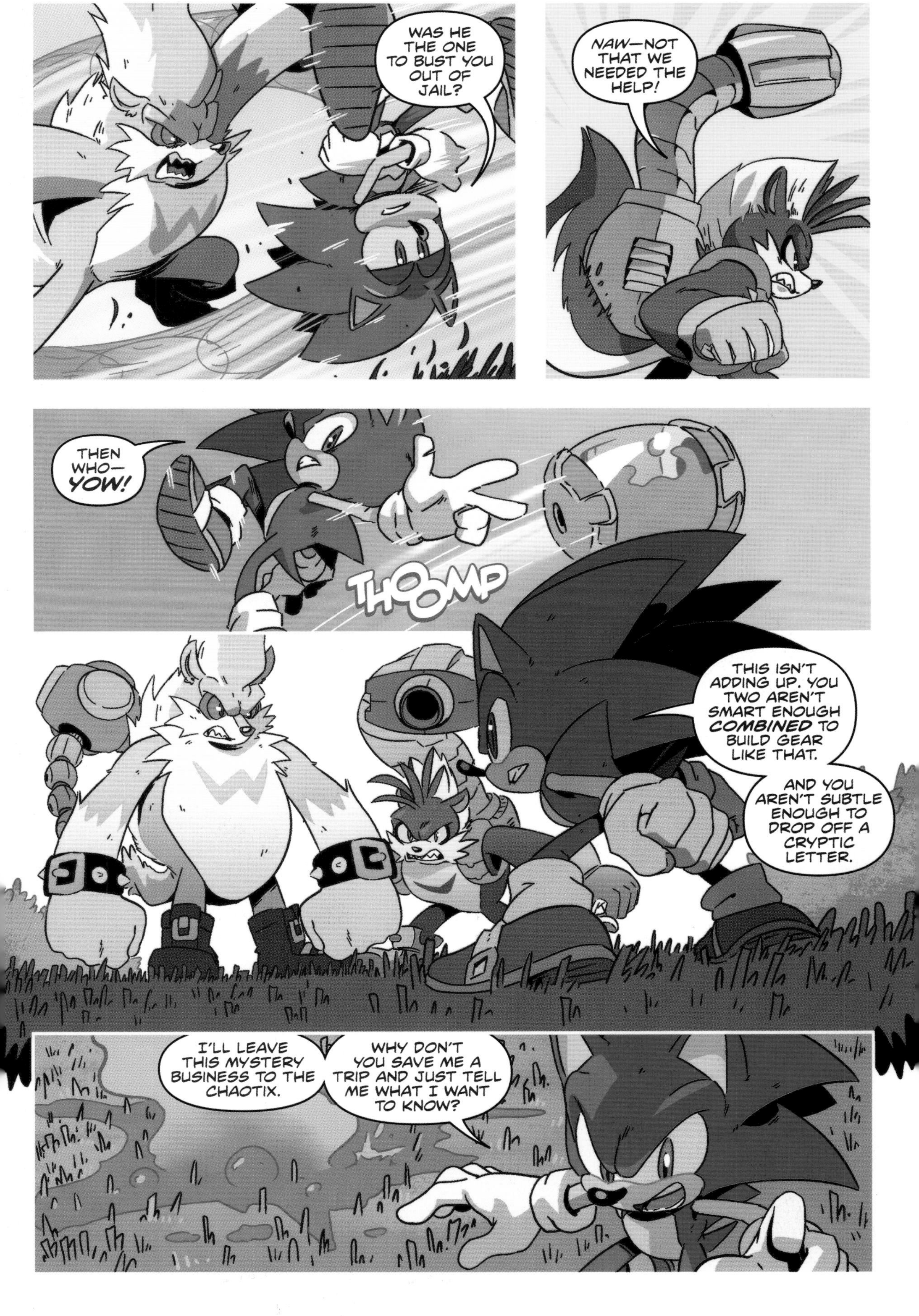
WAS HE THE ONE TO BUST YOU OUT OF JAIL?
NAW—NOT THAT WE NEEDED THE HELP!
THEN WHO—YOW!
THOOMP
THIS ISN'T ADDING UP. YOU TWO AREN'T SMART ENOUGH COMBINED TO BUILD GEAR LIKE THAT.
AND YOU AREN'T SUBTLE ENOUGH TO DROP OFF A CRYPTIC LETTER.
I'LL LEAVE THIS MYSTERY BUSINESS TO THE CHAOTIX.
WHY DON'T YOU SAVE ME A TRIP AND JUST TELL ME WHAT I WANT TO KNOW?

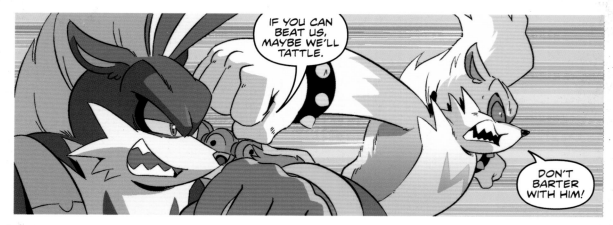

IF YOU CAN BEAT US, MAYBE WE'LL TATTLE.

DON'T BARTER WITH HIM!

CRUSH HIM!

SLAM

CLANK

IT'S ALL RIGHT, EVERYONE! SONIC AND TAILS HAVE COME TO SAVE US!

SWING AND A MISS!

YOU'RE ALL BETTER OFF IN HERE UNTIL THE FIGHT IS DONE. TAKE COVER AND KEEP YOUR HEADS DOWN.

O-OH... ALRIGHT THEN...

TEST TWO! COMMENCING WITH VERTEBRATE SPECIMENS!

JUST LIKE BEFORE! FULL SATURATION LEADS TO IMMEDIATE TRANSMUTATION!

INITIATING TEST THREE!

POCKY! GRAB THE PICKY!

REEE REEE!

GOOD. NOW BACK OFF!

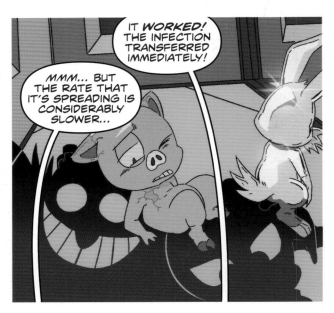

IT *WORKED!* THE INFECTION TRANSFERRED IMMEDIATELY!

MMM... BUT THE RATE THAT IT'S SPREADING IS CONSIDERABLY SLOWER...

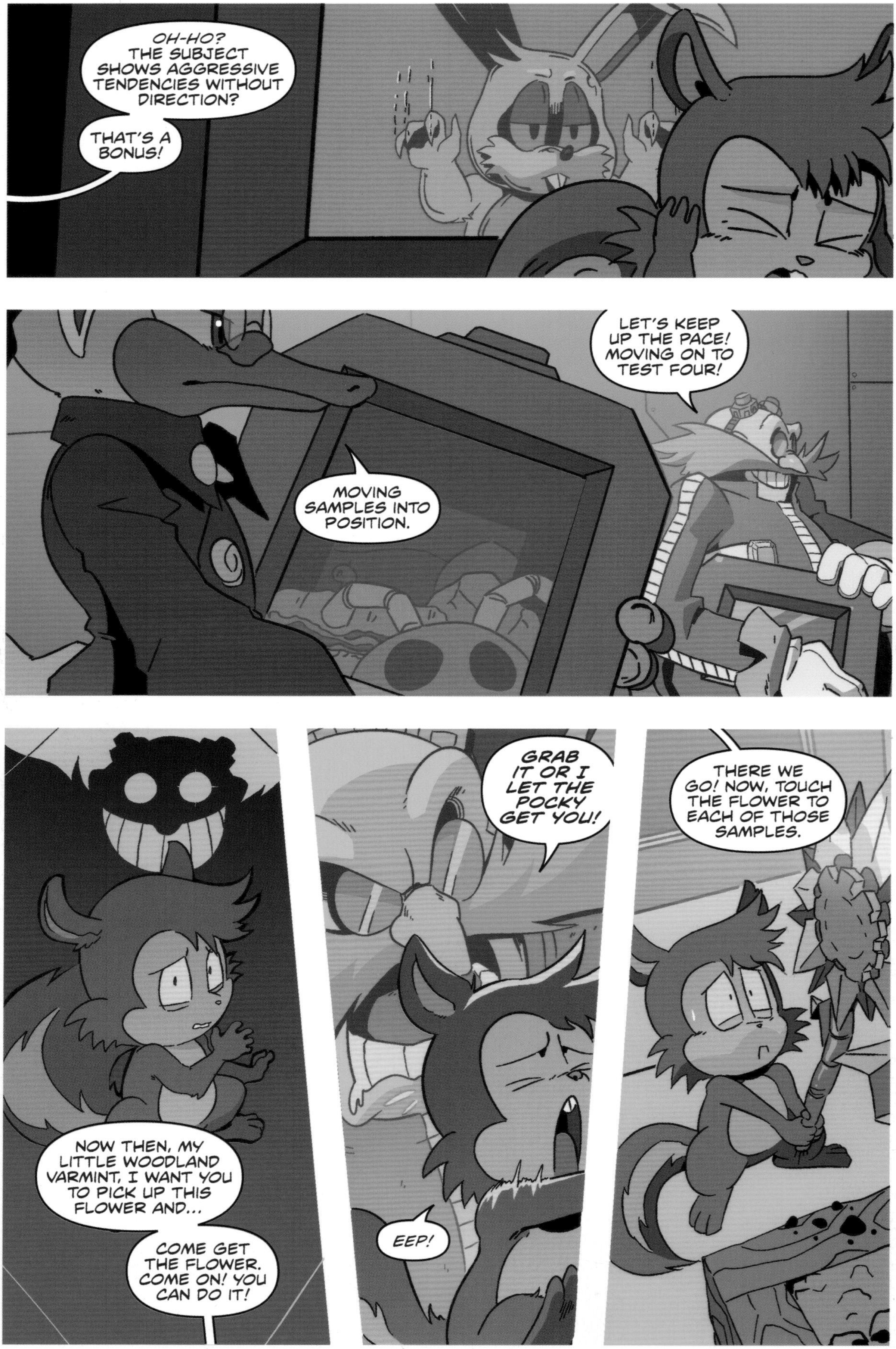

OH-HO? THE SUBJECT SHOWS AGGRESSIVE TENDENCIES WITHOUT DIRECTION?
THAT'S A BONUS!
LET'S KEEP UP THE PACE! MOVING ON TO TEST FOUR!
MOVING SAMPLES INTO POSITION.
NOW THEN, MY LITTLE WOODLAND VARMINT, I WANT YOU TO PICK UP THIS FLOWER AND...
COME GET THE FLOWER. COME ON! YOU CAN DO IT!
GRAB IT OR I LET THE POCKY GET YOU!
EEP!
THERE WE GO! NOW, TOUCH THE FLOWER TO EACH OF THOSE SAMPLES.

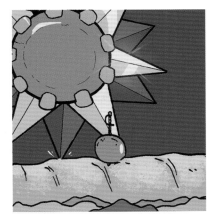
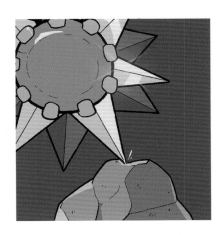

I... DON'T SEE ANY SIGNS OF INFECTION, SIR.

NO, BUT IT *DID* PASS FROM FLORA TO FAUNA. THAT'S TEST FIVE COMPLETE!

MY *METAL VIRUS* IS A COMPLETE SUCCESS!

EVEN WITH THE SLIGHTEST EXPOSURE, MY SYNTHETIC CON-COCTION SPREADS ACROSS ORGANIC TISSUE, CONVERTING IT INTO MY ROBOTIC SLAVE! IT'S AN ARMY THAT BUILDS ITSELF!

INORGANIC OR PROCESSED MATERIAL REMAINS INERT, MEANING MY INFRASTRUCTURE IS SAFE FROM INFECTION OR CORRUPTION!

I'M A GENIUS!

I'M SO HAPPY TO HAVE BEEN A PART OF THIS! I NEVER DREAMED I'D BE SO HONORED WHEN I WAS SEARCHING FOR YOU!

HOW *DID* YOU FIND ME? METAL SONIC HAD HALF MY EMPIRE SCOURING THE GLOBE.

HE SENT SEARCH PARTIES OF BADNIKS. THAT'S A FINITE NUMBER OF SENSORS OVER A LIMITED RANGE, ALL OF WHICH TAKES TIMES.

I HAD THE WARP TOPAZ.

WITH A MODEST CHARGE, I COULD OPEN "WINDOWS" TO THE *WORLD* IN AN INSTANT.

I LOOKED FARTHER AND FURTHER IN HOURS THAN THE BADNIKS COULD DO IN A DAY.

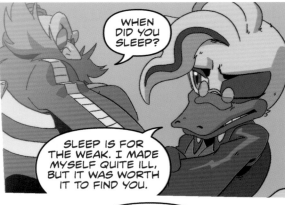

WHEN DID YOU SLEEP?

SLEEP IS FOR THE WEAK. I MADE MYSELF QUITE ILL, BUT IT WAS WORTH IT TO FIND YOU.

≋SNERK≋ I'M... SO GLAD YOU THINK SO. CAN YOU ZOOM IN? I WANT TO SEE SONIC GETTING HIS TEETH KICKED IN.

BY YOUR COMMAND, DOCTOR.

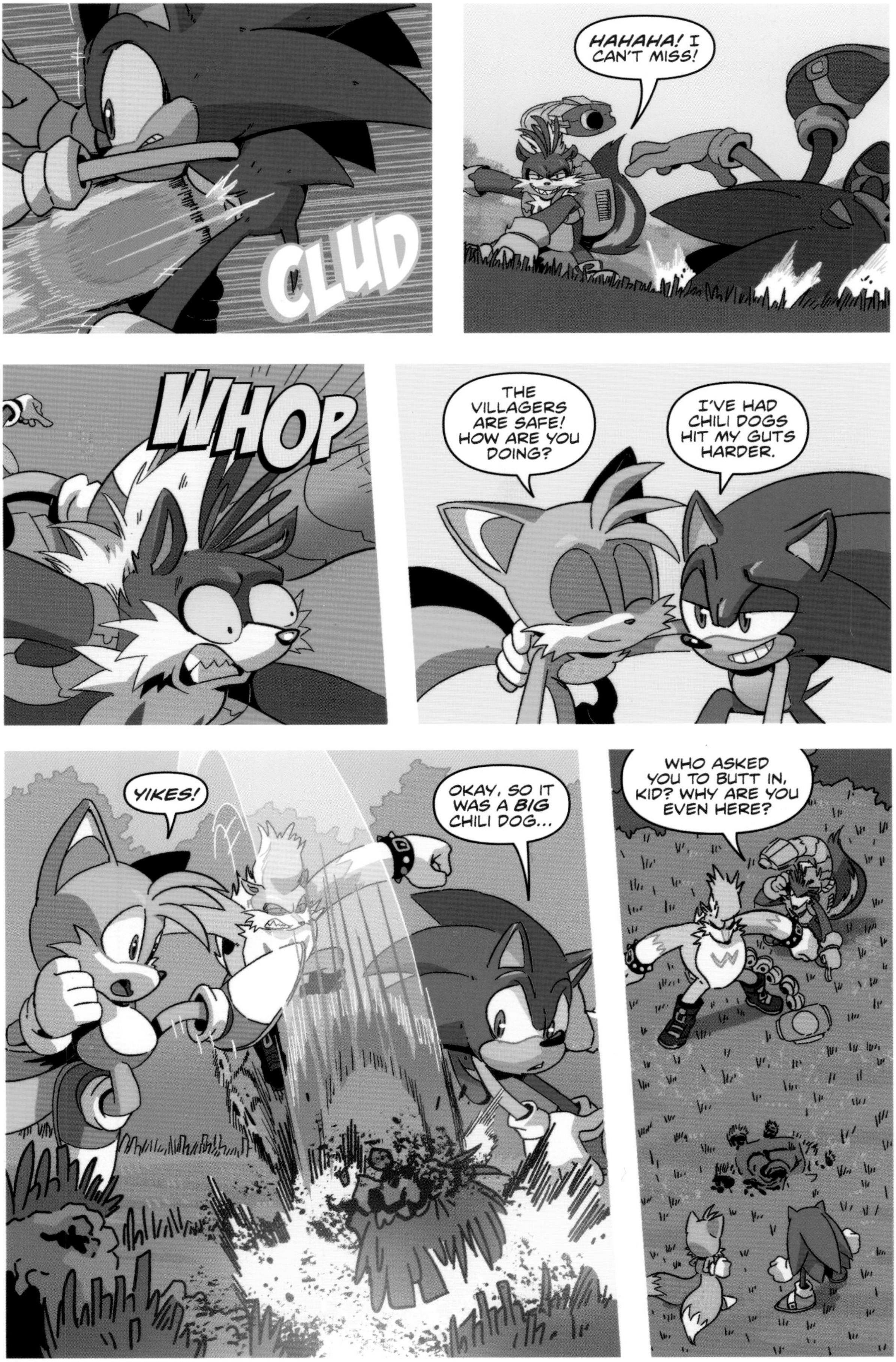
CLUD
HAHAHA! I CAN'T MISS!
WHOP
THE VILLAGERS ARE SAFE! HOW ARE YOU DOING?
I'VE HAD CHILI DOGS HIT MY GUTS HARDER.
YIKES!
OKAY, SO IT WAS A BIG CHILI DOG...
WHO ASKED YOU TO BUTT IN, KID? WHY ARE YOU EVEN HERE?

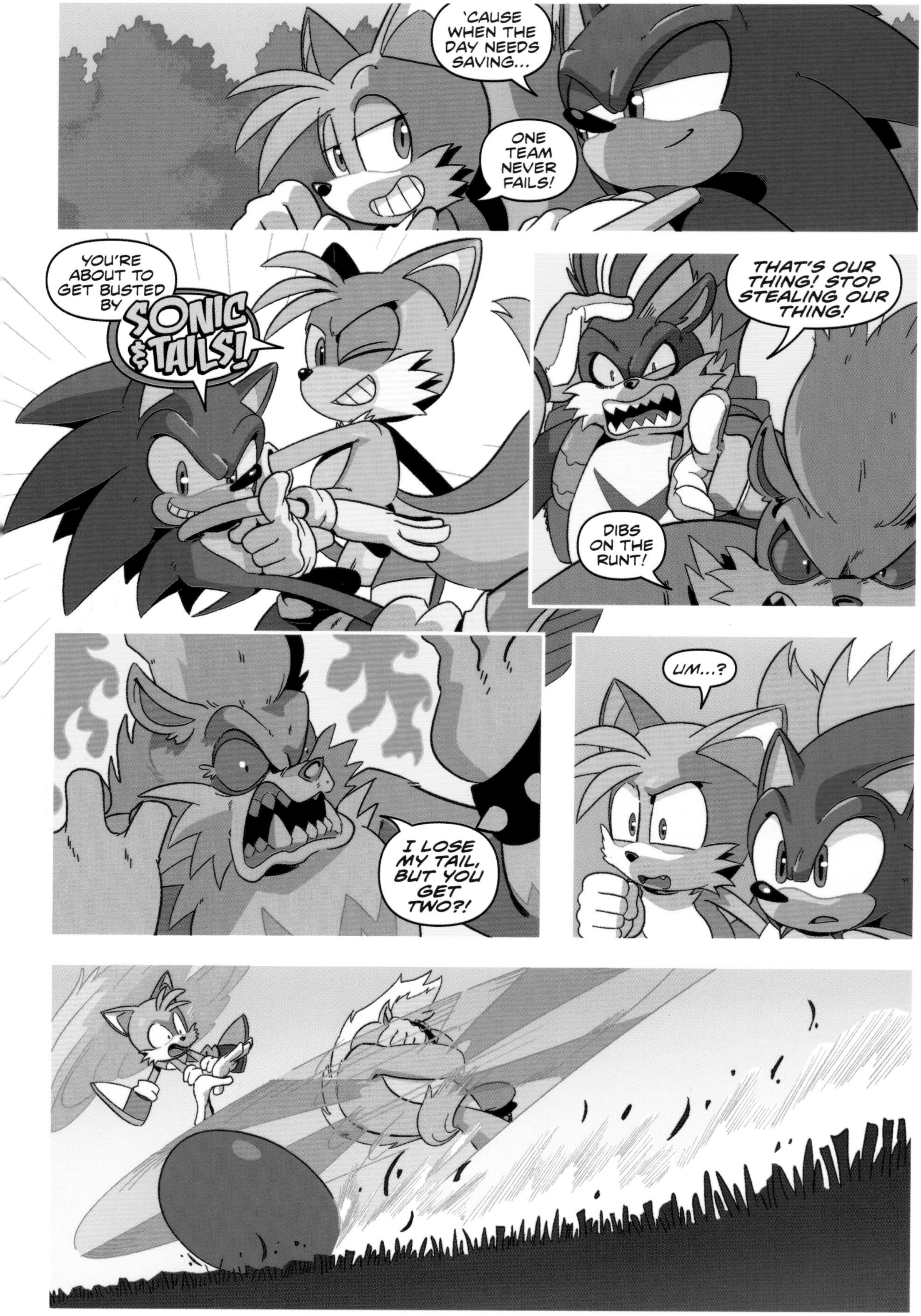
'CAUSE WHEN THE DAY NEEDS SAVING...
ONE TEAM NEVER FAILS!
YOU'RE ABOUT TO GET BUSTED BY SONIC & TAILS!
THAT'S OUR THING! STOP STEALING OUR THING!
DIBS ON THE RUNT!
I LOSE MY TAIL, BUT YOU GET TWO?!
UM...?

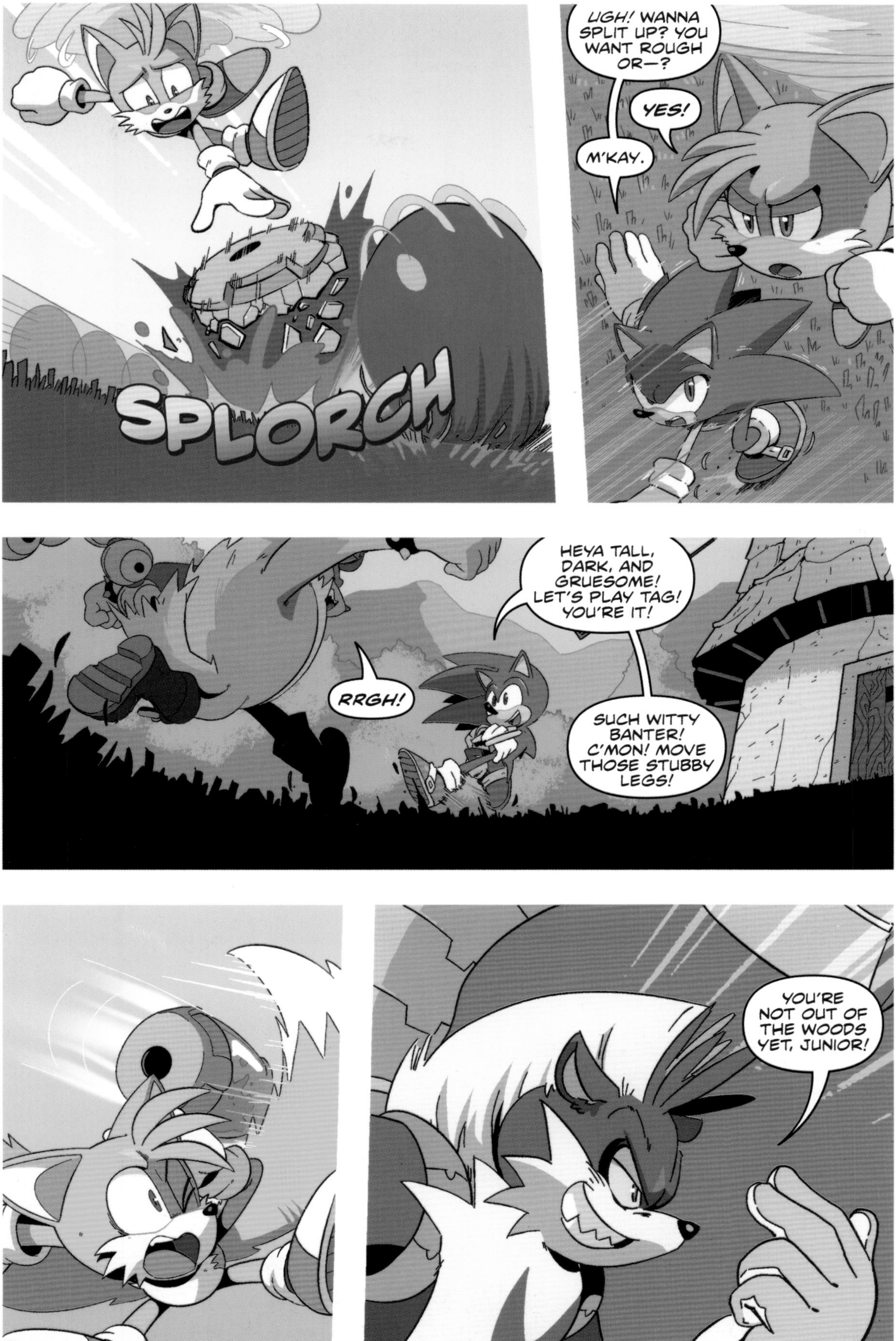
SPLORCH
UGH! WANNA SPLIT UP? YOU WANT ROUGH OR—?
YES!
M'KAY.
HEYA TALL, DARK, AND GRUESOME! LET'S PLAY TAG! YOU'RE IT!
RRGH!
SUCH WITTY BANTER! C'MON! MOVE THOSE STUBBY LEGS!
YOU'RE NOT OUT OF THE WOODS YET, JUNIOR!

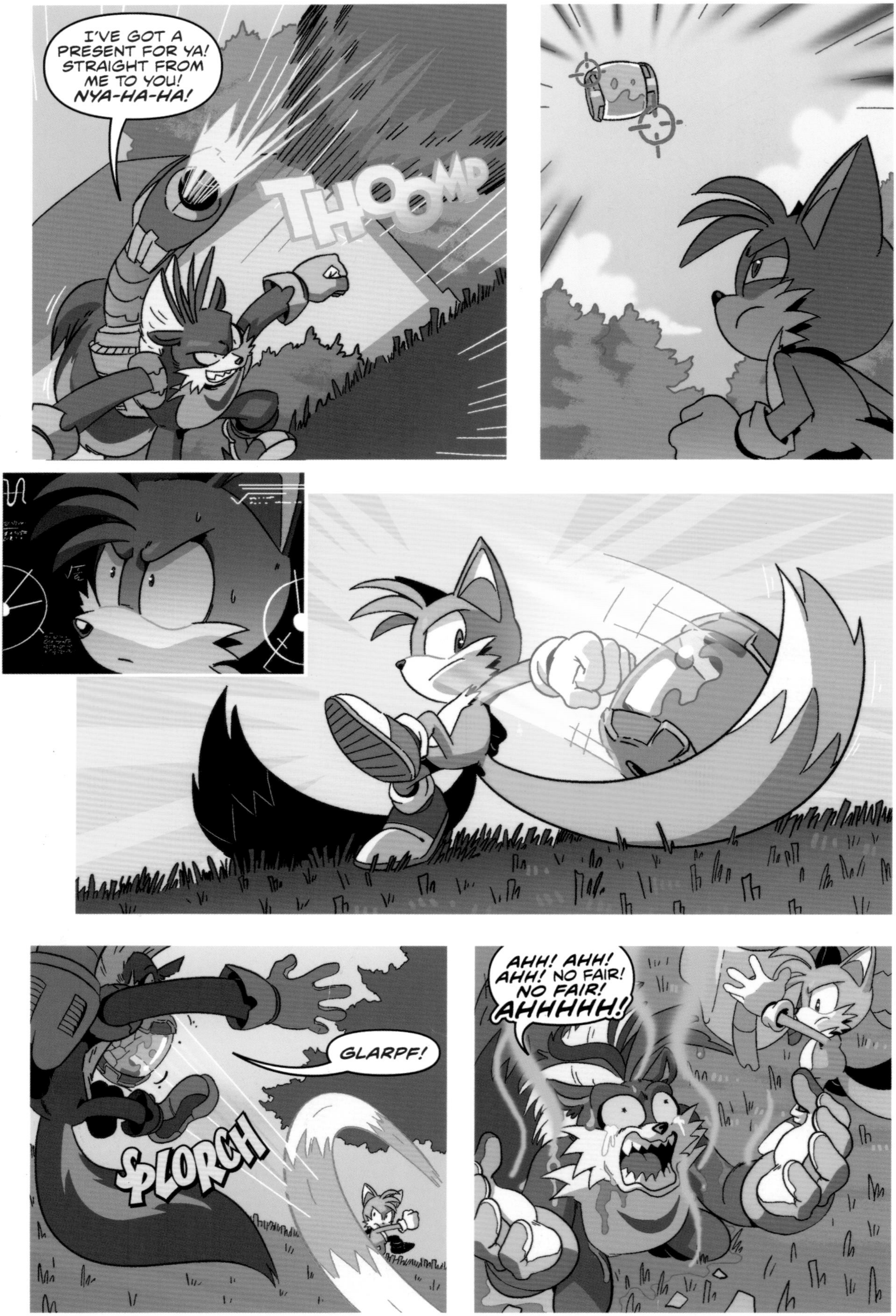
I'VE GOT A PRESENT FOR YA! STRAIGHT FROM ME TO YOU! NYA-HA-HA!
THOOMP
GLARPF!
SPLORCH
AHH! AHH! AHH! NO FAIR! NO FAIR! AHHHHH!

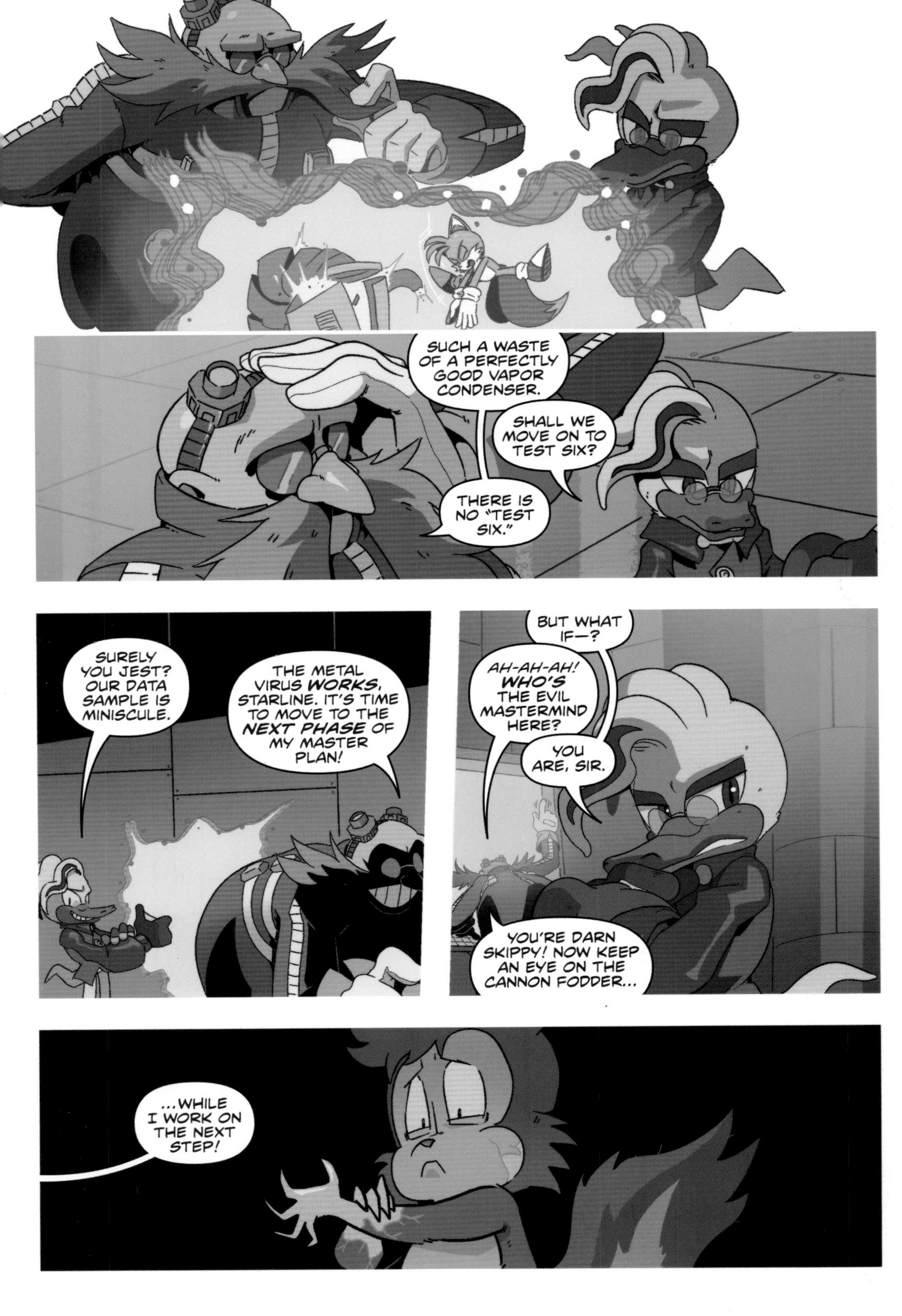
SUCH A WASTE OF A PERFECTLY GOOD VAPOR CONDENSER.
SHALL WE MOVE ON TO TEST SIX?
THERE IS NO "TEST SIX."
SURELY YOU JEST? OUR DATA SAMPLE IS MINISCULE.
THE METAL VIRUS **WORKS**, STARLINE. IT'S TIME TO MOVE TO THE ***NEXT PHASE*** OF MY MASTER PLAN!
BUT WHAT IF—?
AH-AH-AH! ***WHO'S*** THE EVIL MASTERMIND HERE?
YOU ARE, SIR.
YOU'RE DARN SKIPPY! NOW KEEP AN EYE ON THE CANNON FODDER...
...WHILE I WORK ON THE NEXT STEP!

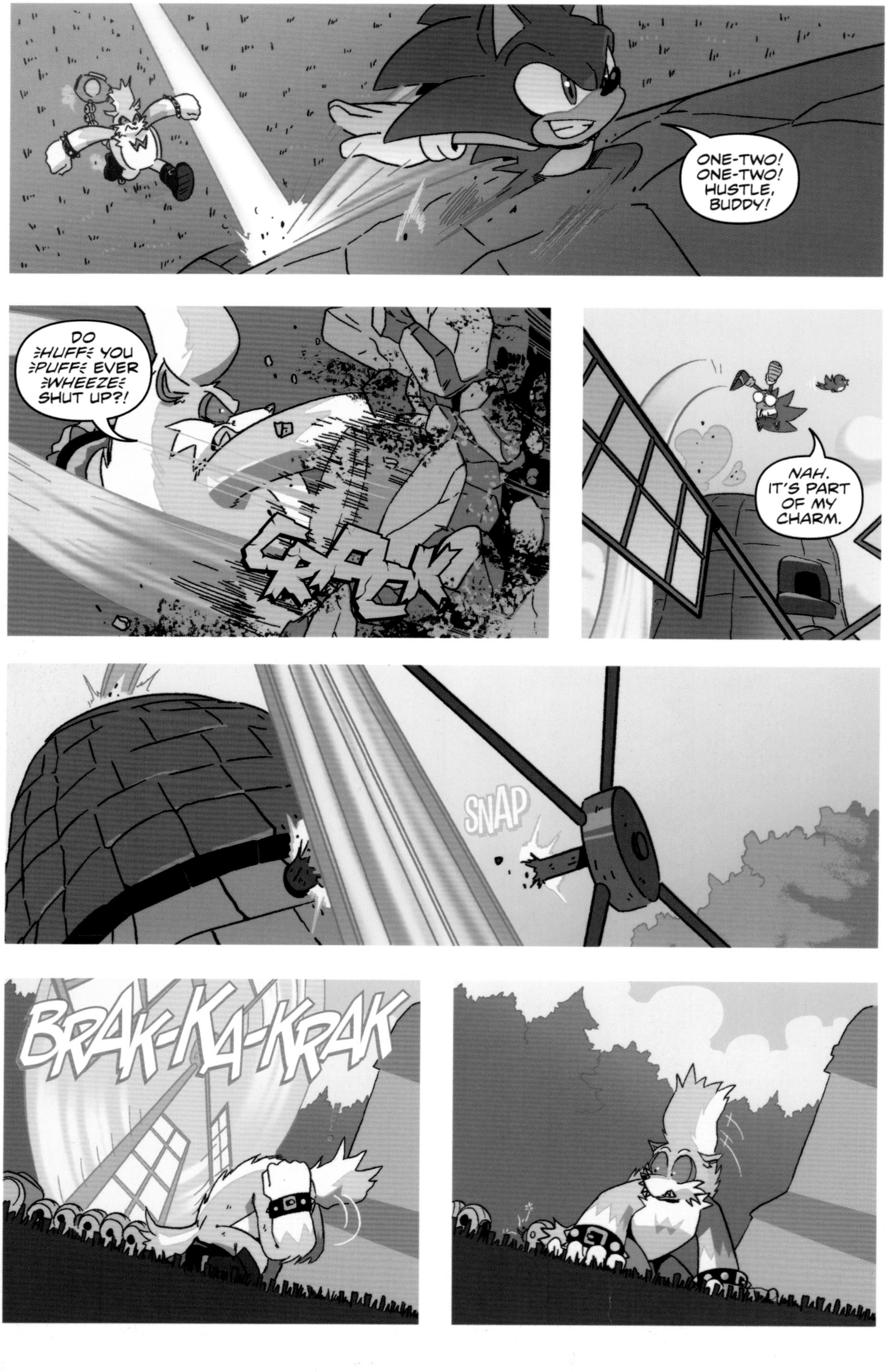
ONE-TWO! ONE-TWO! HUSTLE, BUDDY!
DO ≡HUFF≡ YOU ≡PUFF≡ EVER ≡WHEEZE≡ SHUT UP?!
CRACK
NAH. IT'S PART OF MY CHARM.
SNAP
BRAK-KA-KRAK

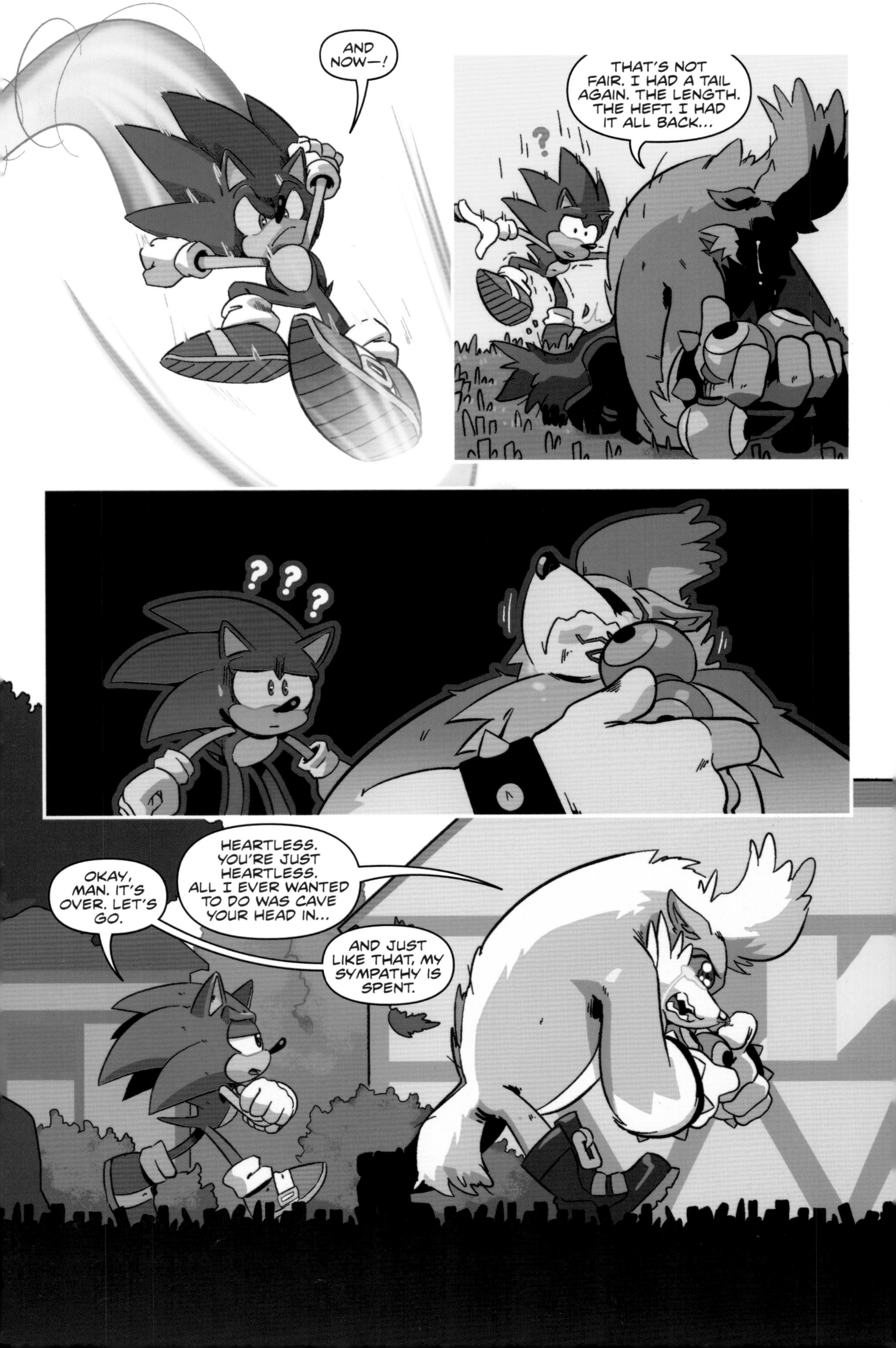
AND NOW—!
THAT'S NOT FAIR. I HAD A TAIL AGAIN. THE LENGTH. THE HEFT. I HAD IT ALL BACK...
?
???
OKAY, MAN. IT'S OVER. LET'S GO.
HEARTLESS. YOU'RE JUST HEARTLESS. ALL I EVER WANTED TO DO WAS CAVE YOUR HEAD IN...
AND JUST LIKE THAT, MY SYMPATHY IS SPENT.

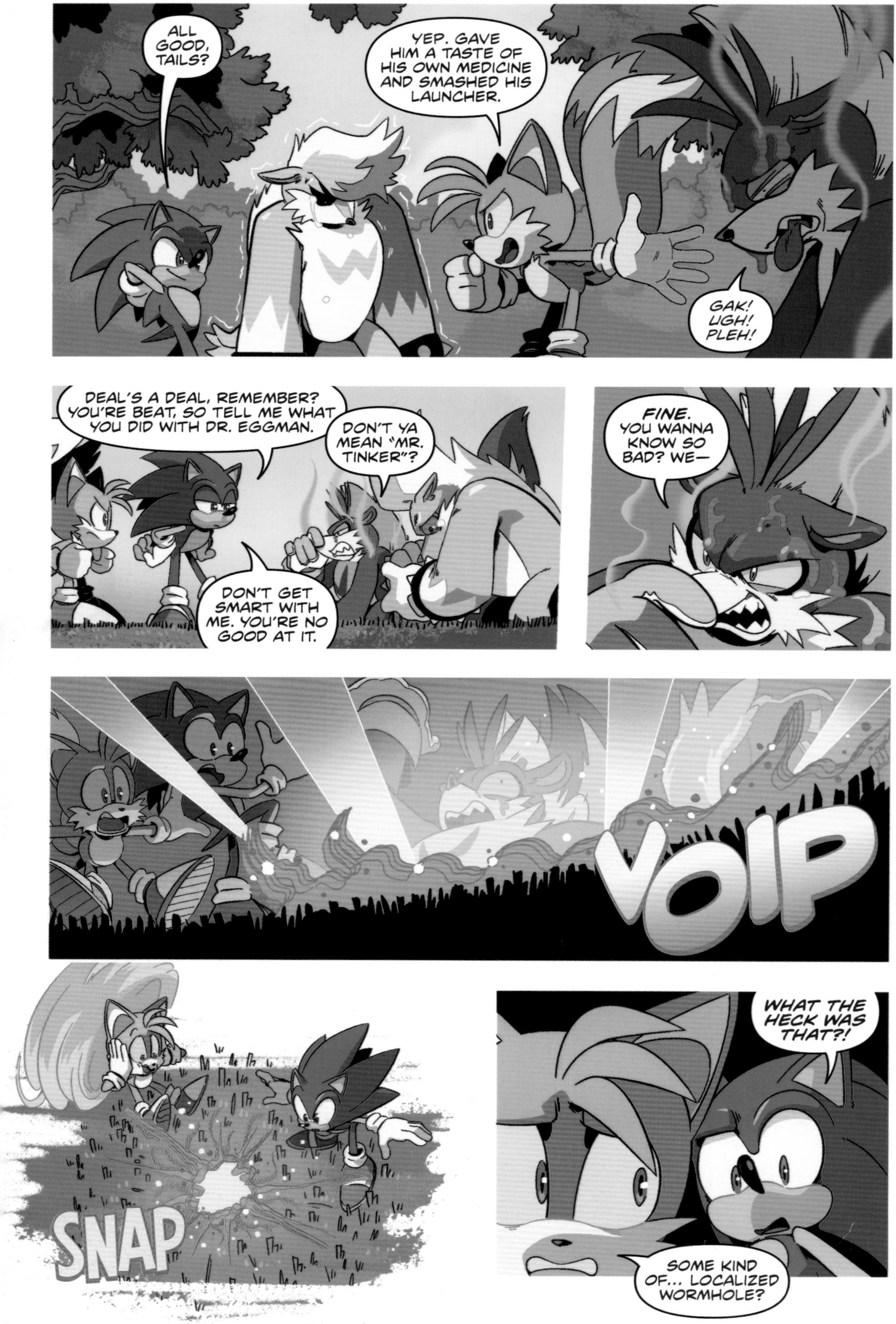
ALL GOOD, TAILS?
YEP. GAVE HIM A TASTE OF HIS OWN MEDICINE AND SMASHED HIS LAUNCHER.
GAK! UGH! PLEH!
DEAL'S A DEAL, REMEMBER? YOU'RE BEAT, SO TELL ME WHAT YOU DID WITH DR. EGGMAN.
DON'T YA MEAN "MR. TINKER"?
DON'T GET SMART WITH ME. YOU'RE NO GOOD AT IT.
FINE. YOU WANNA KNOW SO BAD? WE—
VOIP
SNAP
WHAT THE HECK WAS THAT?!
SOME KIND OF... LOCALIZED WORMHOLE?

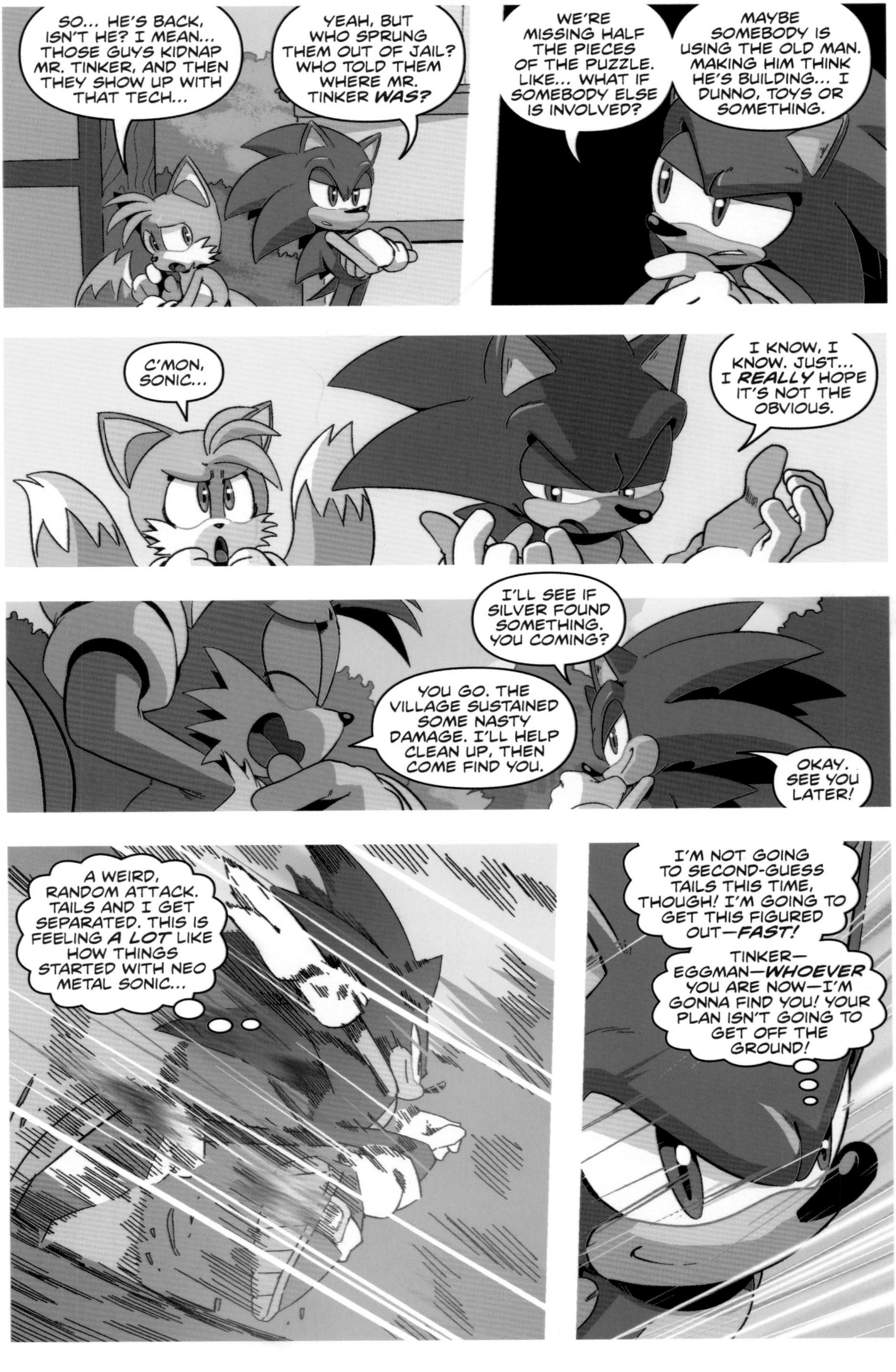

SO... HE'S BACK, ISN'T HE? I MEAN... THOSE GUYS KIDNAP MR. TINKER, AND THEN THEY SHOW UP WITH THAT TECH...
YEAH, BUT WHO SPRUNG THEM OUT OF JAIL? WHO TOLD THEM WHERE MR. TINKER *WAS?*
WE'RE MISSING HALF THE PIECES OF THE PUZZLE. LIKE... WHAT IF SOMEBODY ELSE IS INVOLVED?
MAYBE SOMEBODY IS USING THE OLD MAN. MAKING HIM THINK HE'S BUILDING... I DUNNO, TOYS OR SOMETHING.
C'MON, SONIC...
I KNOW, I KNOW. JUST... I *REALLY* HOPE IT'S NOT THE OBVIOUS.
I'LL SEE IF SILVER FOUND SOMETHING. YOU COMING?
YOU GO. THE VILLAGE SUSTAINED SOME NASTY DAMAGE. I'LL HELP CLEAN UP, THEN COME FIND YOU.
OKAY. SEE YOU LATER!
A WEIRD, RANDOM ATTACK. TAILS AND I GET SEPARATED. THIS IS FEELING *A LOT* LIKE HOW THINGS STARTED WITH NEO METAL SONIC...
I'M NOT GOING TO SECOND-GUESS TAILS THIS TIME, THOUGH! I'M GOING TO GET THIS FIGURED OUT—*FAST!*
TINKER—EGGMAN—*WHOEVER* YOU ARE NOW—I'M GONNA FIND YOU! YOUR PLAN ISN'T GOING TO GET OFF THE GROUND!

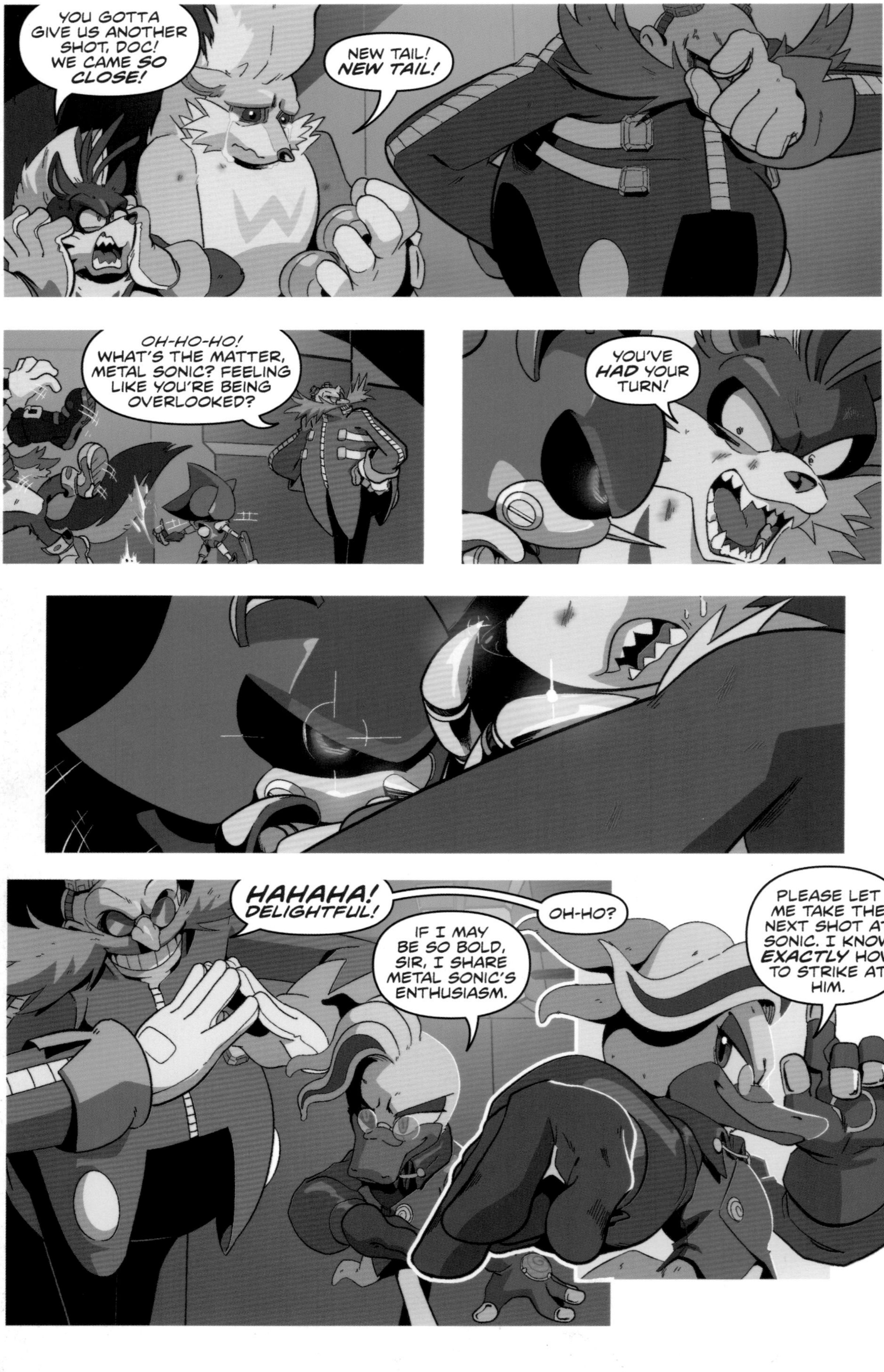
YOU GOTTA GIVE US ANOTHER SHOT, DOC! WE CAME SO CLOSE!
NEW TAIL! NEW TAIL!
OH-HO-HO! WHAT'S THE MATTER, METAL SONIC? FEELING LIKE YOU'RE BEING OVERLOOKED?
YOU'VE HAD YOUR TURN!
HAHAHA! DELIGHTFUL!
OH-HO?
IF I MAY BE SO BOLD, SIR, I SHARE METAL SONIC'S ENTHUSIASM.
PLEASE LET ME TAKE THE NEXT SHOT AT SONIC. I KNOW EXACTLY HOW TO STRIKE AT HIM.

ART BY KIERAN GATES

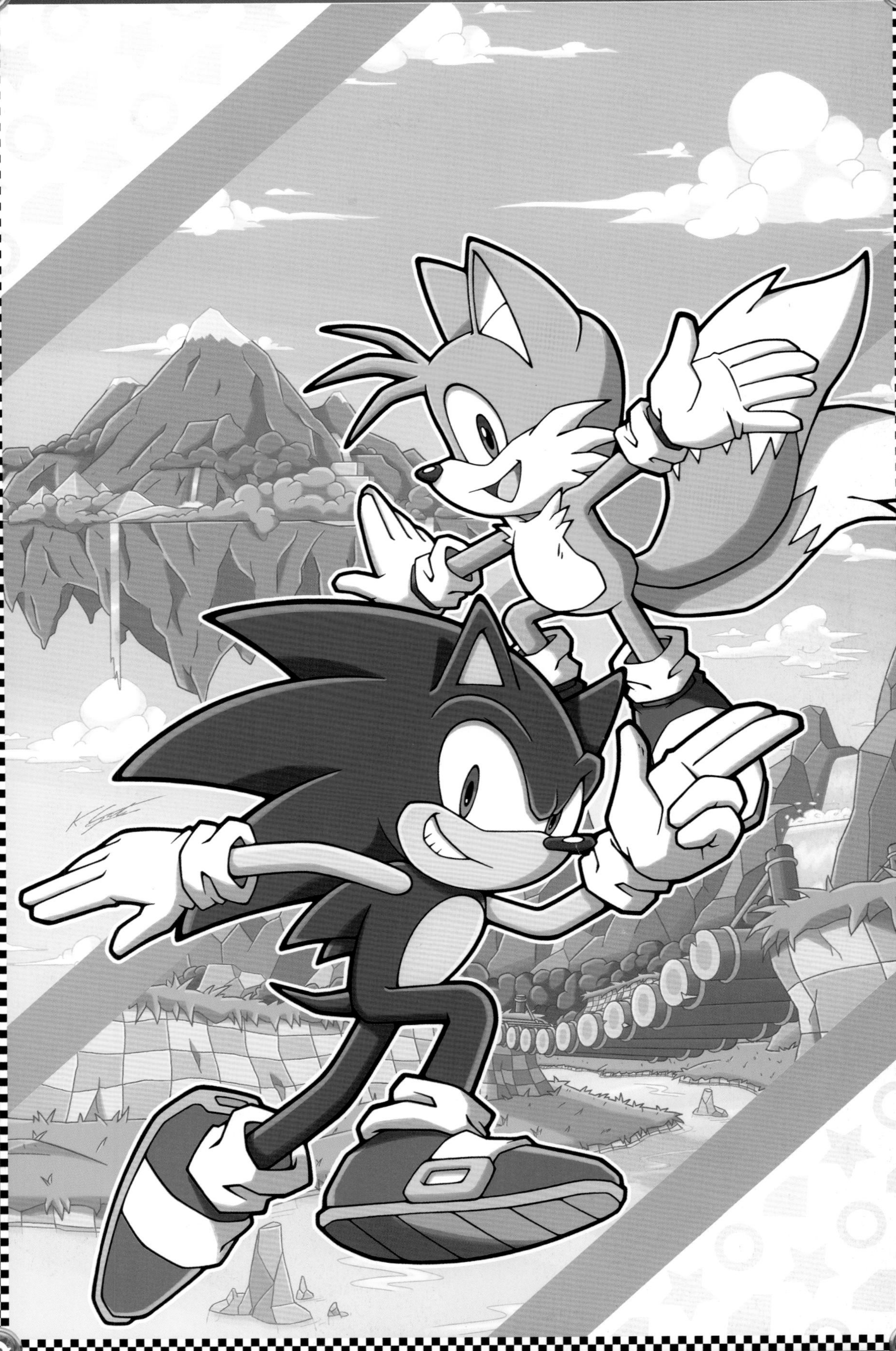

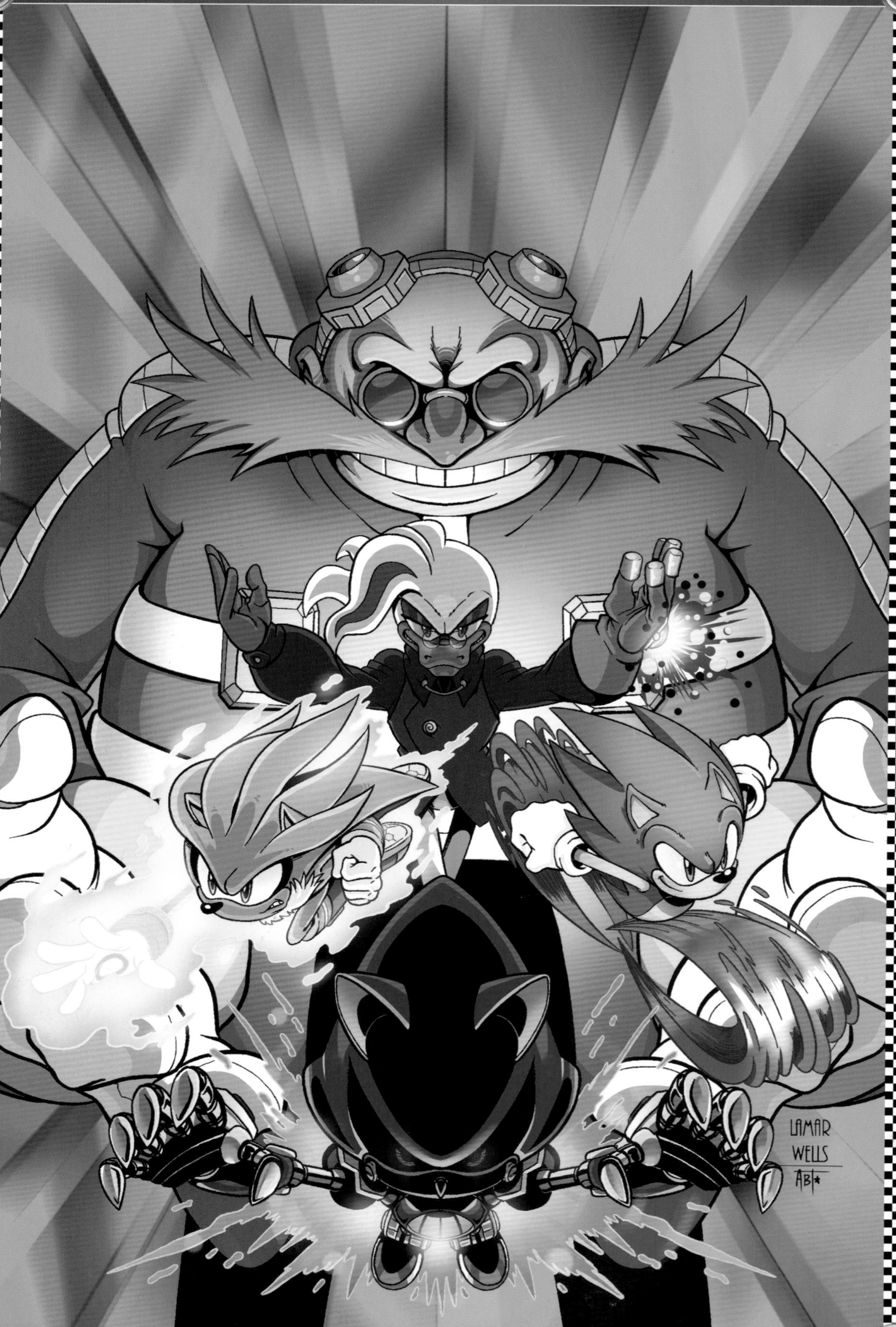
LAMAR
WELLS
ABT

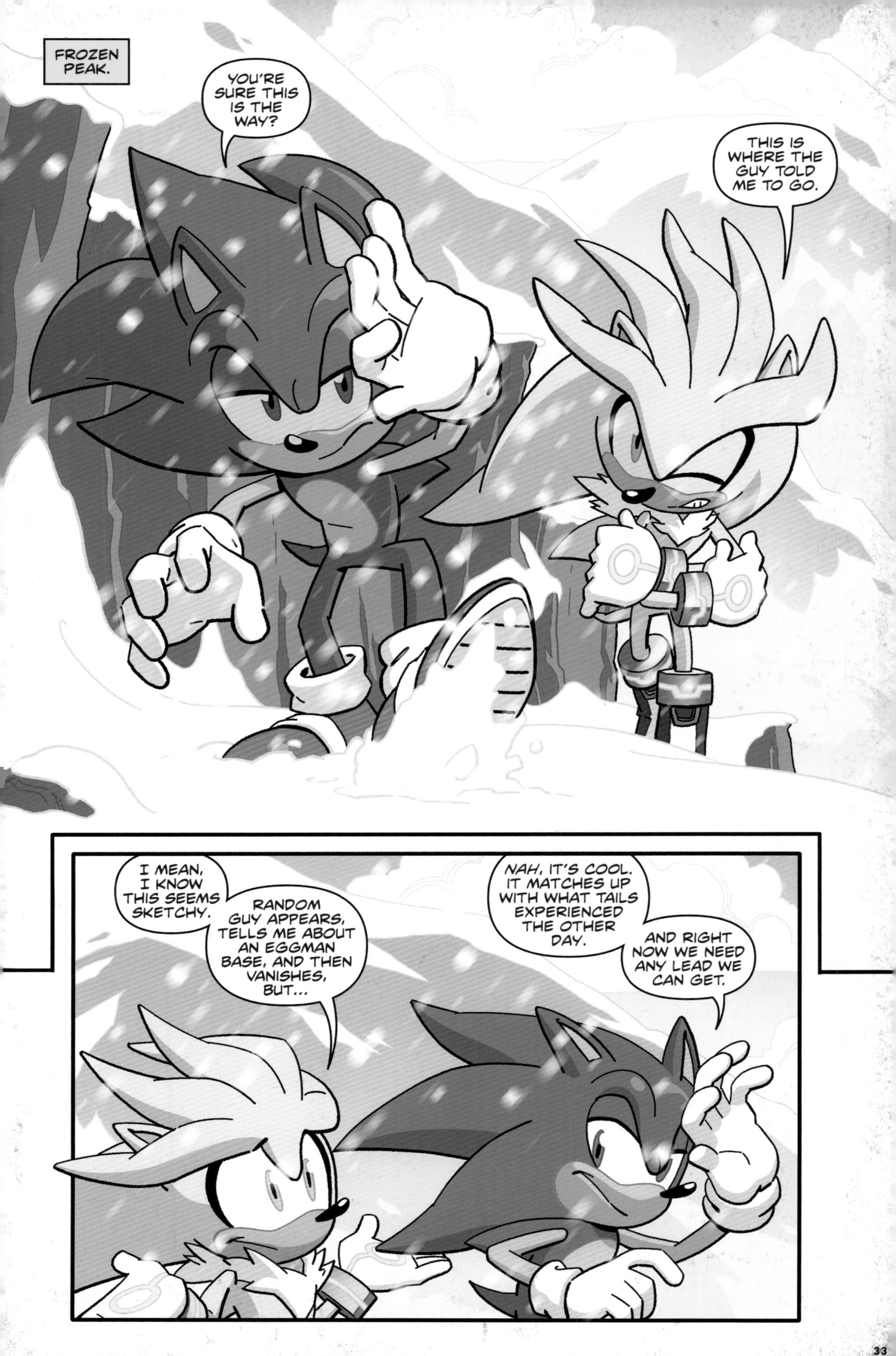
FROZEN PEAK.
YOU'RE SURE THIS IS THE WAY?
THIS IS WHERE THE GUY TOLD ME TO GO.
I MEAN, I KNOW THIS SEEMS SKETCHY.
RANDOM GUY APPEARS, TELLS ME ABOUT AN EGGMAN BASE, AND THEN VANISHES, BUT...
NAH, IT'S COOL. IT MATCHES UP WITH WHAT TAILS EXPERIENCED THE OTHER DAY.
AND RIGHT NOW WE NEED ANY LEAD WE CAN GET.

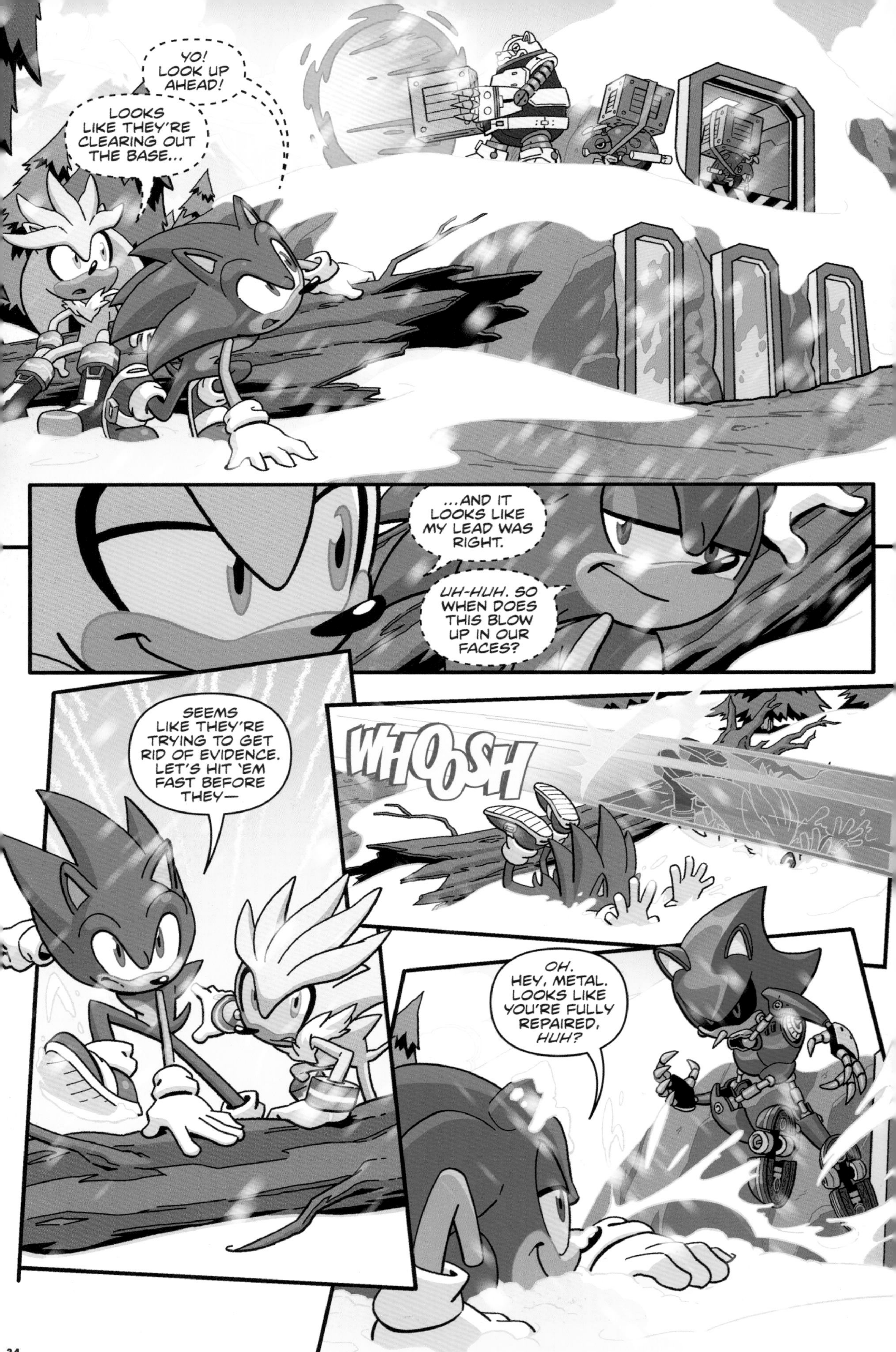
YO! LOOK UP AHEAD!
LOOKS LIKE THEY'RE CLEARING OUT THE BASE...
...AND IT LOOKS LIKE MY LEAD WAS RIGHT.
UH-HUH. SO WHEN DOES THIS BLOW UP IN OUR FACES?
SEEMS LIKE THEY'RE TRYING TO GET RID OF EVIDENCE. LET'S HIT 'EM FAST BEFORE THEY—
WHOOSH
OH. HEY, METAL. LOOKS LIKE YOU'RE FULLY REPAIRED, HUH?

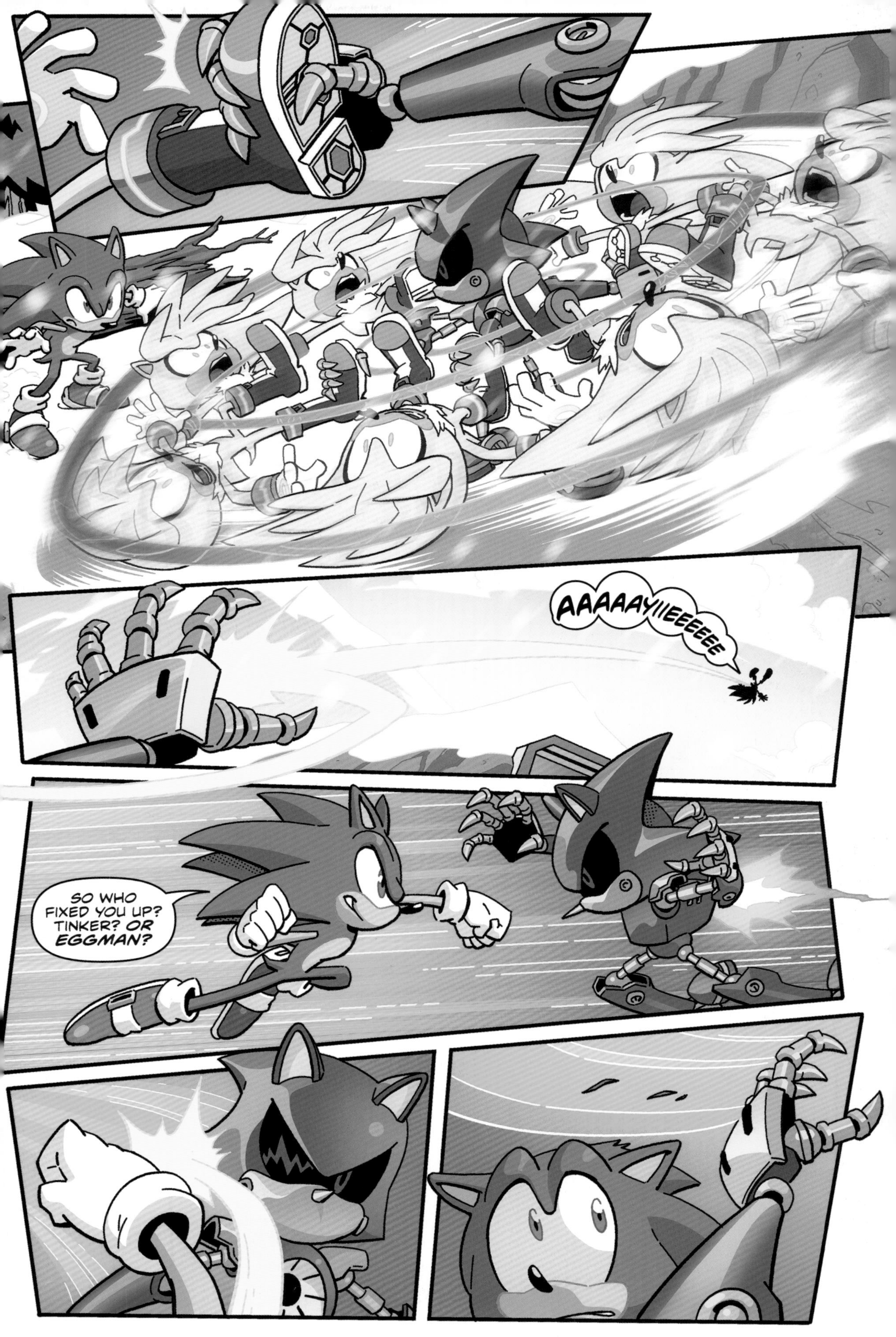
AAAAAYIIEEEEEE
SO WHO FIXED YOU UP? TINKER? OR EGGMAN?

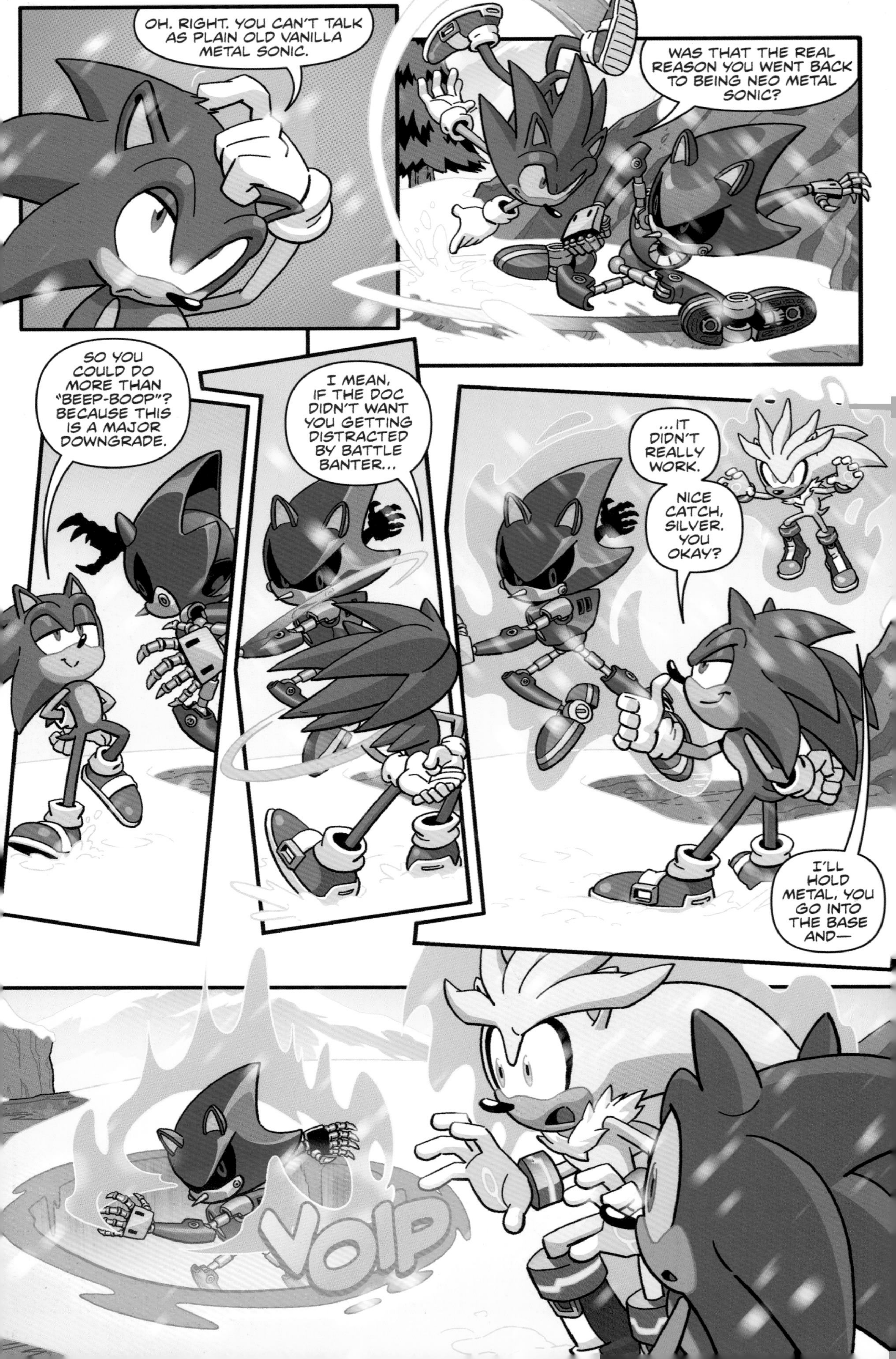
OH. RIGHT. YOU CAN'T TALK AS PLAIN OLD VANILLA METAL SONIC.
WAS THAT THE REAL REASON YOU WENT BACK TO BEING NEO METAL SONIC?
SO YOU COULD DO MORE THAN "BEEP-BOOP"? BECAUSE THIS IS A MAJOR DOWNGRADE.
I MEAN, IF THE DOC DIDN'T WANT YOU GETTING DISTRACTED BY BATTLE BANTER...
...IT DIDN'T REALLY WORK.
NICE CATCH, SILVER. YOU OKAY?
I'LL HOLD METAL, YOU GO INTO THE BASE AND—
VOIP

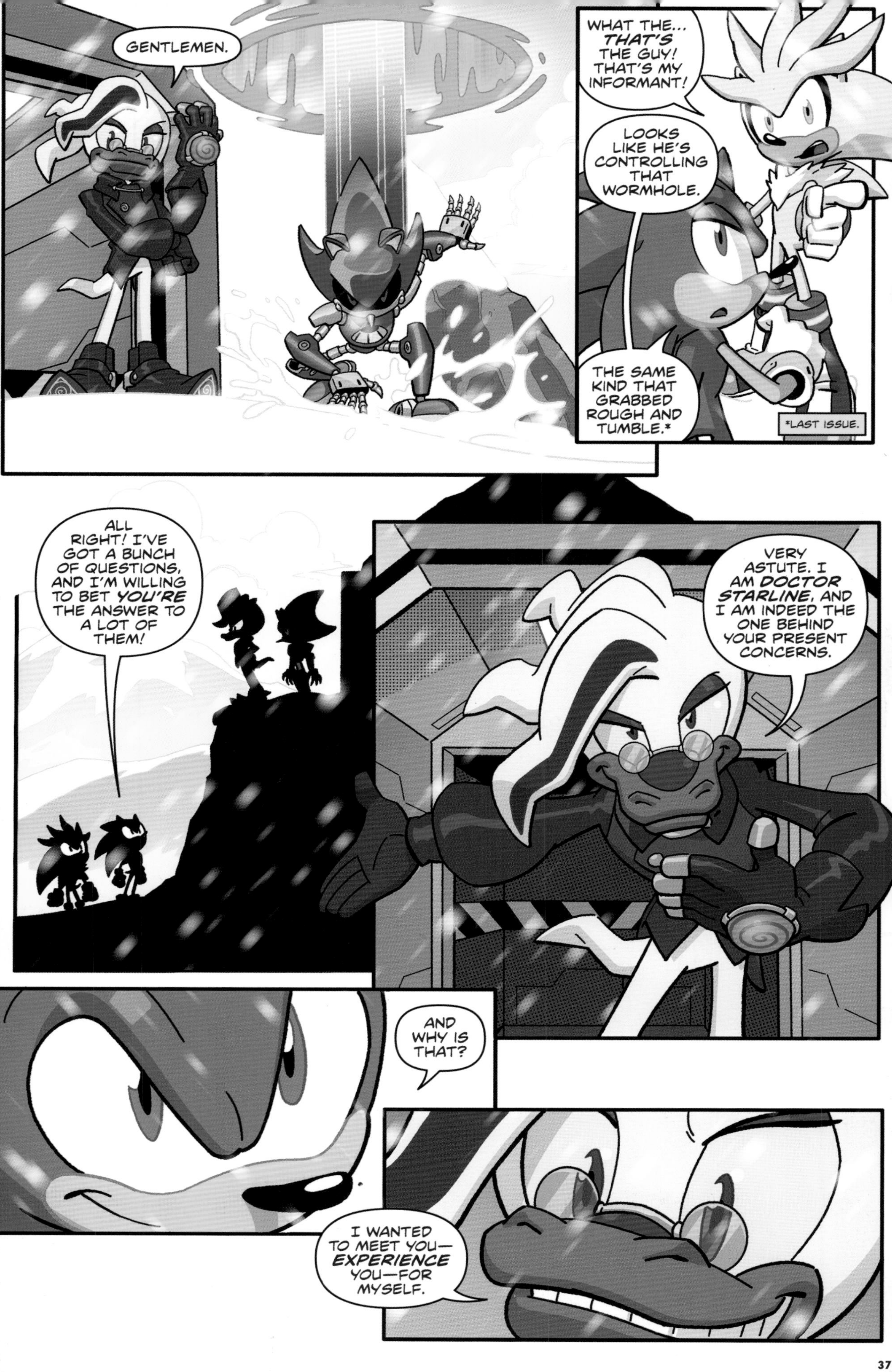
GENTLEMEN.
WHAT THE... *THAT'S* THE GUY! THAT'S MY INFORMANT!
LOOKS LIKE HE'S CONTROLLING THAT WORMHOLE.
THE SAME KIND THAT GRABBED ROUGH AND TUMBLE.*
*LAST ISSUE.
ALL RIGHT! I'VE GOT A BUNCH OF QUESTIONS, AND I'M WILLING TO BET *YOU'RE* THE ANSWER TO A LOT OF THEM!
VERY ASTUTE. I AM *DOCTOR STARLINE*, AND I AM INDEED THE ONE BEHIND YOUR PRESENT CONCERNS.
AND WHY IS THAT?
I WANTED TO MEET YOU— *EXPERIENCE* YOU—FOR MYSELF.

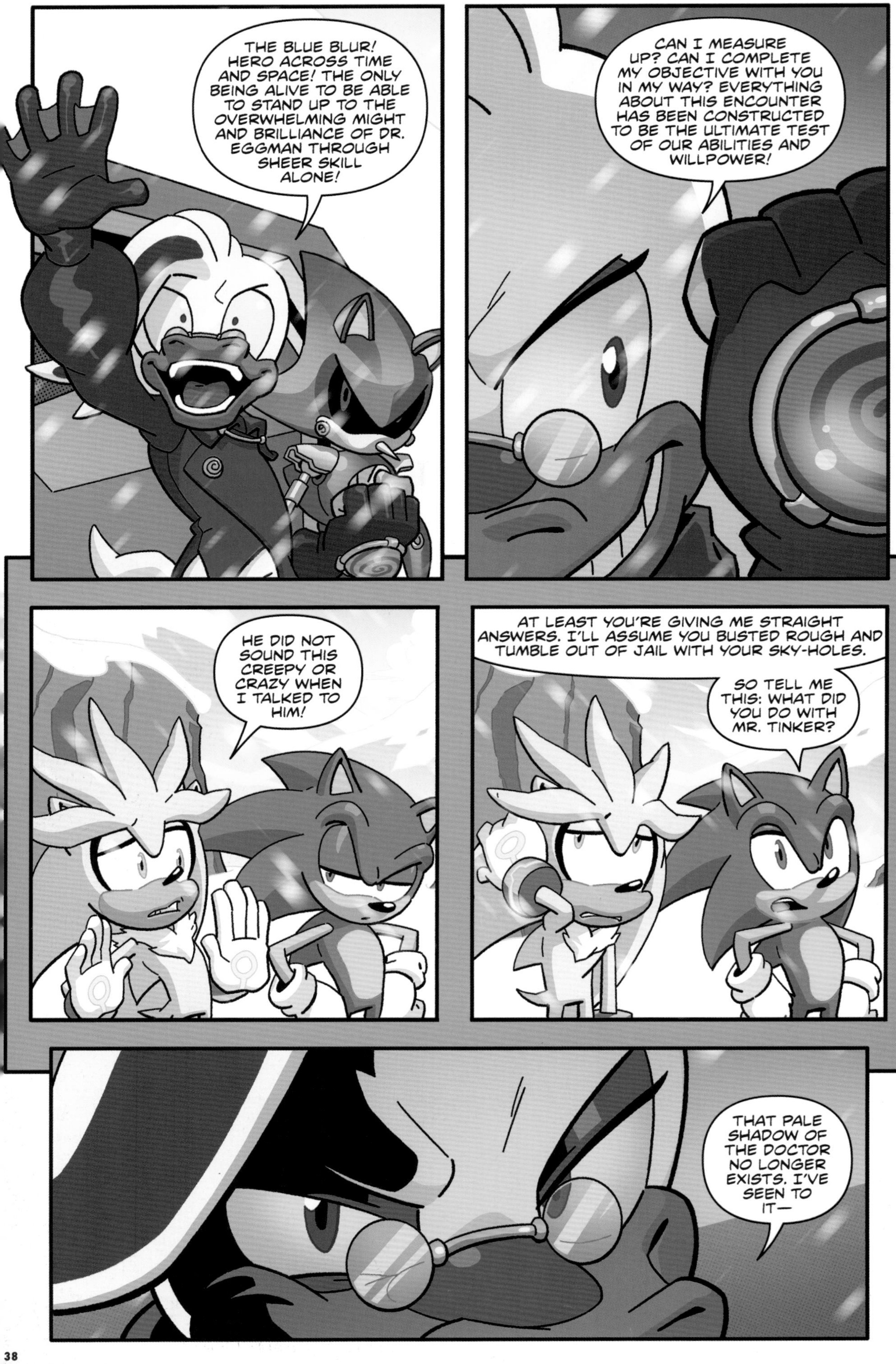
THE BLUE BLUR! HERO ACROSS TIME AND SPACE! THE ONLY BEING ALIVE TO BE ABLE TO STAND UP TO THE OVERWHELMING MIGHT AND BRILLIANCE OF DR. EGGMAN THROUGH SHEER SKILL ALONE!
CAN I MEASURE UP? CAN I COMPLETE MY OBJECTIVE WITH YOU IN MY WAY? EVERYTHING ABOUT THIS ENCOUNTER HAS BEEN CONSTRUCTED TO BE THE ULTIMATE TEST OF OUR ABILITIES AND WILLPOWER!
HE DID NOT SOUND THIS CREEPY OR CRAZY WHEN I TALKED TO HIM!
AT LEAST YOU'RE GIVING ME STRAIGHT ANSWERS. I'LL ASSUME YOU BUSTED ROUGH AND TUMBLE OUT OF JAIL WITH YOUR SKY-HOLES.
SO TELL ME THIS: WHAT DID YOU DO WITH MR. TINKER?
THAT PALE SHADOW OF THE DOCTOR NO LONGER EXISTS. I'VE SEEN TO IT—

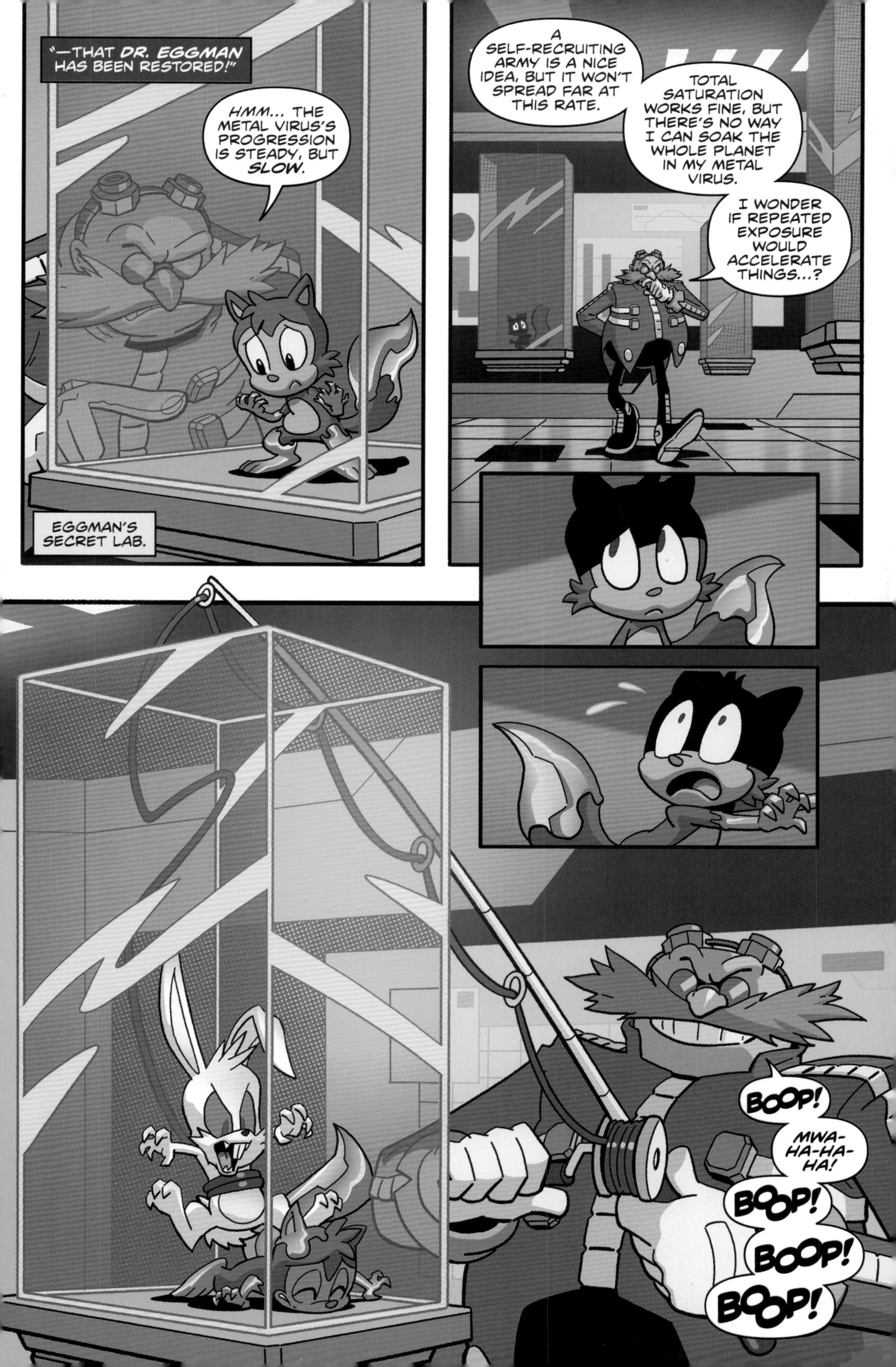
"—THAT DR. EGGMAN HAS BEEN RESTORED!"
HMM... THE METAL VIRUS'S PROGRESSION IS STEADY, BUT SLOW.
EGGMAN'S SECRET LAB.
A SELF-RECRUITING ARMY IS A NICE IDEA, BUT IT WON'T SPREAD FAR AT THIS RATE.
TOTAL SATURATION WORKS FINE, BUT THERE'S NO WAY I CAN SOAK THE WHOLE PLANET IN MY METAL VIRUS.
I WONDER IF REPEATED EXPOSURE WOULD ACCELERATE THINGS...?
BOOP!
MWA-HA-HA-HA!
BOOP!
BOOP!
BOOP!

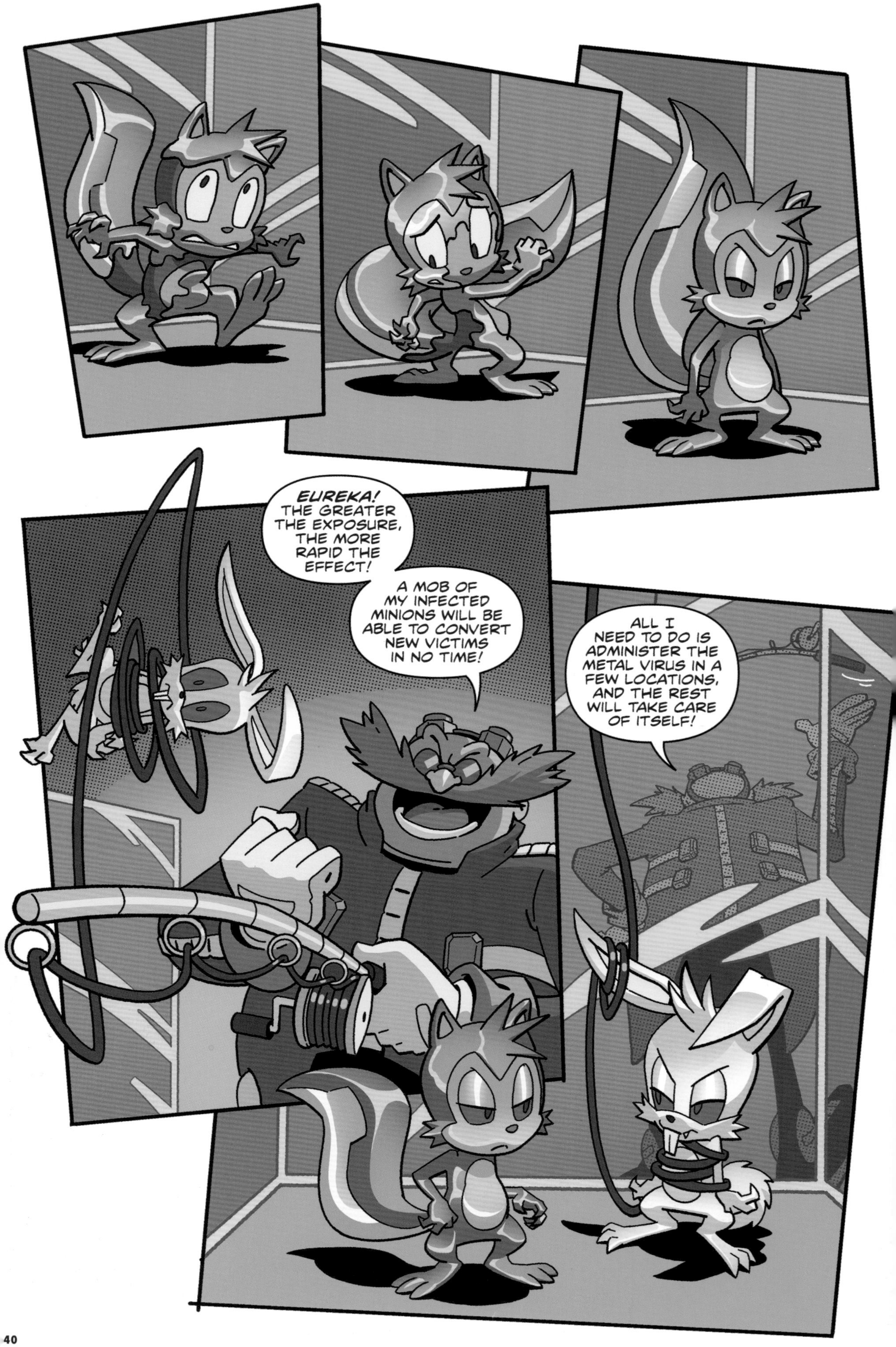
EUREKA! THE GREATER THE EXPOSURE, THE MORE RAPID THE EFFECT!
A MOB OF MY INFECTED MINIONS WILL BE ABLE TO CONVERT NEW VICTIMS IN NO TIME!
ALL I NEED TO DO IS ADMINISTER THE METAL VIRUS IN A FEW LOCATIONS, AND THE REST WILL TAKE CARE OF ITSELF!

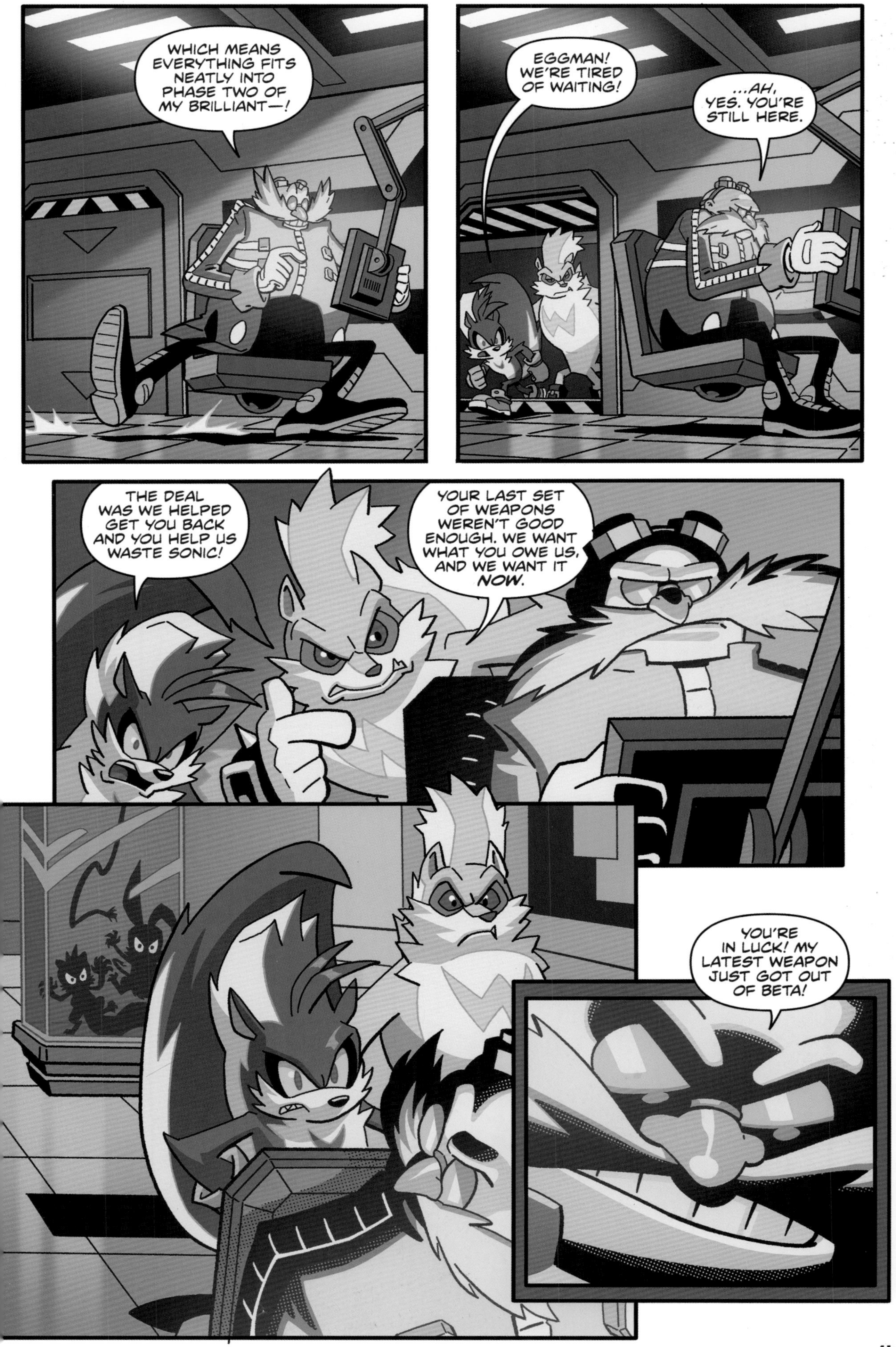
WHICH MEANS EVERYTHING FITS NEATLY INTO PHASE TWO OF MY BRILLIANT—!
EGGMAN! WE'RE TIRED OF WAITING!
...AH, YES. YOU'RE STILL HERE.
THE DEAL WAS WE HELPED GET YOU BACK AND YOU HELP US WASTE SONIC!
YOUR LAST SET OF WEAPONS WEREN'T GOOD ENOUGH. WE WANT WHAT YOU OWE US, AND WE WANT IT NOW.
YOU'RE IN LUCK! MY LATEST WEAPON JUST GOT OUT OF BETA!

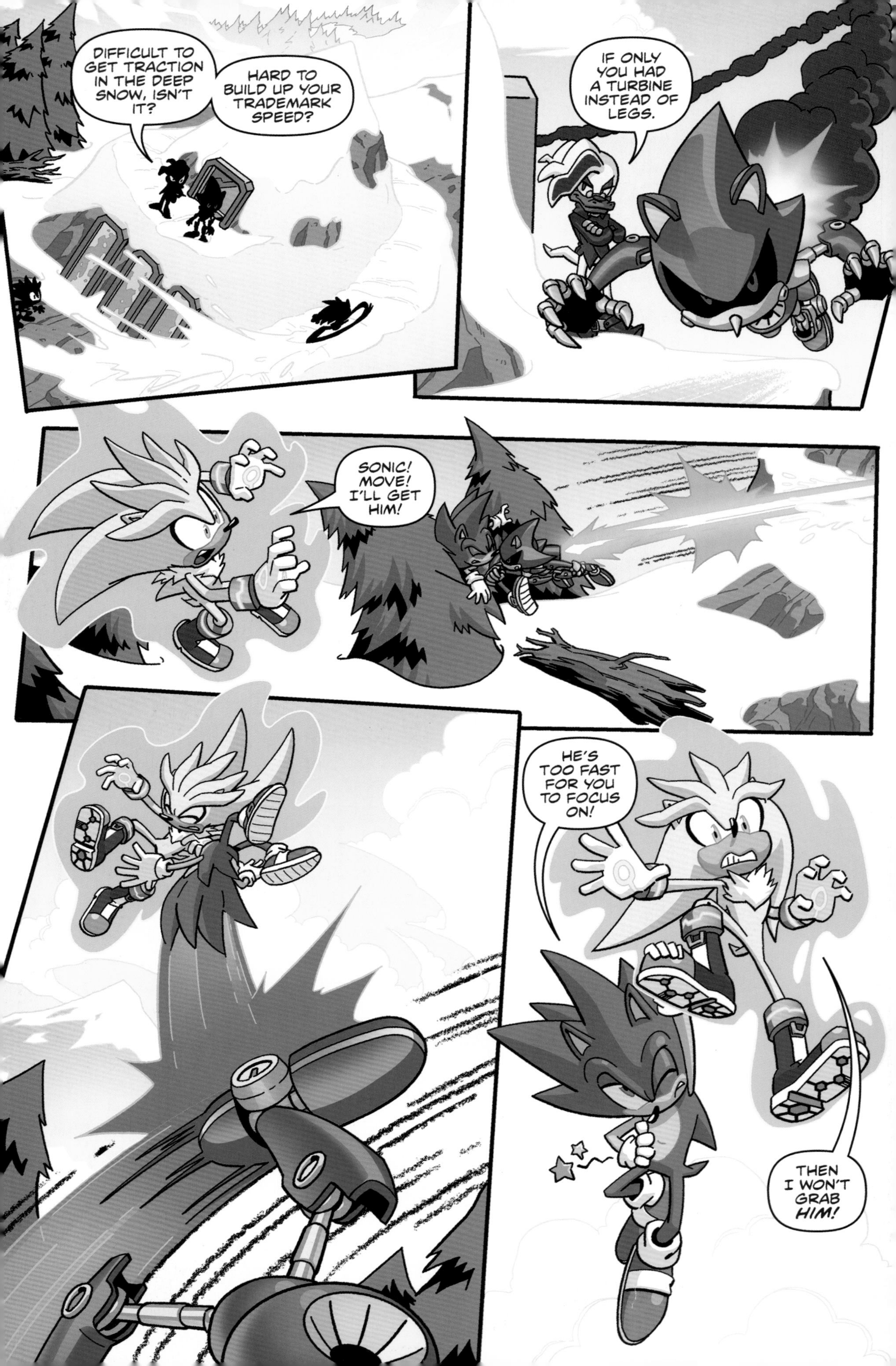
DIFFICULT TO GET TRACTION IN THE DEEP SNOW, ISN'T IT?
HARD TO BUILD UP YOUR TRADEMARK SPEED?
IF ONLY YOU HAD A TURBINE INSTEAD OF LEGS.
SONIC! MOVE! I'LL GET HIM!
HE'S TOO FAST FOR YOU TO FOCUS ON!
THEN I WON'T GRAB *HIM!*

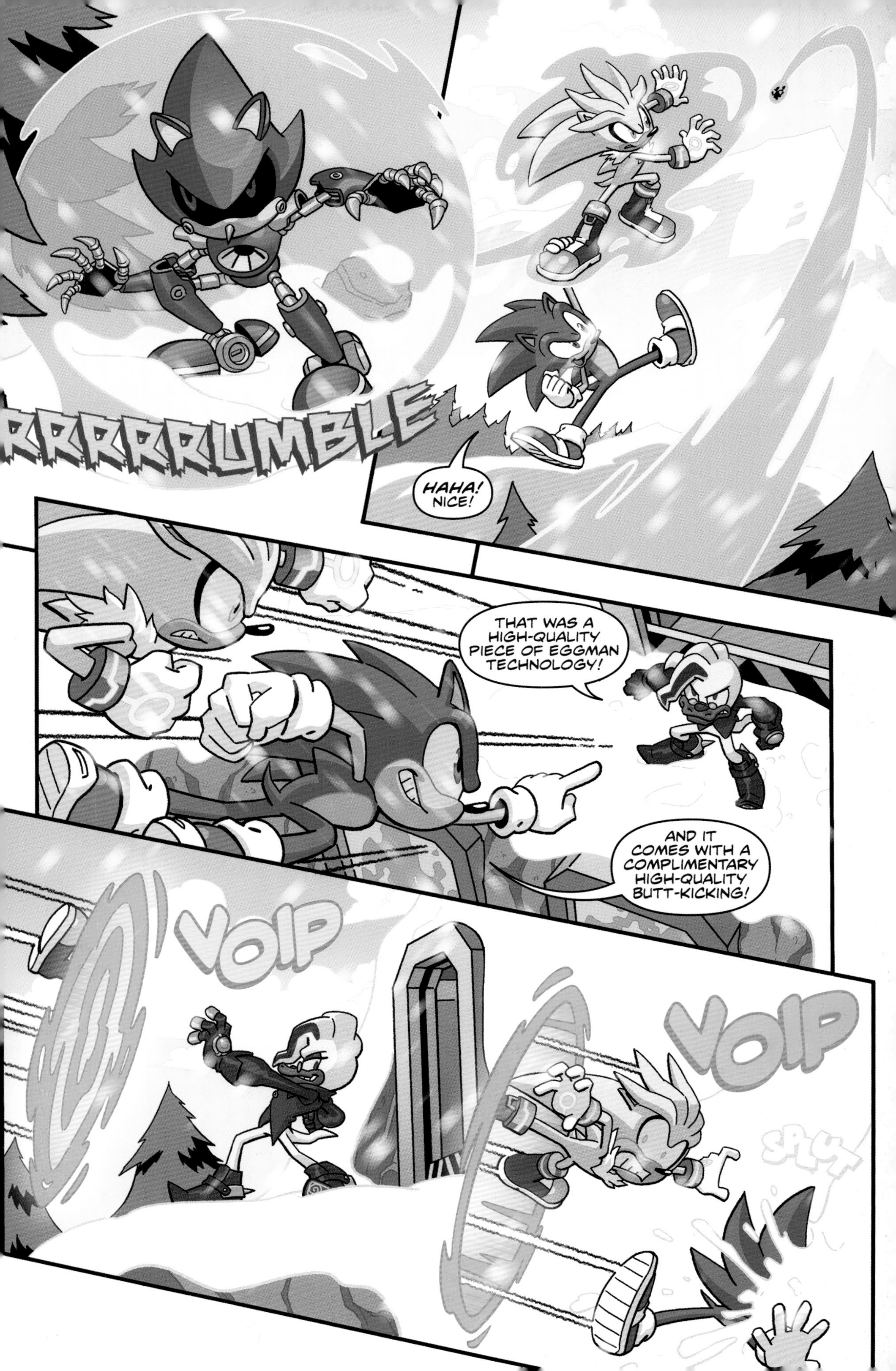
RRRRRRUMBLE
HAHA! NICE!
THAT WAS A HIGH-QUALITY PIECE OF EGGMAN TECHNOLOGY!
AND IT COMES WITH A COMPLIMENTARY HIGH-QUALITY BUTT-KICKING!
VOIP
VOIP

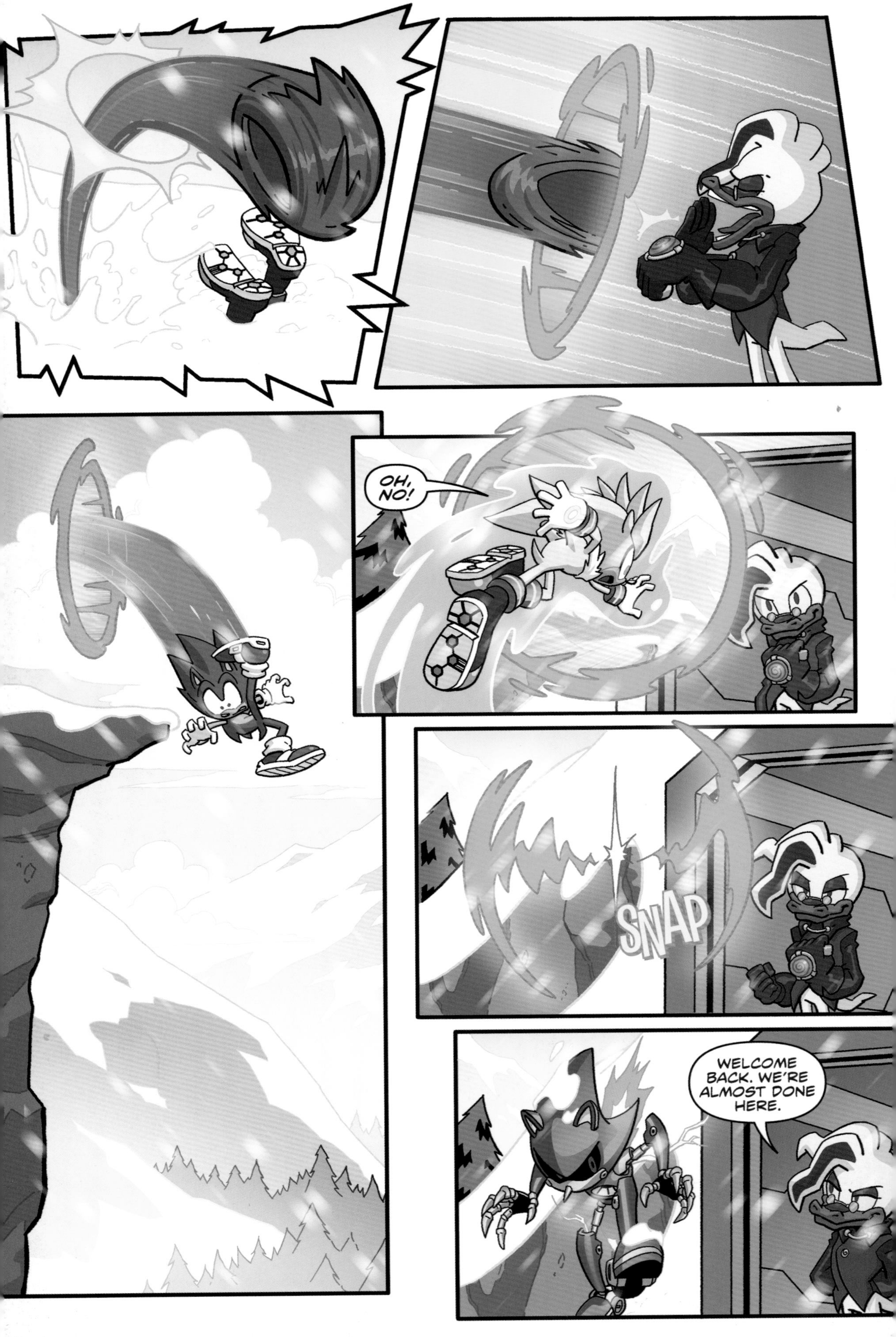
OH, NO!
SNAP
WELCOME BACK. WE'RE ALMOST DONE HERE.

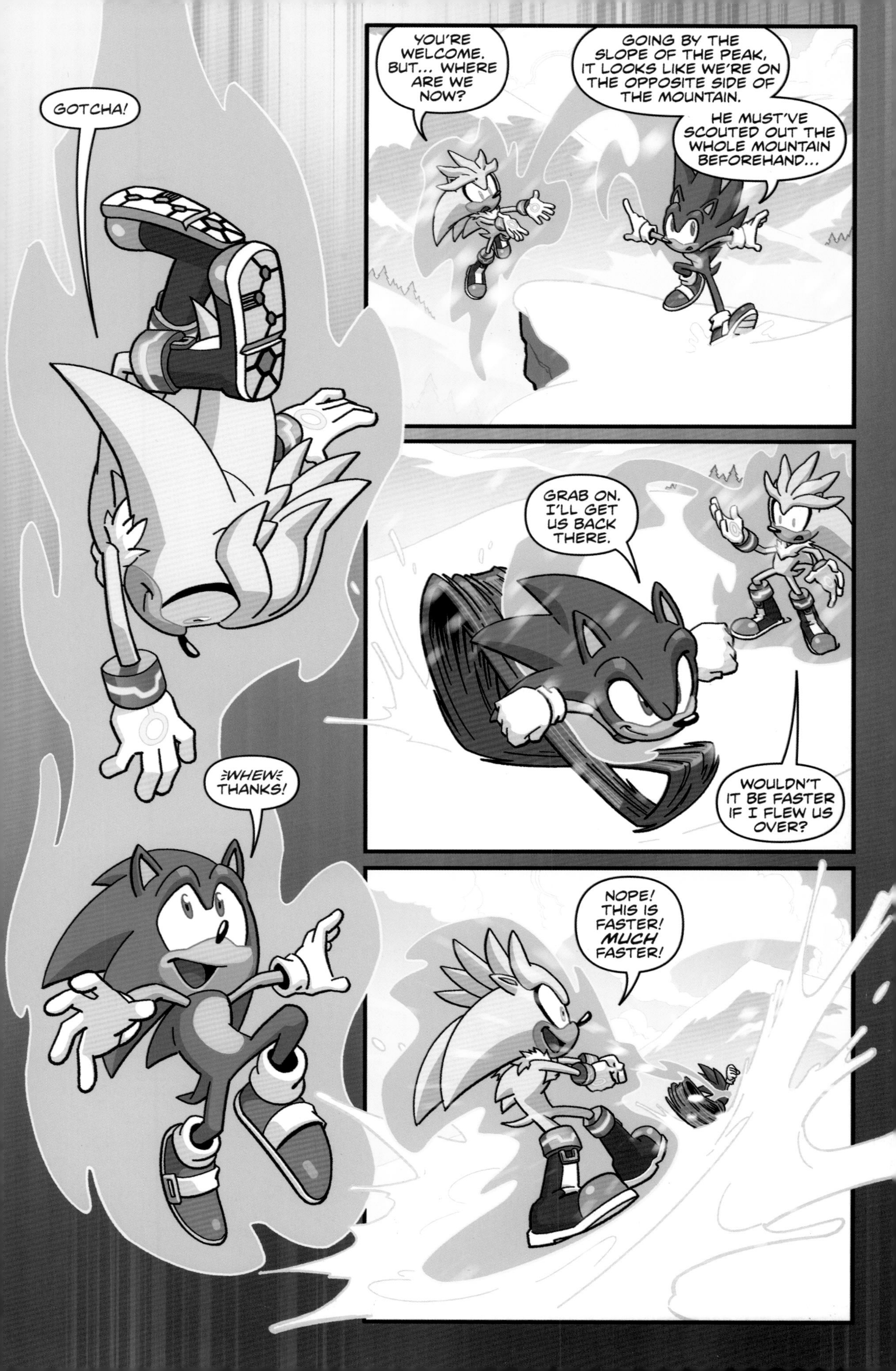
GOTCHA!
YOU'RE WELCOME. BUT... WHERE ARE WE NOW?
GOING BY THE SLOPE OF THE PEAK, IT LOOKS LIKE WE'RE ON THE OPPOSITE SIDE OF THE MOUNTAIN.
HE MUST'VE SCOUTED OUT THE WHOLE MOUNTAIN BEFOREHAND...
GRAB ON. I'LL GET US BACK THERE.
WOULDN'T IT BE FASTER IF I FLEW US OVER?
WHEW THANKS!
NOPE! THIS IS FASTER! MUCH FASTER!

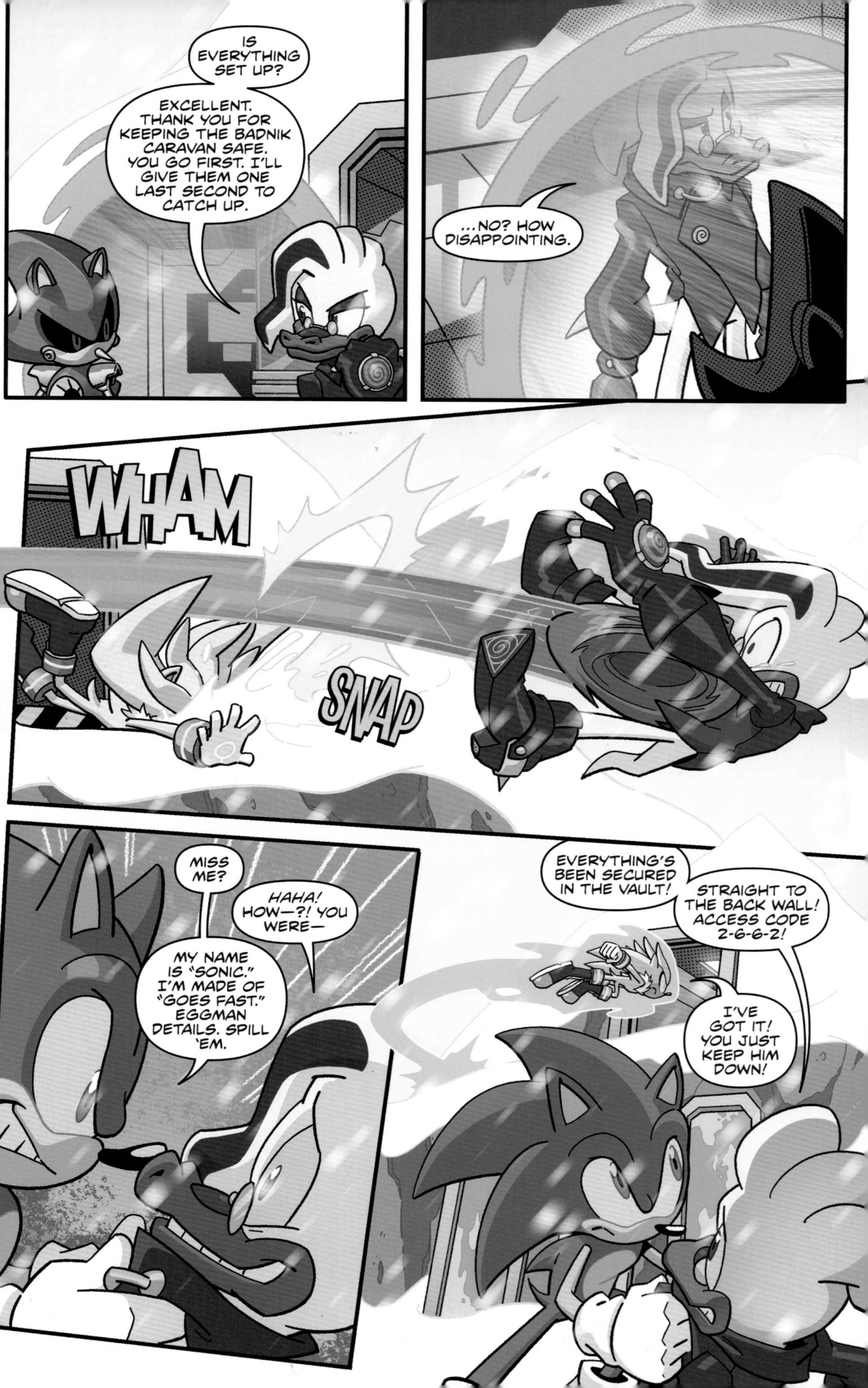
IS EVERYTHING SET UP?
EXCELLENT. THANK YOU FOR KEEPING THE BADNIK CARAVAN SAFE. YOU GO FIRST. I'LL GIVE THEM ONE LAST SECOND TO CATCH UP.
...NO? HOW DISAPPOINTING.
WHAM
SNAP
MISS ME?
HAHA! HOW—?! YOU WERE—
MY NAME IS "SONIC." I'M MADE OF "GOES FAST." EGGMAN DETAILS. SPILL 'EM.
EVERYTHING'S BEEN SECURED IN THE VAULT!
STRAIGHT TO THE BACK WALL! ACCESS CODE 2-6-6-2!
I'VE GOT IT! YOU JUST KEEP HIM DOWN!

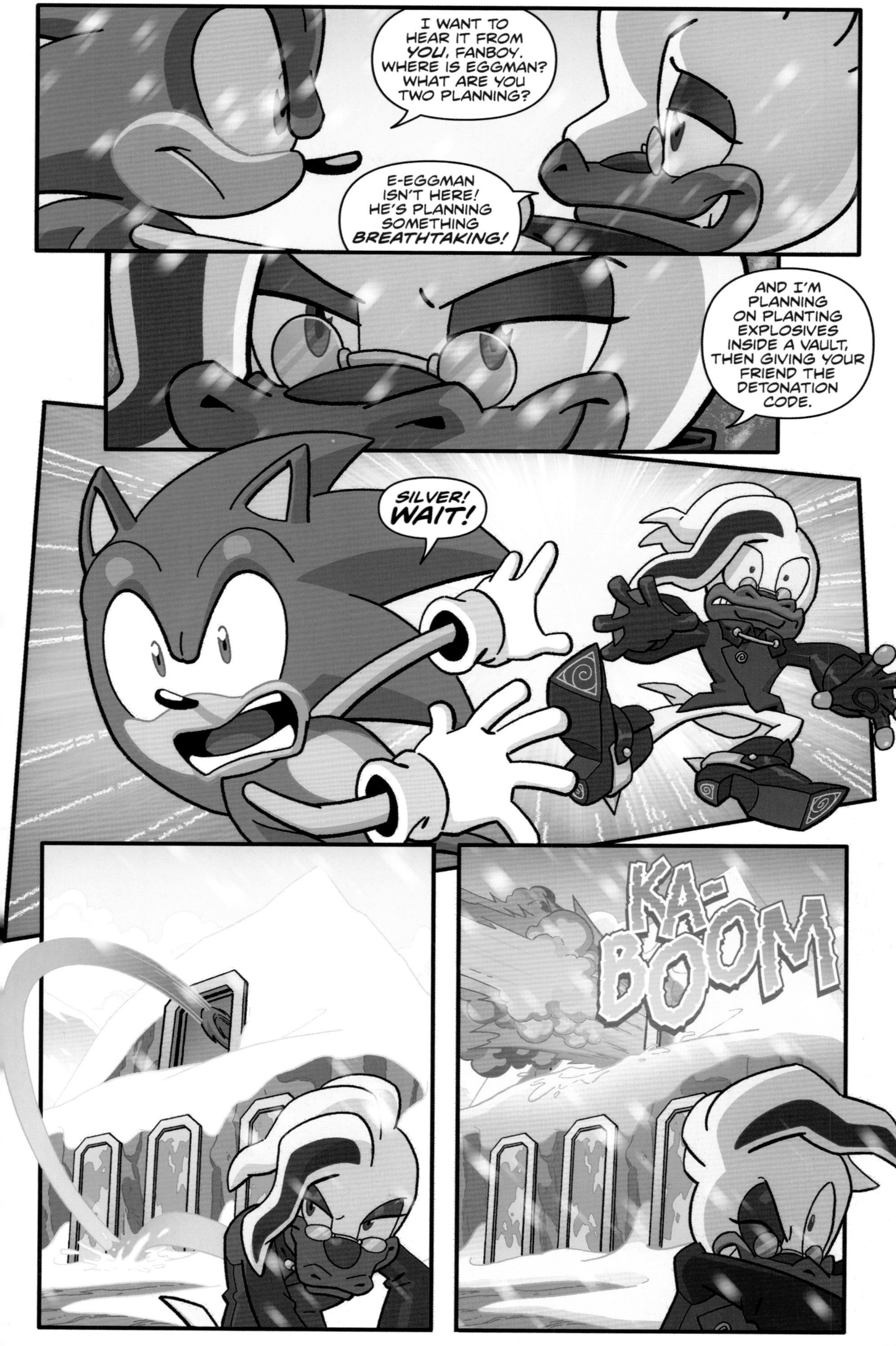
I WANT TO HEAR IT FROM YOU, FANBOY. WHERE IS EGGMAN? WHAT ARE YOU TWO PLANNING?
E-EGGMAN ISN'T HERE! HE'S PLANNING SOMETHING BREATHTAKING!
AND I'M PLANNING ON PLANTING EXPLOSIVES INSIDE A VAULT, THEN GIVING YOUR FRIEND THE DETONATION CODE.
SILVER! WAIT!
KA-BOOM

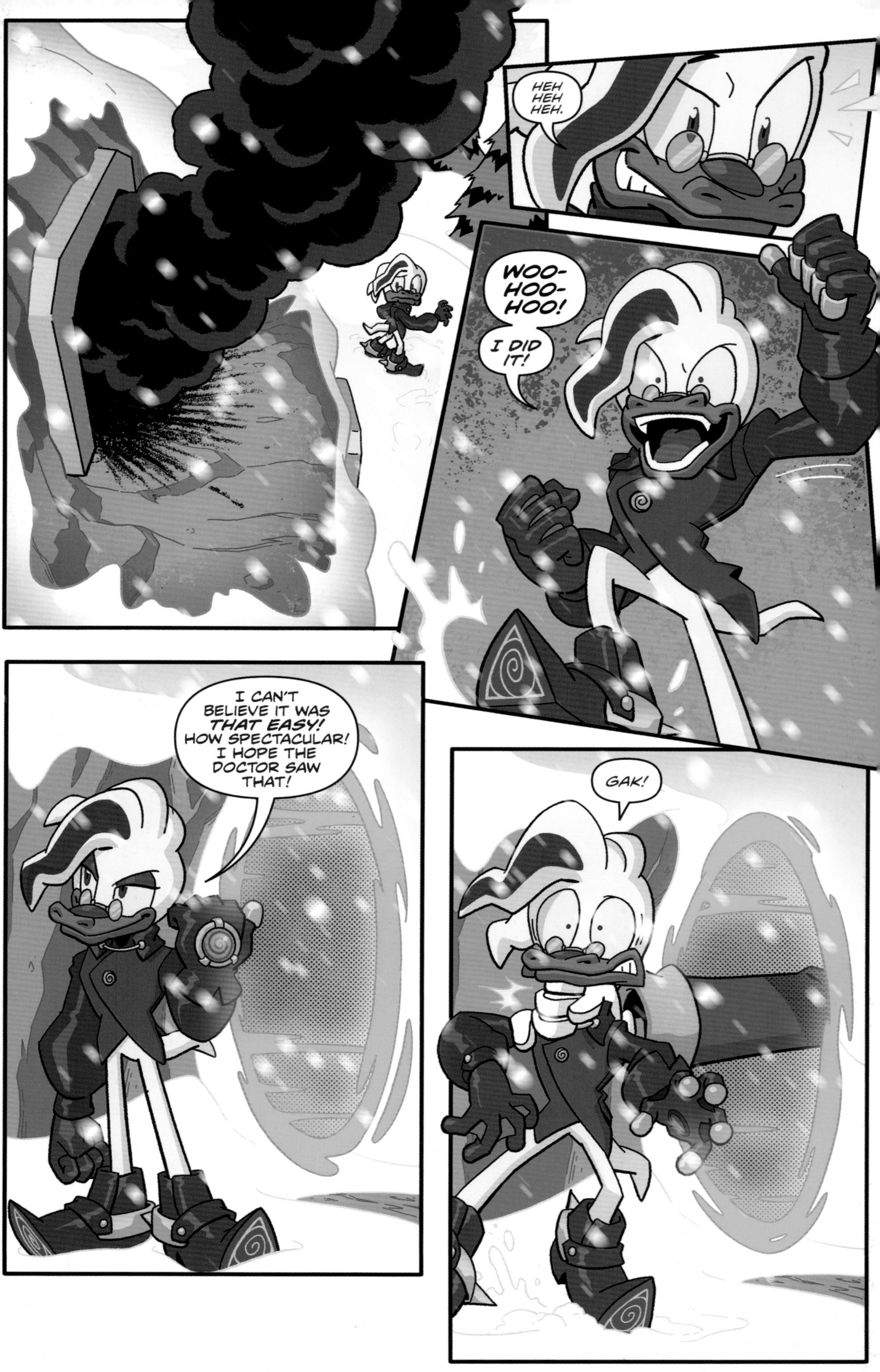
HEH HEH HEH.
WOO-HOO-HOO!
I DID IT!
I CAN'T BELIEVE IT WAS THAT EASY! HOW SPECTACULAR! I HOPE THE DOCTOR SAW THAT!
GAK!

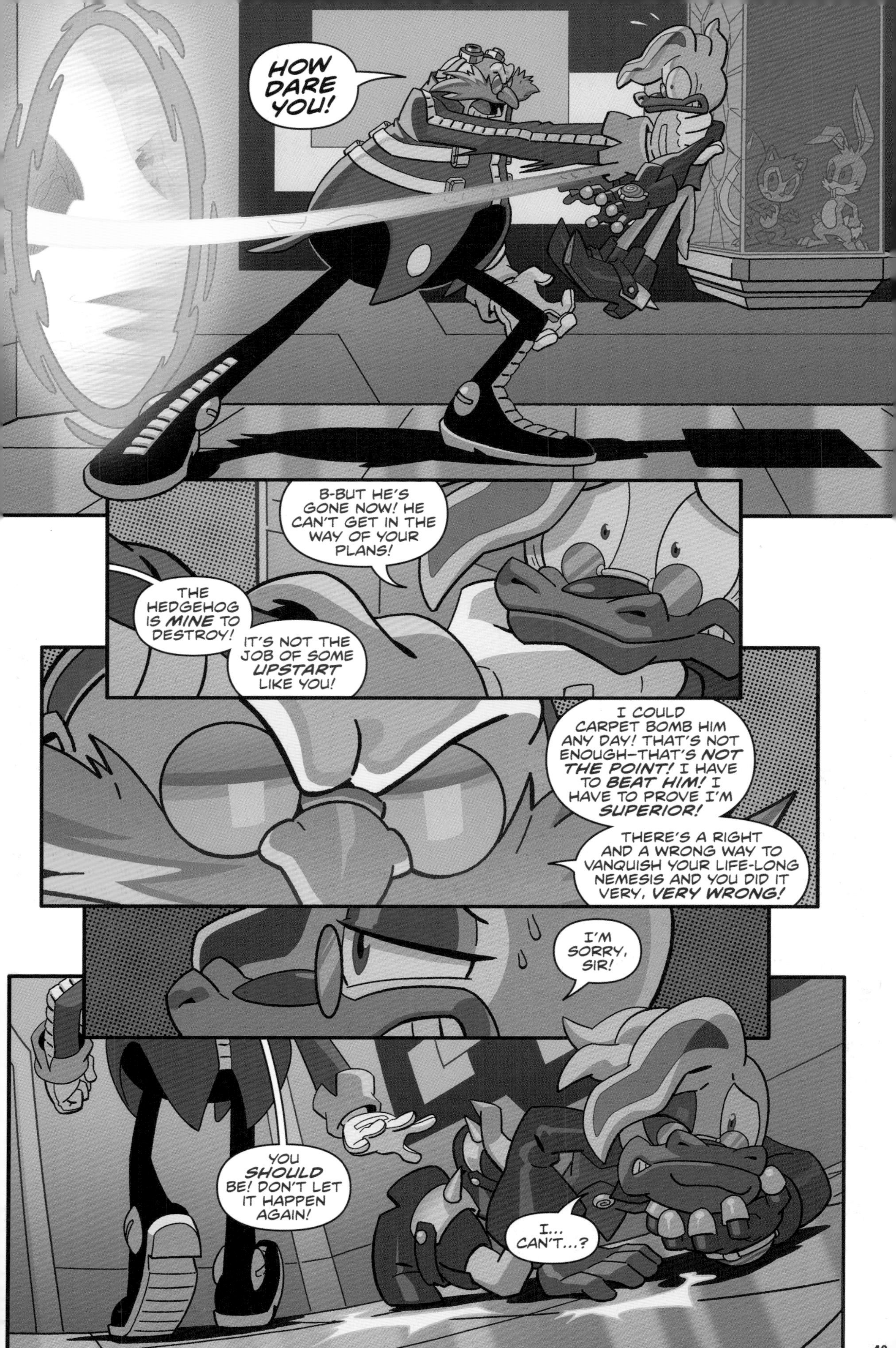
HOW DARE YOU!
B-BUT HE'S GONE NOW! HE CAN'T GET IN THE WAY OF YOUR PLANS!
THE HEDGEHOG IS MINE TO DESTROY!
IT'S NOT THE JOB OF SOME UPSTART LIKE YOU!
I COULD CARPET BOMB HIM ANY DAY! THAT'S NOT ENOUGH–THAT'S NOT THE POINT! I HAVE TO BEAT HIM! I HAVE TO PROVE I'M SUPERIOR!
THERE'S A RIGHT AND A WRONG WAY TO VANQUISH YOUR LIFE-LONG NEMESIS AND YOU DID IT VERY, VERY WRONG!
I'M SORRY, SIR!
YOU SHOULD BE! DON'T LET IT HAPPEN AGAIN!
I... CAN'T...?

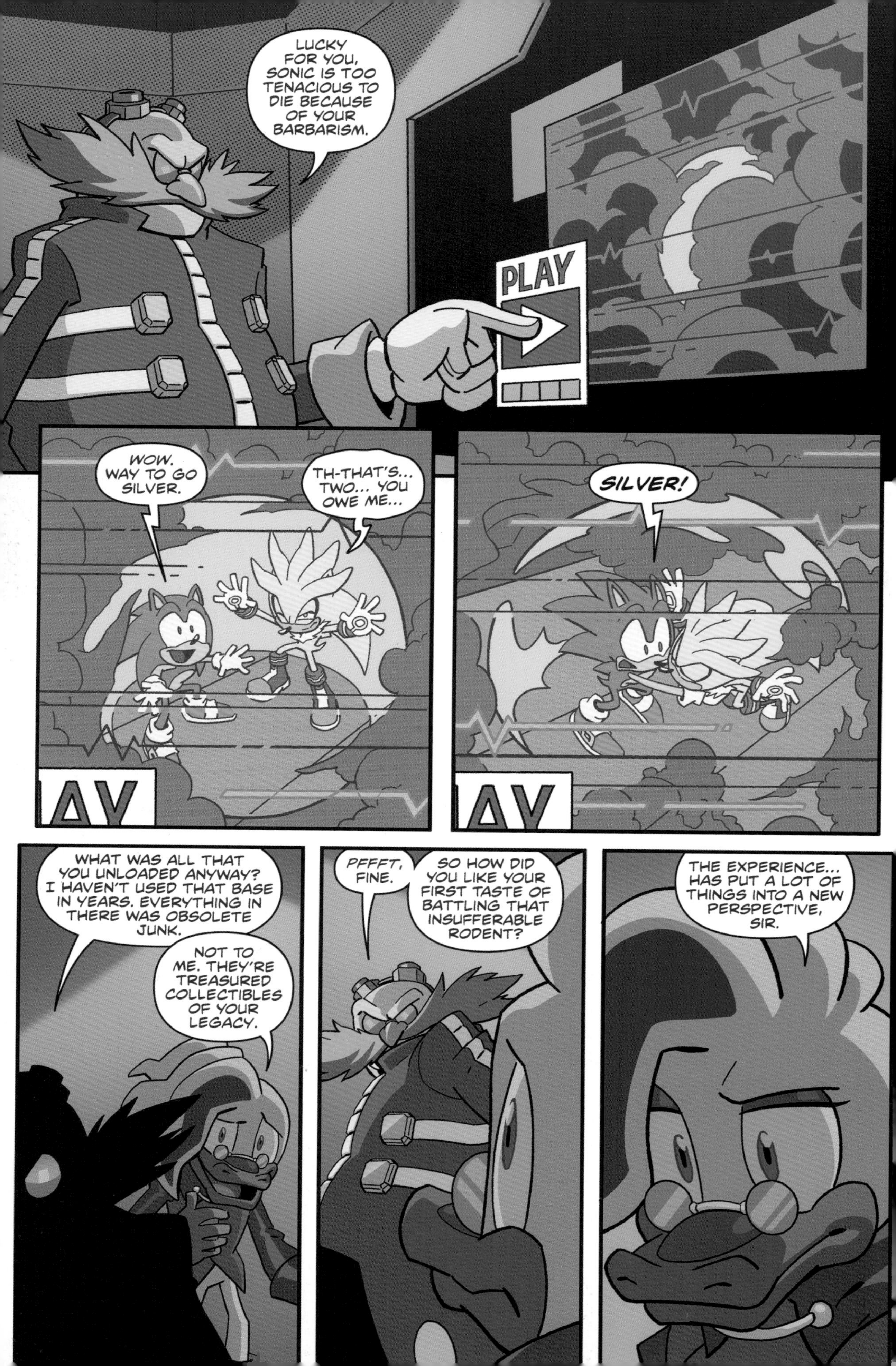
LUCKY FOR YOU, SONIC IS TOO TENACIOUS TO DIE BECAUSE OF YOUR BARBARISM.
PLAY
WOW. WAY TO GO SILVER.
TH-THAT'S... TWO... YOU OWE ME...
AY
SILVER!
AY
WHAT WAS ALL THAT YOU UNLOADED ANYWAY? I HAVEN'T USED THAT BASE IN YEARS. EVERYTHING IN THERE WAS OBSOLETE JUNK.
NOT TO ME. THEY'RE TREASURED COLLECTIBLES OF YOUR LEGACY.
PFFFT, FINE.
SO HOW DID YOU LIKE YOUR FIRST TASTE OF BATTLING THAT INSUFFERABLE RODENT?
THE EXPERIENCE... HAS PUT A LOT OF THINGS INTO A NEW PERSPECTIVE, SIR.

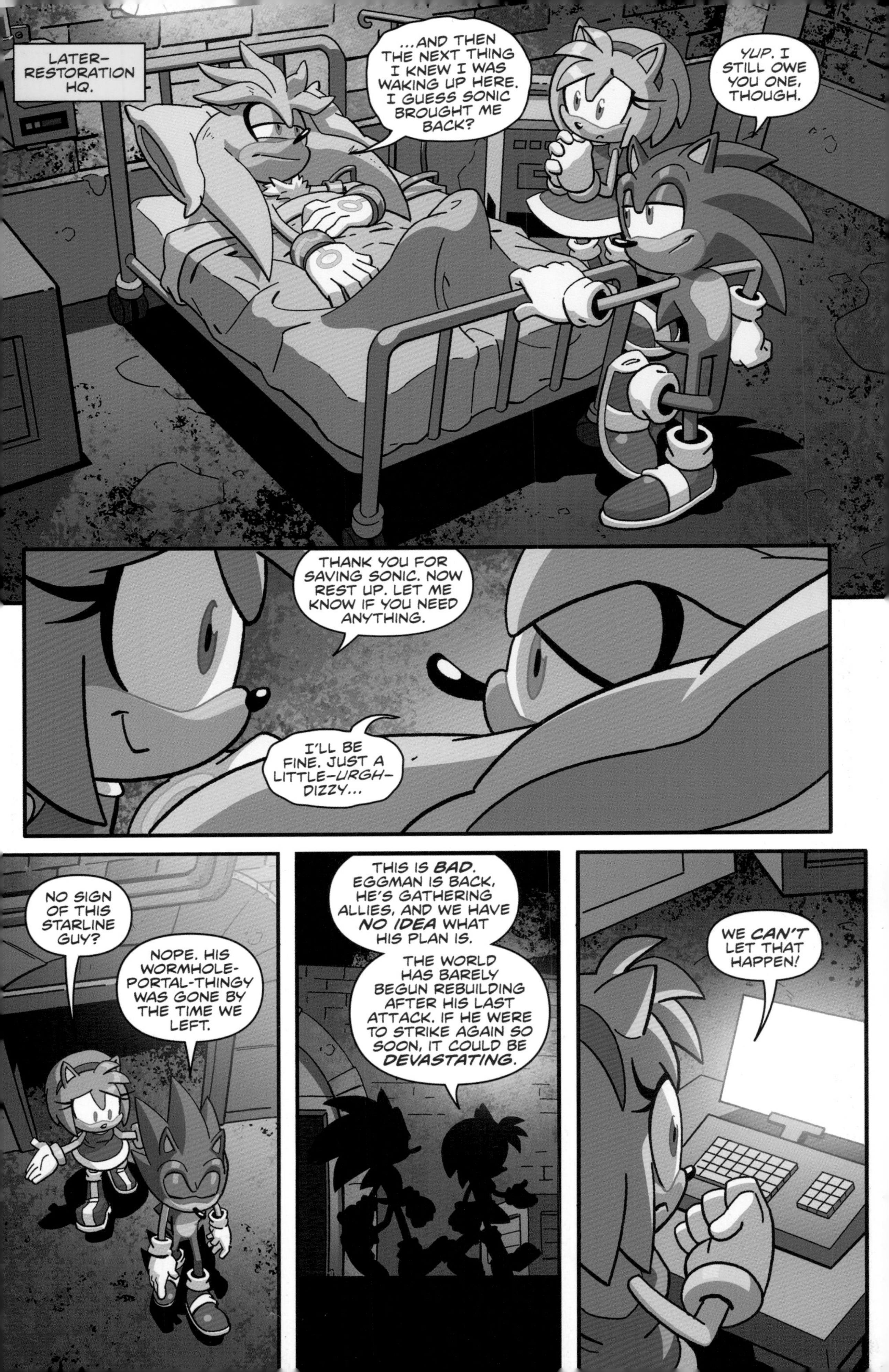
LATER-RESTORATION HQ.
...AND THEN THE NEXT THING I KNEW I WAS WAKING UP HERE. I GUESS SONIC BROUGHT ME BACK?
YUP. I STILL OWE YOU ONE, THOUGH.
THANK YOU FOR SAVING SONIC. NOW REST UP. LET ME KNOW IF YOU NEED ANYTHING.
I'LL BE FINE. JUST A LITTLE-URGH-DIZZY...
NO SIGN OF THIS STARLINE GUY?
NOPE. HIS WORMHOLE-PORTAL-THINGY WAS GONE BY THE TIME WE LEFT.
THIS IS BAD. EGGMAN IS BACK, HE'S GATHERING ALLIES, AND WE HAVE NO IDEA WHAT HIS PLAN IS.
THE WORLD HAS BARELY BEGUN REBUILDING AFTER HIS LAST ATTACK. IF HE WERE TO STRIKE AGAIN SO SOON, IT COULD BE DEVASTATING.
WE CAN'T LET THAT HAPPEN!

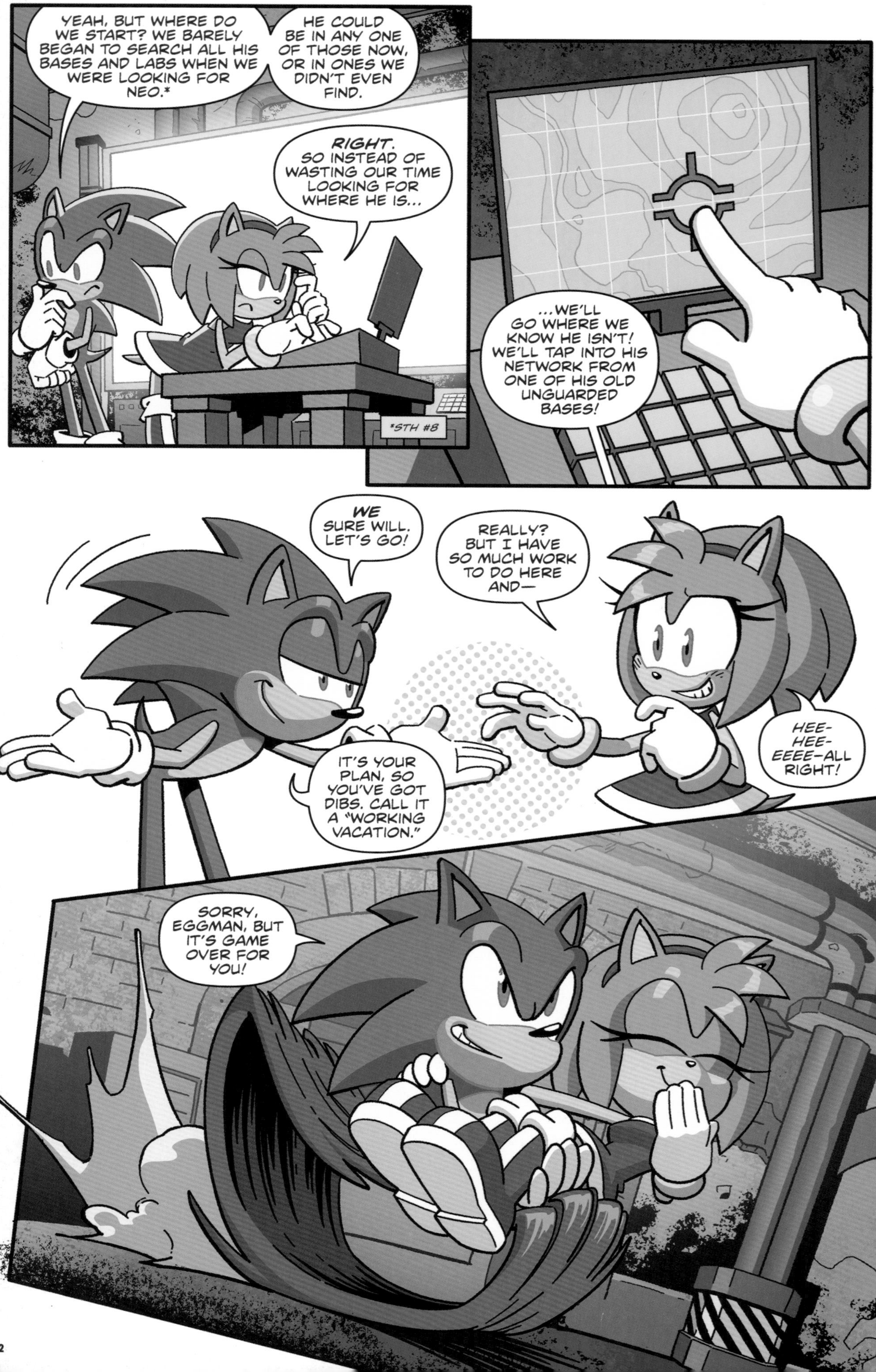
YEAH, BUT WHERE DO WE START? WE BARELY BEGAN TO SEARCH ALL HIS BASES AND LABS WHEN WE WERE LOOKING FOR NEO.*
HE COULD BE IN ANY ONE OF THOSE NOW, OR IN ONES WE DIDN'T EVEN FIND.
RIGHT. SO INSTEAD OF WASTING OUR TIME LOOKING FOR WHERE HE IS...
*STH #8
...WE'LL GO WHERE WE KNOW HE ISN'T! WE'LL TAP INTO HIS NETWORK FROM ONE OF HIS OLD UNGUARDED BASES!
WE SURE WILL. LET'S GO!
REALLY? BUT I HAVE SO MUCH WORK TO DO HERE AND—
IT'S YOUR PLAN, SO YOU'VE GOT DIBS. CALL IT A "WORKING VACATION."
HEE-HEE-EEEE—ALL RIGHT!
SORRY, EGGMAN, BUT IT'S GAME OVER FOR YOU!

ART BY JONATHAN GRAY COLORS BY REGGIE GRAHAM

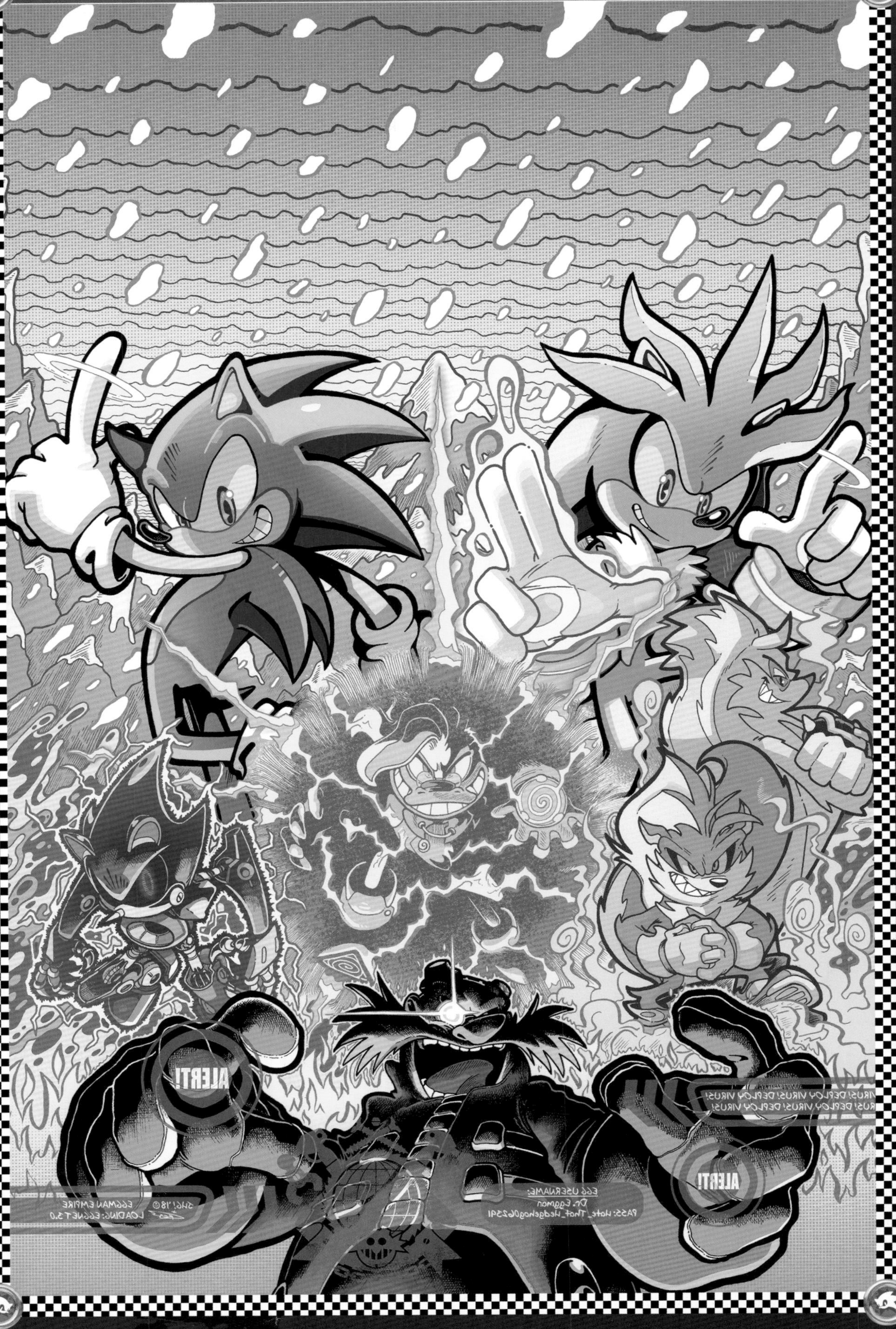
ALERT!
ALERT!

ART BY JACK LAWRENCE COLORS BY MATT HERMS

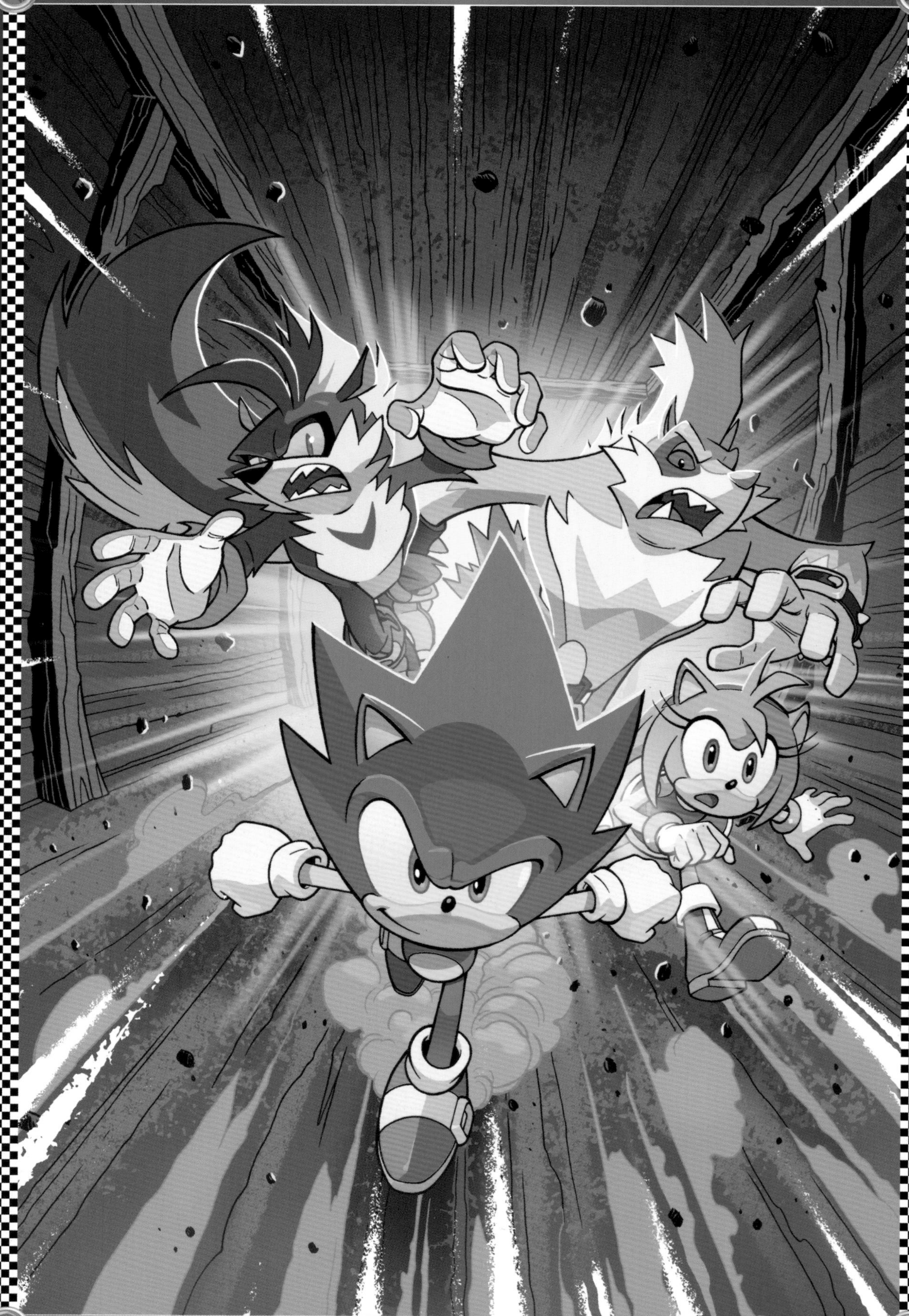

SONIC THE HEDGEHOG #15

ECHO MINE.

Y'KNOW WHAT I LIKE BEST ABOUT EGGMAN?

WHAT'S THAT?

HIS SUBTLETY.

LOOKS LIKE THERE WAS A HECK OF A BATTLE HERE.

THERE WAS! THIS WAS WHERE ONE OF OUR BIGGEST COUNTER-ATTACKS AGAINST DR. EGGMAN'S FORCES HAPPENED BEFORE YOU CAME BACK TO US.

WE WERE ABLE TO LIBERATE A LOT OF PEOPLE THAT DAY.

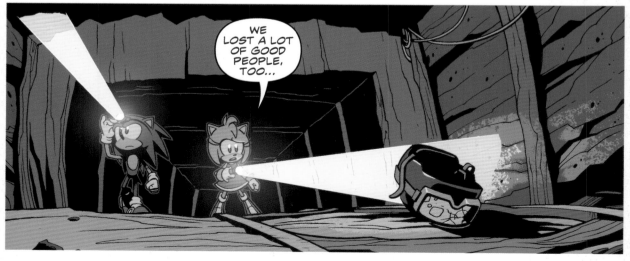

WE LOST A LOT OF GOOD PEOPLE, TOO...

HEY— YOU MADE SURE IT WAS WORTH IT.

YOU WON THE WAR FOR US.

WELL, YEAH. SAVING THE DAY IS WHAT I DO.

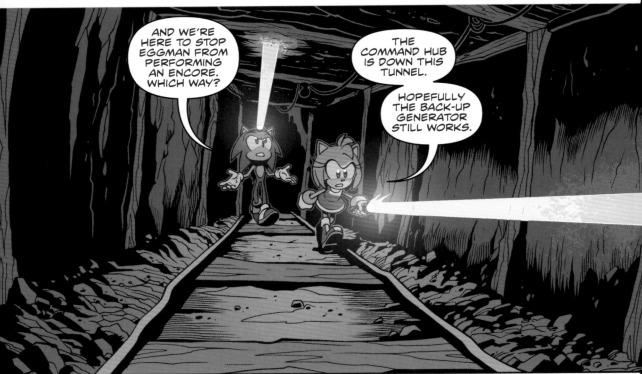

AND WE'RE HERE TO STOP EGGMAN FROM PERFORMING AN ENCORE. WHICH WAY?

THE COMMAND HUB IS DOWN THIS TUNNEL.

HOPEFULLY THE BACK-UP GENERATOR STILL WORKS.

WITH A LITTLE LUCK, WE'LL BE ABLE TO BOOT UP HIS COMPUTER, ACCESS HIS NETWORK, AND FIND OUT WHAT HE'S PLANNING!

SILVER AND I SAW HIS BADNIKS EMPTYING A DEFUNCT LAB, THOUGH.* HOW DO YOU KNOW HE HASN'T DONE THE SAME THING HERE?

I DON'T. BUT THIS IS THE CLOSEST ABANDONED BASE ON FILE, SO IT'S THE BEST PLACE TO START!

*LAST ISSUE.

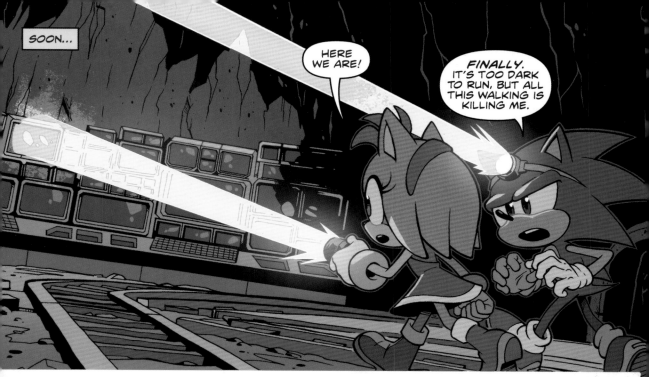

SOON...

HERE WE ARE!

FINALLY. IT'S TOO DARK TO RUN, BUT ALL THIS WALKING IS KILLING ME.

PLEASE-OH-PLEASE WORK...

KA-CHUNK

CLICK-CLICK-HUMMMM

WOO-HOO! WE'RE IN BUSINESS.

MAN, NOT EVEN RESERVE BADNIKS? SNORE-FEST.

eggnet

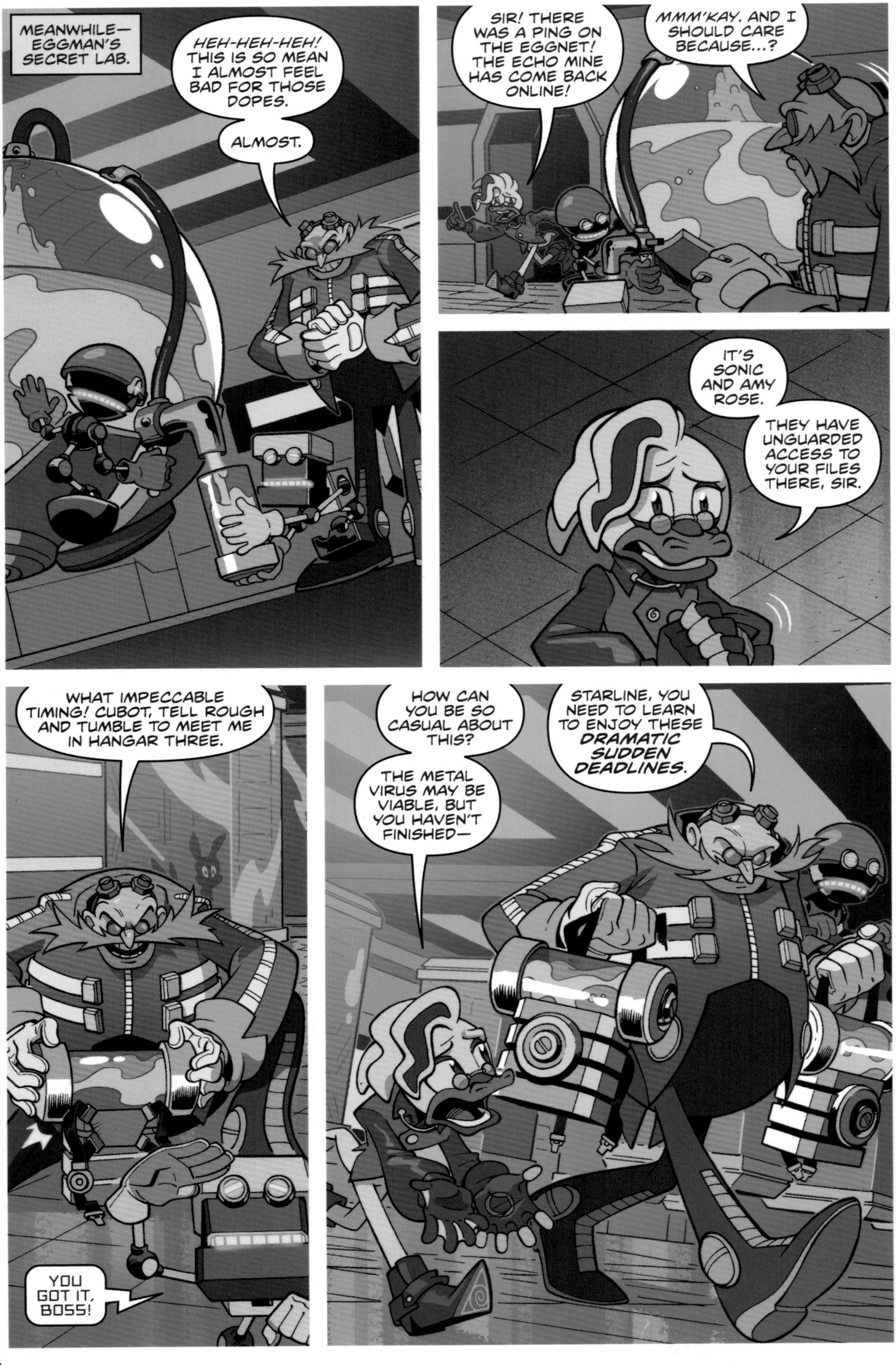
MEANWHILE— EGGMAN'S SECRET LAB.
HEH-HEH-HEH! THIS IS SO MEAN I ALMOST FEEL BAD FOR THOSE DOPES.
ALMOST.
SIR! THERE WAS A PING ON THE EGGNET! THE ECHO MINE HAS COME BACK ONLINE!
MMM'KAY. AND I SHOULD CARE BECAUSE...?
IT'S SONIC AND AMY ROSE.
THEY HAVE UNGUARDED ACCESS TO YOUR FILES THERE, SIR.
WHAT IMPECCABLE TIMING! CUBOT, TELL ROUGH AND TUMBLE TO MEET ME IN HANGAR THREE.
YOU GOT IT, BOSS!
HOW CAN YOU BE SO CASUAL ABOUT THIS?
THE METAL VIRUS MAY BE VIABLE, BUT YOU HAVEN'T FINISHED—
STARLINE, YOU NEED TO LEARN TO ENJOY THESE DRAMATIC SUDDEN DEADLINES.

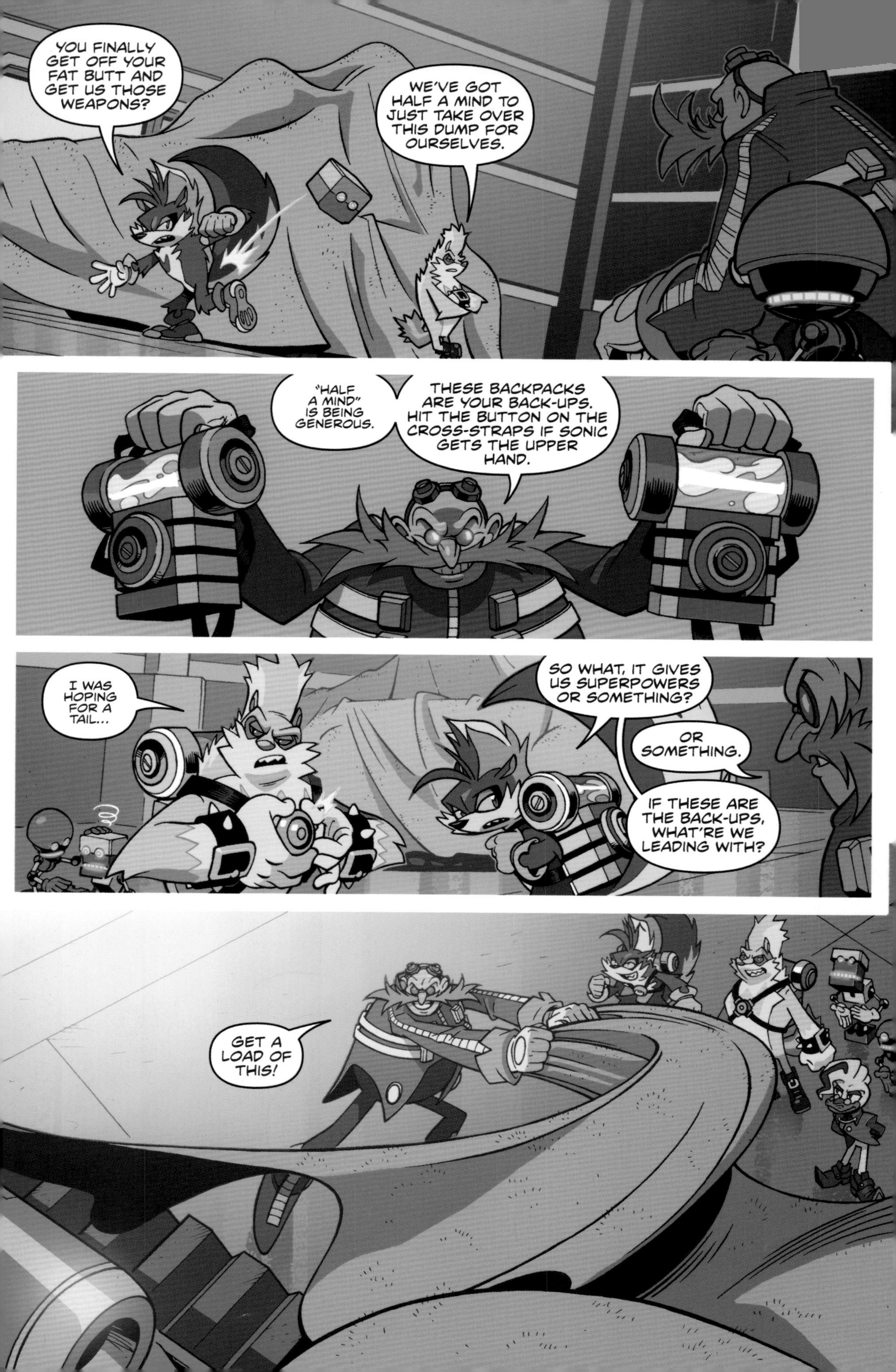
YOU FINALLY GET OFF YOUR FAT BUTT AND GET US THOSE WEAPONS?
WE'VE GOT HALF A MIND TO JUST TAKE OVER THIS DUMP FOR OURSELVES.
"HALF A MIND" IS BEING GENEROUS.
THESE BACKPACKS ARE YOUR BACK-UPS. HIT THE BUTTON ON THE CROSS-STRAPS IF SONIC GETS THE UPPER HAND.
I WAS HOPING FOR A TAIL...
SO WHAT, IT GIVES US SUPERPOWERS OR SOMETHING?
OR SOMETHING.
IF THESE ARE THE BACK-UPS, WHAT'RE WE LEADING WITH?
GET A LOAD OF THIS!

UH-OH— LOGIN SCREEN. DO YOU EVEN REMEMBER ANY OLD PASSWORDS?

IT'S USUALLY A VARIATION ON THIS.

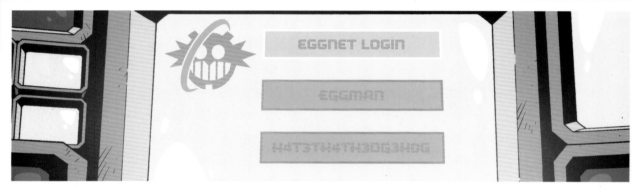

EGGNET LOGIN

EGGMAN

H4T3TH4TH3DG3HDG

I'M IN.

THE MOST RECENT FILES ARE FOR... THIS.

IS THAT THE ARK?

NO, THIS LOOKS TO BE MUCH SMALLER.

I'M SEEING A LOT OF TALK ABOUT "PAYLOAD DISTRIBUTION", BUT OF WHAT...?

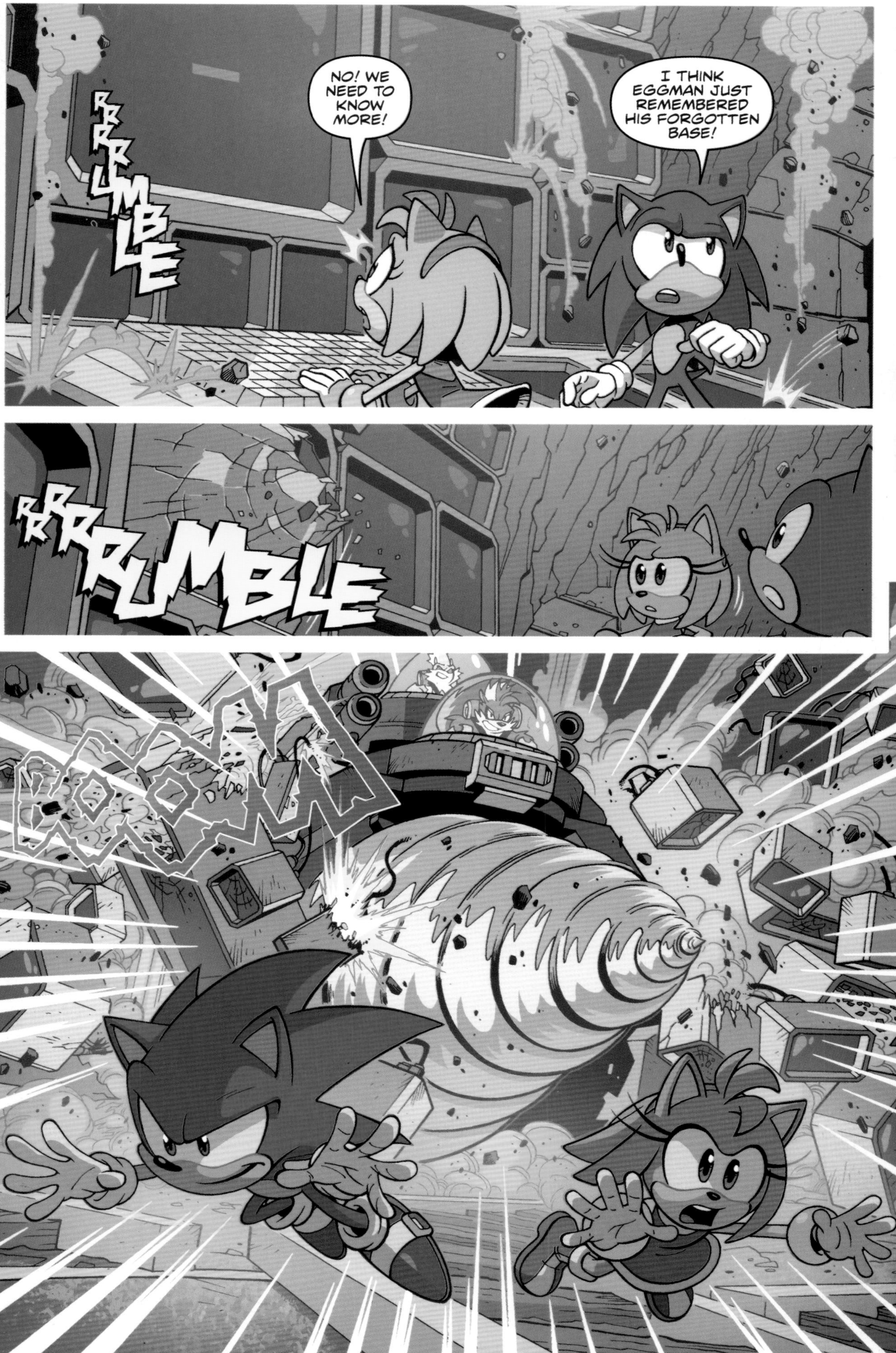
RRRRUMBLE
NO! WE NEED TO KNOW MORE!
I THINK EGGMAN JUST REMEMBERED HIS FORGOTTEN BASE!
RRRRUMBLE
BOOM

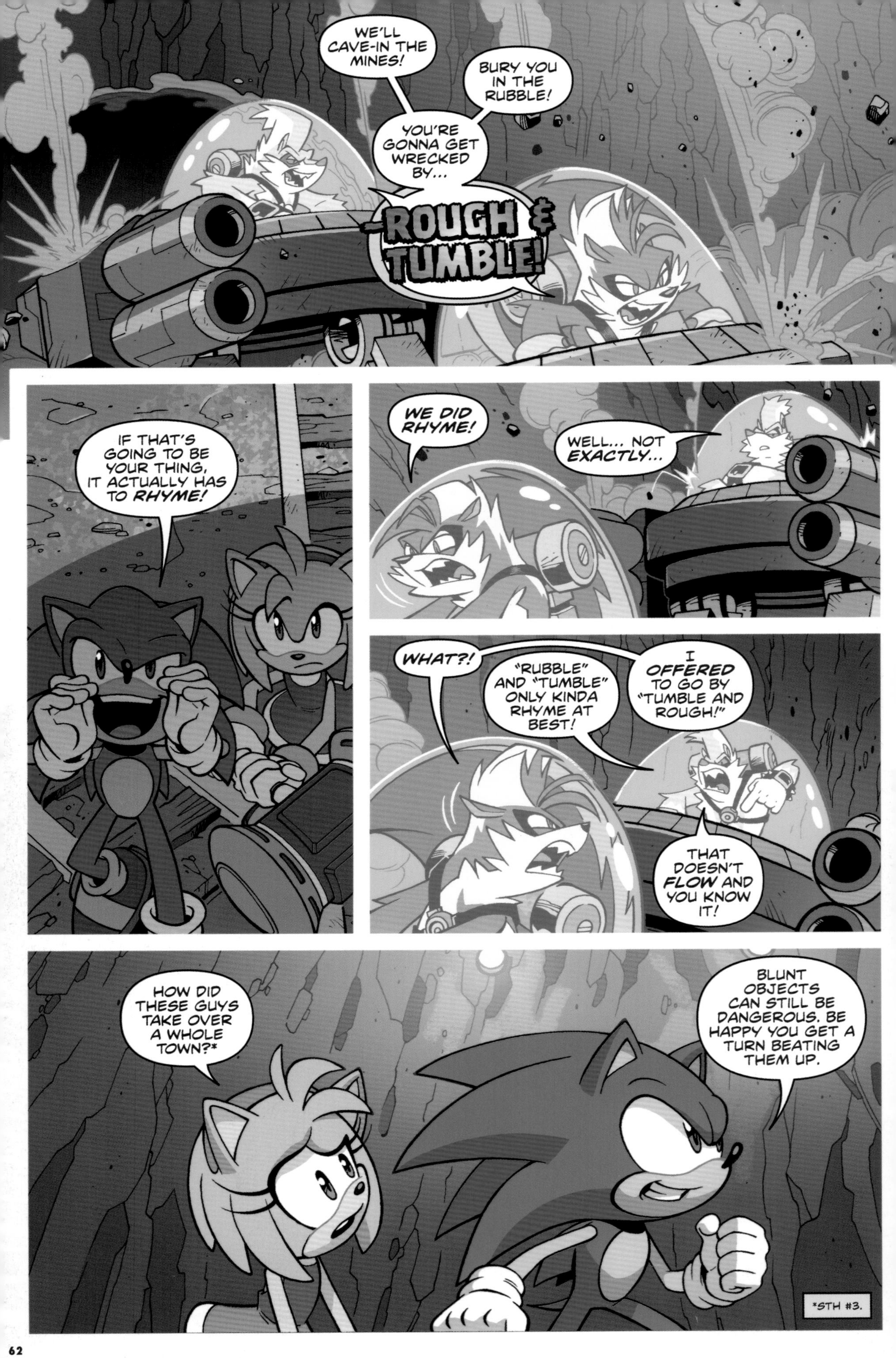
WE'LL CAVE-IN THE MINES!
BURY YOU IN THE RUBBLE!
YOU'RE GONNA GET WRECKED BY...
-ROUGH & TUMBLE!
IF THAT'S GOING TO BE YOUR THING, IT ACTUALLY HAS TO *RHYME!*
WE DID RHYME!
WELL... NOT *EXACTLY*...
WHAT?!
"RUBBLE" AND "TUMBLE" ONLY KINDA RHYME AT BEST!
I *OFFERED* TO GO BY "TUMBLE AND ROUGH!"
THAT DOESN'T *FLOW* AND YOU KNOW IT!
HOW DID THESE GUYS TAKE OVER A WHOLE TOWN?*
BLUNT OBJECTS CAN STILL BE DANGEROUS. BE HAPPY YOU GET A TURN BEATING THEM UP.
*STH #3.

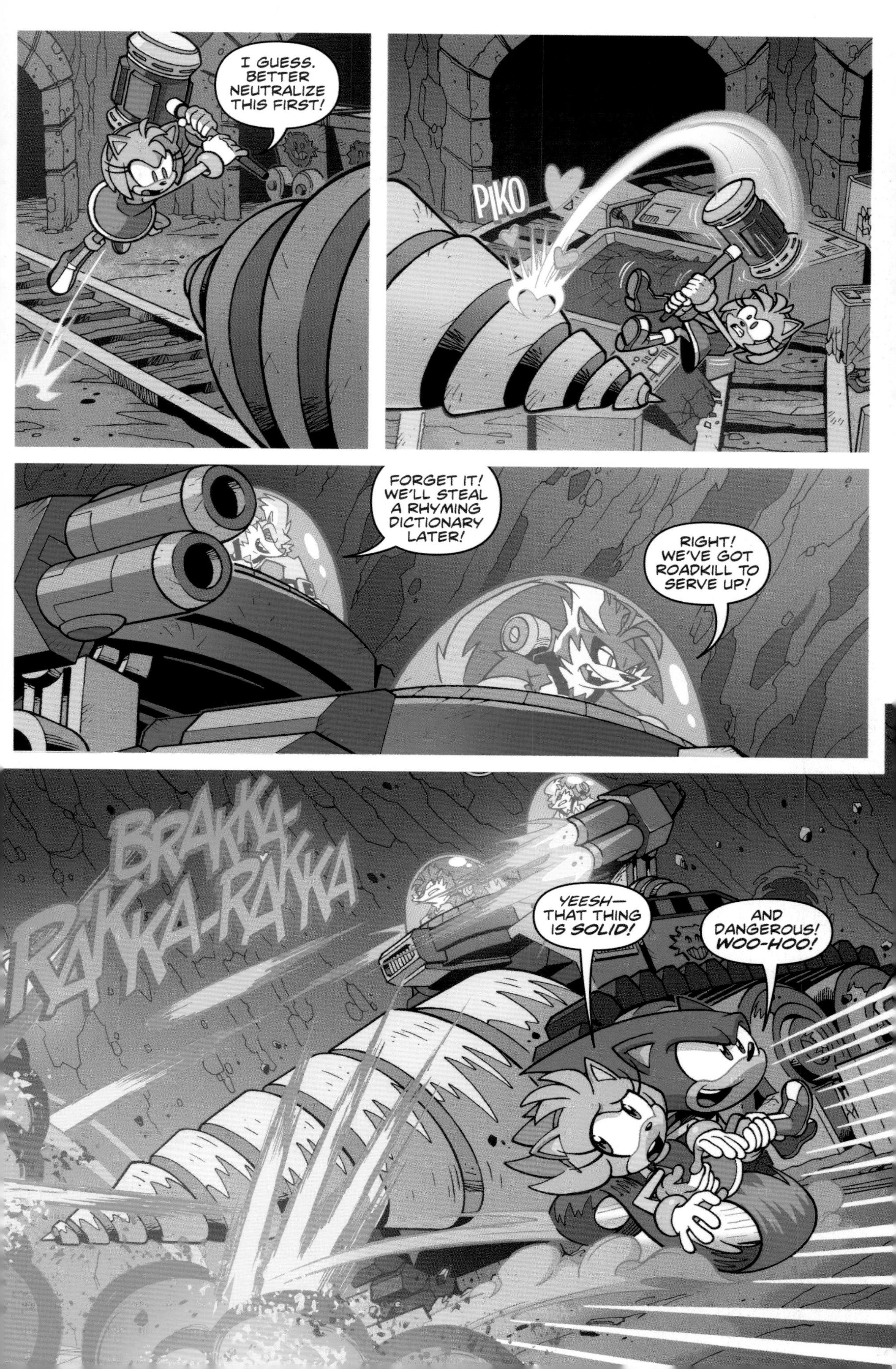
I GUESS. BETTER NEUTRALIZE THIS FIRST!
PIKO
FORGET IT! WE'LL STEAL A RHYMING DICTIONARY LATER!
RIGHT! WE'VE GOT ROADKILL TO SERVE UP!
BRAKKA-RAKKA-RAKKA
YEESH— THAT THING IS SOLID!
AND DANGEROUS! WOO-HOO!

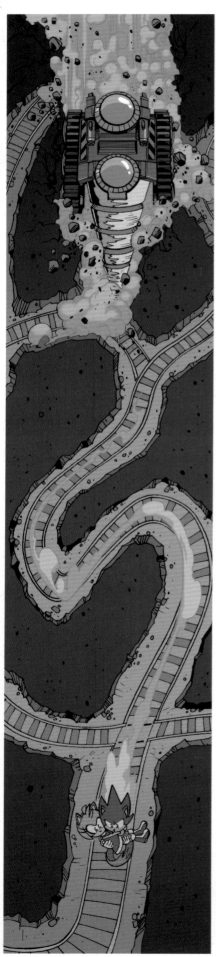

WHOOPS!

CAREFUL!

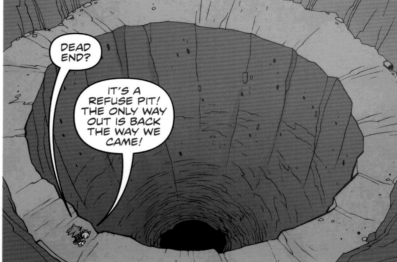

DEAD END?

IT'S A REFUSE PIT! THE ONLY WAY OUT IS BACK THE WAY WE CAME!

HOLD ON—THIS PATH IS BARELY WIDE ENOUGH FOR THEIR TANK.

IF THEY DROVE OUT HERE, THEY WOULDN'T BE ABLE TO TURN AROUND.

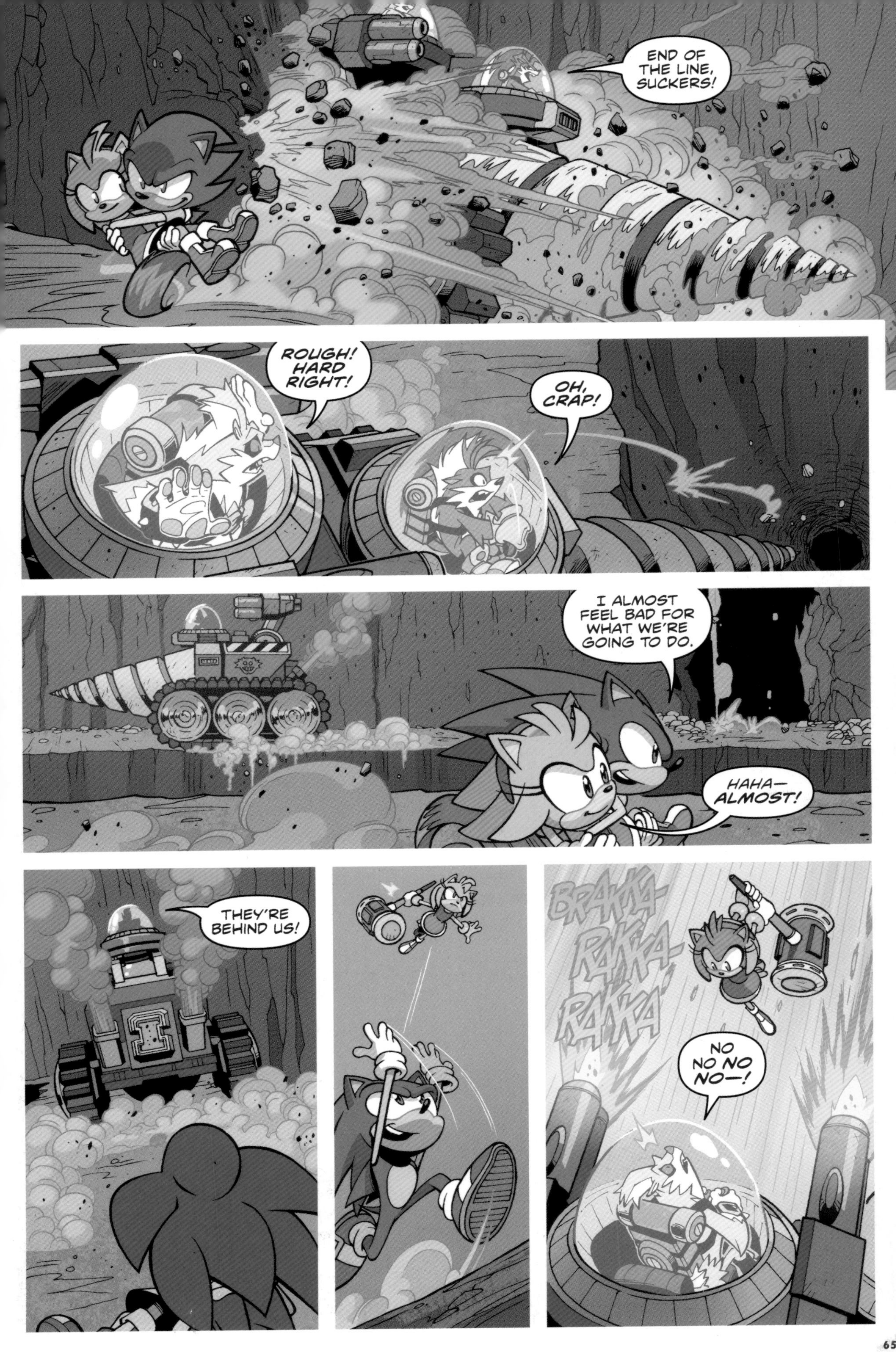
END OF THE LINE, SUCKERS!
ROUGH! HARD RIGHT!
OH, CRAP!
I ALMOST FEEL BAD FOR WHAT WE'RE GOING TO DO.
HAHA— ALMOST!
THEY'RE BEHIND US!
BRAKKA-RAKKA-RAKKA
NO NO NO NO—!

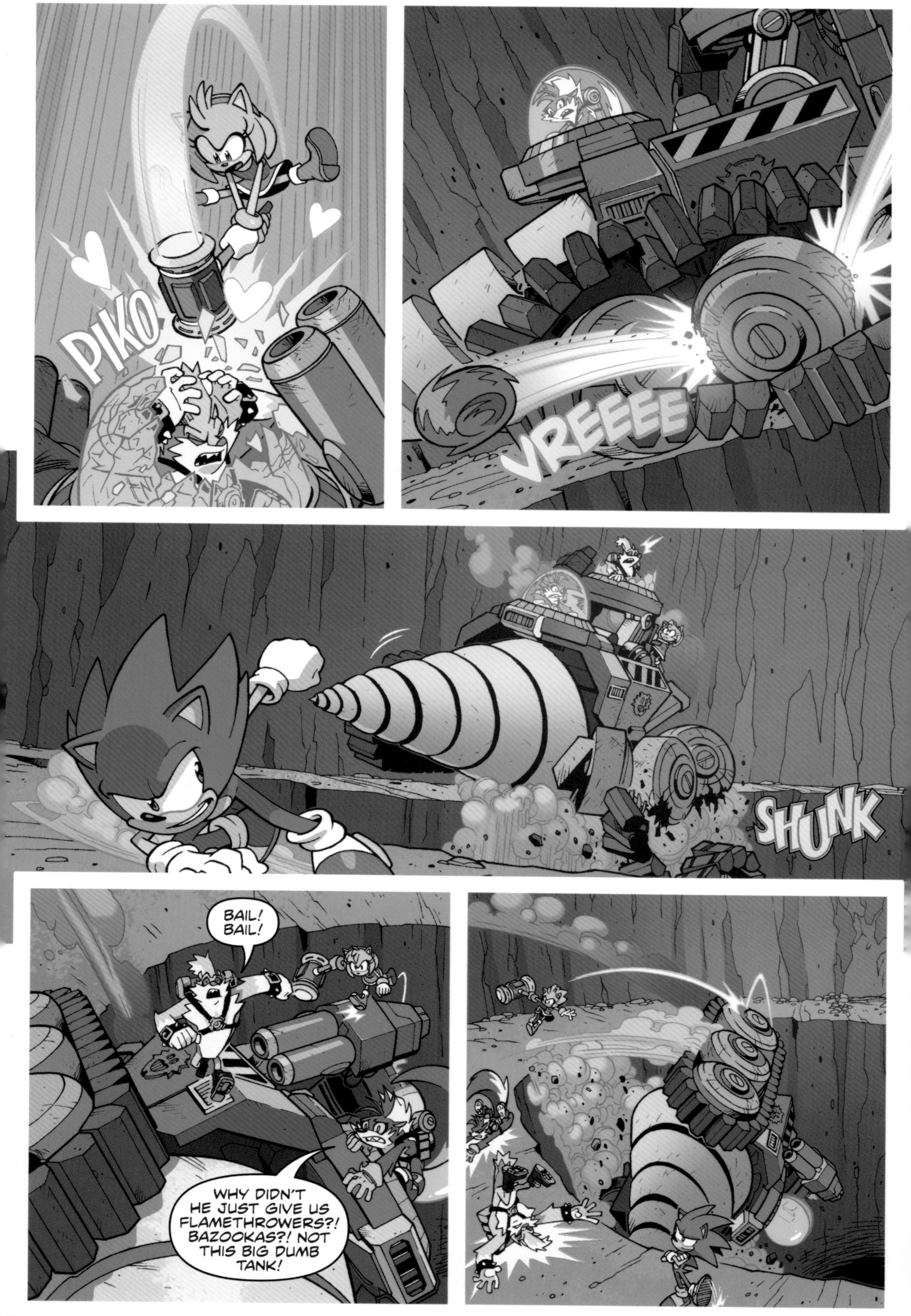
PIKO
VREEEE
SHUNK
BAIL! BAIL!
WHY DIDN'T HE JUST GIVE US FLAMETHROWERS?! BAZOOKAS?! NOT THIS BIG DUMB TANK!

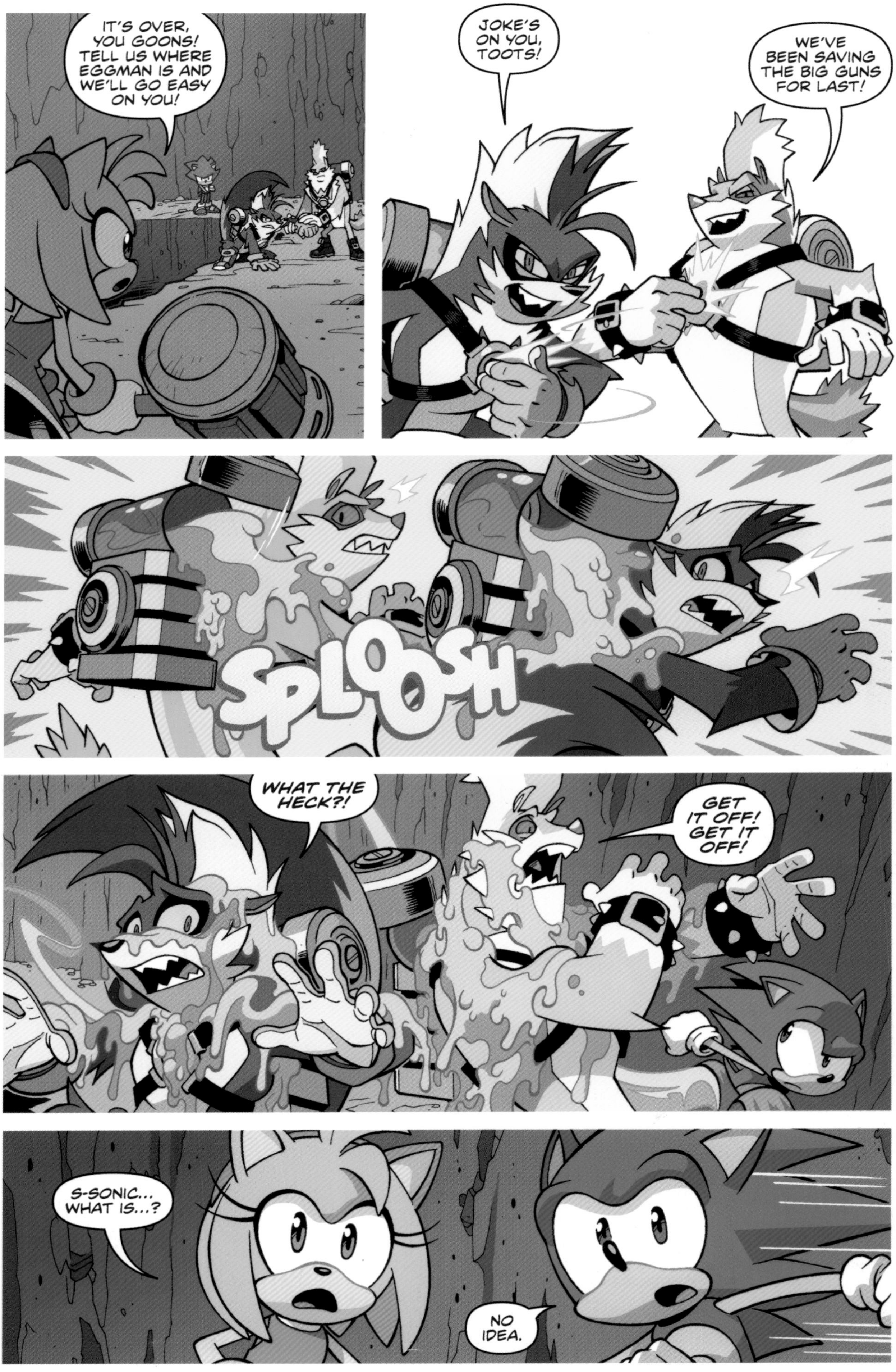
IT'S OVER, YOU GOONS! TELL US WHERE EGGMAN IS AND WE'LL GO EASY ON YOU!
JOKE'S ON YOU, TOOTS!
WE'VE BEEN SAVING THE BIG GUNS FOR LAST!
SPLOOSH
WHAT THE HECK?!
GET IT OFF! GET IT OFF!
S-SONIC... WHAT IS...?
NO IDEA.

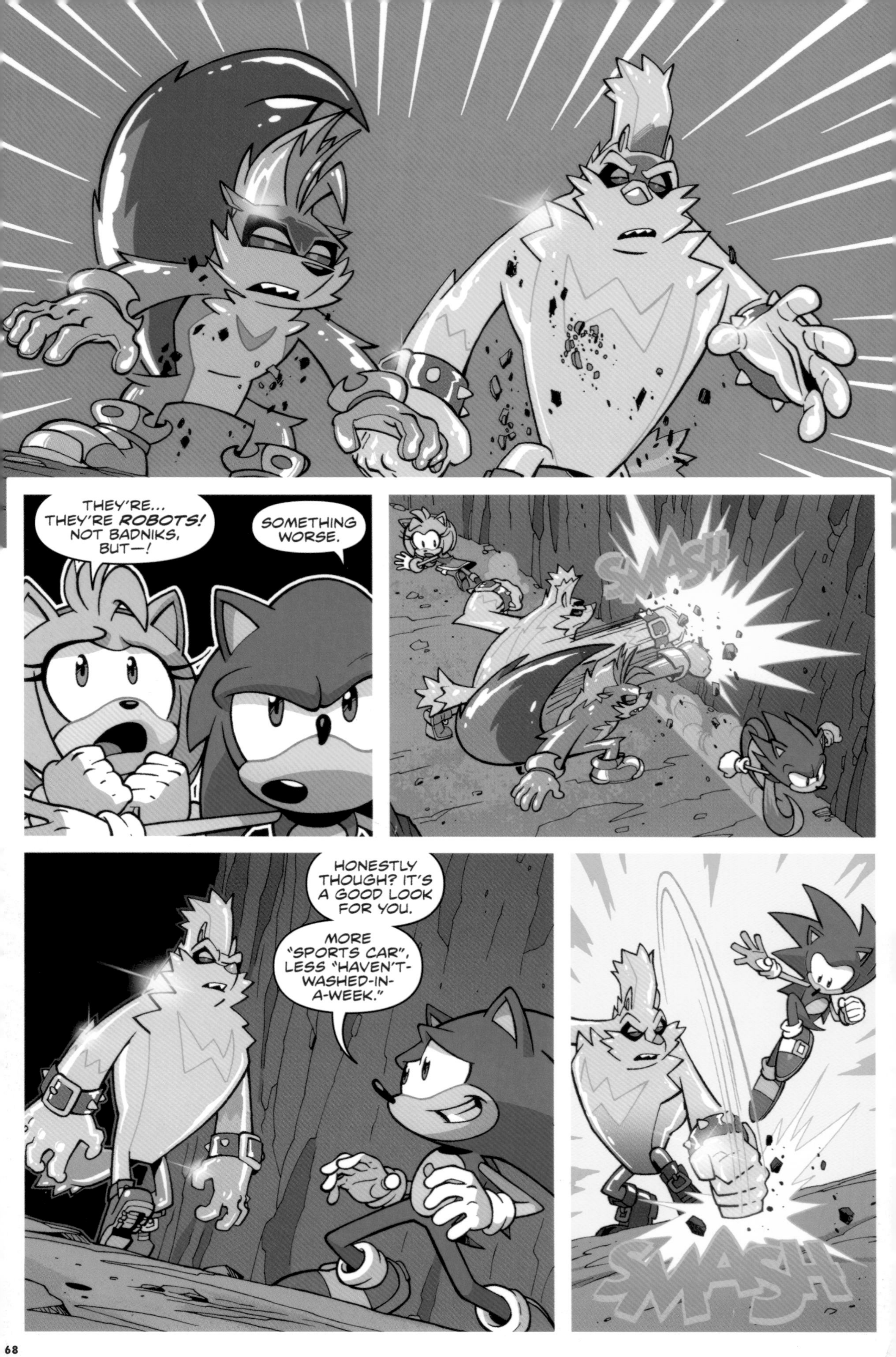

THEY'RE... THEY'RE *ROBOTS!* NOT BADNIKS, BUT—!
SOMETHING WORSE.
SMASH!
HONESTLY THOUGH? IT'S A GOOD LOOK FOR YOU.
MORE "SPORTS CAR", LESS "HAVEN'T-WASHED-IN-A-WEEK."
SMASH

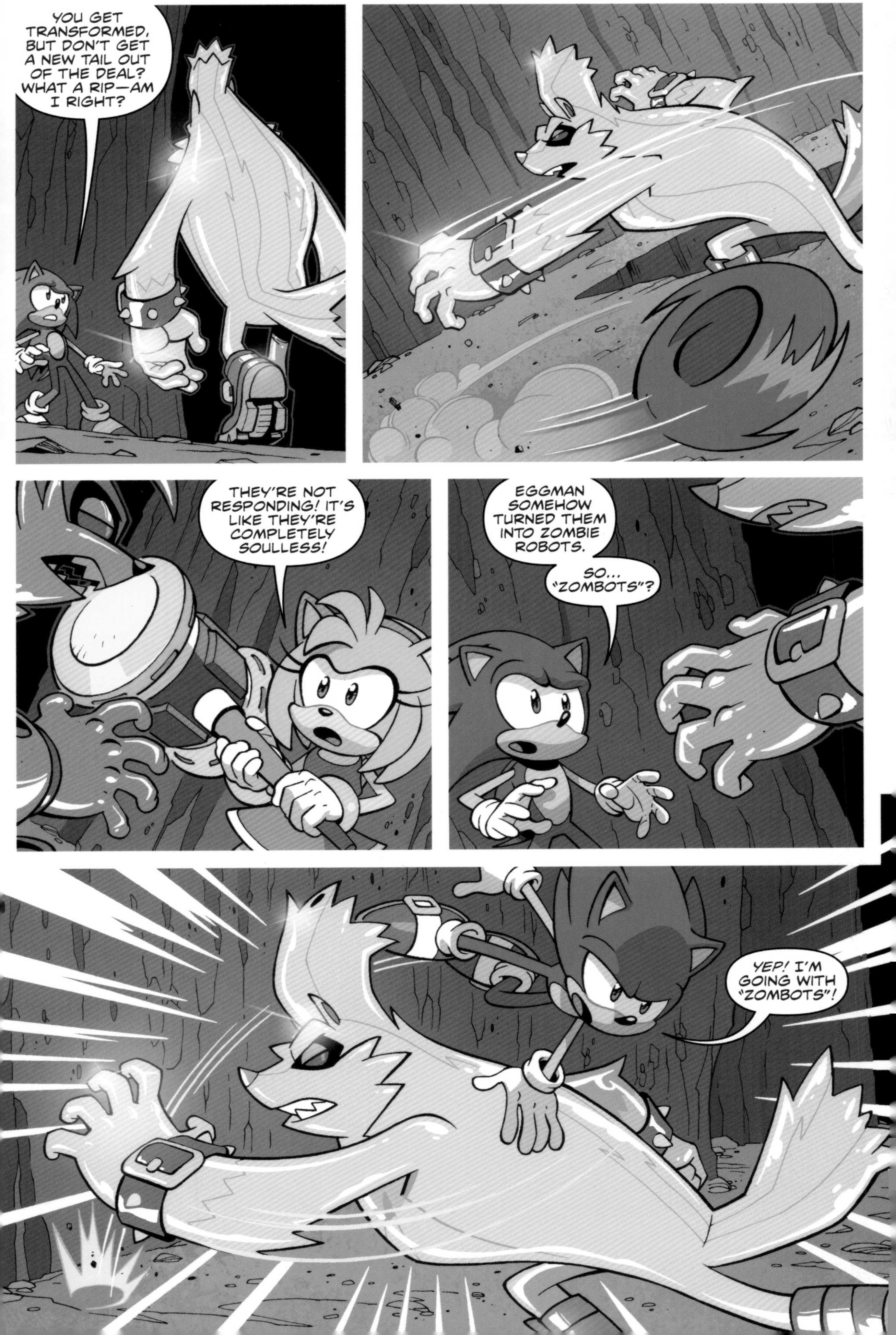
YOU GET TRANSFORMED, BUT DON'T GET A NEW TAIL OUT OF THE DEAL? WHAT A RIP—AM I RIGHT?
THEY'RE NOT RESPONDING! IT'S LIKE THEY'RE COMPLETELY SOULLESS!
EGGMAN SOMEHOW TURNED THEM INTO ZOMBIE ROBOTS.
SO... "ZOMBOTS"?
YEP! I'M GOING WITH "ZOMBOTS"!

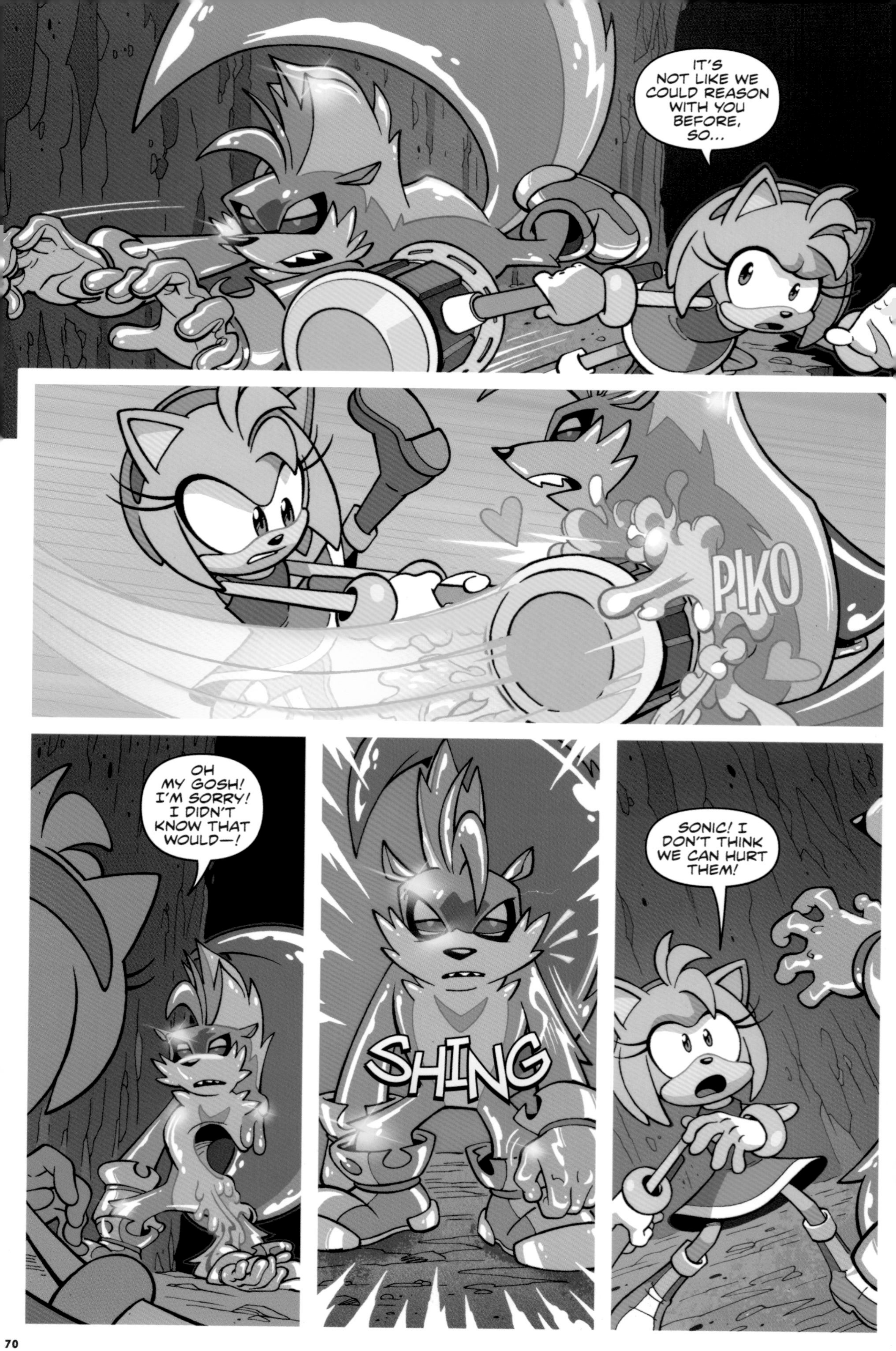
IT'S NOT LIKE WE COULD REASON WITH YOU BEFORE, SO...
PIKO
OH MY GOSH! I'M SORRY! I DIDN'T KNOW THAT WOULD—!
SHING
SONIC! I DON'T THINK WE CAN HURT THEM!

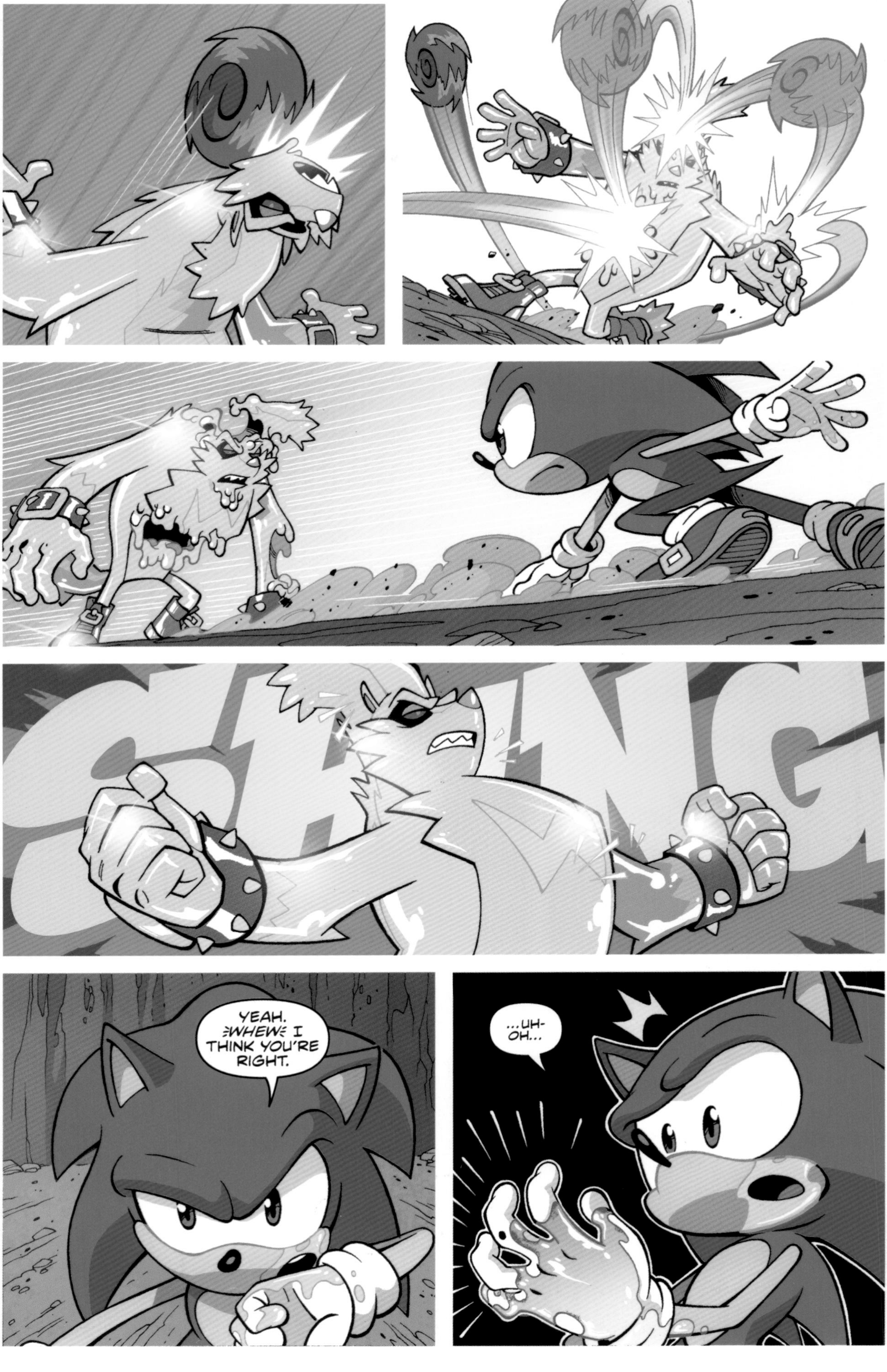
YEAH. *WHEW* I THINK YOU'RE RIGHT.
...UH-OH...

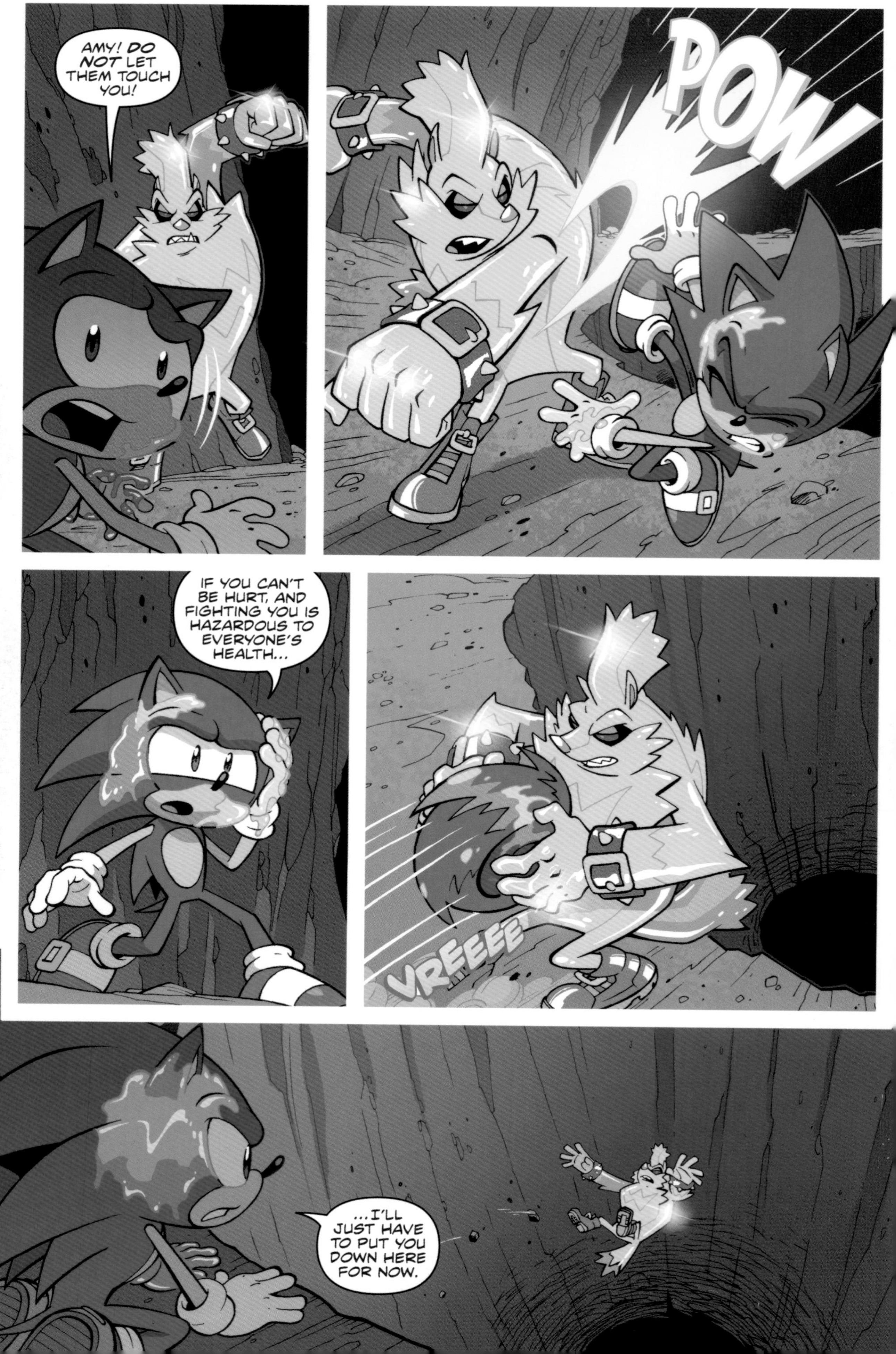
AMY! DO NOT LET THEM TOUCH YOU!
POW
IF YOU CAN'T BE HURT, AND FIGHTING YOU IS HAZARDOUS TO EVERYONE'S HEALTH...
VREEEEE
...I'LL JUST HAVE TO PUT YOU DOWN HERE FOR NOW.

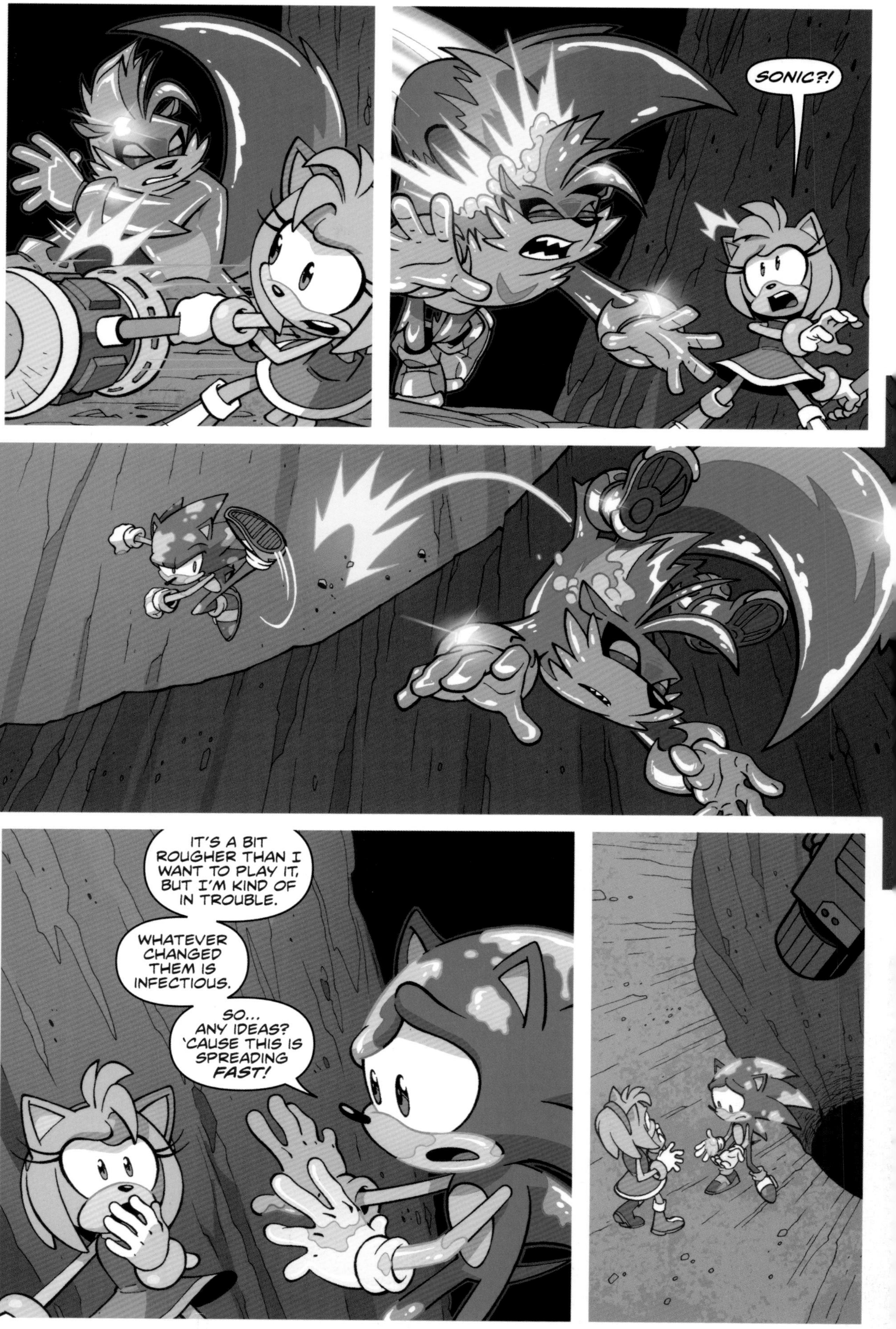
SONIC?!
IT'S A BIT ROUGHER THAN I WANT TO PLAY IT, BUT I'M KIND OF IN TROUBLE.
WHATEVER CHANGED THEM IS INFECTIOUS.
SO... ANY IDEAS? 'CAUSE THIS IS SPREADING FAST!

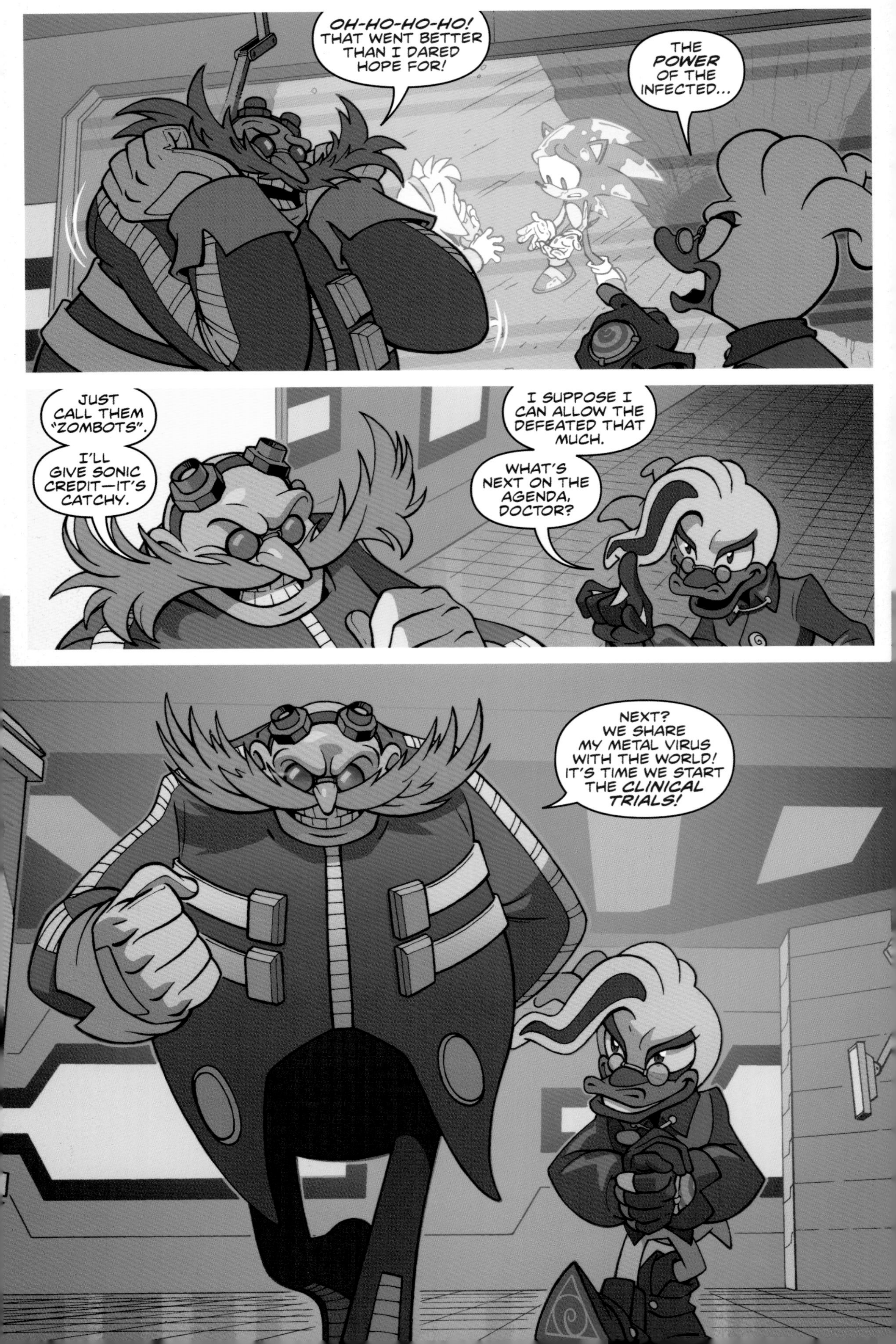
OH-HO-HO-HO! THAT WENT BETTER THAN I DARED HOPE FOR!
THE POWER OF THE INFECTED...
JUST CALL THEM "ZOMBOTS".
I'LL GIVE SONIC CREDIT—IT'S CATCHY.
I SUPPOSE I CAN ALLOW THE DEFEATED THAT MUCH.
WHAT'S NEXT ON THE AGENDA, DOCTOR?
NEXT? WE SHARE MY METAL VIRUS WITH THE WORLD! IT'S TIME WE START THE CLINICAL TRIALS!

ART BY DIANA SKELLY COLORS BY ELAINA UNGER

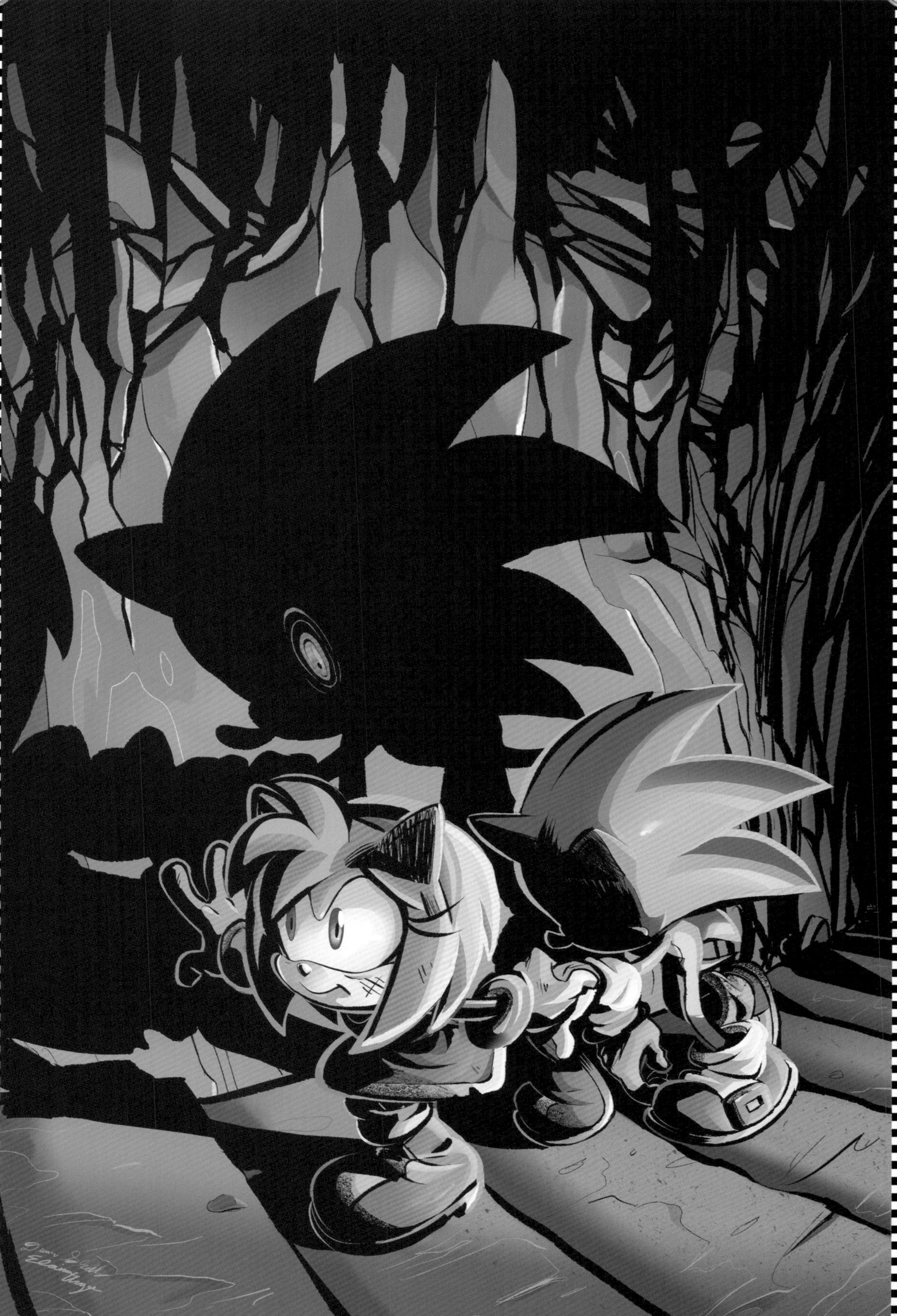

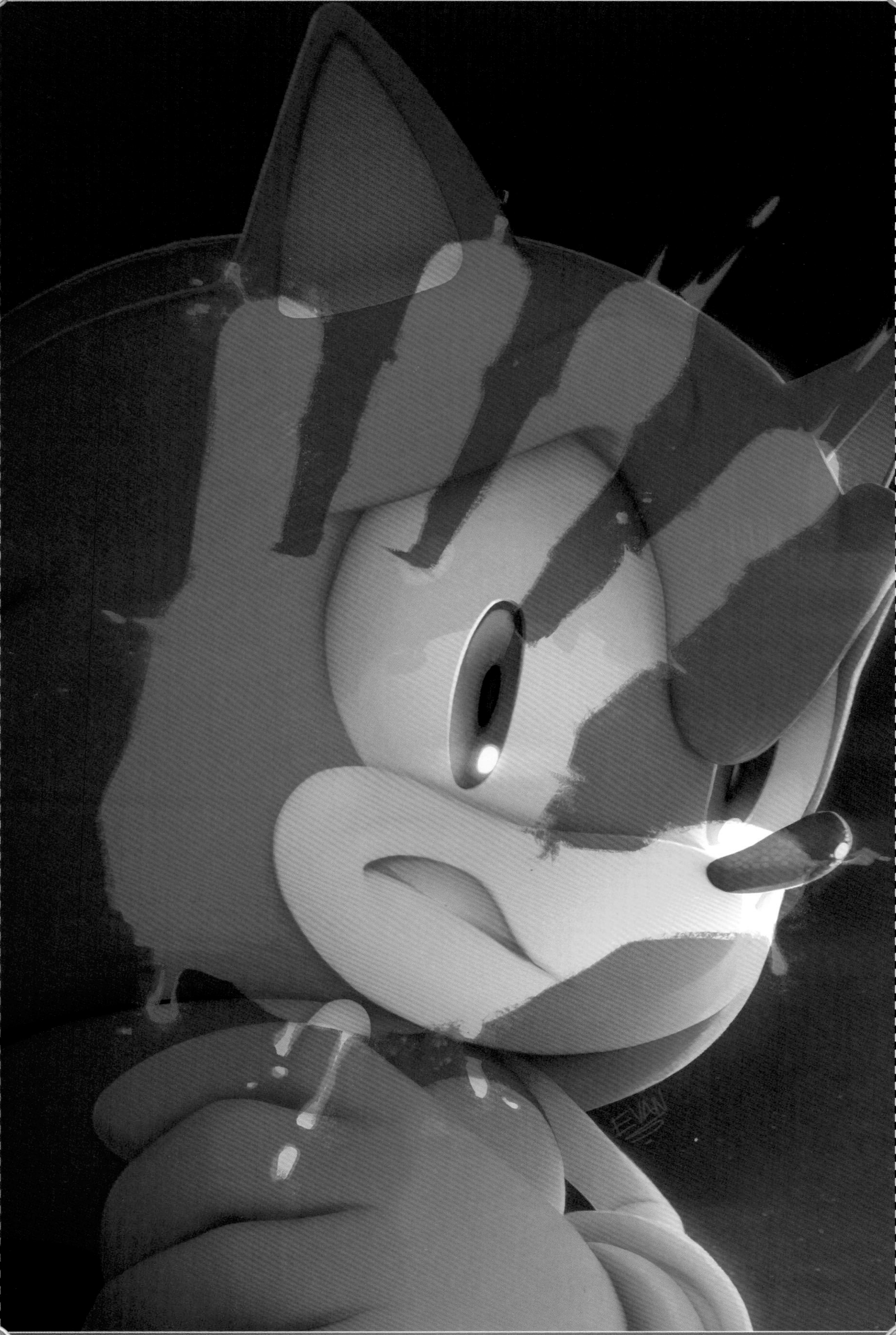

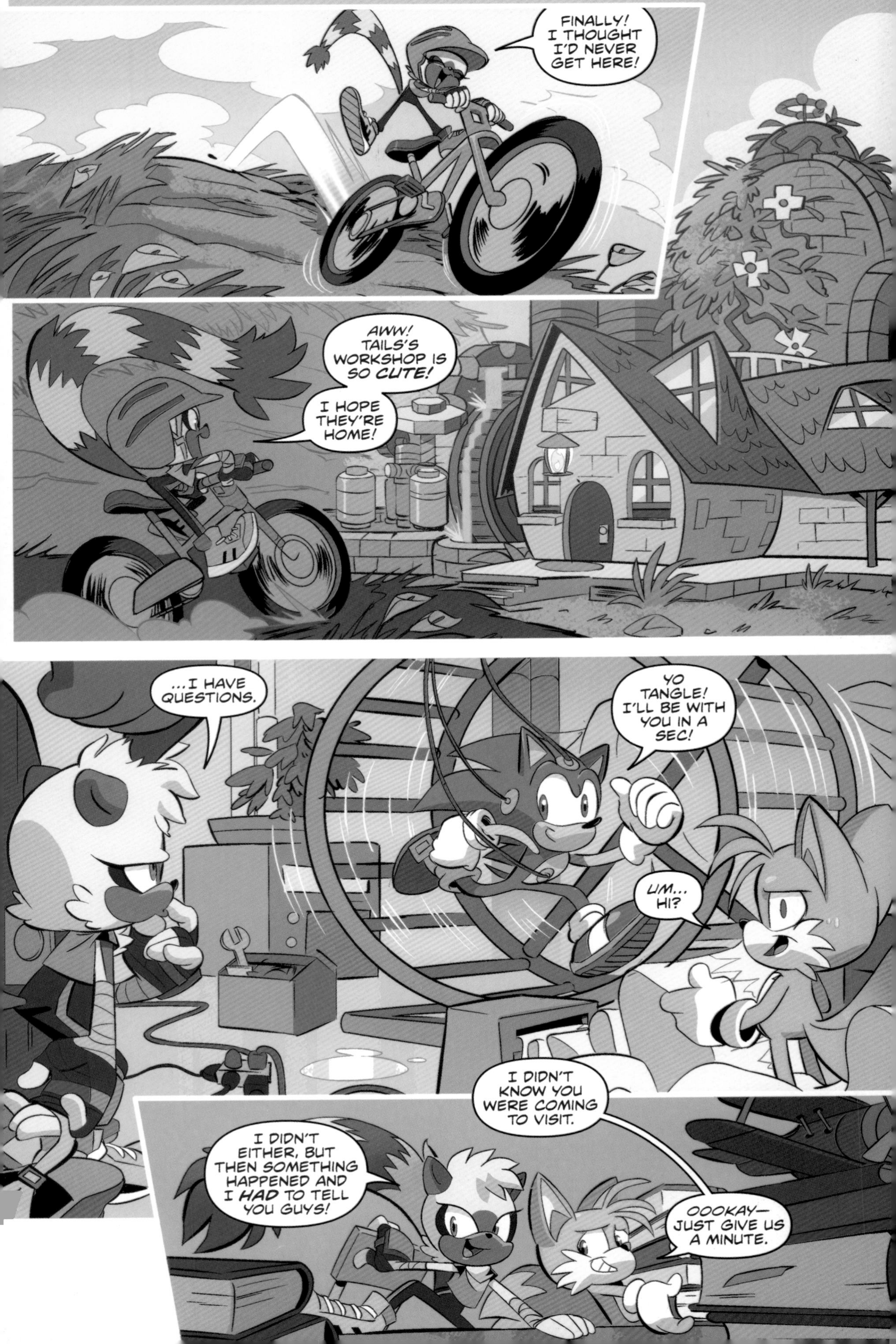
FINALLY! I THOUGHT I'D NEVER GET HERE!
AWW! TAILS'S WORKSHOP IS SO *CUTE!*
I HOPE THEY'RE HOME!
...I HAVE QUESTIONS.
YO TANGLE! I'LL BE WITH YOU IN A SEC!
UM... HI?
I DIDN'T KNOW YOU WERE COMING TO VISIT.
I DIDN'T EITHER, BUT THEN SOMETHING HAPPENED AND I ***HAD*** TO TELL YOU GUYS!
OOOKAY— JUST GIVE US A MINUTE.

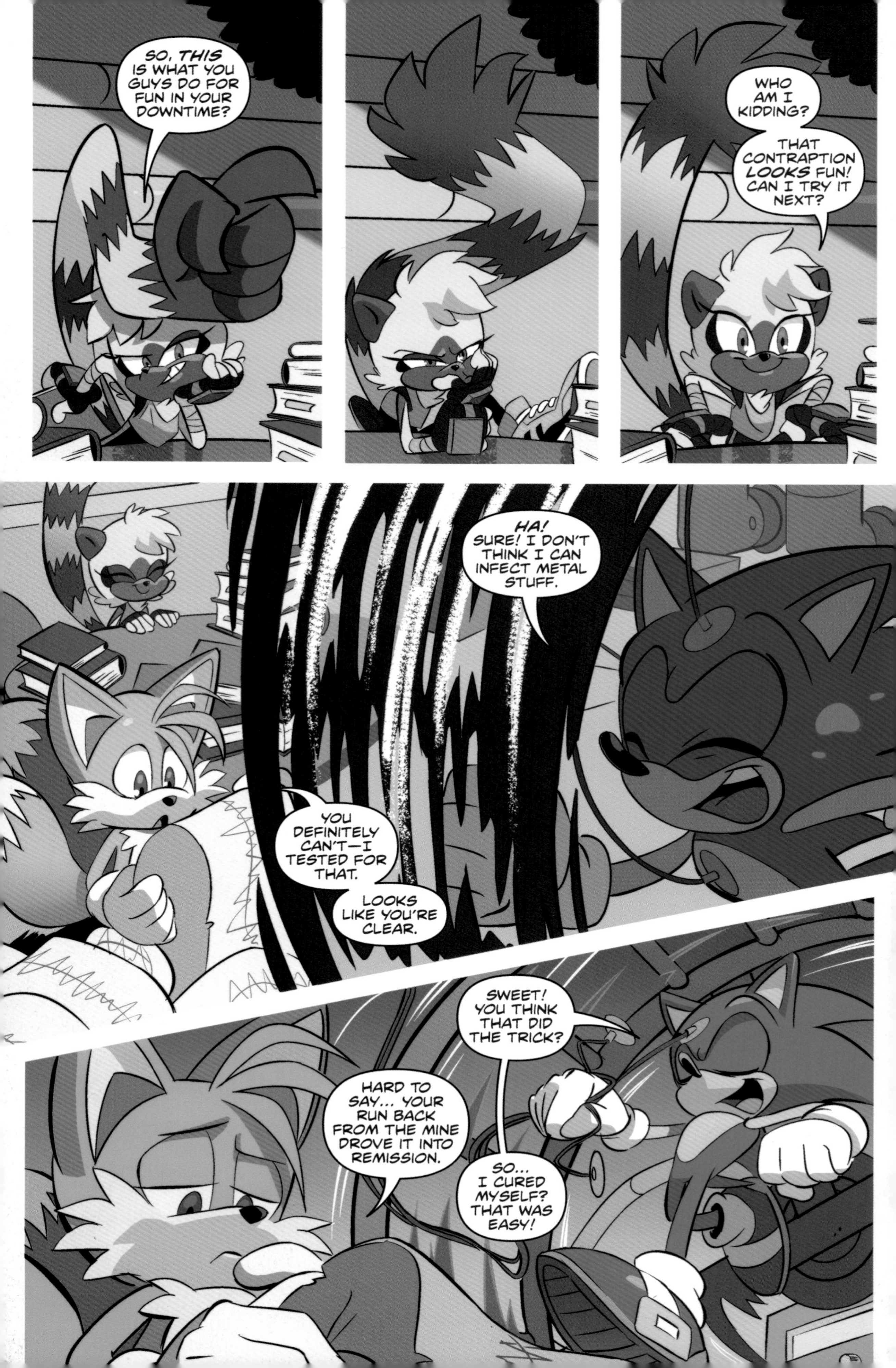
SO, THIS IS WHAT YOU GUYS DO FOR FUN IN YOUR DOWNTIME?
WHO AM I KIDDING?
THAT CONTRAPTION LOOKS FUN! CAN I TRY IT NEXT?
HA! SURE! I DON'T THINK I CAN INFECT METAL STUFF.
YOU DEFINITELY CAN'T—I TESTED FOR THAT.
LOOKS LIKE YOU'RE CLEAR.
SWEET! YOU THINK THAT DID THE TRICK?
HARD TO SAY... YOUR RUN BACK FROM THE MINE DROVE IT INTO REMISSION.
SO... I CURED MYSELF? THAT WAS EASY!

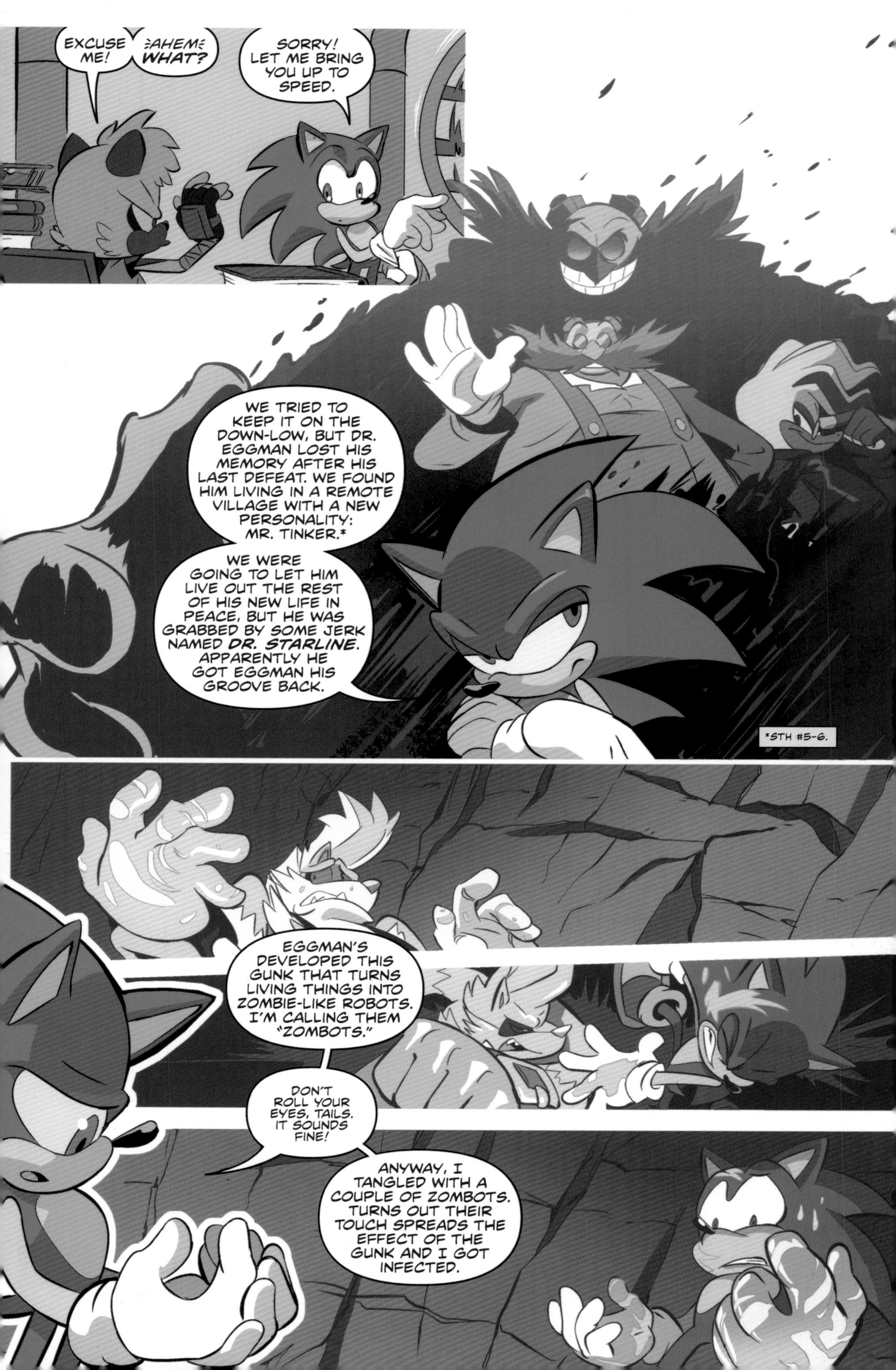
EXCUSE ME!
AHEM WHAT?
SORRY! LET ME BRING YOU UP TO SPEED.
WE TRIED TO KEEP IT ON THE DOWN-LOW, BUT DR. EGGMAN LOST HIS MEMORY AFTER HIS LAST DEFEAT. WE FOUND HIM LIVING IN A REMOTE VILLAGE WITH A NEW PERSONALITY: MR. TINKER.*
WE WERE GOING TO LET HIM LIVE OUT THE REST OF HIS NEW LIFE IN PEACE, BUT HE WAS GRABBED BY SOME JERK NAMED DR. STARLINE. APPARENTLY HE GOT EGGMAN HIS GROOVE BACK.
*STH #5-6.
EGGMAN'S DEVELOPED THIS GUNK THAT TURNS LIVING THINGS INTO ZOMBIE-LIKE ROBOTS. I'M CALLING THEM "ZOMBOTS."
DON'T ROLL YOUR EYES, TAILS. IT SOUNDS FINE!
ANYWAY, I TANGLED WITH A COUPLE OF ZOMBOTS. TURNS OUT THEIR TOUCH SPREADS THE EFFECT OF THE GUNK AND I GOT INFECTED.

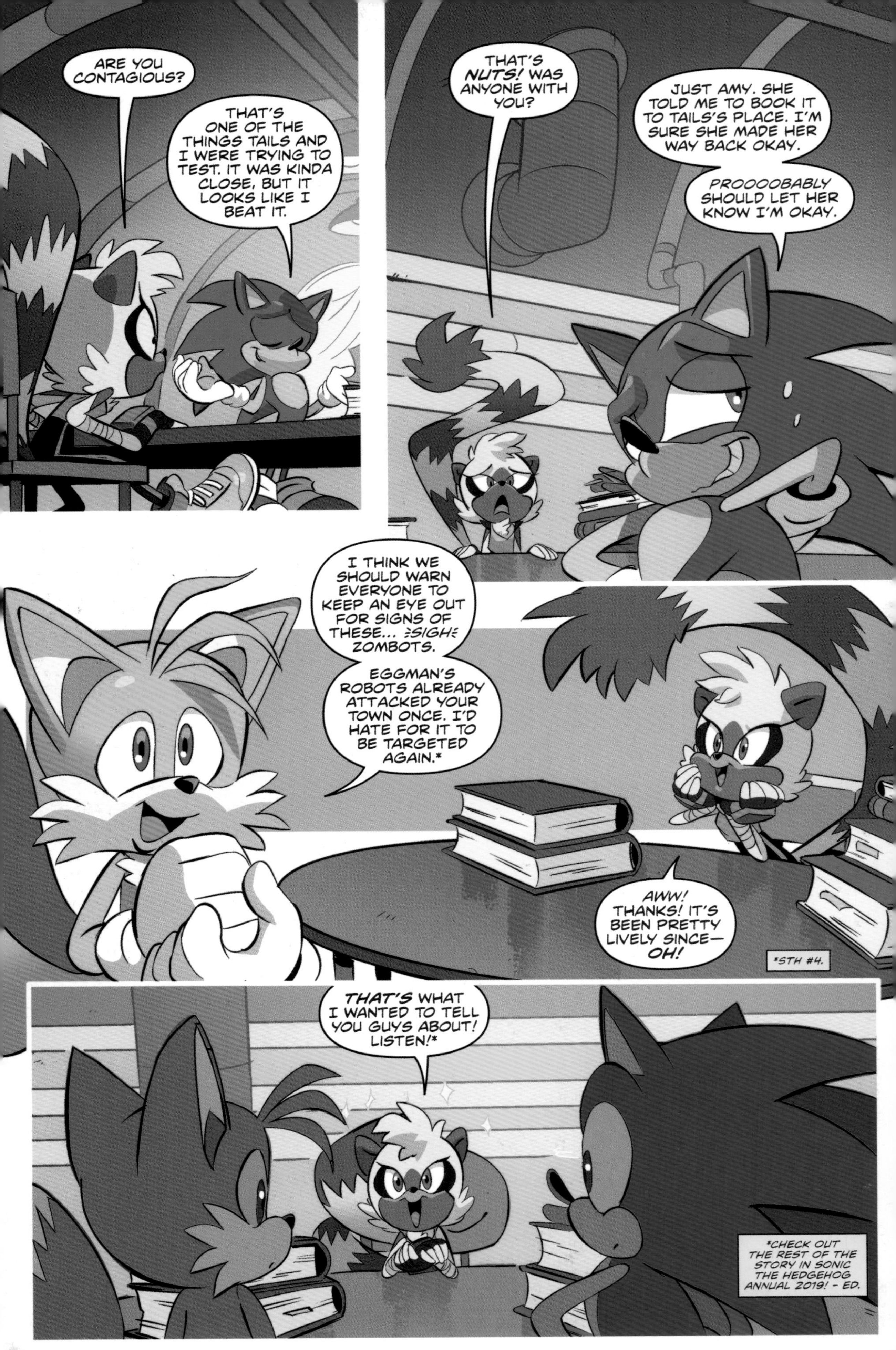
ARE YOU CONTAGIOUS?
THAT'S ONE OF THE THINGS TAILS AND I WERE TRYING TO TEST. IT WAS KINDA CLOSE, BUT IT LOOKS LIKE I BEAT IT.
THAT'S NUTS! WAS ANYONE WITH YOU?
JUST AMY. SHE TOLD ME TO BOOK IT TO TAILS'S PLACE. I'M SURE SHE MADE HER WAY BACK OKAY.
PROOOOBABLY SHOULD LET HER KNOW I'M OKAY.
I THINK WE SHOULD WARN EVERYONE TO KEEP AN EYE OUT FOR SIGNS OF THESE... ≡SIGH≡ ZOMBOTS.
EGGMAN'S ROBOTS ALREADY ATTACKED YOUR TOWN ONCE. I'D HATE FOR IT TO BE TARGETED AGAIN.*
AWW! THANKS! IT'S BEEN PRETTY LIVELY SINCE— OH!
*STH #4.
THAT'S WHAT I WANTED TO TELL YOU GUYS ABOUT! LISTEN!*
*CHECK OUT THE REST OF THE STORY IN SONIC THE HEDGEHOG ANNUAL 2019! - ED.

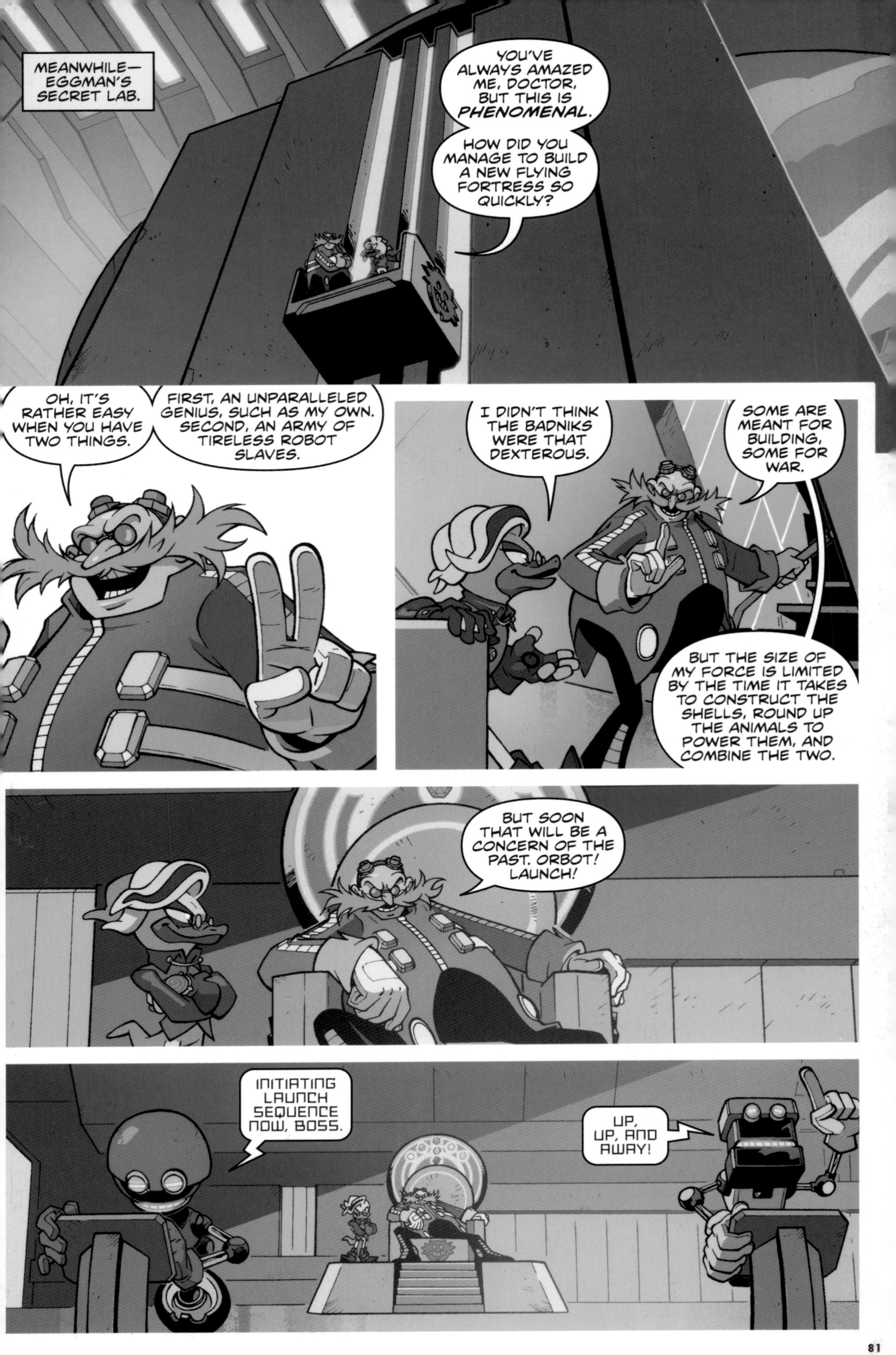
MEANWHILE— EGGMAN'S SECRET LAB.
YOU'VE ALWAYS AMAZED ME, DOCTOR, BUT THIS IS PHENOMENAL.
HOW DID YOU MANAGE TO BUILD A NEW FLYING FORTRESS SO QUICKLY?
OH, IT'S RATHER EASY WHEN YOU HAVE TWO THINGS.
FIRST, AN UNPARALLELED GENIUS, SUCH AS MY OWN. SECOND, AN ARMY OF TIRELESS ROBOT SLAVES.
I DIDN'T THINK THE BADNIKS WERE THAT DEXTEROUS.
SOME ARE MEANT FOR BUILDING, SOME FOR WAR.
BUT THE SIZE OF MY FORCE IS LIMITED BY THE TIME IT TAKES TO CONSTRUCT THE SHELLS, ROUND UP THE ANIMALS TO POWER THEM, AND COMBINE THE TWO.
BUT SOON THAT WILL BE A CONCERN OF THE PAST. ORBOT! LAUNCH!
INITIATING LAUNCH SEQUENCE NOW, BOSS.
UP, UP, AND AWAY!

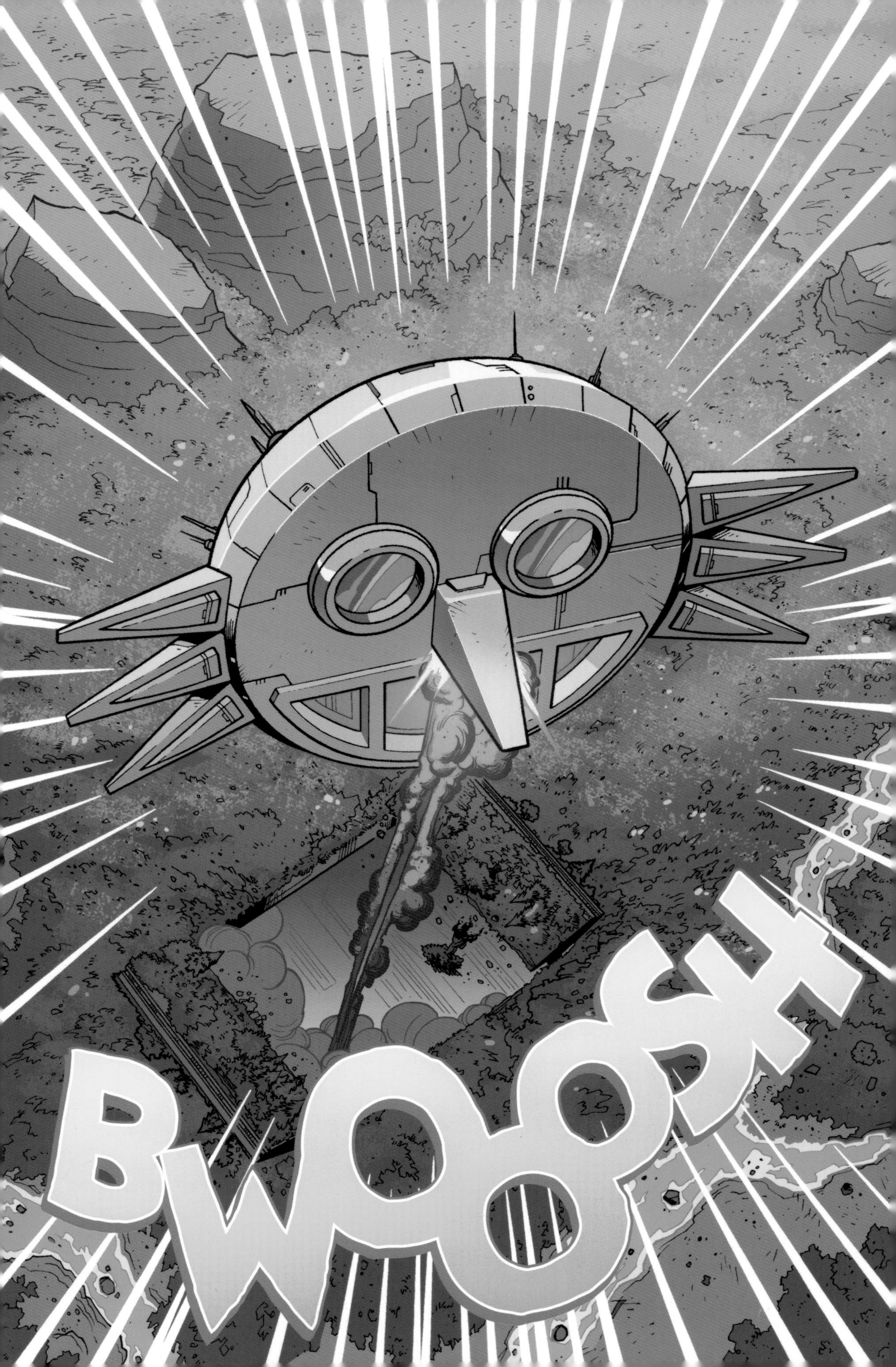
BWOOSH

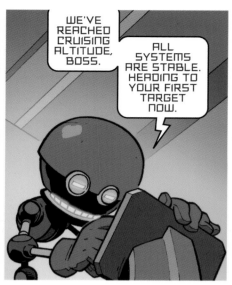

WE'VE REACHED CRUISING ALTITUDE, BOSS.

ALL SYSTEMS ARE STABLE. HEADING TO YOUR FIRST TARGET NOW.

WE HAVE SOME TIME BEFORE WE ARRIVE. CARE FOR A TOUR, DOCTOR?

I'D LOVE ONE, SIR!

VERY WELL! FIRST, I'M SURE YOU'VE NOTICED I'M KEEPING YOUR LITTLE GIFT OF THE CHAOS EMERALDS CLOSE AT HAND!

THIS THRONE DOUBLES AS THE POWER GENERATOR FOR THE ENTIRE FACESHIP.

FACESHIP...

A SHORT WALK AWAY IS THIS LOVELY VIEWING AREA, WHERE I CAN SEE MY BRILLIANT PLAN UNFOLD—ALL FROM A SAFE ALTITUDE.

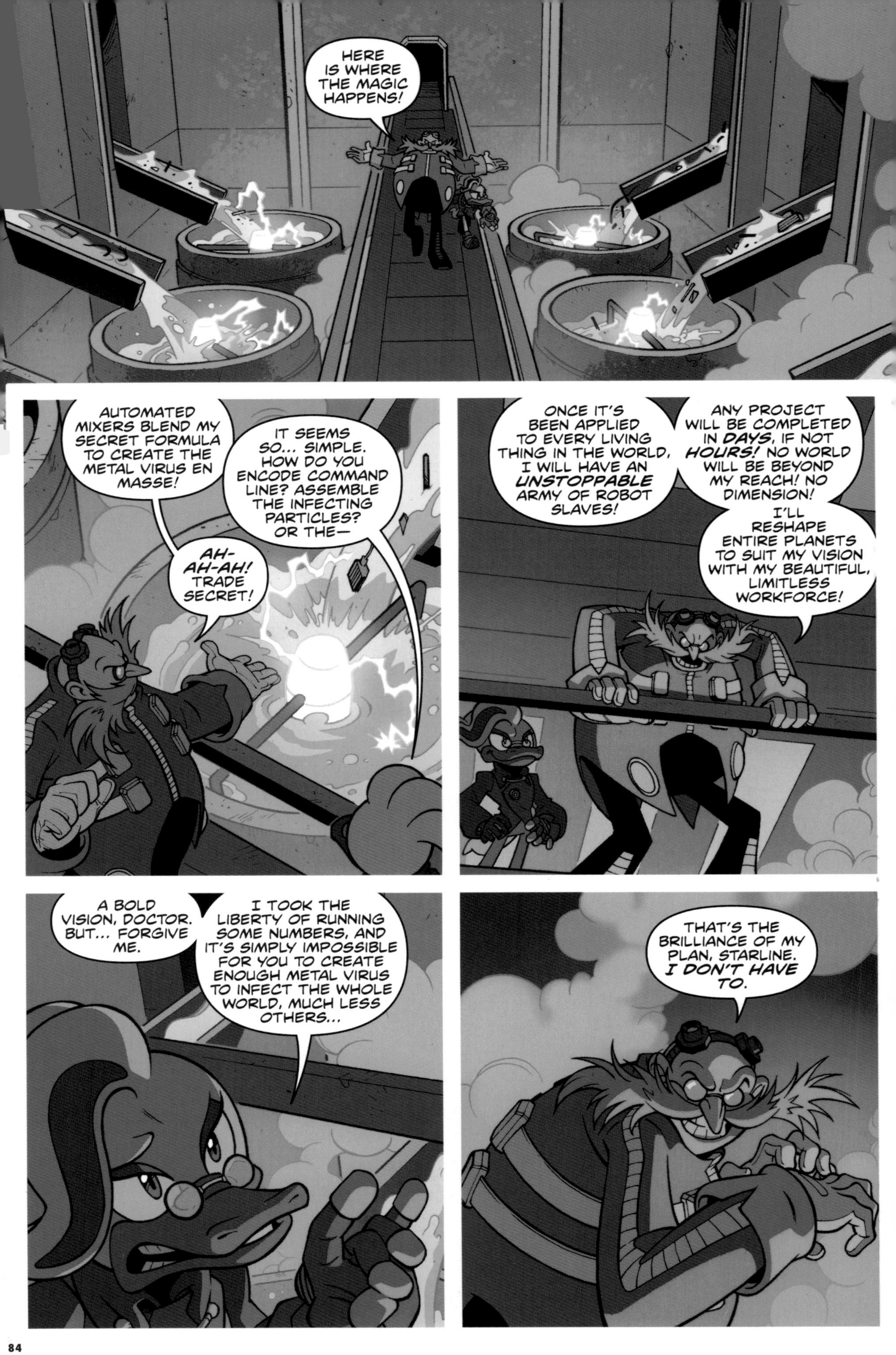
HERE IS WHERE THE MAGIC HAPPENS!
AUTOMATED MIXERS BLEND MY SECRET FORMULA TO CREATE THE METAL VIRUS EN MASSE!
IT SEEMS SO... SIMPLE. HOW DO YOU ENCODE COMMAND LINE? ASSEMBLE THE INFECTING PARTICLES? OR THE—
AH-AH-AH! TRADE SECRET!
ONCE IT'S BEEN APPLIED TO EVERY LIVING THING IN THE WORLD, I WILL HAVE AN *UNSTOPPABLE* ARMY OF ROBOT SLAVES!
ANY PROJECT WILL BE COMPLETED IN *DAYS*, IF NOT *HOURS!* NO WORLD WILL BE BEYOND MY REACH! NO DIMENSION!
I'LL RESHAPE ENTIRE PLANETS TO SUIT MY VISION WITH MY BEAUTIFUL, LIMITLESS WORKFORCE!
A BOLD VISION, DOCTOR. BUT... FORGIVE ME.
I TOOK THE LIBERTY OF RUNNING SOME NUMBERS, AND IT'S SIMPLY IMPOSSIBLE FOR YOU TO CREATE ENOUGH METAL VIRUS TO INFECT THE WHOLE WORLD, MUCH LESS OTHERS...
THAT'S THE BRILLIANCE OF MY PLAN, STARLINE. *I DON'T HAVE TO.*

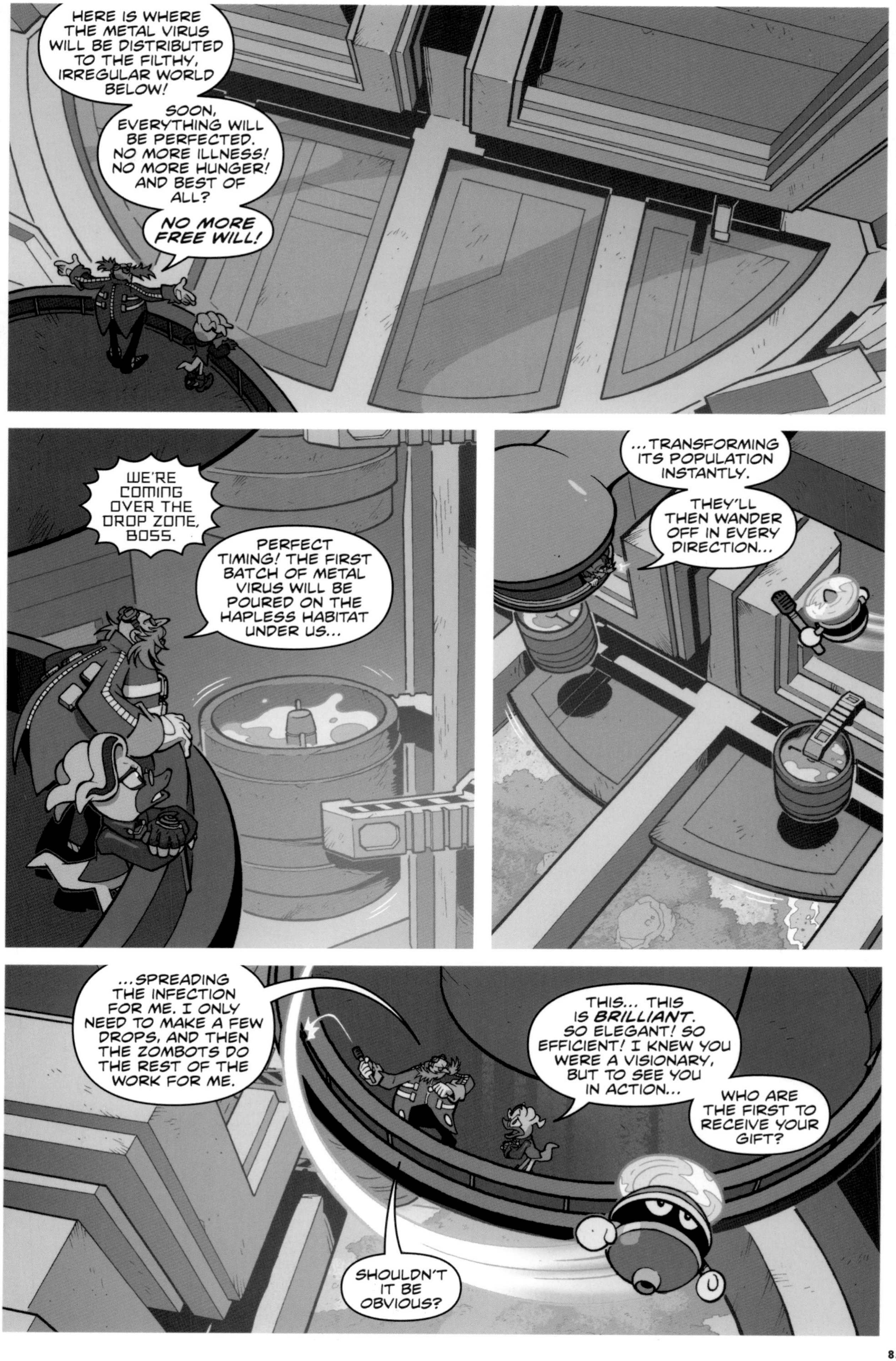
HERE IS WHERE THE METAL VIRUS WILL BE DISTRIBUTED TO THE FILTHY, IRREGULAR WORLD BELOW!
SOON, EVERYTHING WILL BE PERFECTED. NO MORE ILLNESS! NO MORE HUNGER! AND BEST OF ALL?
NO MORE FREE WILL!
WE'RE COMING OVER THE DROP ZONE, BOSS.
PERFECT TIMING! THE FIRST BATCH OF METAL VIRUS WILL BE POURED ON THE HAPLESS HABITAT UNDER US...
...TRANSFORMING ITS POPULATION INSTANTLY.
THEY'LL THEN WANDER OFF IN EVERY DIRECTION...
...SPREADING THE INFECTION FOR ME. I ONLY NEED TO MAKE A FEW DROPS, AND THEN THE ZOMBOTS DO THE REST OF THE WORK FOR ME.
THIS... THIS IS BRILLIANT. SO ELEGANT! SO EFFICIENT! I KNEW YOU WERE A VISIONARY, BUT TO SEE YOU IN ACTION...
WHO ARE THE FIRST TO RECEIVE YOUR GIFT?
SHOULDN'T IT BE OBVIOUS?

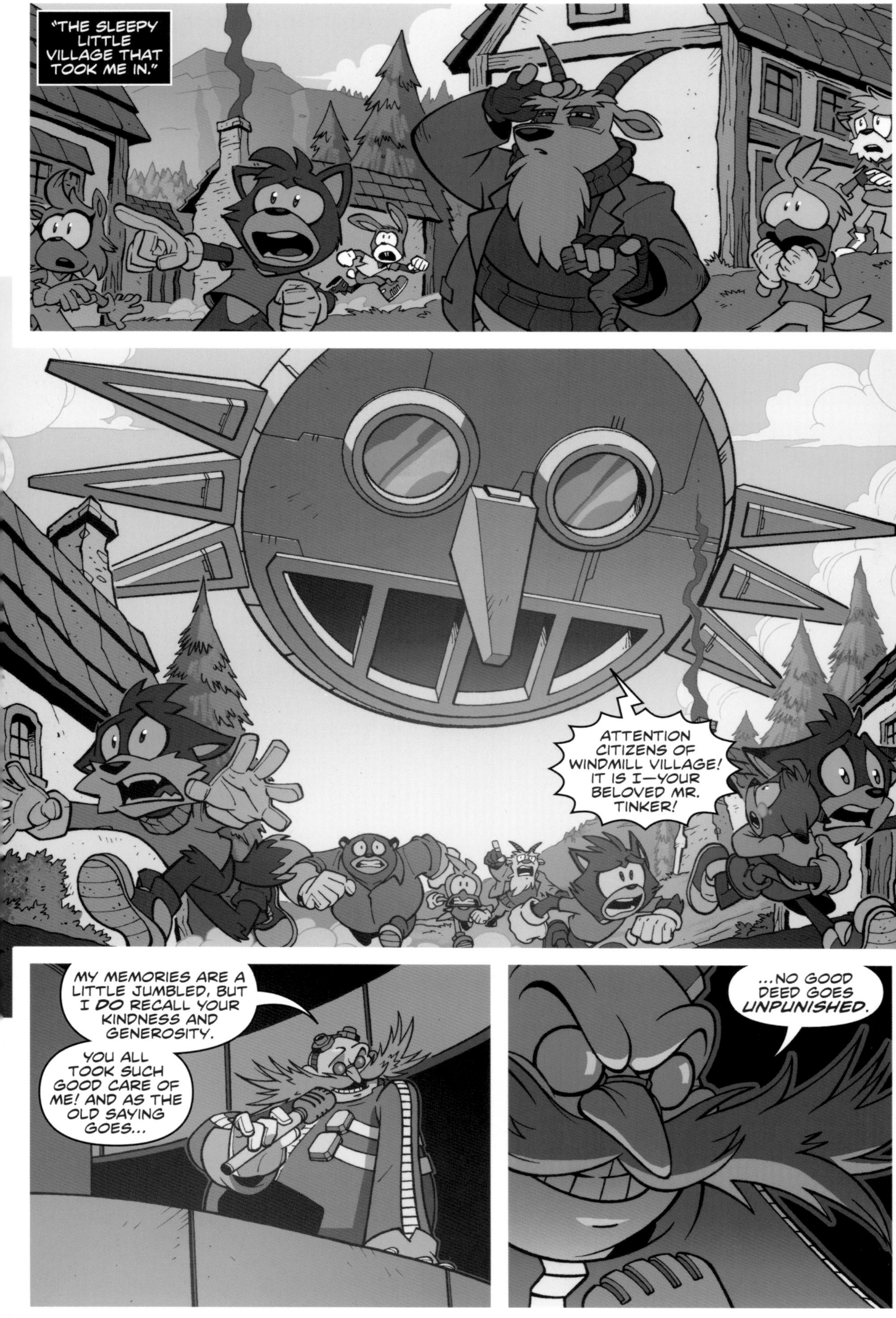
"THE SLEEPY LITTLE VILLAGE THAT TOOK ME IN."
ATTENTION CITIZENS OF WINDMILL VILLAGE! IT IS I—YOUR BELOVED MR. TINKER!
MY MEMORIES ARE A LITTLE JUMBLED, BUT I DO RECALL YOUR KINDNESS AND GENEROSITY.
YOU ALL TOOK SUCH GOOD CARE OF ME! AND AS THE OLD SAYING GOES...
...NO GOOD DEED GOES UNPUNISHED.

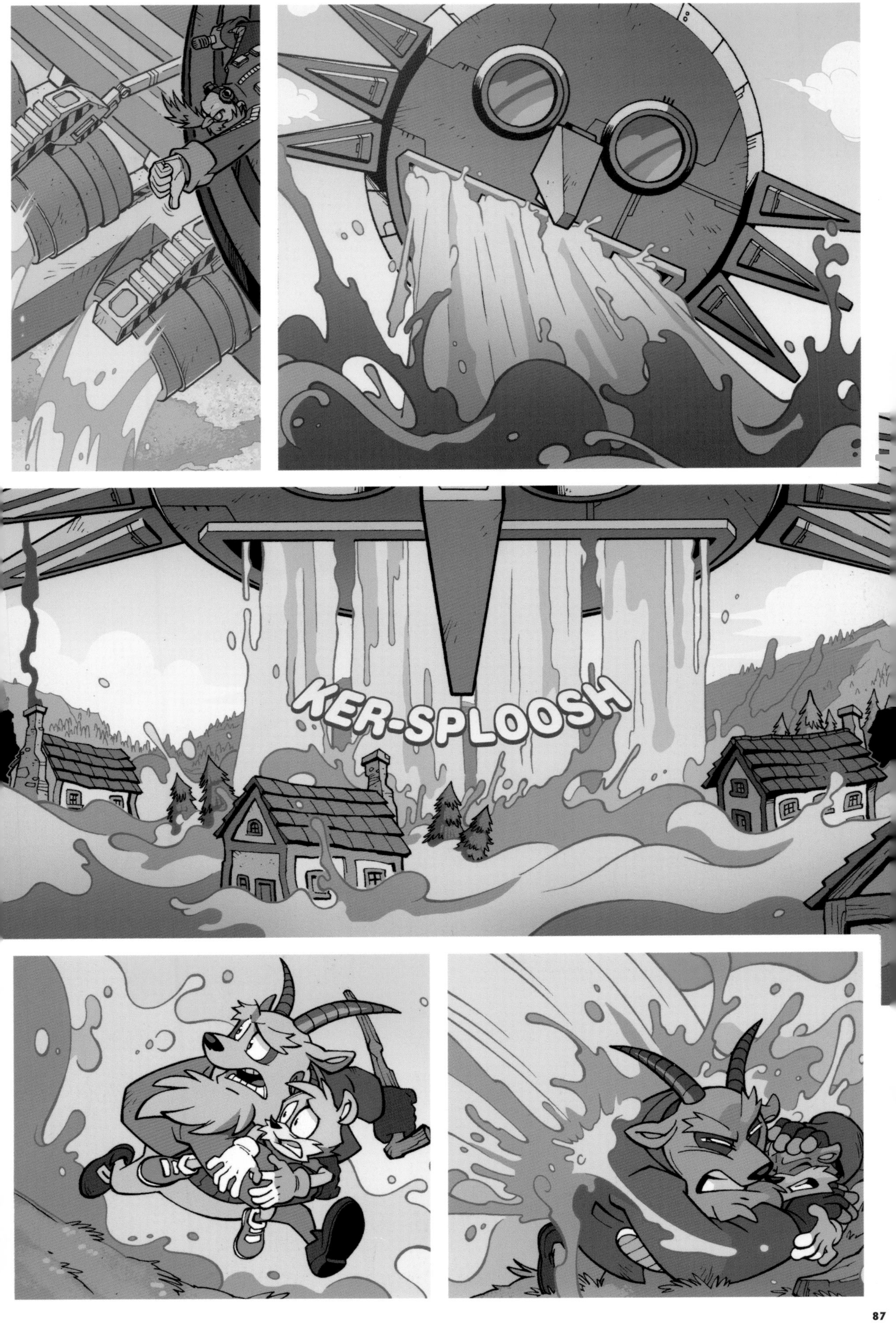
KER-SPLOOSH

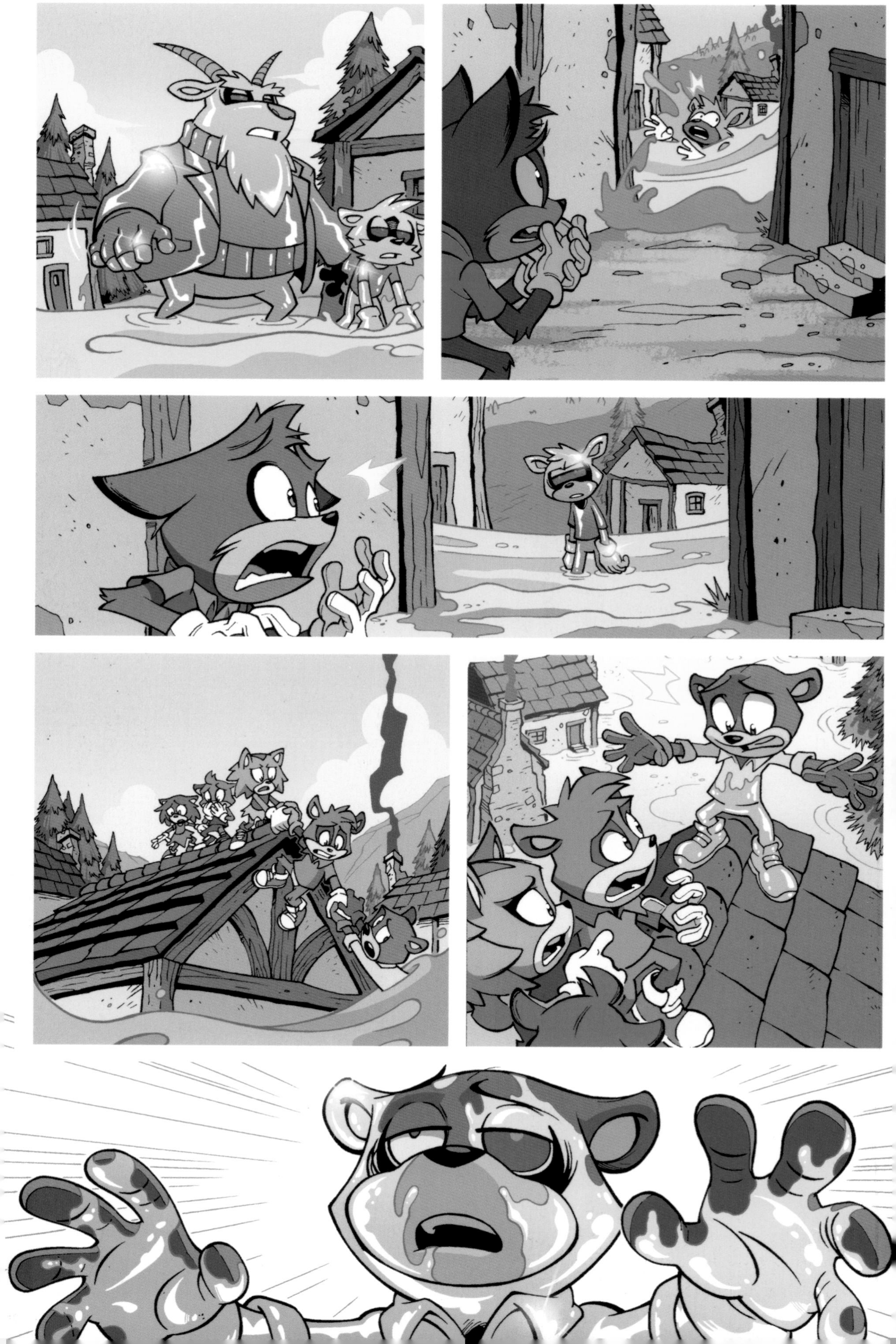

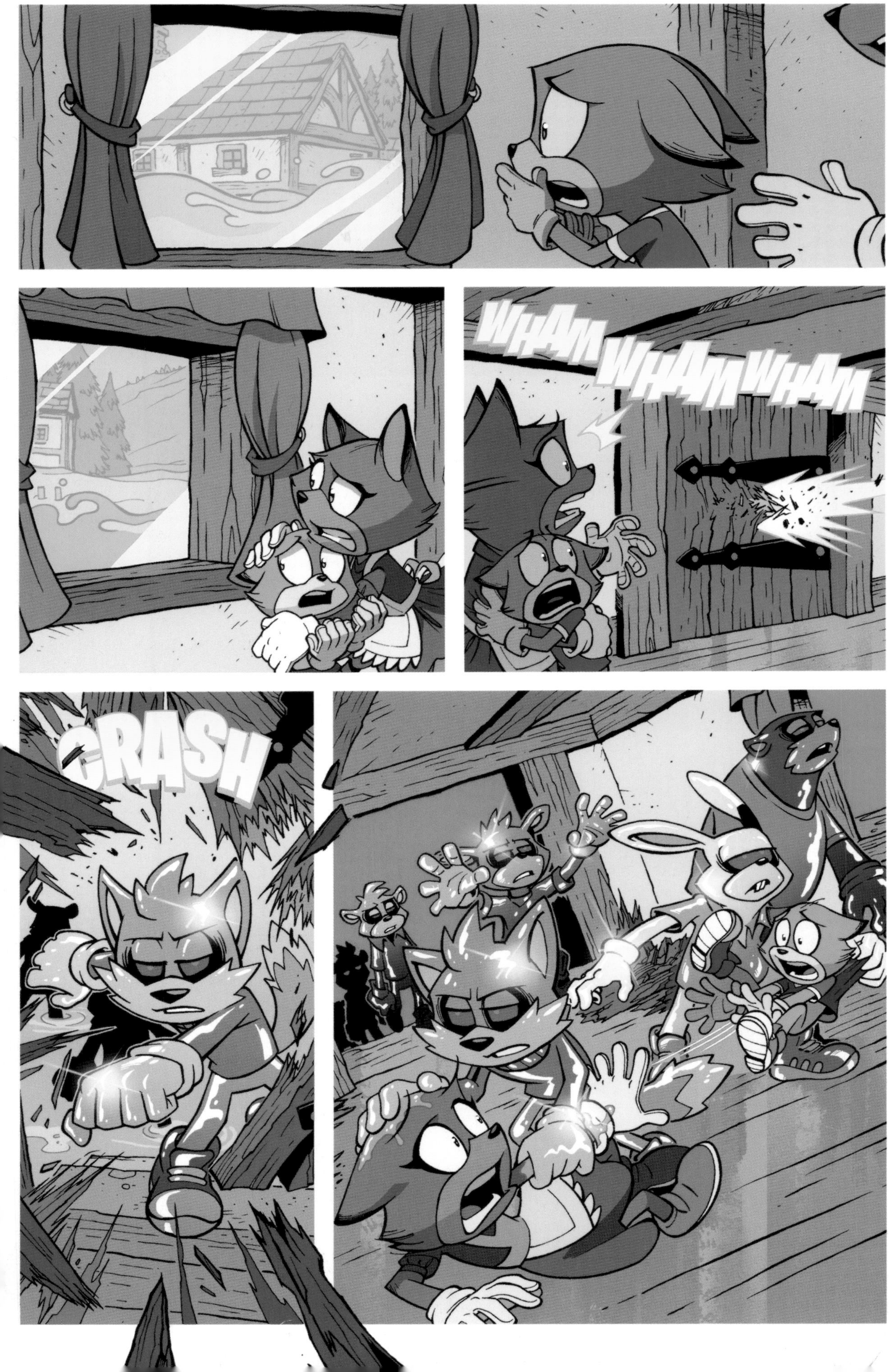
WHAM
WHAM
WHAM
CRASH

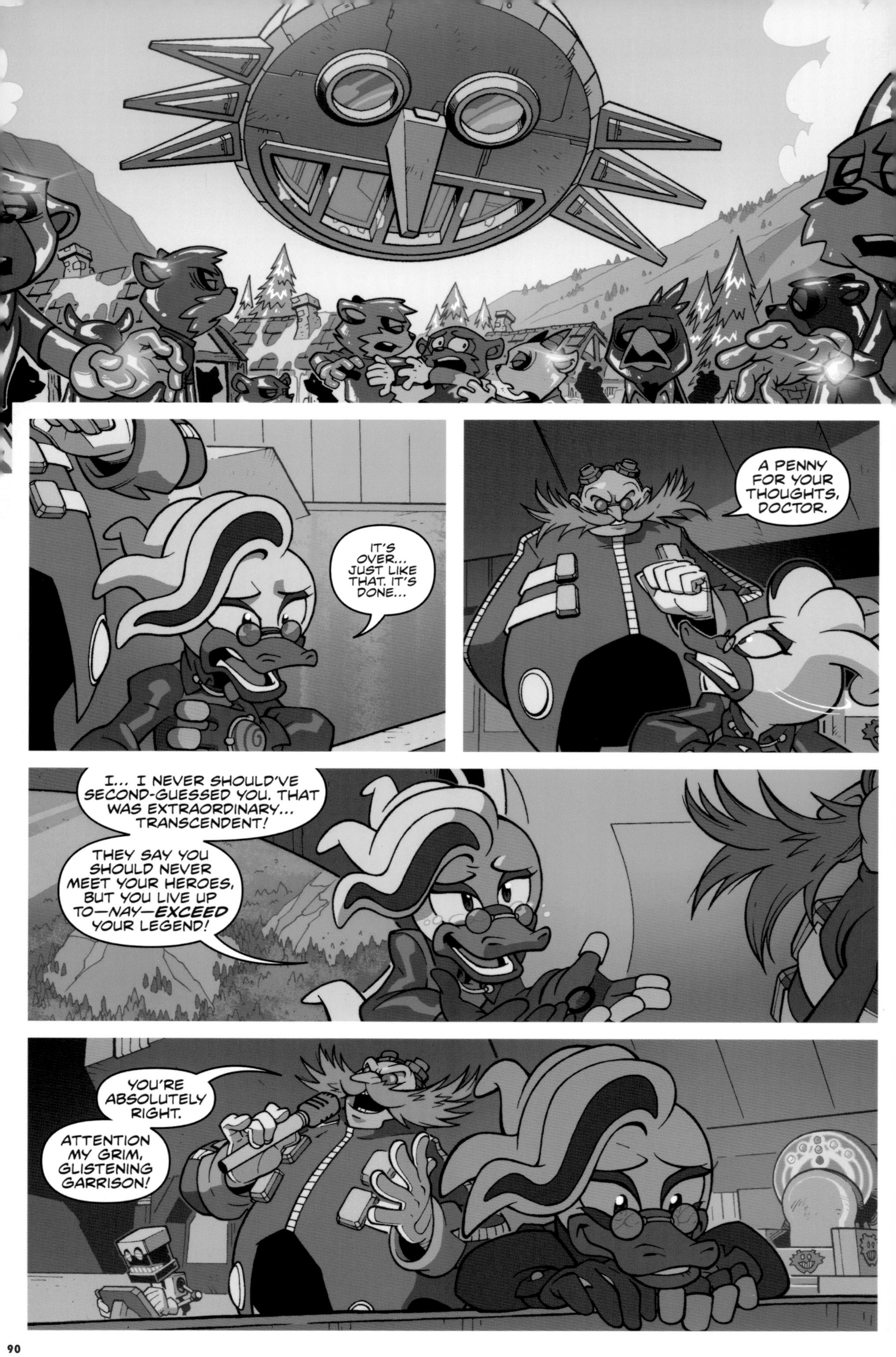
IT'S OVER... JUST LIKE THAT. IT'S DONE...
A PENNY FOR YOUR THOUGHTS, DOCTOR.
I... I NEVER SHOULD'VE SECOND-GUESSED YOU. THAT WAS EXTRAORDINARY... TRANSCENDENT!
THEY SAY YOU SHOULD NEVER MEET YOUR HEROES, BUT YOU LIVE UP TO—NAY—**EXCEED** YOUR LEGEND!
YOU'RE ABSOLUTELY RIGHT.
ATTENTION MY GRIM, GLISTENING GARRISON!

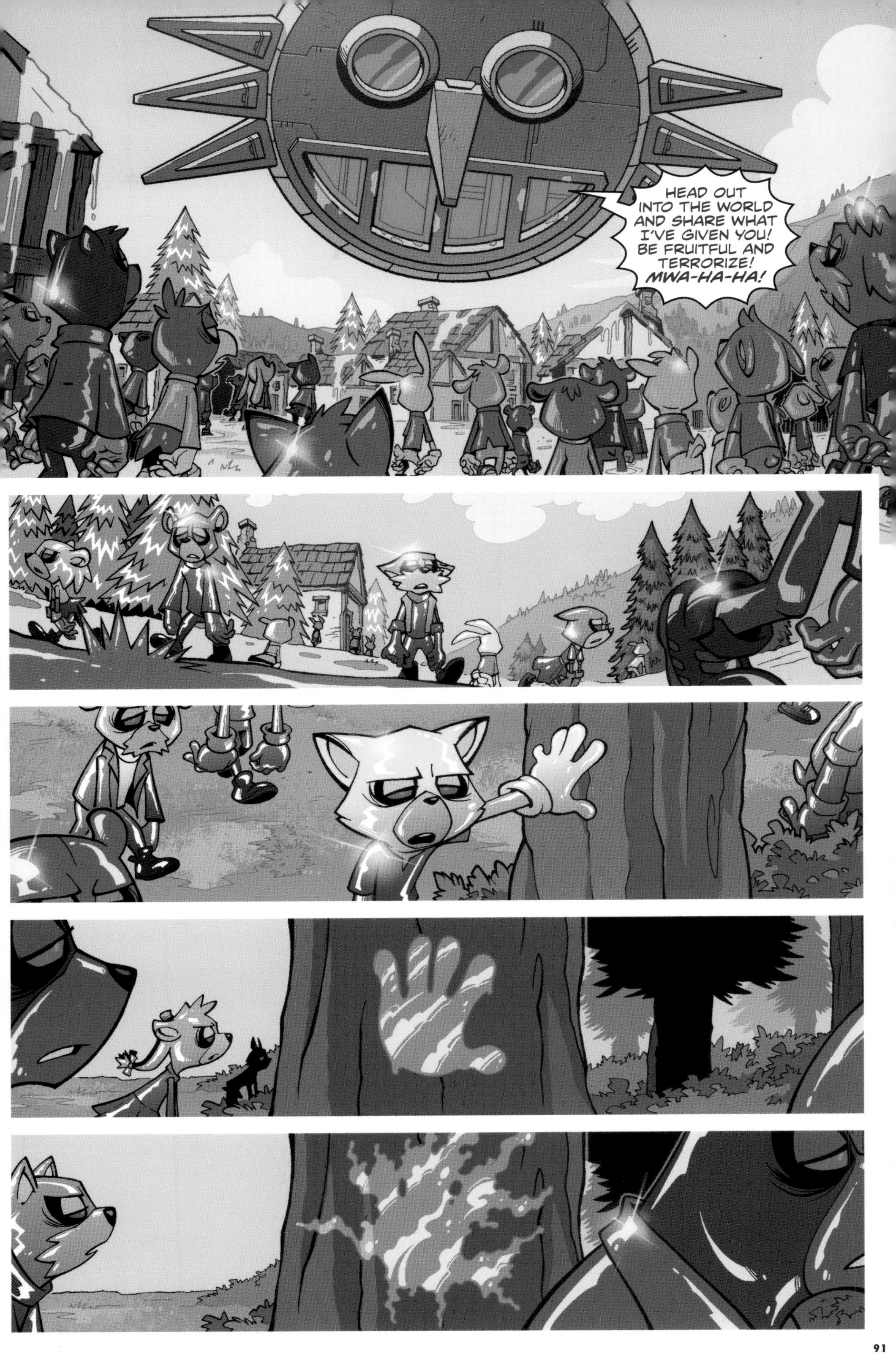
HEAD OUT INTO THE WORLD AND SHARE WHAT I'VE GIVEN YOU! BE FRUITFUL AND TERRORIZE! MWA-HA-HA!

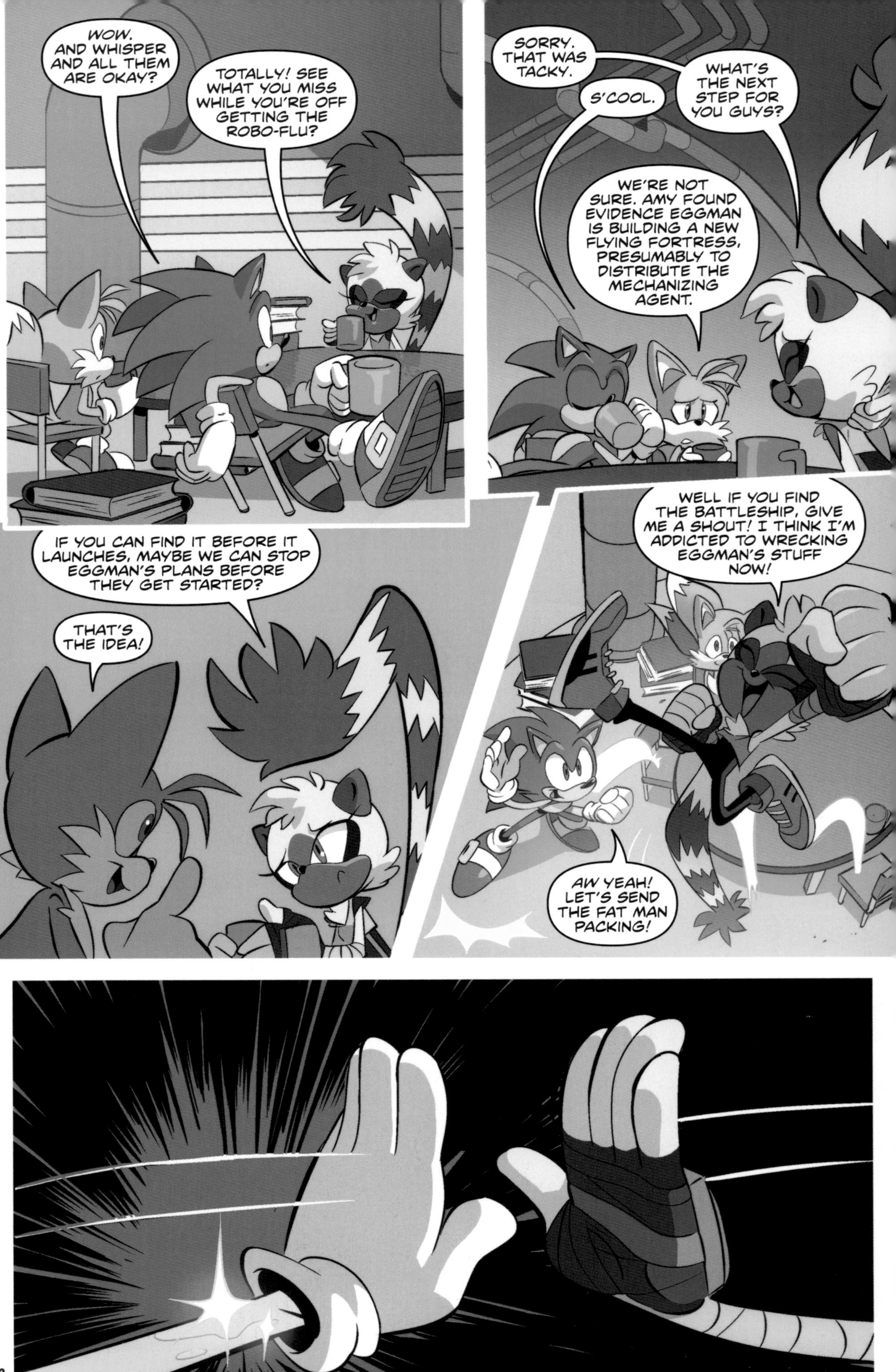
WOW. AND WHISPER AND ALL THEM ARE OKAY?
TOTALLY! SEE WHAT YOU MISS WHILE YOU'RE OFF GETTING THE ROBO-FLU?
SORRY. THAT WAS TACKY.
S'COOL.
WHAT'S THE NEXT STEP FOR YOU GUYS?
WE'RE NOT SURE. AMY FOUND EVIDENCE EGGMAN IS BUILDING A NEW FLYING FORTRESS, PRESUMABLY TO DISTRIBUTE THE MECHANIZING AGENT.
IF YOU CAN FIND IT BEFORE IT LAUNCHES, MAYBE WE CAN STOP EGGMAN'S PLANS BEFORE THEY GET STARTED?
THAT'S THE IDEA!
WELL IF YOU FIND THE BATTLESHIP, GIVE ME A SHOUT! I THINK I'M ADDICTED TO WRECKING EGGMAN'S STUFF NOW!
AW YEAH! LET'S SEND THE FAT MAN PACKING!

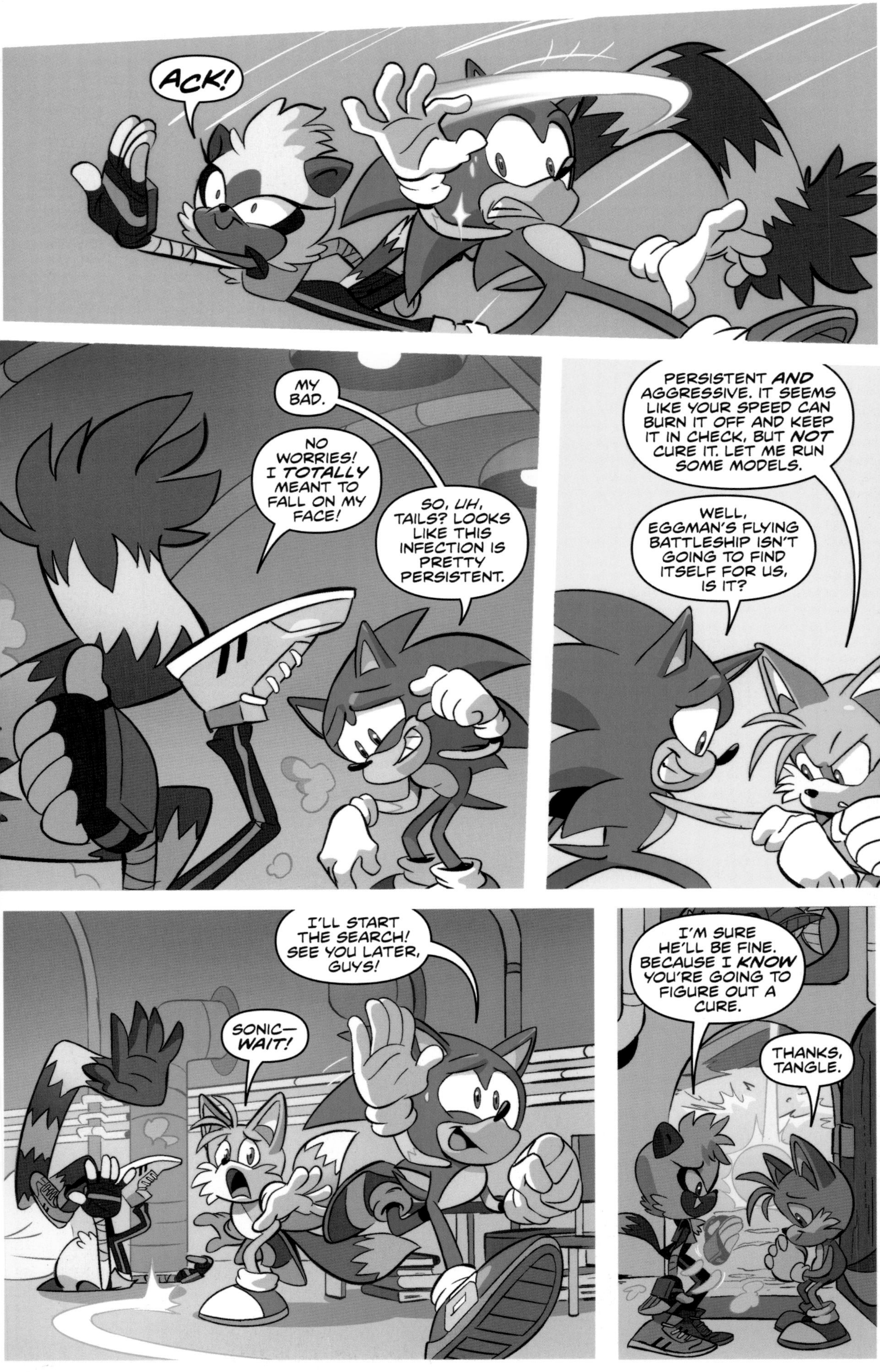
ACK!
MY BAD.
NO WORRIES! I TOTALLY MEANT TO FALL ON MY FACE!
SO, UH, TAILS? LOOKS LIKE THIS INFECTION IS PRETTY PERSISTENT.
PERSISTENT AND AGGRESSIVE. IT SEEMS LIKE YOUR SPEED CAN BURN IT OFF AND KEEP IT IN CHECK, BUT NOT CURE IT. LET ME RUN SOME MODELS.
WELL, EGGMAN'S FLYING BATTLESHIP ISN'T GOING TO FIND ITSELF FOR US, IS IT?
I'LL START THE SEARCH! SEE YOU LATER, GUYS!
SONIC— WAIT!
I'M SURE HE'LL BE FINE. BECAUSE I KNOW YOU'RE GOING TO FIGURE OUT A CURE.
THANKS, TANGLE.

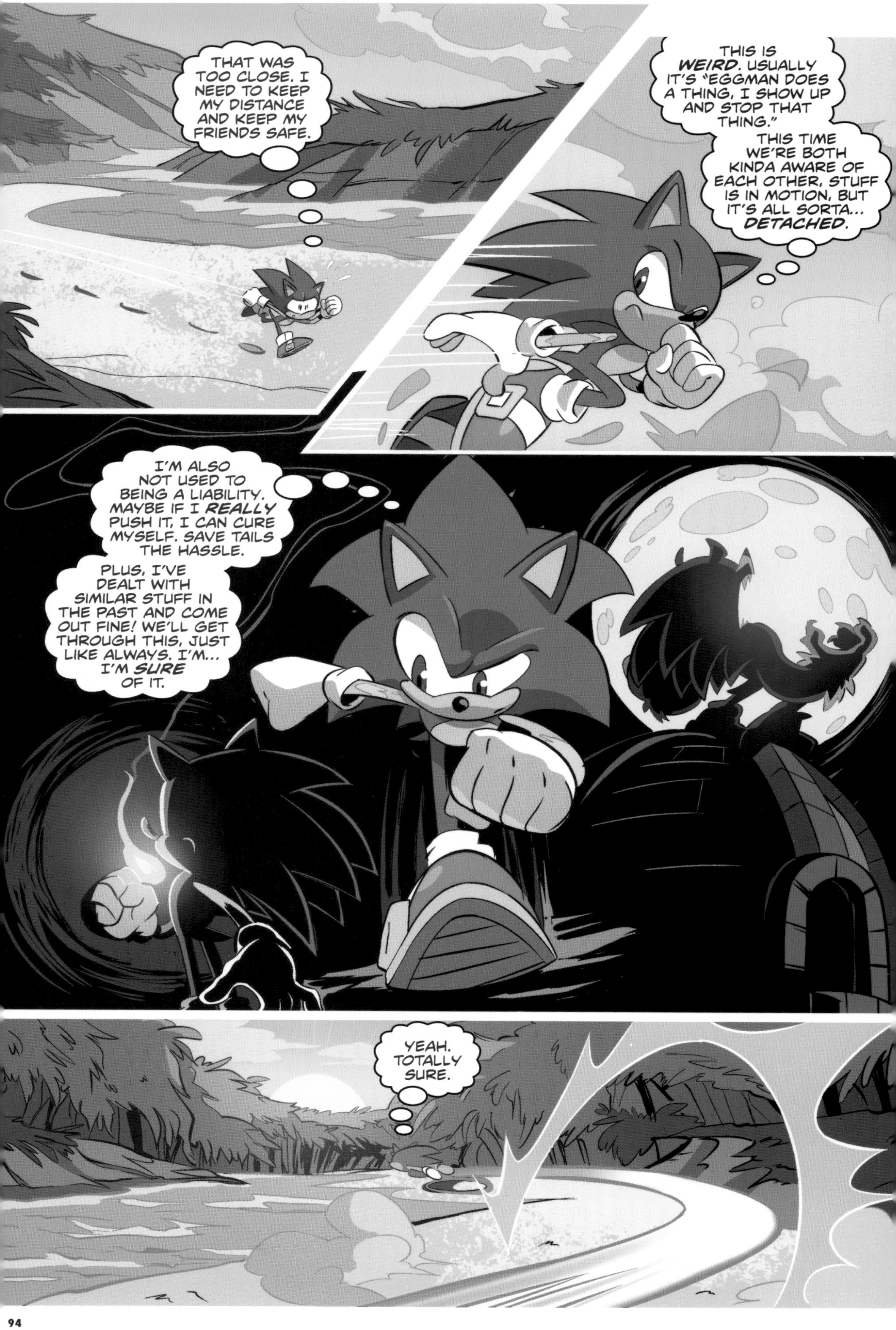
THAT WAS TOO CLOSE. I NEED TO KEEP MY DISTANCE AND KEEP MY FRIENDS SAFE.
THIS IS WEIRD. USUALLY IT'S "EGGMAN DOES A THING, I SHOW UP AND STOP THAT THING."
THIS TIME WE'RE BOTH KINDA AWARE OF EACH OTHER, STUFF IS IN MOTION, BUT IT'S ALL SORTA... DETACHED.
I'M ALSO NOT USED TO BEING A LIABILITY. MAYBE IF I REALLY PUSH IT, I CAN CURE MYSELF. SAVE TAILS THE HASSLE.
PLUS, I'VE DEALT WITH SIMILAR STUFF IN THE PAST AND COME OUT FINE! WE'LL GET THROUGH THIS, JUST LIKE ALWAYS. I'M... I'M SURE OF IT.
YEAH. TOTALLY SURE.

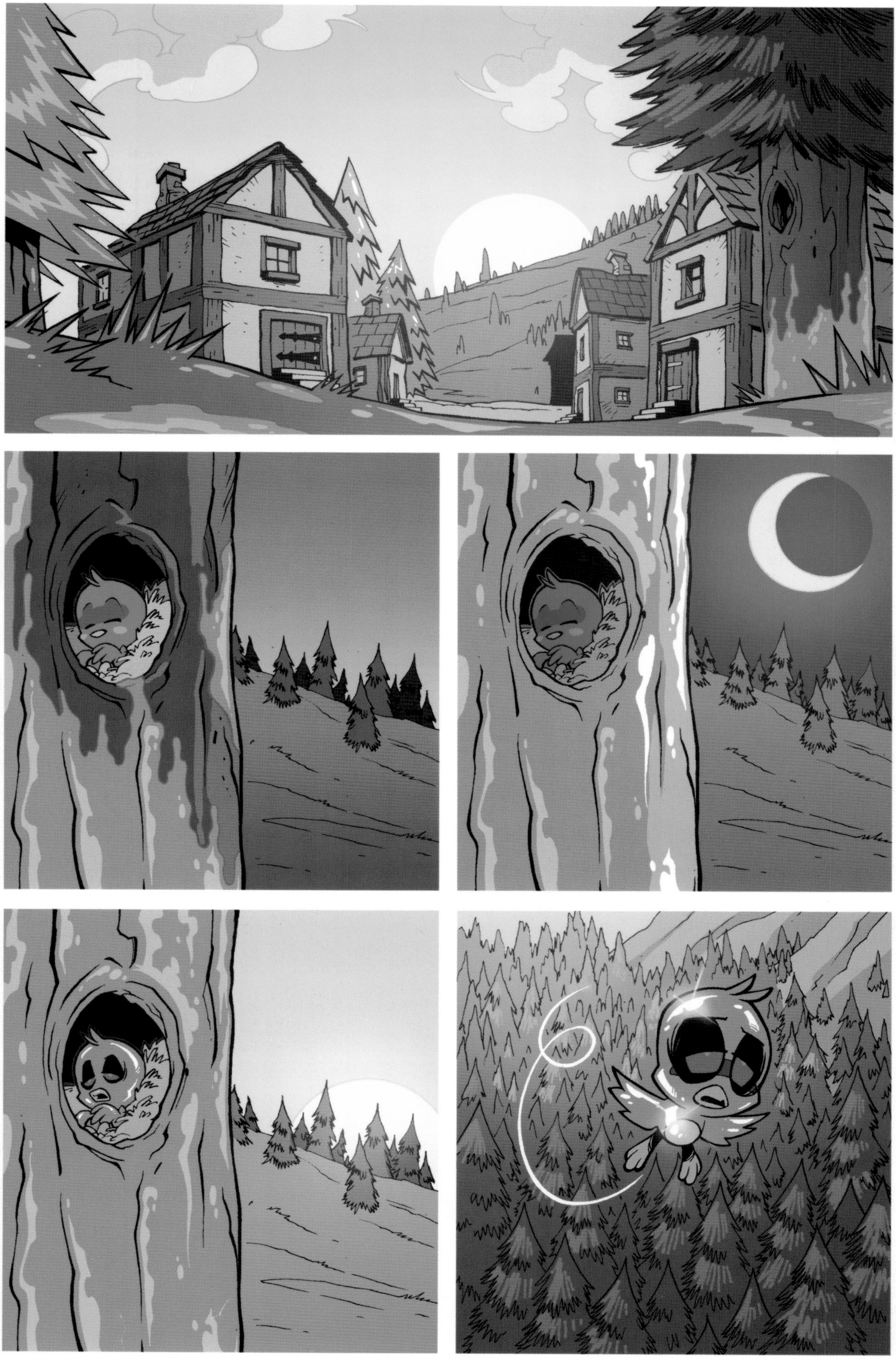

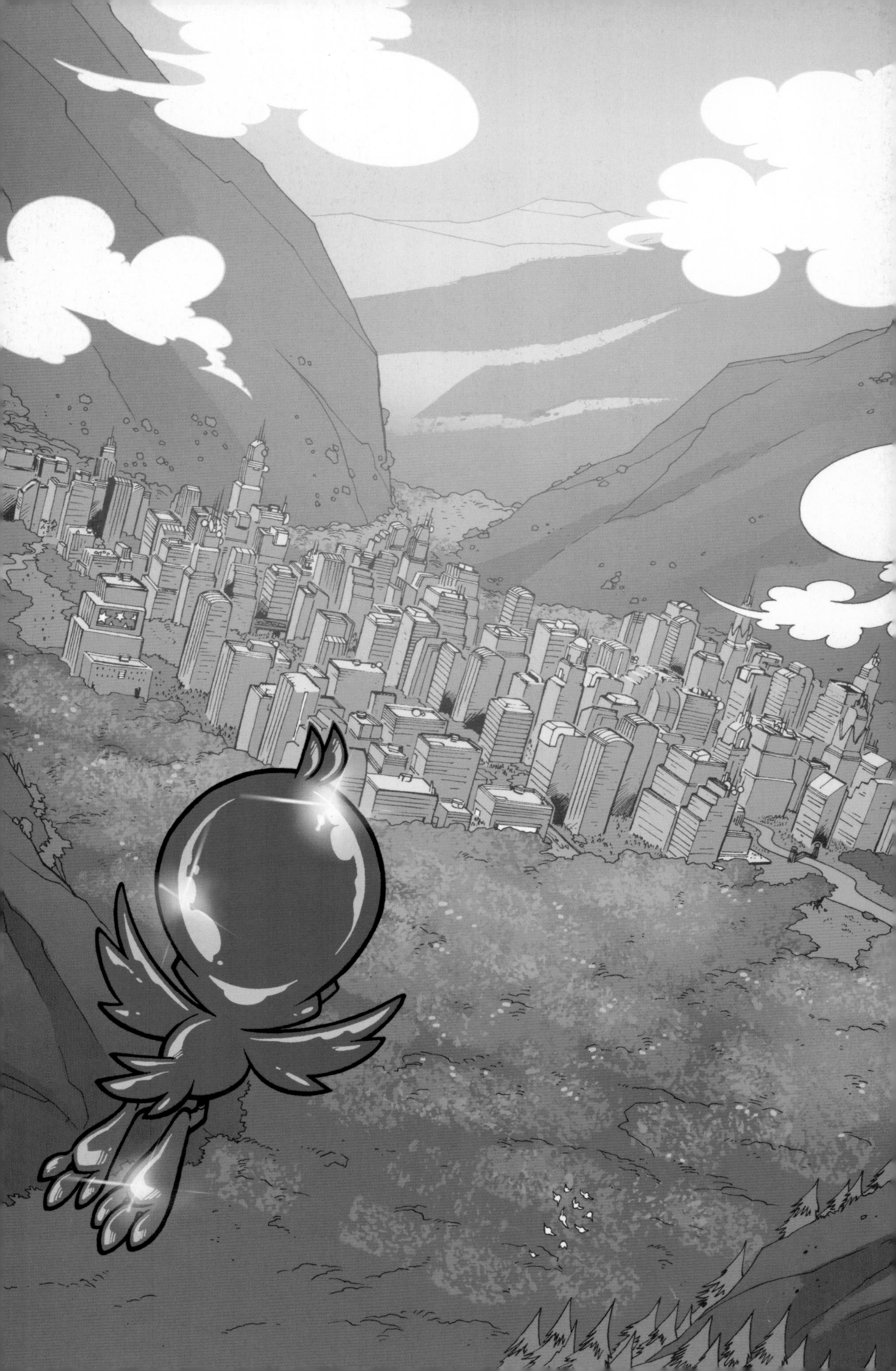

ART BY JONATHAN GRAY COLORS BY MATT HERMS

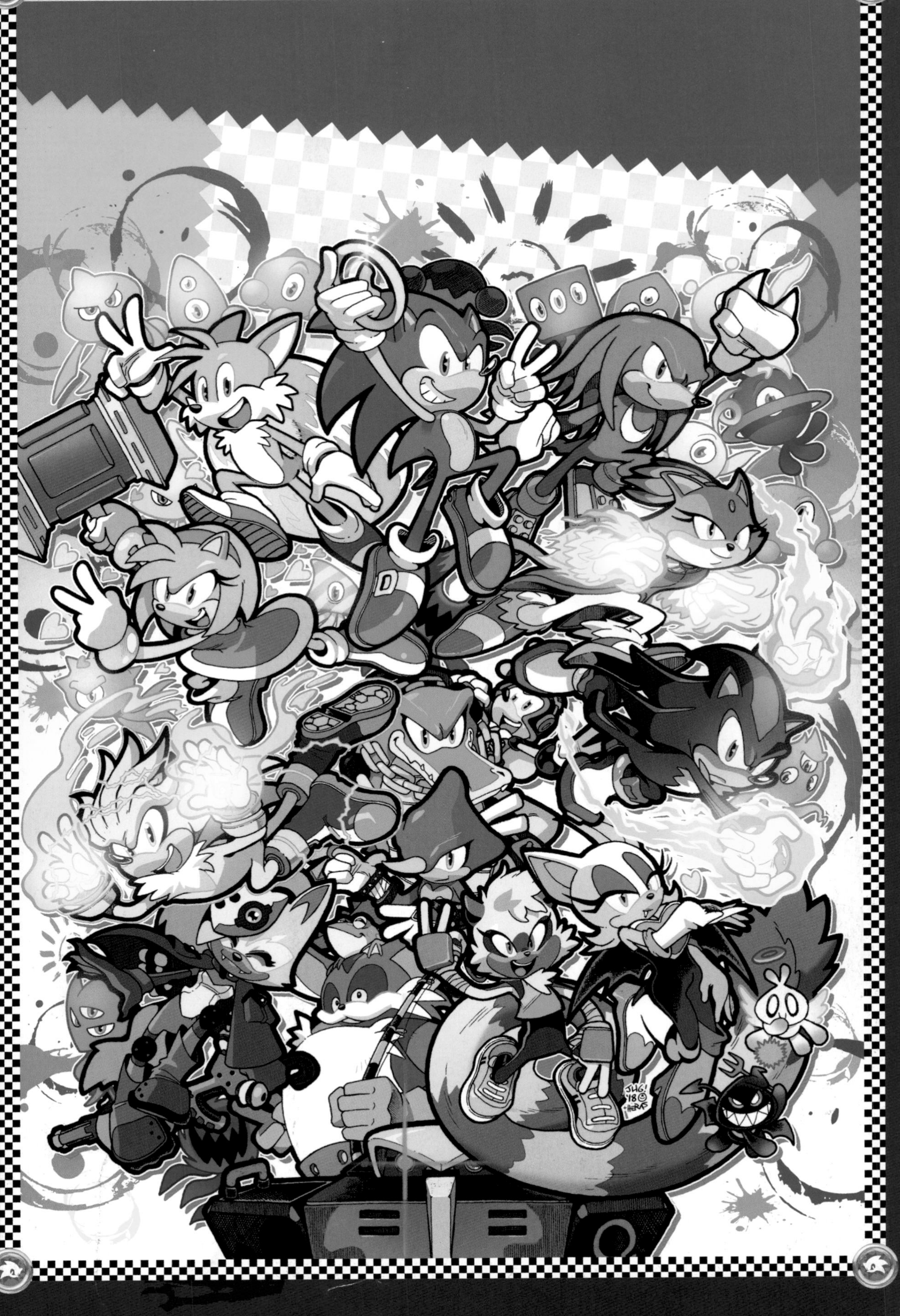

ART BY YUJI UEKAWA OF SONIC TEAM

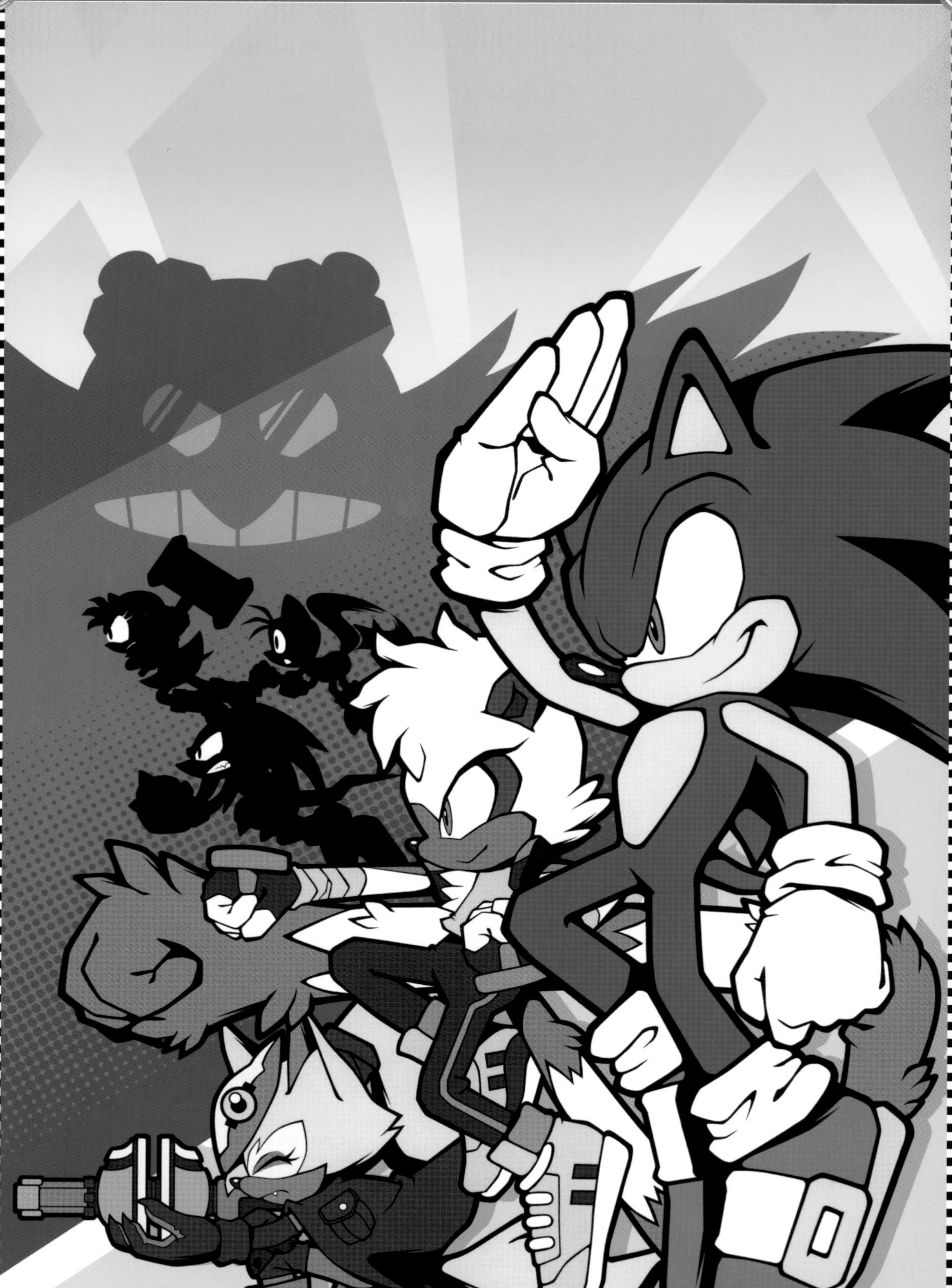

2019 ANNUAL

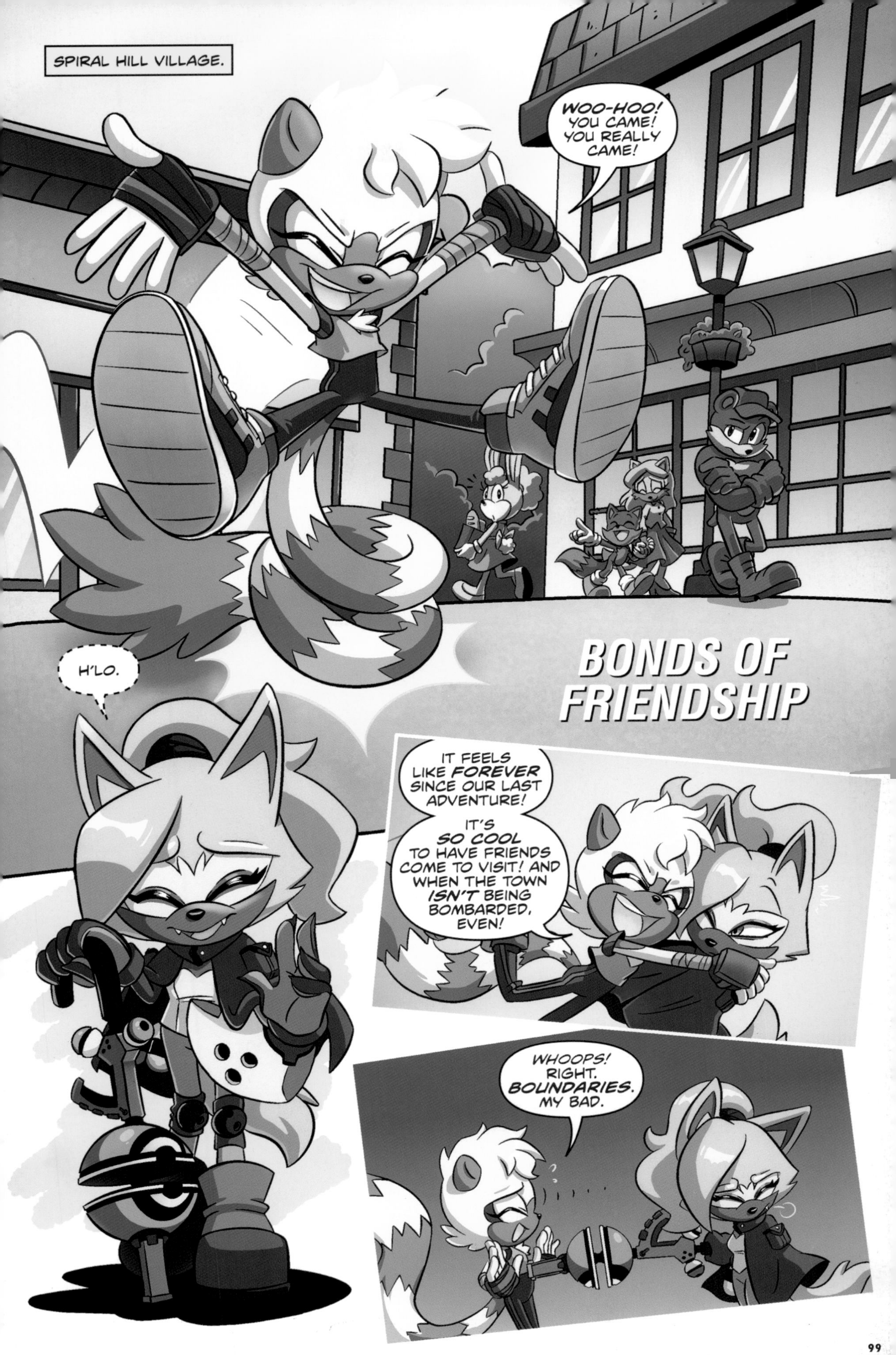
SPIRAL HILL VILLAGE.
WOO-HOO! YOU CAME! YOU REALLY CAME!
H'LO.
BONDS OF FRIENDSHIP
IT FEELS LIKE FOREVER SINCE OUR LAST ADVENTURE!
IT'S SO COOL TO HAVE FRIENDS COME TO VISIT! AND WHEN THE TOWN ISN'T BEING BOMBARDED, EVEN!
WHOOPS! RIGHT. BOUNDARIES. MY BAD.

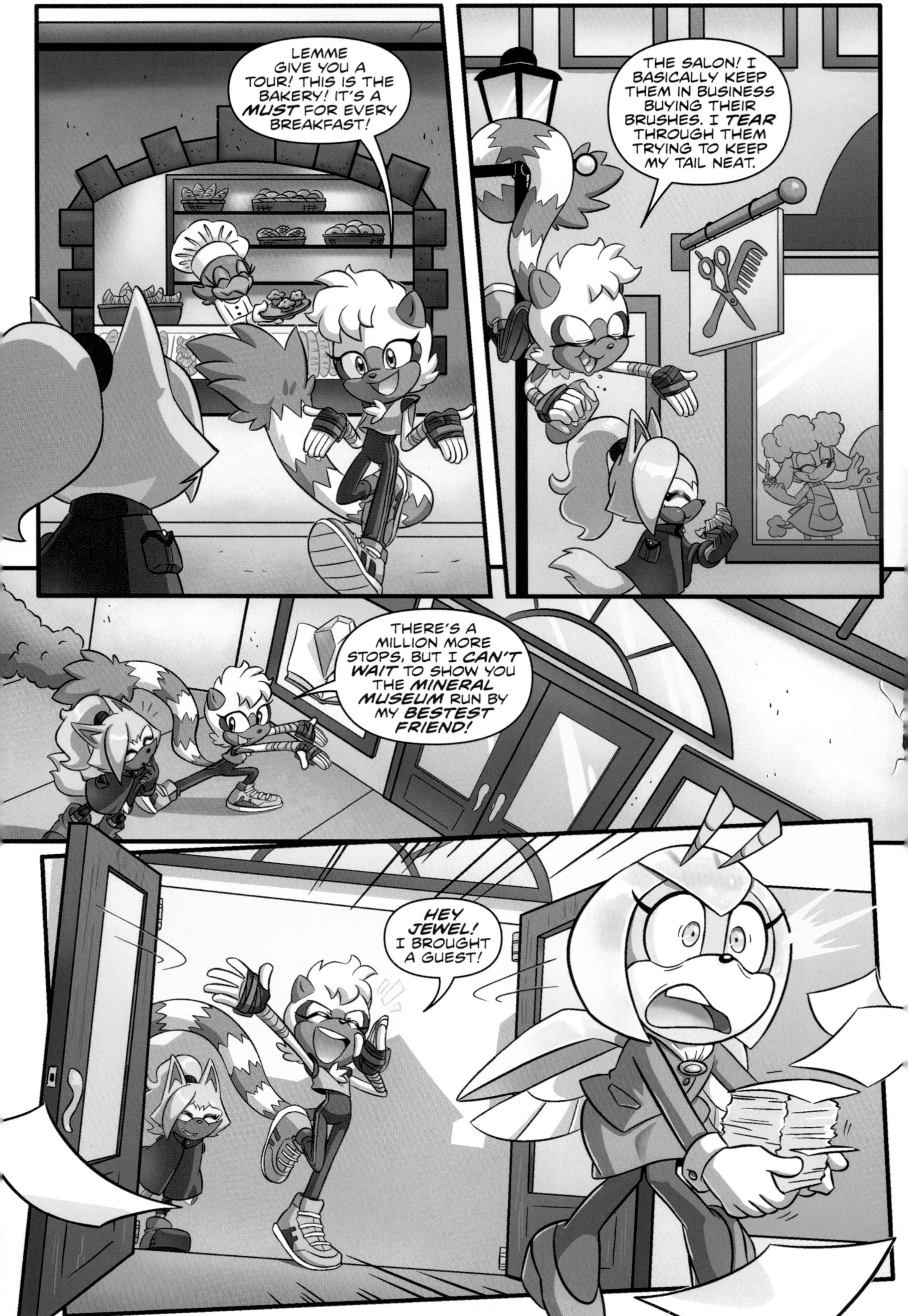
LEMME GIVE YOU A TOUR! THIS IS THE BAKERY! IT'S A MUST FOR EVERY BREAKFAST!
THE SALON! I BASICALLY KEEP THEM IN BUSINESS BUYING THEIR BRUSHES. I TEAR THROUGH THEM TRYING TO KEEP MY TAIL NEAT.
THERE'S A MILLION MORE STOPS, BUT I CAN'T WAIT TO SHOW YOU THE MINERAL MUSEUM RUN BY MY BESTEST FRIEND!
HEY JEWEL! I BROUGHT A GUEST!

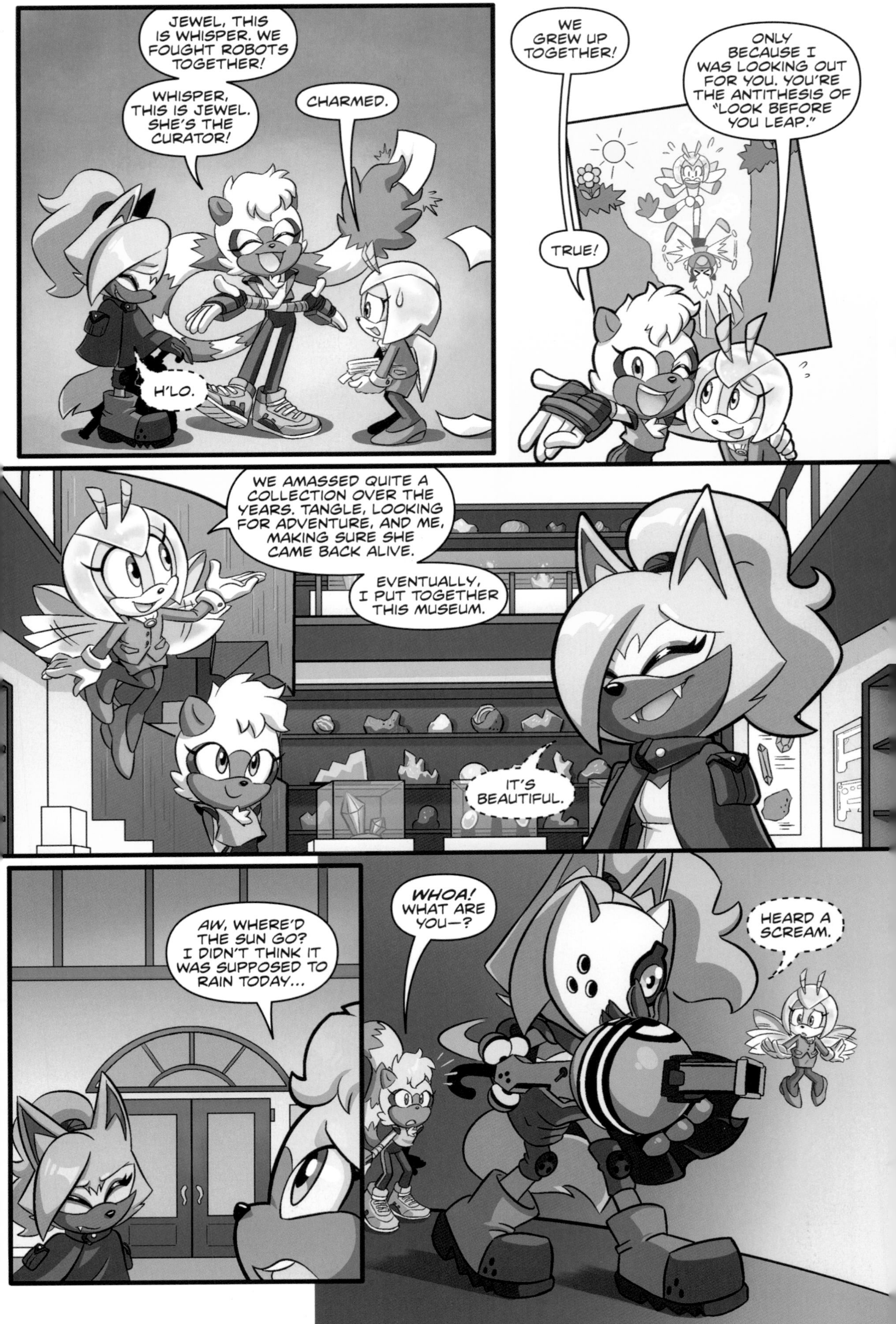
JEWEL, THIS IS WHISPER. WE FOUGHT ROBOTS TOGETHER!
WHISPER, THIS IS JEWEL. SHE'S THE CURATOR!
CHARMED.
H'LO.
WE GREW UP TOGETHER!
ONLY BECAUSE I WAS LOOKING OUT FOR YOU. YOU'RE THE ANTITHESIS OF "LOOK BEFORE YOU LEAP."
TRUE!
WE AMASSED QUITE A COLLECTION OVER THE YEARS. TANGLE, LOOKING FOR ADVENTURE, AND ME, MAKING SURE SHE CAME BACK ALIVE.
EVENTUALLY, I PUT TOGETHER THIS MUSEUM.
IT'S BEAUTIFUL.
AW, WHERE'D THE SUN GO? I DIDN'T THINK IT WAS SUPPOSED TO RAIN TODAY...
WHOA! WHAT ARE YOU—?
HEARD A SCREAM.

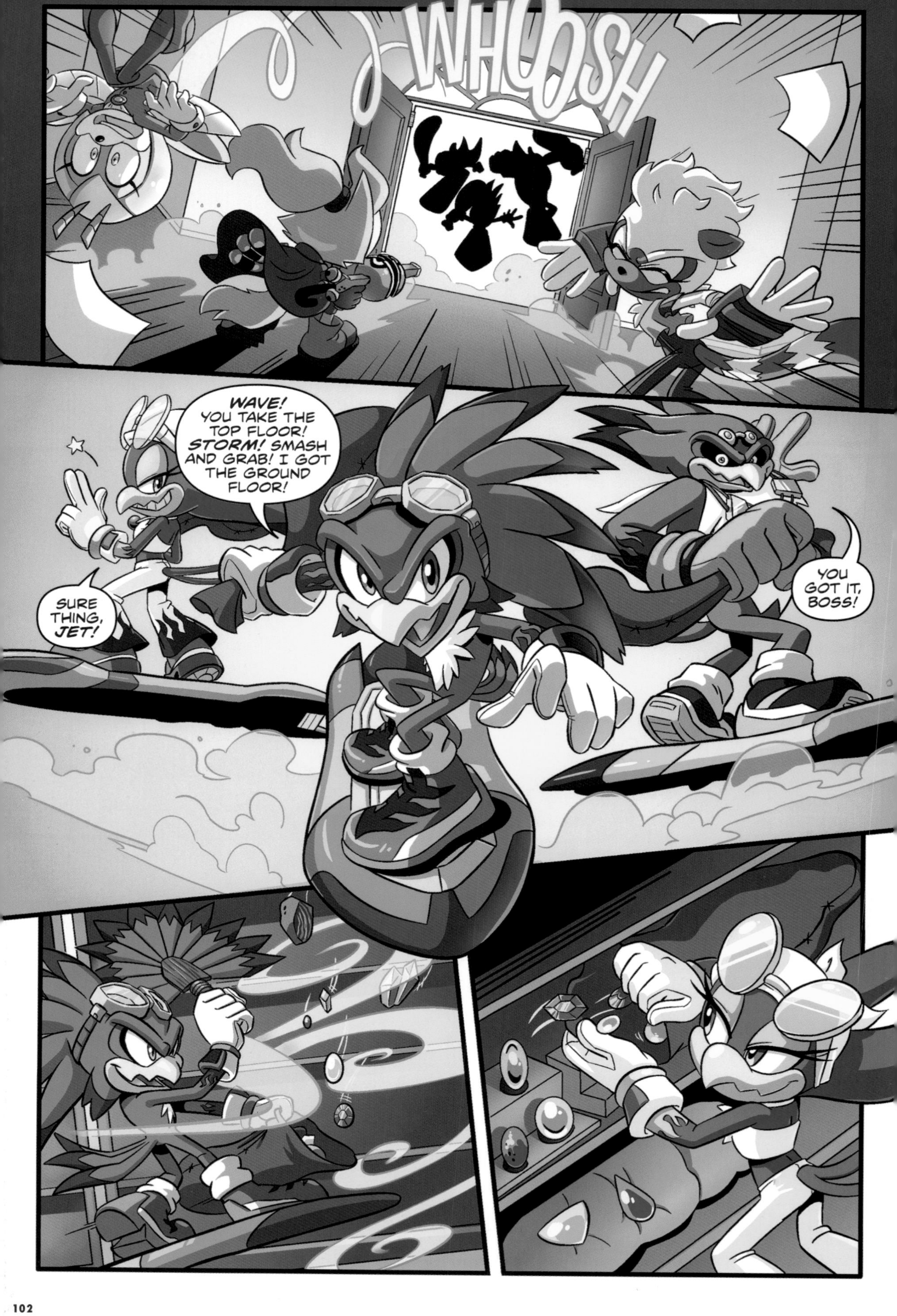
WHOOOSH
WAVE! YOU TAKE THE TOP FLOOR! STORM! SMASH AND GRAB! I GOT THE GROUND FLOOR!
SURE THING, JET!
YOU GOT IT, BOSS!

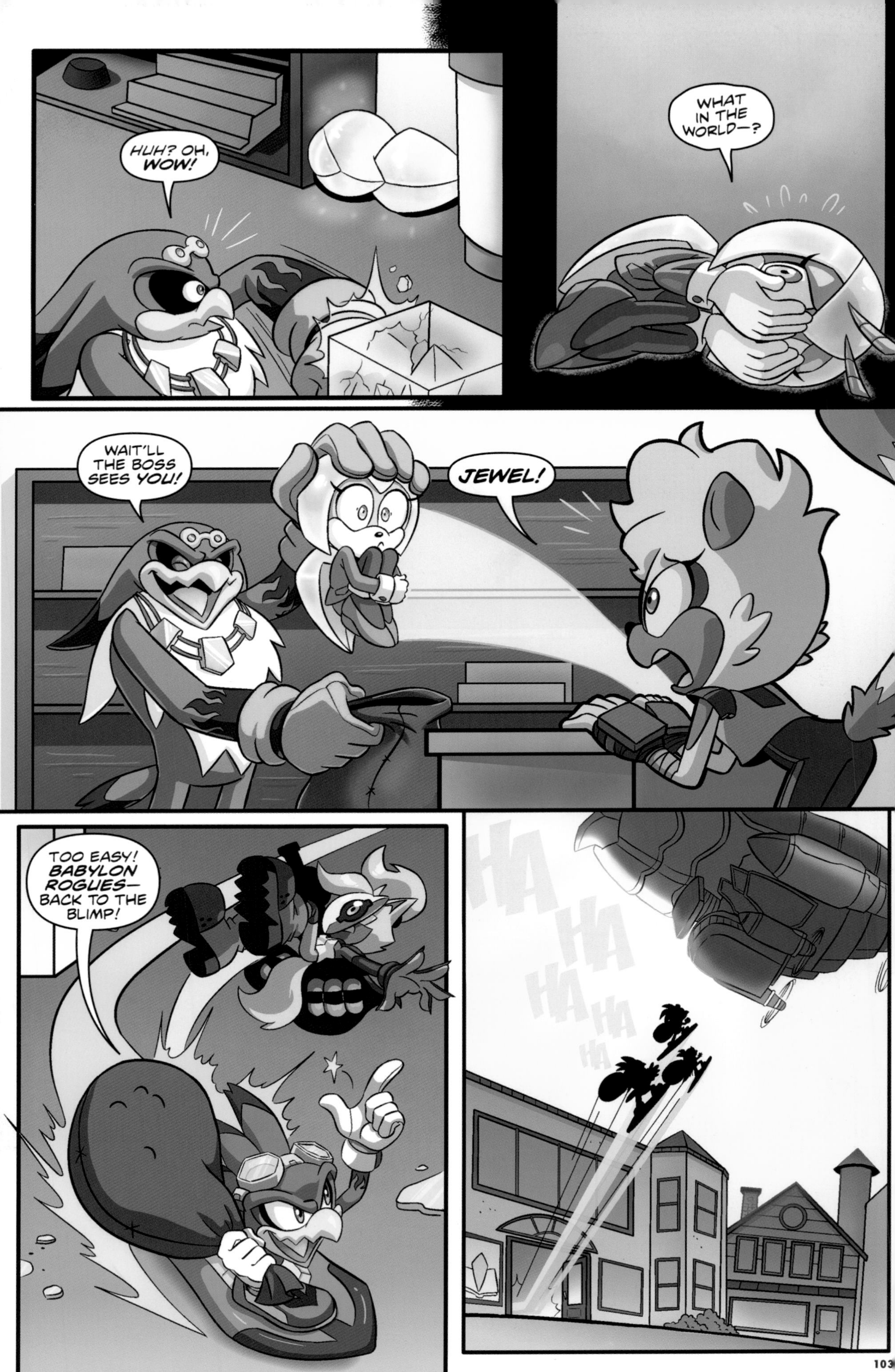
HUH? OH, WOW!
WHAT IN THE WORLD—?
WAIT'LL THE BOSS SEES YOU!
JEWEL!
TOO EASY! BABYLON ROGUES— BACK TO THE BLIMP!
HA HA HA HA HA

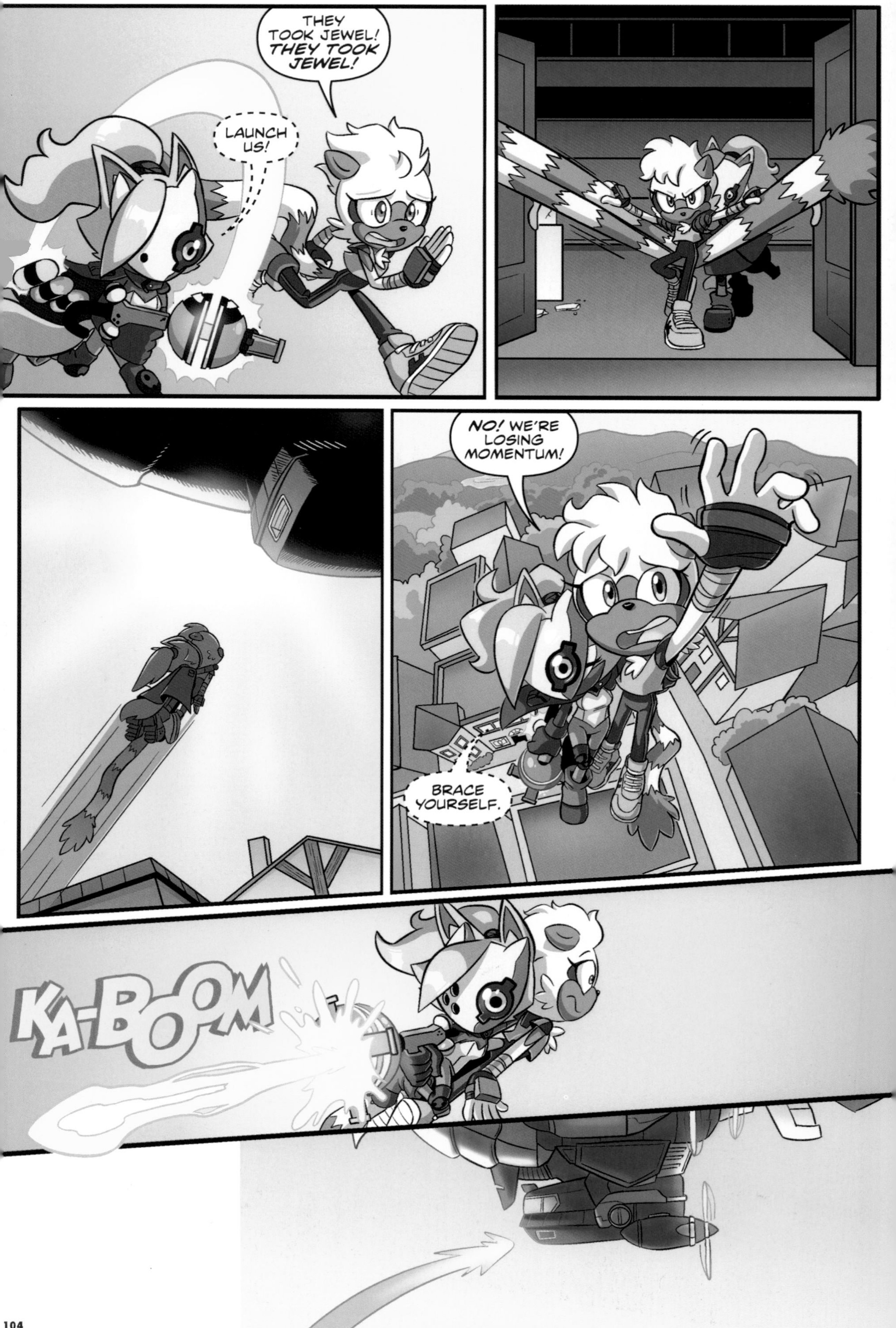
THEY TOOK JEWEL! THEY TOOK JEWEL!
LAUNCH US!
NO! WE'RE LOSING MOMENTUM!
BRACE YOURSELF.
KA-BOOM

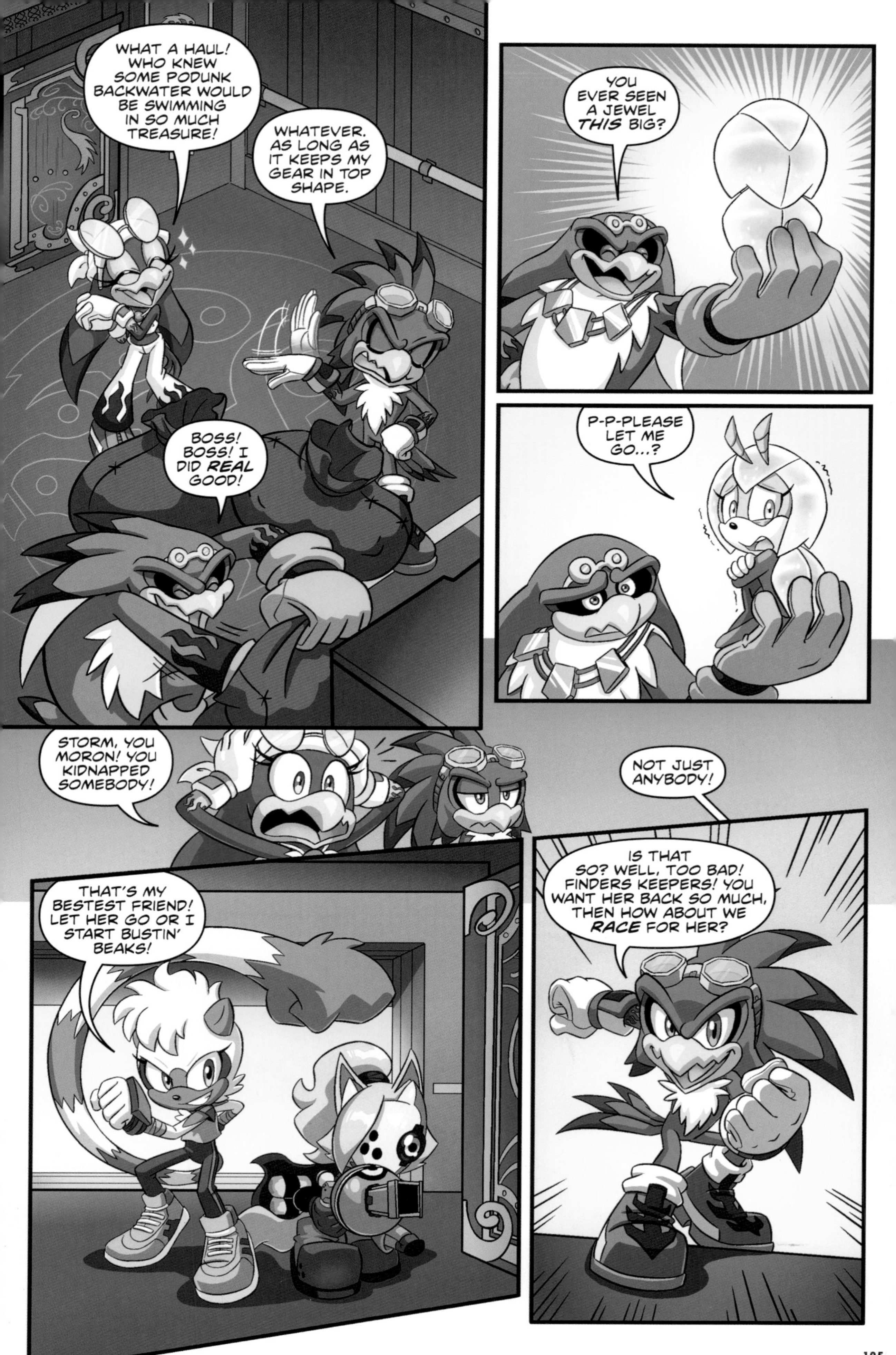
WHAT A HAUL! WHO KNEW SOME PODUNK BACKWATER WOULD BE SWIMMING IN SO MUCH TREASURE!
WHATEVER. AS LONG AS IT KEEPS MY GEAR IN TOP SHAPE.
BOSS! BOSS! I DID REAL GOOD!
YOU EVER SEEN A JEWEL THIS BIG?
P-P-PLEASE LET ME GO...?
STORM, YOU MORON! YOU KIDNAPPED SOMEBODY!
NOT JUST ANYBODY!
THAT'S MY BESTEST FRIEND! LET HER GO OR I START BUSTIN' BEAKS!
IS THAT SO? WELL, TOO BAD! FINDERS KEEPERS! YOU WANT HER BACK SO MUCH, THEN HOW ABOUT WE RACE FOR HER?

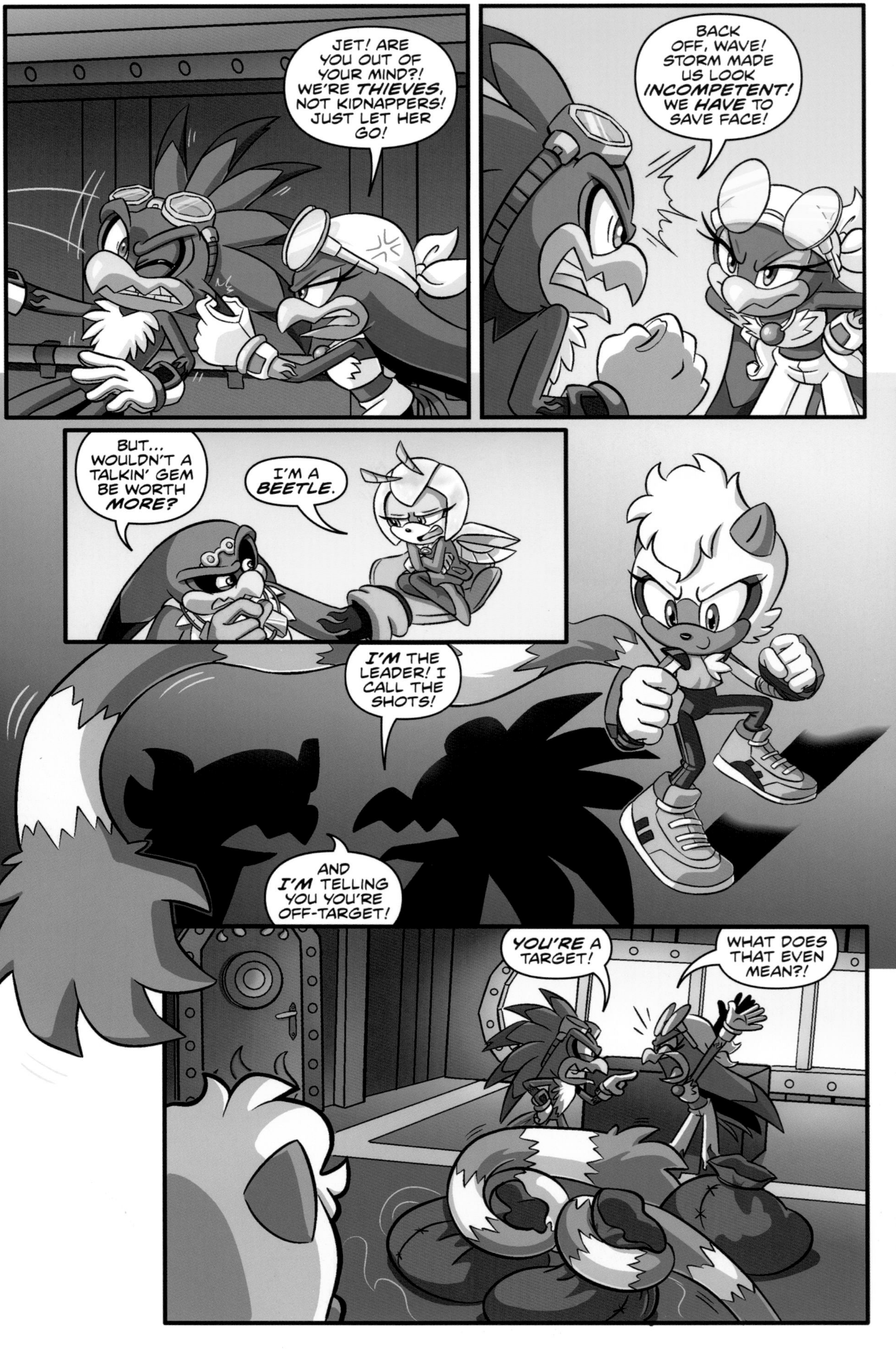
JET! ARE YOU OUT OF YOUR MIND?! WE'RE THIEVES, NOT KIDNAPPERS! JUST LET HER GO!
BACK OFF, WAVE! STORM MADE US LOOK INCOMPETENT! WE HAVE TO SAVE FACE!
BUT... WOULDN'T A TALKIN' GEM BE WORTH MORE?
I'M A BEETLE.
I'M THE LEADER! I CALL THE SHOTS!
AND I'M TELLING YOU YOU'RE OFF-TARGET!
YOU'RE A TARGET!
WHAT DOES THAT EVEN MEAN?!

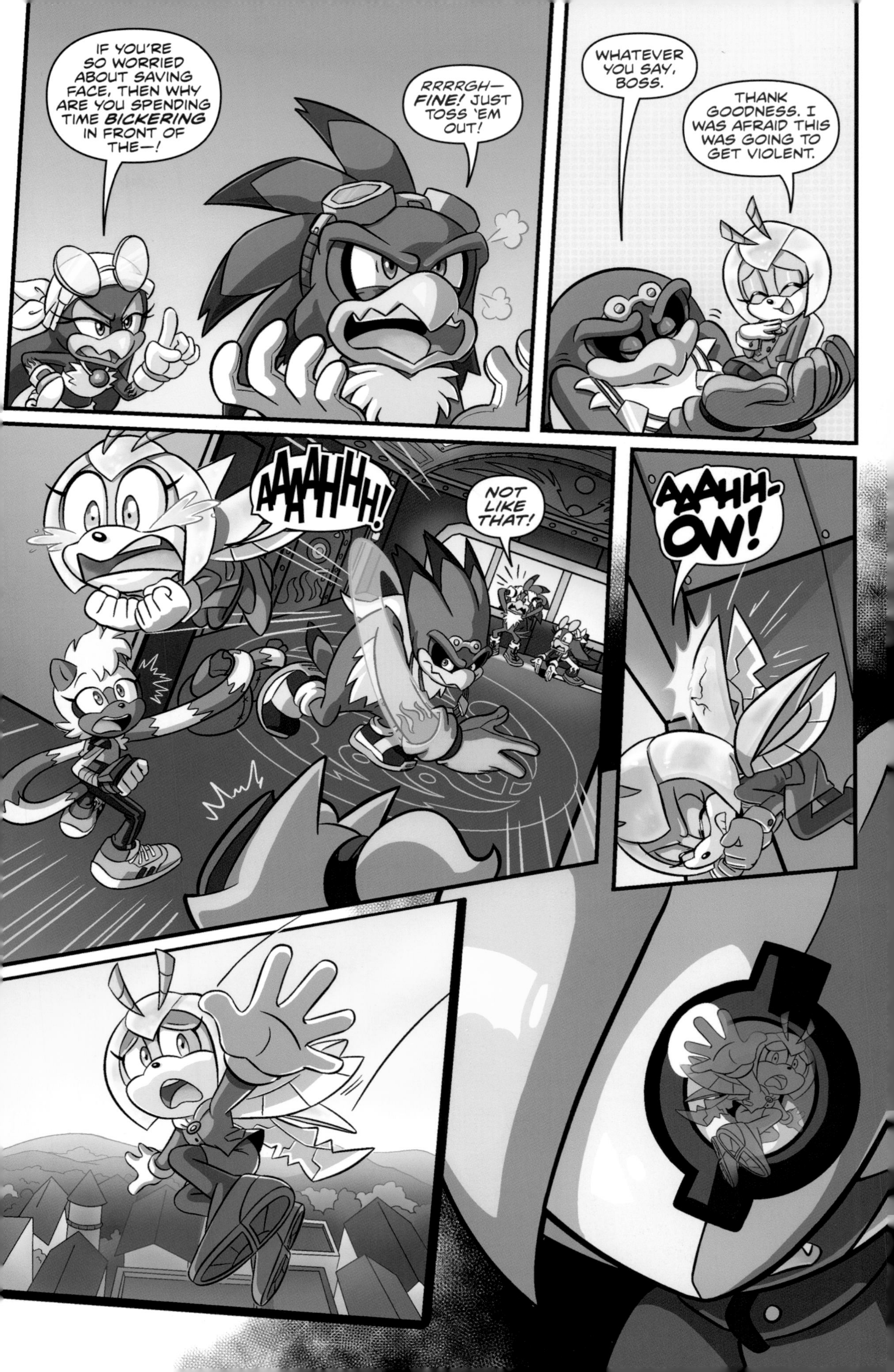

IF YOU'RE SO WORRIED ABOUT SAVING FACE, THEN WHY ARE YOU SPENDING TIME BICKERING IN FRONT OF THE—!
RRRRGH— FINE! JUST TOSS 'EM OUT!
WHATEVER YOU SAY, BOSS.
THANK GOODNESS. I WAS AFRAID THIS WAS GOING TO GET VIOLENT.
AAAAHHHH!
NOT LIKE THAT!
AAAHH-OW!

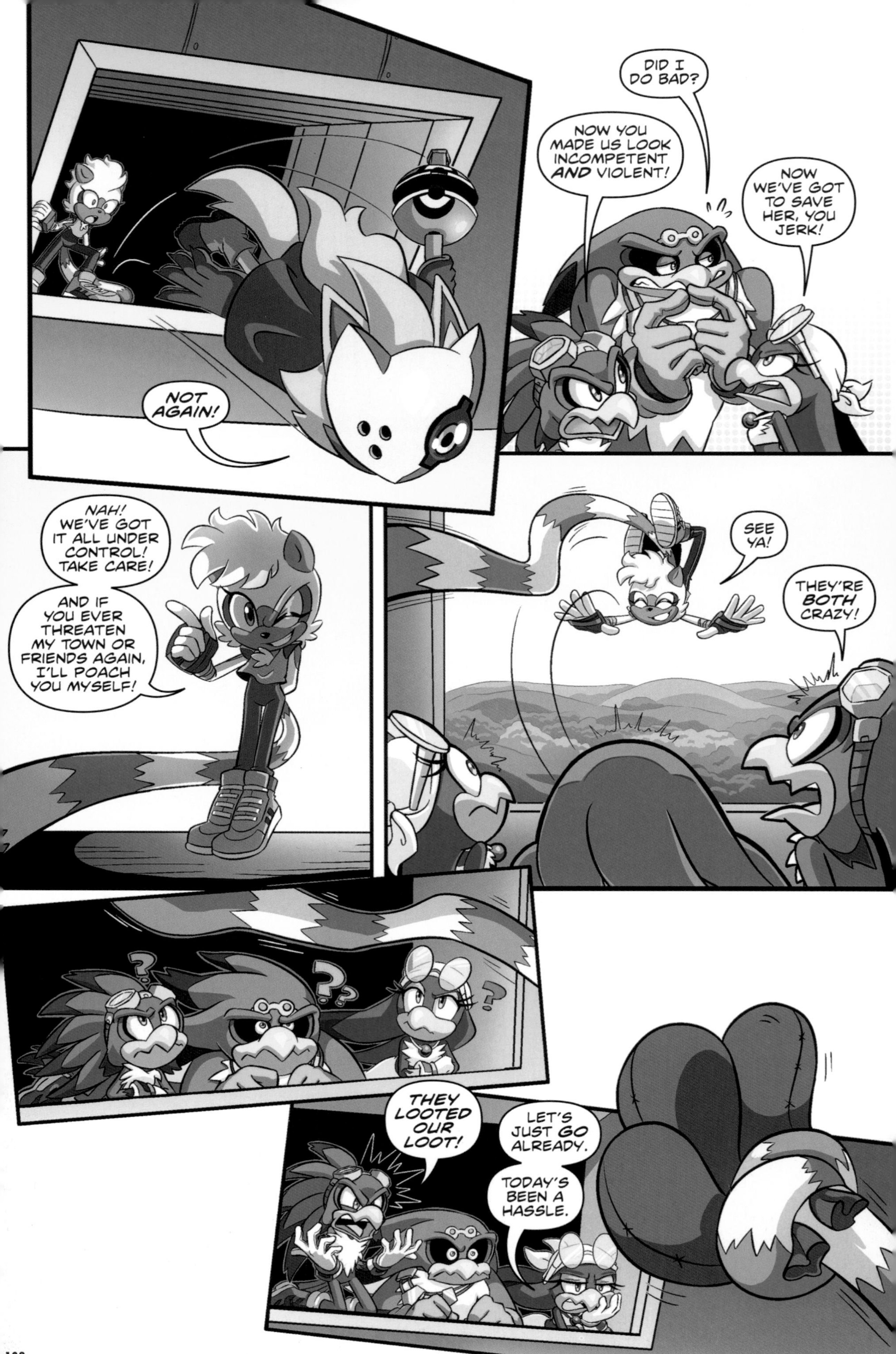
NOT AGAIN!
NOW YOU MADE US LOOK INCOMPETENT AND VIOLENT!
DID I DO BAD?
NOW WE'VE GOT TO SAVE HER, YOU JERK!
NAH! WE'VE GOT IT ALL UNDER CONTROL! TAKE CARE!
AND IF YOU EVER THREATEN MY TOWN OR FRIENDS AGAIN, I'LL POACH YOU MYSELF!
SEE YA!
THEY'RE BOTH CRAZY!
?
??
?
THEY LOOTED OUR LOOT!
LET'S JUST GO ALREADY.
TODAY'S BEEN A HASSLE.

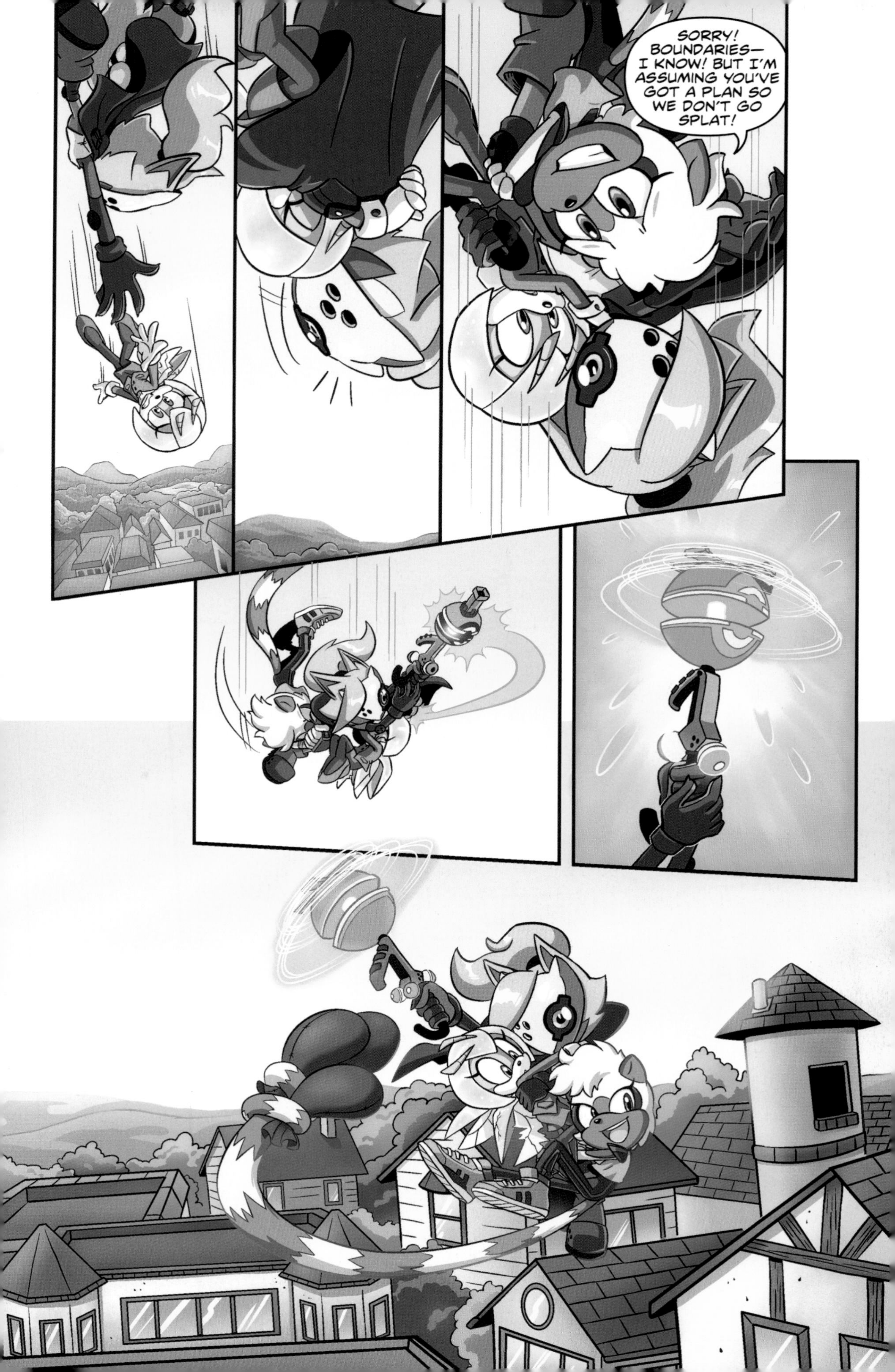
SORRY! BOUNDARIES— I KNOW! BUT I'M ASSUMING YOU'VE GOT A PLAN SO WE DON'T GO SPLAT!

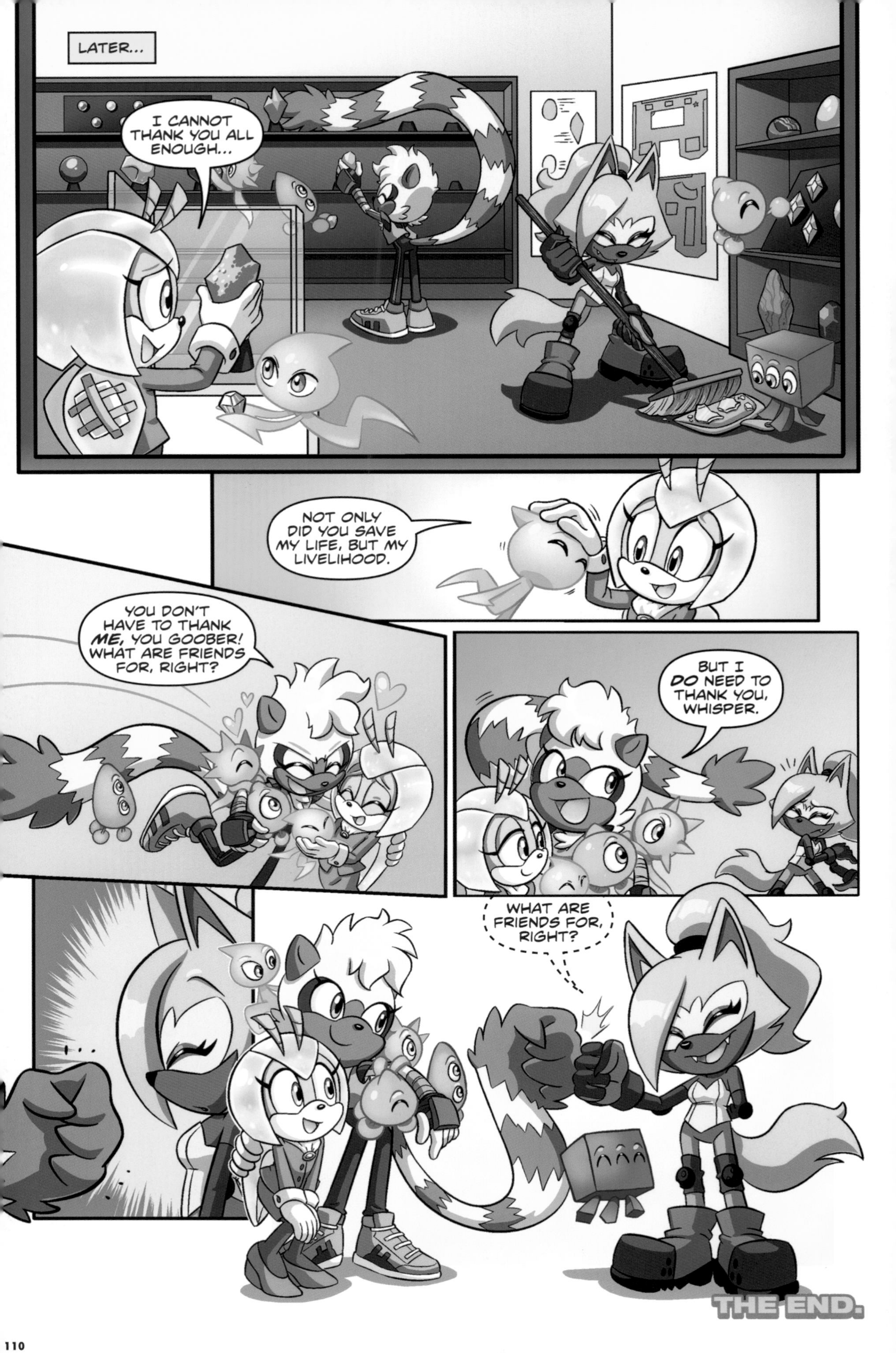
LATER...
I CANNOT THANK YOU ALL ENOUGH...
NOT ONLY DID YOU SAVE MY LIFE, BUT MY LIVELIHOOD.
YOU DON'T HAVE TO THANK ME, YOU GOOBER! WHAT ARE FRIENDS FOR, RIGHT?
BUT I DO NEED TO THANK YOU, WHISPER.
...
WHAT ARE FRIENDS FOR, RIGHT?
THE END.

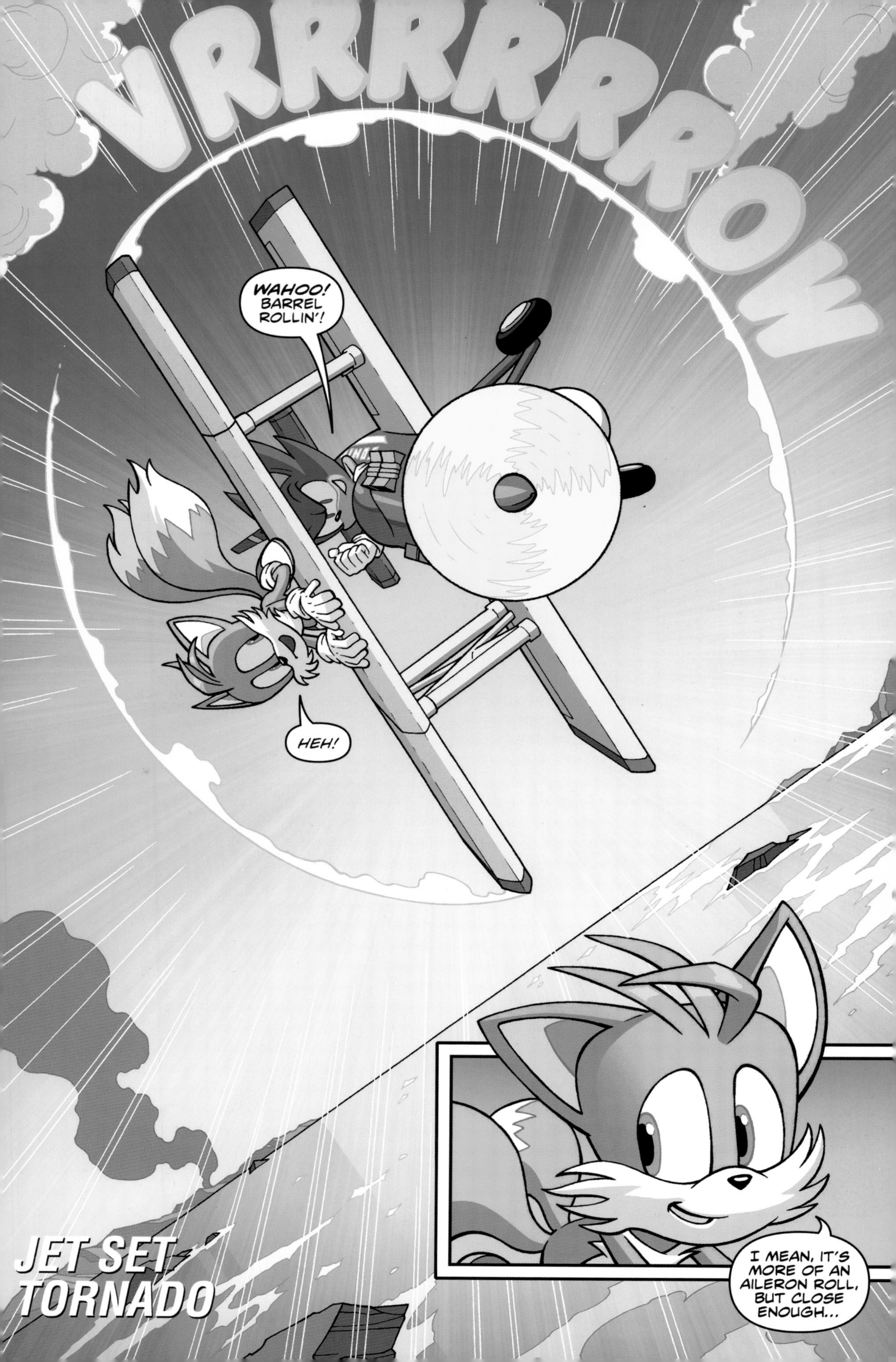
VRRRRRROW
WAHOO! BARREL ROLLIN'!
HEH!
I MEAN, IT'S MORE OF AN AILERON ROLL, BUT CLOSE ENOUGH...
JET SET TORNADO

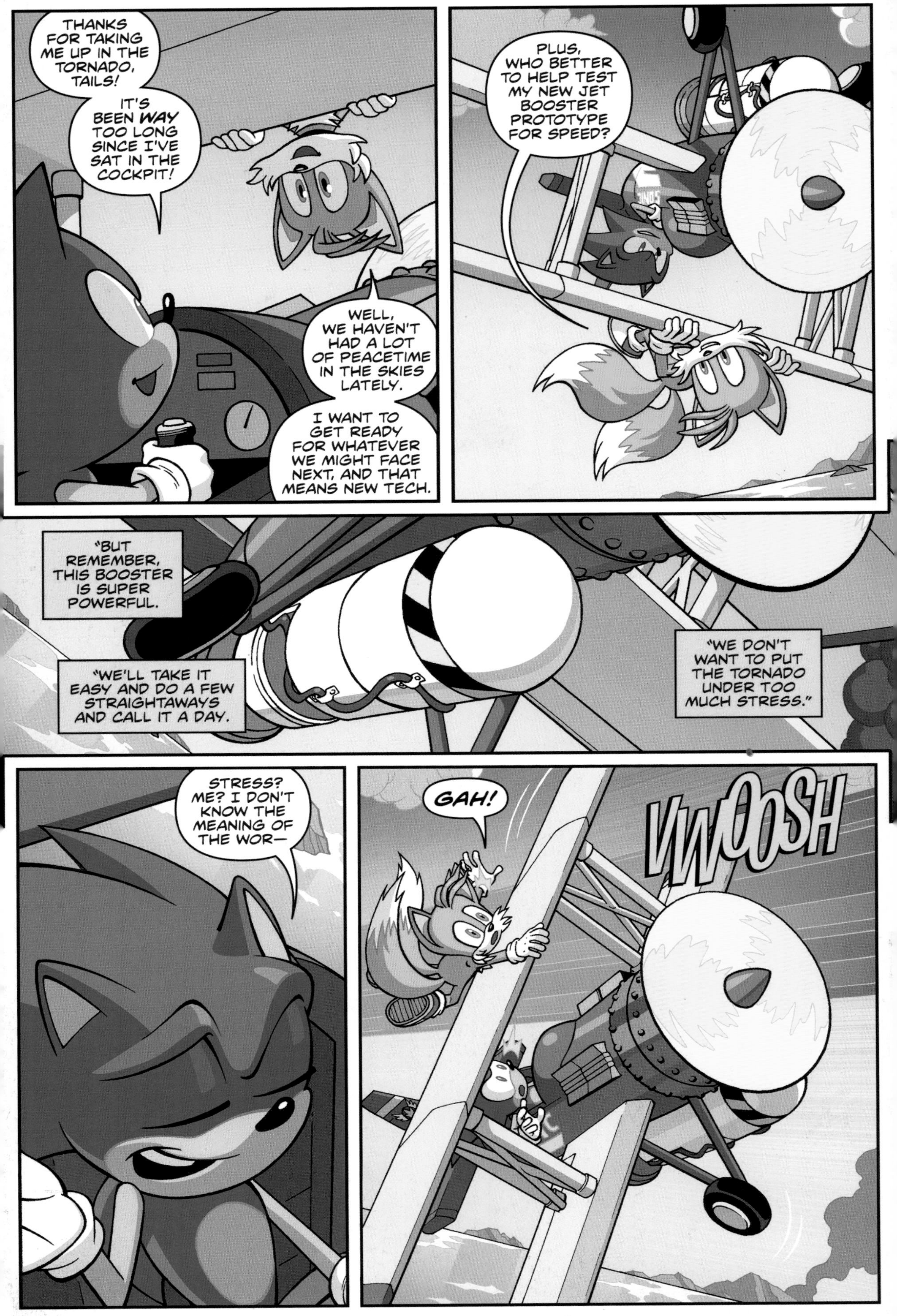
THANKS FOR TAKING ME UP IN THE TORNADO, TAILS!
IT'S BEEN **WAY** TOO LONG SINCE I'VE SAT IN THE COCKPIT!
WELL, WE HAVEN'T HAD A LOT OF PEACETIME IN THE SKIES LATELY.
I WANT TO GET READY FOR WHATEVER WE MIGHT FACE NEXT, AND THAT MEANS NEW TECH.
PLUS, WHO BETTER TO HELP TEST MY NEW JET BOOSTER PROTOTYPE FOR SPEED?
"BUT REMEMBER, THIS BOOSTER IS SUPER POWERFUL.
"WE'LL TAKE IT EASY AND DO A FEW STRAIGHTAWAYS AND CALL IT A DAY.
"WE DON'T WANT TO PUT THE TORNADO UNDER TOO MUCH STRESS."
STRESS? ME? I DON'T KNOW THE MEANING OF THE WOR—
GAH!
VWOOSH

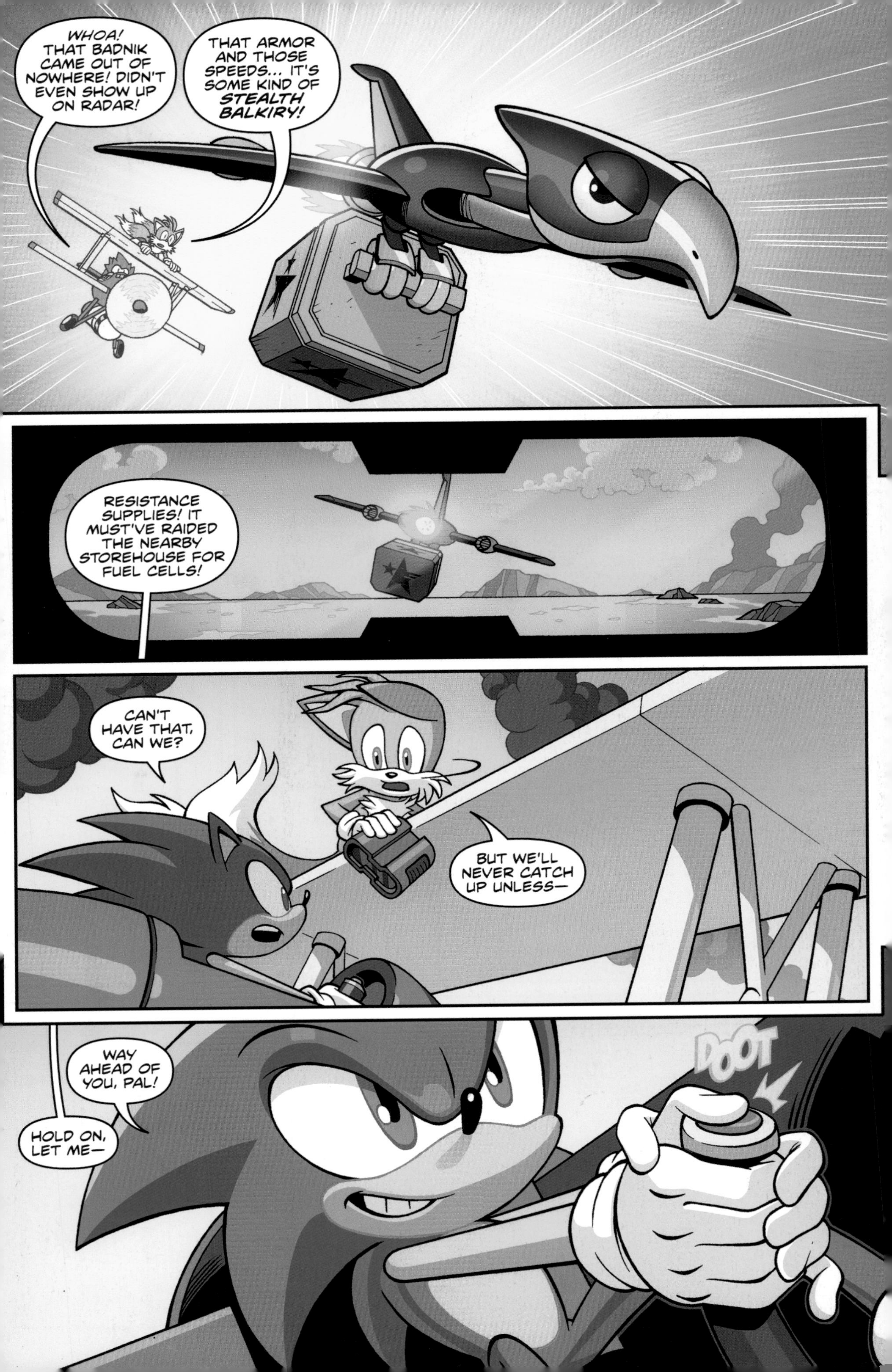
WHOA! THAT BADNIK CAME OUT OF NOWHERE! DIDN'T EVEN SHOW UP ON RADAR!
THAT ARMOR AND THOSE SPEEDS... IT'S SOME KIND OF STEALTH BALKIRY!
RESISTANCE SUPPLIES! IT MUST'VE RAIDED THE NEARBY STOREHOUSE FOR FUEL CELLS!
CAN'T HAVE THAT, CAN WE?
BUT WE'LL NEVER CATCH UP UNLESS—
HOLD ON, LET ME—
WAY AHEAD OF YOU, PAL!
DOOT

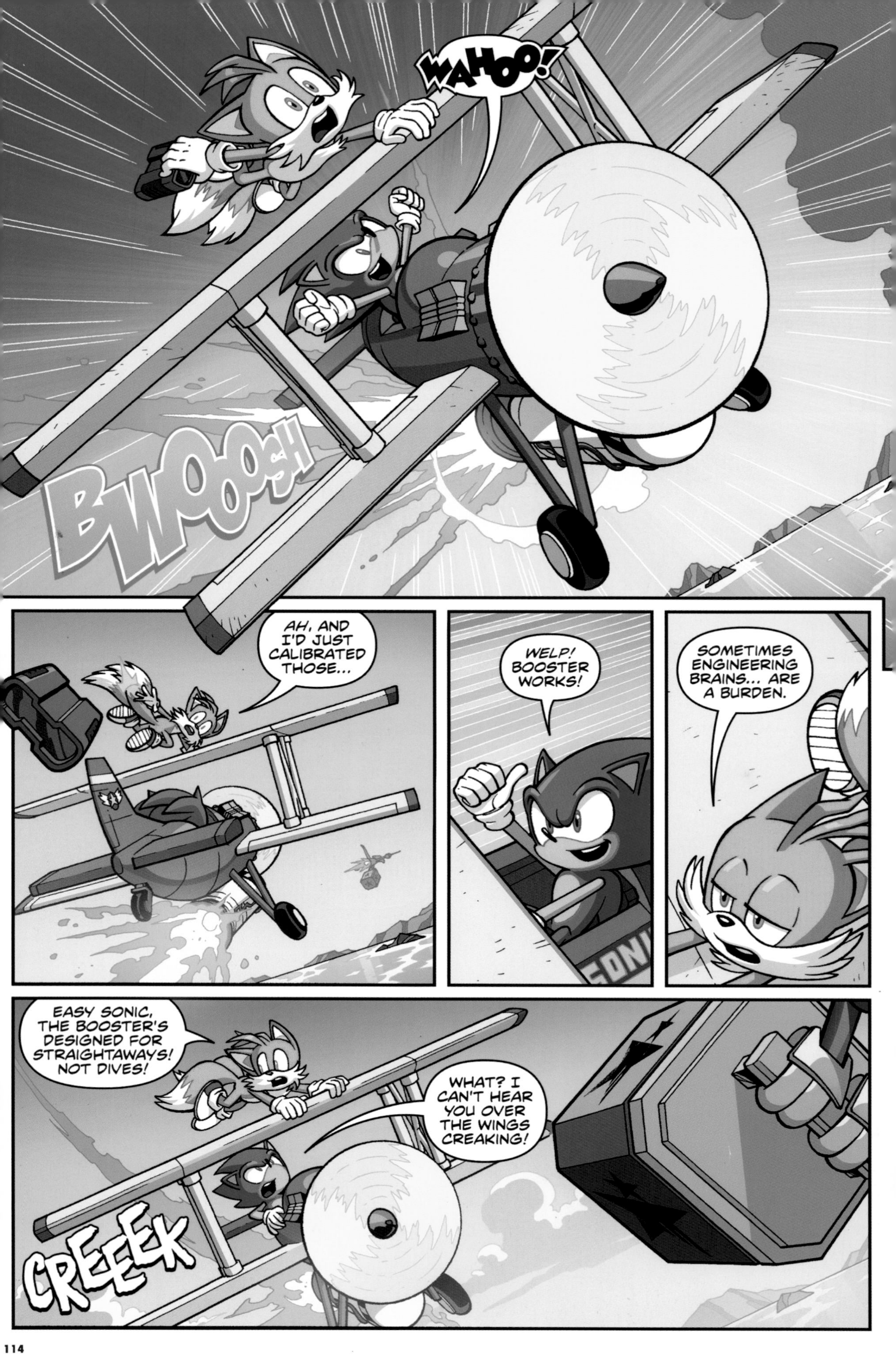
WAHOO!
BWOOOSH
AH, AND I'D JUST CALIBRATED THOSE...
WELP! BOOSTER WORKS!
SOMETIMES ENGINEERING BRAINS... ARE A BURDEN.
EASY SONIC, THE BOOSTER'S DESIGNED FOR STRAIGHTAWAYS! NOT DIVES!
WHAT? I CAN'T HEAR YOU OVER THE WINGS CREAKING!
CREEEK

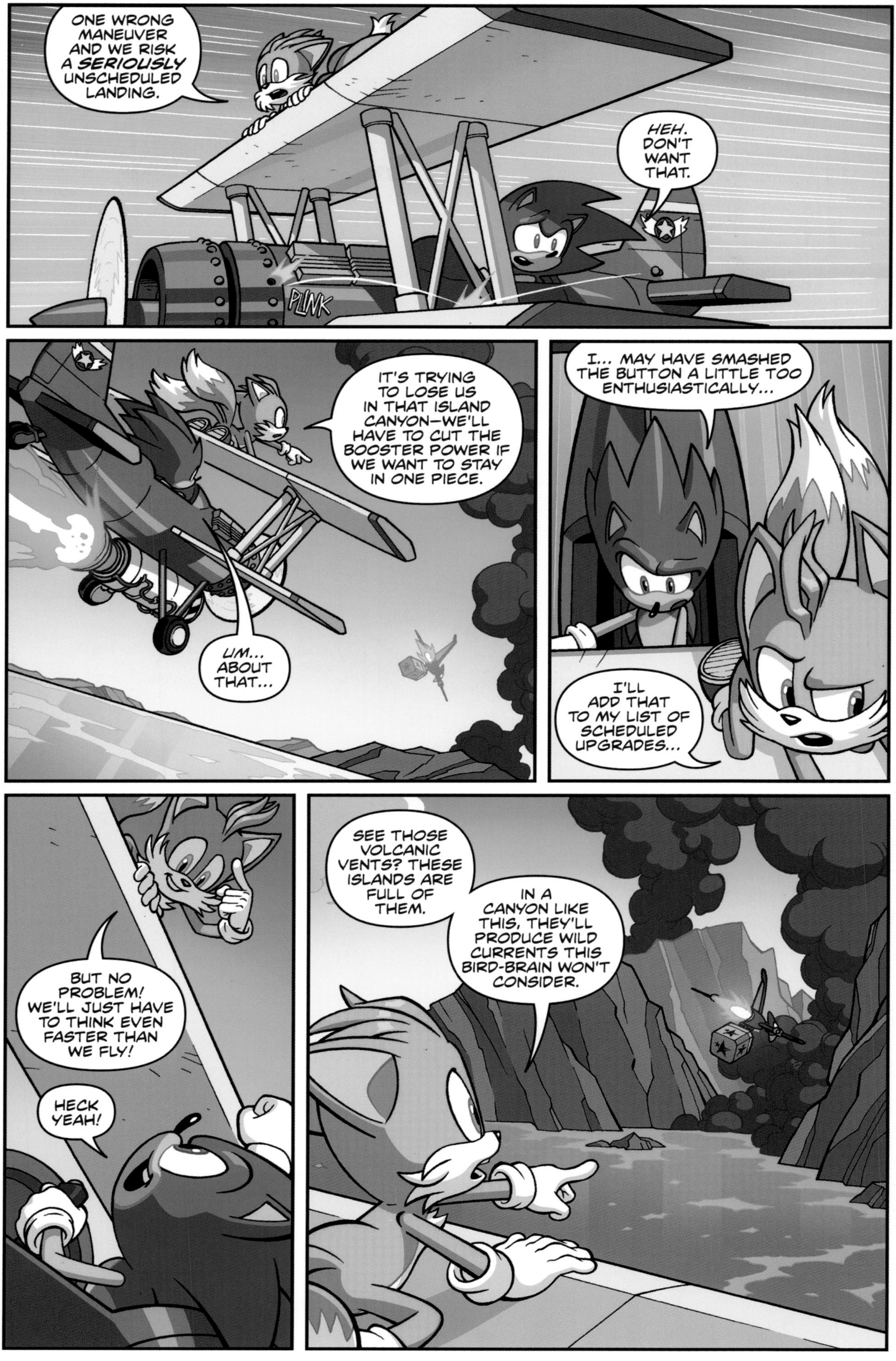
ONE WRONG MANEUVER AND WE RISK A *SERIOUSLY* UNSCHEDULED LANDING.
HEH. DON'T WANT THAT.
PLINK
IT'S TRYING TO LOSE US IN THAT ISLAND CANYON—WE'LL HAVE TO CUT THE BOOSTER POWER IF WE WANT TO STAY IN ONE PIECE.
UM... ABOUT THAT...
I... MAY HAVE SMASHED THE BUTTON A LITTLE TOO ENTHUSIASTICALLY...
I'LL ADD THAT TO MY LIST OF SCHEDULED UPGRADES...
BUT NO PROBLEM! WE'LL JUST HAVE TO THINK EVEN FASTER THAN WE FLY!
HECK YEAH!
SEE THOSE VOLCANIC VENTS? THESE ISLANDS ARE FULL OF THEM.
IN A CANYON LIKE THIS, THEY'LL PRODUCE WILD CURRENTS THIS BIRD-BRAIN WON'T CONSIDER.

PLUS, WHERE THERE'RE VENTS, THERE'RE GEYSERS! STAY ON ITS TAIL UNTIL WE CAN RIDE AN UPDRAFT AND GET THE DROP ON IT.

RIGHT. THAT WAY I WON'T STRESS OUT THE TORNADO AGAIN!

ON MY SIGNAL, PULL UP—GENTLY—UNTIL WE'RE IN POSITION TO DROP OUR PAYLOAD.

YOU DON'T MEAN—

≋SIGH≋ YEAH, BUT I CAN ALWAYS BUILD ANOTHER ONE.

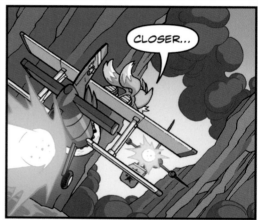

CLOSER...

...CLOSER...

NOW!

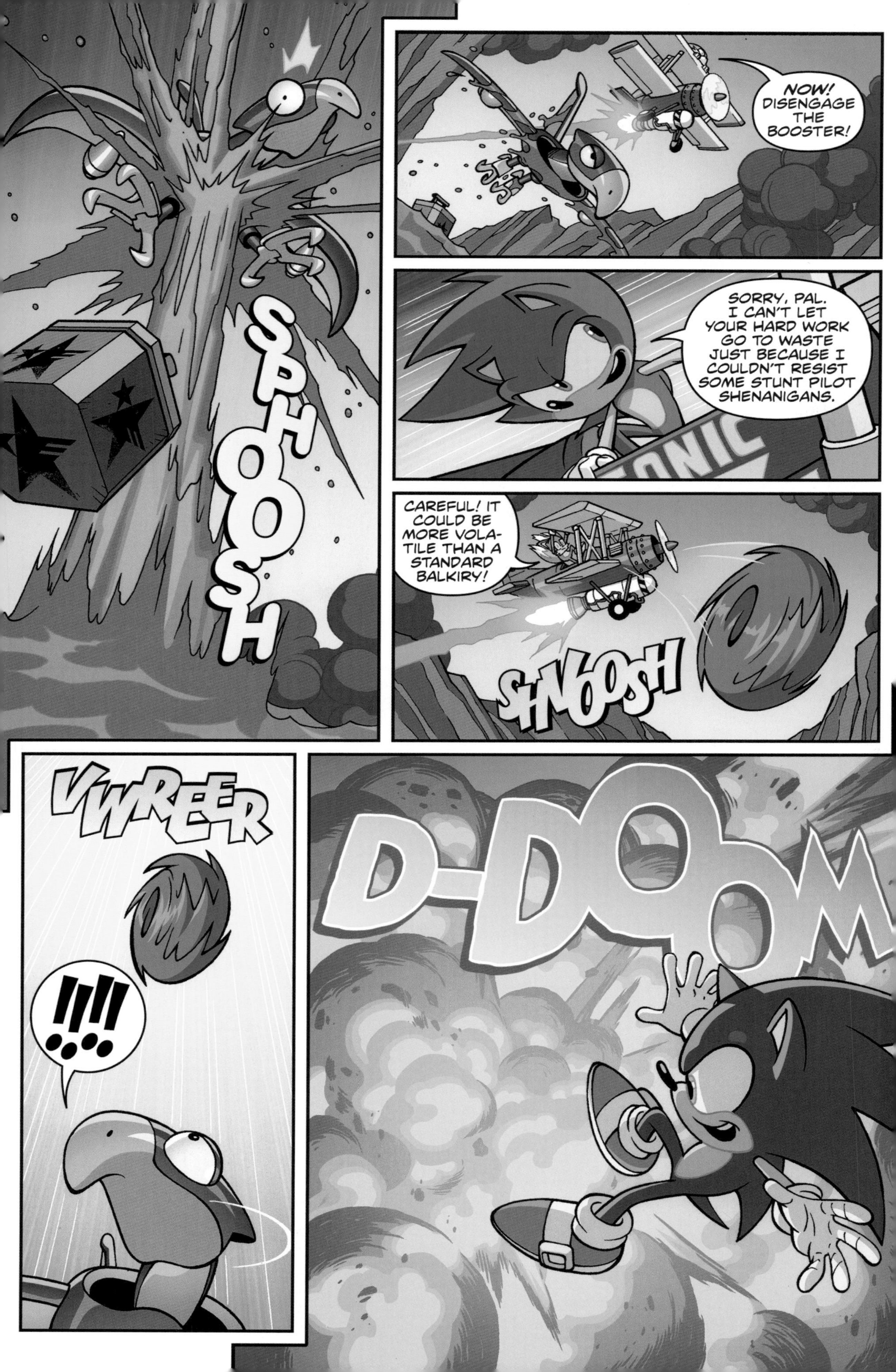
SPHOOSH
NOW! DISENGAGE THE BOOSTER!
SORRY, PAL. I CAN'T LET YOUR HARD WORK GO TO WASTE JUST BECAUSE I COULDN'T RESIST SOME STUNT PILOT SHENANIGANS.
SONIC
CAREFUL! IT COULD BE MORE VOLATILE THAN A STANDARD BALKIRY!
SHNOOSH
VWREER
!!!!....
D-DOOM

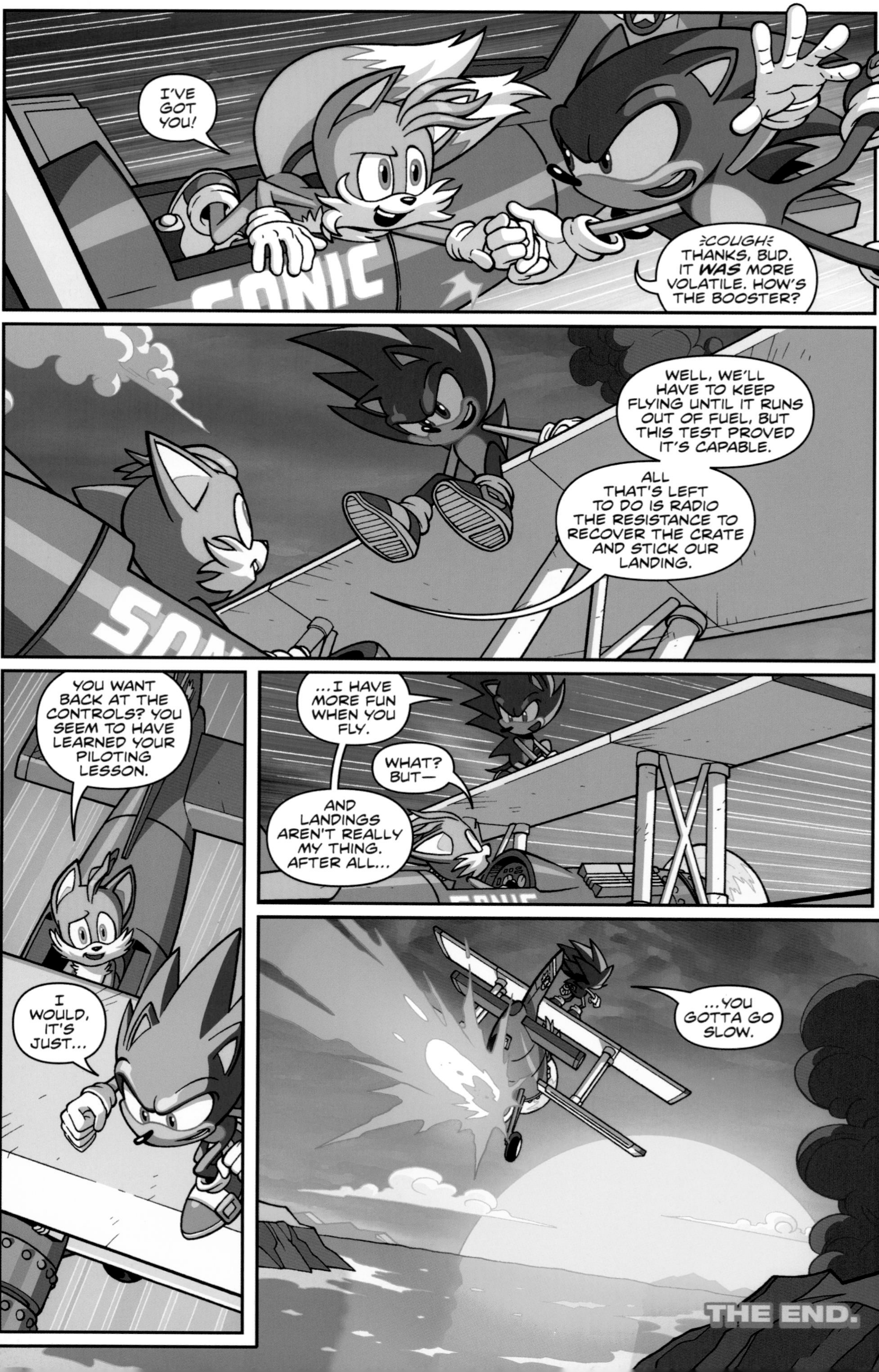

I'VE GOT YOU!
≷COUGH≶ THANKS, BUD. IT **WAS** MORE VOLATILE. HOW'S THE BOOSTER?
SONIC
WELL, WE'LL HAVE TO KEEP FLYING UNTIL IT RUNS OUT OF FUEL, BUT THIS TEST PROVED IT'S CAPABLE.
ALL THAT'S LEFT TO DO IS RADIO THE RESISTANCE TO RECOVER THE CRATE AND STICK OUR LANDING.
YOU WANT BACK AT THE CONTROLS? YOU SEEM TO HAVE LEARNED YOUR PILOTING LESSON.
I WOULD, IT'S JUST...
...I HAVE MORE FUN WHEN YOU FLY.
WHAT? BUT—
AND LANDINGS AREN'T REALLY MY THING. AFTER ALL...
...YOU GOTTA GO SLOW.
THE END.

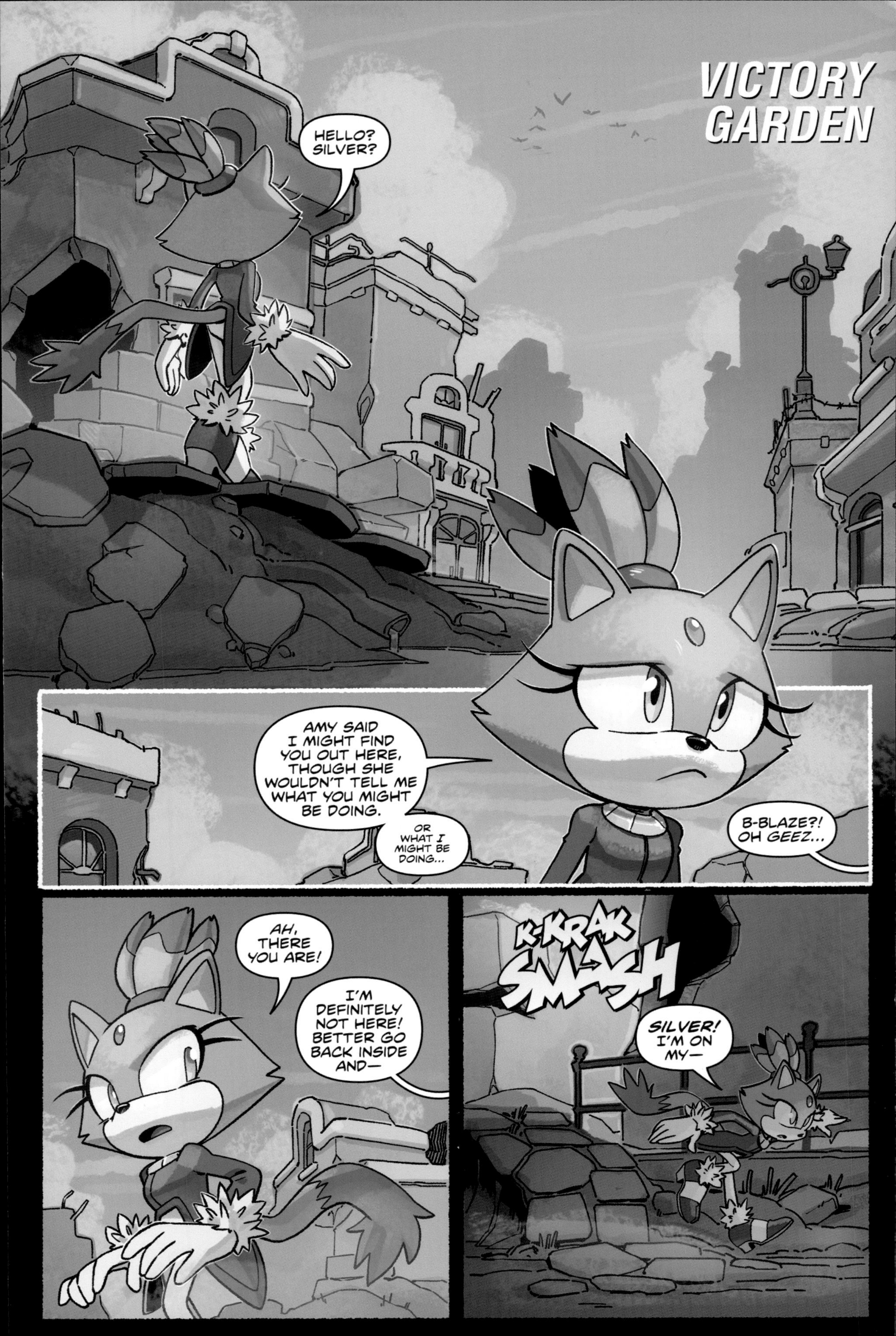
VICTORY GARDEN
HELLO? SILVER?
AMY SAID I MIGHT FIND YOU OUT HERE, THOUGH SHE WOULDN'T TELL ME WHAT YOU MIGHT BE DOING.
OR WHAT I MIGHT BE DOING...
B-BLAZE?! OH GEEZ...
AH, THERE YOU ARE!
I'M DEFINITELY NOT HERE! BETTER GO BACK INSIDE AND—
K-KRAK SMASH
SILVER! I'M ON MY—

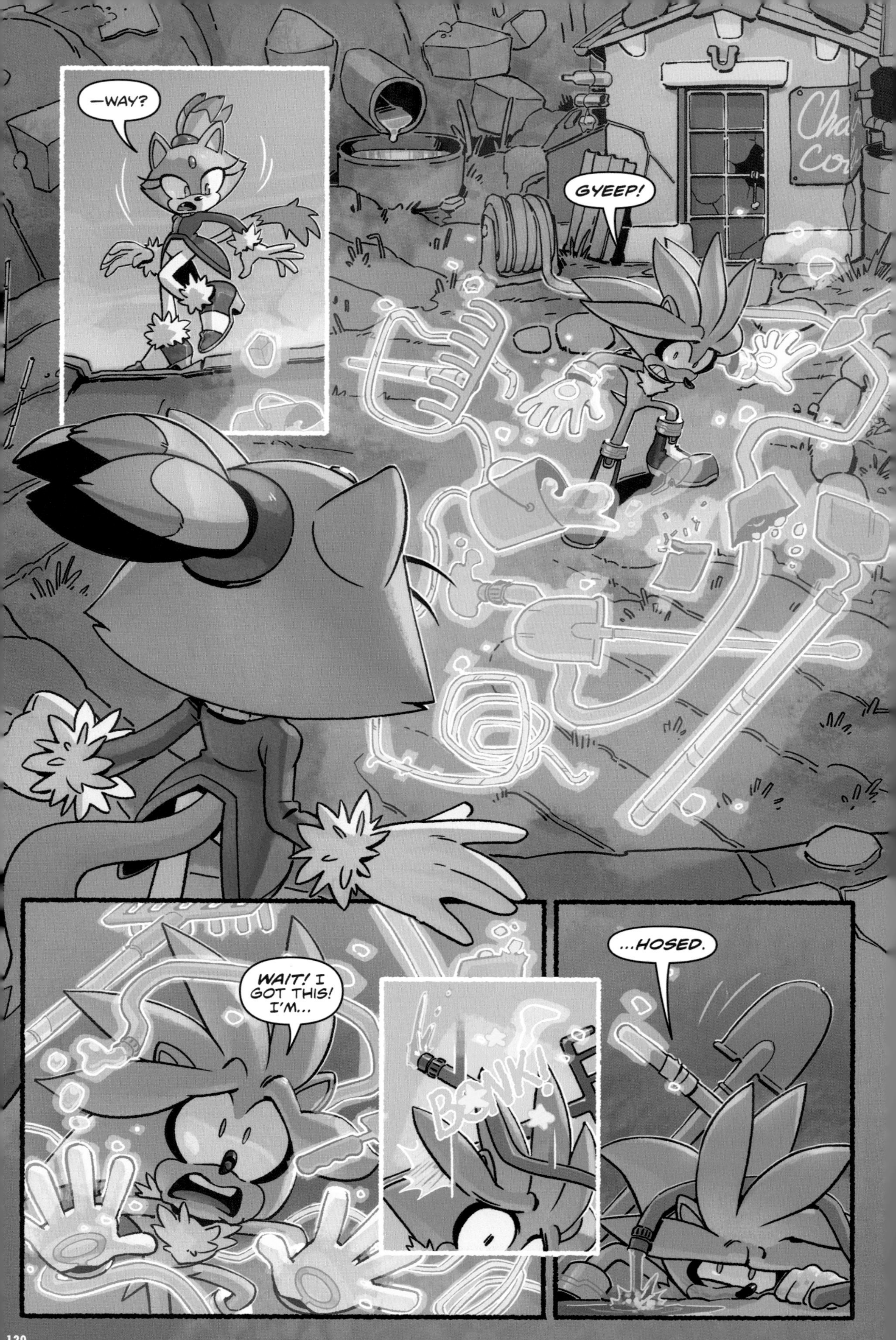
—WAY?
GYEEP!
WAIT! I GOT THIS! I'M...
BONK!
...HOSED.

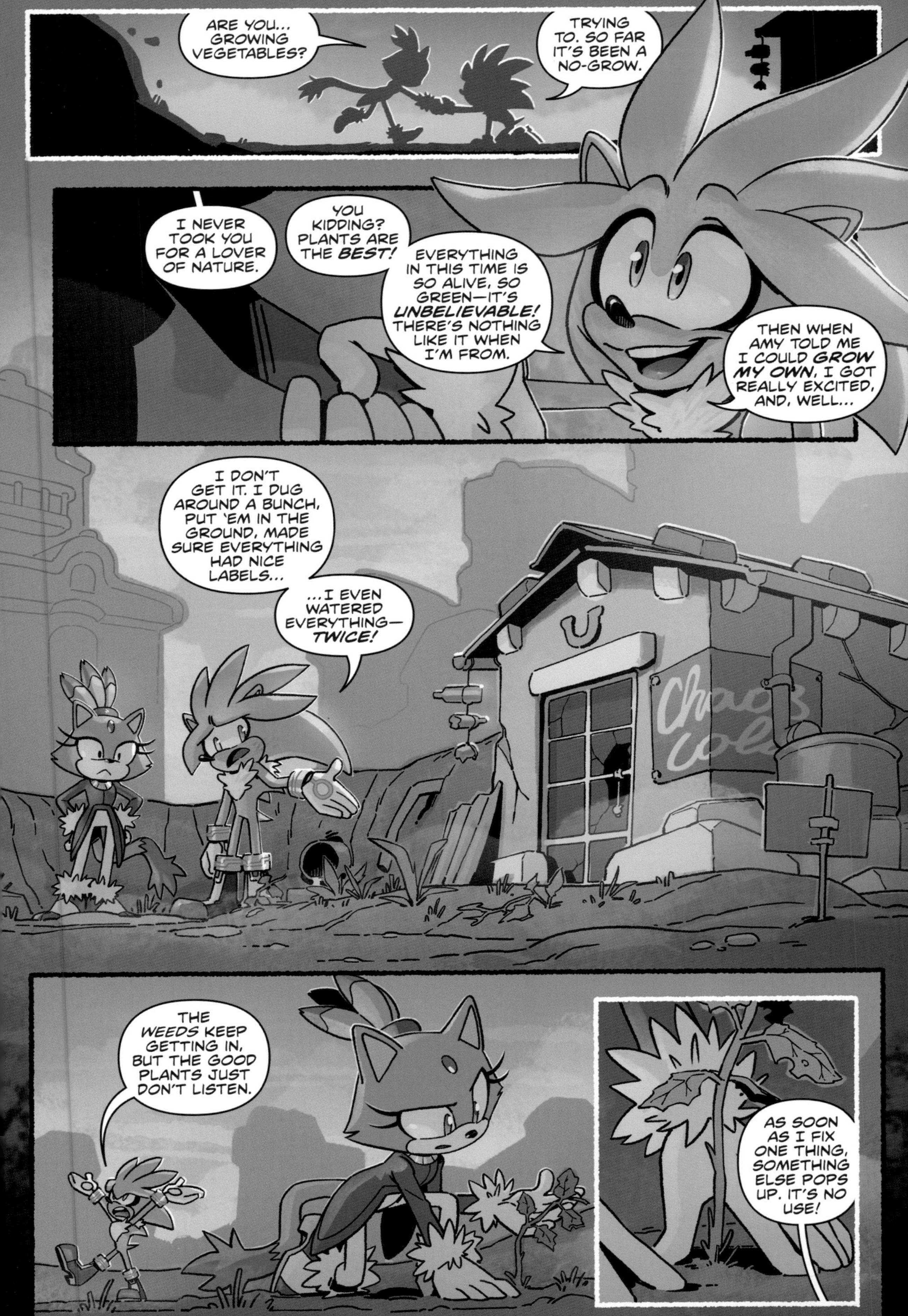

ARE YOU... GROWING VEGETABLES?
TRYING TO. SO FAR IT'S BEEN A NO-GROW.
I NEVER TOOK YOU FOR A LOVER OF NATURE.
YOU KIDDING? PLANTS ARE THE *BEST!*
EVERYTHING IN THIS TIME IS SO ALIVE, SO GREEN—IT'S *UNBELIEVABLE!* THERE'S NOTHING LIKE IT WHEN I'M FROM.
THEN WHEN AMY TOLD ME I COULD *GROW MY OWN*, I GOT REALLY EXCITED, AND, WELL...
I DON'T GET IT. I DUG AROUND A BUNCH, PUT 'EM IN THE GROUND, MADE SURE EVERYTHING HAD NICE LABELS...
...I EVEN WATERED EVERYTHING—*TWICE!*
THE *WEEDS* KEEP GETTING IN, BUT THE GOOD PLANTS JUST DON'T LISTEN.
AS SOON AS I FIX ONE THING, SOMETHING ELSE POPS UP. IT'S NO USE!

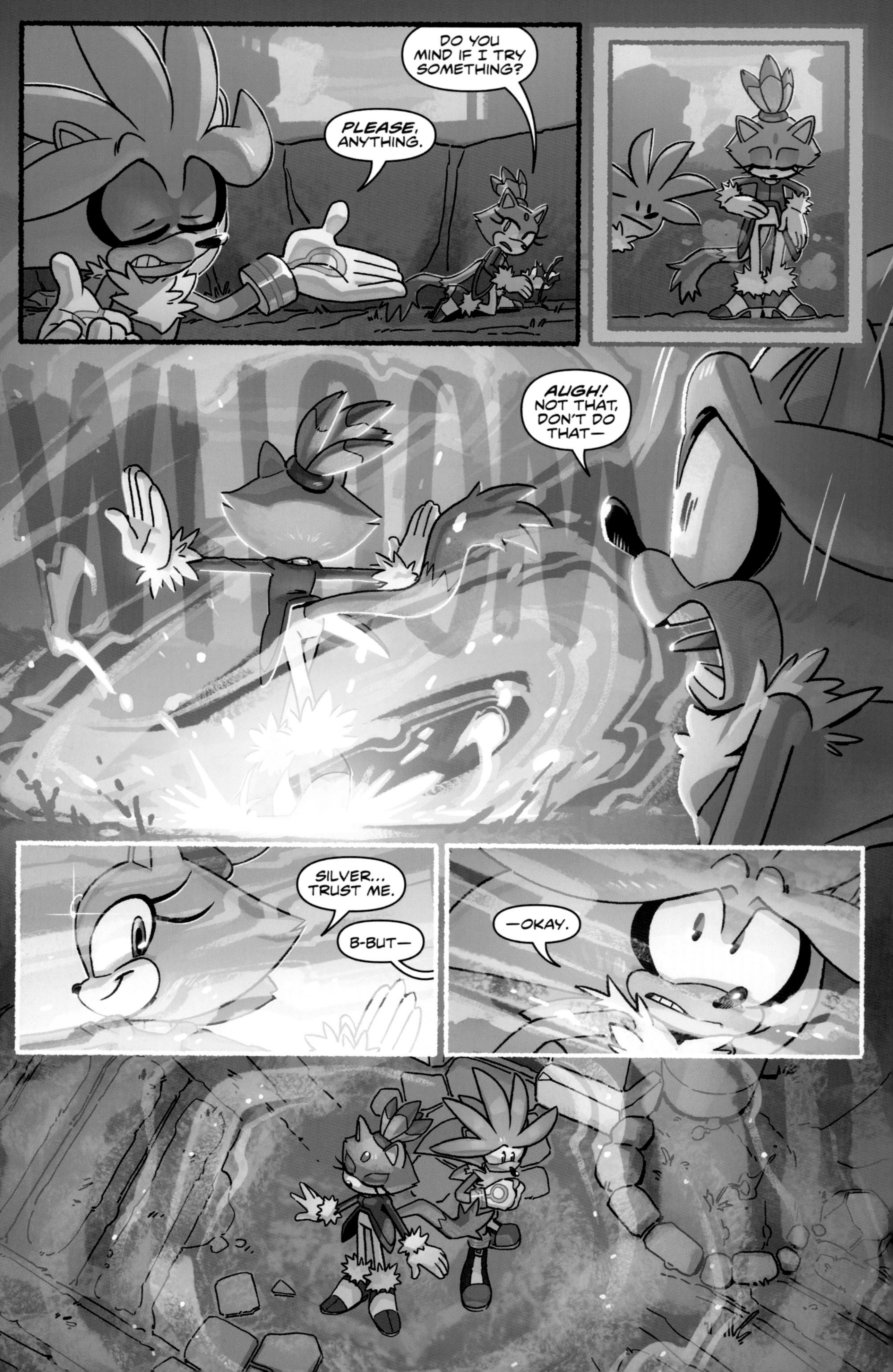
DO YOU MIND IF I TRY SOMETHING?
PLEASE, ANYTHING.
AUGH! NOT THAT, DON'T DO THAT—
SILVER... TRUST ME.
B-BUT—
—OKAY.

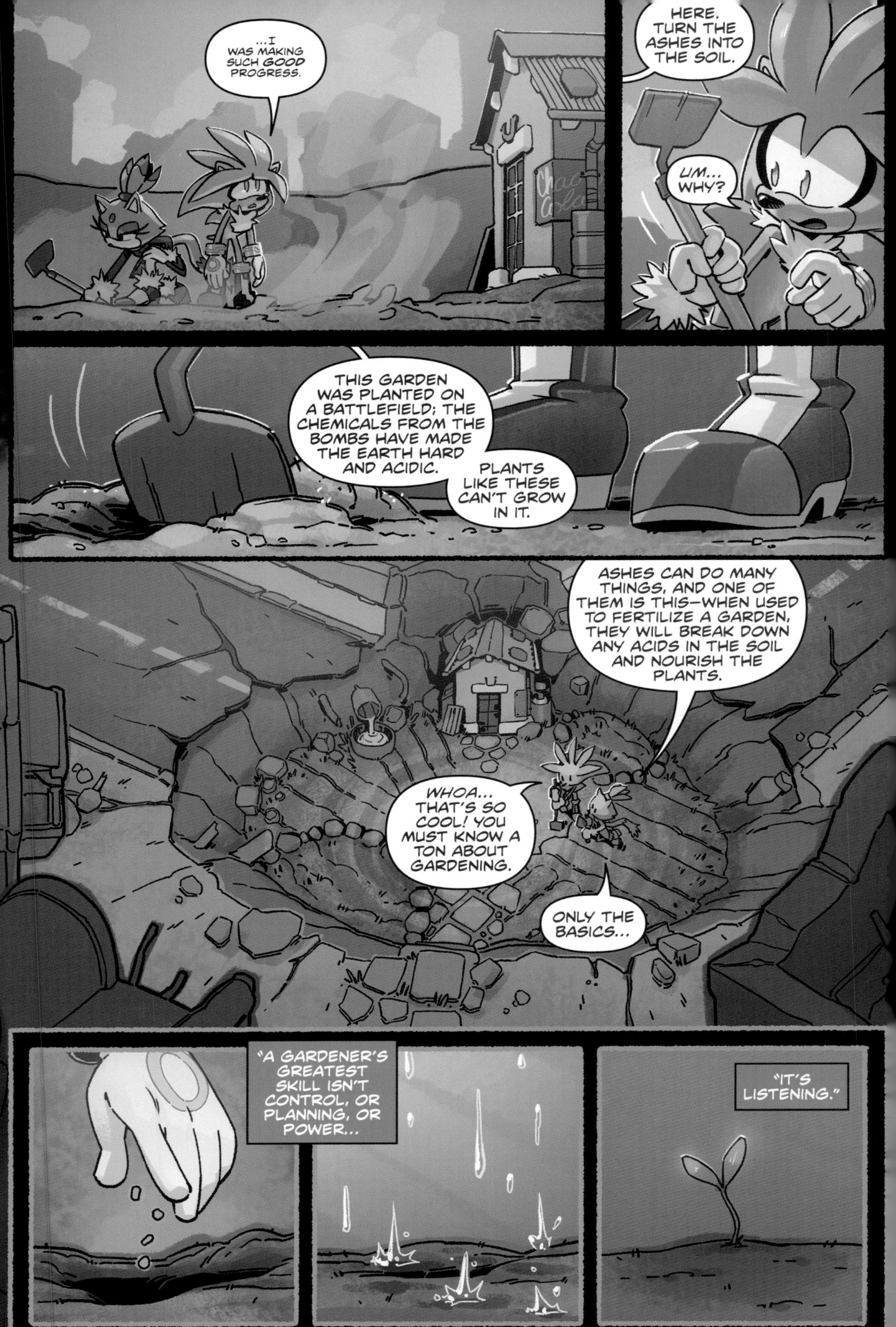
...I WAS MAKING SUCH GOOD PROGRESS.
HERE. TURN THE ASHES INTO THE SOIL.
UM... WHY?
THIS GARDEN WAS PLANTED ON A BATTLEFIELD; THE CHEMICALS FROM THE BOMBS HAVE MADE THE EARTH HARD AND ACIDIC.
PLANTS LIKE THESE CAN'T GROW IN IT.
ASHES CAN DO MANY THINGS, AND ONE OF THEM IS THIS—WHEN USED TO FERTILIZE A GARDEN, THEY WILL BREAK DOWN ANY ACIDS IN THE SOIL AND NOURISH THE PLANTS.
WHOA... THAT'S SO COOL! YOU MUST KNOW A TON ABOUT GARDENING.
ONLY THE BASICS...
"A GARDENER'S GREATEST SKILL ISN'T CONTROL, OR PLANNING, OR POWER...
"IT'S LISTENING."

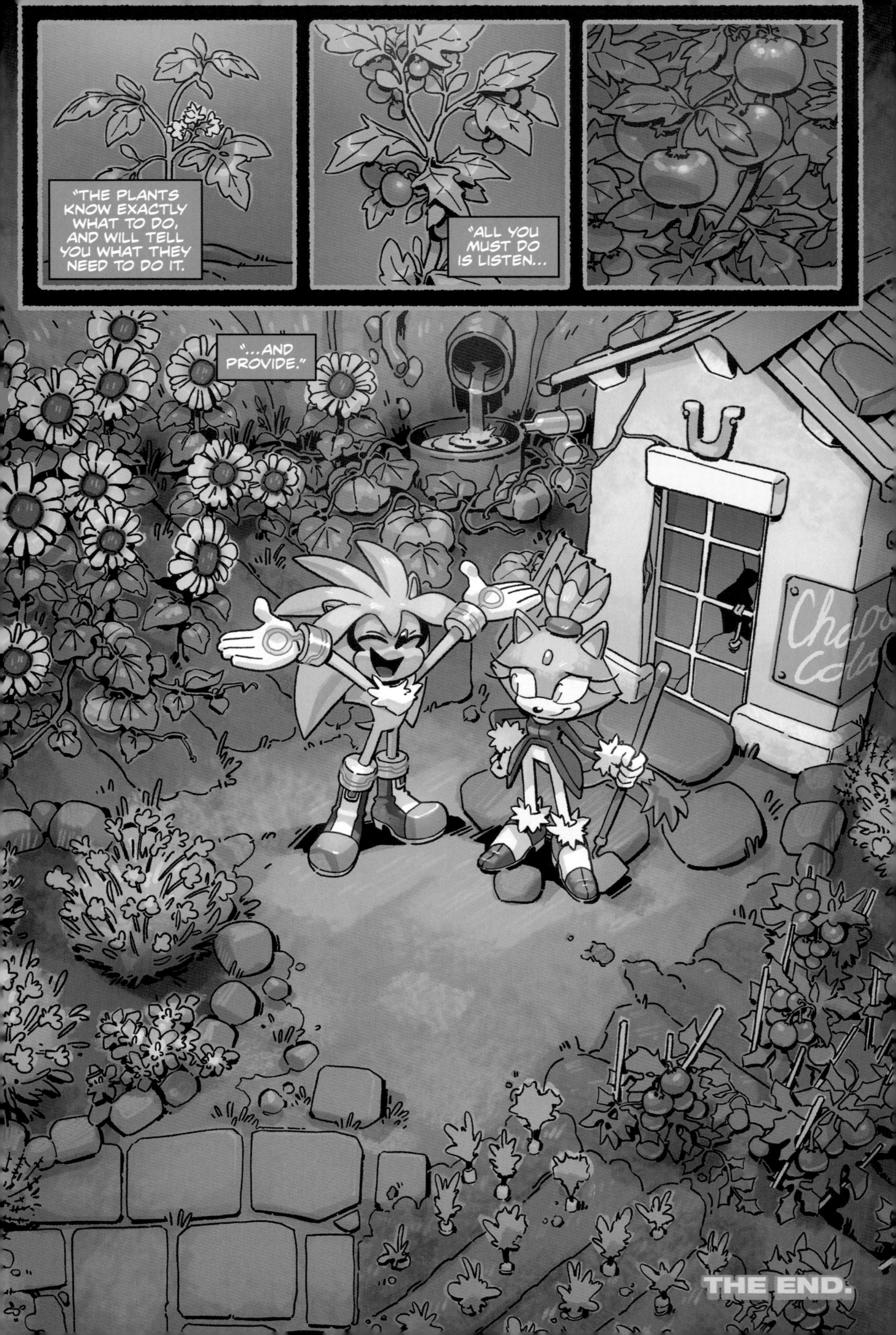
"THE PLANTS KNOW EXACTLY WHAT TO DO, AND WILL TELL YOU WHAT THEY NEED TO DO IT.
"ALL YOU MUST DO IS LISTEN...
"...AND PROVIDE."
THE END.

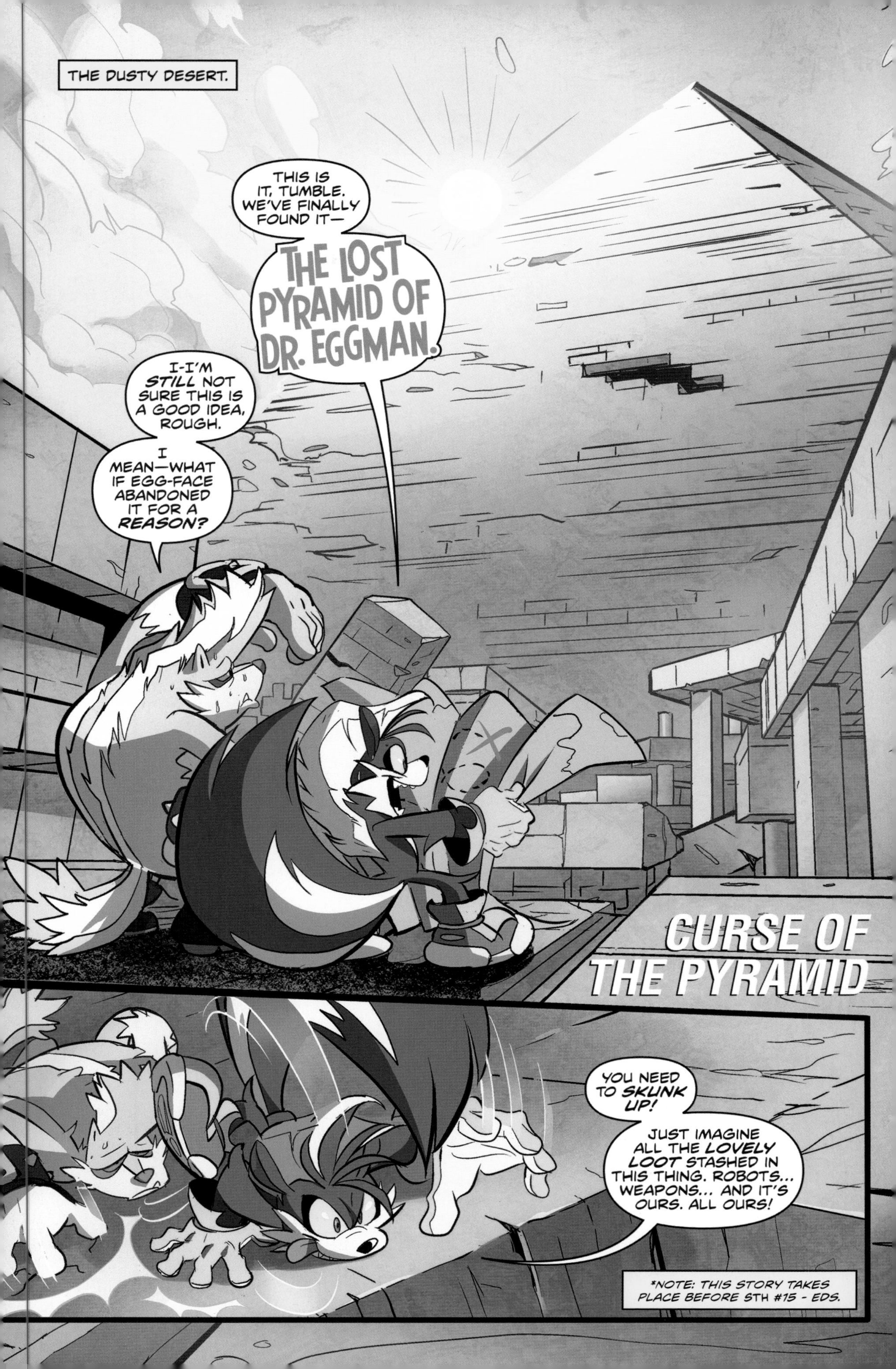
THE DUSTY DESERT.
THIS IS IT, TUMBLE. WE'VE FINALLY FOUND IT—
THE LOST PYRAMID OF DR. EGGMAN.
I-I'M STILL NOT SURE THIS IS A GOOD IDEA, ROUGH.
I MEAN—WHAT IF EGG-FACE ABANDONED IT FOR A REASON?
CURSE OF THE PYRAMID
YOU NEED TO SKUNK UP!
JUST IMAGINE ALL THE LOVELY LOOT STASHED IN THIS THING. ROBOTS... WEAPONS... AND IT'S OURS. ALL OURS!
*NOTE: THIS STORY TAKES PLACE BEFORE STH #15 - EDS.

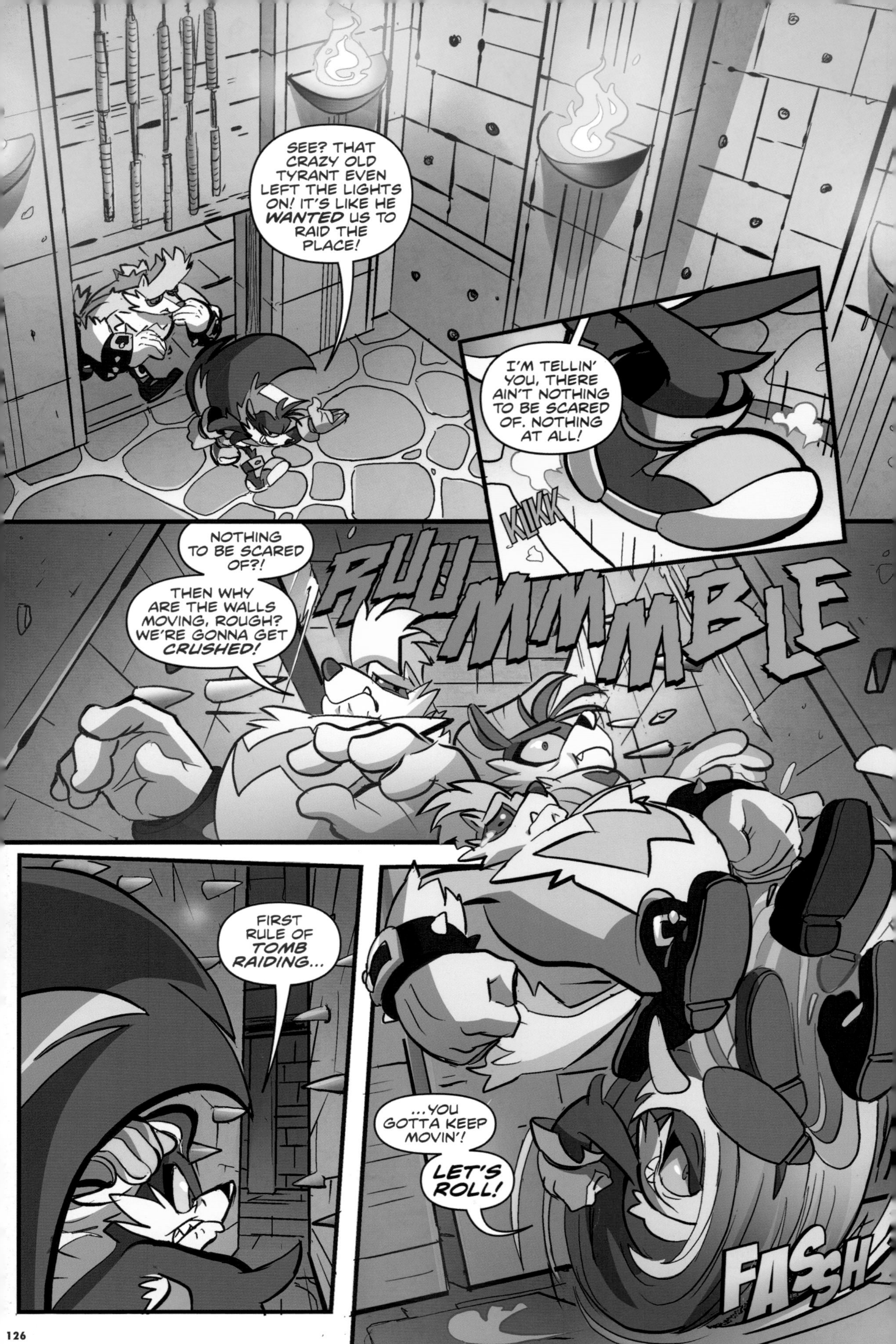
SEE? THAT CRAZY OLD TYRANT EVEN LEFT THE LIGHTS ON! IT'S LIKE HE *WANTED* US TO RAID THE PLACE!
I'M TELLIN' YOU, THERE AIN'T NOTHING TO BE SCARED OF. NOTHING AT ALL!
KLIKK
NOTHING TO BE SCARED OF?!
THEN WHY ARE THE WALLS MOVING, ROUGH? WE'RE GONNA GET *CRUSHED!*
RUUMMMBLE
FIRST RULE OF *TOMB RAIDING*...
...YOU GOTTA KEEP MOVIN'!
LET'S ROLL!
FASSH

WHAMM

THERE. WHAT DID I TELL YOU?

WE'RE *UNSTOPPABLE!*

YEAH, B-BUT WHAT ABOUT ALL THE *LEGENDS?* THEY SAY THIS PLACE IS *CURSED!*

I'M *S-SCARED,* ROUGH. REAL SCARED.

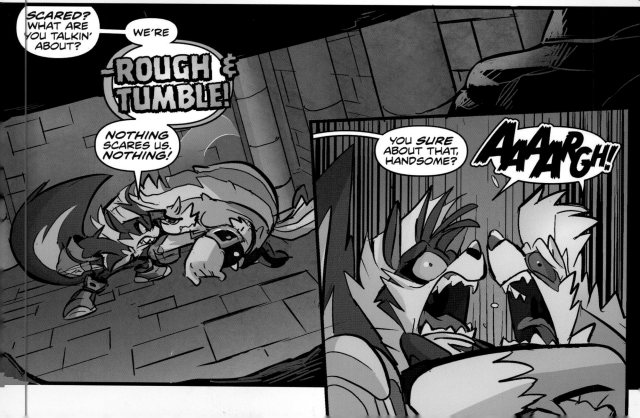

SCARED? WHAT ARE YOU TALKIN' ABOUT?

WE'RE *ROUGH & TUMBLE!*

NOTHING SCARES US. NOTHING!

YOU *SURE* ABOUT THAT, HANDSOME?

AAARGH!

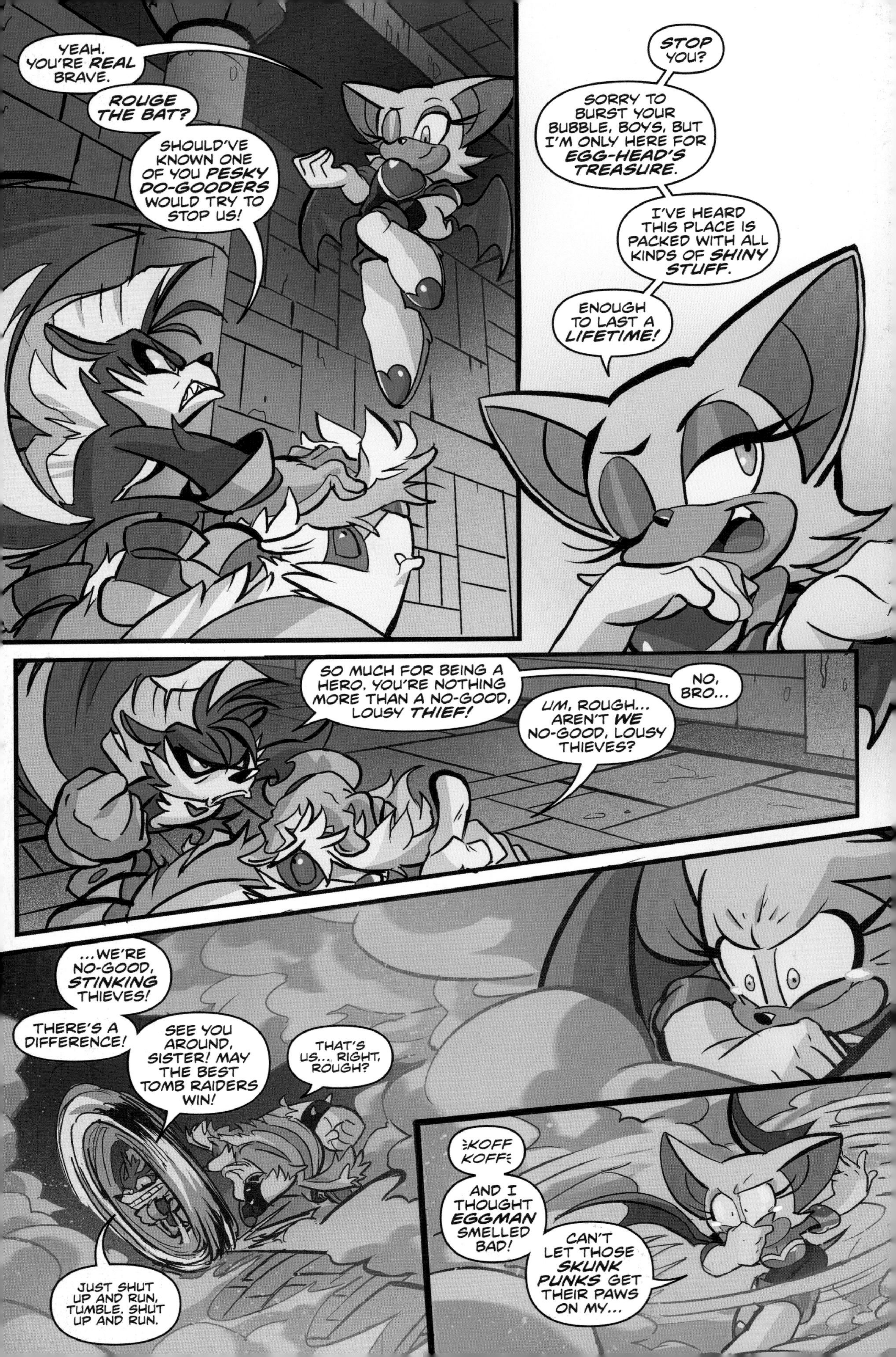
YEAH. YOU'RE REAL BRAVE.
ROUGE THE BAT?
SHOULD'VE KNOWN ONE OF YOU PESKY DO-GOODERS WOULD TRY TO STOP US!
STOP YOU?
SORRY TO BURST YOUR BUBBLE, BOYS, BUT I'M ONLY HERE FOR EGG-HEAD'S TREASURE.
I'VE HEARD THIS PLACE IS PACKED WITH ALL KINDS OF SHINY STUFF.
ENOUGH TO LAST A LIFETIME!
SO MUCH FOR BEING A HERO. YOU'RE NOTHING MORE THAN A NO-GOOD, LOUSY THIEF!
UM, ROUGH... AREN'T WE NO-GOOD, LOUSY THIEVES?
NO, BRO...
...WE'RE NO-GOOD, STINKING THIEVES!
THERE'S A DIFFERENCE!
SEE YOU AROUND, SISTER! MAY THE BEST TOMB RAIDERS WIN!
THAT'S US... RIGHT, ROUGH?
JUST SHUT UP AND RUN, TUMBLE. SHUT UP AND RUN.
KOFF KOFF
AND I THOUGHT EGGMAN SMELLED BAD!
CAN'T LET THOSE SKUNK PUNKS GET THEIR PAWS ON MY...

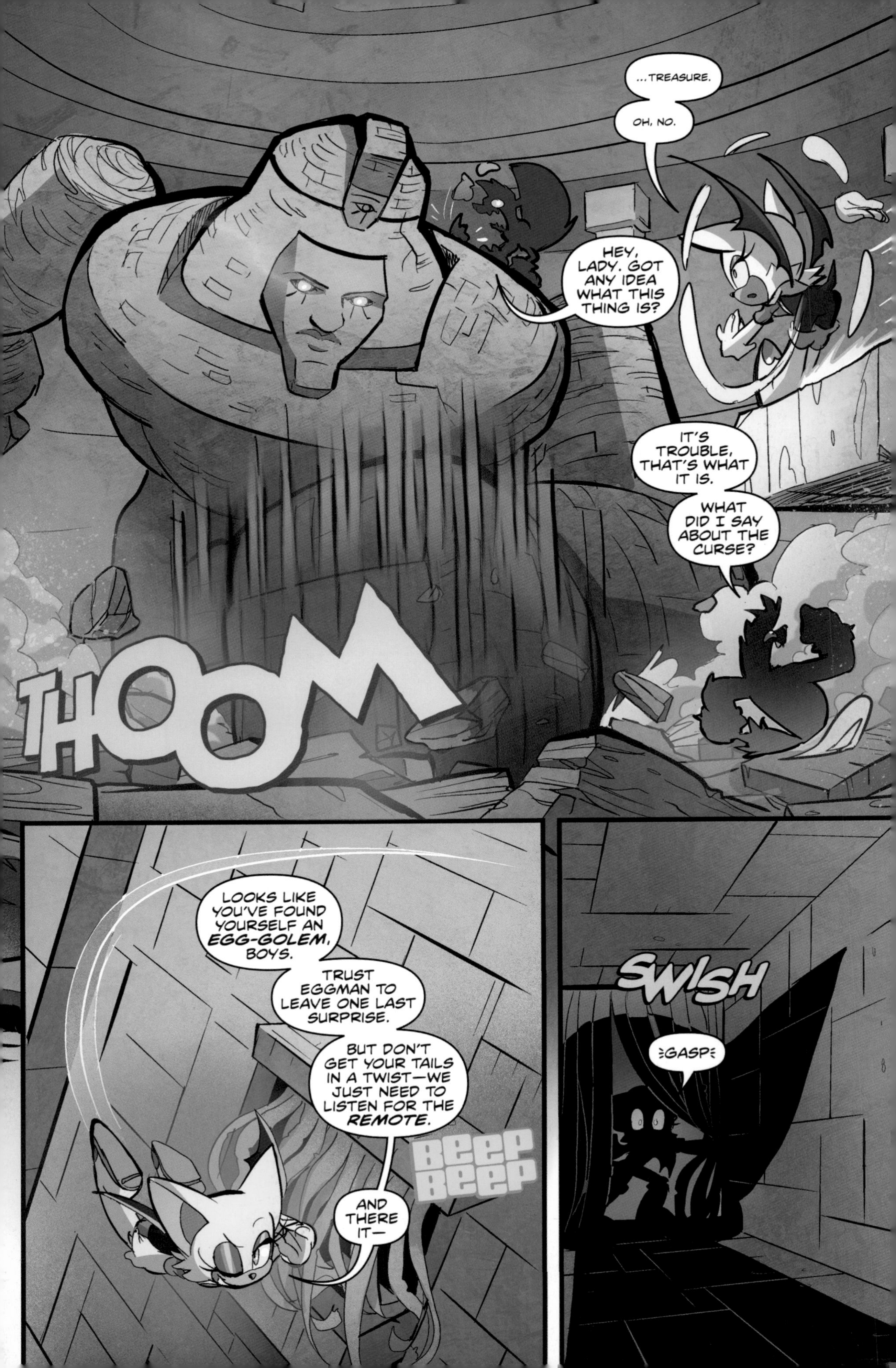
...TREASURE.
OH, NO.
HEY, LADY. GOT ANY IDEA WHAT THIS THING IS?
IT'S TROUBLE, THAT'S WHAT IT IS.
WHAT DID I SAY ABOUT THE CURSE?
THOOM
LOOKS LIKE YOU'VE FOUND YOURSELF AN ***EGG-GOLEM***, BOYS.
TRUST EGGMAN TO LEAVE ONE LAST SURPRISE.
BUT DON'T GET YOUR TAILS IN A TWIST—WE JUST NEED TO LISTEN FOR THE ***REMOTE***.
BEEP BEEP
AND THERE IT—
SWISH
GASP

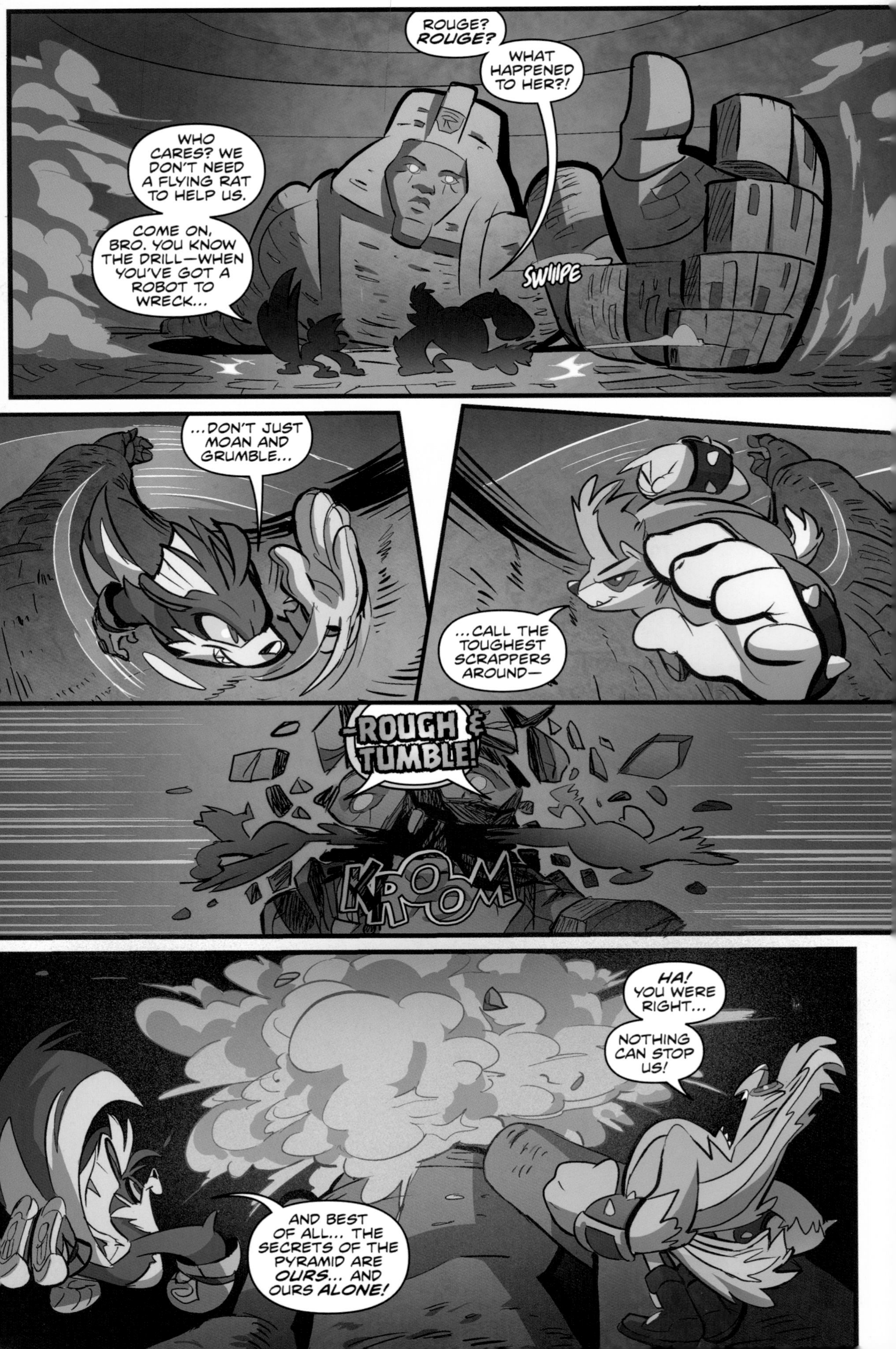
ROUGE? ROUGE?
WHAT HAPPENED TO HER?!
WHO CARES? WE DON'T NEED A FLYING RAT TO HELP US.
COME ON, BRO. YOU KNOW THE DRILL—WHEN YOU'VE GOT A ROBOT TO WRECK...
SWIIPE
...DON'T JUST MOAN AND GRUMBLE...
...CALL THE TOUGHEST SCRAPPERS AROUND—
ROUGH & TUMBLE!
KROOM
HA! YOU WERE RIGHT...
NOTHING CAN STOP US!
AND BEST OF ALL... THE SECRETS OF THE PYRAMID ARE OURS... AND OURS ALONE!

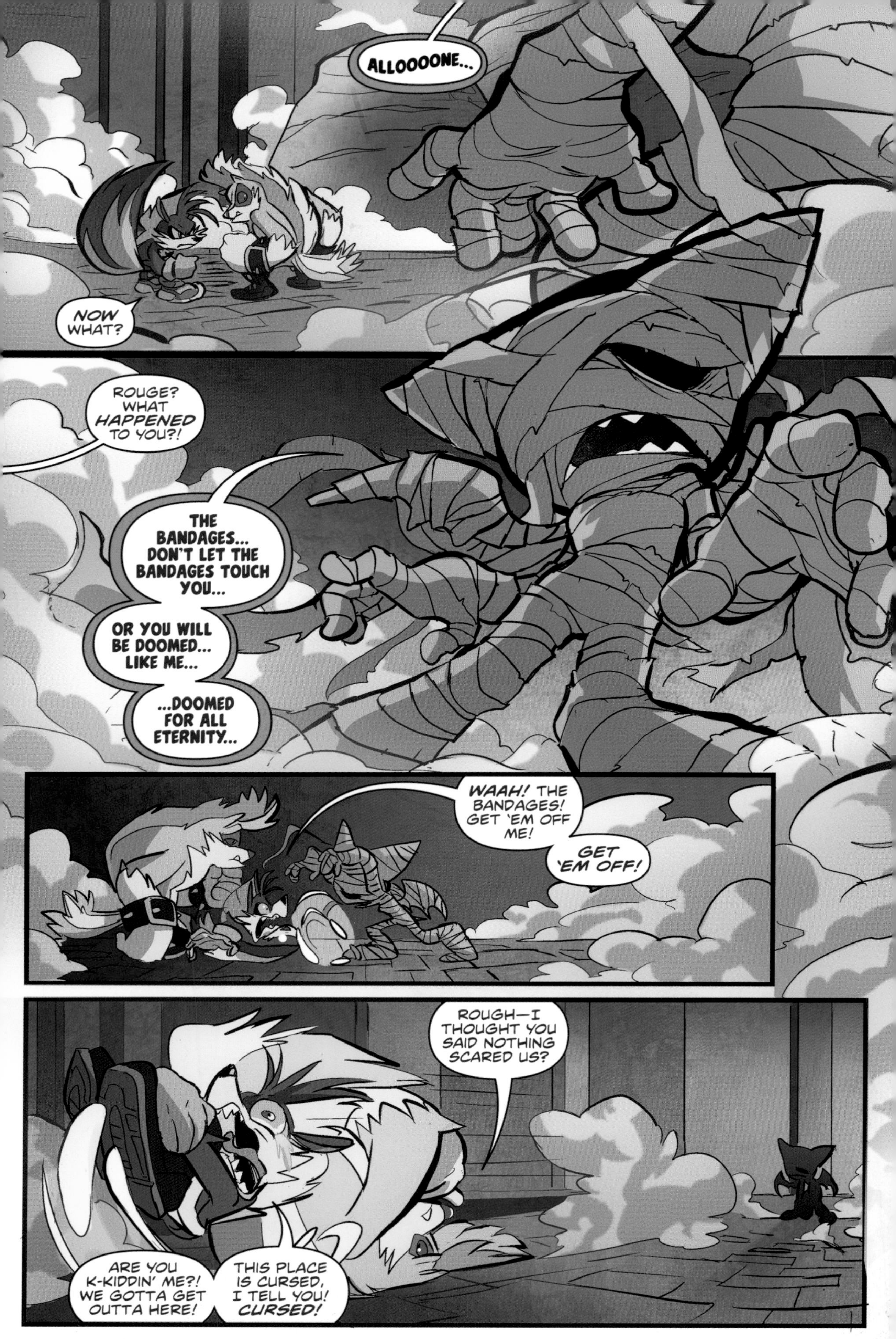
ALLOOOONE...
NOW WHAT?
ROUGE? WHAT HAPPENED TO YOU?!
THE BANDAGES... DON'T LET THE BANDAGES TOUCH YOU...
OR YOU WILL BE DOOMED... LIKE ME...
...DOOMED FOR ALL ETERNITY...
WAAH! THE BANDAGES! GET 'EM OFF ME!
GET 'EM OFF!
ROUGH—I THOUGHT YOU SAID NOTHING SCARED US?
ARE YOU K-KIDDIN' ME?! WE GOTTA GET OUTTA HERE!
THIS PLACE IS CURSED, I TELL YOU! CURSED!

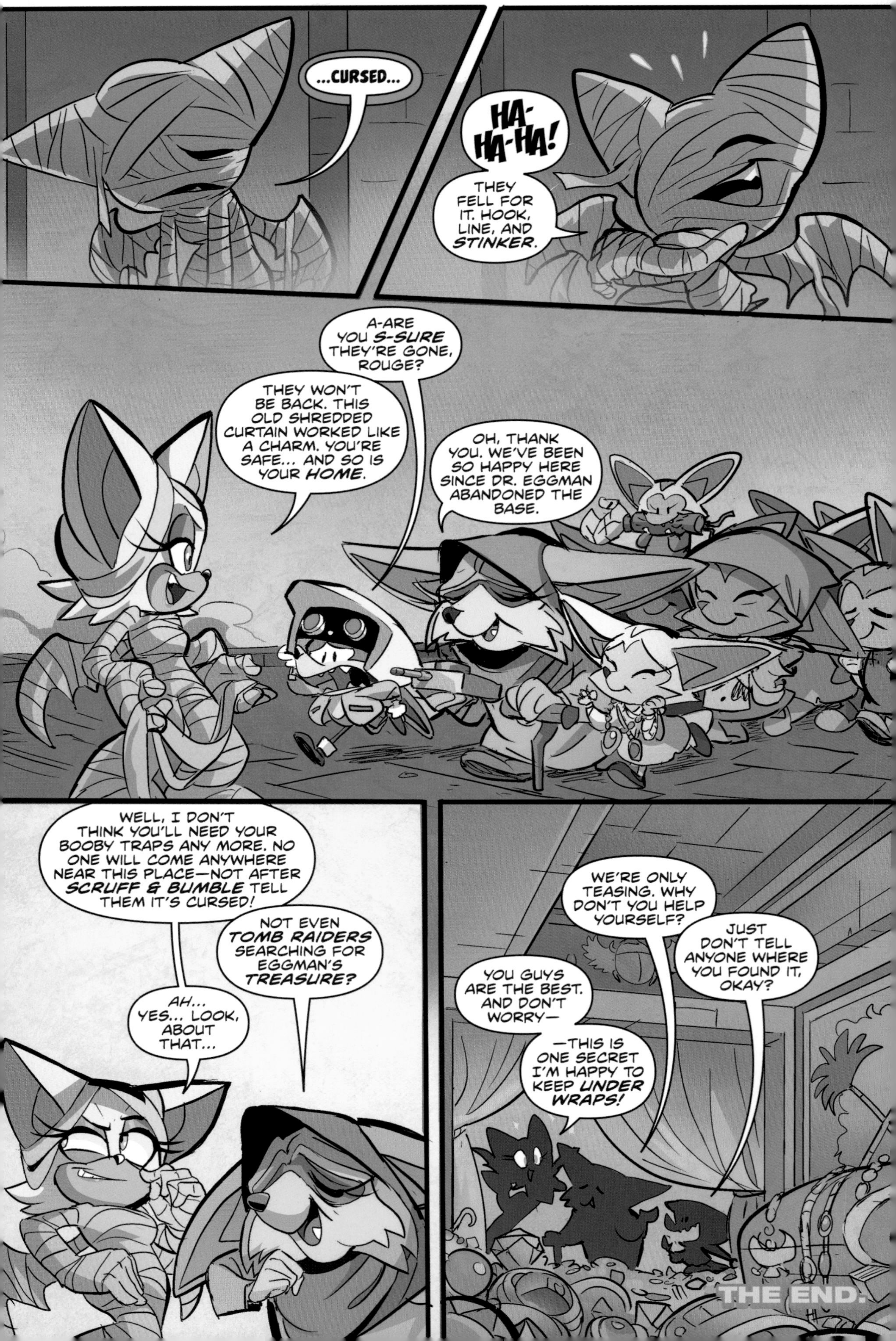
...CURSED...
HA-HA-HA!
THEY FELL FOR IT. HOOK, LINE, AND STINKER.
A-ARE YOU S-SURE THEY'RE GONE, ROUGE?
THEY WON'T BE BACK. THIS OLD SHREDDED CURTAIN WORKED LIKE A CHARM. YOU'RE SAFE... AND SO IS YOUR HOME.
OH, THANK YOU. WE'VE BEEN SO HAPPY HERE SINCE DR. EGGMAN ABANDONED THE BASE.
WELL, I DON'T THINK YOU'LL NEED YOUR BOOBY TRAPS ANY MORE. NO ONE WILL COME ANYWHERE NEAR THIS PLACE—NOT AFTER SCRUFF & BUMBLE TELL THEM IT'S CURSED!
NOT EVEN TOMB RAIDERS SEARCHING FOR EGGMAN'S TREASURE?
AH... YES... LOOK, ABOUT THAT...
WE'RE ONLY TEASING. WHY DON'T YOU HELP YOURSELF?
JUST DON'T TELL ANYONE WHERE YOU FOUND IT, OKAY?
YOU GUYS ARE THE BEST. AND DON'T WORRY—
—THIS IS ONE SECRET I'M HAPPY TO KEEP UNDER WRAPS!
THE END.

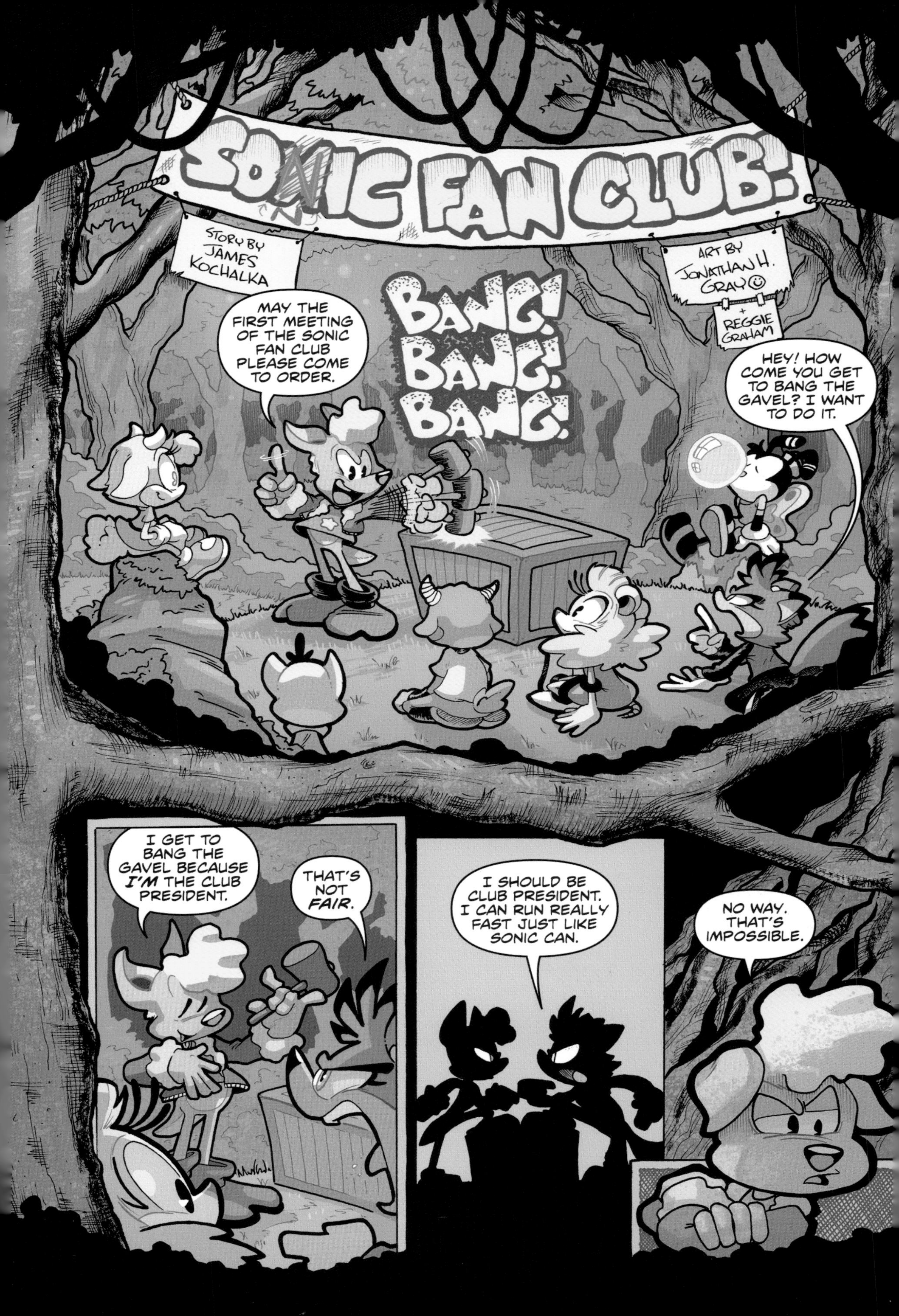
SONIC FAN CLUB!
STORY BY JAMES KOCHALKA
ART BY JONATHAN H. GRAY + REGGIE GRAHAM
MAY THE FIRST MEETING OF THE SONIC FAN CLUB PLEASE COME TO ORDER.
BANG! BANG! BANG!
HEY! HOW COME YOU GET TO BANG THE GAVEL? I WANT TO DO IT.
I GET TO BANG THE GAVEL BECAUSE *I'M* THE CLUB PRESIDENT.
THAT'S NOT *FAIR*.
I SHOULD BE CLUB PRESIDENT. I CAN RUN REALLY FAST JUST LIKE SONIC CAN.
NO WAY. THAT'S IMPOSSIBLE.

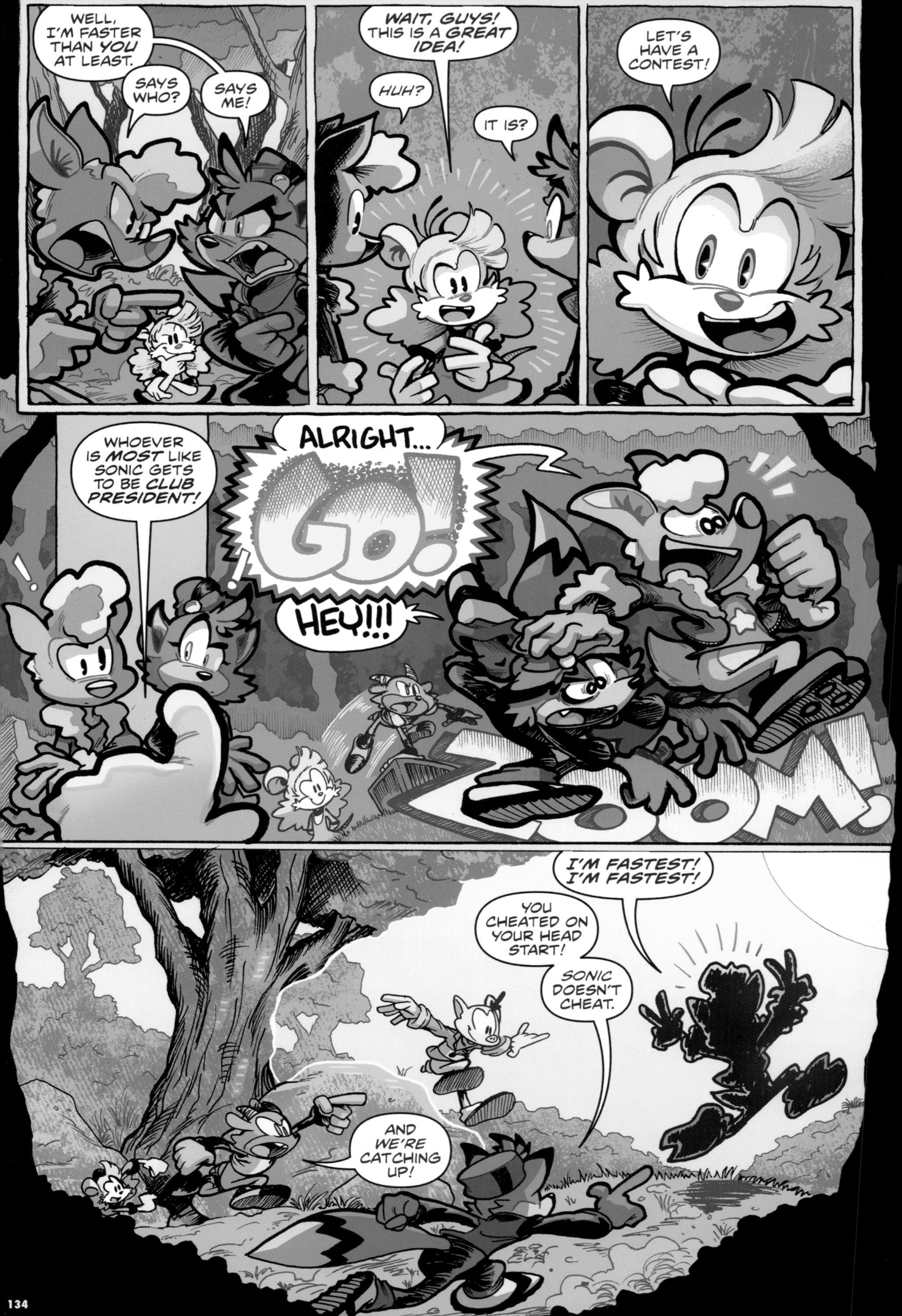
WELL, I'M FASTER THAN YOU AT LEAST.
SAYS WHO?
SAYS ME!
WAIT, GUYS! THIS IS A GREAT IDEA!
HUH?
IT IS?
LET'S HAVE A CONTEST!
WHOEVER IS MOST LIKE SONIC GETS TO BE CLUB PRESIDENT!
ALRIGHT...
GO!
HEY!!!
I'M FASTEST! I'M FASTEST!
YOU CHEATED ON YOUR HEAD START!
SONIC DOESN'T CHEAT.
AND WE'RE CATCHING UP!

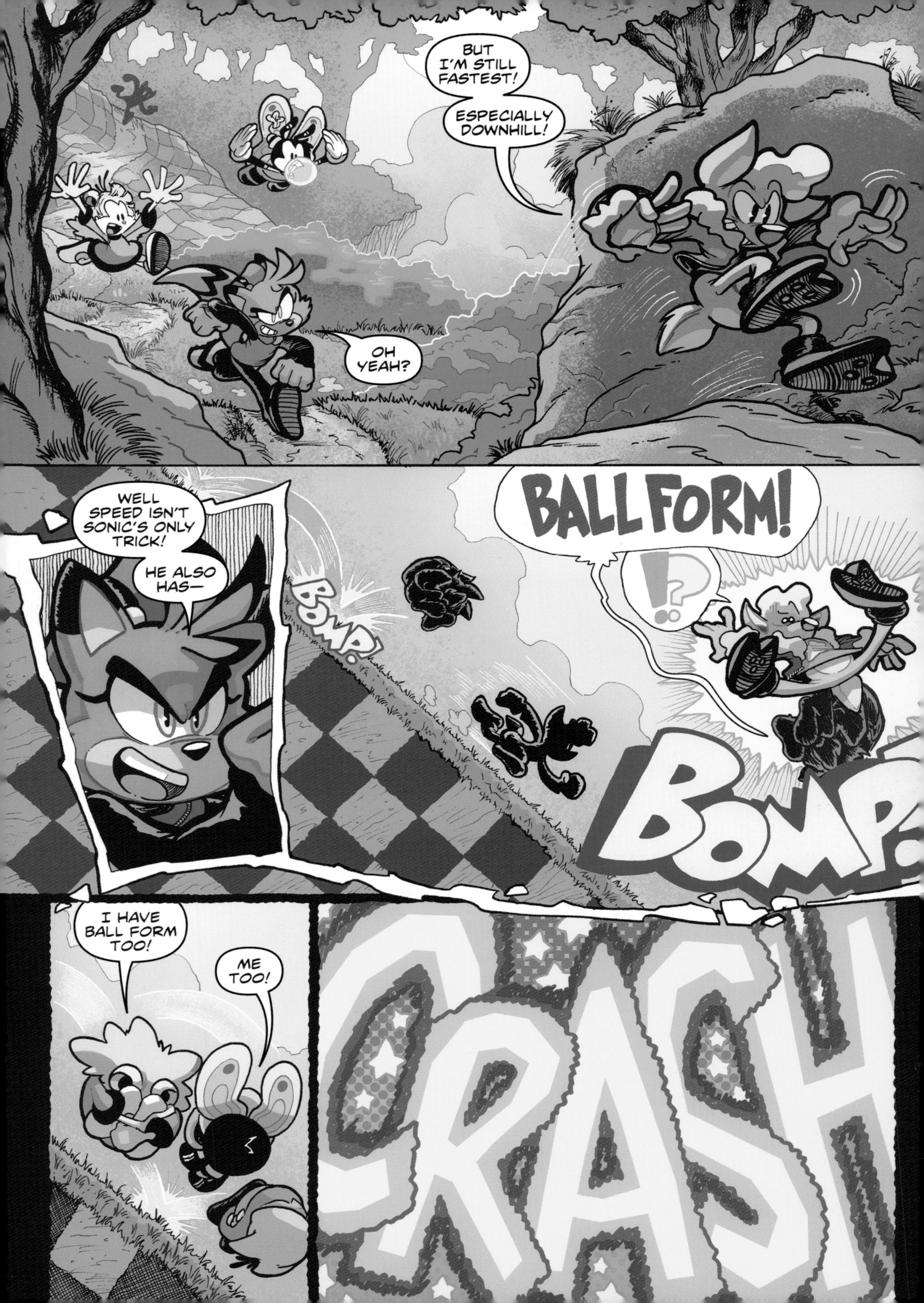
BUT I'M STILL FASTEST!
ESPECIALLY DOWNHILL!
OH YEAH?
WELL SPEED ISN'T SONIC'S ONLY TRICK!
HE ALSO HAS—
BOMP!
BALL FORM!
!?
BOMP
I HAVE BALL FORM TOO!
ME TOO!
CRASH

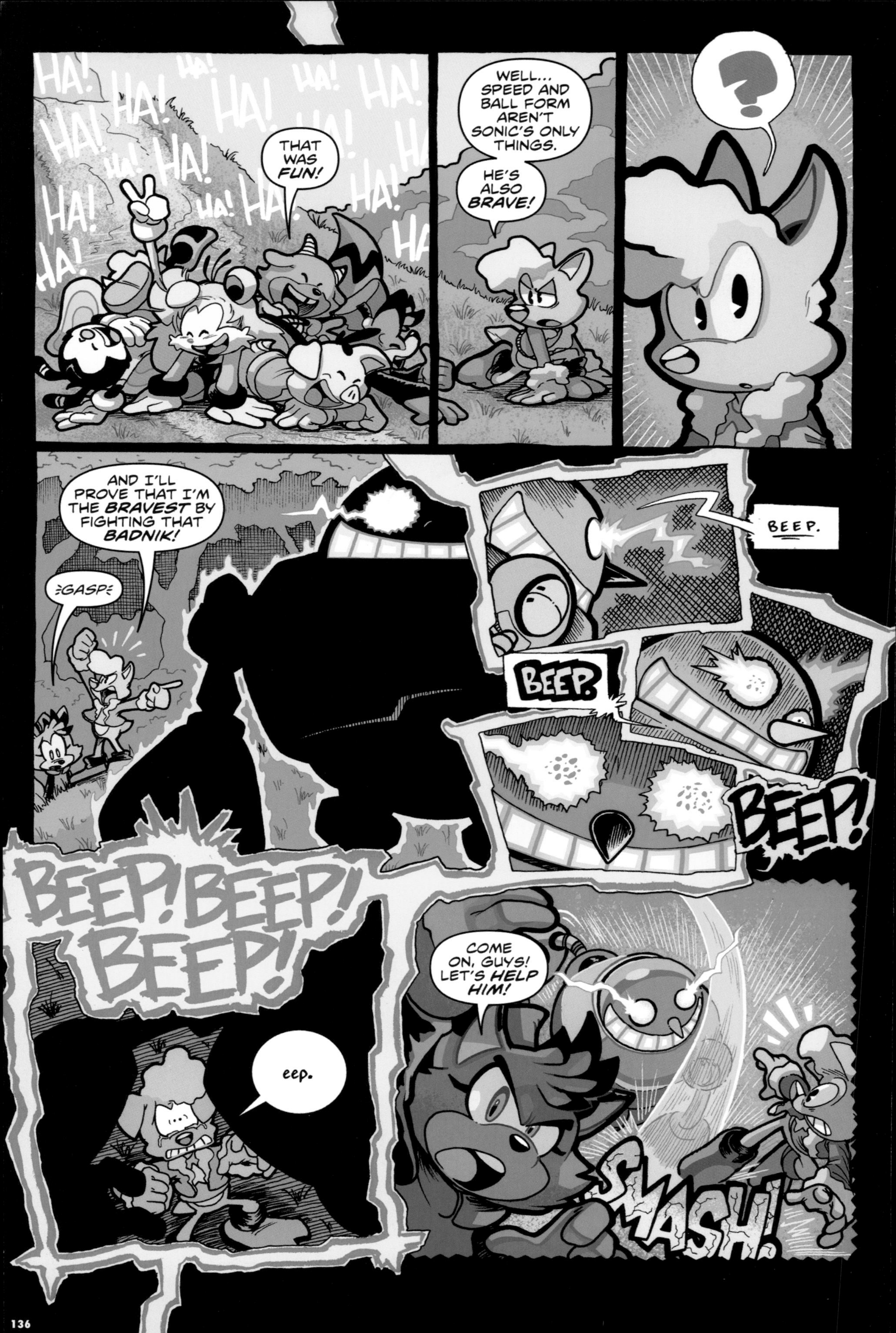
HA! HA! HA! HA! HA! HA! HA! HA! HA! HA! HA! HA! HA! HA!
THAT WAS FUN!
WELL... SPEED AND BALL FORM AREN'T SONIC'S ONLY THINGS.
HE'S ALSO BRAVE!
?
AND I'LL PROVE THAT I'M THE BRAVEST BY FIGHTING THAT BADNIK!
GASP
BEEP.
BEEP.
BEEP!
BEEP! BEEP! BEEP!
eep.
COME ON, GUYS! LET'S HELP HIM!
SMASH!

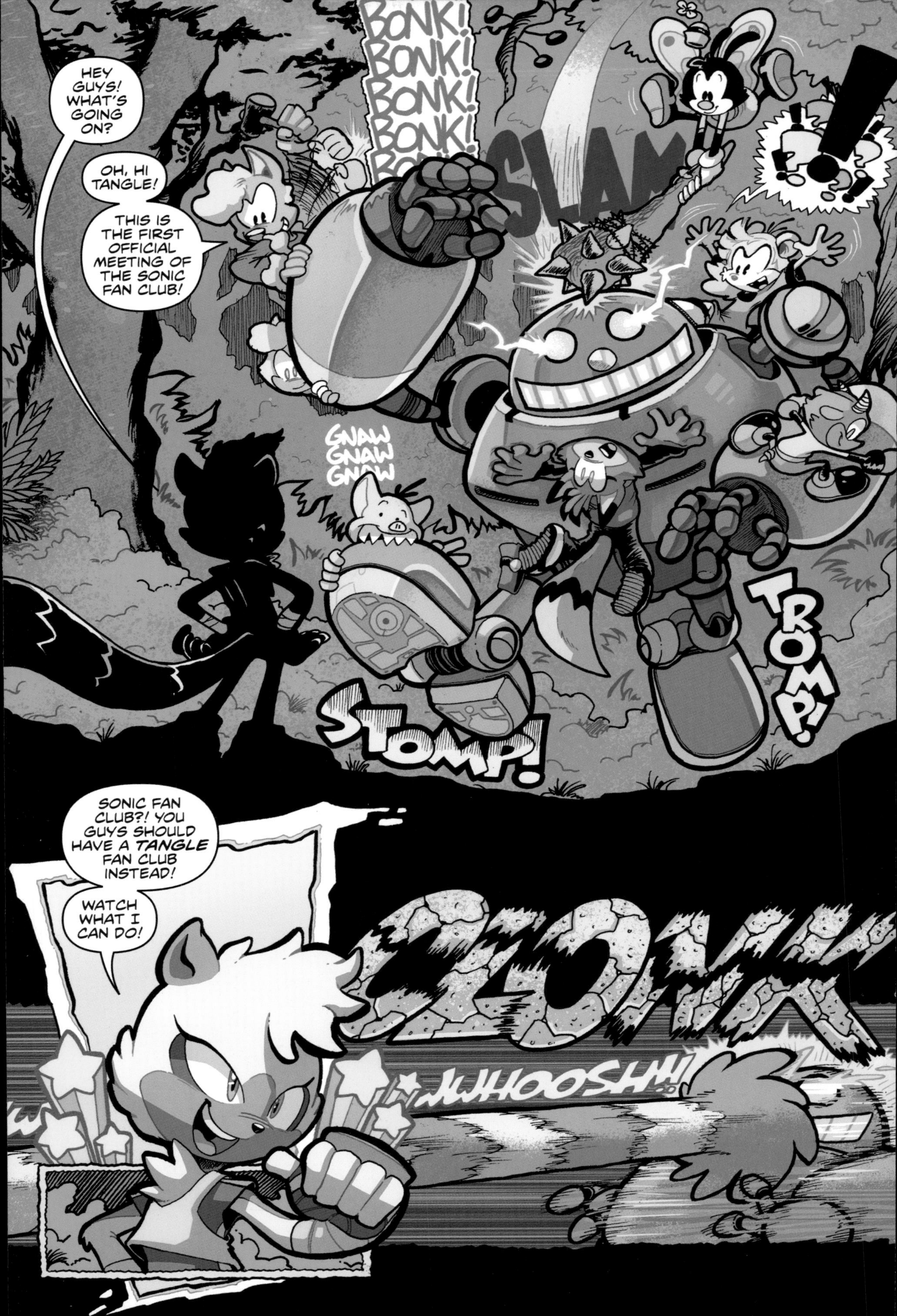
HEY GUYS! WHAT'S GOING ON?
OH, HI TANGLE!
THIS IS THE FIRST OFFICIAL MEETING OF THE SONIC FAN CLUB!
BONK! BONK! BONK! BONK!
SLAM
GNAW GNAW GNAW
STOMP!
TROMP!
SONIC FAN CLUB?! YOU GUYS SHOULD HAVE A *TANGLE* FAN CLUB INSTEAD!
WATCH WHAT I CAN DO!
WHOOSH!

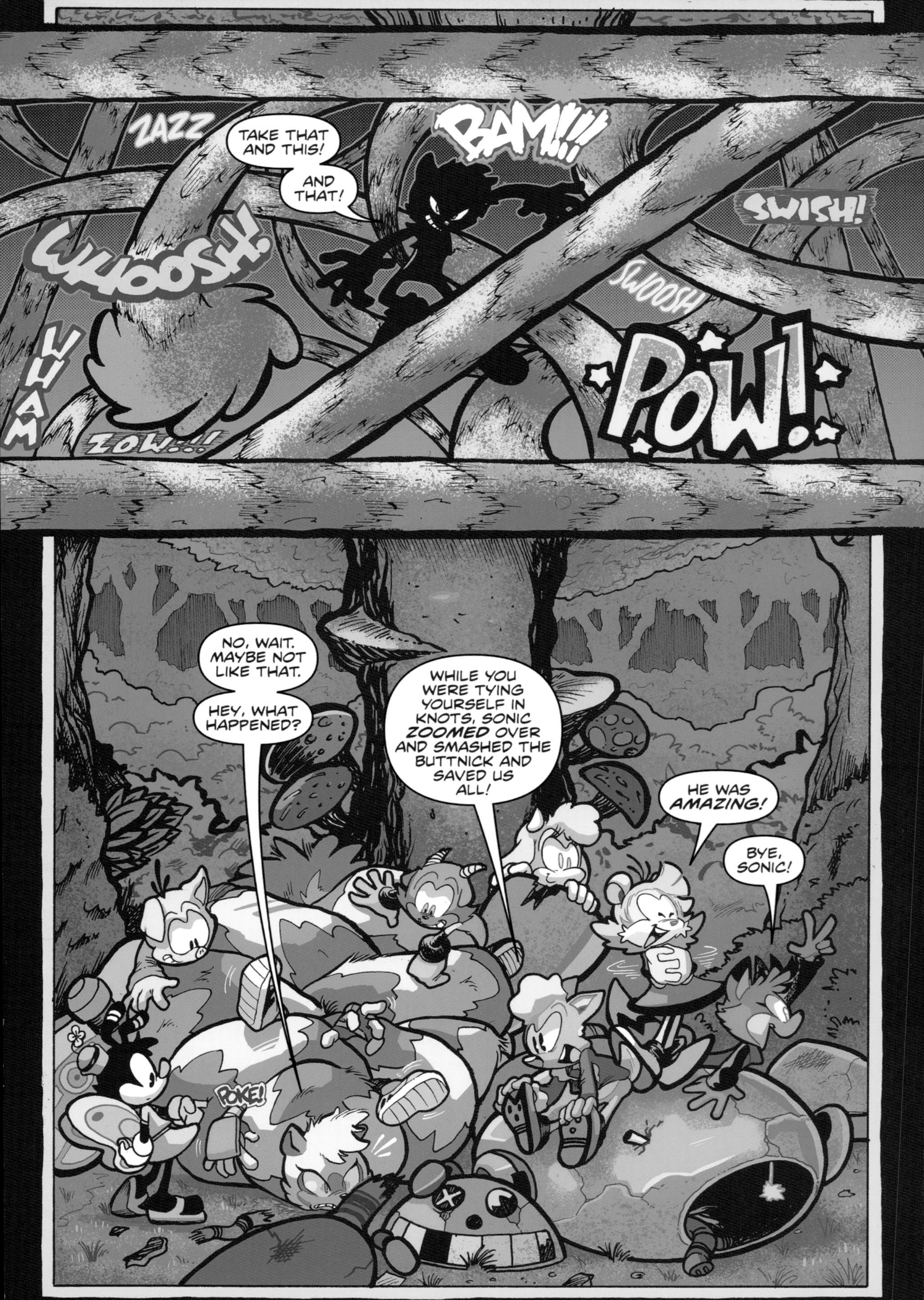
ZAZZ
TAKE THAT AND THIS!
AND THAT!
BAM!!!!
SWISH!
WHOOSH!
SWOOSH
WHAM
ZOW!!!
POW!
NO, WAIT. MAYBE NOT LIKE THAT.
HEY, WHAT HAPPENED?
WHILE YOU WERE TYING YOURSELF IN KNOTS, SONIC ZOOMED OVER AND SMASHED THE BUTTNICK AND SAVED US ALL!
HE WAS AMAZING!
BYE, SONIC!
POKE!

* the end *

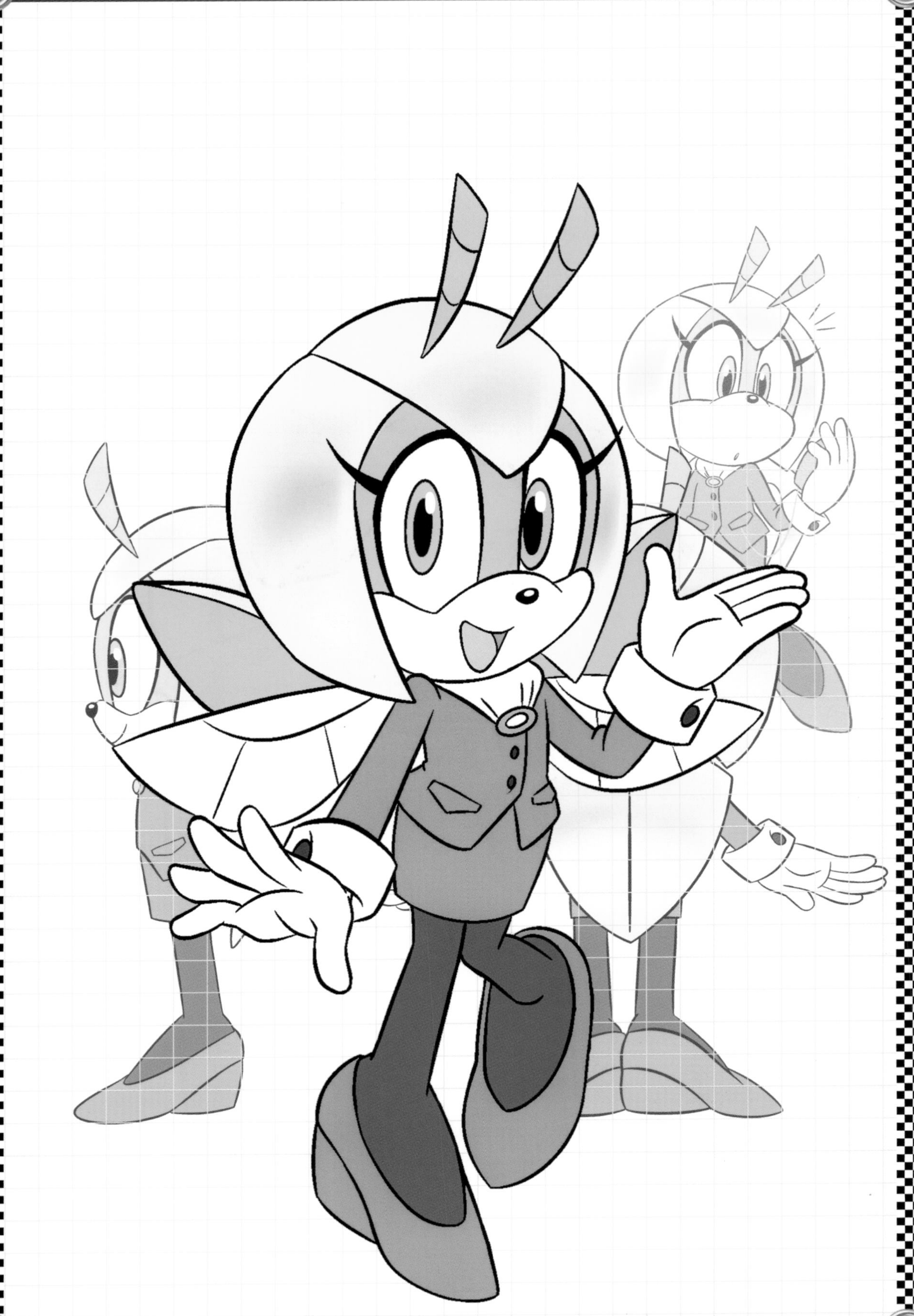

ART BY **EVAN STANLEY**

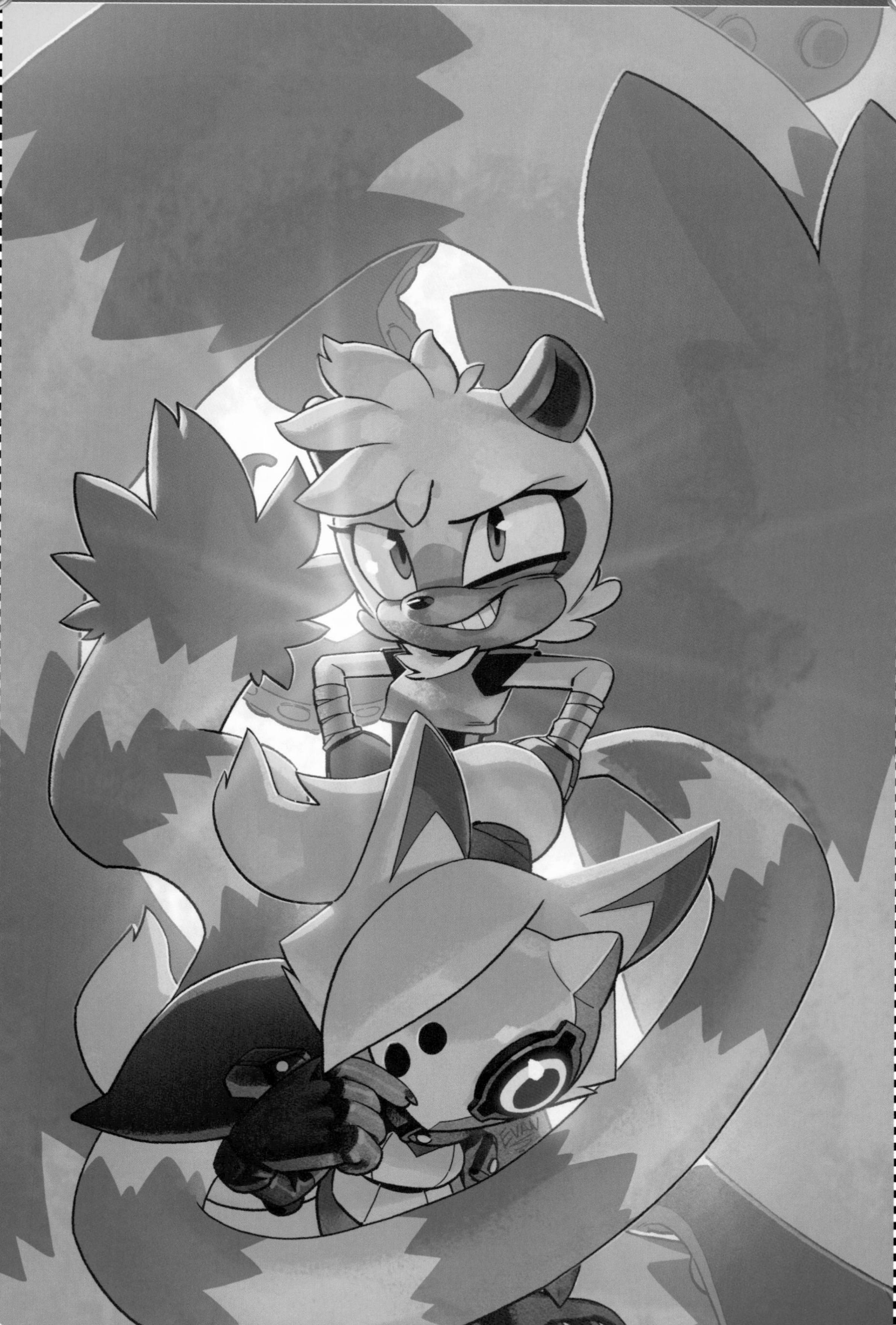
EVAN

TANGLE & WHISPER #1

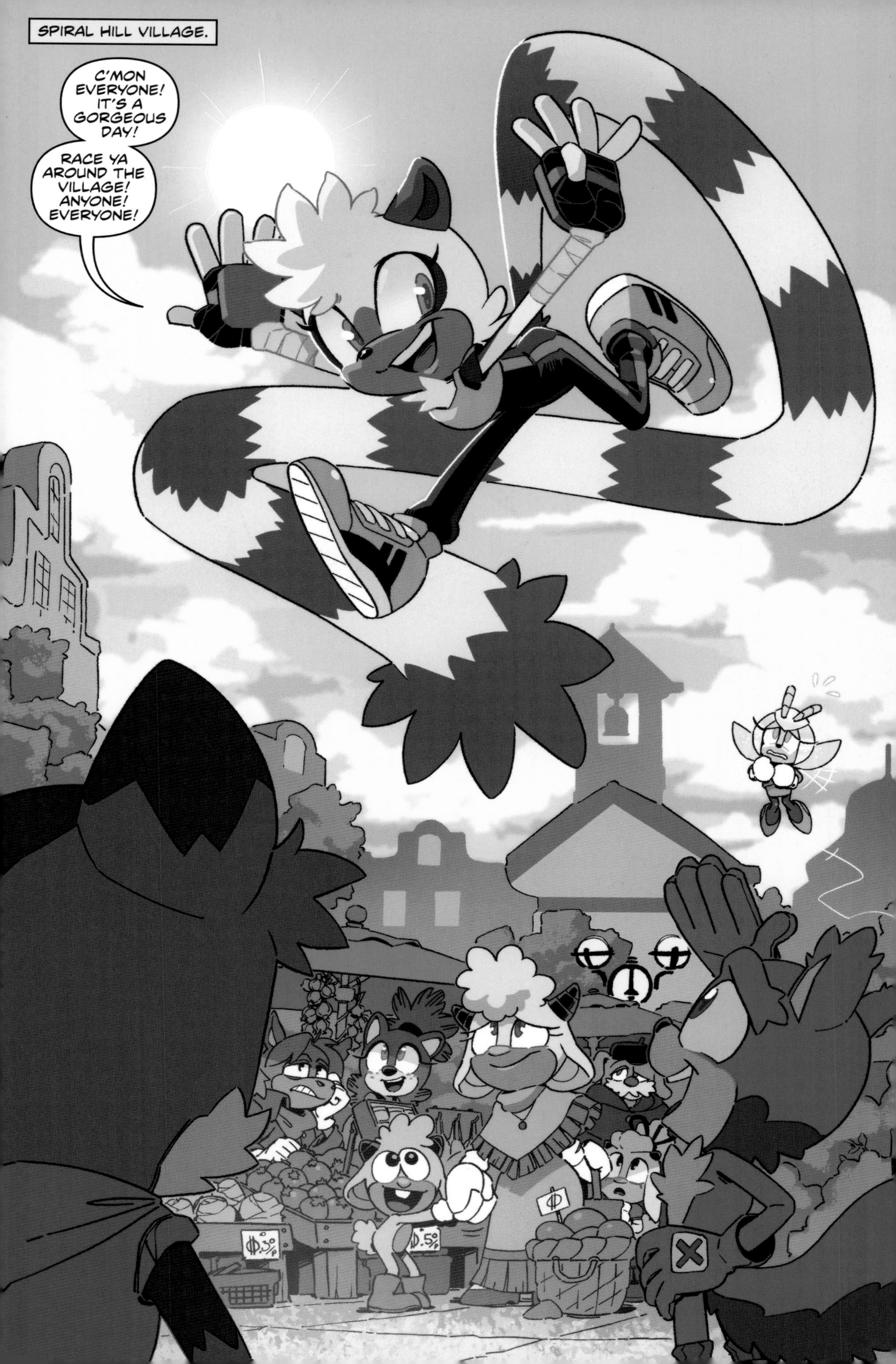
SPIRAL HILL VILLAGE.
C'MON EVERYONE! IT'S A GORGEOUS DAY!
RACE YA AROUND THE VILLAGE! ANYONE! EVERYONE!

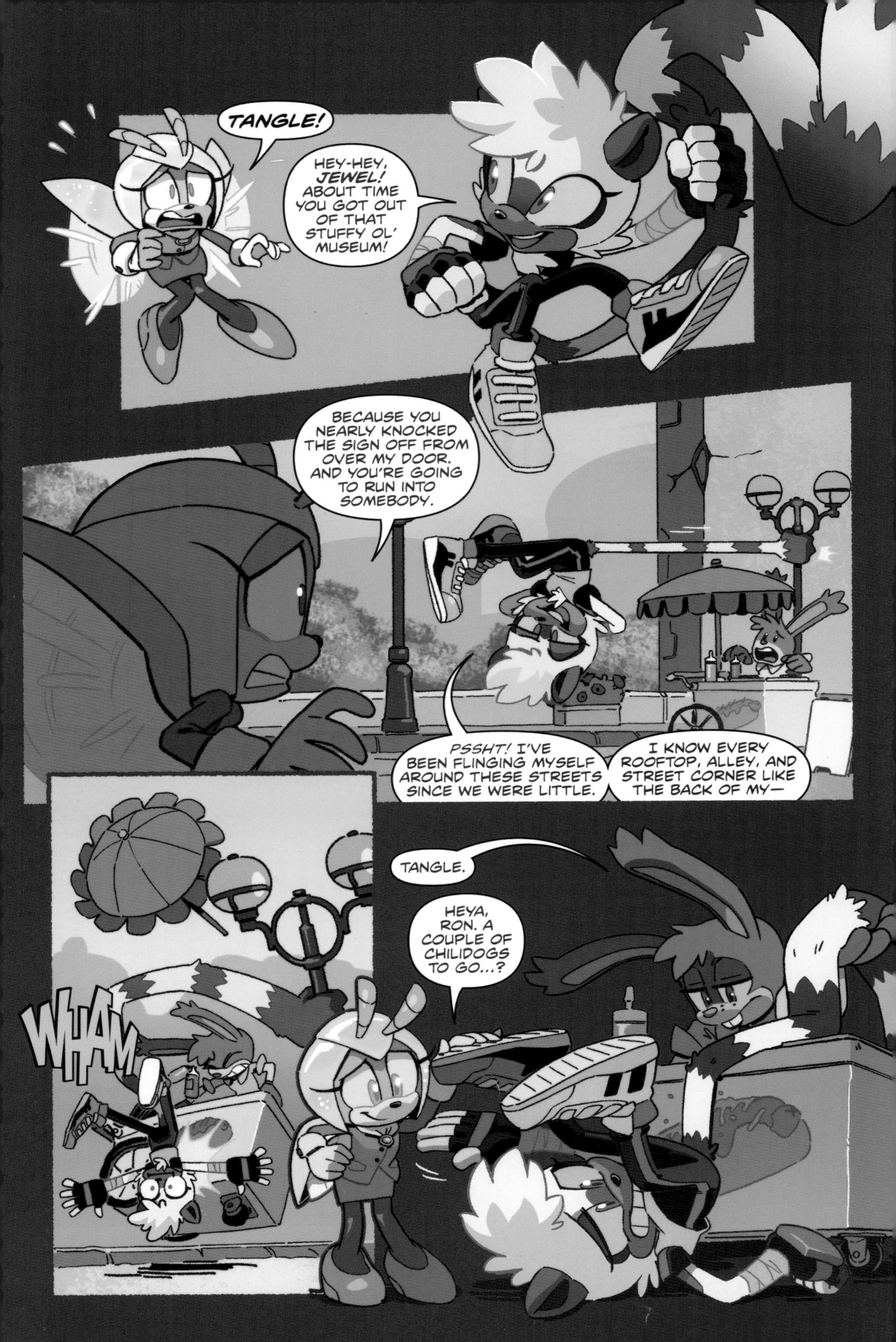
TANGLE!
HEY-HEY, JEWEL! ABOUT TIME YOU GOT OUT OF THAT STUFFY OL' MUSEUM!
BECAUSE YOU NEARLY KNOCKED THE SIGN OFF FROM OVER MY DOOR. AND YOU'RE GOING TO RUN INTO SOMEBODY.
PSSHT! I'VE BEEN FLINGING MYSELF AROUND THESE STREETS SINCE WE WERE LITTLE.
I KNOW EVERY ROOFTOP, ALLEY, AND STREET CORNER LIKE THE BACK OF MY—
WHAM
TANGLE.
HEYA, RON. A COUPLE OF CHILIDOGS TO GO...?

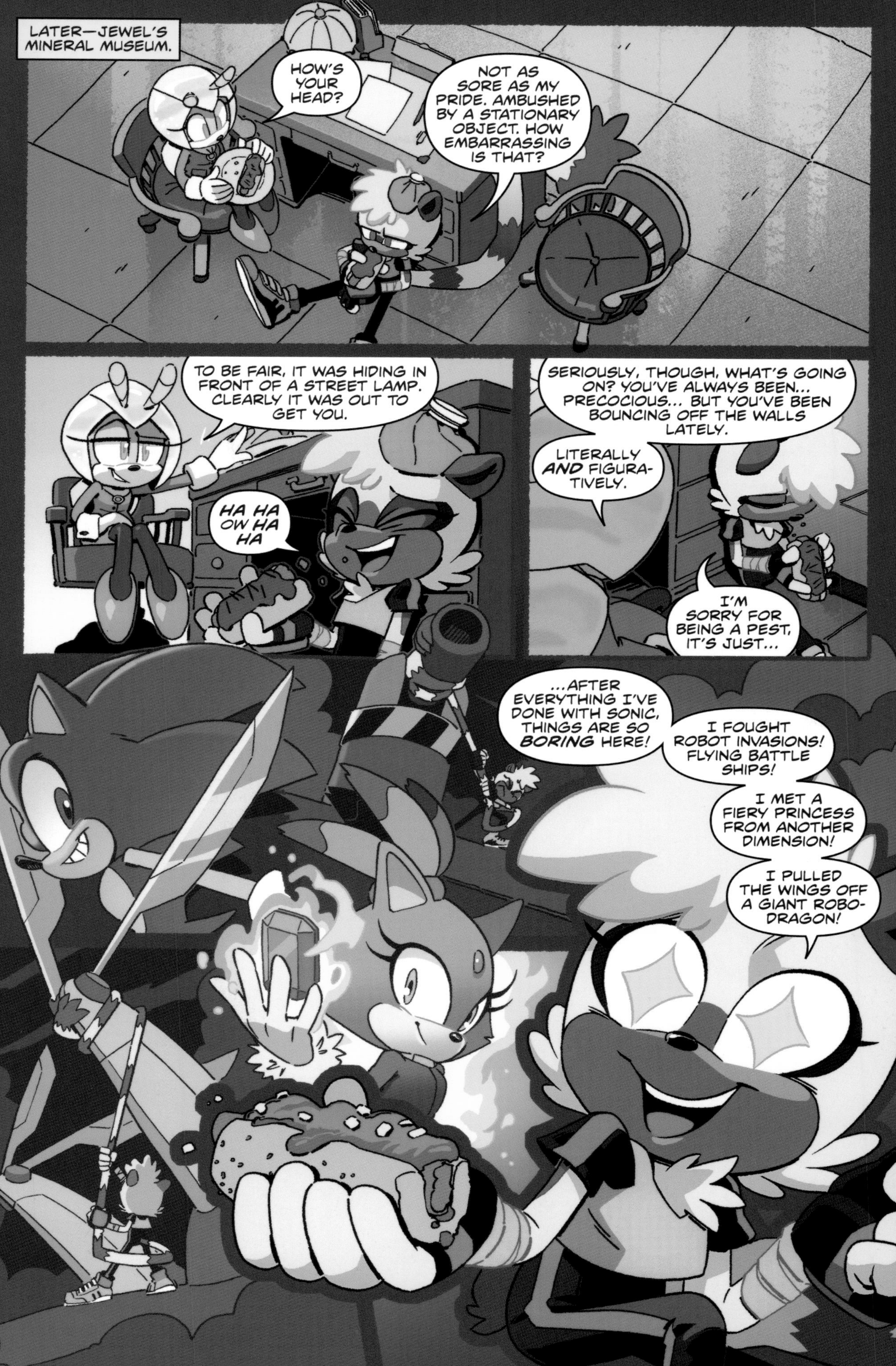

LATER—JEWEL'S MINERAL MUSEUM.
HOW'S YOUR HEAD?
NOT AS SORE AS MY PRIDE. AMBUSHED BY A STATIONARY OBJECT. HOW EMBARRASSING IS THAT?
TO BE FAIR, IT WAS HIDING IN FRONT OF A STREET LAMP. CLEARLY IT WAS OUT TO GET YOU.
HA HA OW HA HA
SERIOUSLY, THOUGH, WHAT'S GOING ON? YOU'VE ALWAYS BEEN... PRECOCIOUS... BUT YOU'VE BEEN BOUNCING OFF THE WALLS LATELY.
LITERALLY AND FIGURATIVELY.
I'M SORRY FOR BEING A PEST, IT'S JUST...
...AFTER EVERYTHING I'VE DONE WITH SONIC, THINGS ARE SO BORING HERE!
I FOUGHT ROBOT INVASIONS! FLYING BATTLE SHIPS!
I MET A FIERY PRINCESS FROM ANOTHER DIMENSION!
I PULLED THE WINGS OFF A GIANT ROBO-DRAGON!

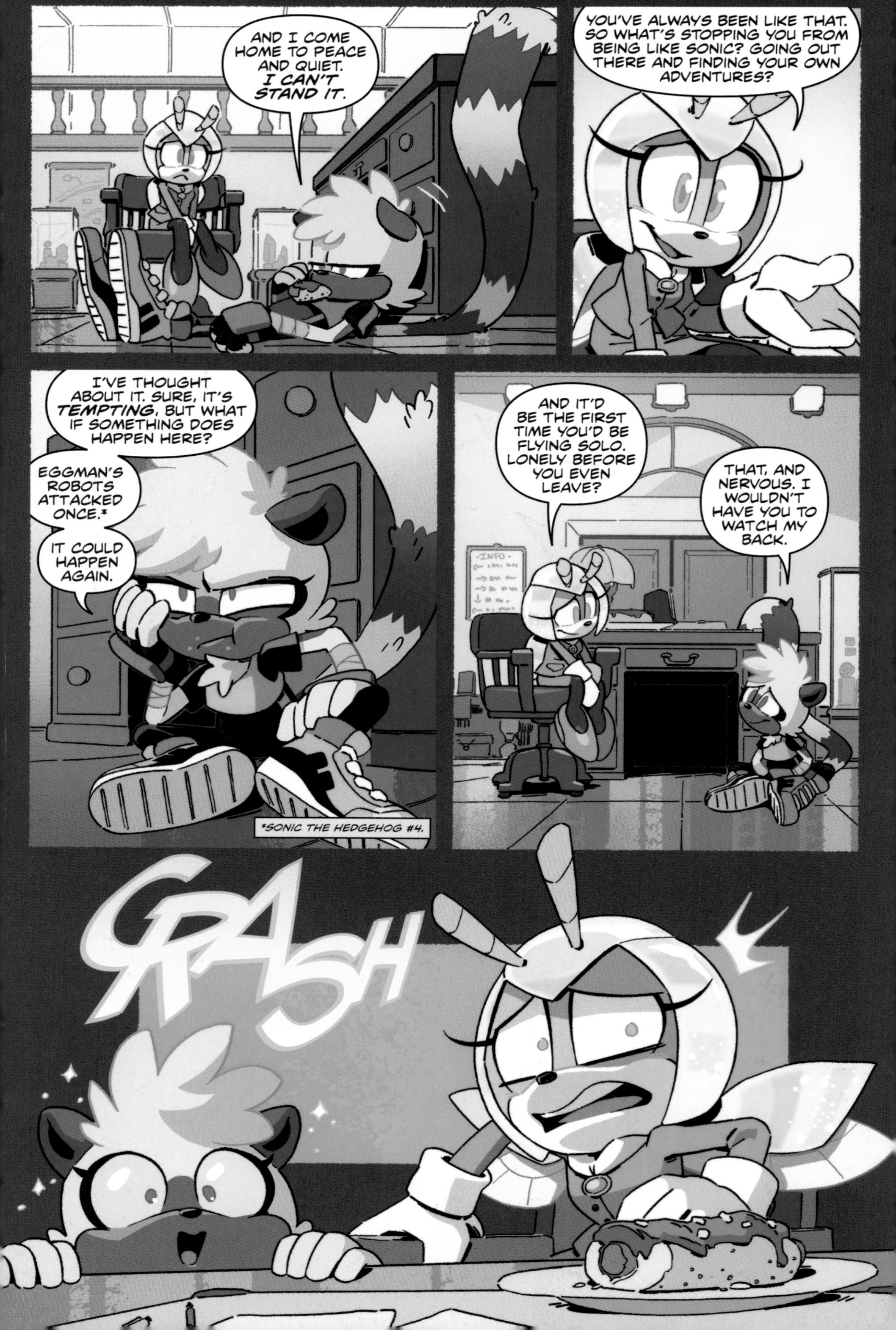
AND I COME HOME TO PEACE AND QUIET. I CAN'T STAND IT.
YOU'VE ALWAYS BEEN LIKE THAT. SO WHAT'S STOPPING YOU FROM BEING LIKE SONIC? GOING OUT THERE AND FINDING YOUR OWN ADVENTURES?
I'VE THOUGHT ABOUT IT. SURE, IT'S TEMPTING, BUT WHAT IF SOMETHING DOES HAPPEN HERE?
EGGMAN'S ROBOTS ATTACKED ONCE.*
IT COULD HAPPEN AGAIN.
*SONIC THE HEDGEHOG #4.
AND IT'D BE THE FIRST TIME YOU'D BE FLYING SOLO. LONELY BEFORE YOU EVEN LEAVE?
THAT, AND NERVOUS. I WOULDN'T HAVE YOU TO WATCH MY BACK.
INFO
CRASH

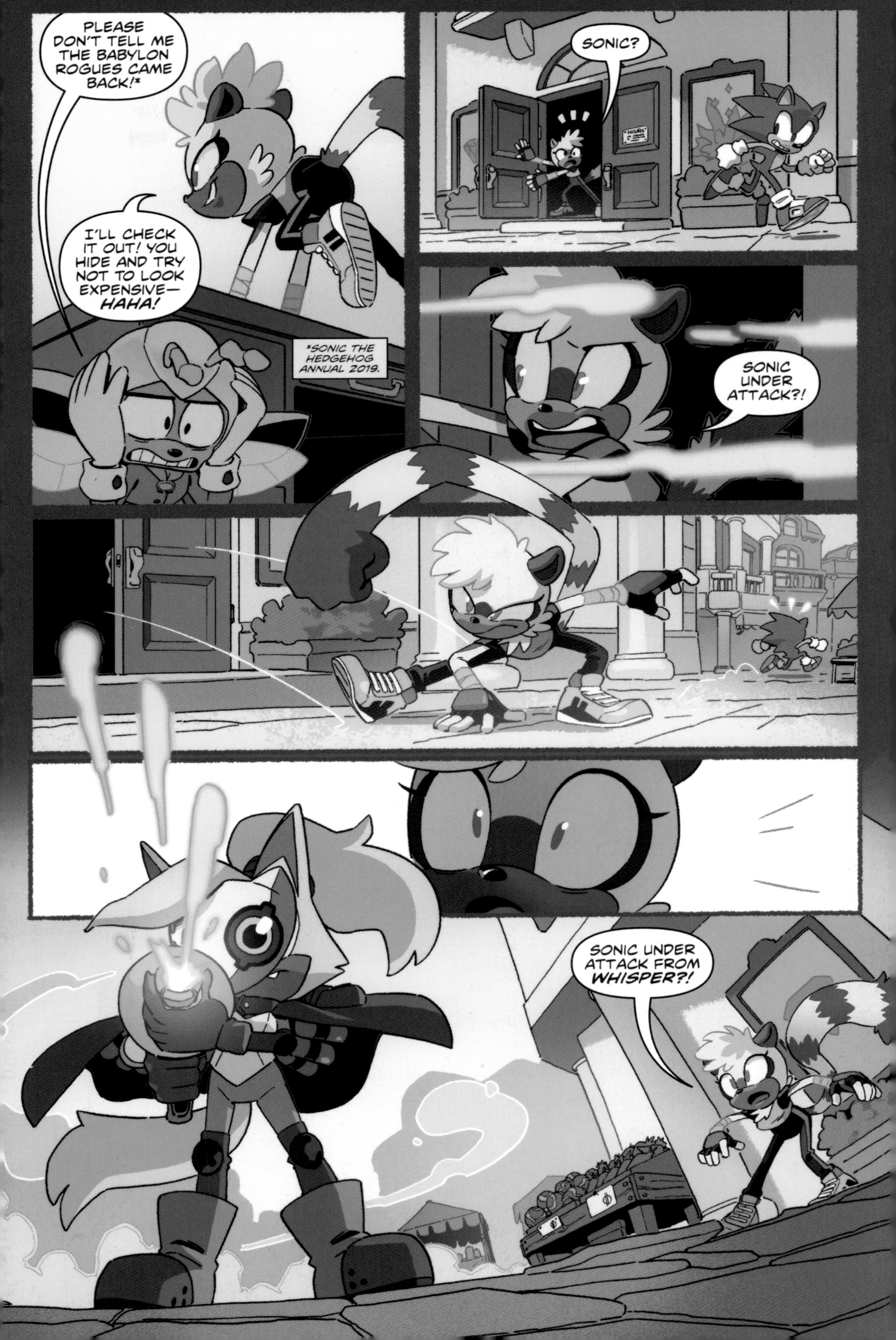
PLEASE DON'T TELL ME THE BABYLON ROGUES CAME BACK!*
I'LL CHECK IT OUT! YOU HIDE AND TRY NOT TO LOOK EXPENSIVE— HAHA!
*SONIC THE HEDGEHOG ANNUAL 2019.
SONIC?
SONIC UNDER ATTACK?!
SONIC UNDER ATTACK FROM WHISPER?!

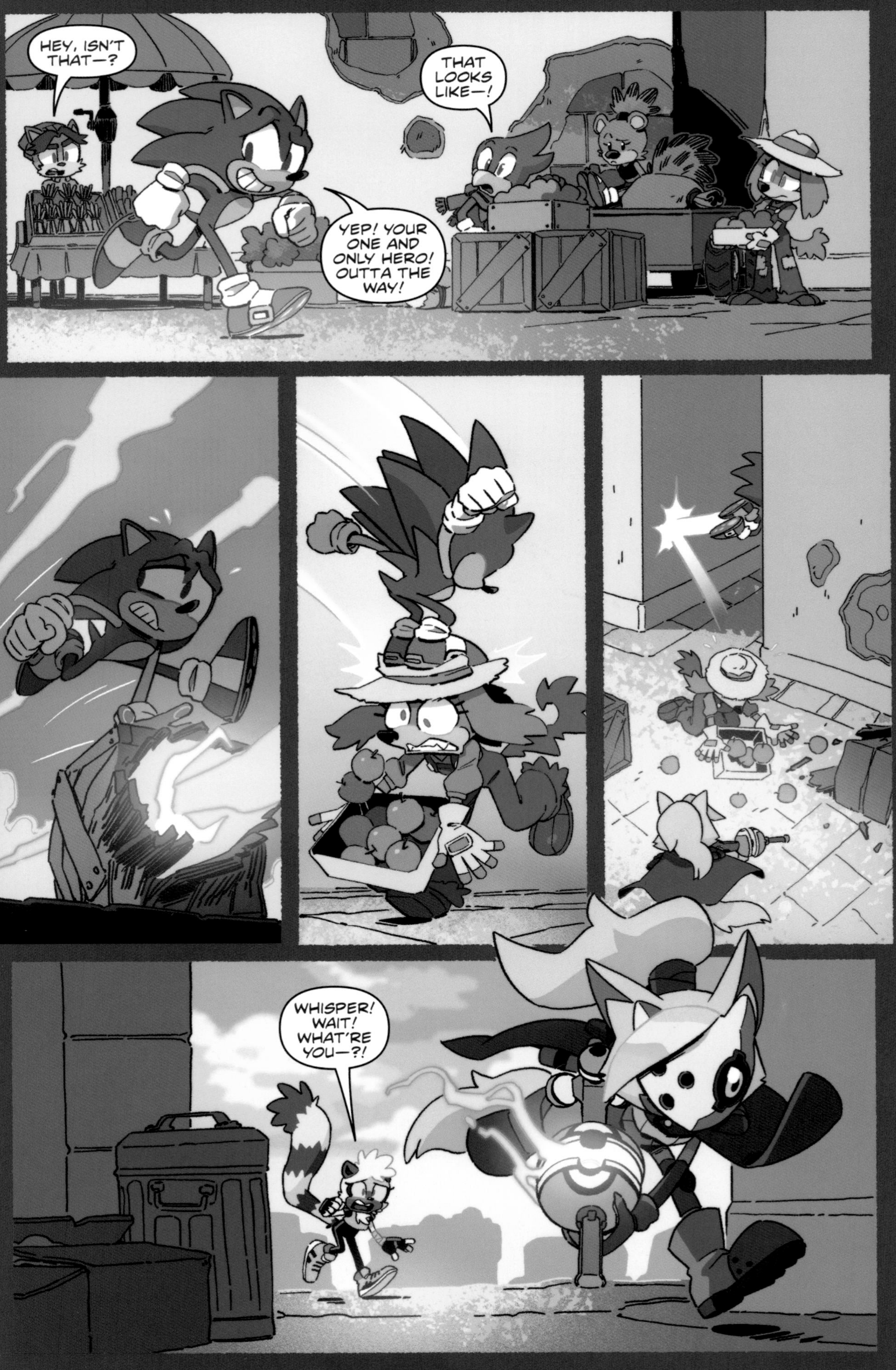
HEY, ISN'T THAT—?
THAT LOOKS LIKE—!
YEP! YOUR ONE AND ONLY HERO! OUTTA THE WAY!
WHISPER! WAIT! WHAT'RE YOU—?!

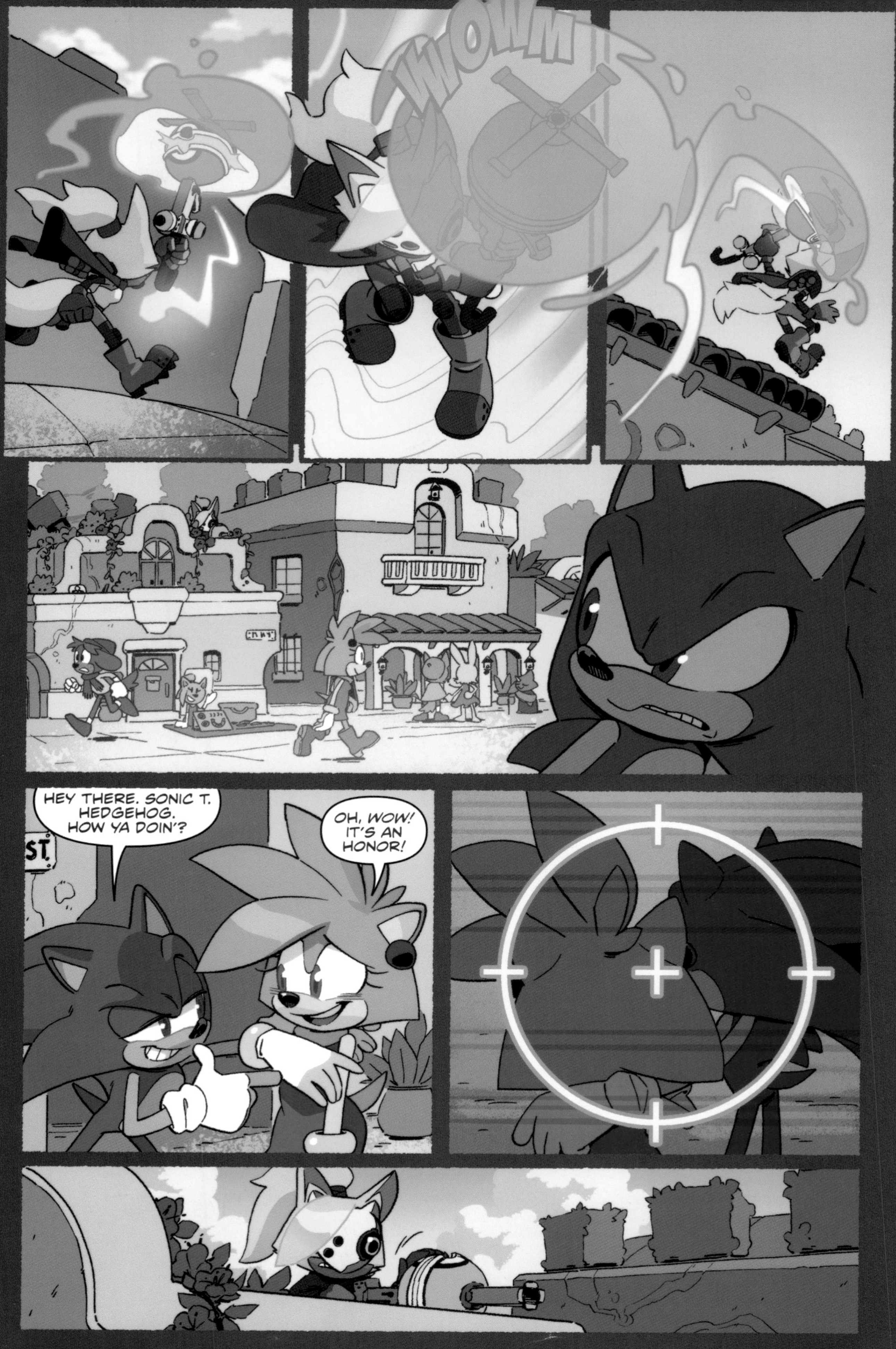
WOWM
HEY THERE. SONIC T. HEDGEHOG. HOW YA DOIN'?
OH, WOW! IT'S AN HONOR!

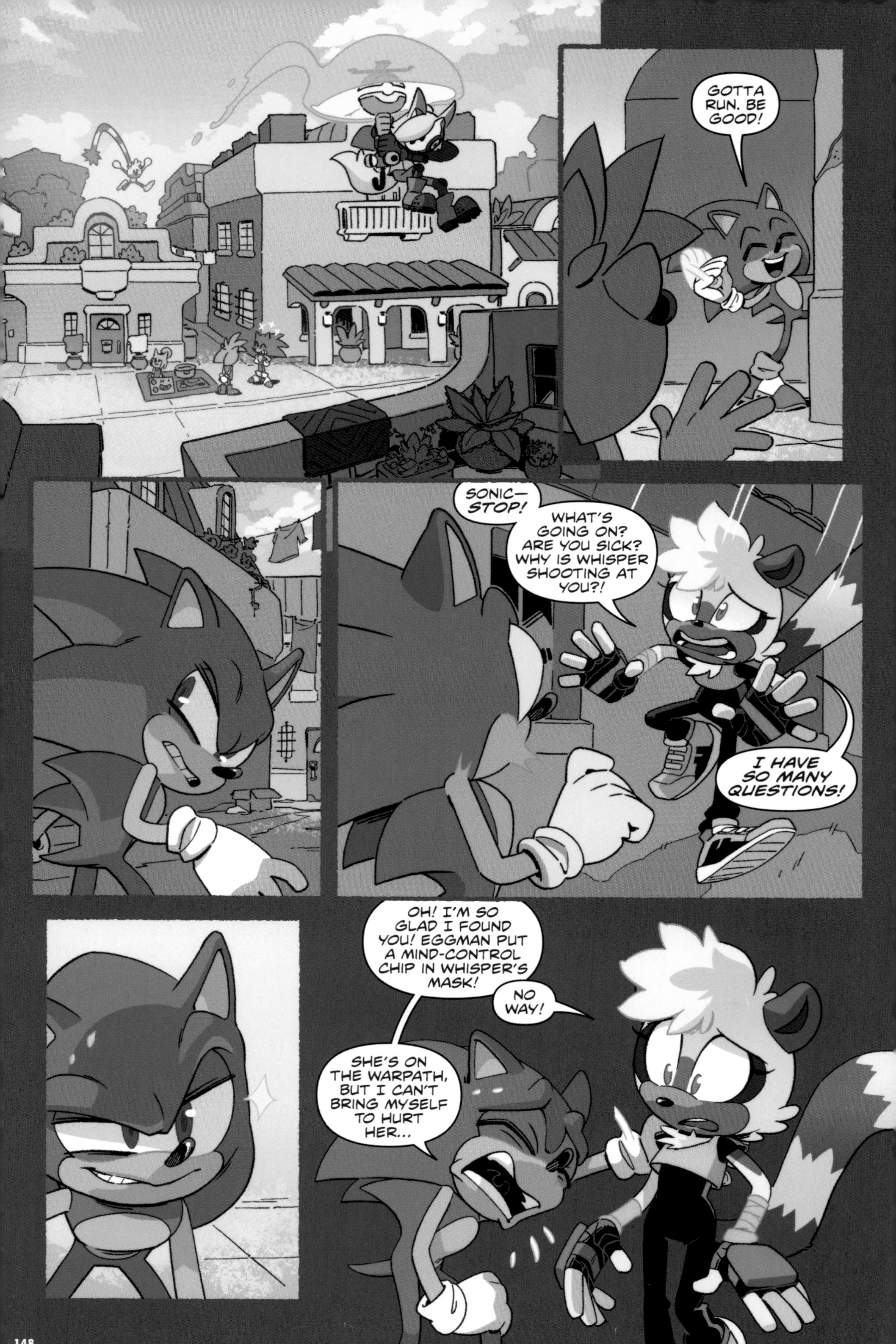
GOTTA RUN. BE GOOD!
SONIC— STOP!
WHAT'S GOING ON? ARE YOU SICK? WHY IS WHISPER SHOOTING AT YOU?!
I HAVE SO MANY QUESTIONS!
OH! I'M SO GLAD I FOUND YOU! EGGMAN PUT A MIND-CONTROL CHIP IN WHISPER'S MASK!
NO WAY!
SHE'S ON THE WARPATH, BUT I CAN'T BRING MYSELF TO HURT HER...

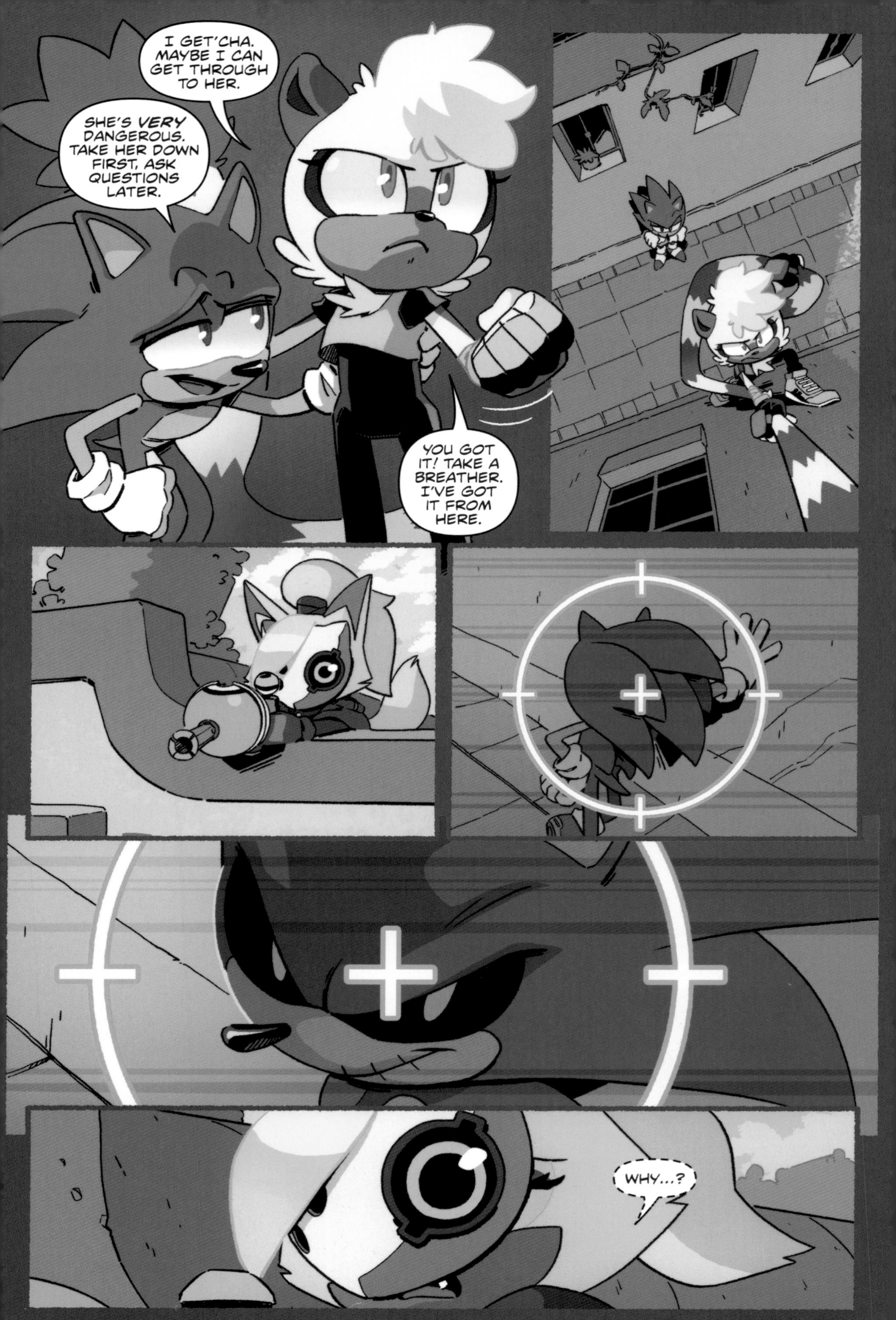

I GET'CHA. MAYBE I CAN GET THROUGH TO HER.
SHE'S *VERY* DANGEROUS. TAKE HER DOWN FIRST, ASK QUESTIONS LATER.
YOU GOT IT! TAKE A BREATHER. I'VE GOT IT FROM HERE.
WHY...?

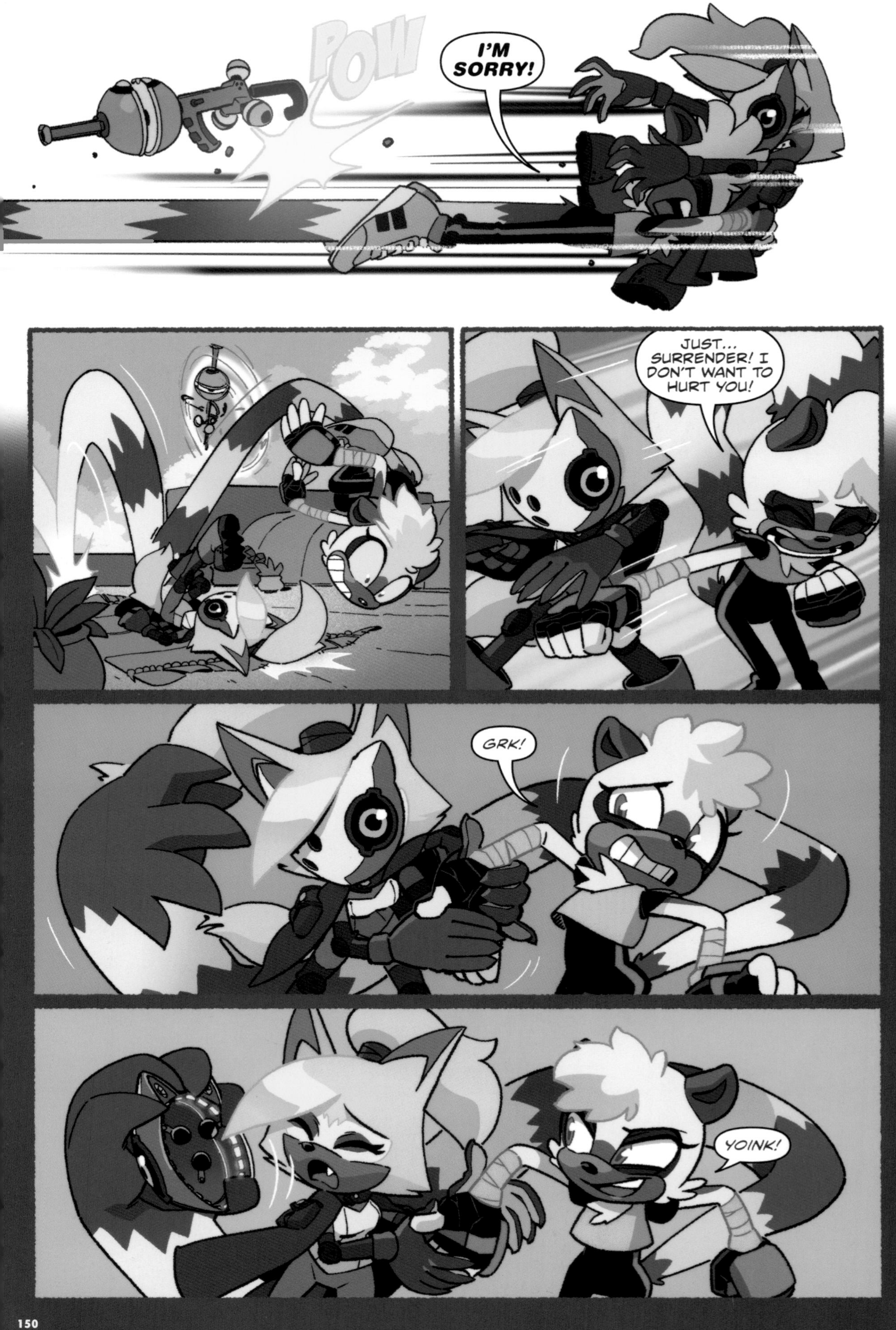
POW
I'M SORRY!
JUST... SURRENDER! I DON'T WANT TO HURT YOU!
GRK!
YOINK!

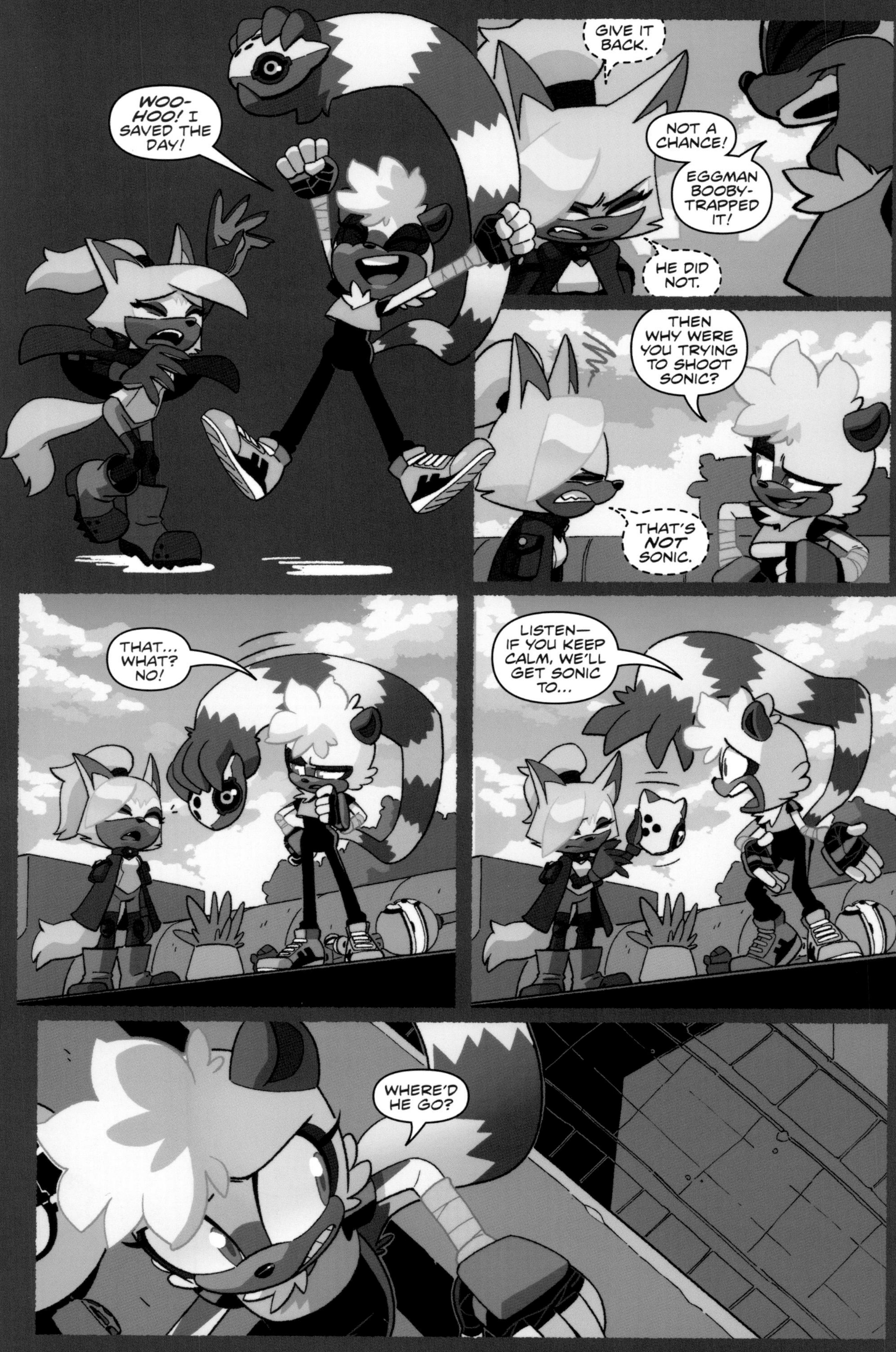
WOO-HOO! I SAVED THE DAY!
GIVE IT BACK.
NOT A CHANCE!
EGGMAN BOOBY-TRAPPED IT!
HE DID NOT.
THEN WHY WERE YOU TRYING TO SHOOT SONIC?
THAT'S *NOT* SONIC.
THAT... WHAT? NO!
LISTEN—IF YOU KEEP CALM, WE'LL GET SONIC TO...
WHERE'D HE GO?

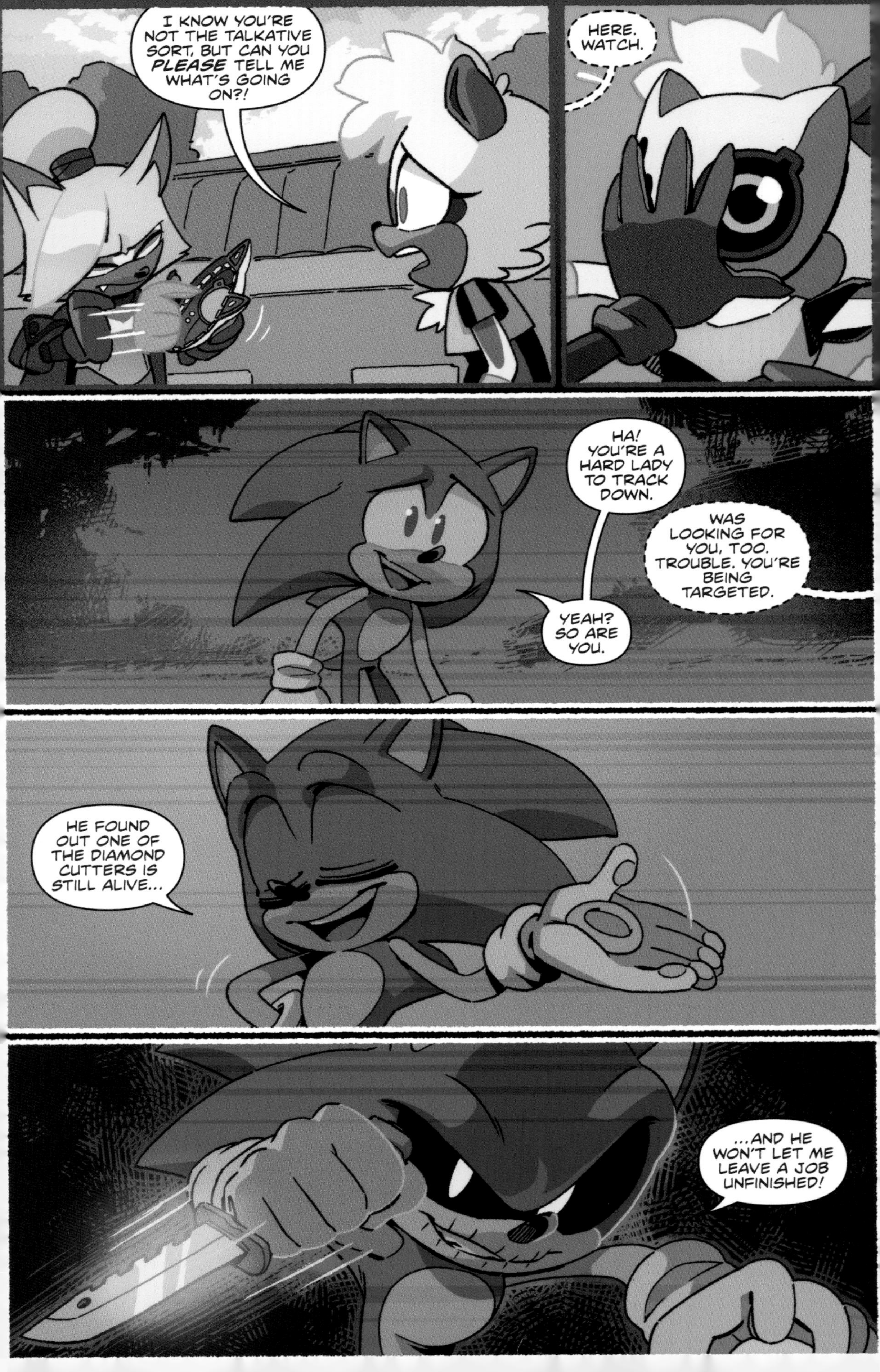
I KNOW YOU'RE NOT THE TALKATIVE SORT, BUT CAN YOU *PLEASE* TELL ME WHAT'S GOING ON?!
HERE. WATCH.
HA! YOU'RE A HARD LADY TO TRACK DOWN.
WAS LOOKING FOR YOU, TOO. TROUBLE. YOU'RE BEING TARGETED.
YEAH? SO ARE YOU.
HE FOUND OUT ONE OF THE DIAMOND CUTTERS IS STILL ALIVE...
...AND HE WON'T LET ME LEAVE A JOB UNFINISHED!

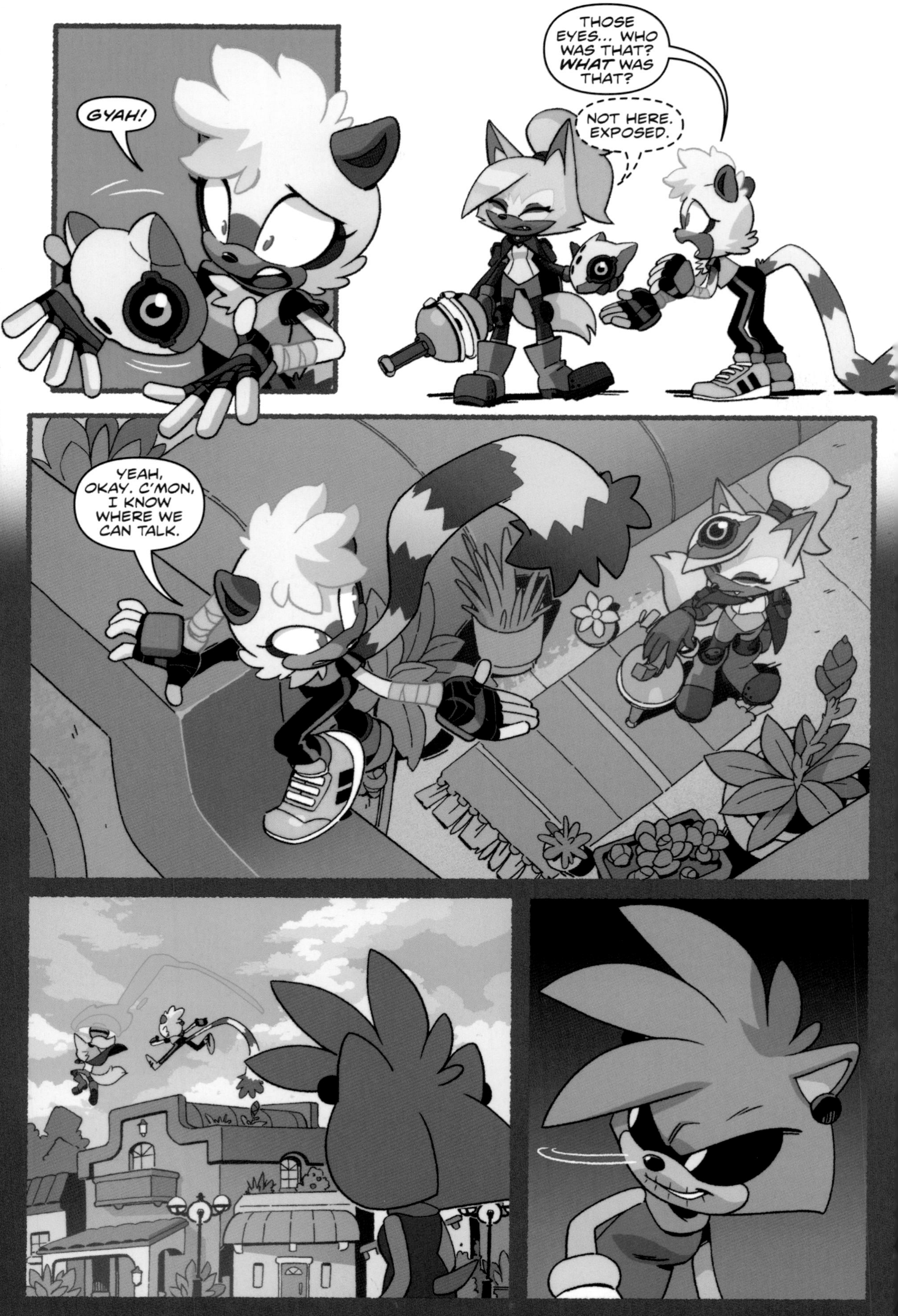
GYAH!
THOSE EYES... WHO WAS THAT? WHAT WAS THAT?
NOT HERE. EXPOSED.
YEAH, OKAY. C'MON, I KNOW WHERE WE CAN TALK.

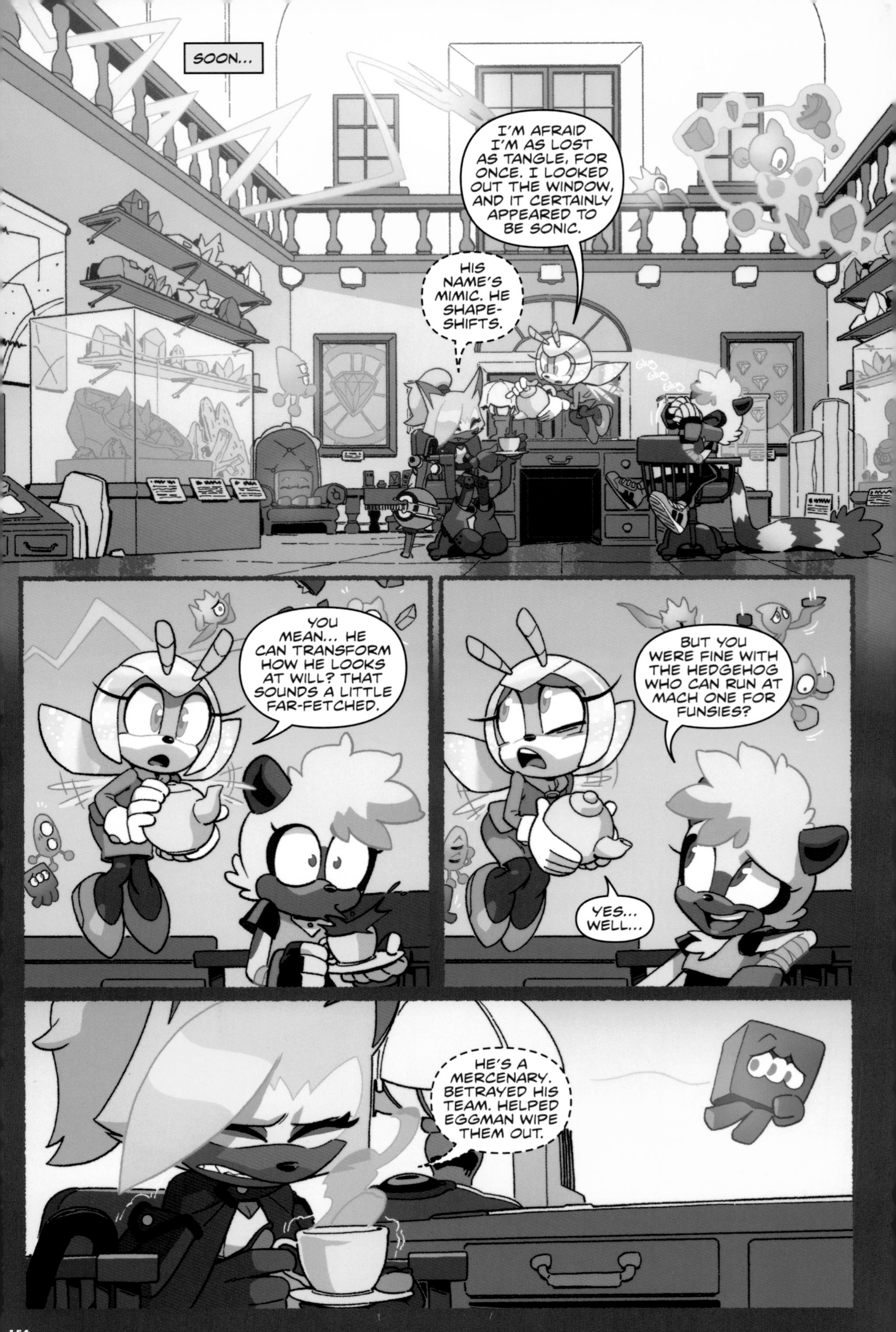
SOON...
HIS NAME'S MIMIC. HE SHAPE-SHIFTS.
I'M AFRAID I'M AS LOST AS TANGLE, FOR ONCE. I LOOKED OUT THE WINDOW, AND IT CERTAINLY APPEARED TO BE SONIC.
Glug Glug Glug
YOU MEAN... HE CAN TRANSFORM HOW HE LOOKS AT WILL? THAT SOUNDS A LITTLE FAR-FETCHED.
BUT YOU WERE FINE WITH THE HEDGEHOG WHO CAN RUN AT MACH ONE FOR FUNSIES?
YES... WELL...
HE'S A MERCENARY. BETRAYED HIS TEAM. HELPED EGGMAN WIPE THEM OUT.

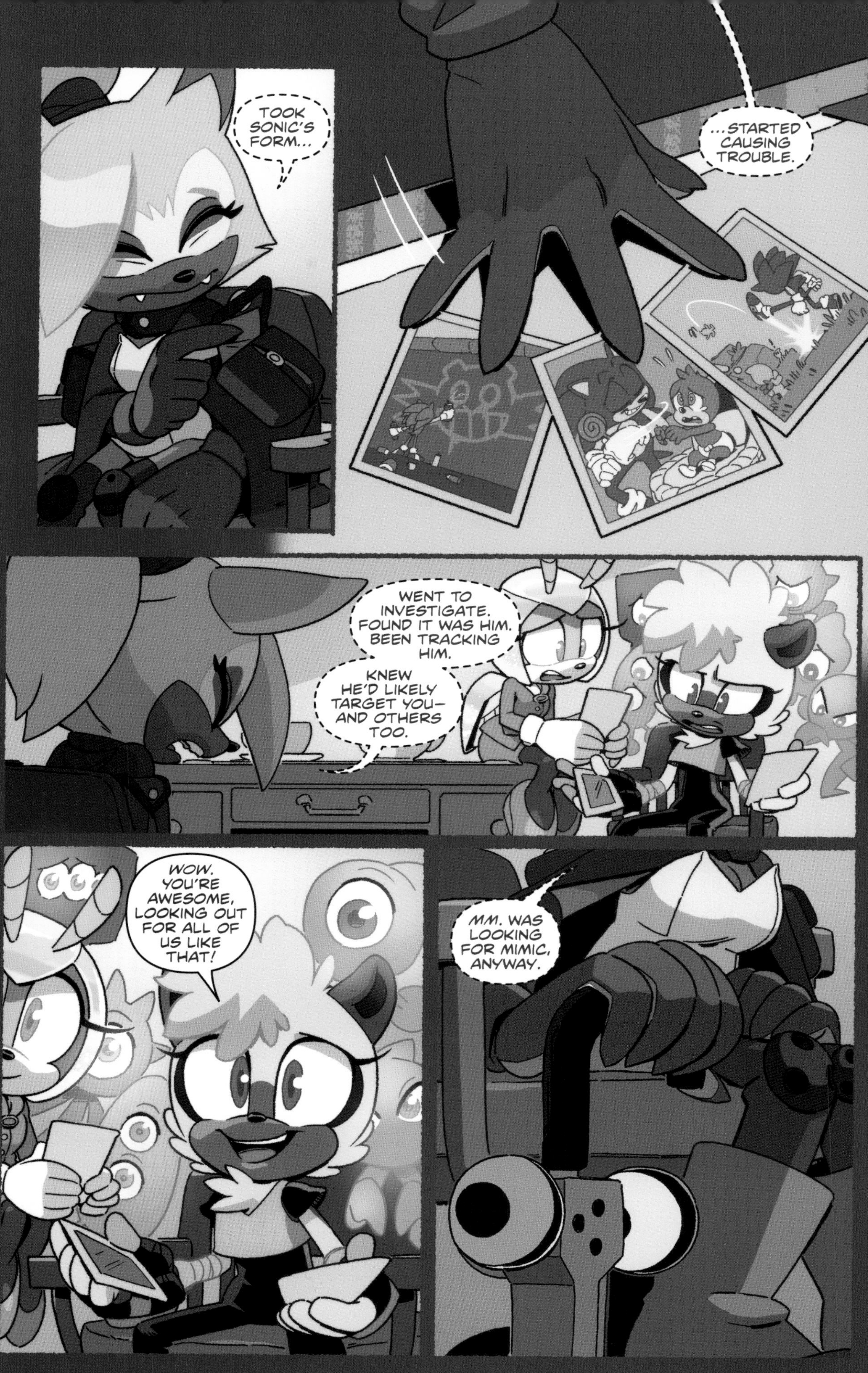
TOOK SONIC'S FORM...
...STARTED CAUSING TROUBLE.
WENT TO INVESTIGATE. FOUND IT WAS HIM. BEEN TRACKING HIM.
KNEW HE'D LIKELY TARGET YOU— AND OTHERS TOO.
WOW. YOU'RE AWESOME, LOOKING OUT FOR ALL OF US LIKE THAT!
MM. WAS LOOKING FOR MIMIC, ANYWAY.

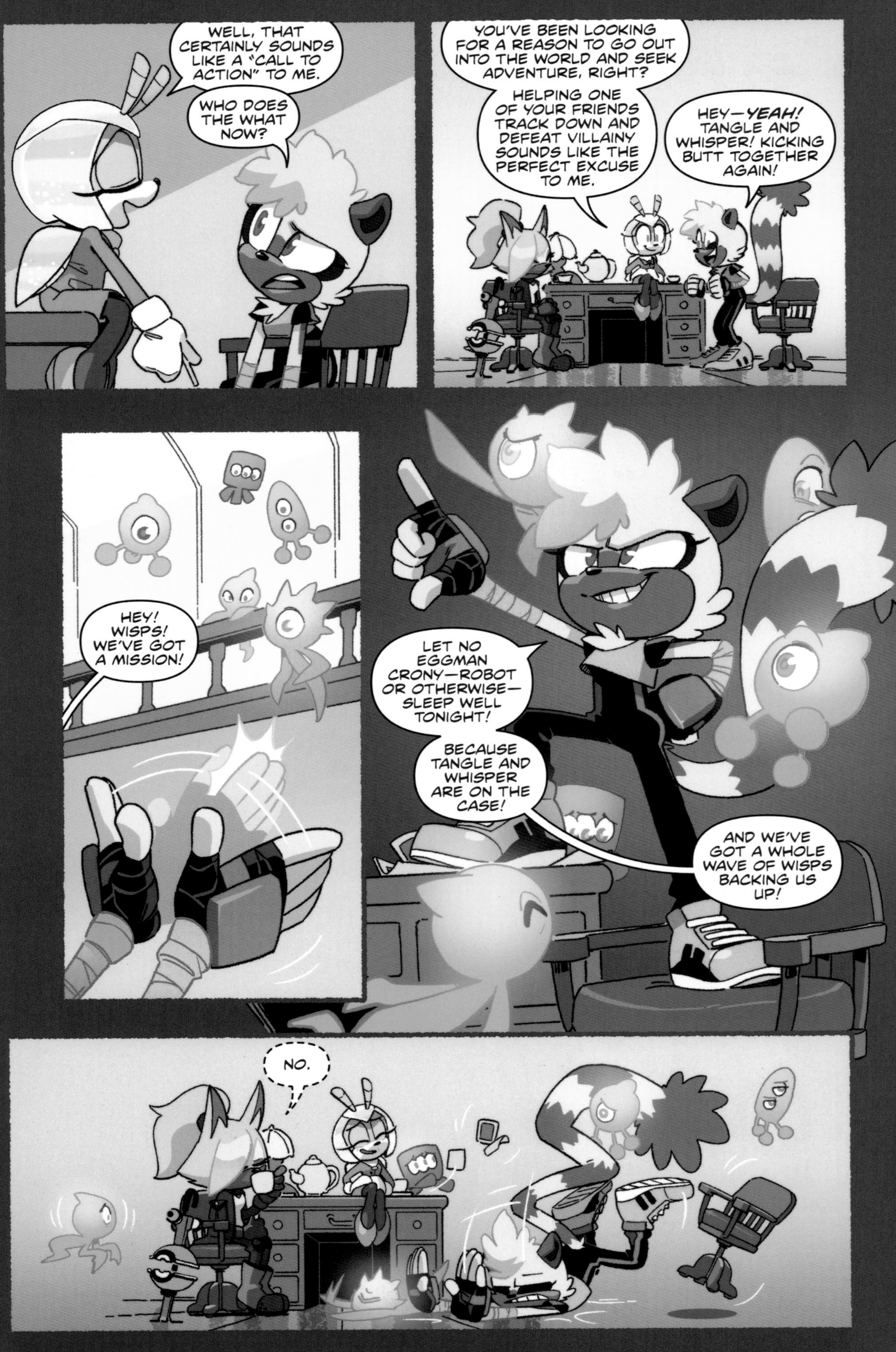
WELL, THAT CERTAINLY SOUNDS LIKE A "CALL TO ACTION" TO ME.
WHO DOES THE WHAT NOW?
YOU'VE BEEN LOOKING FOR A REASON TO GO OUT INTO THE WORLD AND SEEK ADVENTURE, RIGHT?
HELPING ONE OF YOUR FRIENDS TRACK DOWN AND DEFEAT VILLAINY SOUNDS LIKE THE PERFECT EXCUSE TO ME.
HEY—YEAH! TANGLE AND WHISPER! KICKING BUTT TOGETHER AGAIN!
HEY! WISPS! WE'VE GOT A MISSION!
LET NO EGGMAN CRONY—ROBOT OR OTHERWISE—SLEEP WELL TONIGHT!
BECAUSE TANGLE AND WHISPER ARE ON THE CASE!
AND WE'VE GOT A WHOLE WAVE OF WISPS BACKING US UP!
NO.

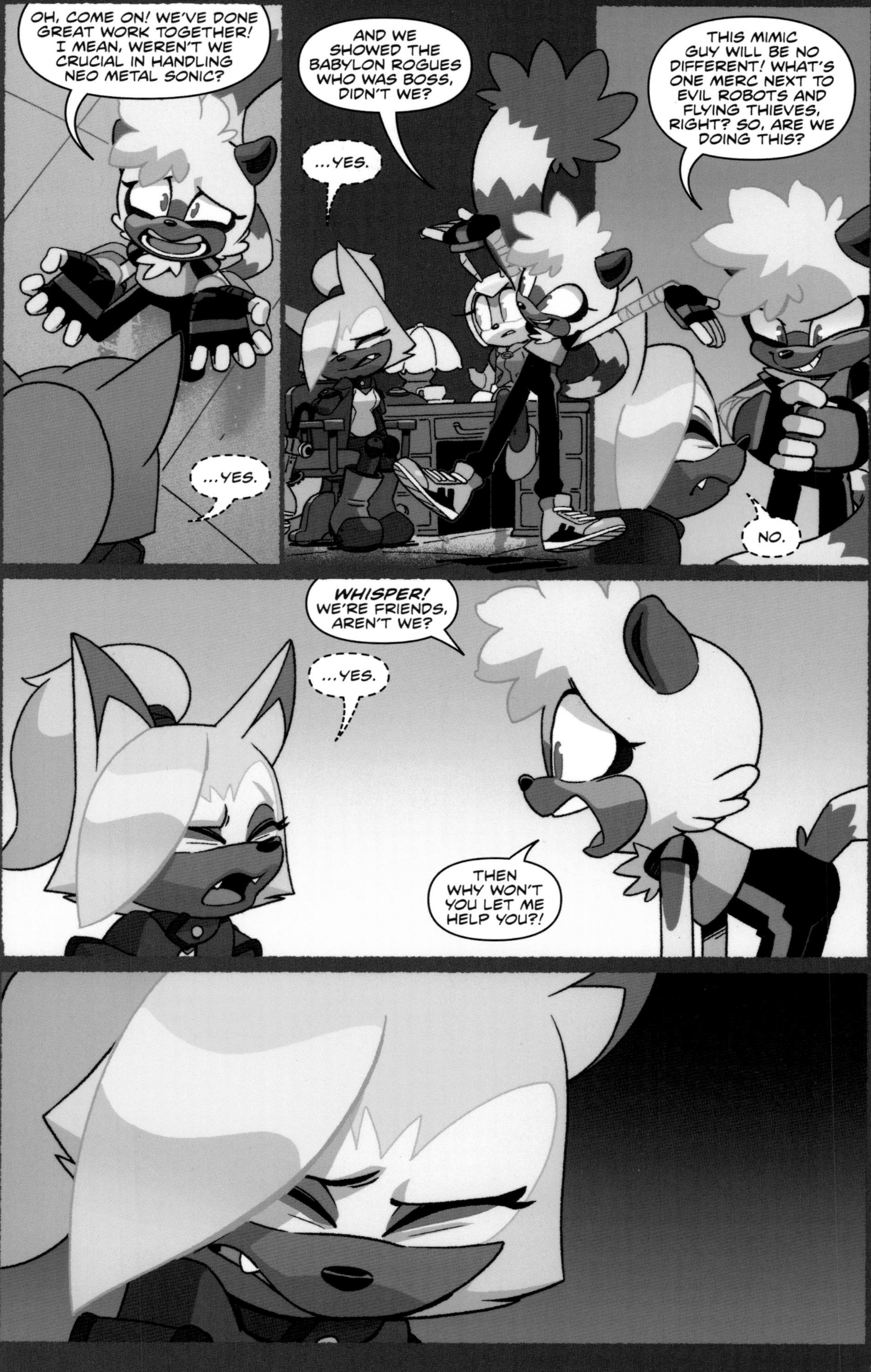
OH, COME ON! WE'VE DONE GREAT WORK TOGETHER! I MEAN, WEREN'T WE CRUCIAL IN HANDLING NEO METAL SONIC?
...YES.
AND WE SHOWED THE BABYLON ROGUES WHO WAS BOSS, DIDN'T WE?
...YES.
THIS MIMIC GUY WILL BE NO DIFFERENT! WHAT'S ONE MERC NEXT TO EVIL ROBOTS AND FLYING THIEVES, RIGHT? SO, ARE WE DOING THIS?
NO.
WHISPER! WE'RE FRIENDS, AREN'T WE?
...YES.
THEN WHY WON'T YOU LET ME HELP YOU?!

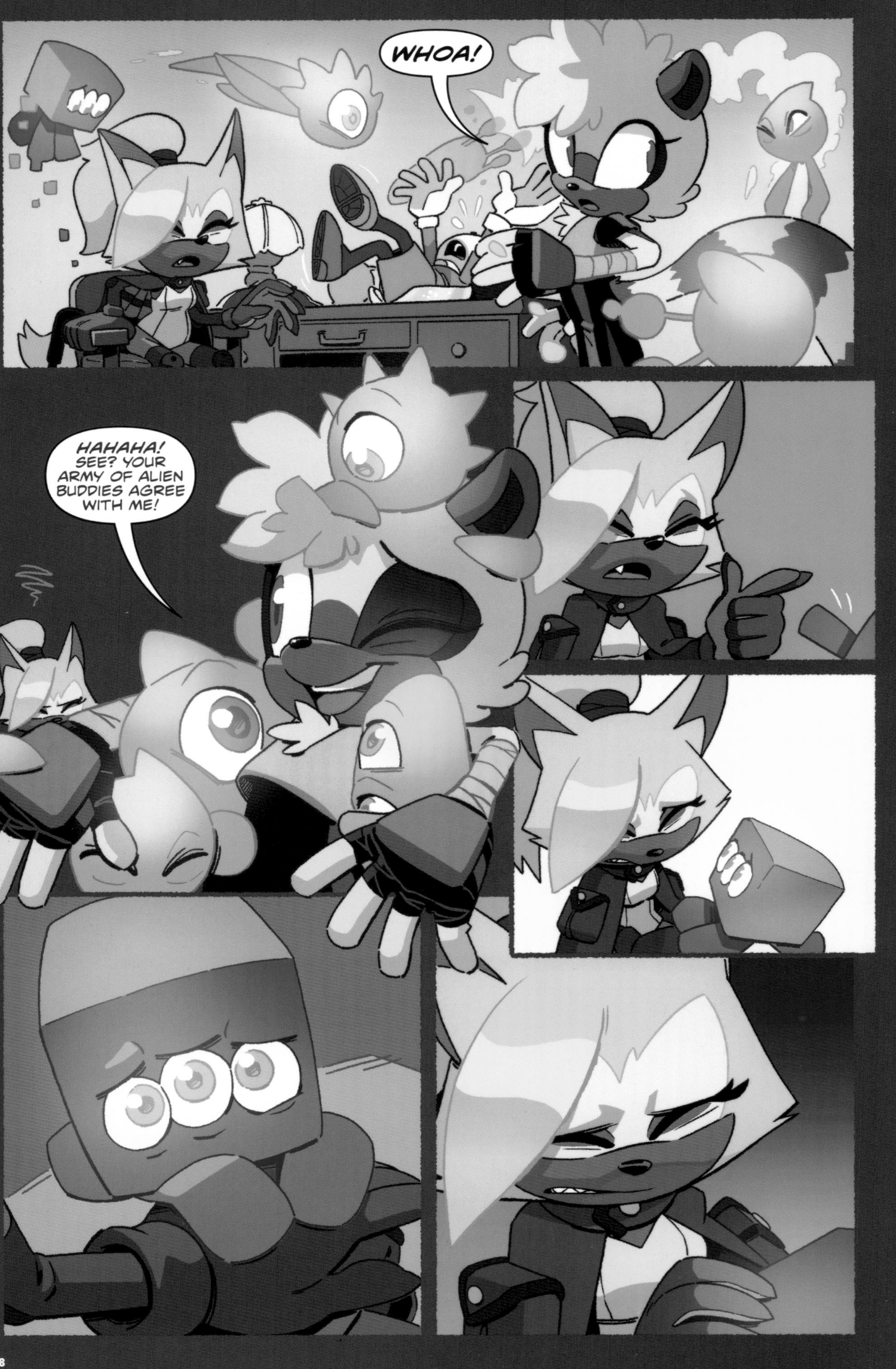
WHOA!
HAHAHA! SEE? YOUR ARMY OF ALIEN BUDDIES AGREE WITH ME!

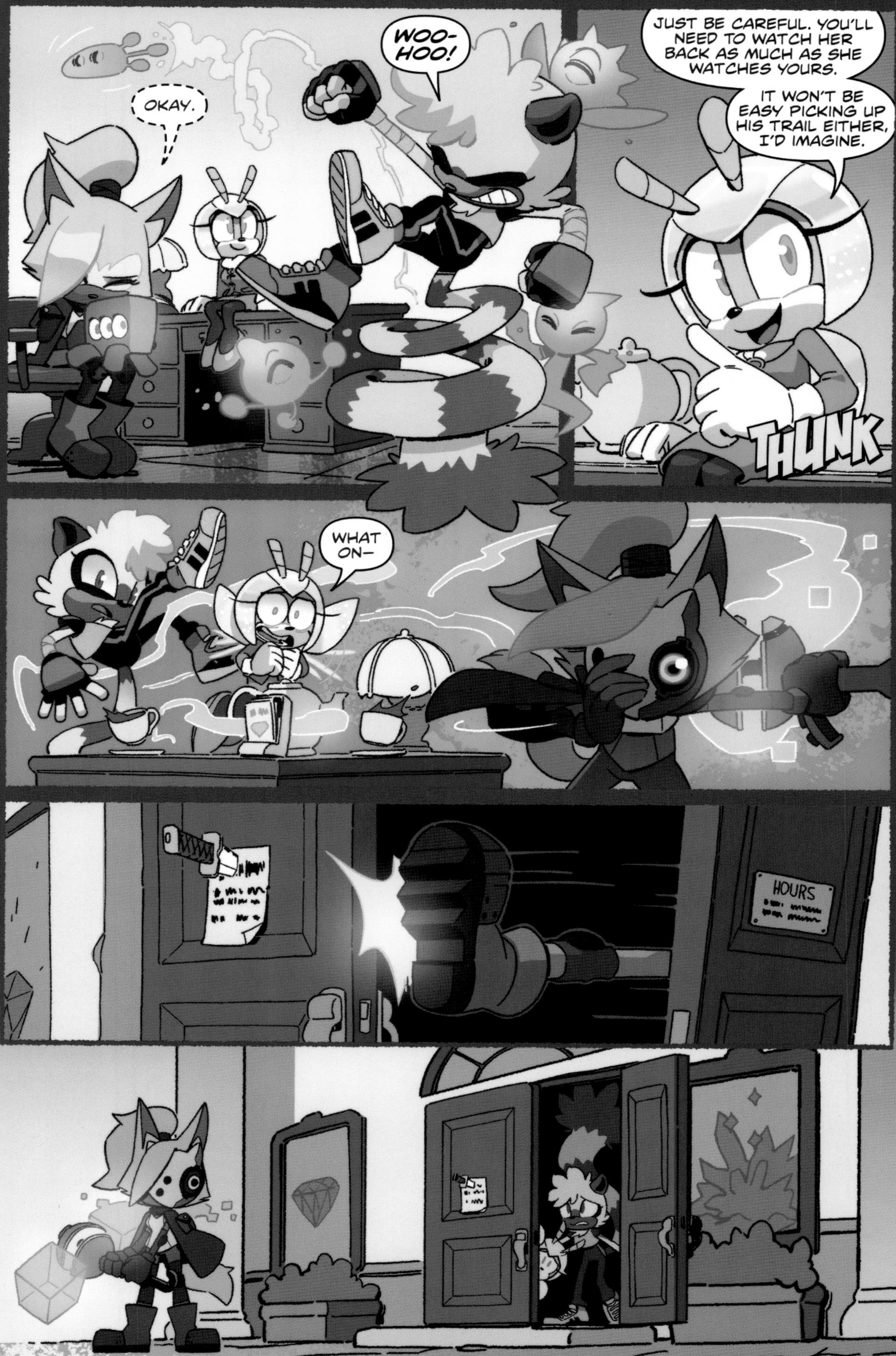
OKAY.
WOO-HOO!
JUST BE CAREFUL. YOU'LL NEED TO WATCH HER BACK AS MUCH AS SHE WATCHES YOURS.
IT WON'T BE EASY PICKING UP HIS TRAIL EITHER, I'D IMAGINE.
THUNK
WHAT ON–
HOURS

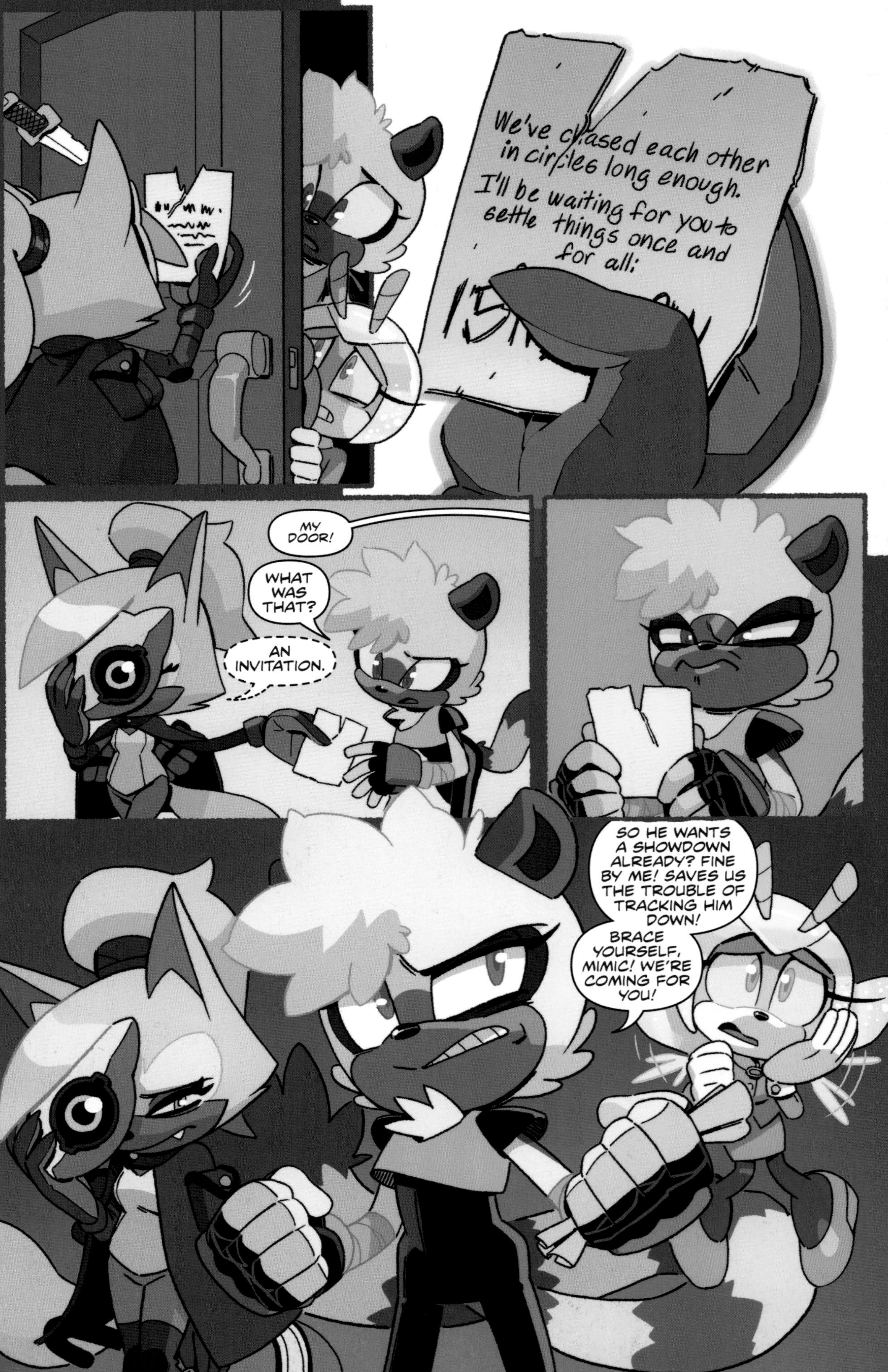
We've chased each other in circles long enough.
I'll be waiting for you to settle things once and for all:
MY DOOR!
WHAT WAS THAT?
AN INVITATION.
SO HE WANTS A SHOWDOWN ALREADY? FINE BY ME! SAVES US THE TROUBLE OF TRACKING HIM DOWN!
BRACE YOURSELF, MIMIC! WE'RE COMING FOR YOU!

ART BY NATHALIE FOURDRAINE

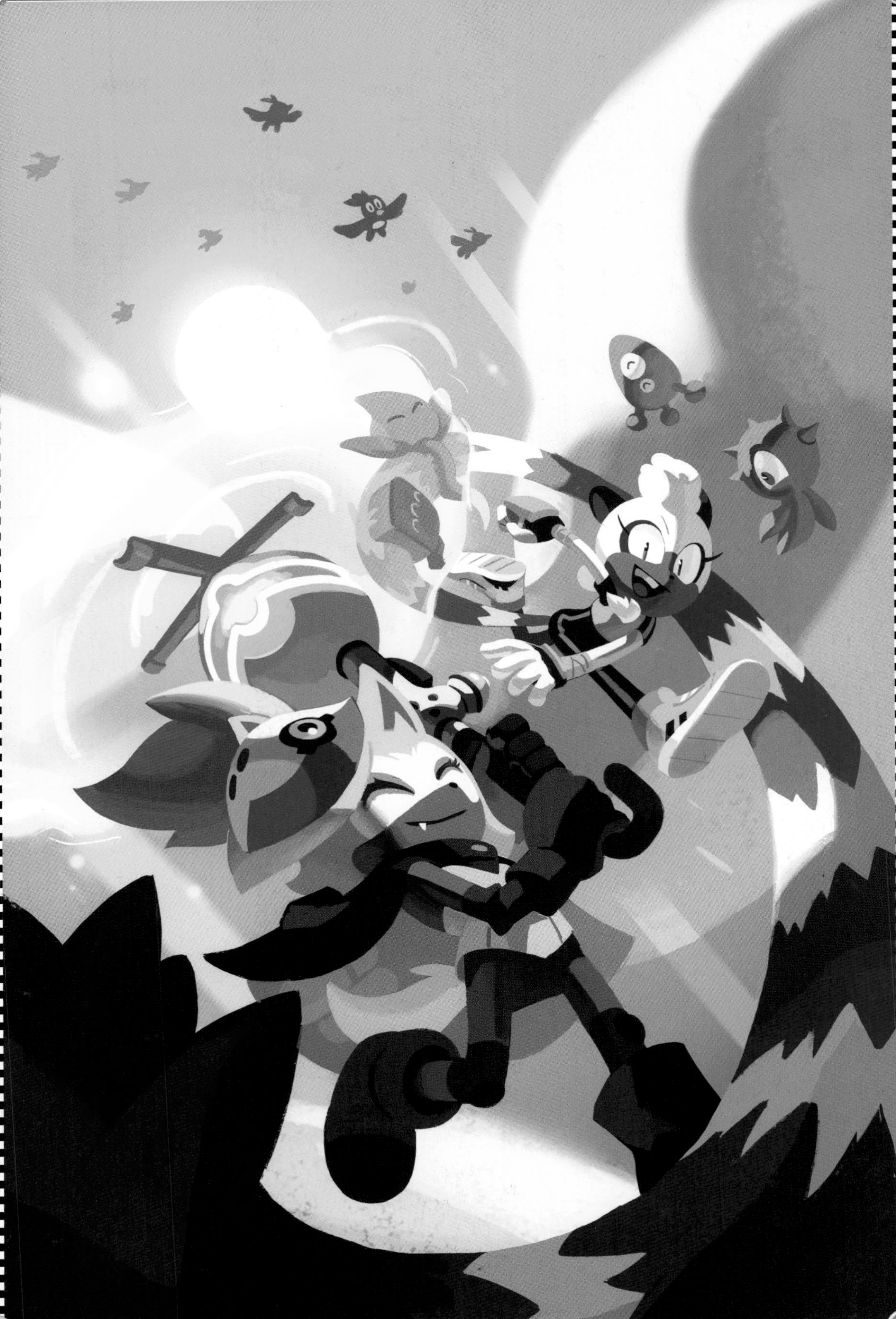

ART BY EVAN STANLEY

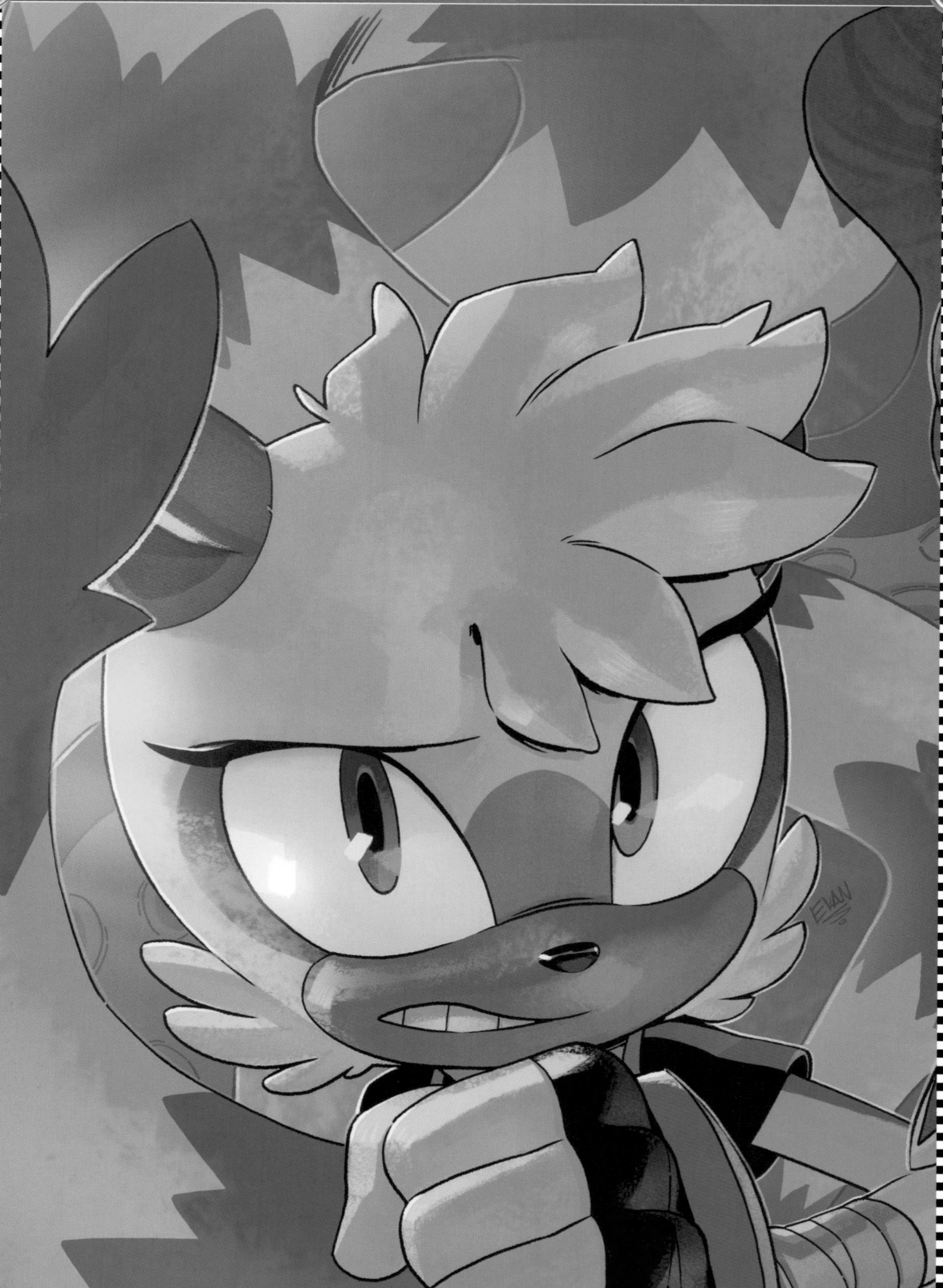

TANGLE & WHISPER #2

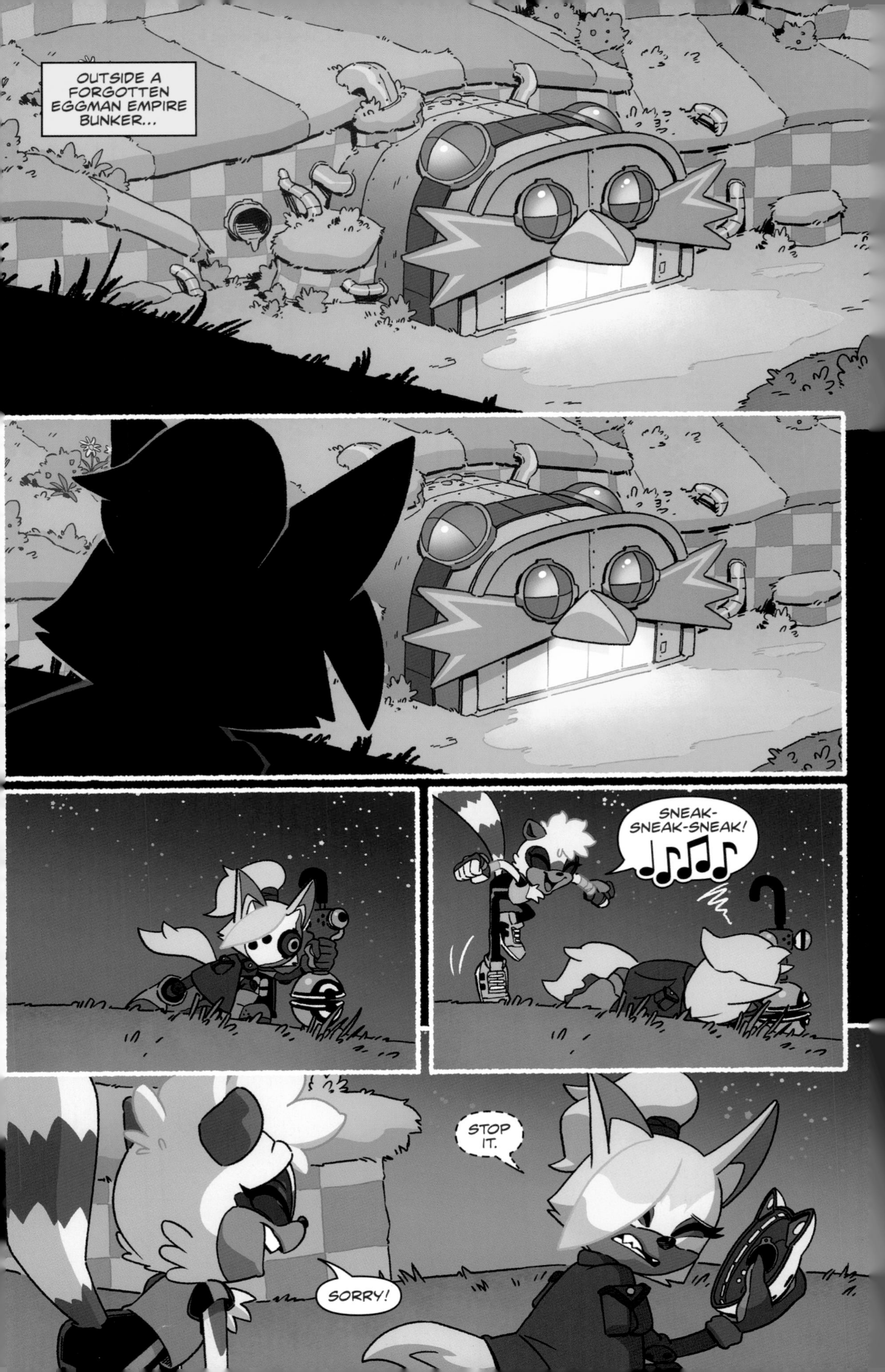
OUTSIDE A FORGOTTEN EGGMAN EMPIRE BUNKER...
SNEAK-SNEAK-SNEAK!
STOP IT.
SORRY!

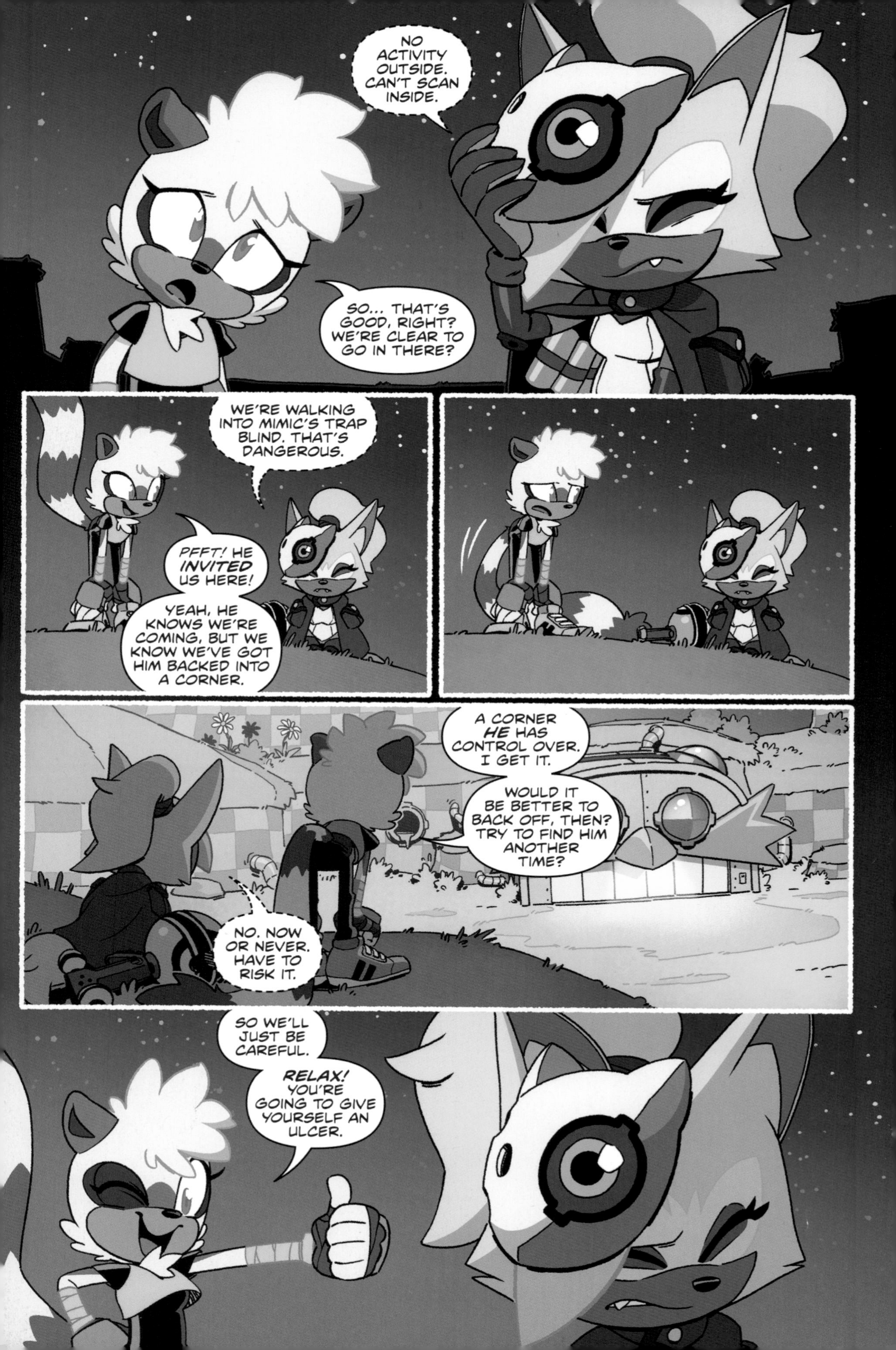
NO ACTIVITY OUTSIDE. CAN'T SCAN INSIDE.
SO... THAT'S GOOD, RIGHT? WE'RE CLEAR TO GO IN THERE?
WE'RE WALKING INTO MIMIC'S TRAP BLIND. THAT'S DANGEROUS.
PFFT! HE *INVITED* US HERE!
YEAH, HE KNOWS WE'RE COMING, BUT WE KNOW WE'VE GOT HIM BACKED INTO A CORNER.
A CORNER *HE* HAS CONTROL OVER. I GET IT.
WOULD IT BE BETTER TO BACK OFF, THEN? TRY TO FIND HIM ANOTHER TIME?
NO. NOW OR NEVER. HAVE TO RISK IT.
SO WE'LL JUST BE CAREFUL.
RELAX! YOU'RE GOING TO GIVE YOURSELF AN ULCER.

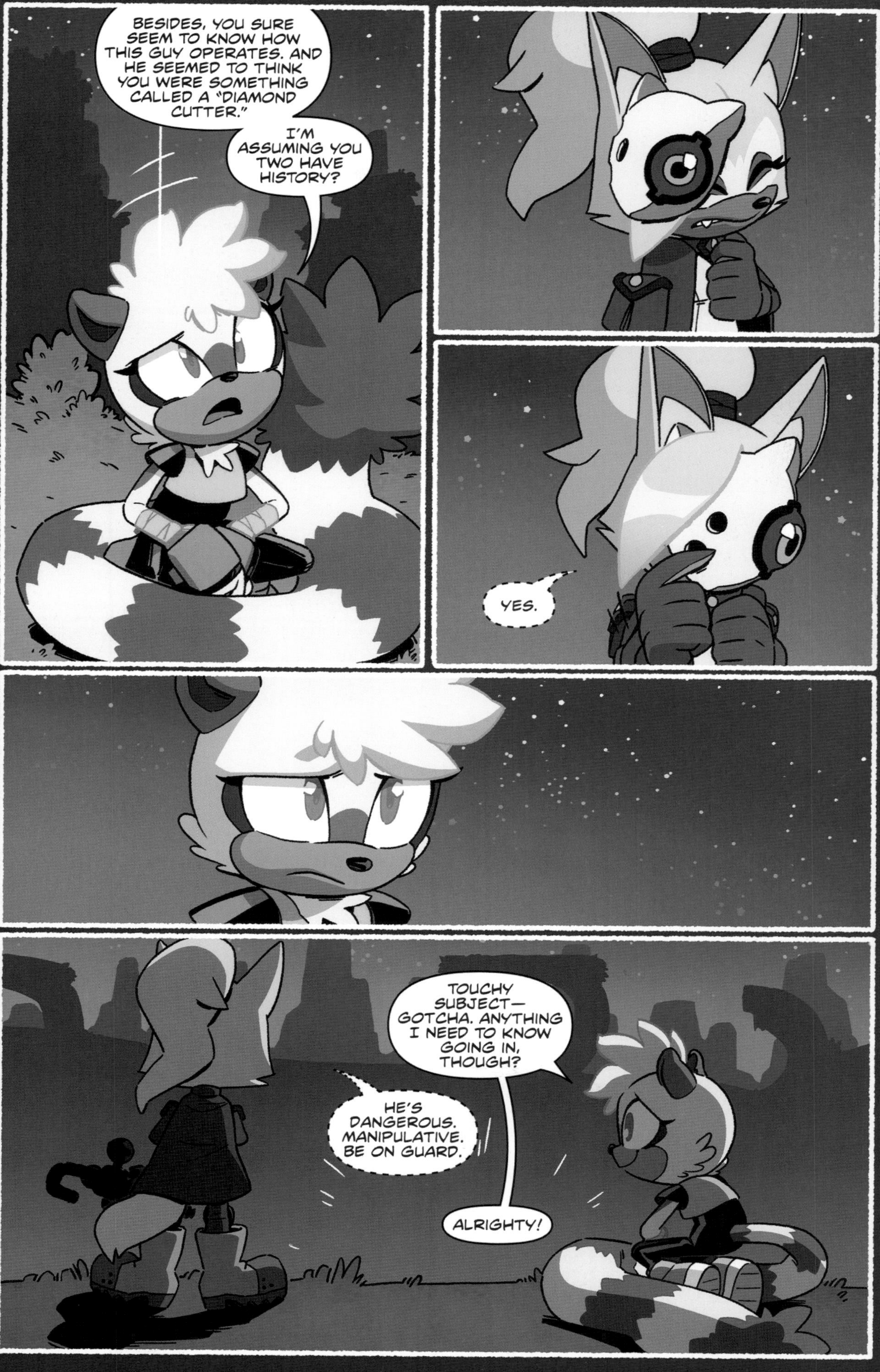
BESIDES, YOU SURE SEEM TO KNOW HOW THIS GUY OPERATES. AND HE SEEMED TO THINK YOU WERE SOMETHING CALLED A "DIAMOND CUTTER."
I'M ASSUMING YOU TWO HAVE HISTORY?
YES.
TOUCHY SUBJECT— GOTCHA. ANYTHING I NEED TO KNOW GOING IN, THOUGH?
HE'S DANGEROUS. MANIPULATIVE. BE ON GUARD.
ALRIGHTY!

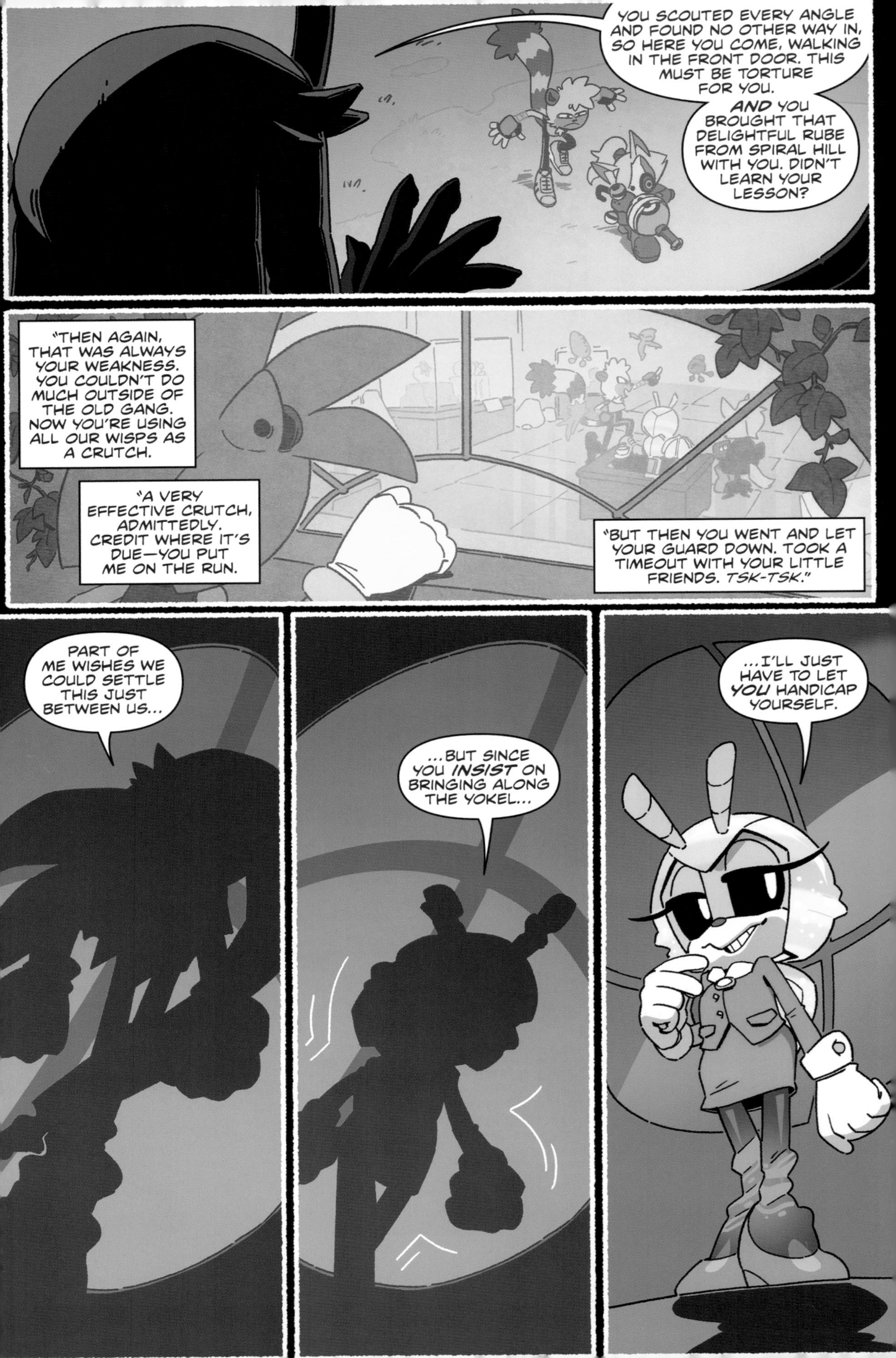

YOU SCOUTED EVERY ANGLE AND FOUND NO OTHER WAY IN, SO HERE YOU COME, WALKING IN THE FRONT DOOR. THIS MUST BE TORTURE FOR YOU.
AND YOU BROUGHT THAT DELIGHTFUL RUBE FROM SPIRAL HILL WITH YOU. DIDN'T LEARN YOUR LESSON?
"THEN AGAIN, THAT WAS ALWAYS YOUR WEAKNESS. YOU COULDN'T DO MUCH OUTSIDE OF THE OLD GANG. NOW YOU'RE USING ALL OUR WISPS AS A CRUTCH.
"A VERY EFFECTIVE CRUTCH, ADMITTEDLY. CREDIT WHERE IT'S DUE—YOU PUT ME ON THE RUN.
"BUT THEN YOU WENT AND LET YOUR GUARD DOWN. TOOK A TIMEOUT WITH YOUR LITTLE FRIENDS. TSK-TSK."
PART OF ME WISHES WE COULD SETTLE THIS JUST BETWEEN US...
...BUT SINCE YOU INSIST ON BRINGING ALONG THE YOKEL...
...I'LL JUST HAVE TO LET YOU HANDICAP YOURSELF.

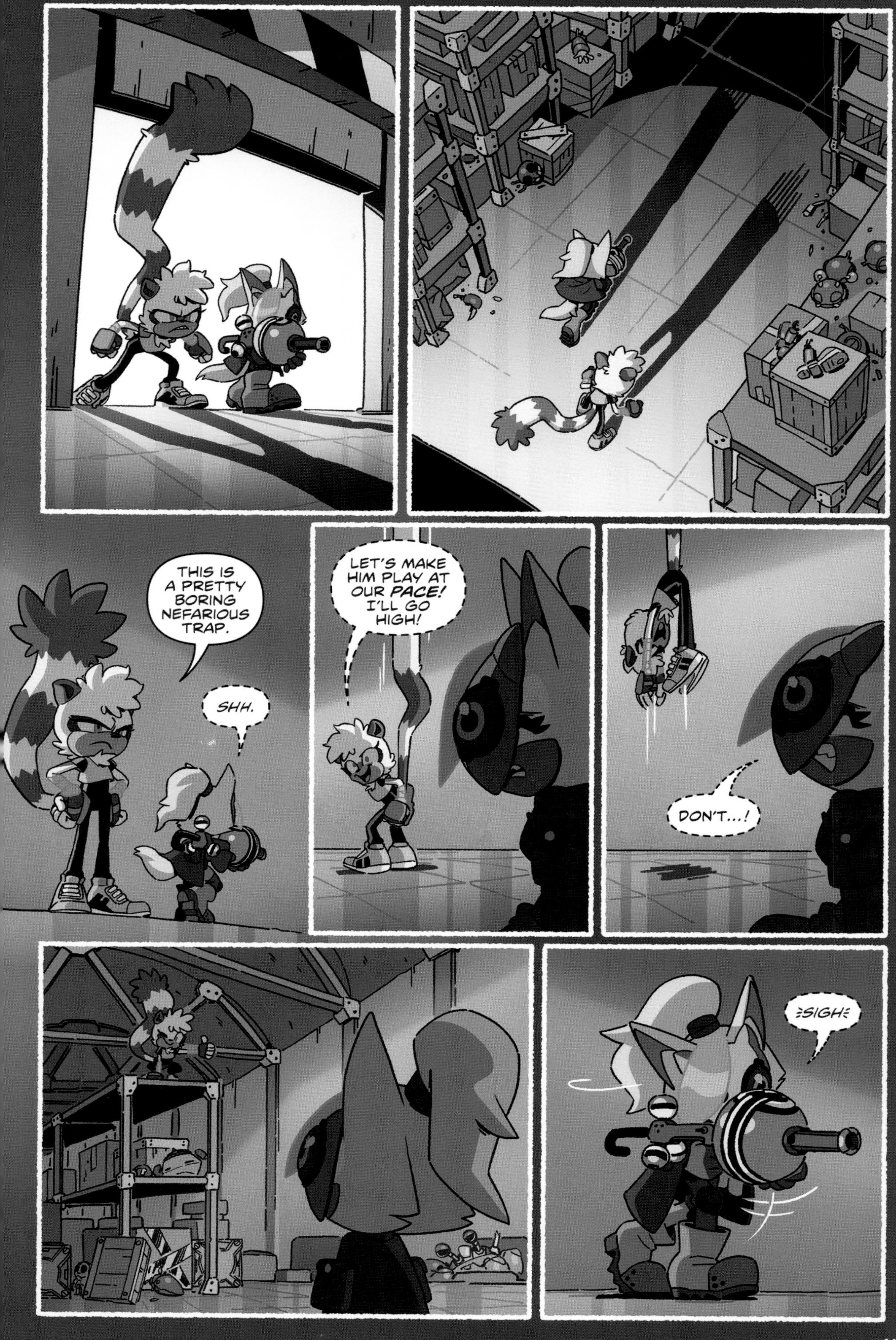
THIS IS A PRETTY BORING NEFARIOUS TRAP.
SHH.
LET'S MAKE HIM PLAY AT OUR *PACE!* I'LL GO HIGH!
DON'T...!
SIGH

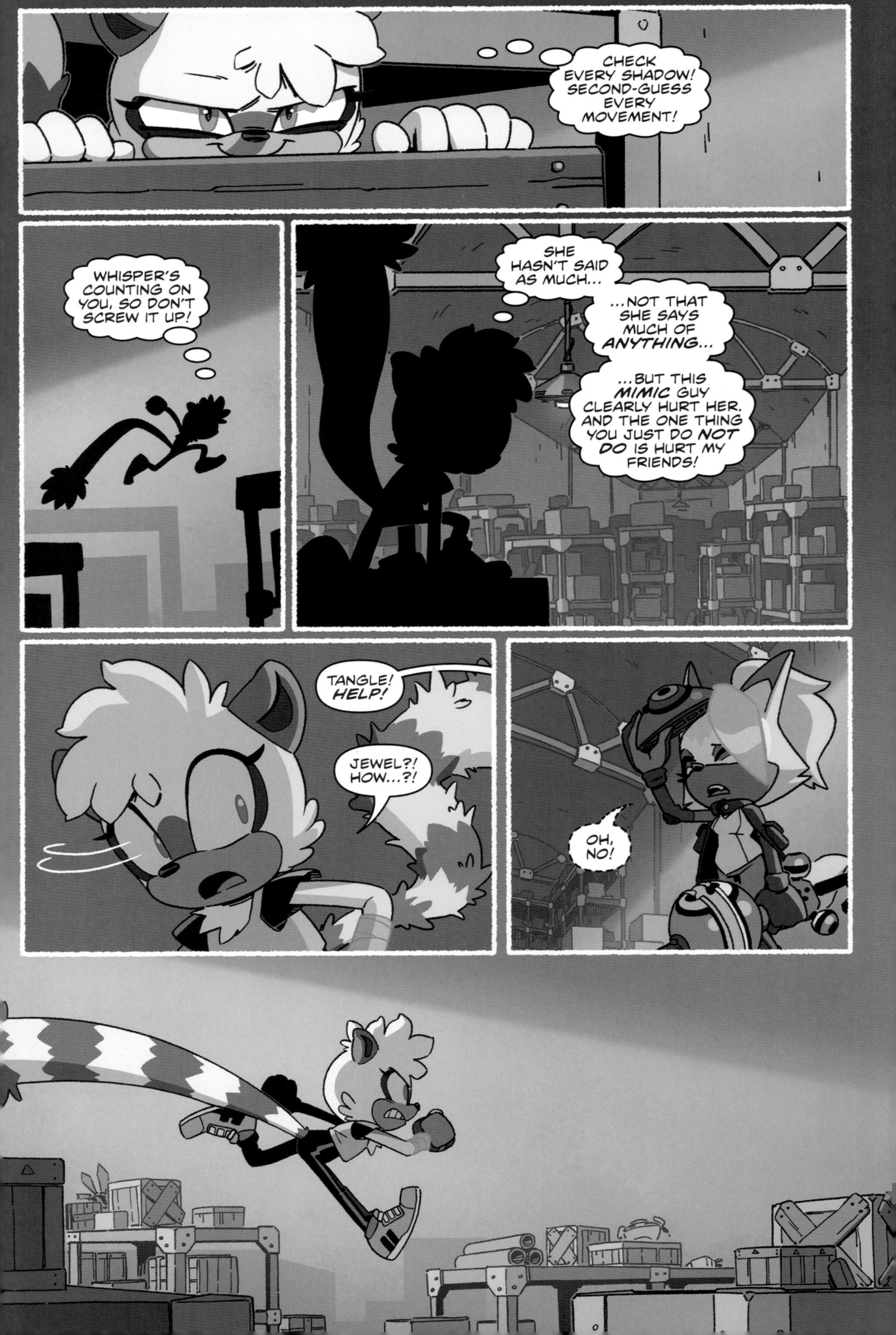
CHECK EVERY SHADOW! SECOND-GUESS EVERY MOVEMENT!
WHISPER'S COUNTING ON YOU, SO DON'T SCREW IT UP!
SHE HASN'T SAID AS MUCH...
...NOT THAT SHE SAYS MUCH OF ANYTHING...
...BUT THIS MIMIC GUY CLEARLY HURT HER. AND THE ONE THING YOU JUST DO NOT DO IS HURT MY FRIENDS!
TANGLE! HELP!
JEWEL?! HOW...?!
OH, NO!

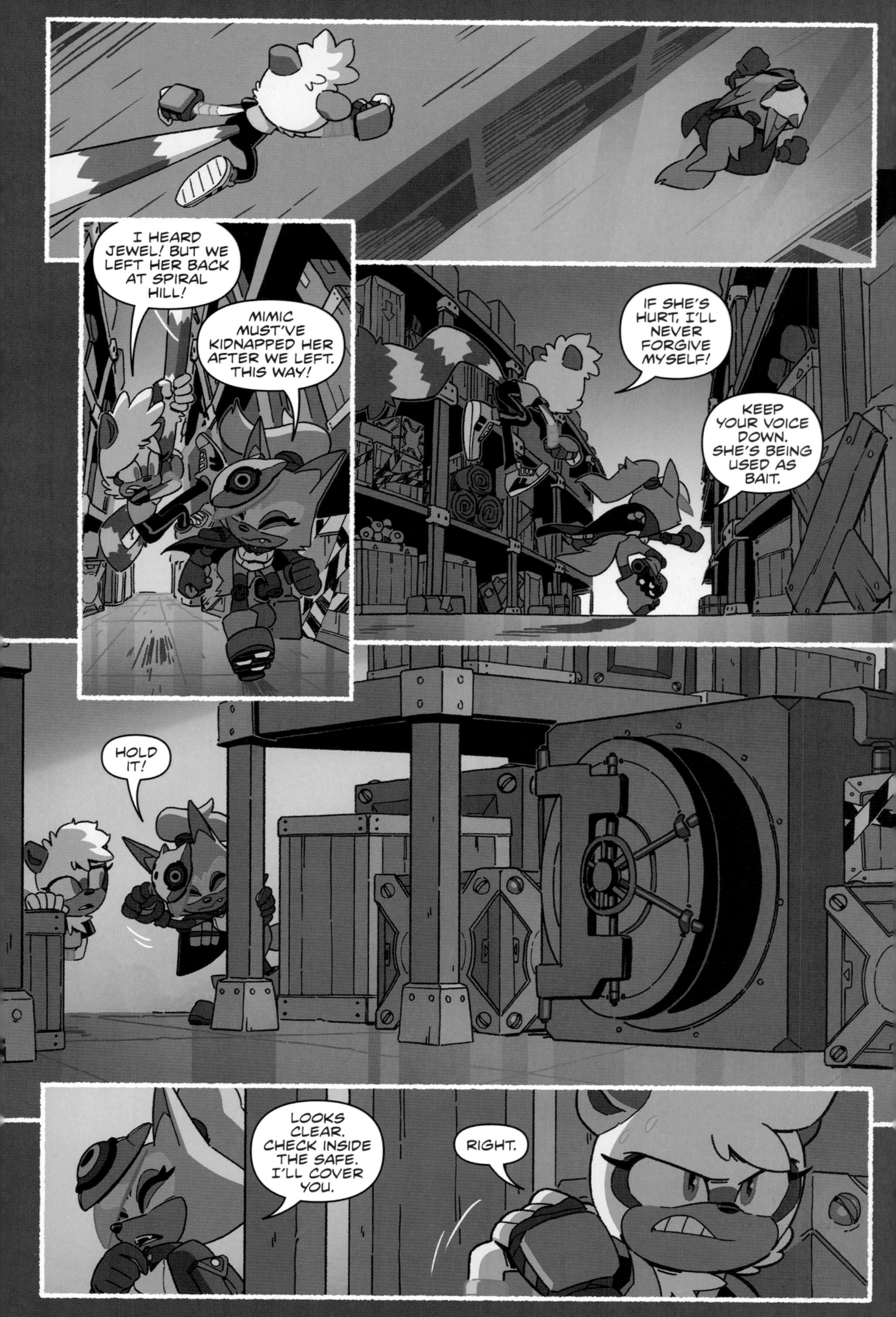
I HEARD JEWEL! BUT WE LEFT HER BACK AT SPIRAL HILL!
MIMIC MUST'VE KIDNAPPED HER AFTER WE LEFT. THIS WAY!
IF SHE'S HURT, I'LL NEVER FORGIVE MYSELF!
KEEP YOUR VOICE DOWN. SHE'S BEING USED AS BAIT.
HOLD IT!
LOOKS CLEAR. CHECK INSIDE THE SAFE. I'LL COVER YOU.
RIGHT.

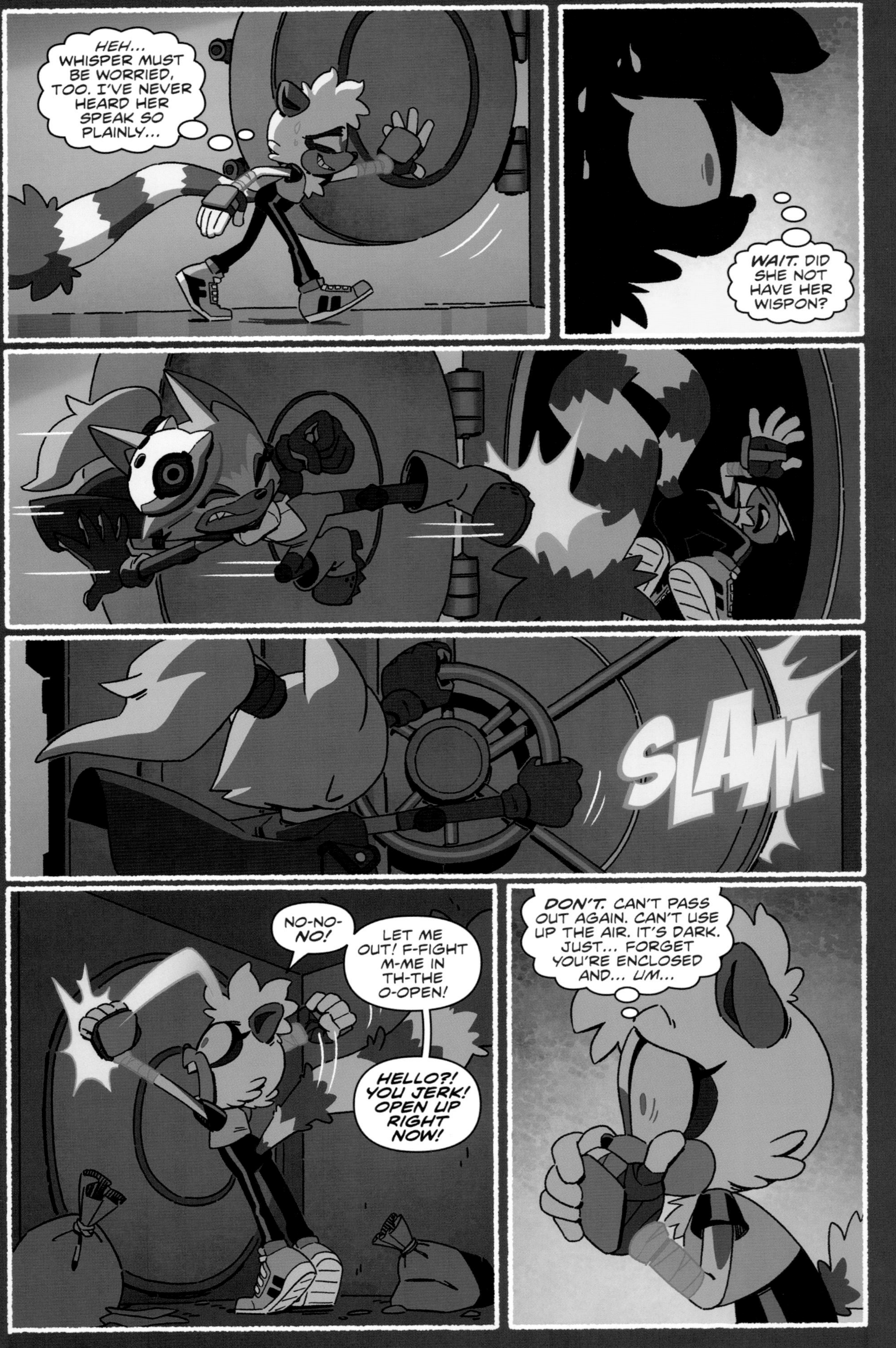
HEH... WHISPER MUST BE WORRIED, TOO. I'VE NEVER HEARD HER SPEAK SO PLAINLY...
WAIT. DID SHE NOT HAVE HER WISPON?
SLAM
NO-NO-NO!
LET ME OUT! F-FIGHT M-ME IN TH-THE O-OPEN!
HELLO?! YOU JERK! OPEN UP RIGHT NOW!
DON'T. CAN'T PASS OUT AGAIN. CAN'T USE UP THE AIR. IT'S DARK. JUST... FORGET YOU'RE ENCLOSED AND... UM...

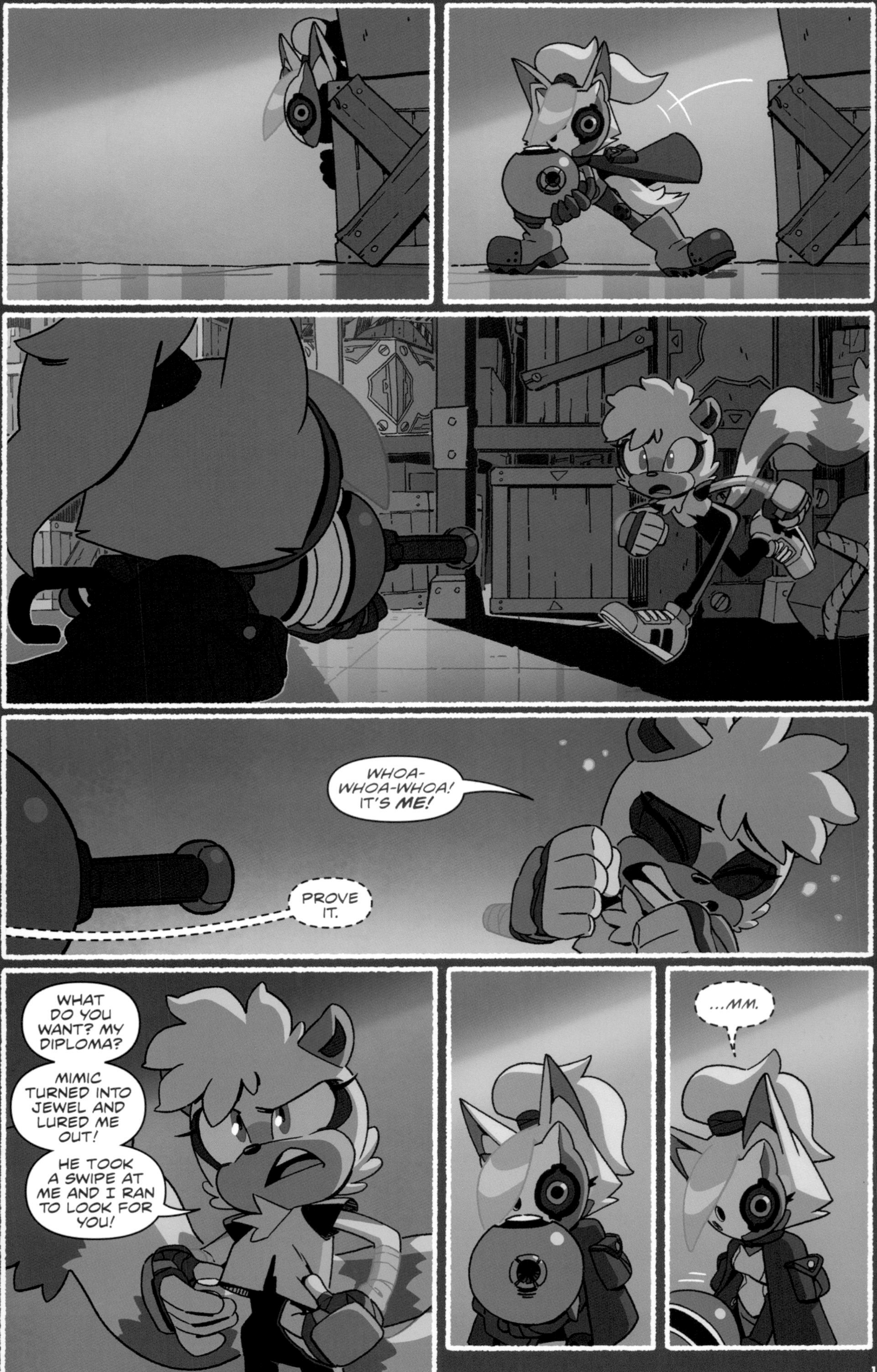
WHOA-WHOA-WHOA! IT'S ME!
PROVE IT.
WHAT DO YOU WANT? MY DIPLOMA?
MIMIC TURNED INTO JEWEL AND LURED ME OUT!
HE TOOK A SWIPE AT ME AND I RAN TO LOOK FOR YOU!
...MM.

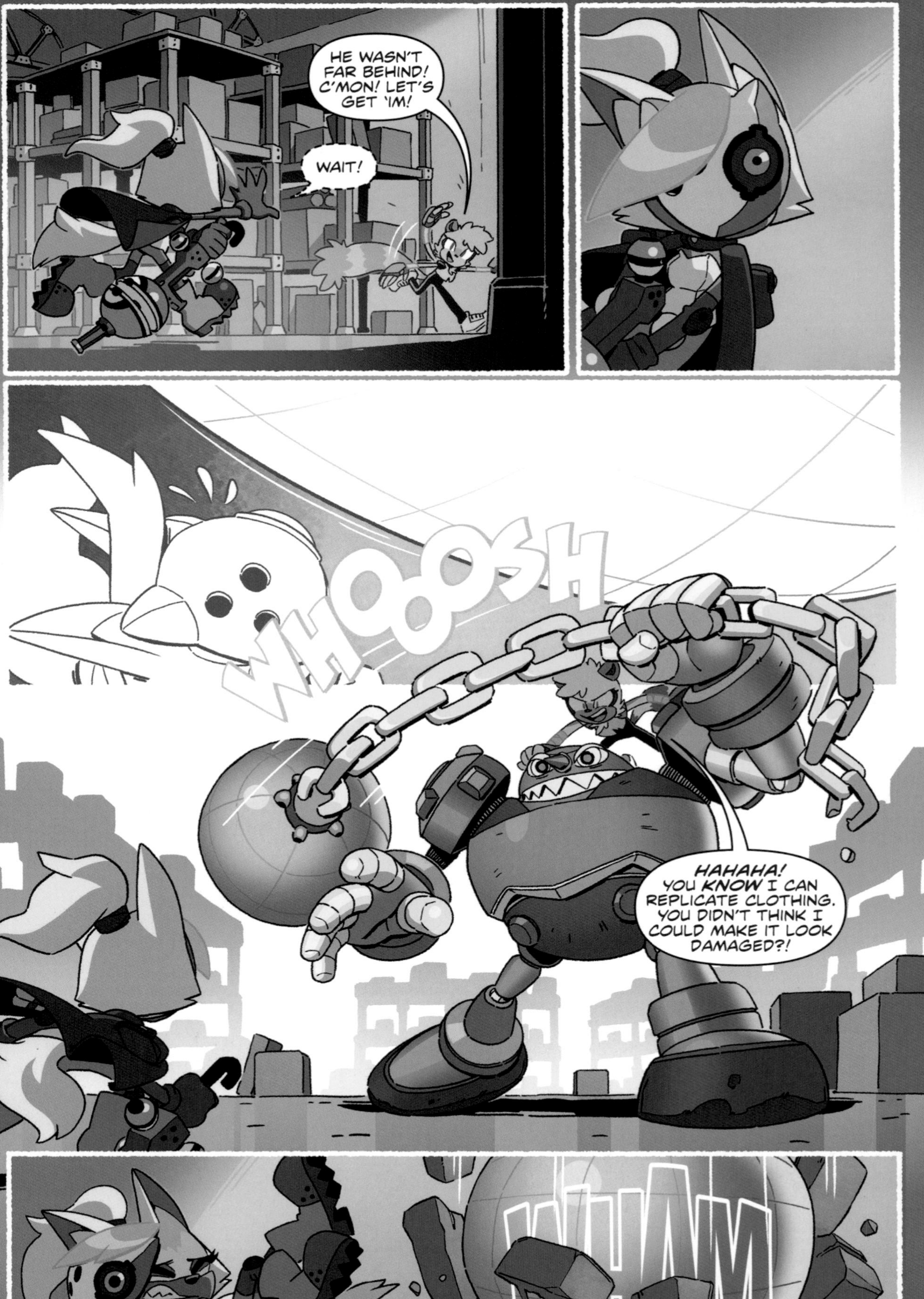
HE WASN'T FAR BEHIND! C'MON! LET'S GET 'IM!
WAIT!
WHOOOSH
HAHAHA! YOU KNOW I CAN REPLICATE CLOTHING. YOU DIDN'T THINK I COULD MAKE IT LOOK DAMAGED?!
WHAM

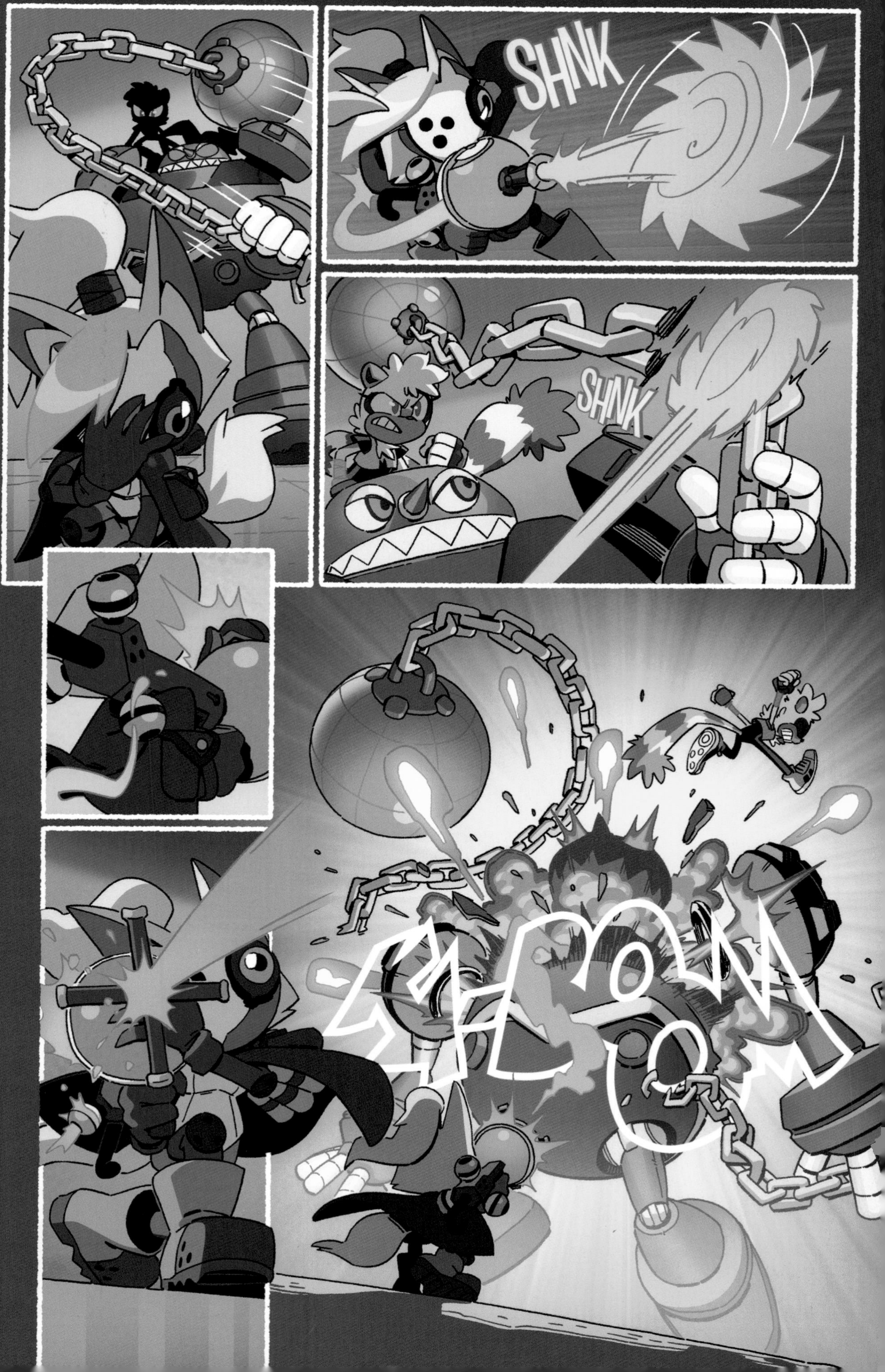
SHNK
SHNK

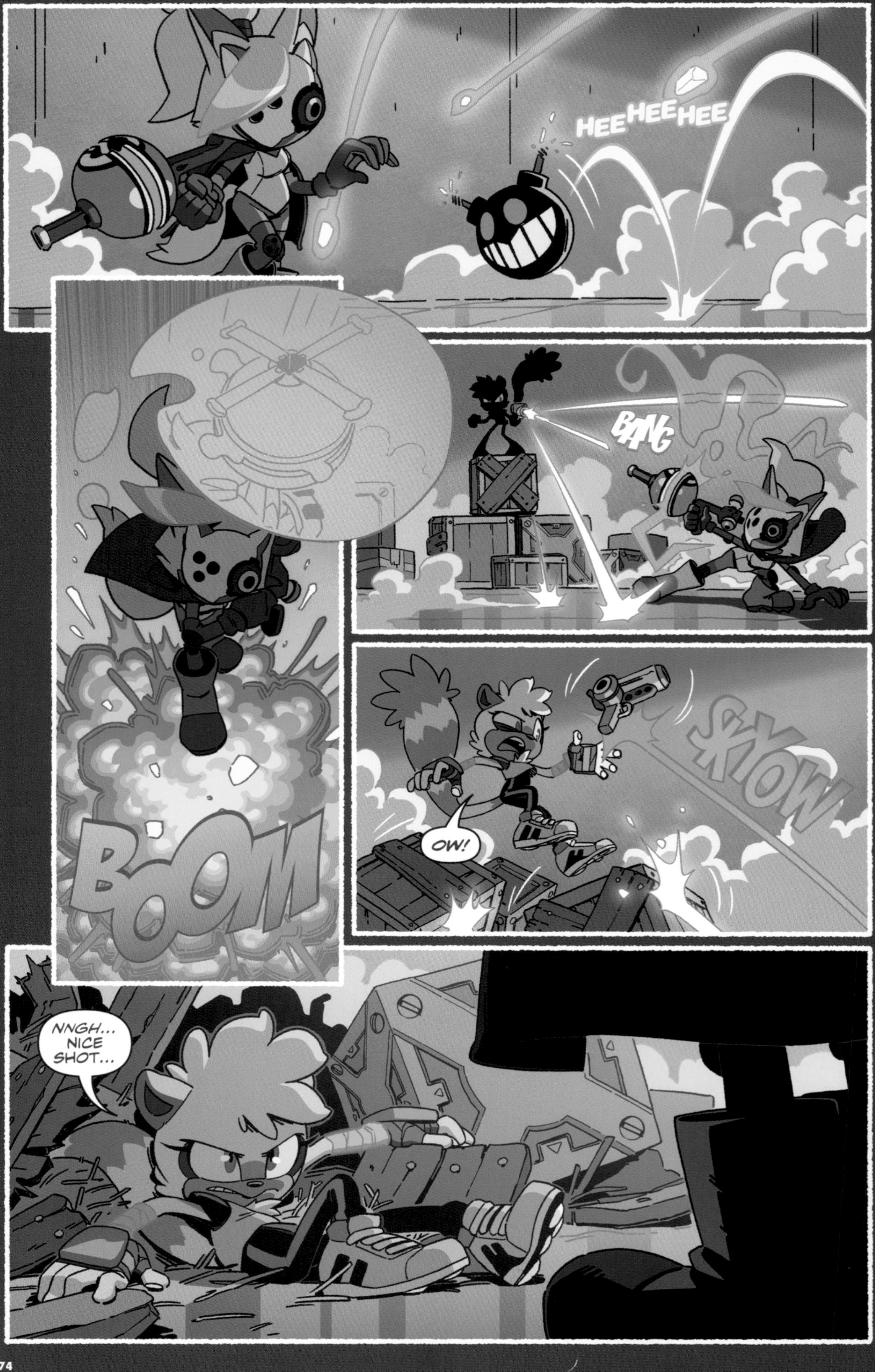
HEE HEE HEE
BANG
BOOM
SKYOW
OW!
NNGH... NICE SHOT...

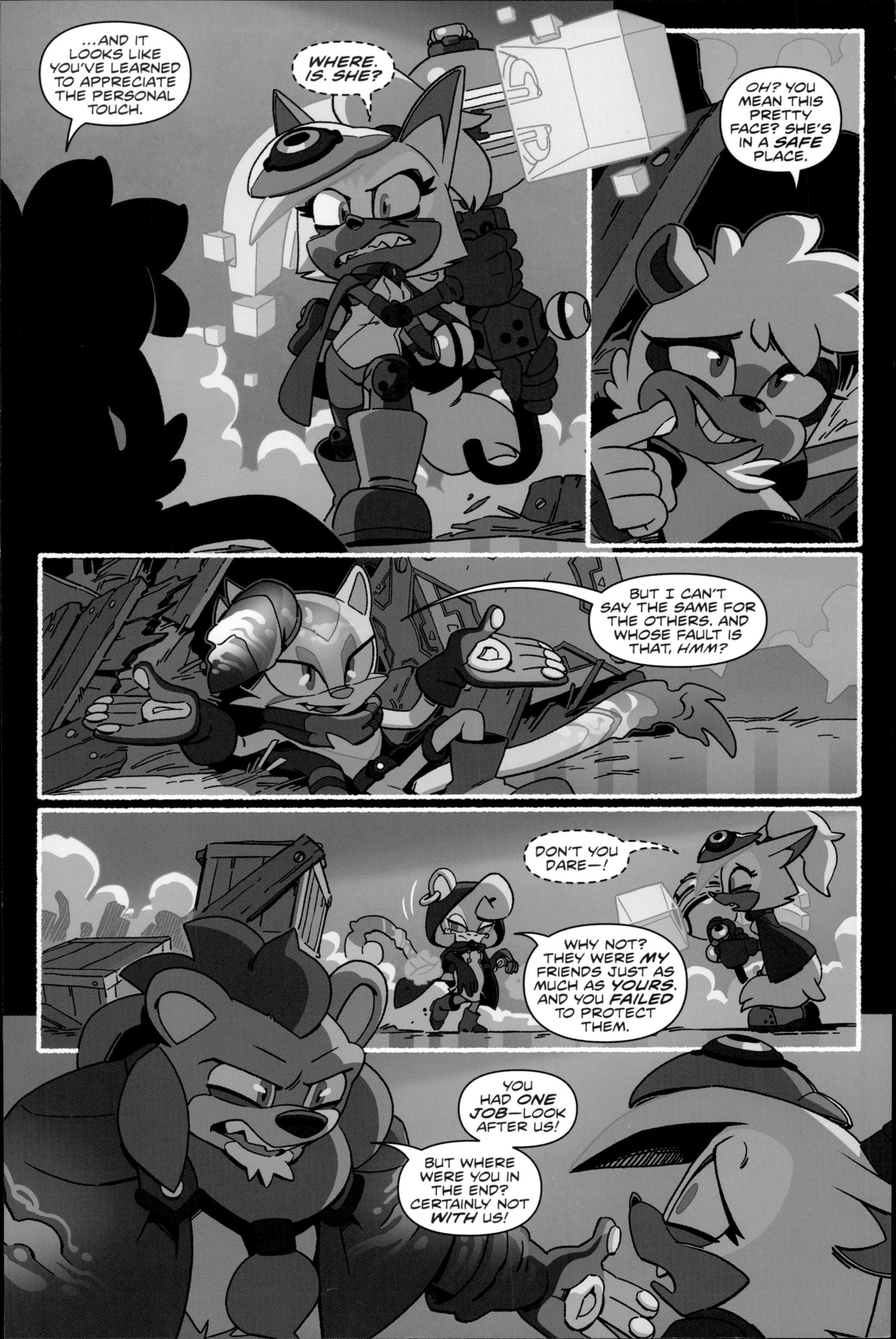
...AND IT LOOKS LIKE YOU'VE LEARNED TO APPRECIATE THE PERSONAL TOUCH.
WHERE. IS. SHE?
OH? YOU MEAN THIS PRETTY FACE? SHE'S IN A SAFE PLACE.
BUT I CAN'T SAY THE SAME FOR THE OTHERS. AND WHOSE FAULT IS THAT, HMM?
DON'T YOU DARE—!
WHY NOT? THEY WERE MY FRIENDS JUST AS MUCH AS YOURS. AND YOU FAILED TO PROTECT THEM.
YOU HAD ONE JOB—LOOK AFTER US!
BUT WHERE WERE YOU IN THE END? CERTAINLY NOT WITH US!

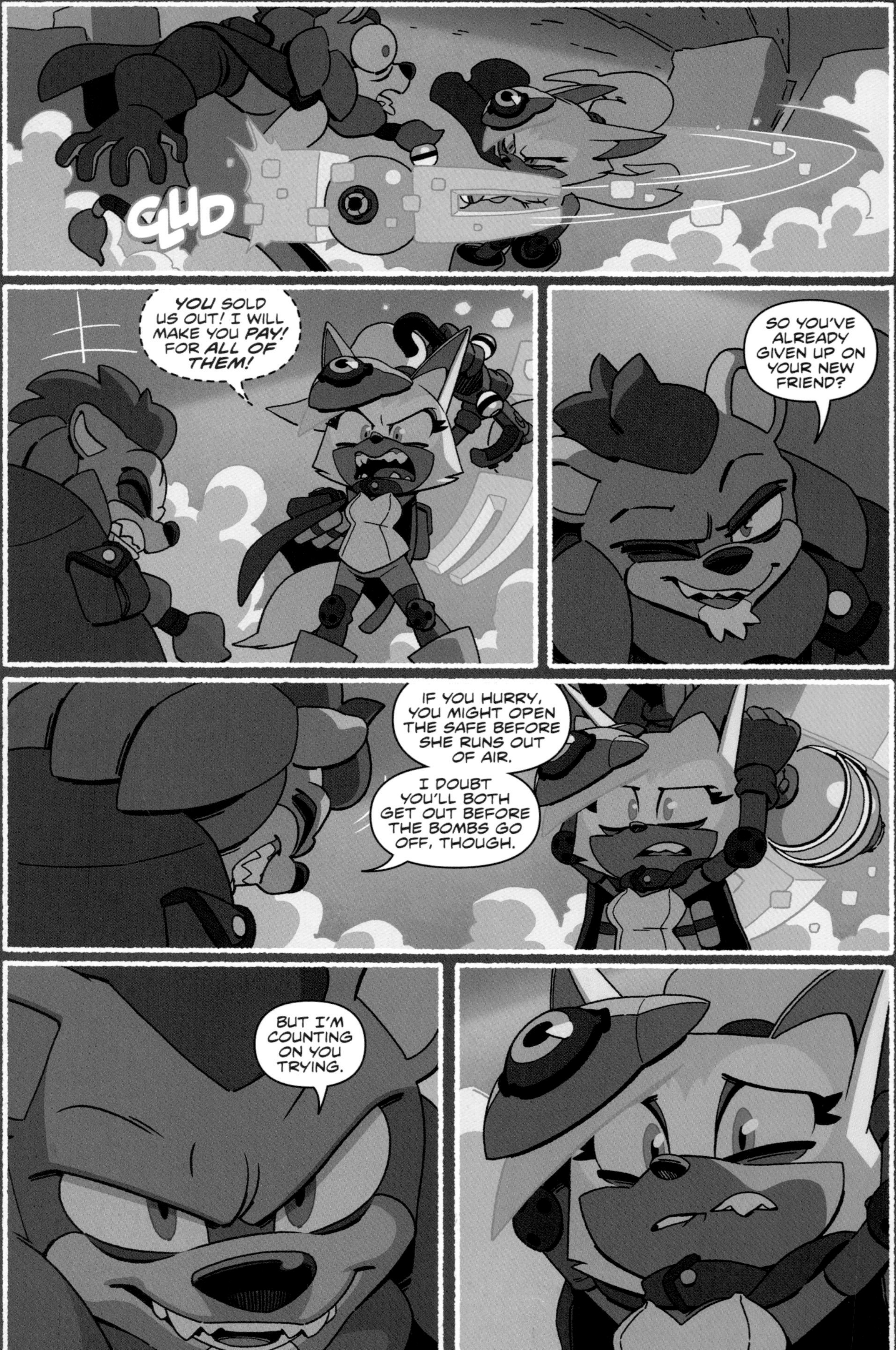

CLUD
YOU SOLD US OUT! I WILL MAKE YOU PAY! FOR ALL OF THEM!
SO YOU'VE ALREADY GIVEN UP ON YOUR NEW FRIEND?
IF YOU HURRY, YOU MIGHT OPEN THE SAFE BEFORE SHE RUNS OUT OF AIR.
I DOUBT YOU'LL BOTH GET OUT BEFORE THE BOMBS GO OFF, THOUGH.
BUT I'M COUNTING ON YOU TRYING.

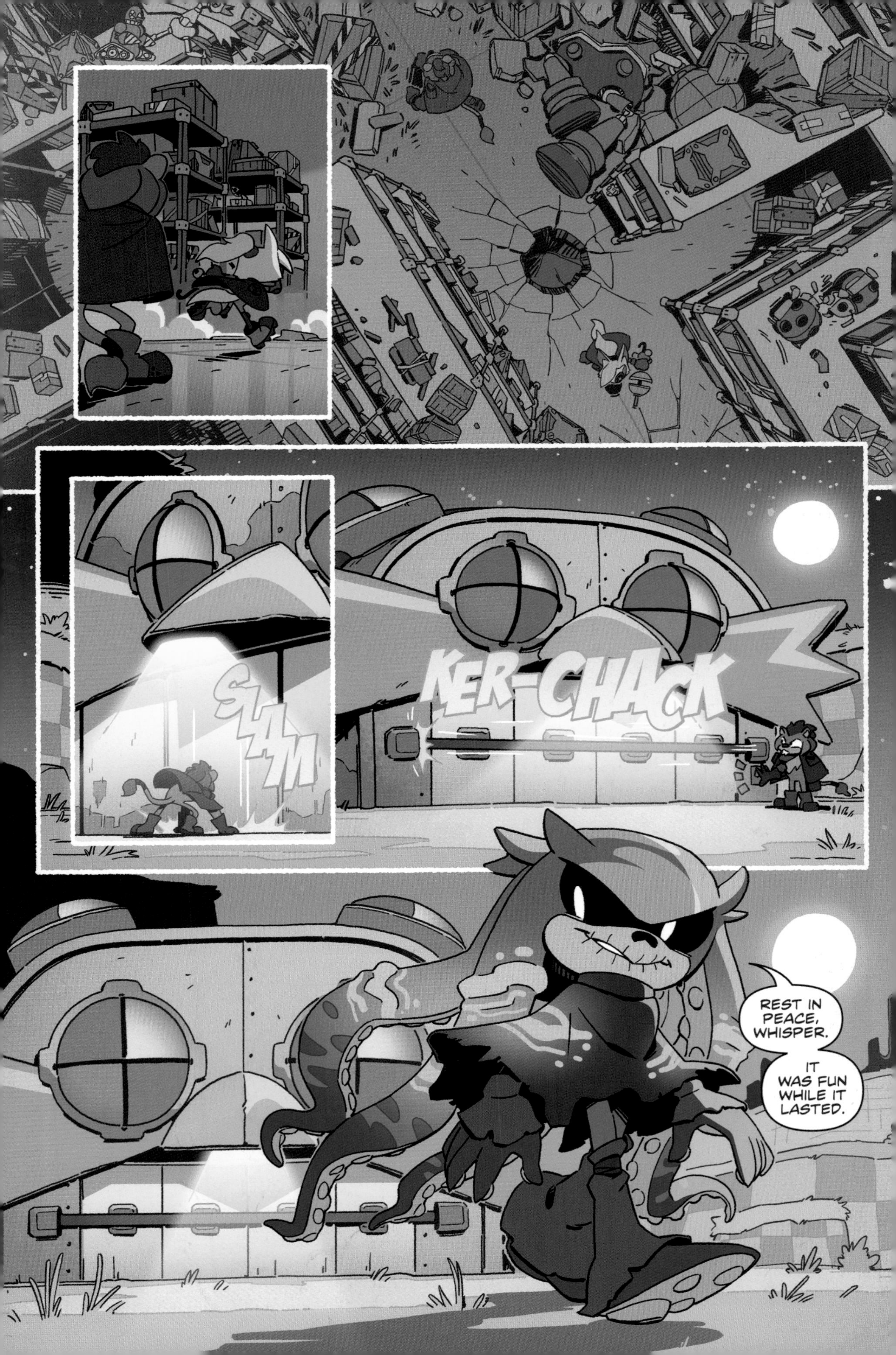
KER-CHACK
SLAM
REST IN PEACE, WHISPER.
IT WAS FUN WHILE IT LASTED.

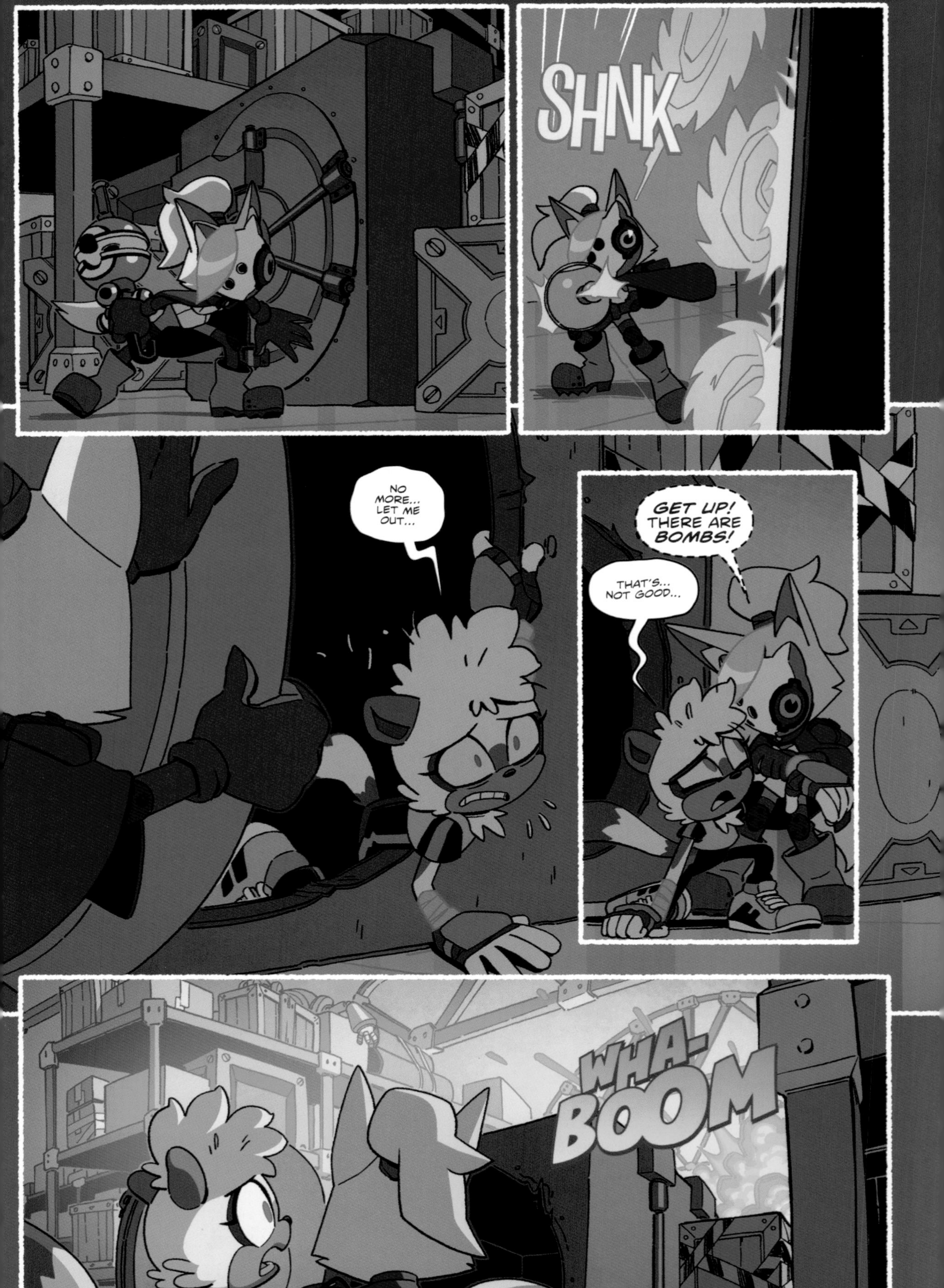
SHNK
NO MORE... LET ME OUT...
GET UP! THERE ARE BOMBS!
THAT'S... NOT GOOD...
WHA-BOOM

WELP...
I'M GONNA
HATE THIS,
BUT...

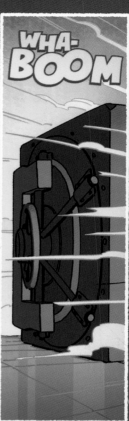

WHA-
BOOM

KRA-KA-KOOM

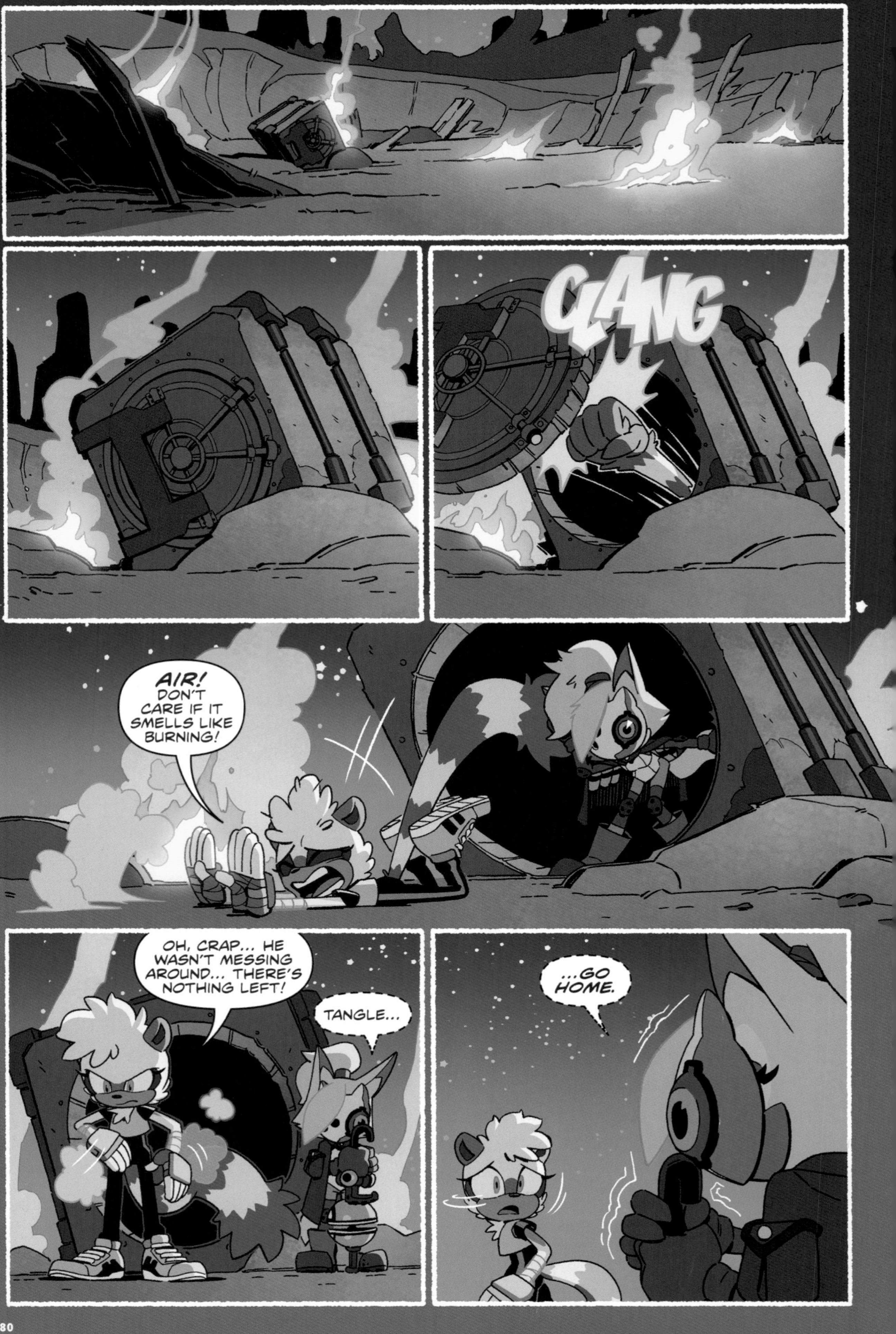
CLANG
AIR! DON'T CARE IF IT SMELLS LIKE BURNING!
OH, CRAP... HE WASN'T MESSING AROUND... THERE'S NOTHING LEFT!
TANGLE...
...GO HOME.

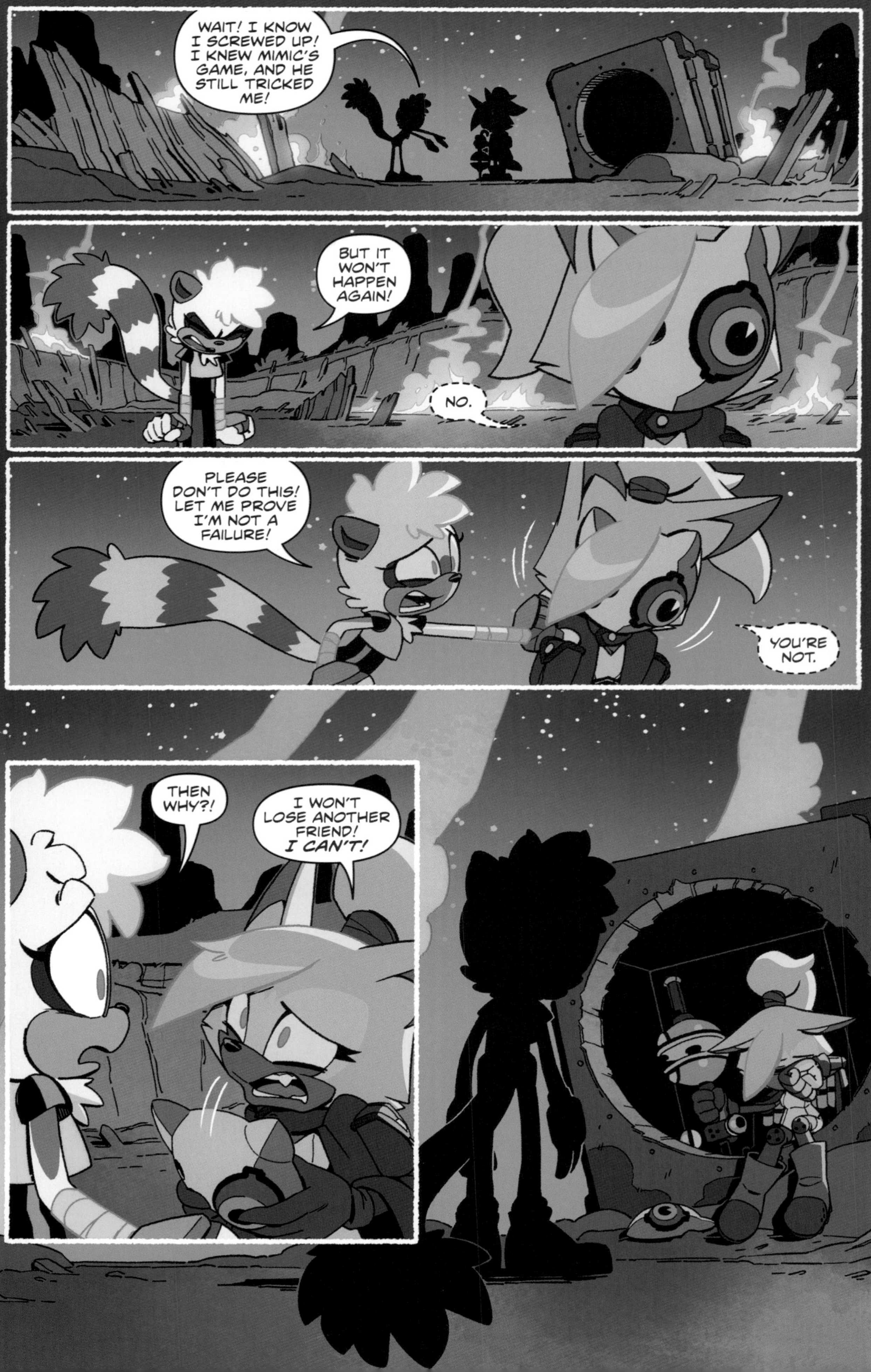
WAIT! I KNOW I SCREWED UP! I KNEW MIMIC'S GAME, AND HE STILL TRICKED ME!
BUT IT WON'T HAPPEN AGAIN!
NO.
PLEASE DON'T DO THIS! LET ME PROVE I'M NOT A FAILURE!
YOU'RE NOT.
THEN WHY?!
I WON'T LOSE ANOTHER FRIEND! *I CAN'T!*

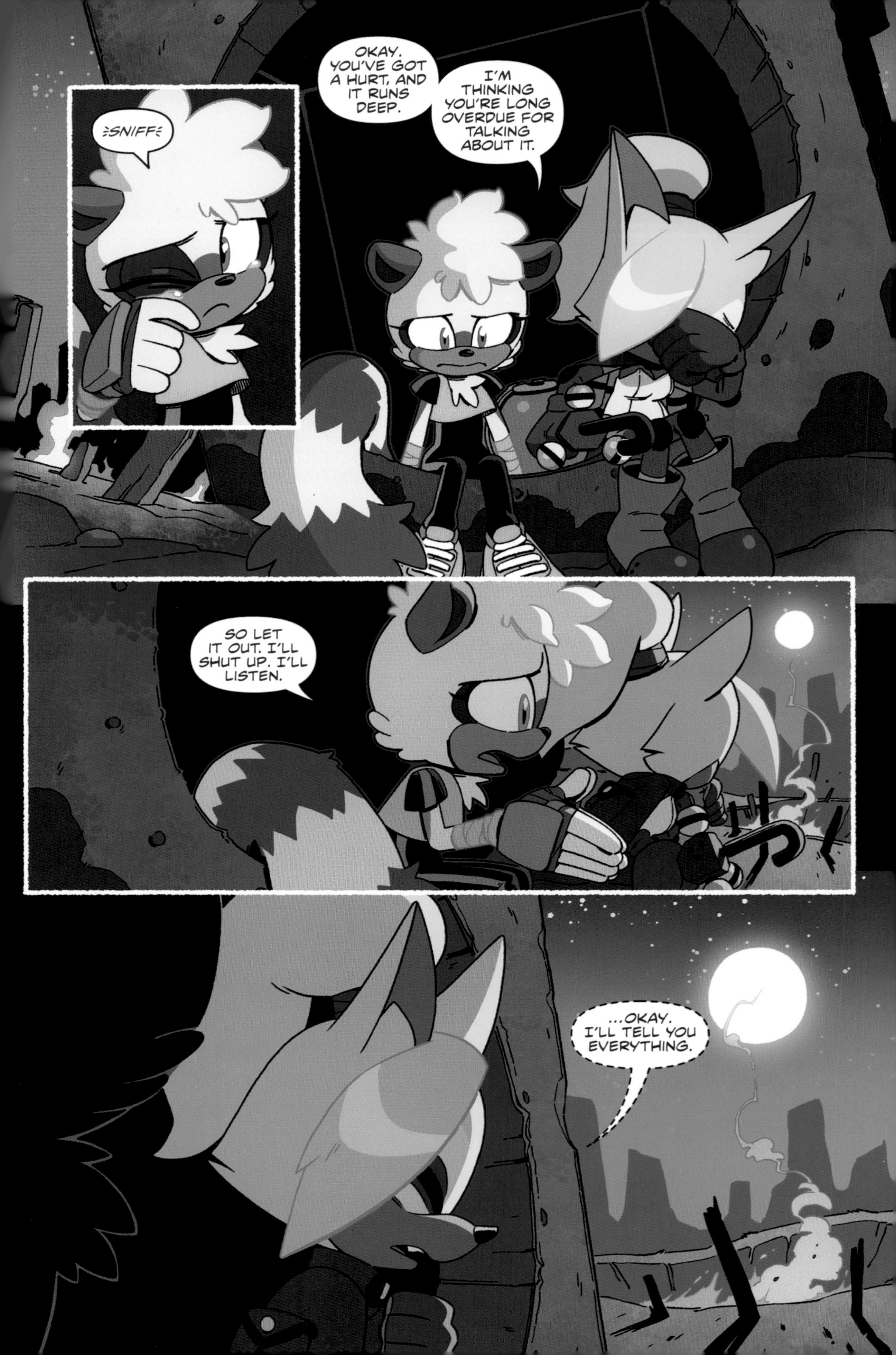

SNIFF
OKAY. YOU'VE GOT A HURT, AND IT RUNS DEEP.
I'M THINKING YOU'RE LONG OVERDUE FOR TALKING ABOUT IT.
SO LET IT OUT. I'LL SHUT UP. I'LL LISTEN.
...OKAY. I'LL TELL YOU EVERYTHING.

ART BY NATHALIE FOURDRAINE

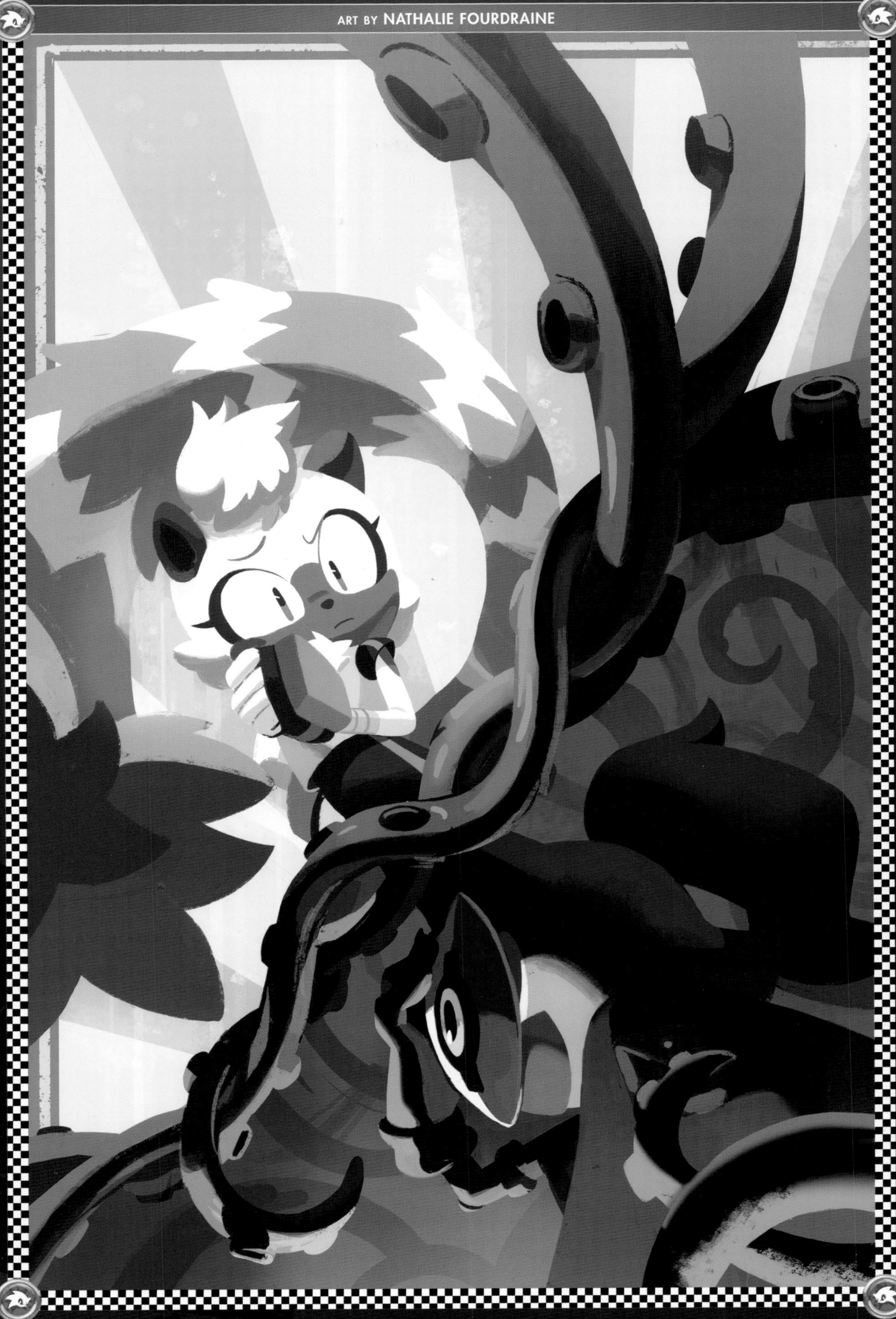

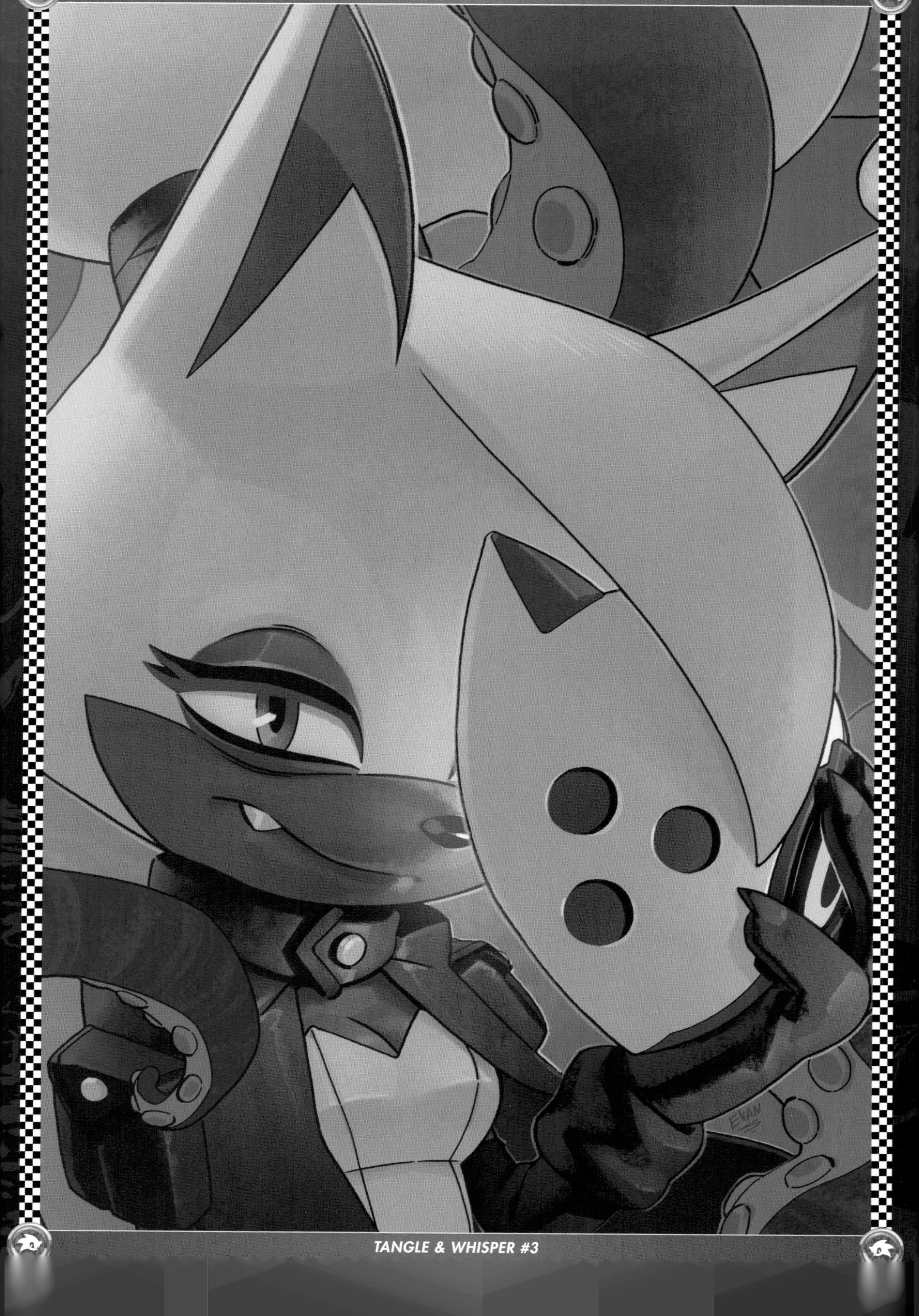
EVAN

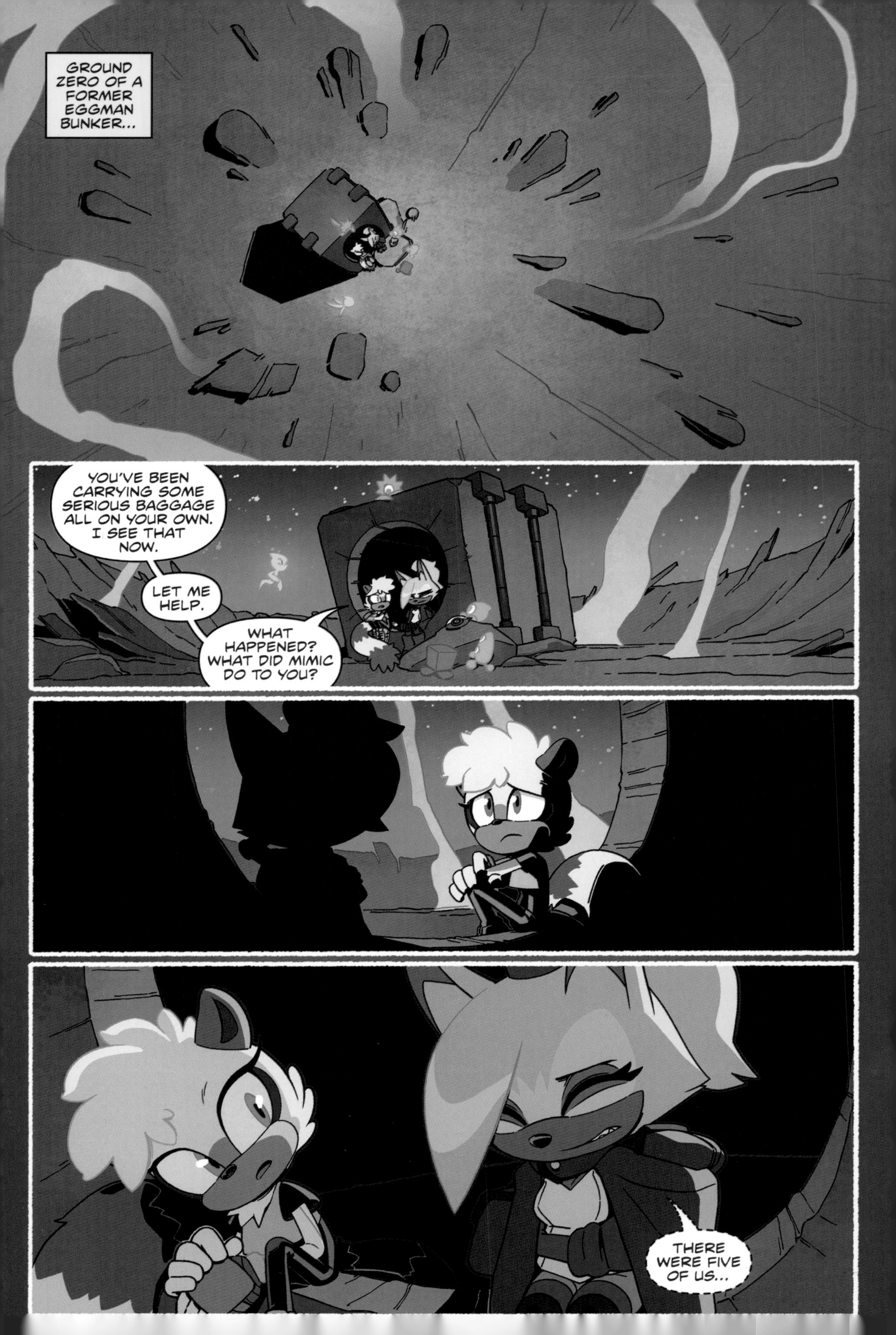
GROUND ZERO OF A FORMER EGGMAN BUNKER...
YOU'VE BEEN CARRYING SOME SERIOUS BAGGAGE ALL ON YOUR OWN. I SEE THAT NOW.
LET ME HELP.
WHAT HAPPENED? WHAT DID MIMIC DO TO YOU?
THERE WERE FIVE OF US...

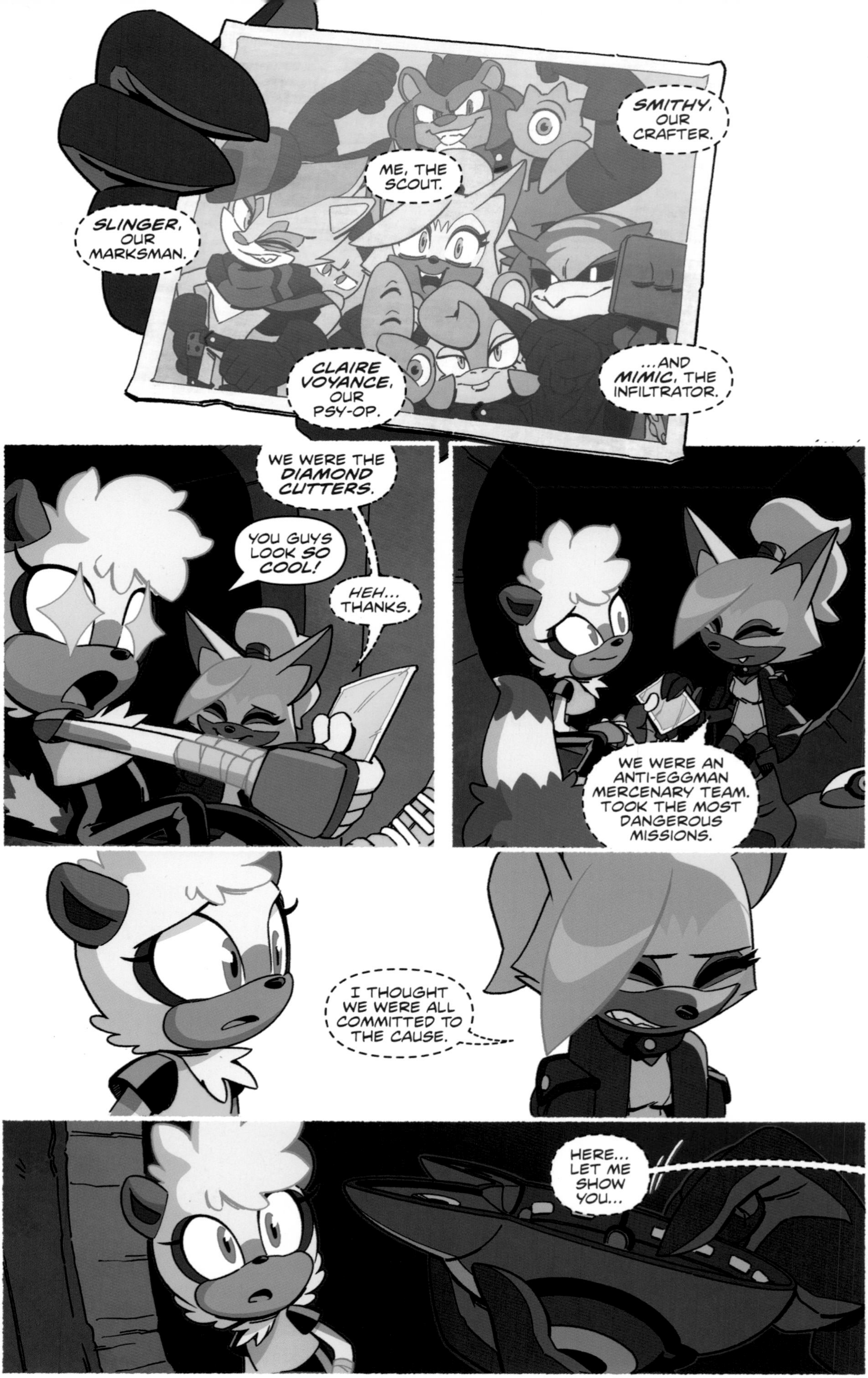
SMITHY, OUR CRAFTER.
ME, THE SCOUT.
SLINGER, OUR MARKSMAN.
CLAIRE VOYANCE, OUR PSY-OP.
...AND MIMIC, THE INFILTRATOR.
WE WERE THE DIAMOND CUTTERS.
YOU GUYS LOOK SO COOL!
HEH... THANKS.
WE WERE AN ANTI-EGGMAN MERCENARY TEAM. TOOK THE MOST DANGEROUS MISSIONS.
I THOUGHT WE WERE ALL COMMITTED TO THE CAUSE.
HERE... LET ME SHOW YOU...

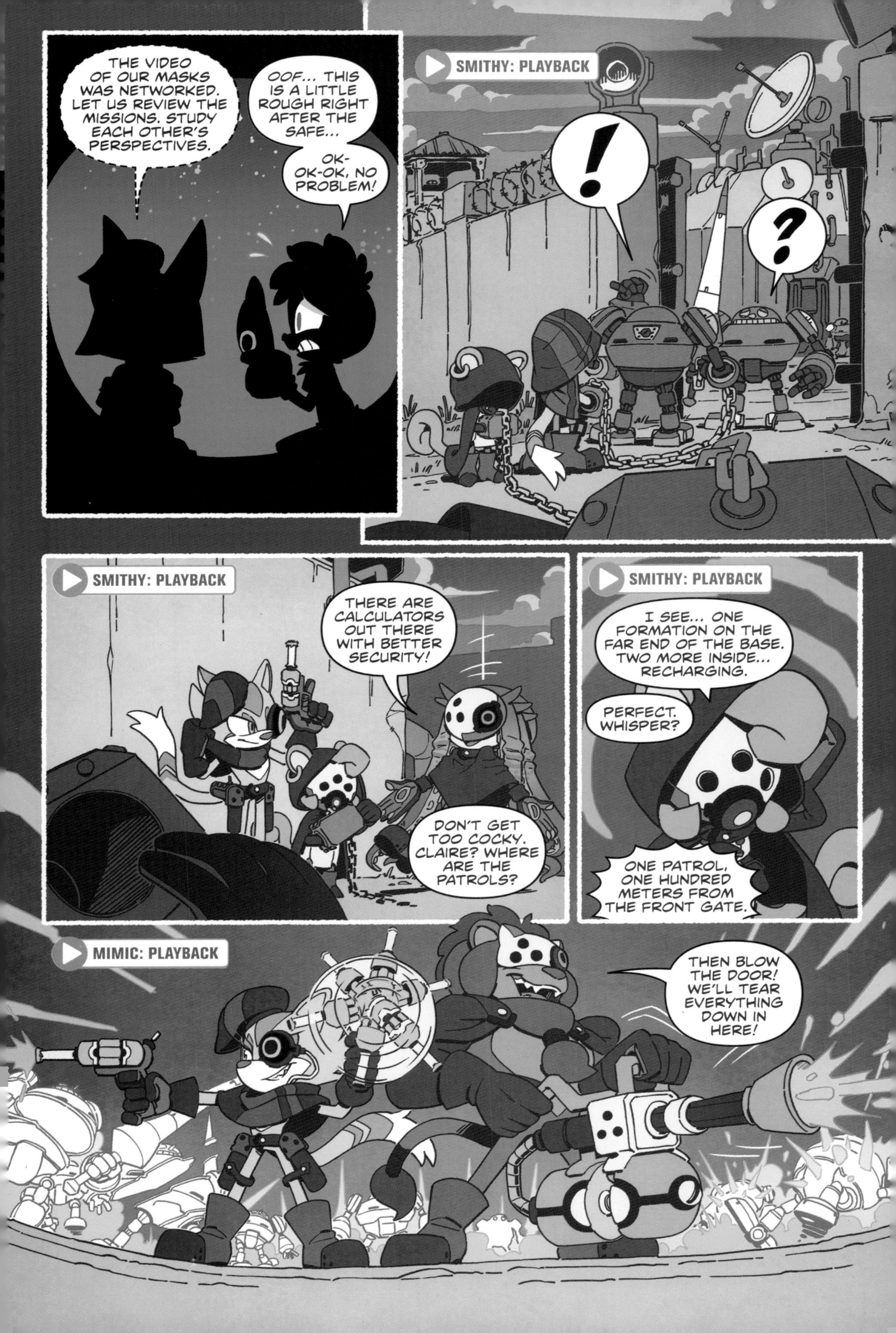
THE VIDEO OF OUR MASKS WAS NETWORKED. LET US REVIEW THE MISSIONS. STUDY EACH OTHER'S PERSPECTIVES.
OOF... THIS IS A LITTLE ROUGH RIGHT AFTER THE SAFE...
OK-OK-OK, NO PROBLEM!
SMITHY: PLAYBACK
!
?
SMITHY: PLAYBACK
THERE ARE CALCULATORS OUT THERE WITH BETTER SECURITY!
DON'T GET TOO COCKY. CLAIRE? WHERE ARE THE PATROLS?
SMITHY: PLAYBACK
I SEE... ONE FORMATION ON THE FAR END OF THE BASE. TWO MORE INSIDE... RECHARGING.
PERFECT. WHISPER?
ONE PATROL, ONE HUNDRED METERS FROM THE FRONT GATE.
MIMIC: PLAYBACK
THEN BLOW THE DOOR! WE'LL TEAR EVERYTHING DOWN IN HERE!

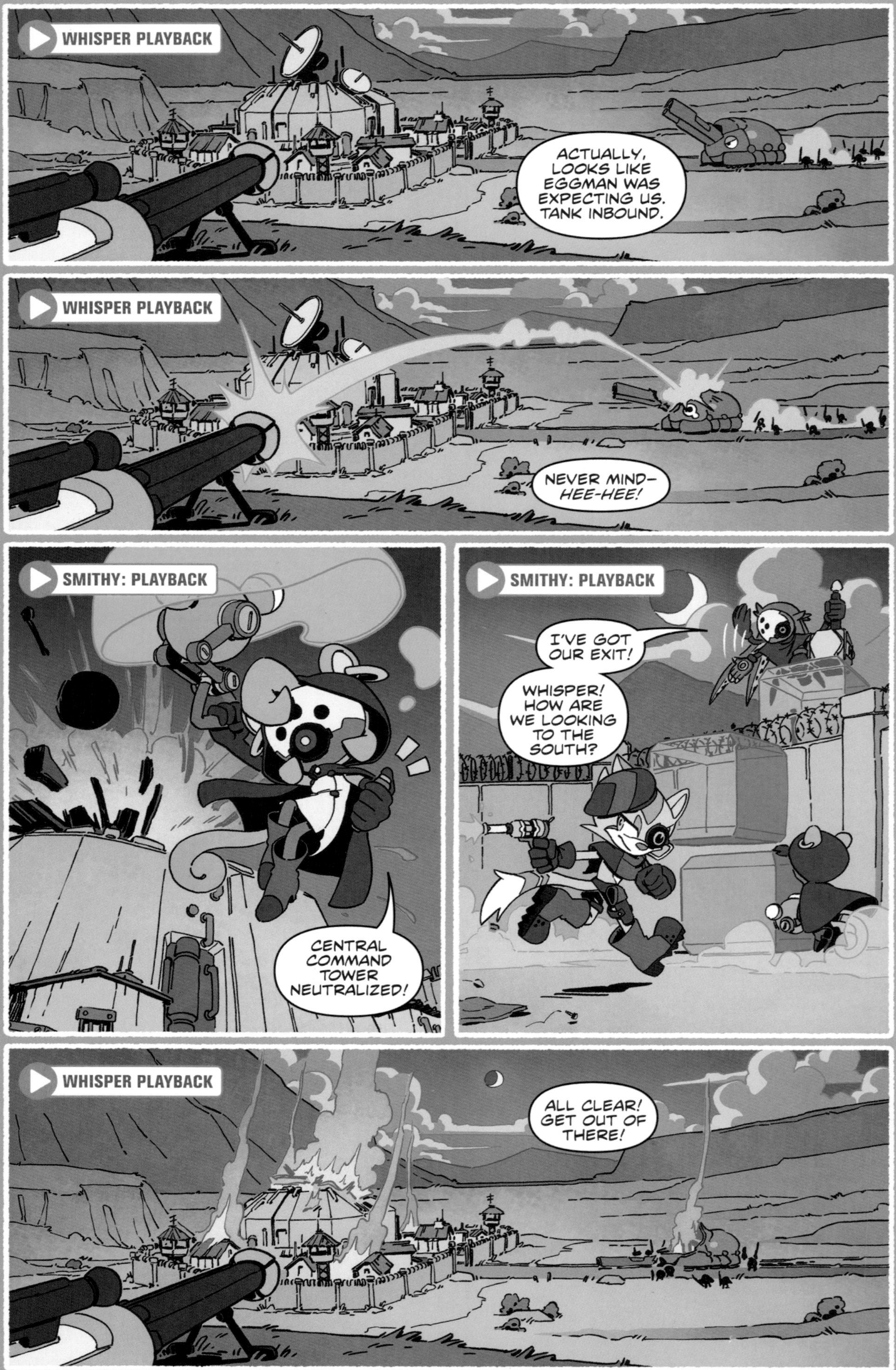
WHISPER PLAYBACK
ACTUALLY, LOOKS LIKE EGGMAN WAS EXPECTING US. TANK INBOUND.
WHISPER PLAYBACK
NEVER MIND—HEE-HEE!
SMITHY: PLAYBACK
CENTRAL COMMAND TOWER NEUTRALIZED!
SMITHY: PLAYBACK
I'VE GOT OUR EXIT!
WHISPER! HOW ARE WE LOOKING TO THE SOUTH?
WHISPER PLAYBACK
ALL CLEAR! GET OUT OF THERE!

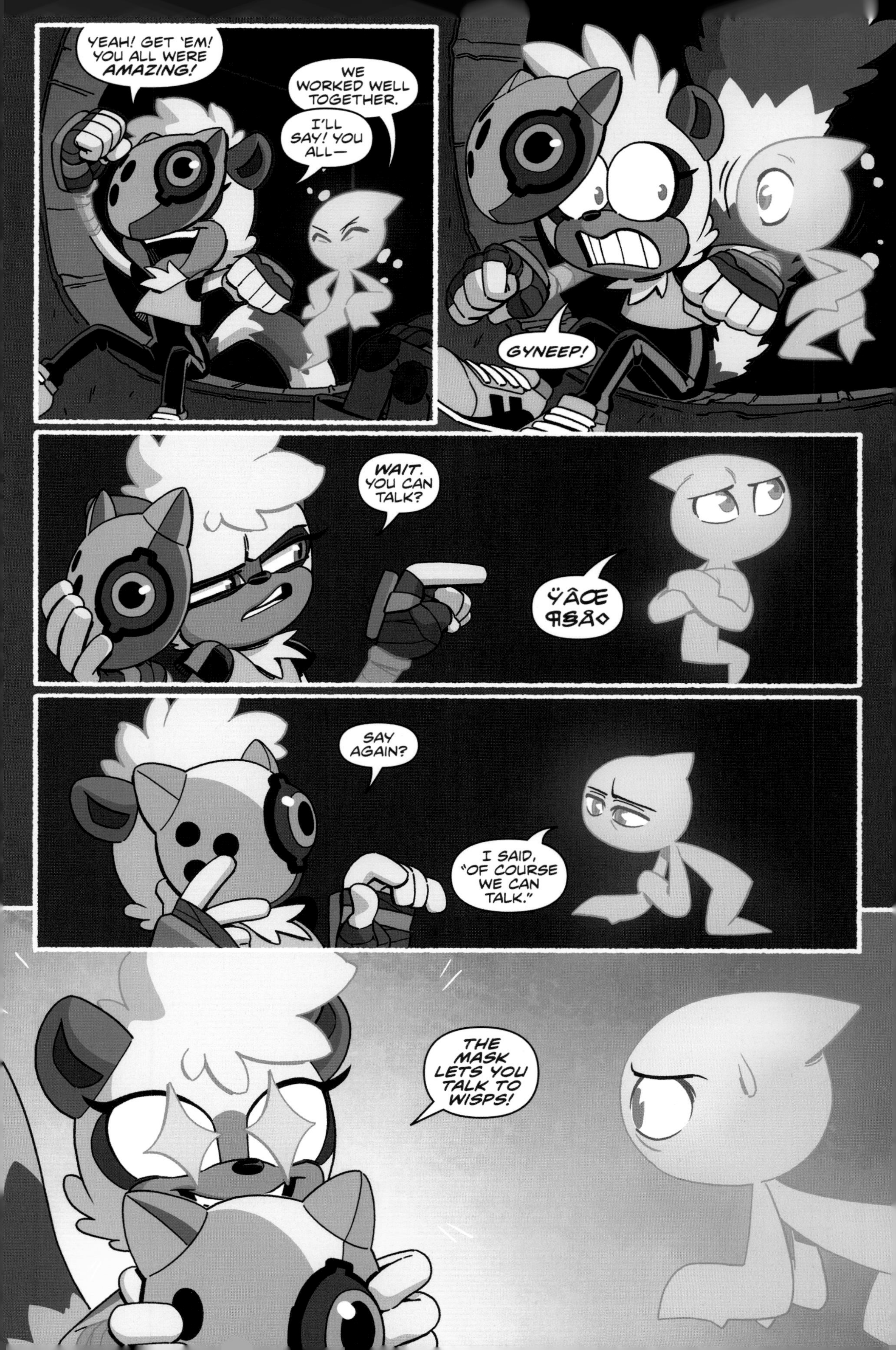
YEAH! GET 'EM! YOU ALL WERE AMAZING!
WE WORKED WELL TOGETHER.
I'LL SAY! YOU ALL—
GYNEEP!
WAIT. YOU CAN TALK?
SAY AGAIN?
I SAID, "OF COURSE WE CAN TALK."
THE MASK LETS YOU TALK TO WISPS!

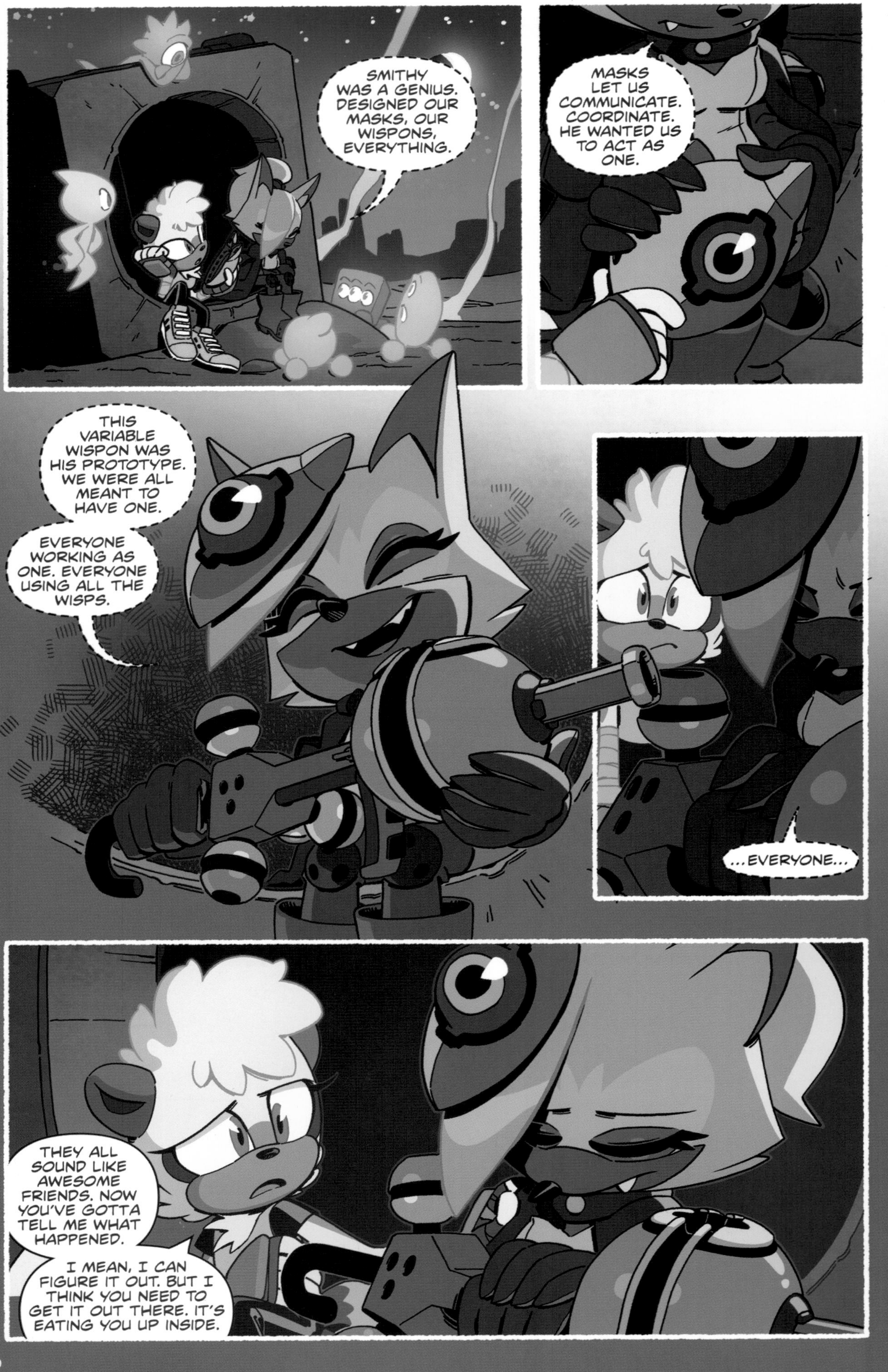
SMITHY WAS A GENIUS. DESIGNED OUR MASKS, OUR WISPONS, EVERYTHING.
MASKS LET US COMMUNICATE. COORDINATE. HE WANTED US TO ACT AS ONE.
THIS VARIABLE WISPON WAS HIS PROTOTYPE. WE WERE ALL MEANT TO HAVE ONE.
EVERYONE WORKING AS ONE. EVERYONE USING ALL THE WISPS.
...EVERYONE...
THEY ALL SOUND LIKE AWESOME FRIENDS. NOW YOU'VE GOTTA TELL ME WHAT HAPPENED.
I MEAN, I CAN FIGURE IT OUT. BUT I THINK YOU NEED TO GET IT OUT THERE. IT'S EATING YOU UP INSIDE.

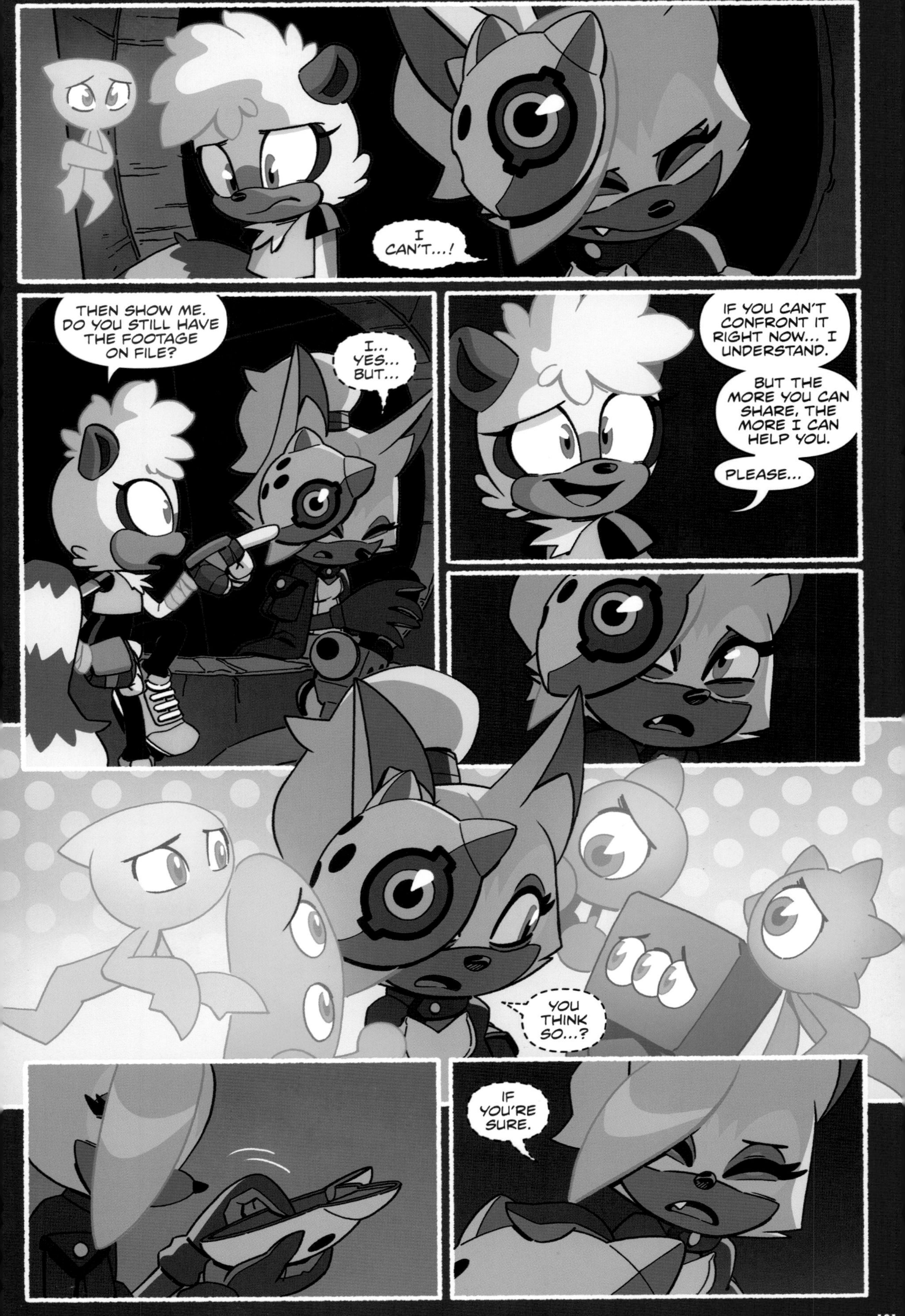
I CAN'T...!
THEN SHOW ME. DO YOU STILL HAVE THE FOOTAGE ON FILE?
I... YES... BUT...
IF YOU CAN'T CONFRONT IT RIGHT NOW... I UNDERSTAND.
BUT THE MORE YOU CAN SHARE, THE MORE I CAN HELP YOU.
PLEASE...
YOU THINK SO...?
IF YOU'RE SURE.

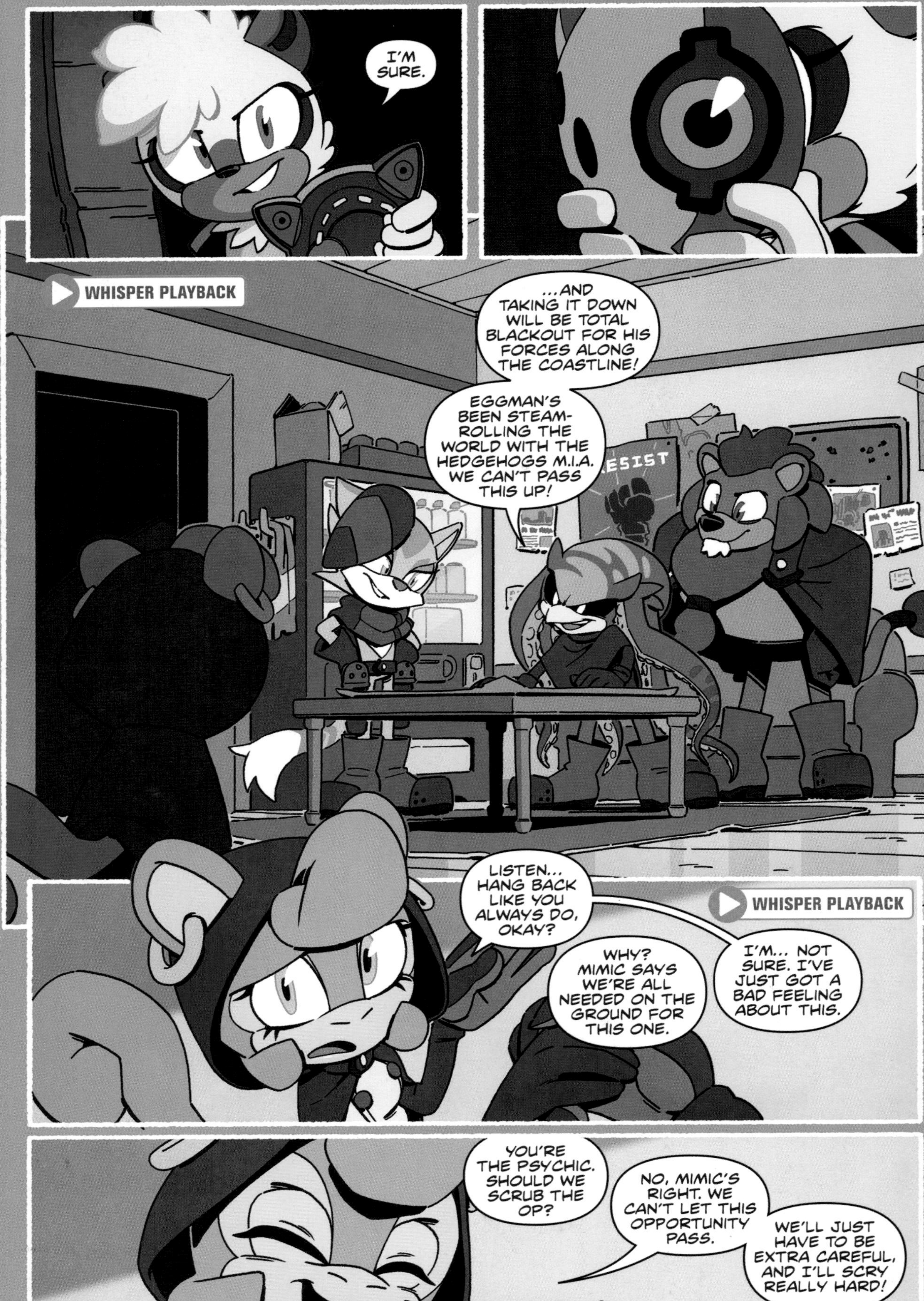
I'M SURE.
WHISPER PLAYBACK
...AND TAKING IT DOWN WILL BE TOTAL BLACKOUT FOR HIS FORCES ALONG THE COASTLINE!
EGGMAN'S BEEN STEAM-ROLLING THE WORLD WITH THE HEDGEHOGS M.I.A. WE CAN'T PASS THIS UP!
RESIST
LISTEN... HANG BACK LIKE YOU ALWAYS DO, OKAY?
WHISPER PLAYBACK
WHY? MIMIC SAYS WE'RE ALL NEEDED ON THE GROUND FOR THIS ONE.
I'M... NOT SURE. I'VE JUST GOT A BAD FEELING ABOUT THIS.
YOU'RE THE PSYCHIC. SHOULD WE SCRUB THE OP?
NO, MIMIC'S RIGHT. WE CAN'T LET THIS OPPORTUNITY PASS.
WE'LL JUST HAVE TO BE EXTRA CAREFUL, AND I'LL SCRY REALLY HARD!
HA HA HA!

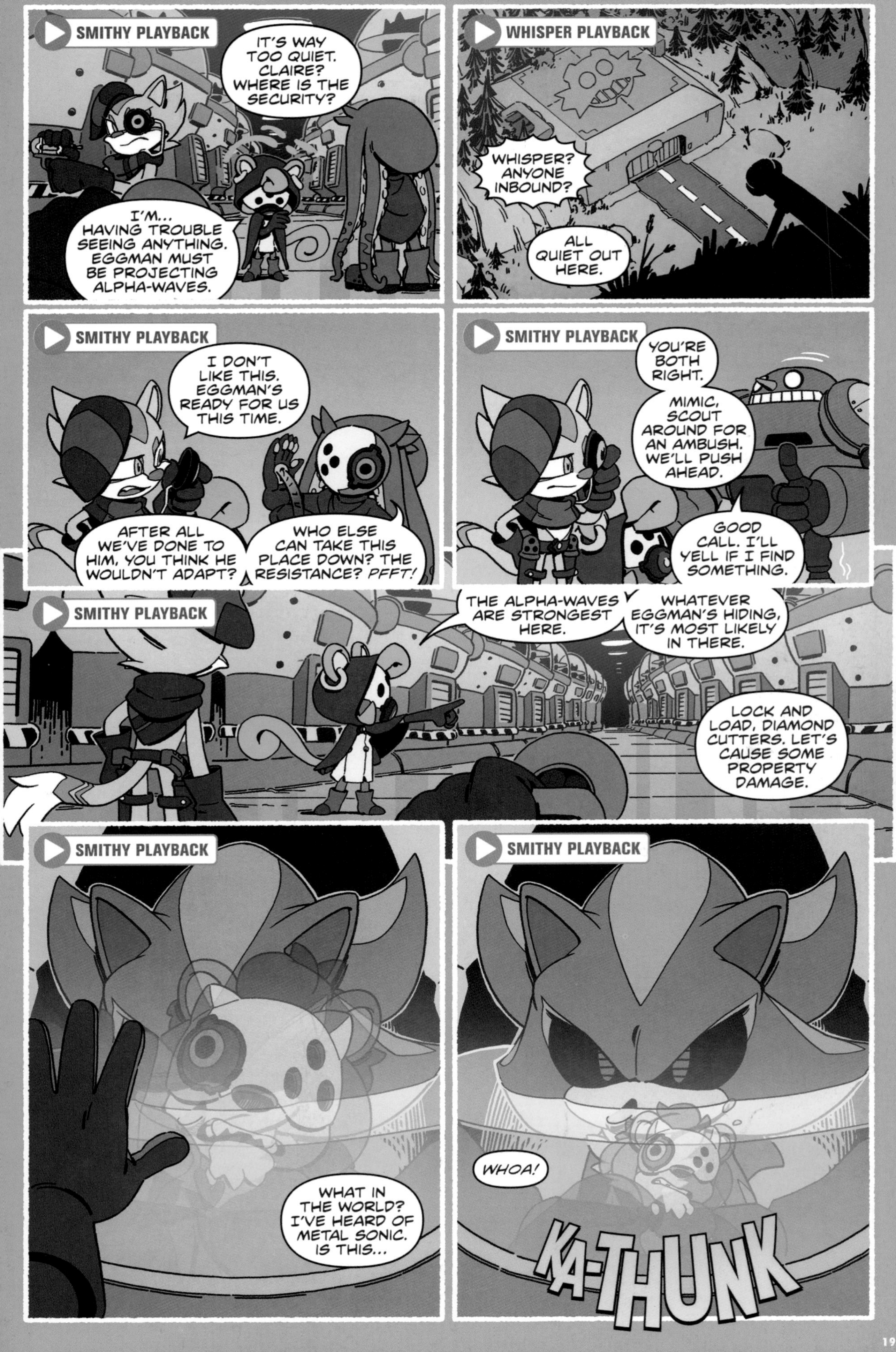
SMITHY PLAYBACK
IT'S WAY TOO QUIET. CLAIRE? WHERE IS THE SECURITY?
I'M... HAVING TROUBLE SEEING ANYTHING. EGGMAN MUST BE PROJECTING ALPHA-WAVES.
WHISPER PLAYBACK
WHISPER? ANYONE INBOUND?
ALL QUIET OUT HERE.
SMITHY PLAYBACK
I DON'T LIKE THIS. EGGMAN'S READY FOR US THIS TIME.
AFTER ALL WE'VE DONE TO HIM, YOU THINK HE WOULDN'T ADAPT?
WHO ELSE CAN TAKE THIS PLACE DOWN? THE RESISTANCE? PFFT!
SMITHY PLAYBACK
YOU'RE BOTH RIGHT.
MIMIC, SCOUT AROUND FOR AN AMBUSH. WE'LL PUSH AHEAD.
GOOD CALL. I'LL YELL IF I FIND SOMETHING.
SMITHY PLAYBACK
THE ALPHA-WAVES ARE STRONGEST HERE.
WHATEVER EGGMAN'S HIDING, IT'S MOST LIKELY IN THERE.
LOCK AND LOAD, DIAMOND CUTTERS. LET'S CAUSE SOME PROPERTY DAMAGE.
SMITHY PLAYBACK
WHAT IN THE WORLD? I'VE HEARD OF METAL SONIC. IS THIS...
SMITHY PLAYBACK
WHOA!
KA-THUNK

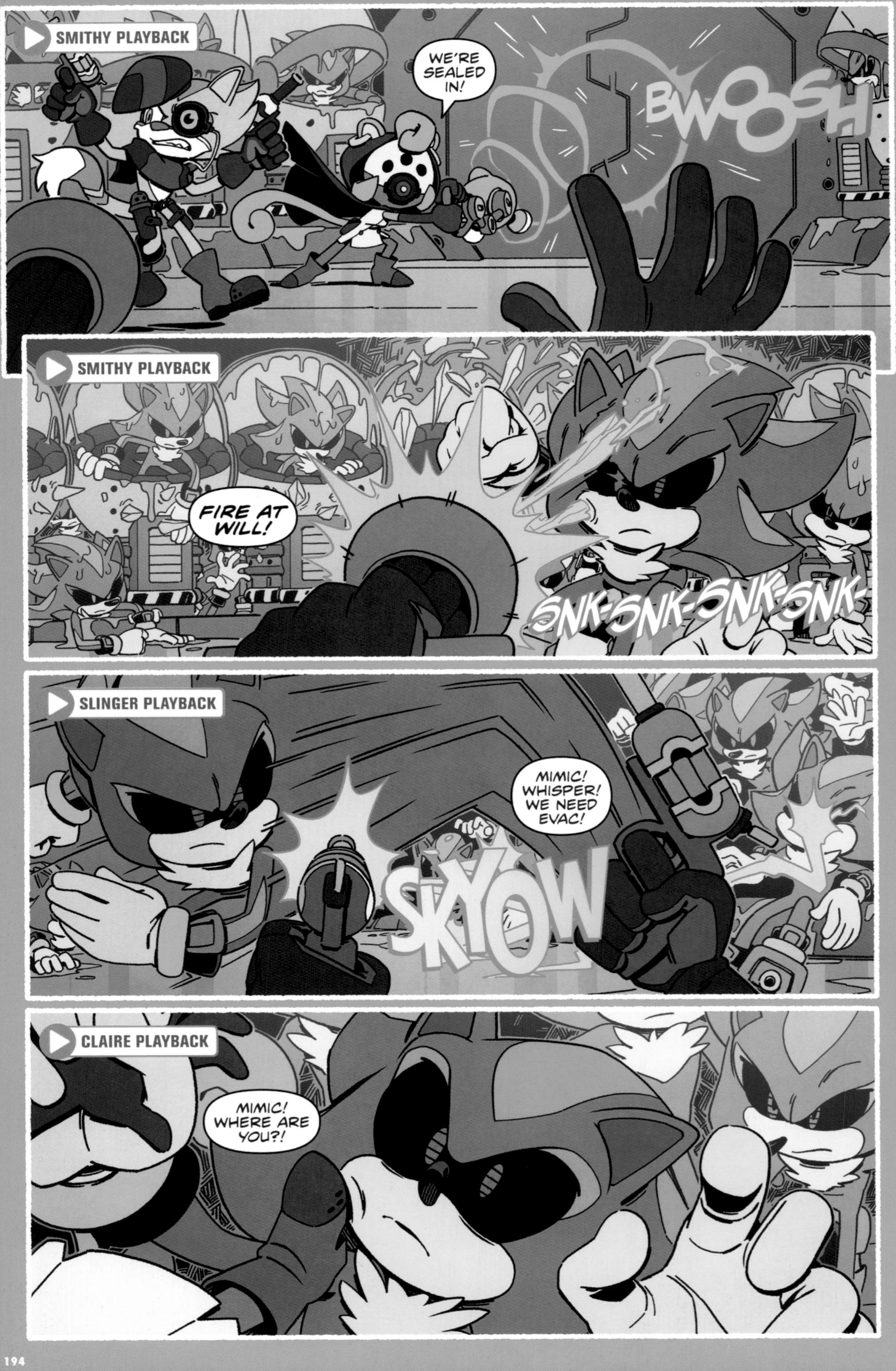
SMITHY PLAYBACK
WE'RE SEALED IN!
BWOOSH
SMITHY PLAYBACK
FIRE AT WILL!
SNK-SNK-SNK-SNK
SLINGER PLAYBACK
MIMIC! WHISPER! WE NEED EVAC!
SKYOW
CLAIRE PLAYBACK
MIMIC! WHERE ARE YOU?!

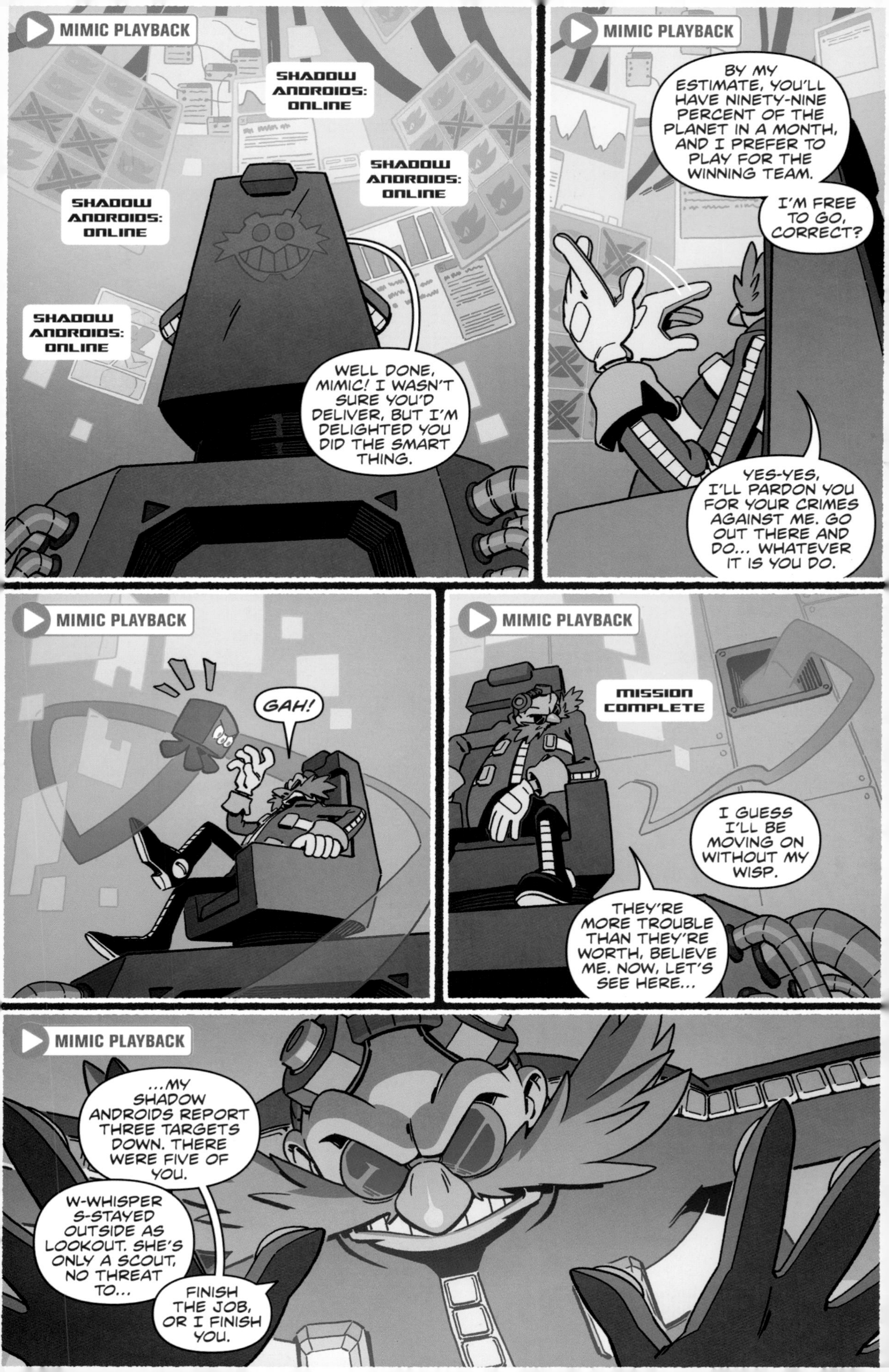
MIMIC PLAYBACK
SHADOW ANDROIDS: ONLINE
SHADOW ANDROIDS: ONLINE
SHADOW ANDROIDS: ONLINE
SHADOW ANDROIDS: ONLINE
WELL DONE, MIMIC! I WASN'T SURE YOU'D DELIVER, BUT I'M DELIGHTED YOU DID THE SMART THING.
MIMIC PLAYBACK
BY MY ESTIMATE, YOU'LL HAVE NINETY-NINE PERCENT OF THE PLANET IN A MONTH, AND I PREFER TO PLAY FOR THE WINNING TEAM.
I'M FREE TO GO, CORRECT?
YES-YES, I'LL PARDON YOU FOR YOUR CRIMES AGAINST ME. GO OUT THERE AND DO... WHATEVER IT IS YOU DO.
MIMIC PLAYBACK
GAH!
MIMIC PLAYBACK
MISSION COMPLETE
I GUESS I'LL BE MOVING ON WITHOUT MY WISP.
THEY'RE MORE TROUBLE THAN THEY'RE WORTH, BELIEVE ME. NOW, LET'S SEE HERE...
MIMIC PLAYBACK
...MY SHADOW ANDROIDS REPORT THREE TARGETS DOWN. THERE WERE FIVE OF YOU.
W-WHISPER S-STAYED OUTSIDE AS LOOKOUT. SHE'S ONLY A SCOUT, NO THREAT TO...
FINISH THE JOB, OR I FINISH YOU.

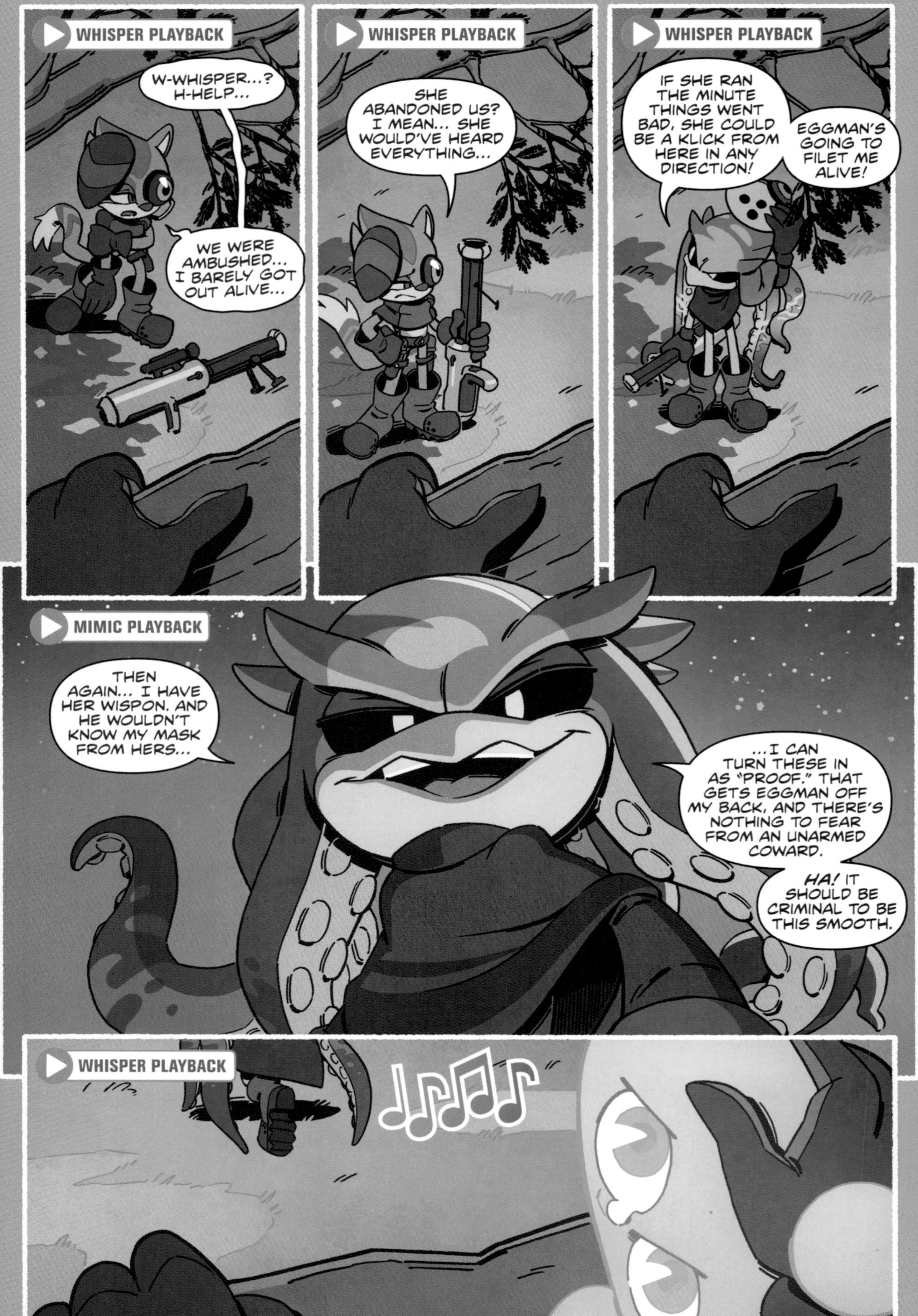
WHISPER PLAYBACK
W-WHISPER...? H-HELP...
WE WERE AMBUSHED... I BARELY GOT OUT ALIVE...
WHISPER PLAYBACK
SHE ABANDONED US? I MEAN... SHE WOULD'VE HEARD EVERYTHING...
WHISPER PLAYBACK
IF SHE RAN THE MINUTE THINGS WENT BAD, SHE COULD BE A KLICK FROM HERE IN ANY DIRECTION!
EGGMAN'S GOING TO FILET ME ALIVE!
MIMIC PLAYBACK
THEN AGAIN... I HAVE HER WISPON. AND HE WOULDN'T KNOW MY MASK FROM HERS...
...I CAN TURN THESE IN AS "PROOF." THAT GETS EGGMAN OFF MY BACK, AND THERE'S NOTHING TO FEAR FROM AN UNARMED COWARD.
HA! IT SHOULD BE CRIMINAL TO BE THIS SMOOTH.
WHISPER PLAYBACK

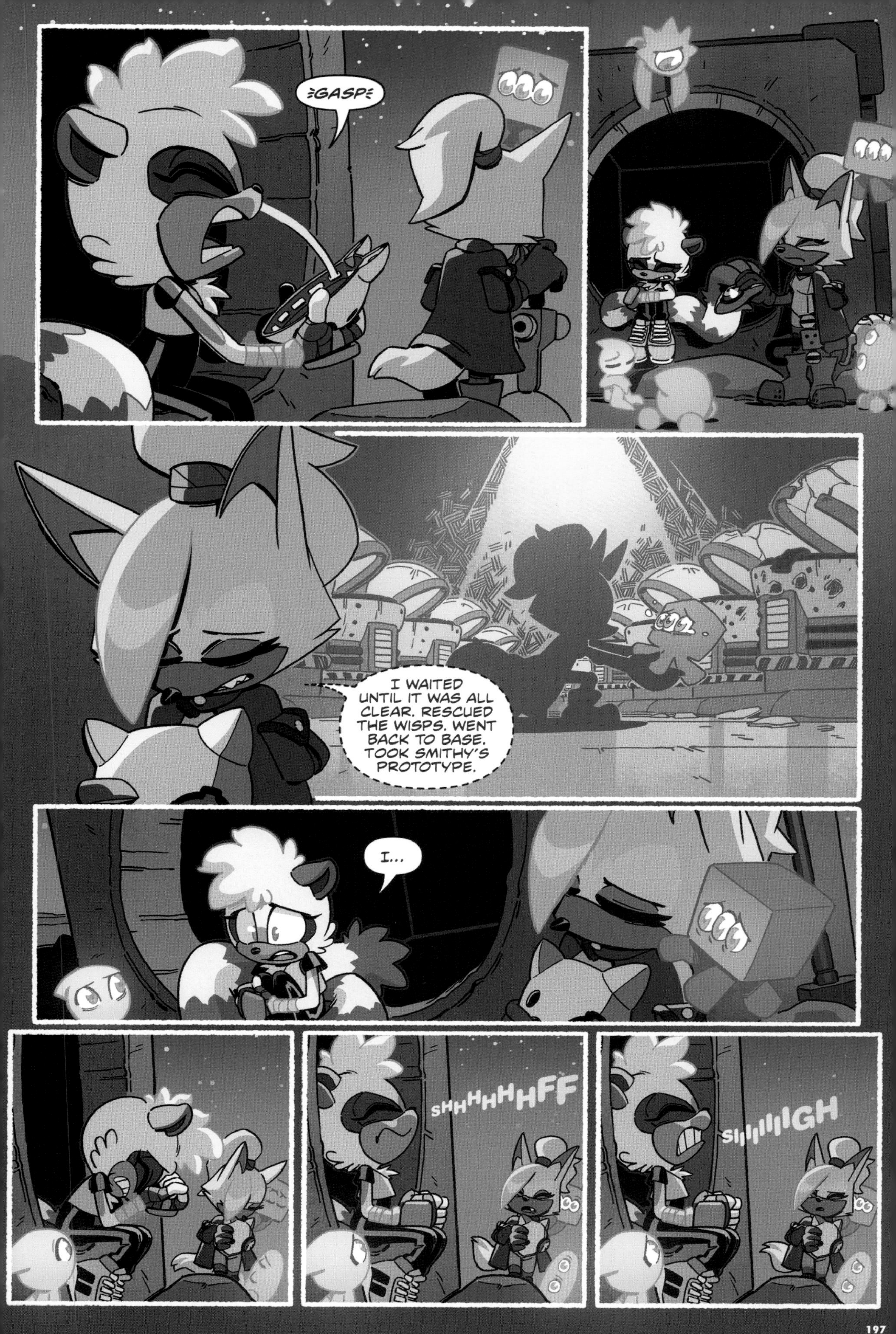
GASP
I WAITED UNTIL IT WAS ALL CLEAR. RESCUED THE WISPS. WENT BACK TO BASE. TOOK SMITHY'S PROTOTYPE.
I...
SHHHHHHHFF
SIIIIIIGH

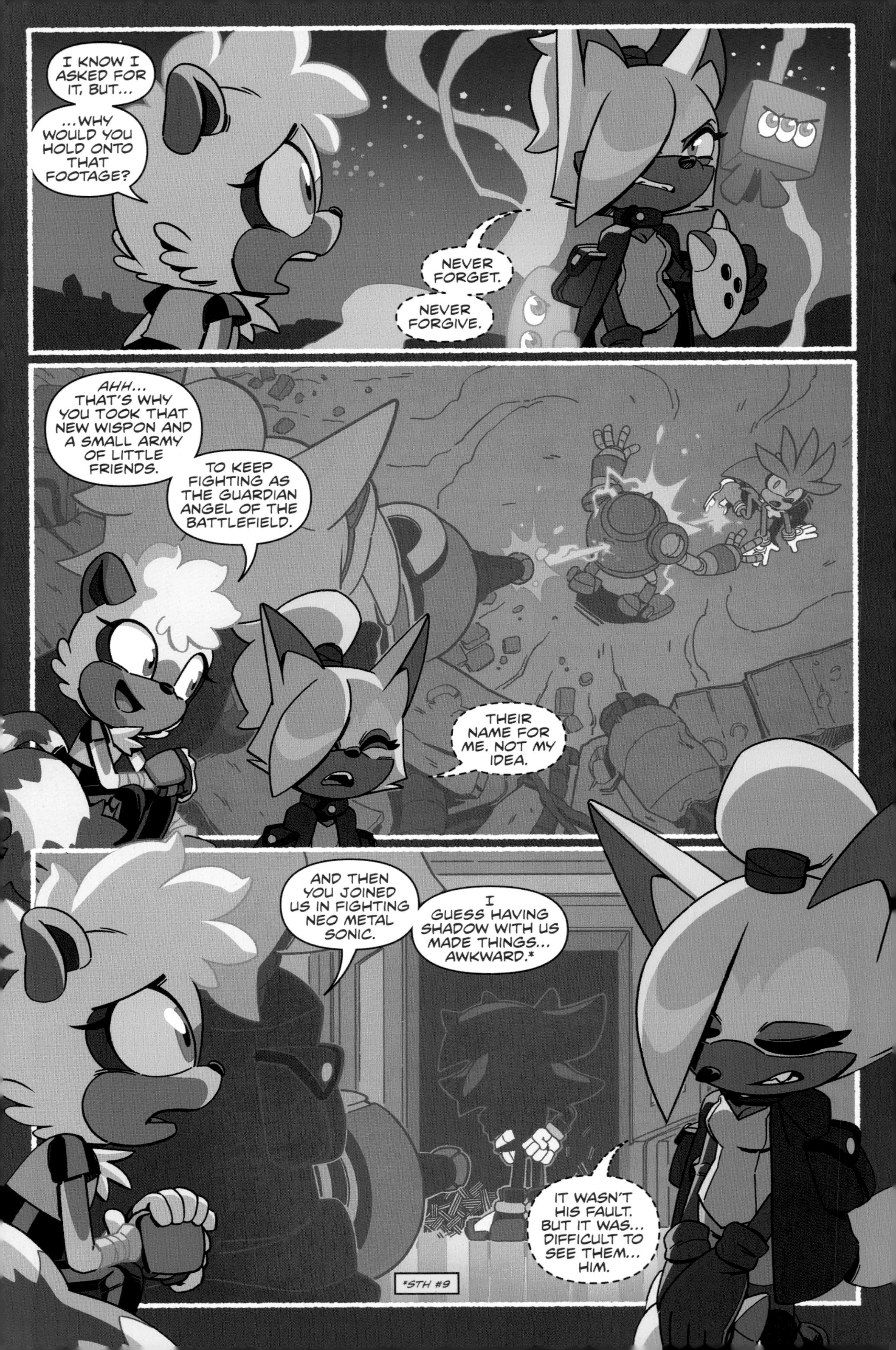
I KNOW I ASKED FOR IT, BUT...
...WHY WOULD YOU HOLD ONTO THAT FOOTAGE?
NEVER FORGET.
NEVER FORGIVE.
AHH... THAT'S WHY YOU TOOK THAT NEW WISPON AND A SMALL ARMY OF LITTLE FRIENDS.
TO KEEP FIGHTING AS THE GUARDIAN ANGEL OF THE BATTLEFIELD.
THEIR NAME FOR ME. NOT MY IDEA.
AND THEN YOU JOINED US IN FIGHTING NEO METAL SONIC.
I GUESS HAVING SHADOW WITH US MADE THINGS... AWKWARD.*
IT WASN'T HIS FAULT. BUT IT WAS... DIFFICULT TO SEE THEM... HIM.
*STH #9

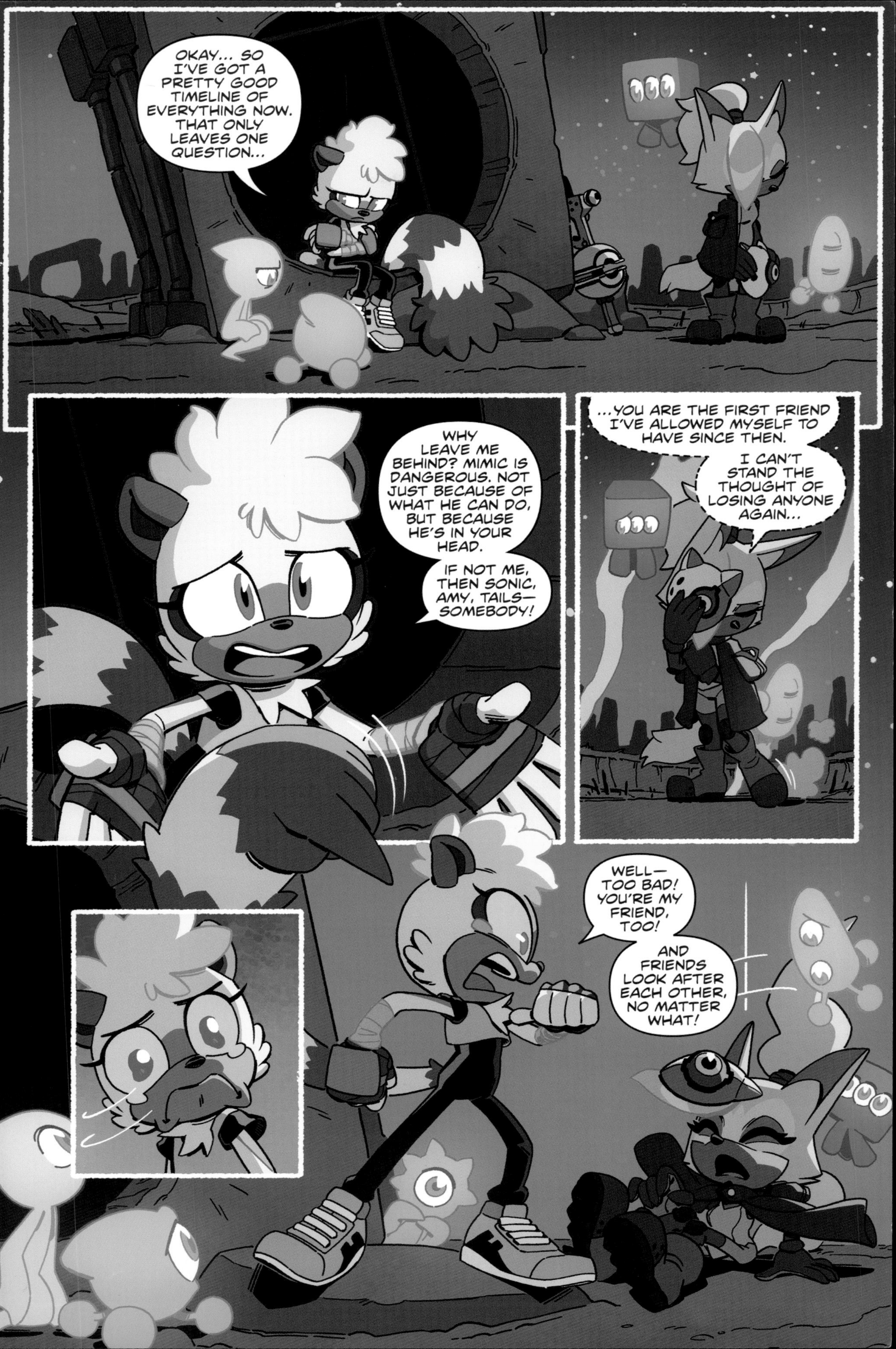
OKAY... SO I'VE GOT A PRETTY GOOD TIMELINE OF EVERYTHING NOW. THAT ONLY LEAVES ONE QUESTION...
WHY LEAVE ME BEHIND? MIMIC IS DANGEROUS. NOT JUST BECAUSE OF WHAT HE CAN DO, BUT BECAUSE HE'S IN YOUR HEAD.
IF NOT ME, THEN SONIC, AMY, TAILS— SOMEBODY!
...YOU ARE THE FIRST FRIEND I'VE ALLOWED MYSELF TO HAVE SINCE THEN.
I CAN'T STAND THE THOUGHT OF LOSING ANYONE AGAIN...
WELL— TOO BAD! YOU'RE MY FRIEND, TOO!
AND FRIENDS LOOK AFTER EACH OTHER, NO MATTER WHAT!

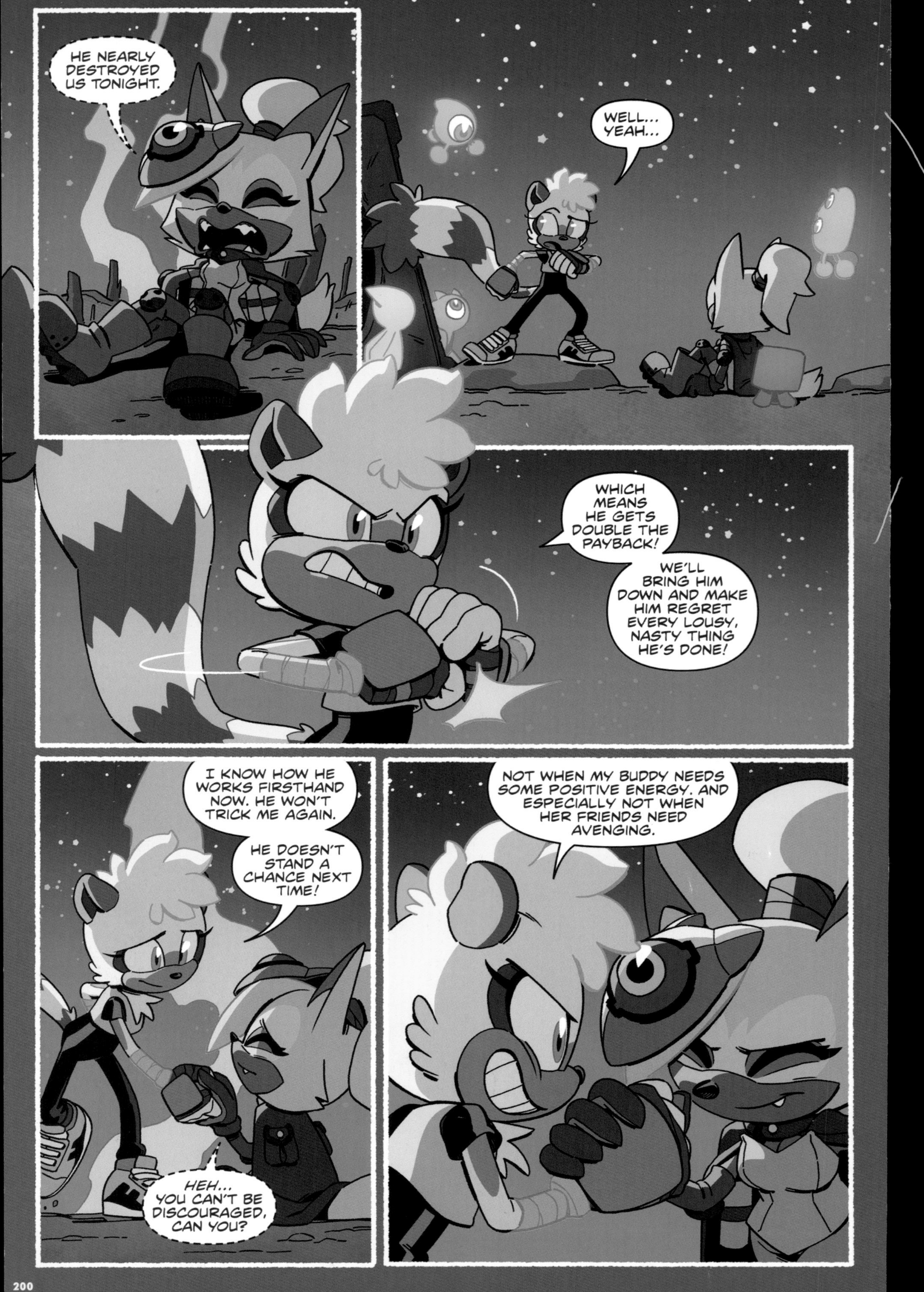

HE NEARLY DESTROYED US TONIGHT.
WELL... YEAH...
WHICH MEANS HE GETS DOUBLE THE PAYBACK!
WE'LL BRING HIM DOWN AND MAKE HIM REGRET EVERY LOUSY, NASTY THING HE'S DONE!
I KNOW HOW HE WORKS FIRSTHAND NOW. HE WON'T TRICK ME AGAIN.
HE DOESN'T STAND A CHANCE NEXT TIME!
HEH... YOU CAN'T BE DISCOURAGED, CAN YOU?
NOT WHEN MY BUDDY NEEDS SOME POSITIVE ENERGY. AND ESPECIALLY NOT WHEN HER FRIENDS NEED AVENGING.

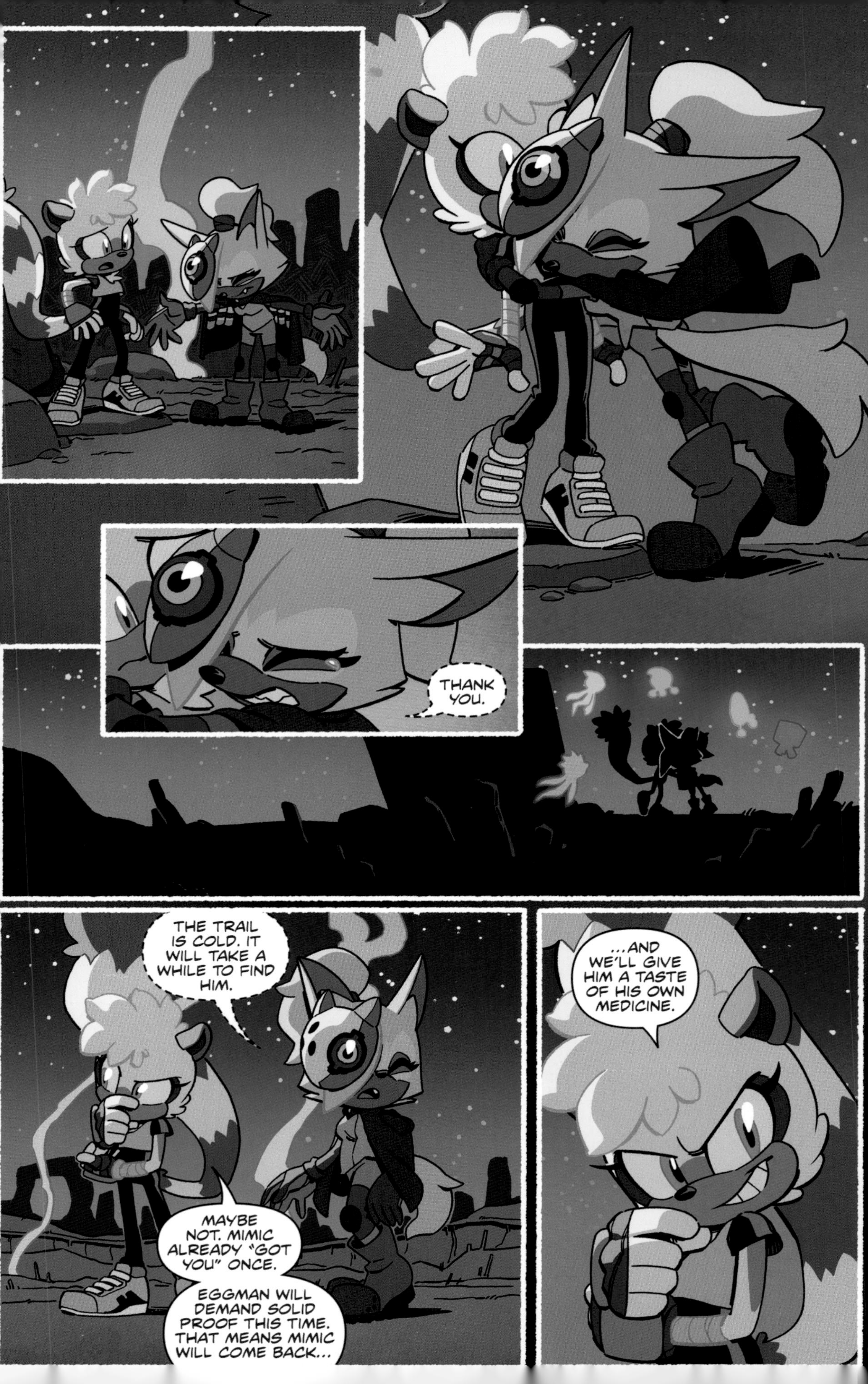
THANK YOU.
THE TRAIL IS COLD. IT WILL TAKE A WHILE TO FIND HIM.
MAYBE NOT. MIMIC ALREADY "GOT YOU" ONCE.
EGGMAN WILL DEMAND SOLID PROOF THIS TIME. THAT MEANS MIMIC WILL COME BACK...
...AND WE'LL GIVE HIM A TASTE OF HIS OWN MEDICINE.

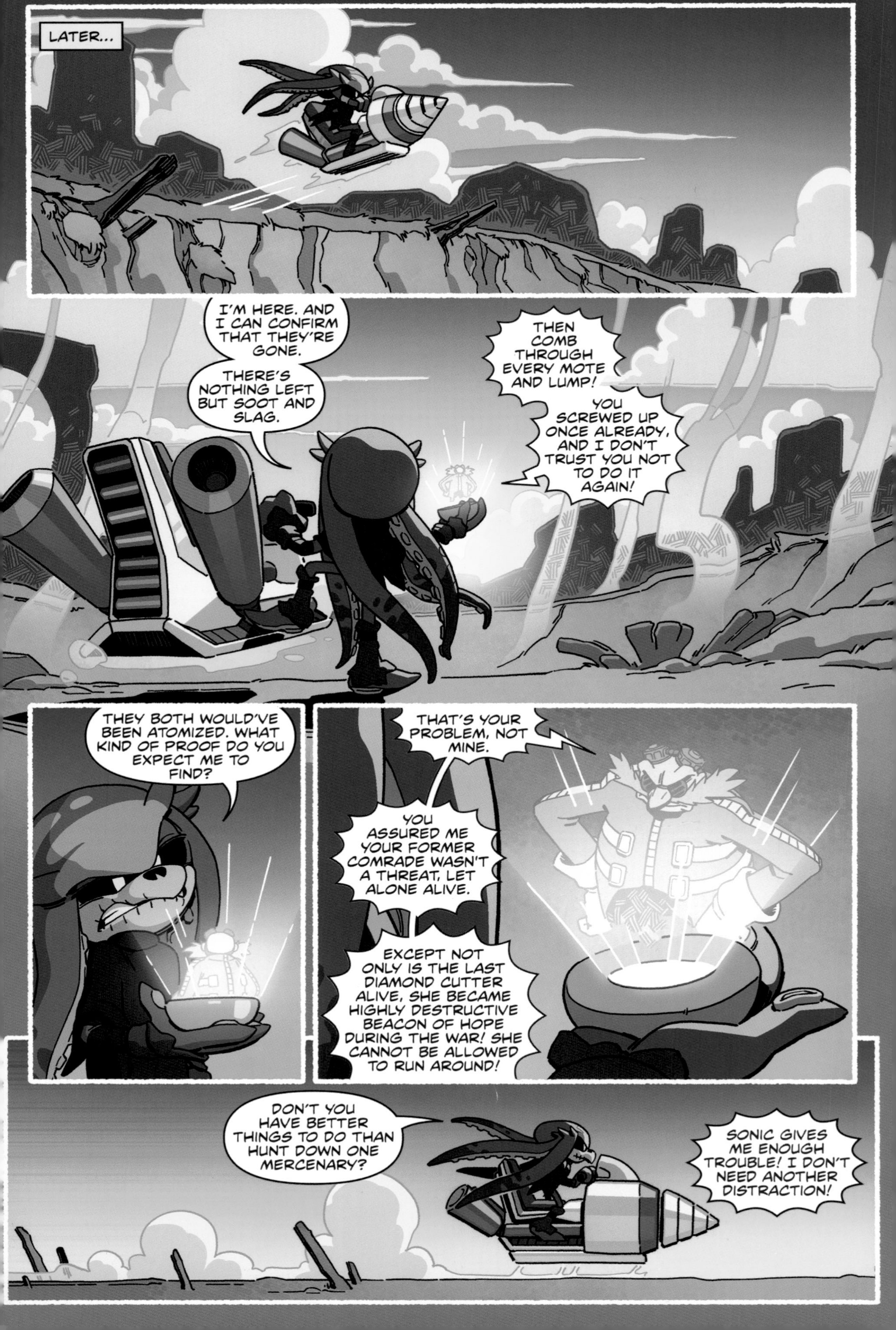
LATER...
I'M HERE. AND I CAN CONFIRM THAT THEY'RE GONE.
THERE'S NOTHING LEFT BUT SOOT AND SLAG.
THEN COMB THROUGH EVERY MOTE AND LUMP!
YOU SCREWED UP ONCE ALREADY, AND I DON'T TRUST YOU NOT TO DO IT AGAIN!
THEY BOTH WOULD'VE BEEN ATOMIZED. WHAT KIND OF PROOF DO YOU EXPECT ME TO FIND?
THAT'S YOUR PROBLEM, NOT MINE.
YOU ASSURED ME YOUR FORMER COMRADE WASN'T A THREAT, LET ALONE ALIVE.
EXCEPT NOT ONLY IS THE LAST DIAMOND CUTTER ALIVE, SHE BECAME HIGHLY DESTRUCTIVE BEACON OF HOPE DURING THE WAR! SHE CANNOT BE ALLOWED TO RUN AROUND!
DON'T YOU HAVE BETTER THINGS TO DO THAN HUNT DOWN ONE MERCENARY?
SONIC GIVES ME ENOUGH TROUBLE! I DON'T NEED ANOTHER DISTRACTION!

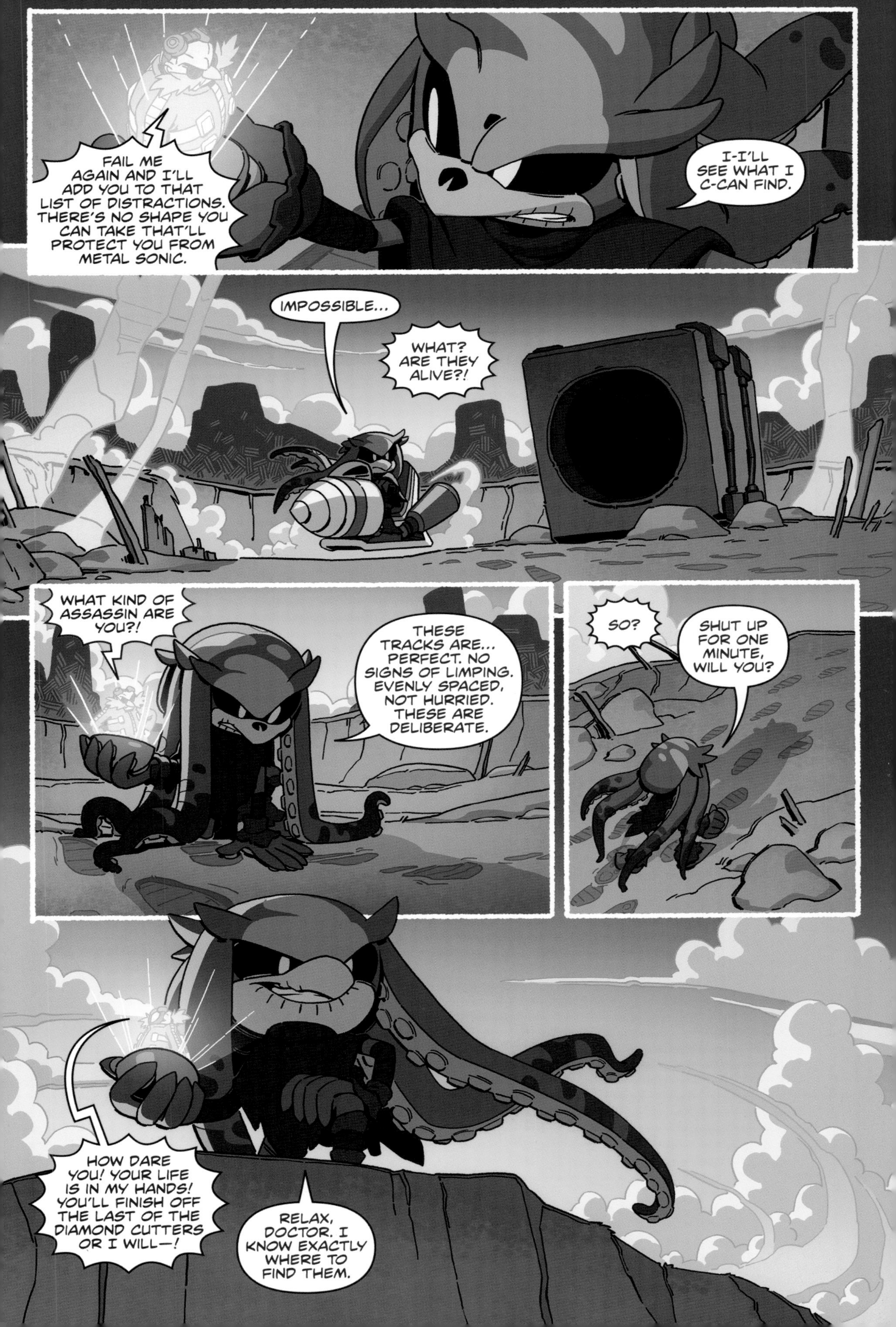
FAIL ME AGAIN AND I'LL ADD YOU TO THAT LIST OF DISTRACTIONS. THERE'S NO SHAPE YOU CAN TAKE THAT'LL PROTECT YOU FROM METAL SONIC.
I-I'LL SEE WHAT I C-CAN FIND.
IMPOSSIBLE...
WHAT? ARE THEY ALIVE?!
WHAT KIND OF ASSASSIN ARE YOU?!
THESE TRACKS ARE... PERFECT. NO SIGNS OF LIMPING. EVENLY SPACED, NOT HURRIED. THESE ARE DELIBERATE.
SO?
SHUT UP FOR ONE MINUTE, WILL YOU?
HOW DARE YOU! YOUR LIFE IS IN MY HANDS! YOU'LL FINISH OFF THE LAST OF THE DIAMOND CUTTERS OR I WILL—!
RELAX, DOCTOR. I KNOW EXACTLY WHERE TO FIND THEM.

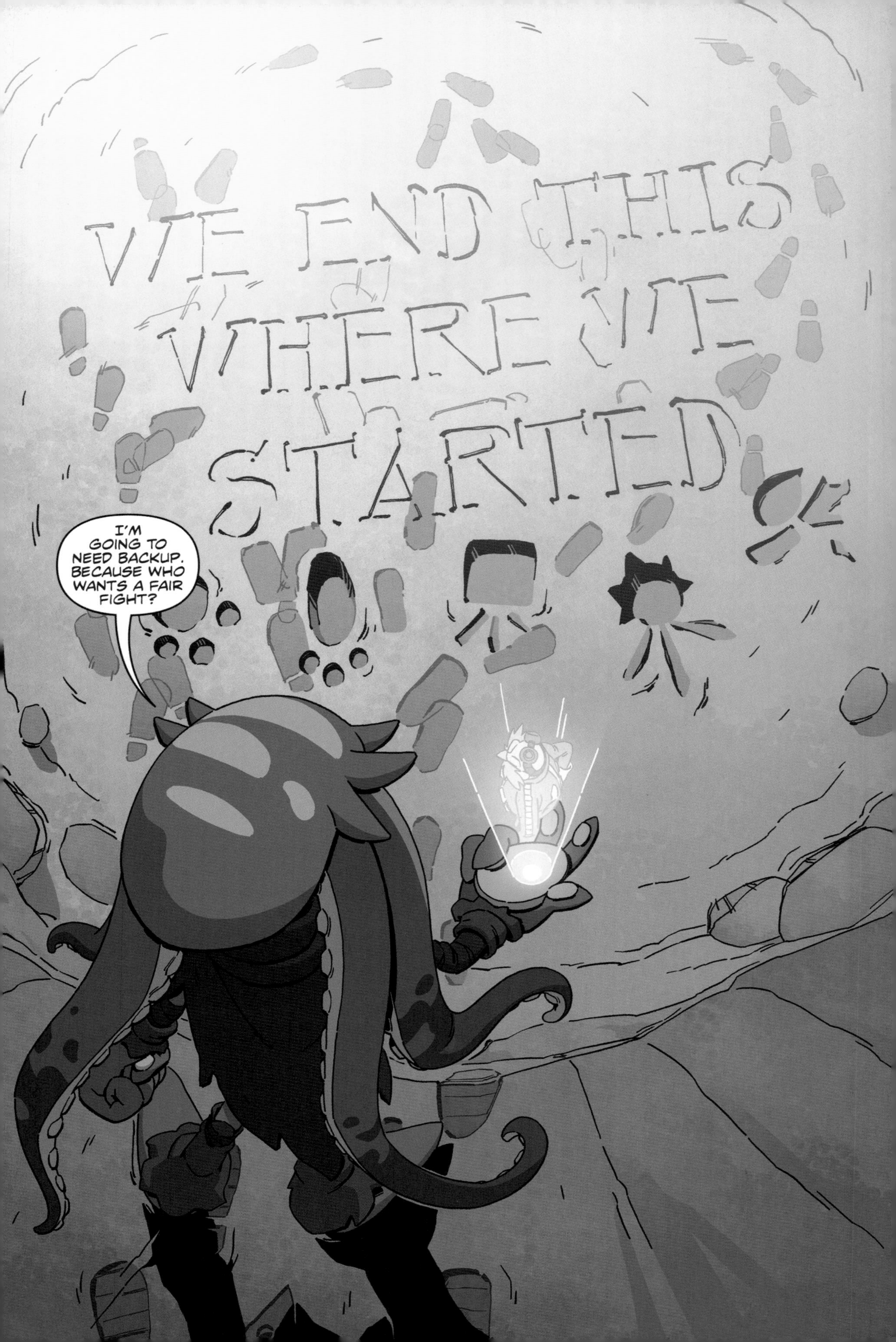
WE END THIS WHERE WE STARTED
I'M GOING TO NEED BACKUP. BECAUSE WHO WANTS A FAIR FIGHT?

ART BY NATHALIE FOURDRAINE

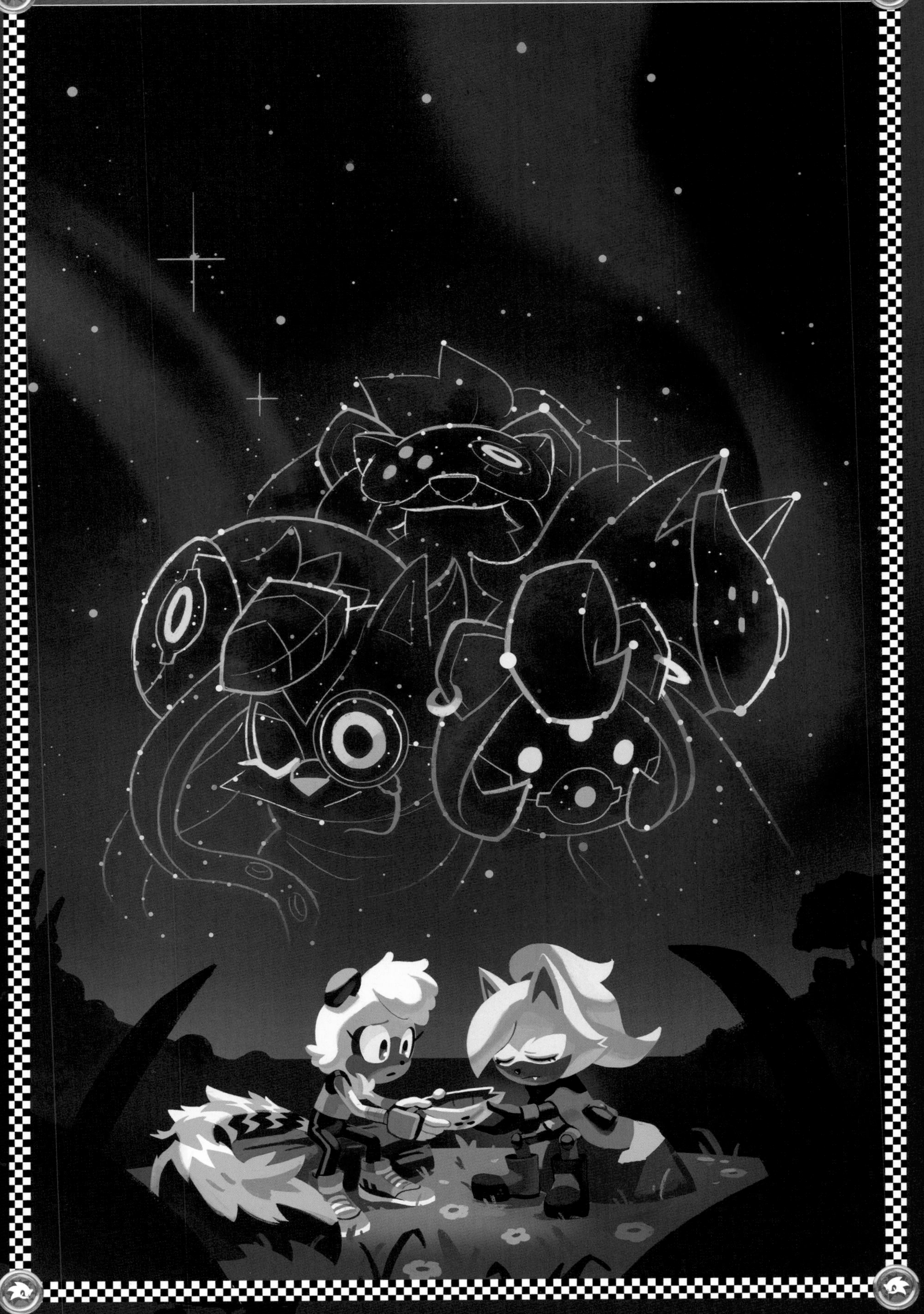

ART BY EVAN STANLEY

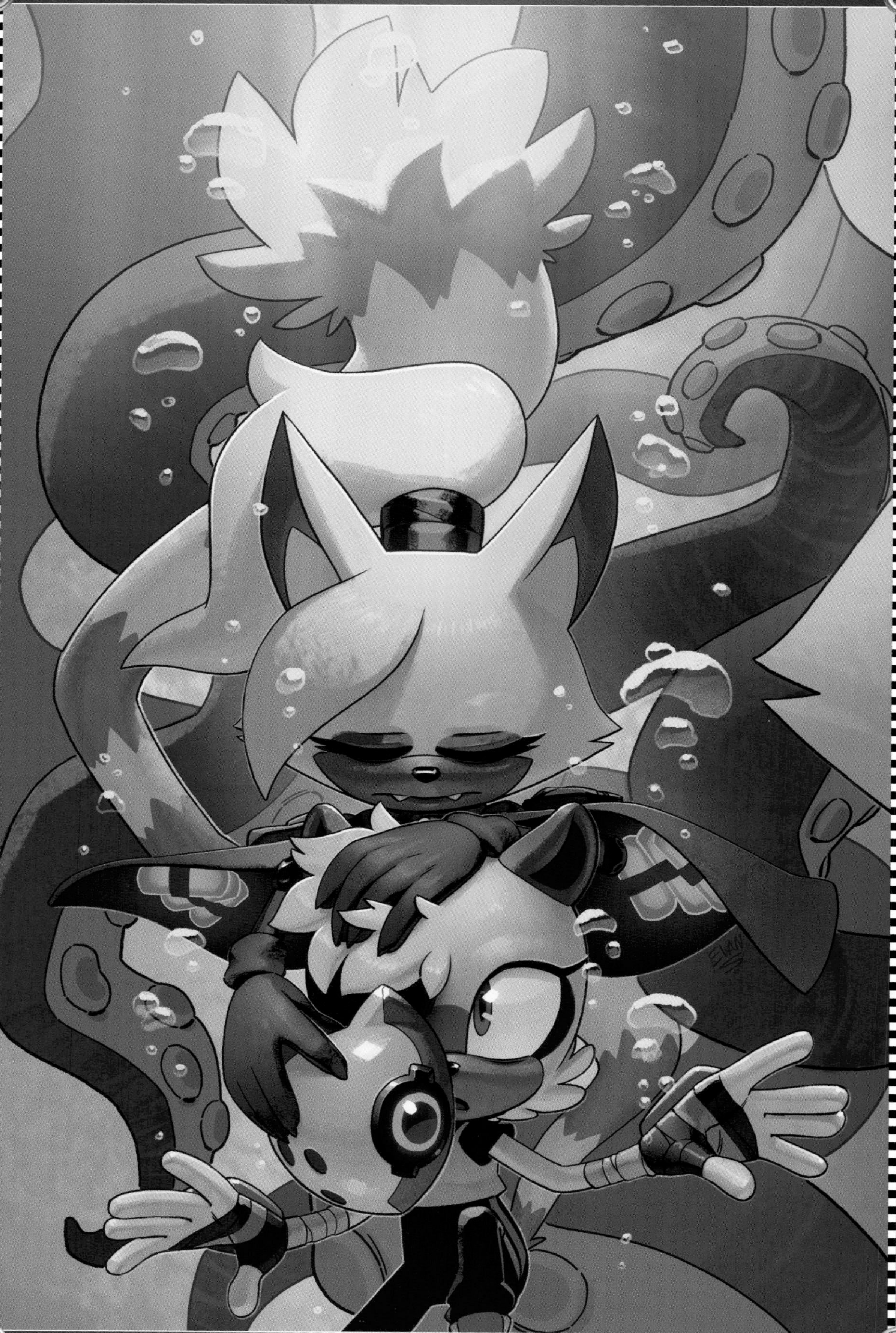

TANGLE & WHISPER #4

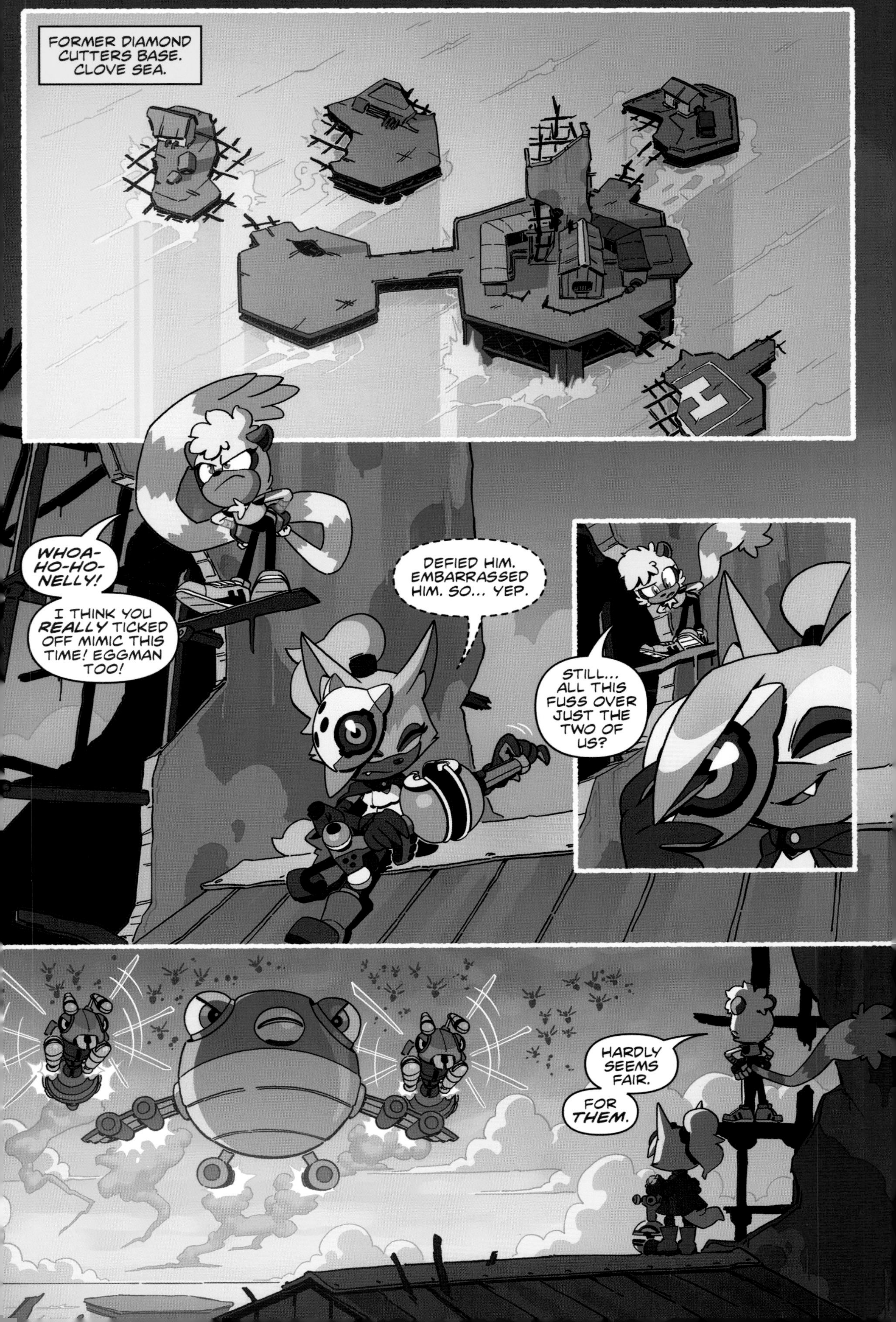
FORMER DIAMOND CUTTERS BASE. CLOVE SEA.
WHOA-HO-HO-NELLY!
I THINK YOU *REALLY* TICKED OFF MIMIC THIS TIME! EGGMAN TOO!
DEFIED HIM. EMBARRASSED HIM. SO... YEP.
STILL... ALL THIS FUSS OVER JUST THE TWO OF US?
HARDLY SEEMS FAIR.
FOR *THEM*.

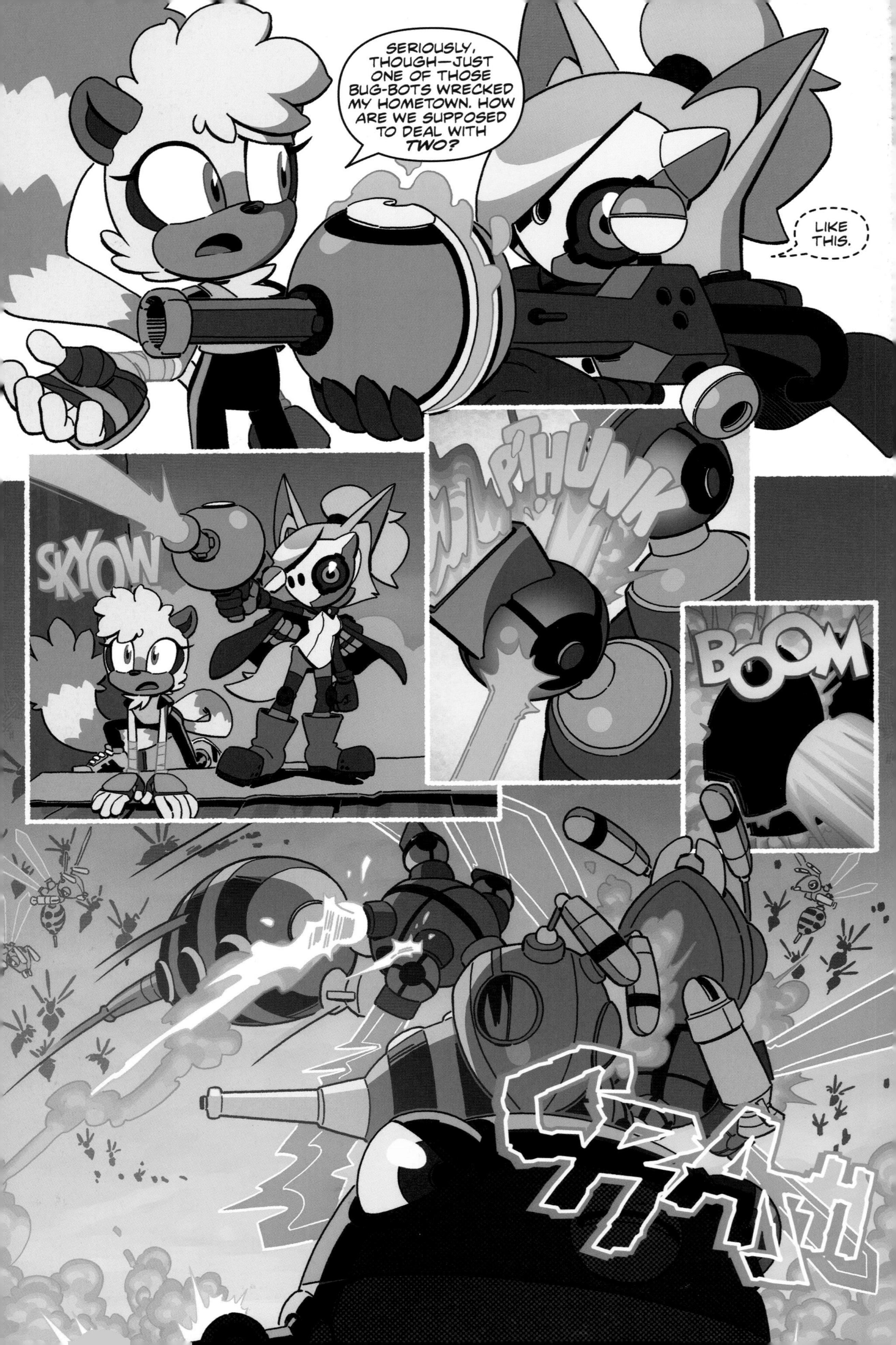
SERIOUSLY, THOUGH—JUST ONE OF THOSE BUG-BOTS WRECKED MY HOMETOWN. HOW ARE WE SUPPOSED TO DEAL WITH *TWO?*
LIKE THIS.
SKYOW
P'THUNK
BOOM

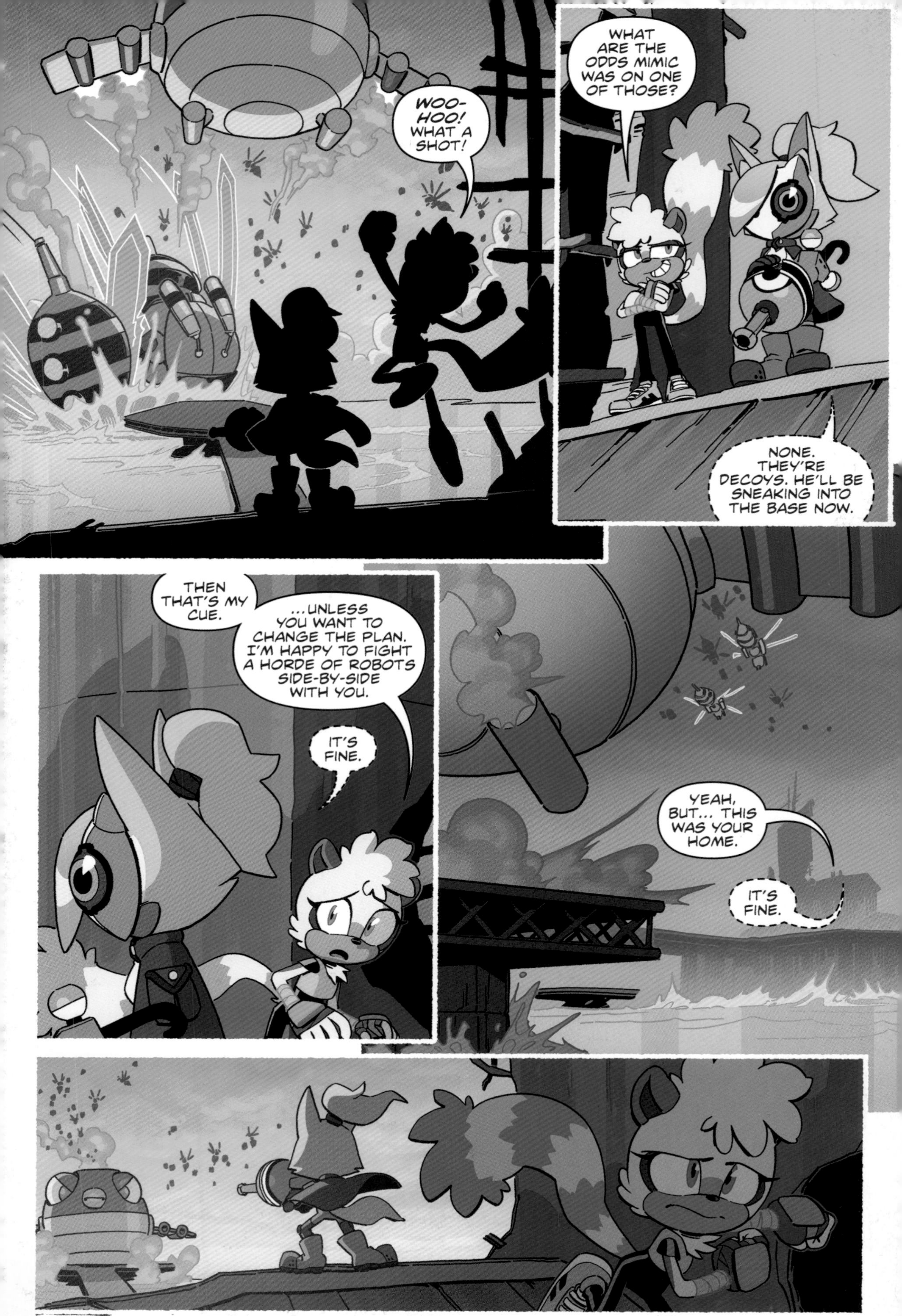
WOO-HOO! WHAT A SHOT!
WHAT ARE THE ODDS MIMIC WAS ON ONE OF THOSE?
NONE. THEY'RE DECOYS. HE'LL BE SNEAKING INTO THE BASE NOW.
THEN THAT'S MY CUE.
...UNLESS YOU WANT TO CHANGE THE PLAN. I'M HAPPY TO FIGHT A HORDE OF ROBOTS SIDE-BY-SIDE WITH YOU.
IT'S FINE.
YEAH, BUT... THIS WAS YOUR HOME.
IT'S FINE.

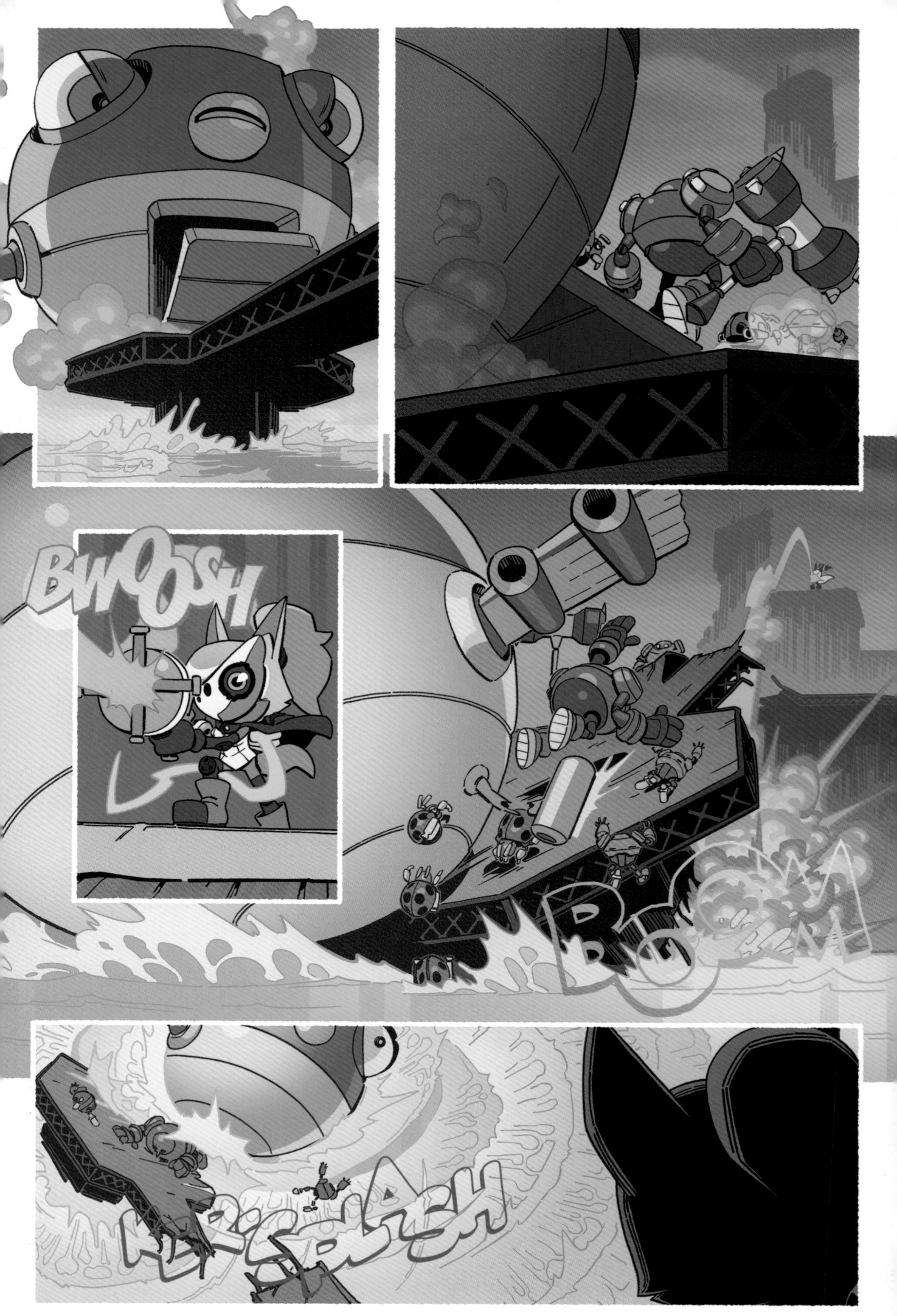
BWOOSH
BOOM
KRASPLASH

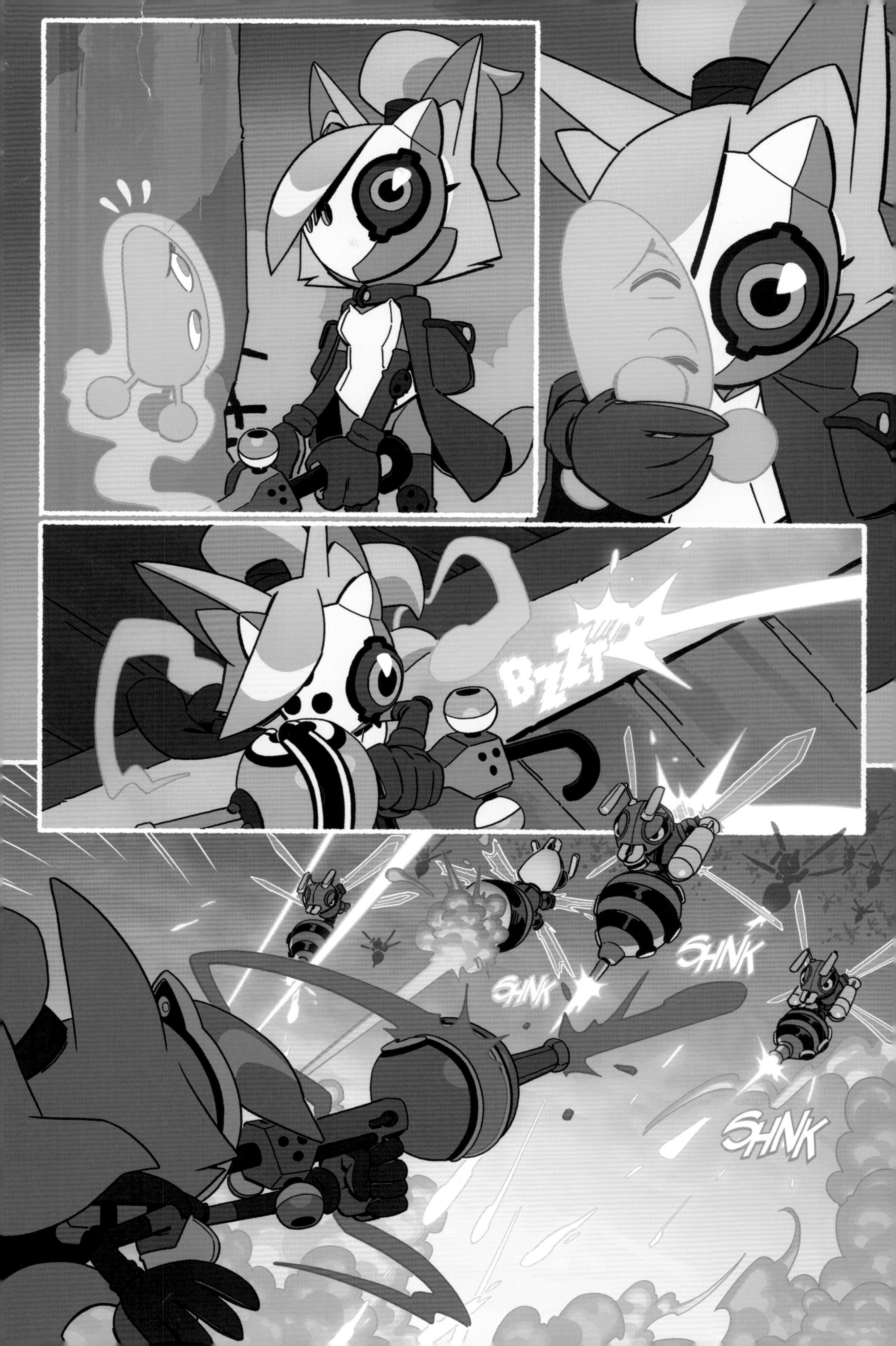
BZZZT
SHNK
SHNK
SHNK

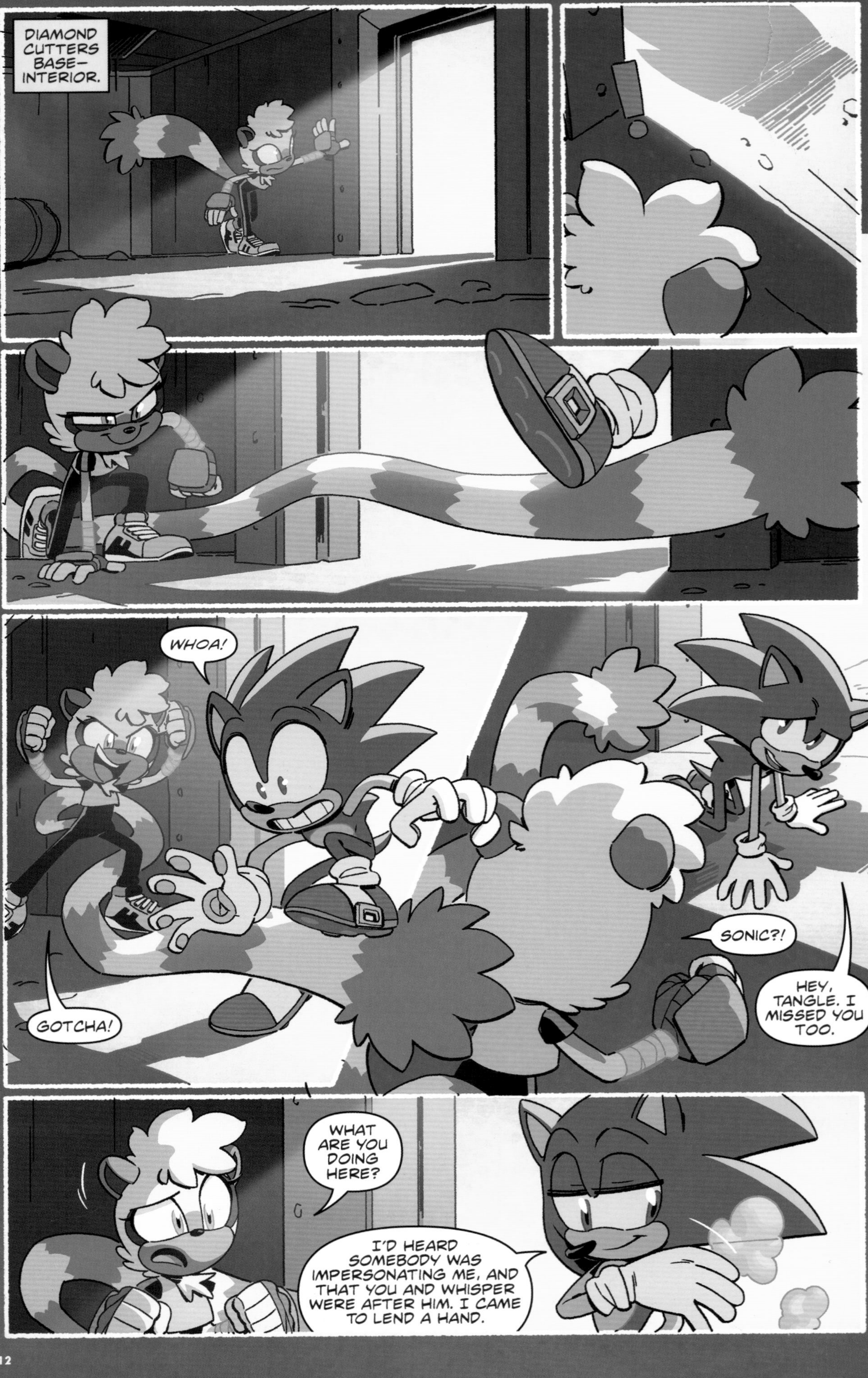
DIAMOND CUTTERS BASE— INTERIOR.
WHOA!
GOTCHA!
SONIC?!
HEY, TANGLE. I MISSED YOU TOO.
WHAT ARE YOU DOING HERE?
I'D HEARD SOMEBODY WAS IMPERSONATING ME, AND THAT YOU AND WHISPER WERE AFTER HIM. I CAME TO LEND A HAND.

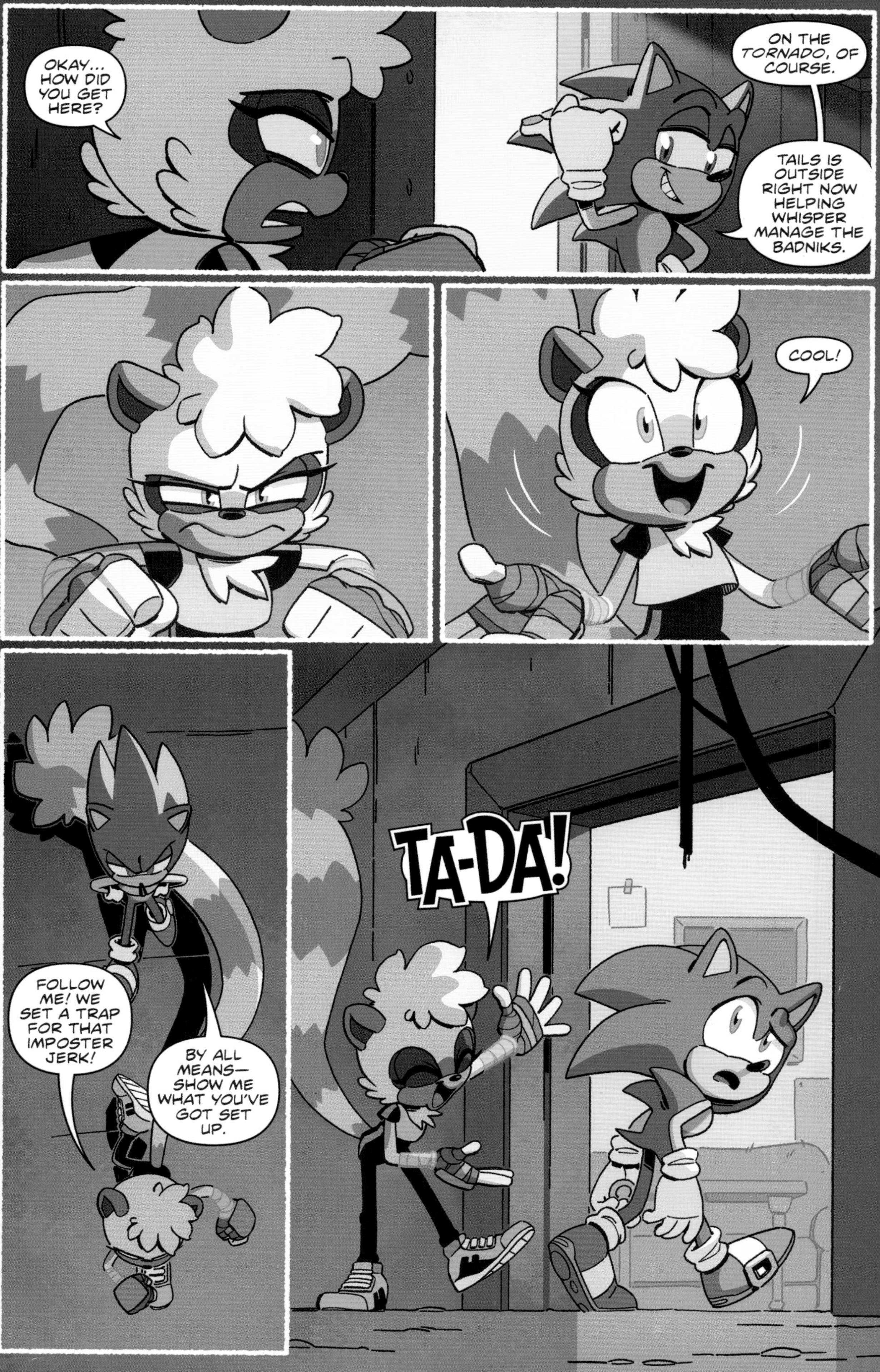
OKAY... HOW DID YOU GET HERE?
ON THE TORNADO, OF COURSE.
TAILS IS OUTSIDE RIGHT NOW HELPING WHISPER MANAGE THE BADNIKS.
COOL!
TA-DA!
FOLLOW ME! WE SET A TRAP FOR THAT IMPOSTER JERK!
BY ALL MEANS— SHOW ME WHAT YOU'VE GOT SET UP.

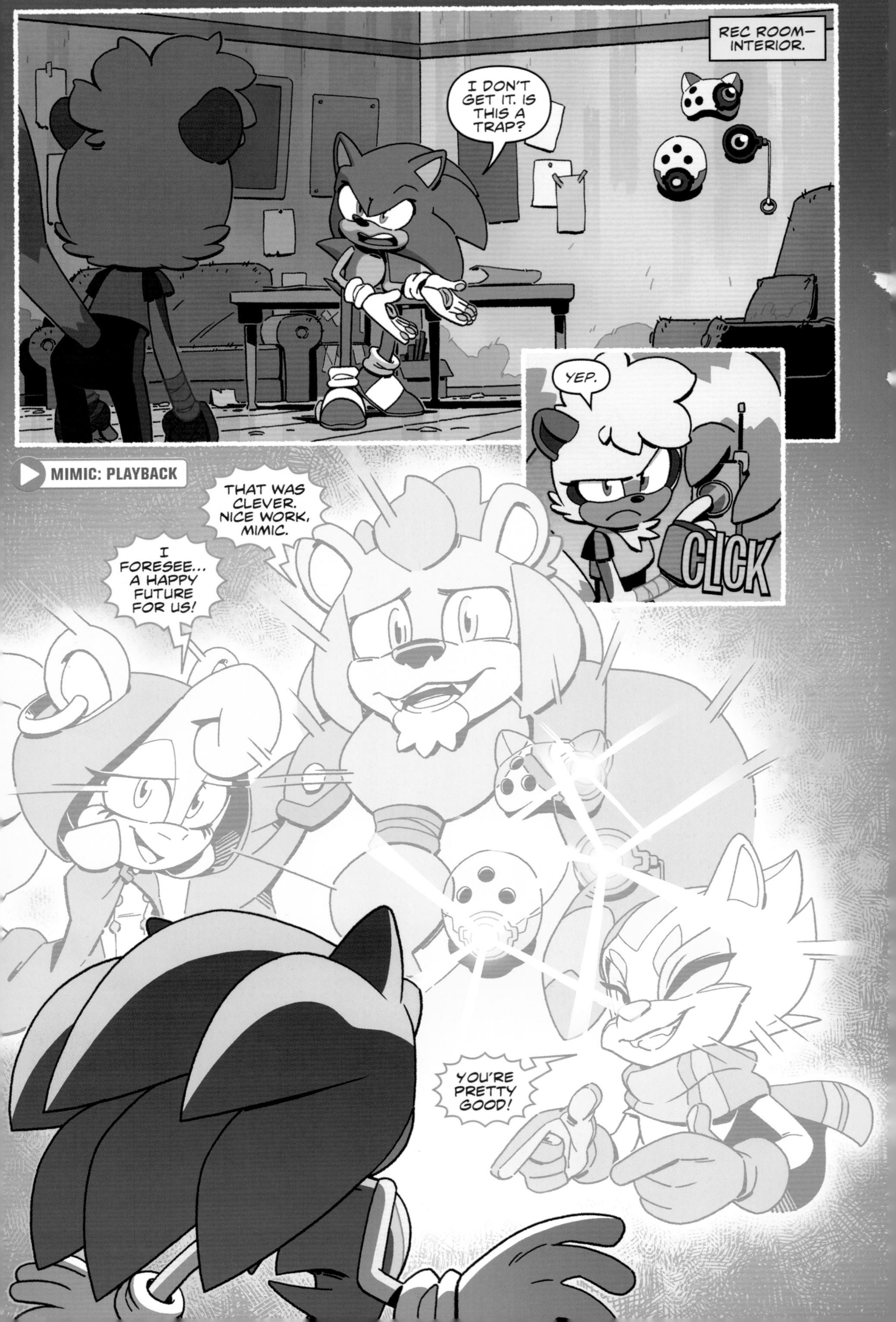
REC ROOM—
INTERIOR.
I DON'T GET IT. IS THIS A TRAP?
YEP.
CLICK
MIMIC: PLAYBACK
THAT WAS CLEVER. NICE WORK, MIMIC.
I FORESEE... A HAPPY FUTURE FOR US!
YOU'RE PRETTY GOOD!

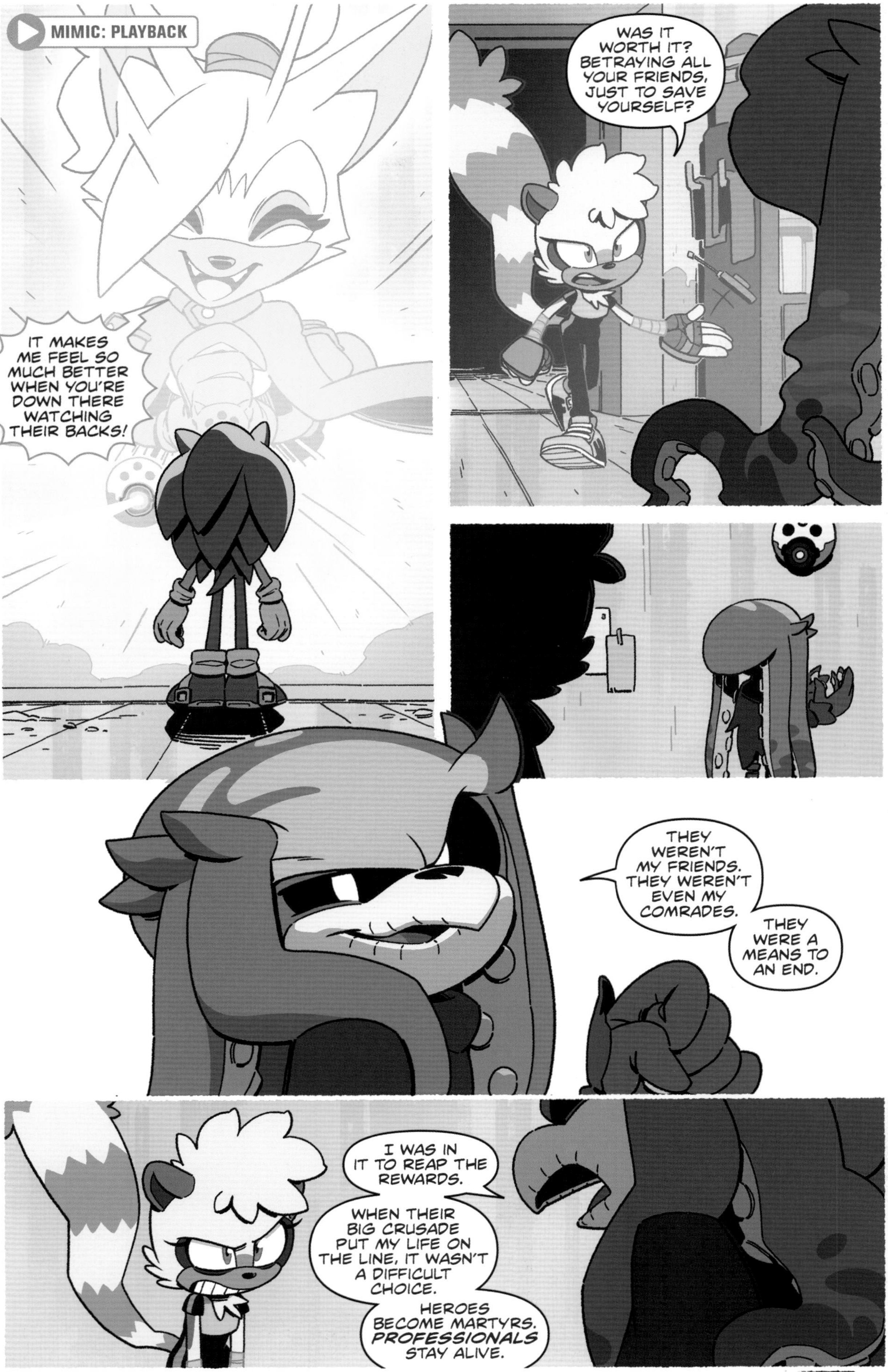
MIMIC: PLAYBACK
IT MAKES ME FEEL SO MUCH BETTER WHEN YOU'RE DOWN THERE WATCHING THEIR BACKS!
WAS IT WORTH IT? BETRAYING ALL YOUR FRIENDS, JUST TO SAVE YOURSELF?
THEY WEREN'T MY FRIENDS. THEY WEREN'T EVEN MY COMRADES.
THEY WERE A MEANS TO AN END.
I WAS IN IT TO REAP THE REWARDS.
WHEN THEIR BIG CRUSADE PUT MY LIFE ON THE LINE, IT WASN'T A DIFFICULT CHOICE.
HEROES BECOME MARTYRS. *PROFESSIONALS* STAY ALIVE.

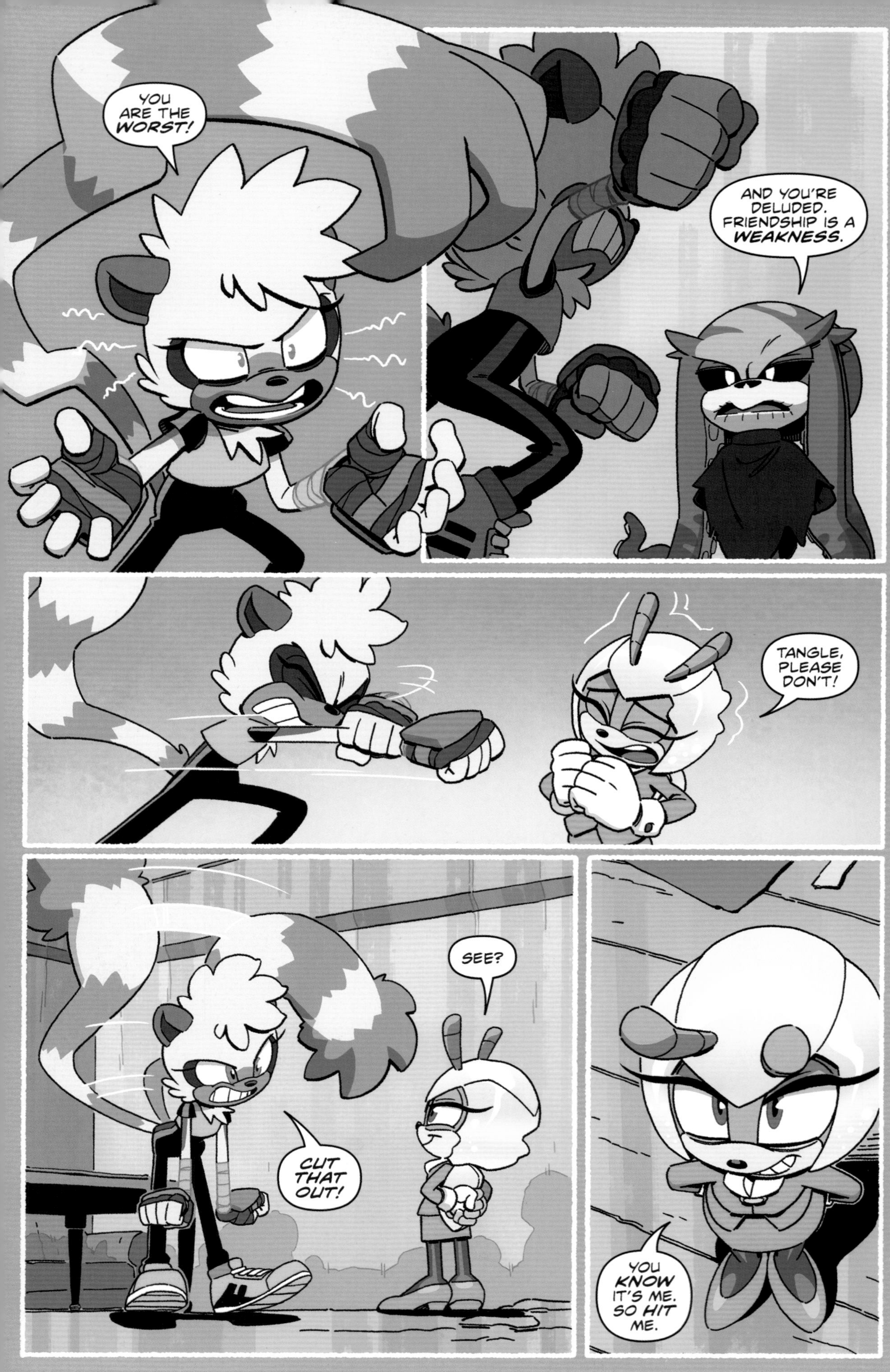
YOU ARE THE WORST!
AND YOU'RE DELUDED. FRIENDSHIP IS A WEAKNESS.
TANGLE, PLEASE DON'T!
SEE?
CUT THAT OUT!
YOU KNOW IT'S ME. SO HIT ME.

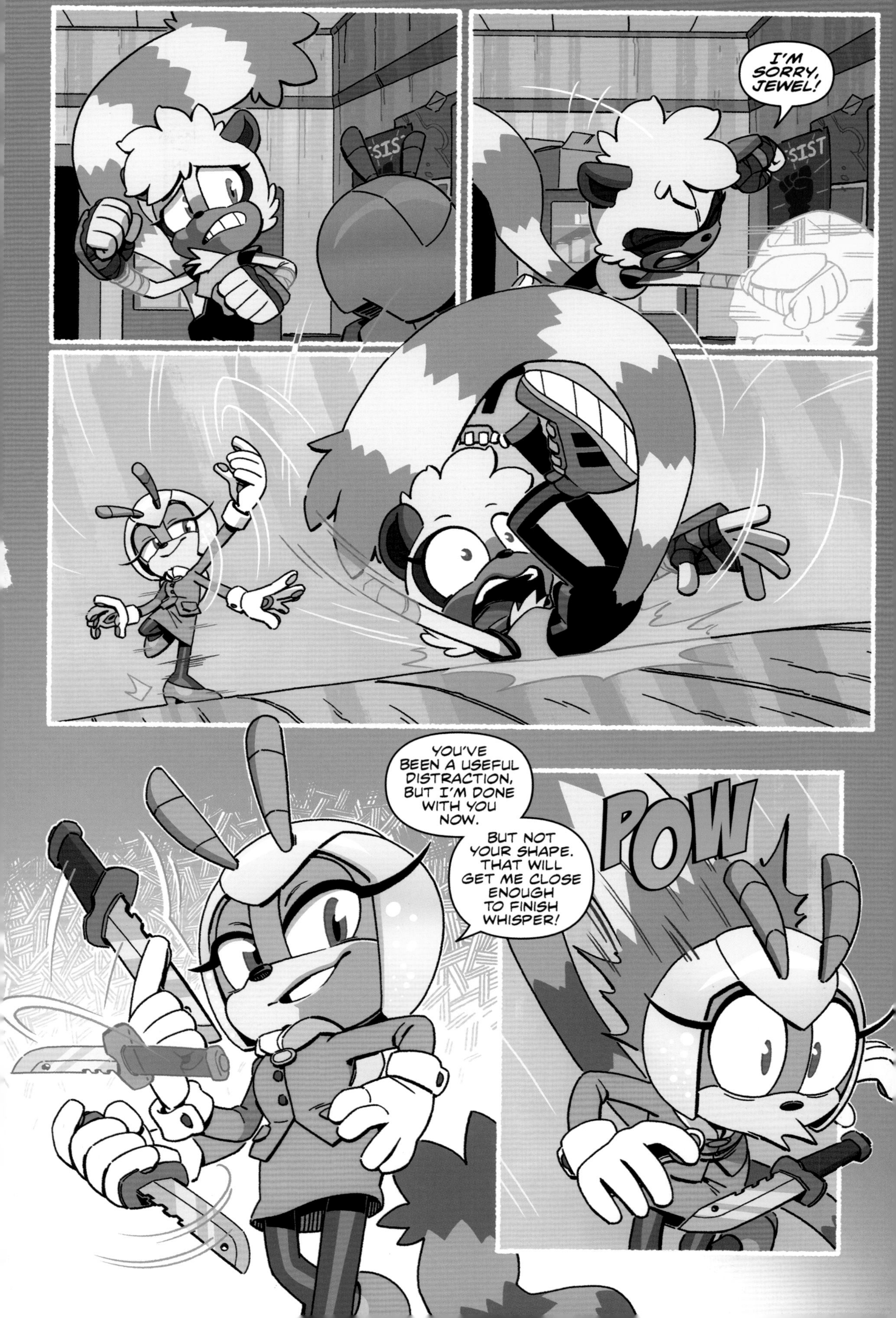
SIST
I'M SORRY, JEWEL!
SIST
YOU'VE BEEN A USEFUL DISTRACTION, BUT I'M DONE WITH YOU NOW.
BUT NOT YOUR SHAPE. THAT WILL GET ME CLOSE ENOUGH TO FINISH WHISPER!
POW

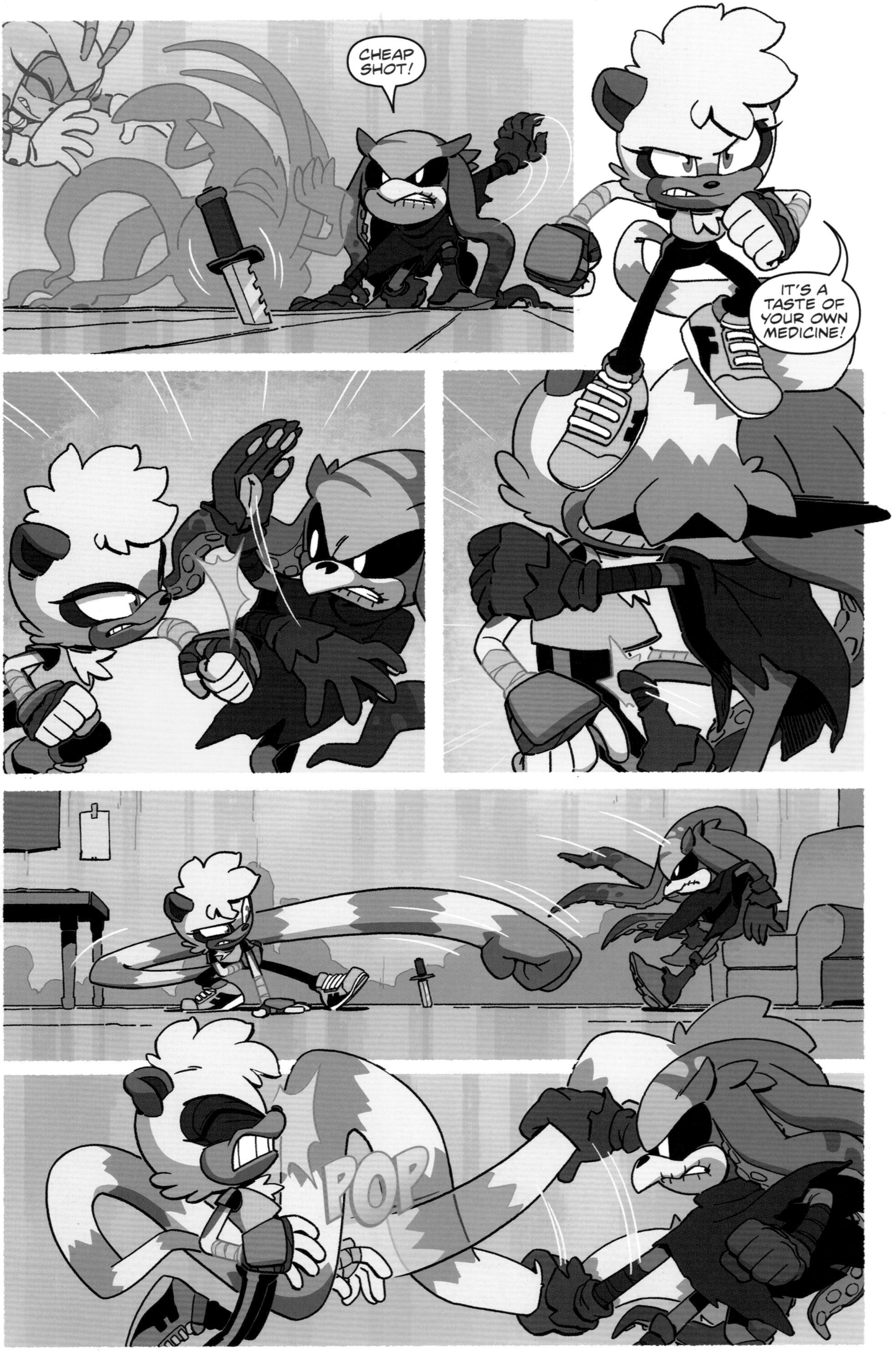
CHEAP SHOT!
IT'S A TASTE OF YOUR OWN MEDICINE!
POP

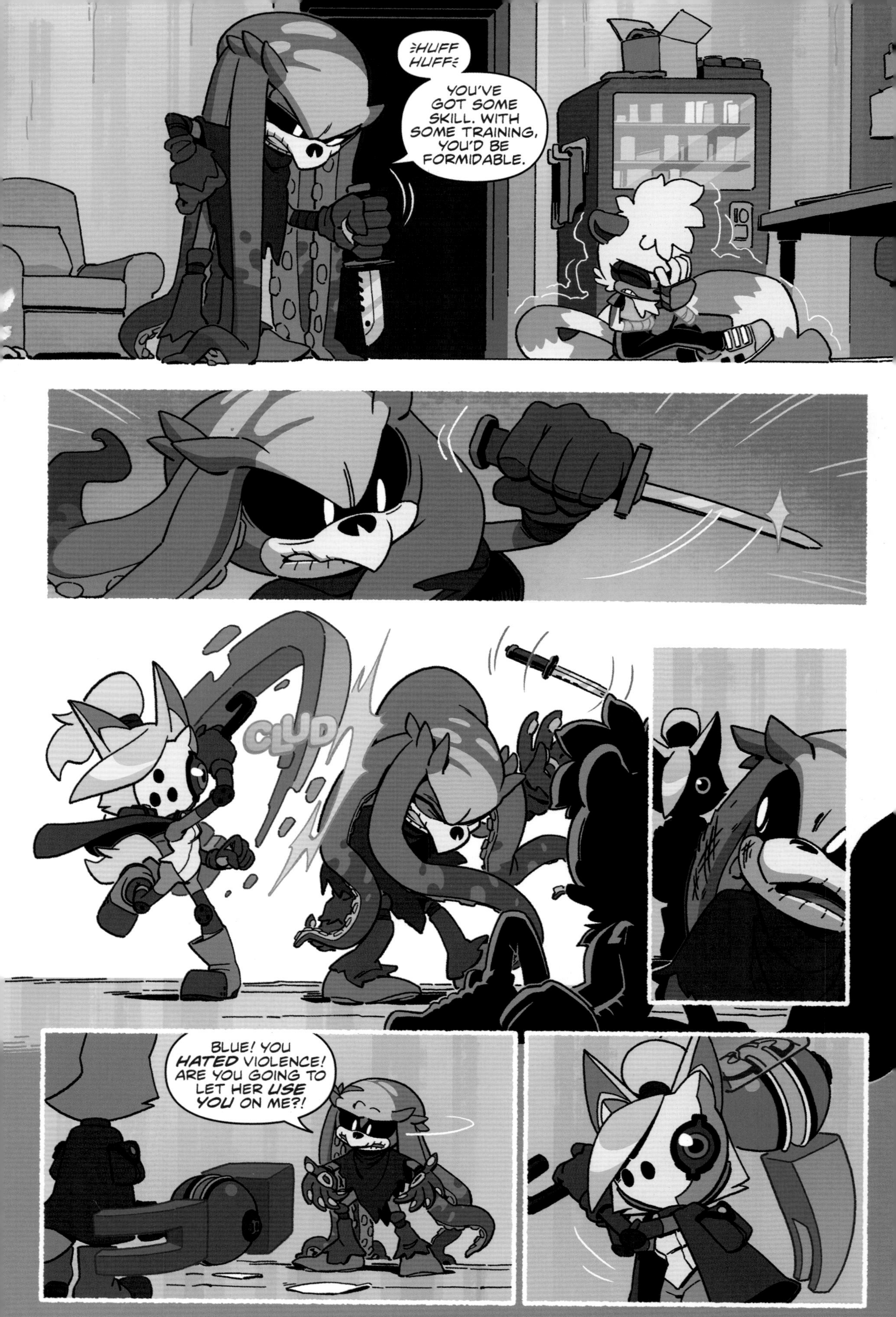

HUFF HUFF
YOU'VE GOT SOME SKILL. WITH SOME TRAINING, YOU'D BE FORMIDABLE.
CLUD
BLUE! YOU HATED VIOLENCE! ARE YOU GOING TO LET HER USE YOU ON ME?!

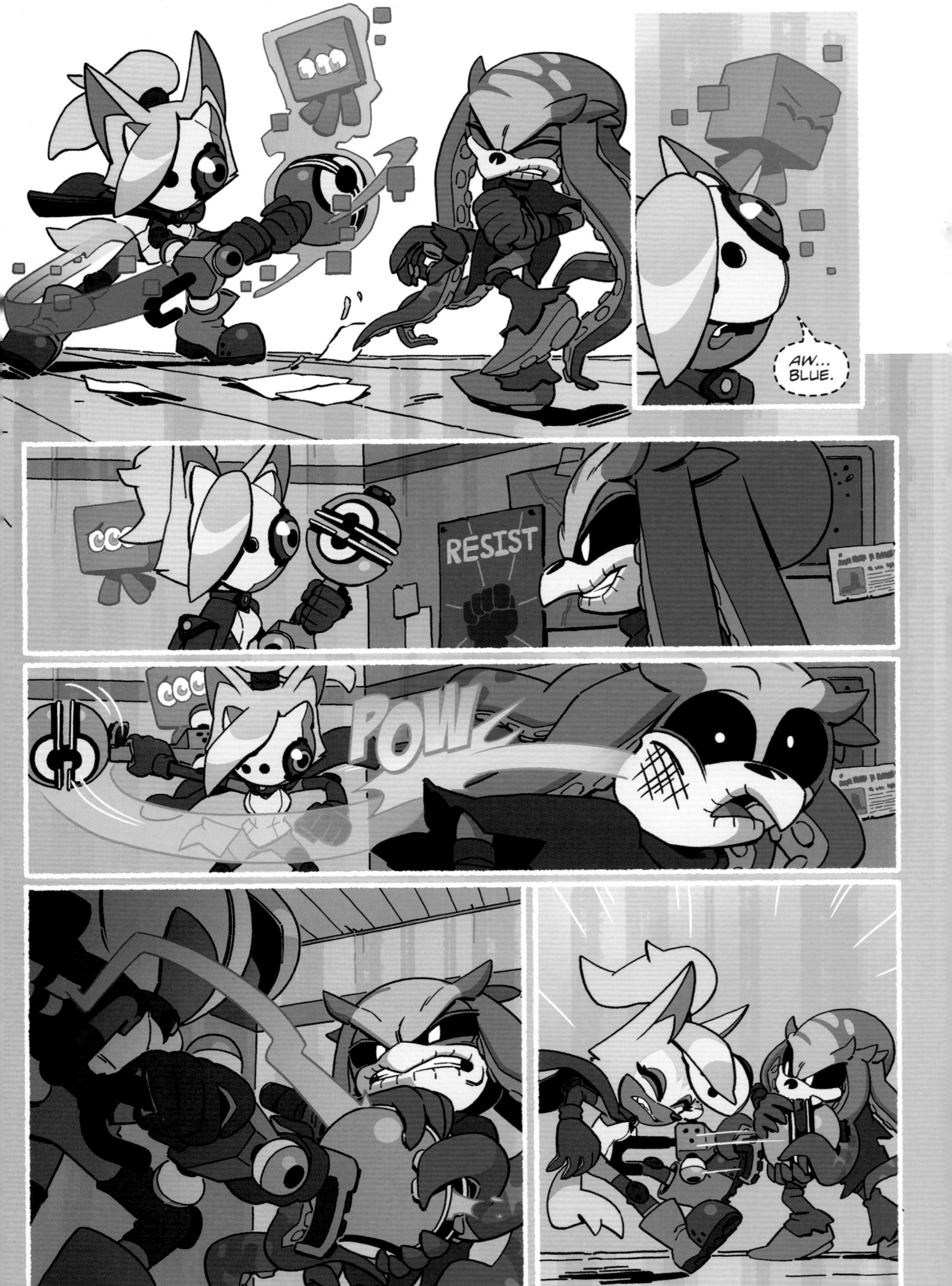
AW... BLUE.
RESIST
POW

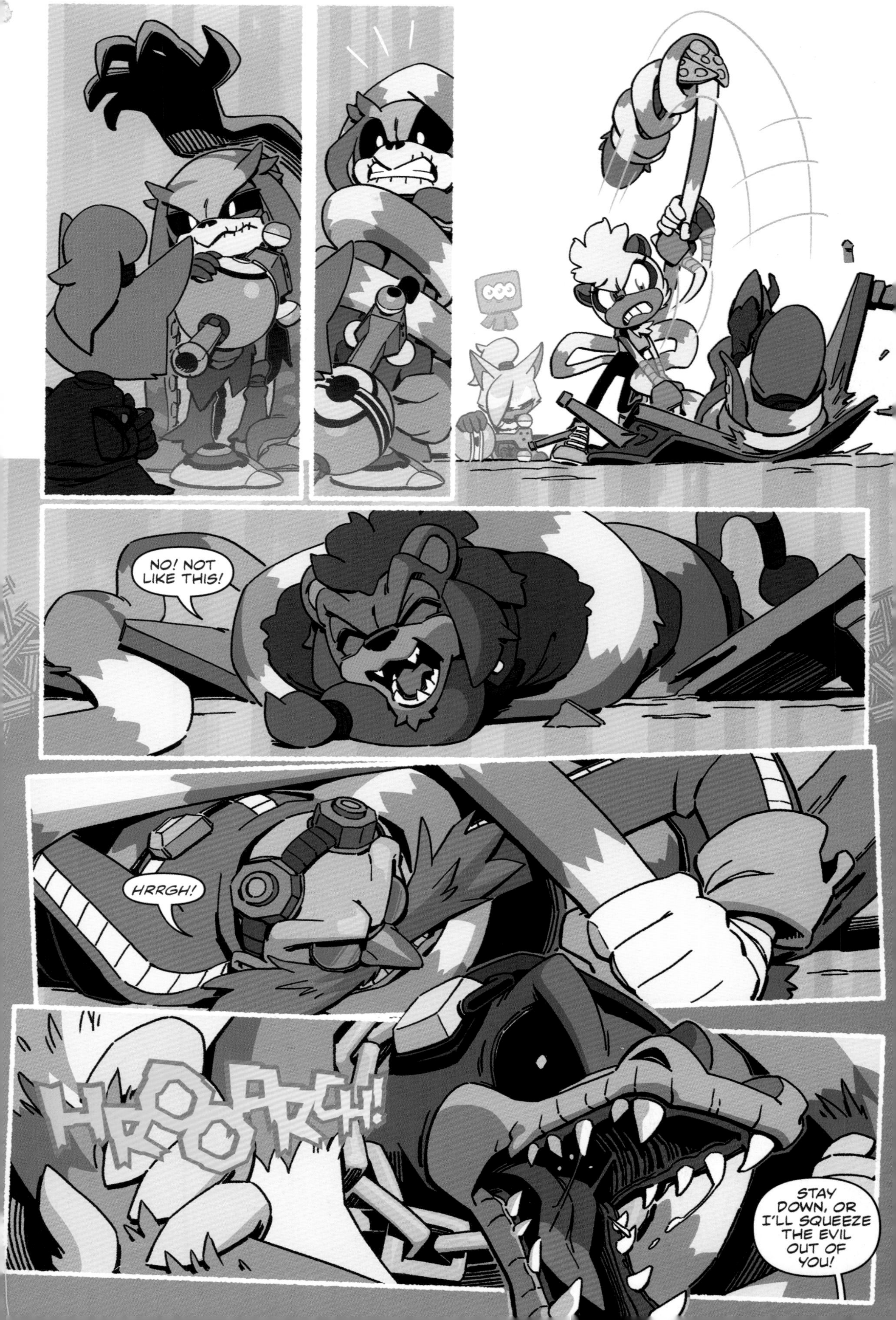
NO! NOT LIKE THIS!
HRRGH!
HROOARGH!
STAY DOWN, OR I'LL SQUEEZE THE EVIL OUT OF YOU!

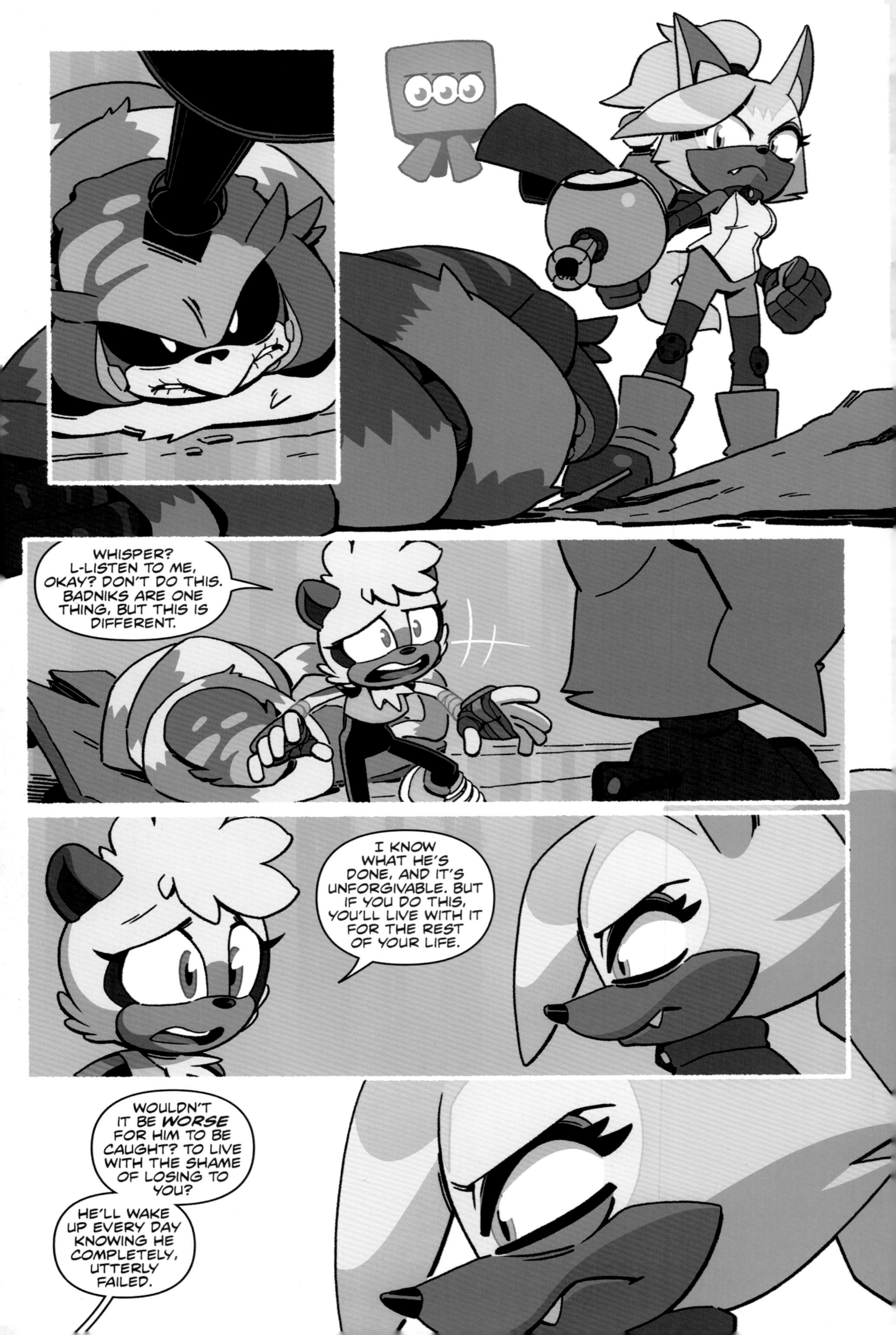
WHISPER? L-LISTEN TO ME, OKAY? DON'T DO THIS. BADNIKS ARE ONE THING, BUT THIS IS DIFFERENT.
I KNOW WHAT HE'S DONE, AND IT'S UNFORGIVABLE. BUT IF YOU DO THIS, YOU'LL LIVE WITH IT FOR THE REST OF YOUR LIFE.
WOULDN'T IT BE *WORSE* FOR HIM TO BE CAUGHT? TO LIVE WITH THE SHAME OF LOSING TO YOU?
HE'LL WAKE UP EVERY DAY KNOWING HE COMPLETELY, UTTERLY FAILED.

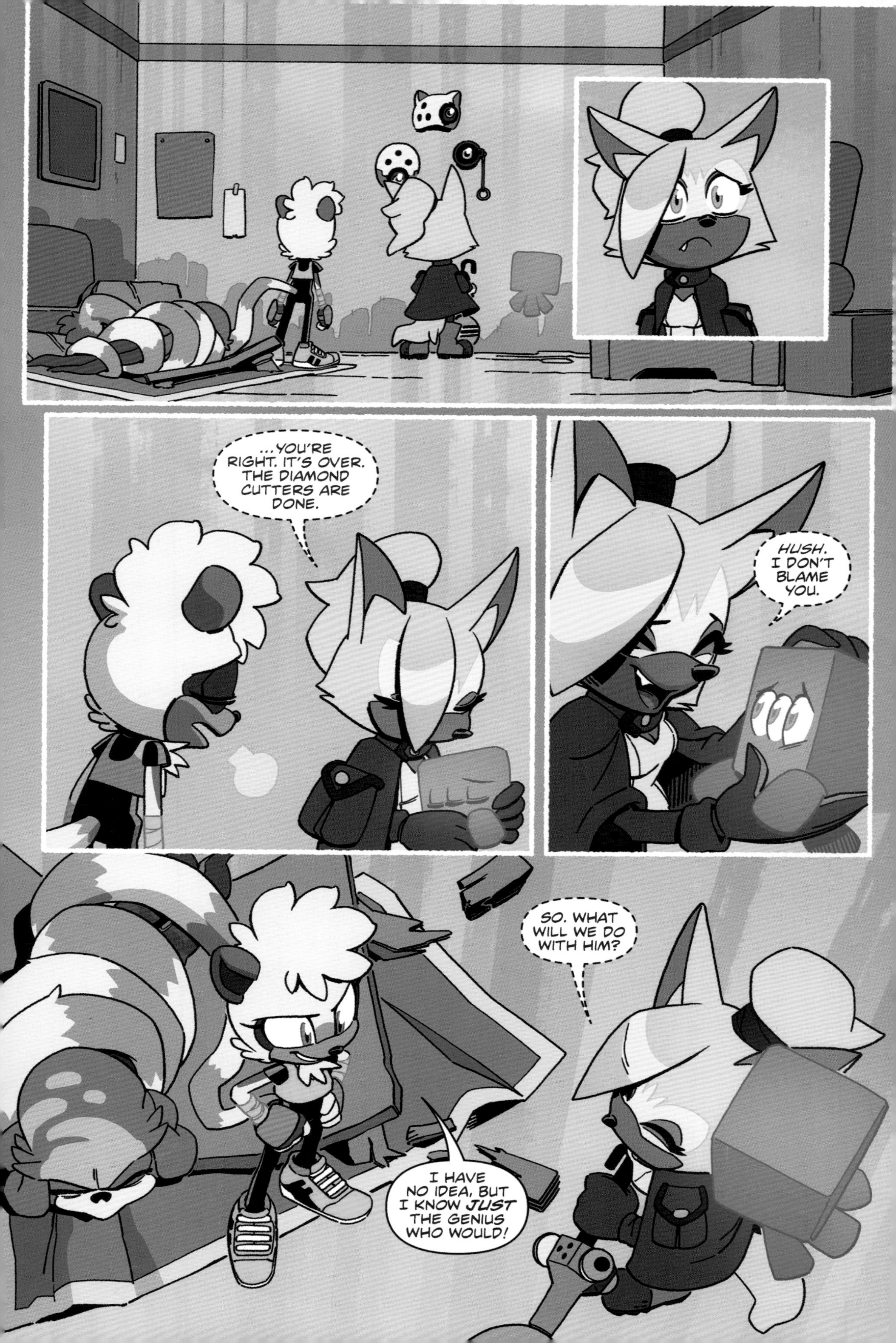
...YOU'RE RIGHT. IT'S OVER. THE DIAMOND CUTTERS ARE DONE.
HUSH. I DON'T BLAME YOU.
SO. WHAT WILL WE DO WITH HIM?
I HAVE NO IDEA, BUT I KNOW JUST THE GENIUS WHO WOULD!

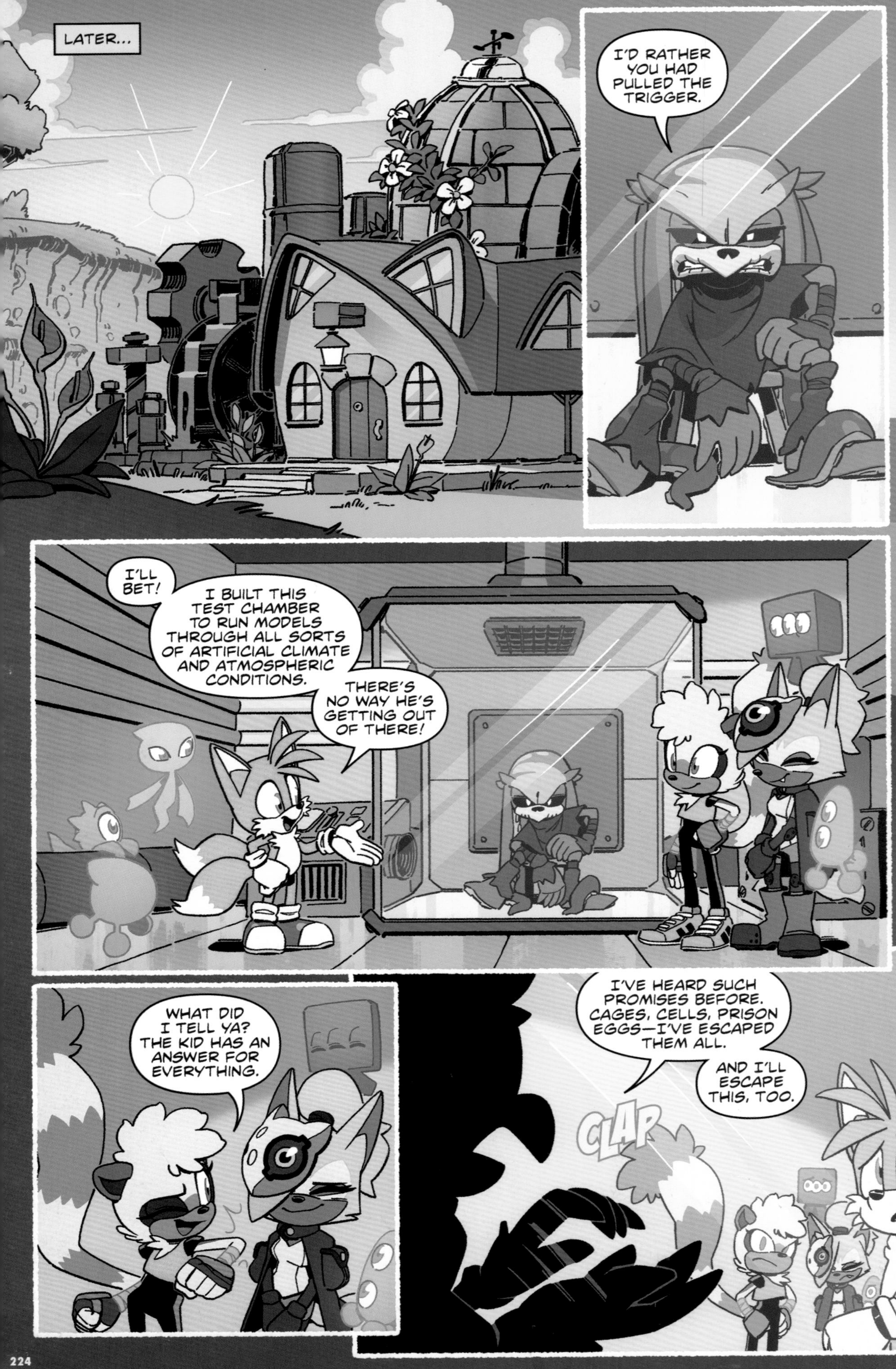
LATER...
I'D RATHER YOU HAD PULLED THE TRIGGER.
I'LL BET!
I BUILT THIS TEST CHAMBER TO RUN MODELS THROUGH ALL SORTS OF ARTIFICIAL CLIMATE AND ATMOSPHERIC CONDITIONS.
THERE'S NO WAY HE'S GETTING OUT OF THERE!
WHAT DID I TELL YA? THE KID HAS AN ANSWER FOR EVERYTHING.
I'VE HEARD SUCH PROMISES BEFORE. CAGES, CELLS, PRISON EGGS—I'VE ESCAPED THEM ALL.
AND I'LL ESCAPE THIS, TOO.
CLAP

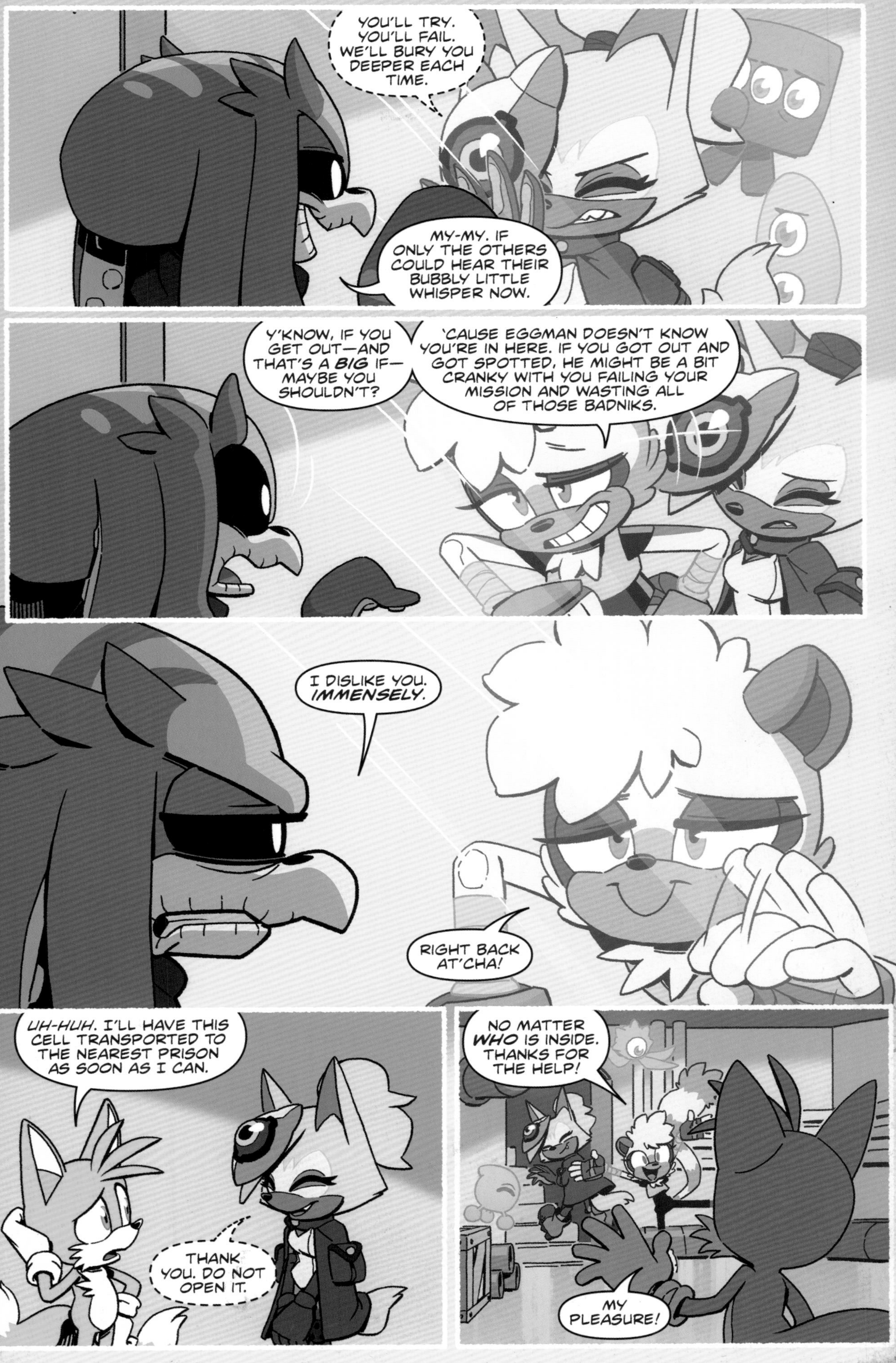
YOU'LL TRY. YOU'LL FAIL. WE'LL BURY YOU DEEPER EACH TIME.
MY-MY. IF ONLY THE OTHERS COULD HEAR THEIR BUBBLY LITTLE WHISPER NOW.
Y'KNOW, IF YOU GET OUT—AND THAT'S A *BIG* IF—MAYBE YOU SHOULDN'T?
'CAUSE EGGMAN DOESN'T KNOW YOU'RE IN HERE. IF YOU GOT OUT AND GOT SPOTTED, HE MIGHT BE A BIT CRANKY WITH YOU FAILING YOUR MISSION AND WASTING ALL OF THOSE BADNIKS.
I DISLIKE YOU. ***IMMENSELY***.
RIGHT BACK AT'CHA!
UH-HUH. I'LL HAVE THIS CELL TRANSPORTED TO THE NEAREST PRISON AS SOON AS I CAN.
THANK YOU. DO NOT OPEN IT.
NO MATTER ***WHO*** IS INSIDE. THANKS FOR THE HELP!
MY PLEASURE!

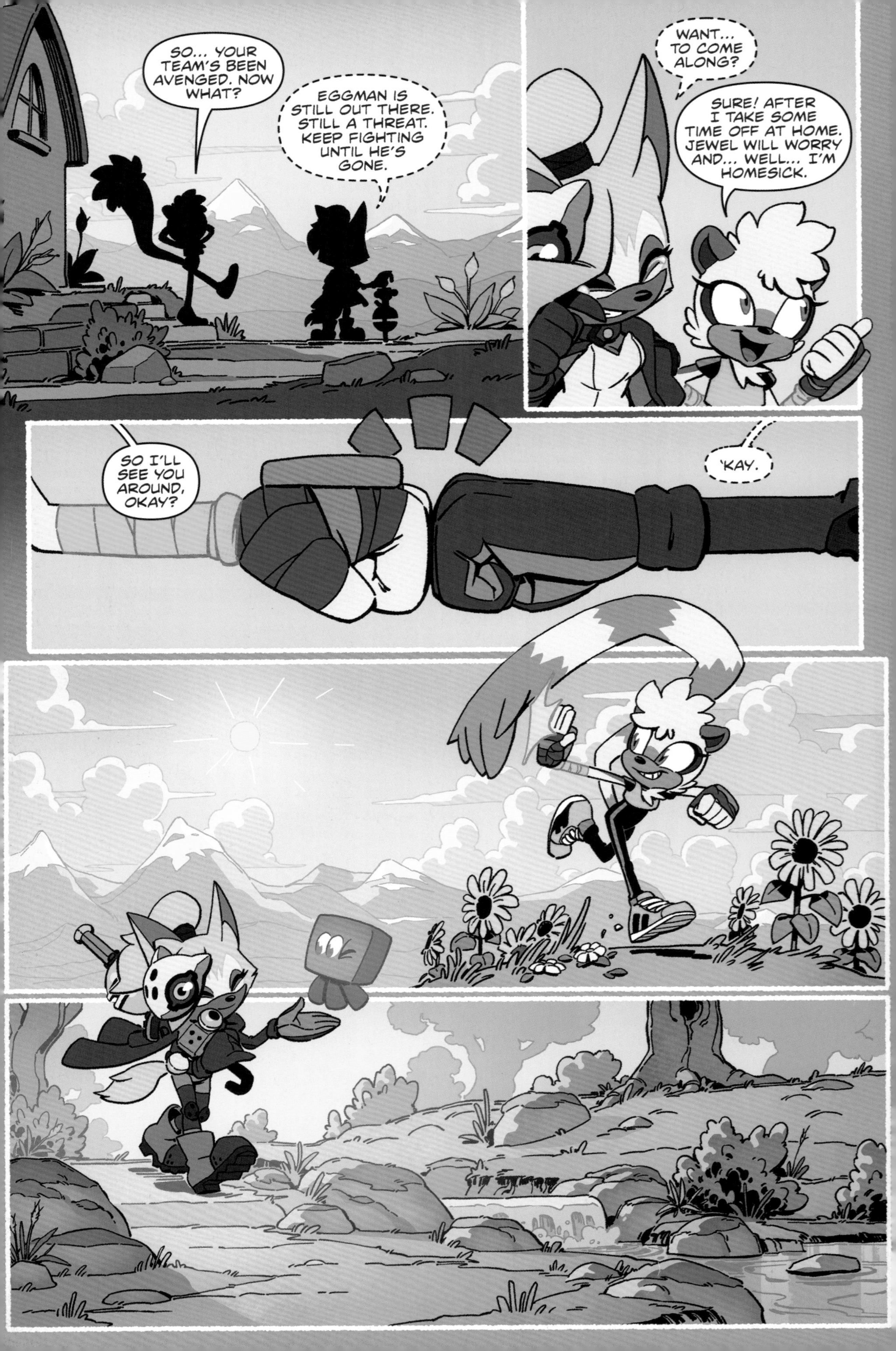
SO... YOUR TEAM'S BEEN AVENGED. NOW WHAT?
EGGMAN IS STILL OUT THERE. STILL A THREAT. KEEP FIGHTING UNTIL HE'S GONE.
WANT... TO COME ALONG?
SURE! AFTER I TAKE SOME TIME OFF AT HOME. JEWEL WILL WORRY AND... WELL... I'M HOMESICK.
SO I'LL SEE YOU AROUND, OKAY?
'KAY.

ART BY NATHALIE FOURDRAINE

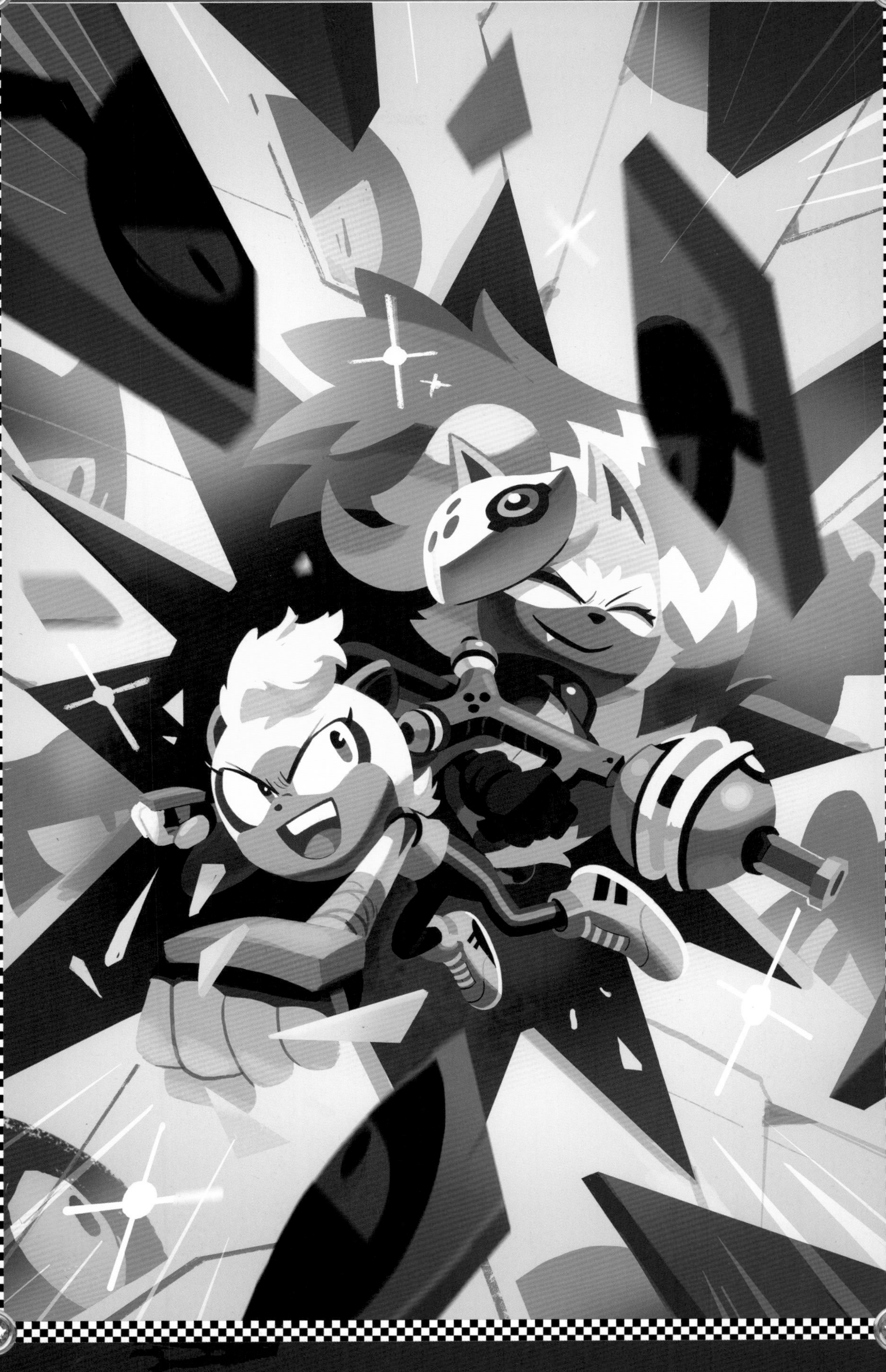

ART BY JACK LAWRENCE COLORS BY MATT HERMS

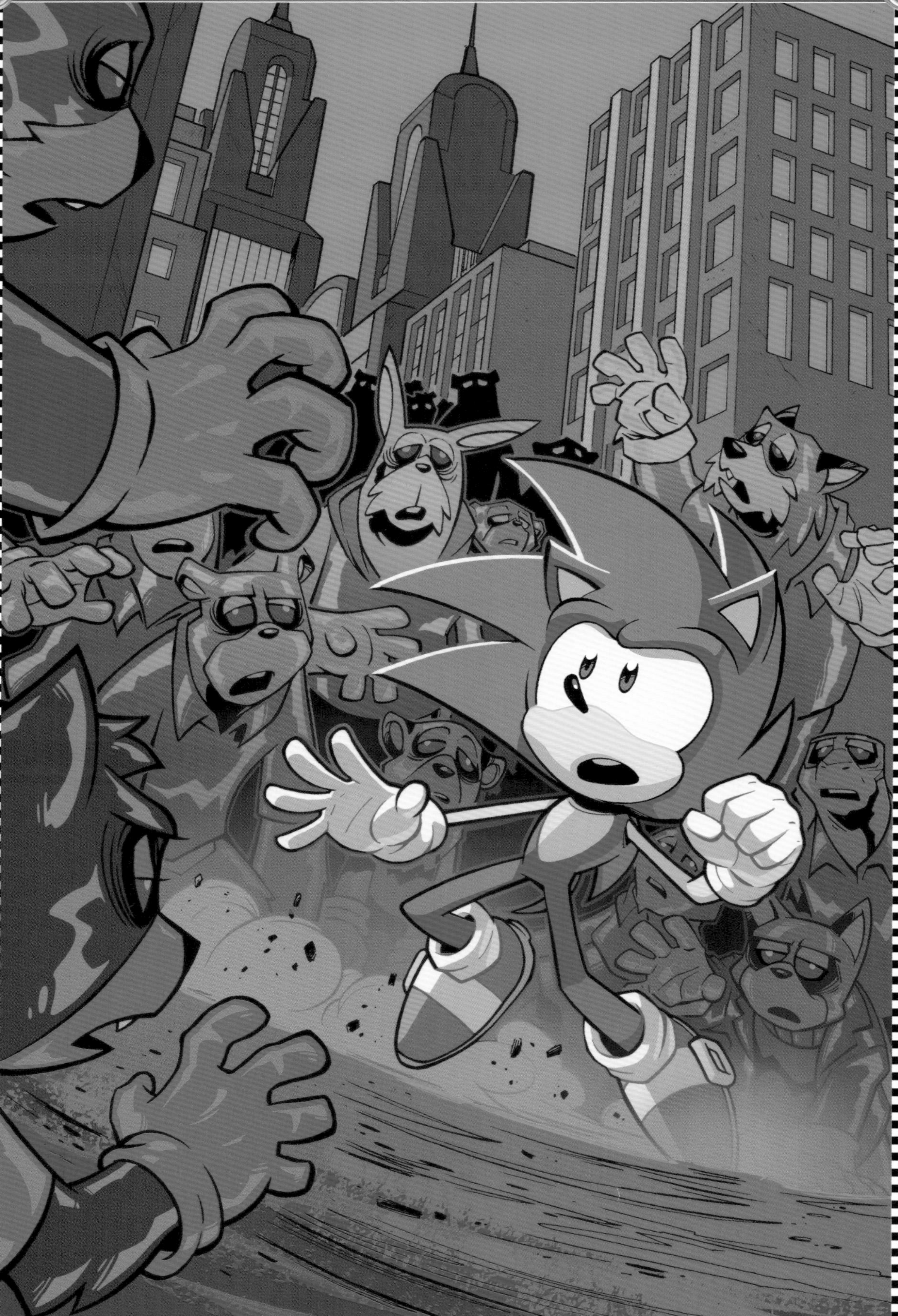

SONIC THE HEDGEHOG #17

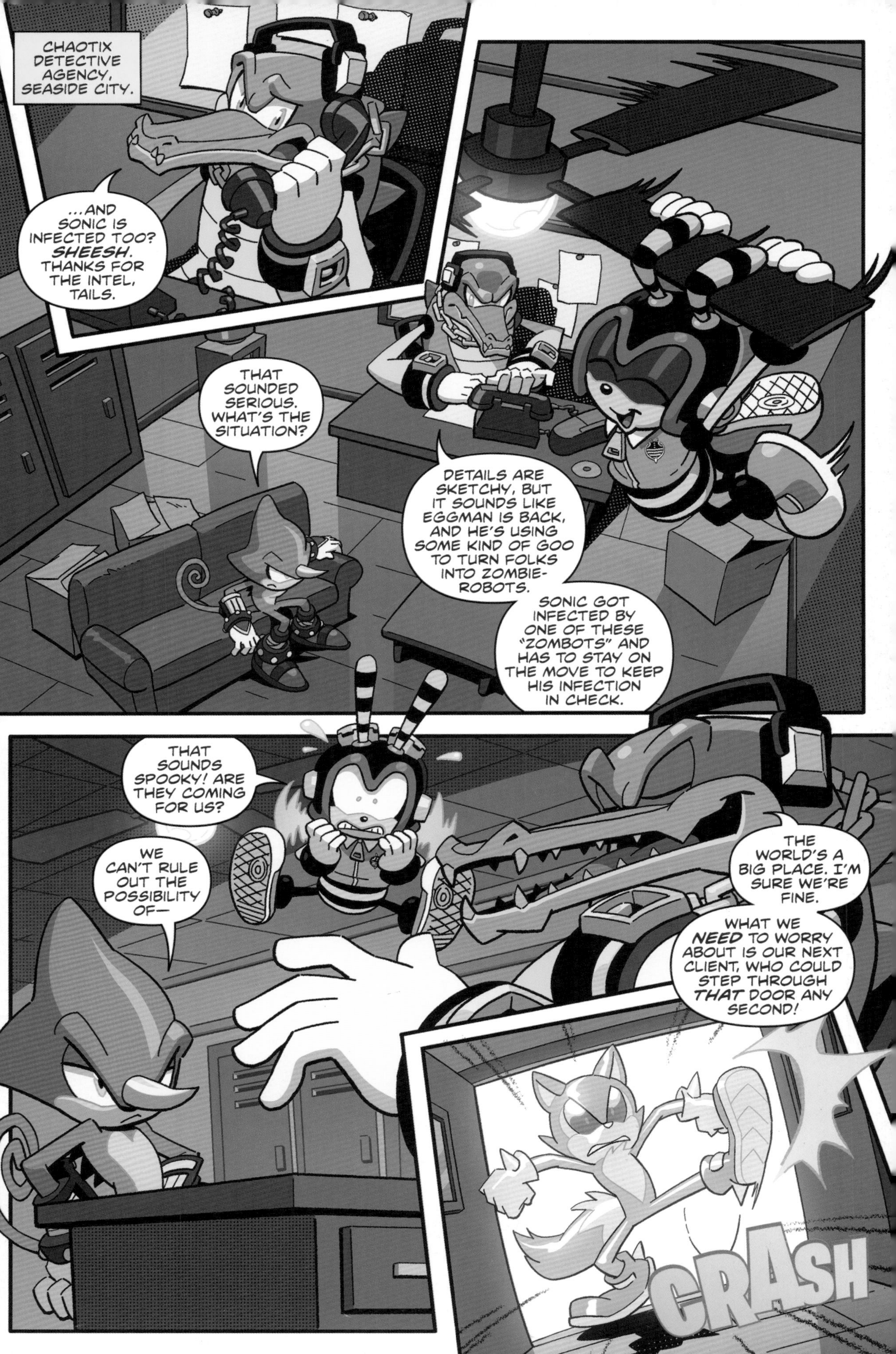
CHAOTIX DETECTIVE AGENCY, SEASIDE CITY.
...AND SONIC IS INFECTED TOO? SHEESH. THANKS FOR THE INTEL, TAILS.
THAT SOUNDED SERIOUS. WHAT'S THE SITUATION?
DETAILS ARE SKETCHY, BUT IT SOUNDS LIKE EGGMAN IS BACK, AND HE'S USING SOME KIND OF GOO TO TURN FOLKS INTO ZOMBIE-ROBOTS.
SONIC GOT INFECTED BY ONE OF THESE "ZOMBOTS" AND HAS TO STAY ON THE MOVE TO KEEP HIS INFECTION IN CHECK.
THAT SOUNDS SPOOKY! ARE THEY COMING FOR US?
WE CAN'T RULE OUT THE POSSIBILITY OF—
THE WORLD'S A BIG PLACE. I'M SURE WE'RE FINE.
WHAT WE NEED TO WORRY ABOUT IS OUR NEXT CLIENT, WHO COULD STEP THROUGH THAT DOOR ANY SECOND!
CRASH

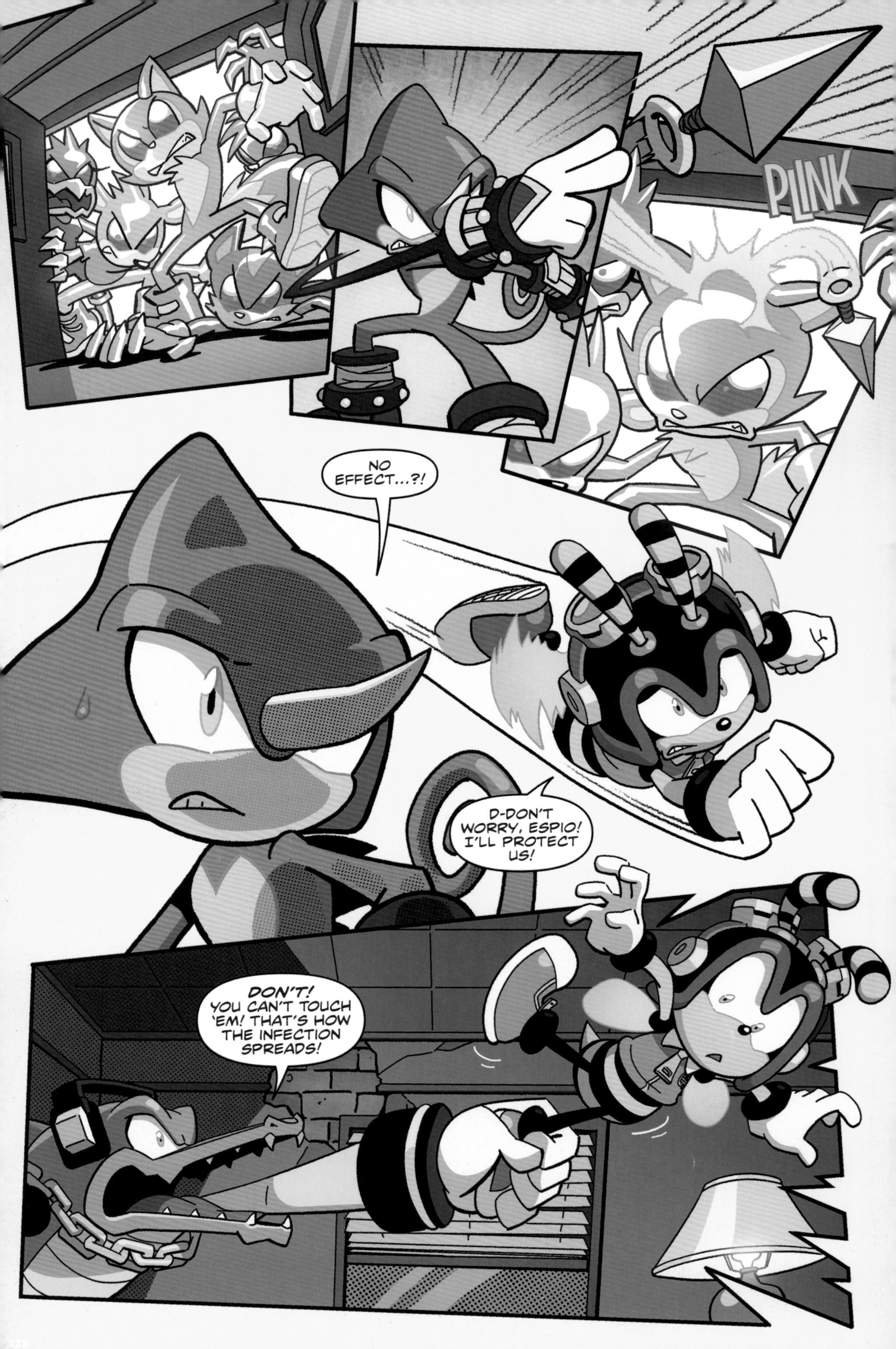
PLINK
NO EFFECT...?!
D-DON'T WORRY, ESPIO! I'LL PROTECT US!
DON'T! YOU CAN'T TOUCH 'EM! THAT'S HOW THE INFECTION SPREADS!

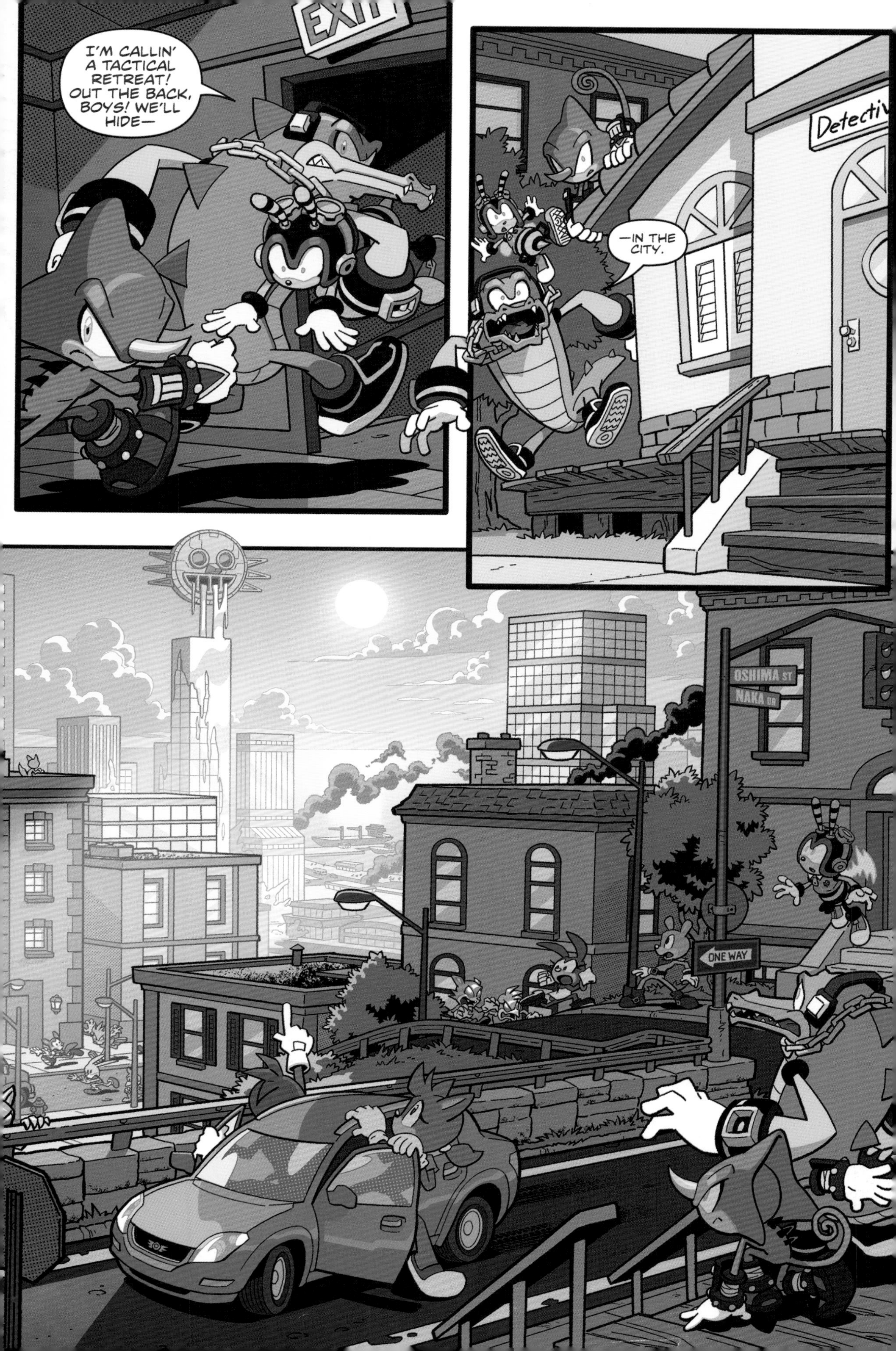
EXIT
I'M CALLIN' A TACTICAL RETREAT! OUT THE BACK, BOYS! WE'LL HIDE—
Detectiv
—IN THE CITY.
OSHIMA ST
NAKA DR
ONE WAY

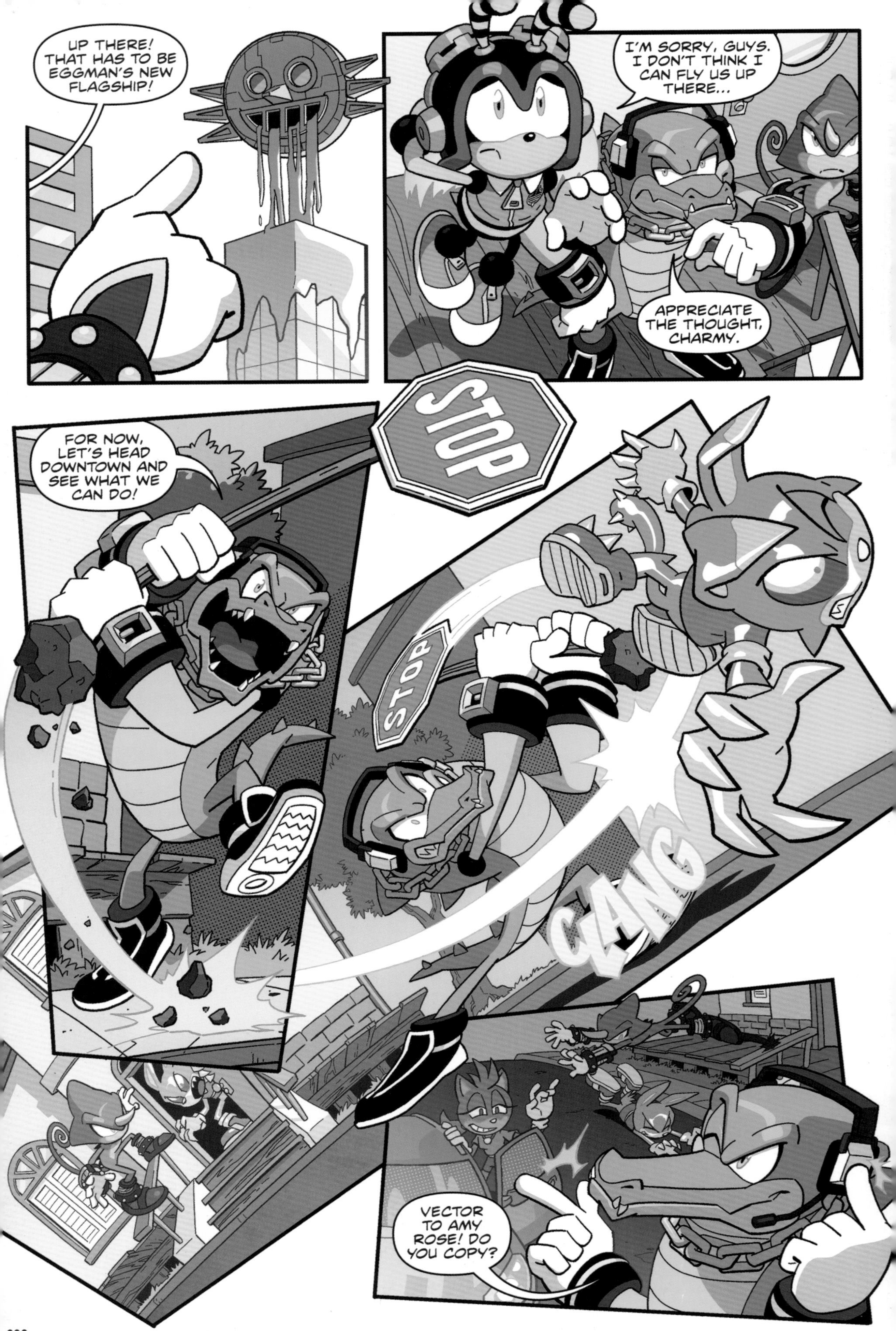
UP THERE! THAT HAS TO BE EGGMAN'S NEW FLAGSHIP!
I'M SORRY, GUYS. I DON'T THINK I CAN FLY US UP THERE...
APPRECIATE THE THOUGHT, CHARMY.
STOP
FOR NOW, LET'S HEAD DOWNTOWN AND SEE WHAT WE CAN DO!
STOP
CLANG
VECTOR TO AMY ROSE! DO YOU COPY?

RESTORATION HQ.

SO MUCH PAPERWORK... WHY DID I AGREE TO THIS...?

MISS ROSE? AN URGENT CALL FOR YOU FROM VECTOR.

OH, *NOW* WHAT...?

SEASIDE CITY JUST GOT HIT BY EGGMAN! THERE'S ZOMBOTS EVERYWHERE!

OH, NO! I'LL SEND A RESCUE SHUTTLE RIGHT AWAY!

WE NEED BACK-UP! CAN YOU SEND SONIC? ANYONE?

I'LL PUT OUT A CALL TO EVERYONE IN THE AREA. HOPEFULLY SONIC WILL HEAR, OR SOMEONE WILL SEE HIM.

BE CAREFUL!

WELL?

HELP'S ON THE WAY, BUT WHO KNOWS HOW MUCH OR HOW SOON.

WE'RE ON OUR OWN, BOYS.

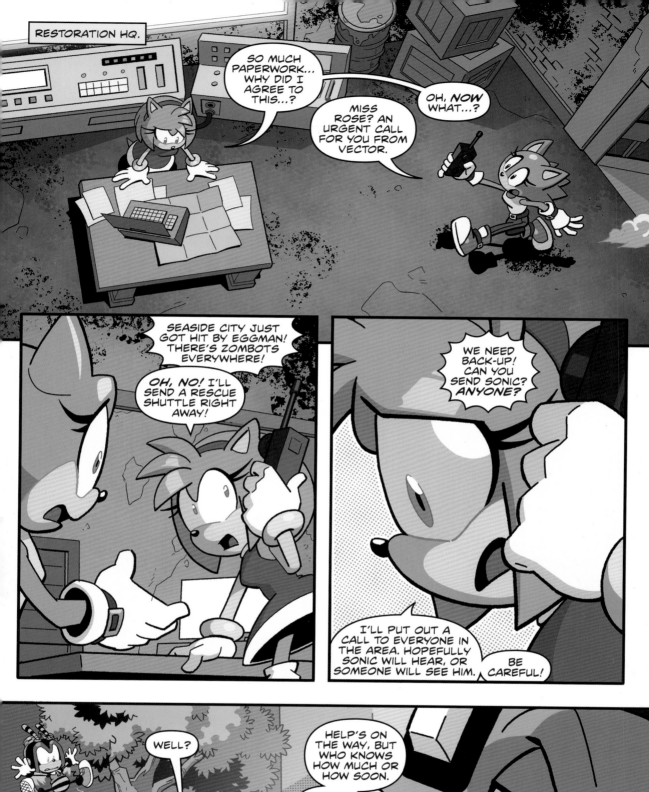

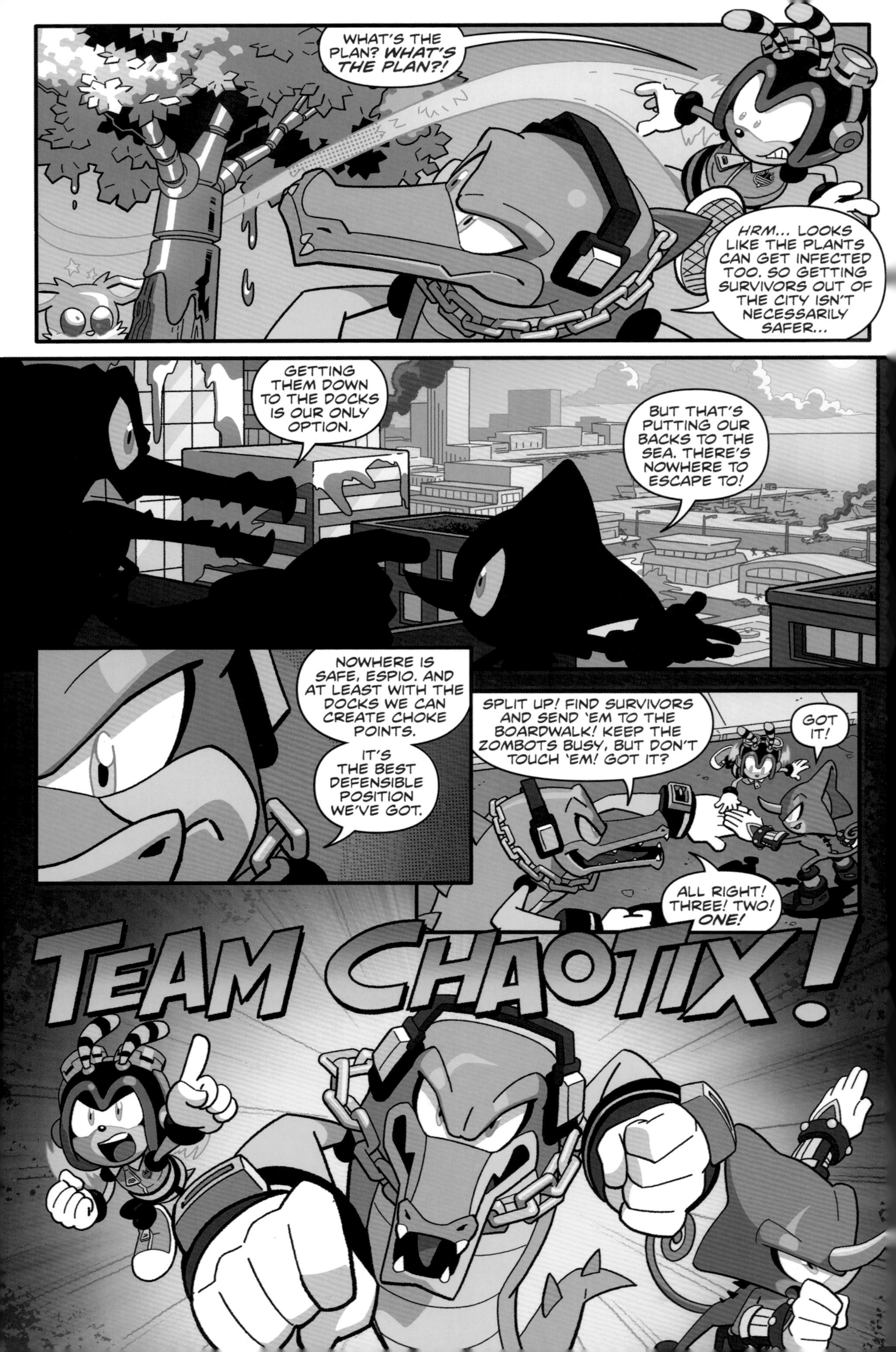
WHAT'S THE PLAN? *WHAT'S THE PLAN?!*
HRM... LOOKS LIKE THE PLANTS CAN GET INFECTED TOO. SO GETTING SURVIVORS OUT OF THE CITY ISN'T NECESSARILY SAFER...
GETTING THEM DOWN TO THE DOCKS IS OUR ONLY OPTION.
BUT THAT'S PUTTING OUR BACKS TO THE SEA. THERE'S NOWHERE TO ESCAPE TO!
NOWHERE IS SAFE, ESPIO. AND AT LEAST WITH THE DOCKS WE CAN CREATE CHOKE POINTS.
IT'S THE BEST DEFENSIBLE POSITION WE'VE GOT.
SPLIT UP! FIND SURVIVORS AND SEND 'EM TO THE BOARDWALK! KEEP THE ZOMBOTS BUSY, BUT DON'T TOUCH 'EM! GOT IT?
GOT IT!
ALL RIGHT! THREE! TWO! *ONE!*
TEAM CHAOTIX!

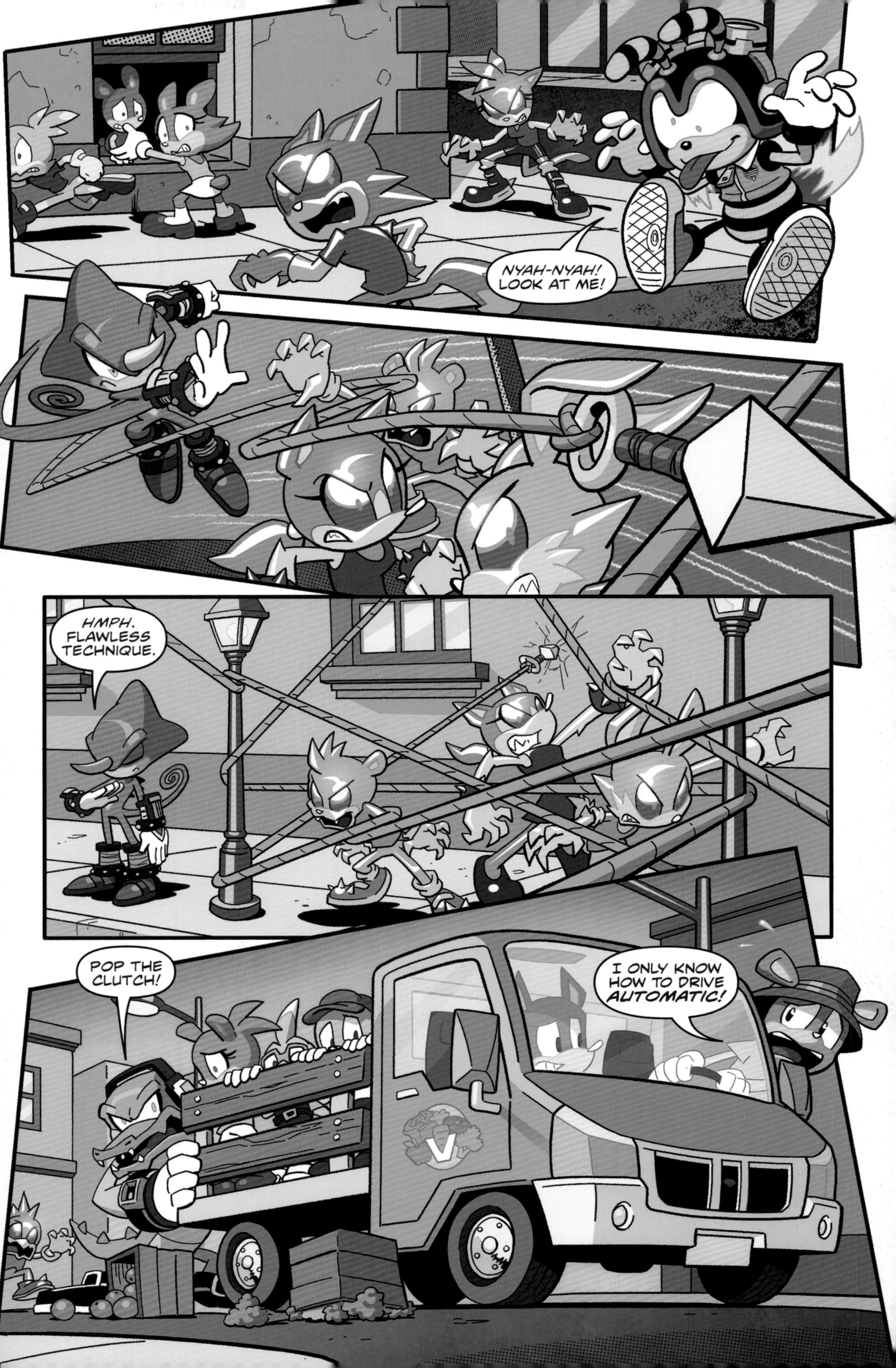
NYAH-NYAH! LOOK AT ME!
HMPH. FLAWLESS TECHNIQUE.
POP THE CLUTCH!
I ONLY KNOW HOW TO DRIVE AUTOMATIC!

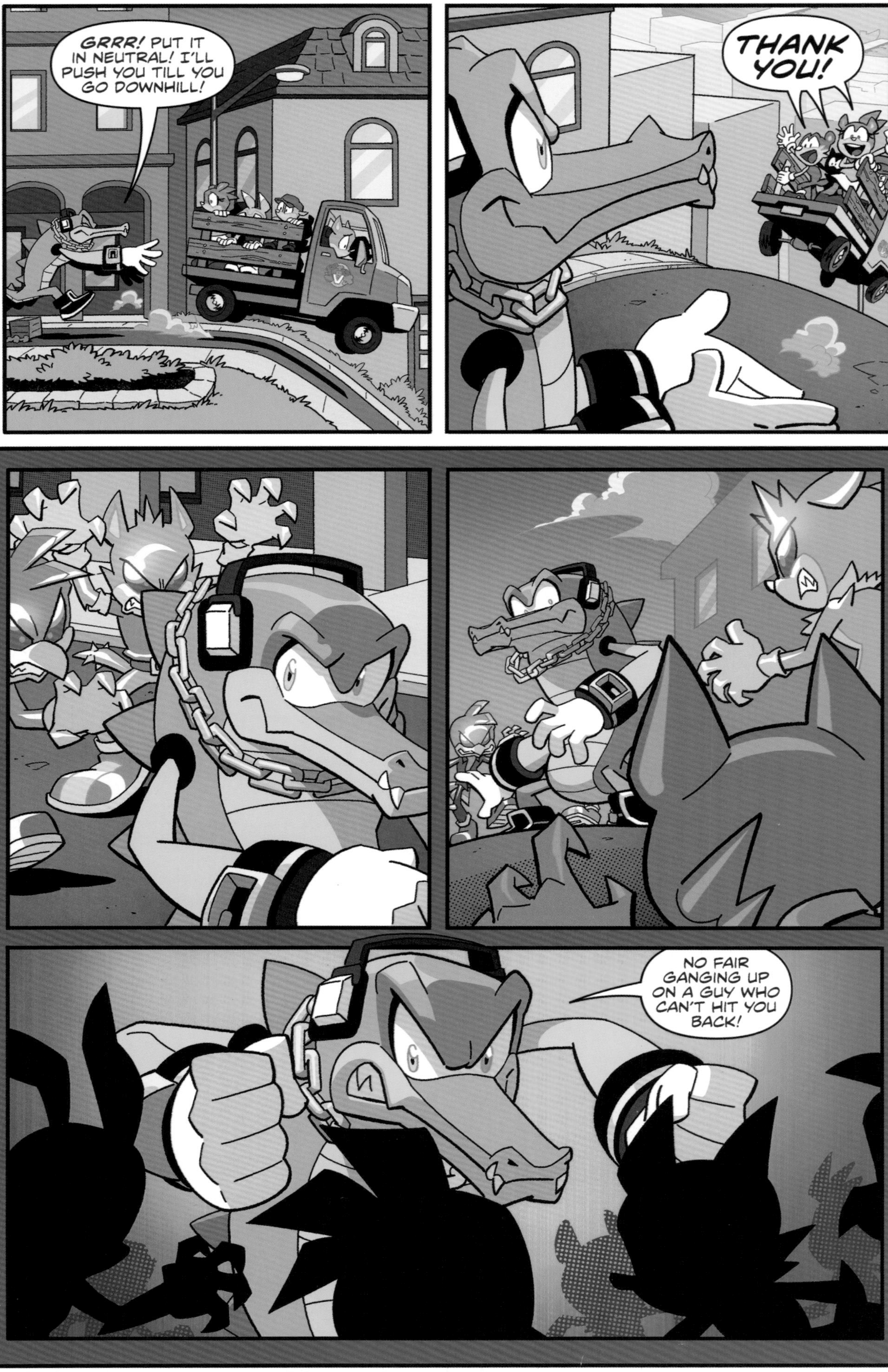
GRRR! PUT IT IN NEUTRAL! I'LL PUSH YOU TILL YOU GO DOWNHILL!
THANK YOU!
NO FAIR GANGING UP ON A GUY WHO CAN'T HIT YOU BACK!

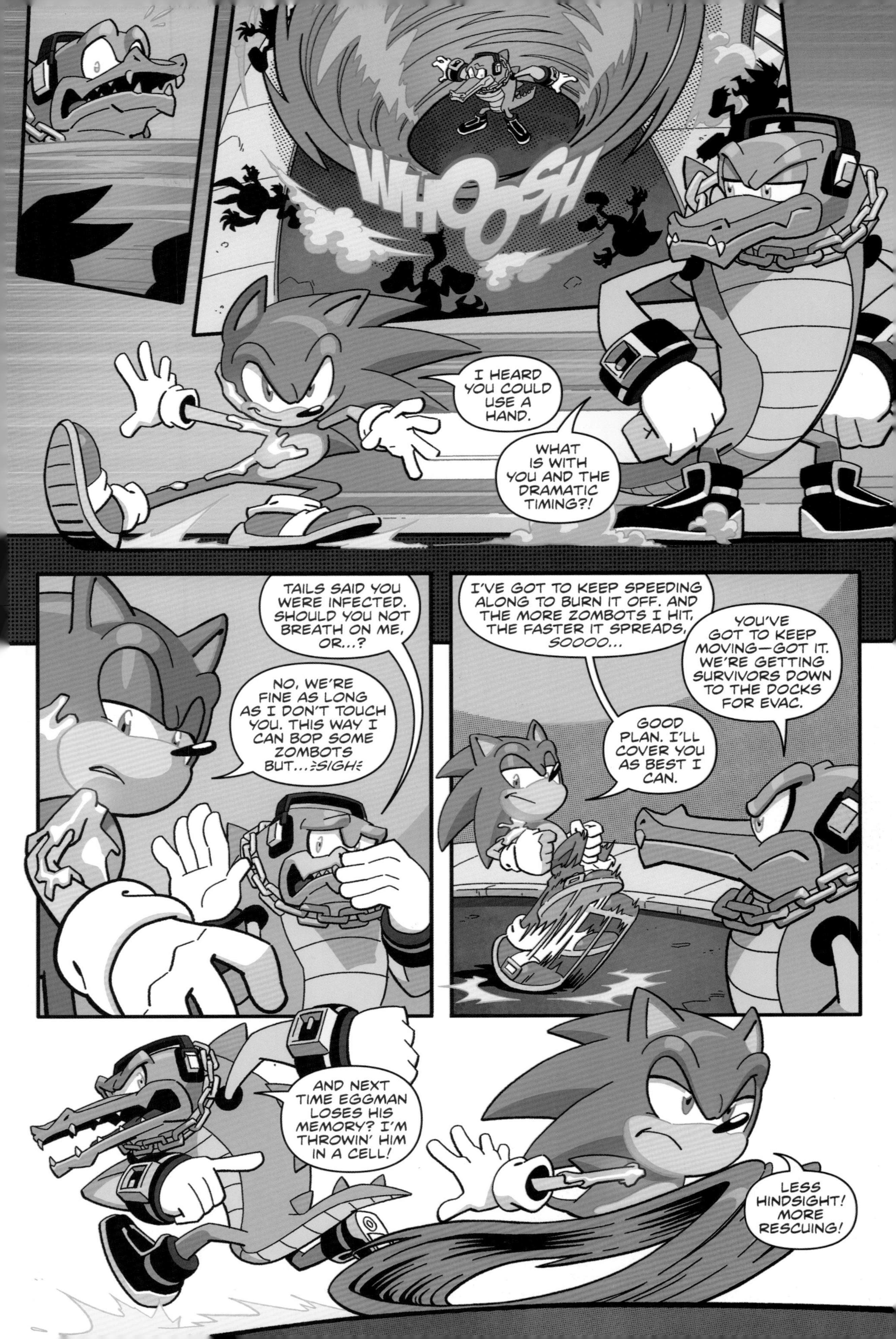
WHOOSH
I HEARD YOU COULD USE A HAND.
WHAT IS WITH YOU AND THE DRAMATIC TIMING?!
TAILS SAID YOU WERE INFECTED. SHOULD YOU NOT BREATH ON ME, OR...?
NO, WE'RE FINE AS LONG AS I DON'T TOUCH YOU. THIS WAY I CAN BOP SOME ZOMBOTS BUT... SIGH
I'VE GOT TO KEEP SPEEDING ALONG TO BURN IT OFF. AND THE MORE ZOMBOTS I HIT, THE FASTER IT SPREADS, SOOOO...
YOU'VE GOT TO KEEP MOVING—GOT IT. WE'RE GETTING SURVIVORS DOWN TO THE DOCKS FOR EVAC.
GOOD PLAN. I'LL COVER YOU AS BEST I CAN.
AND NEXT TIME EGGMAN LOSES HIS MEMORY? I'M THROWIN' HIM IN A CELL!
LESS HINDSIGHT! MORE RESCUING!

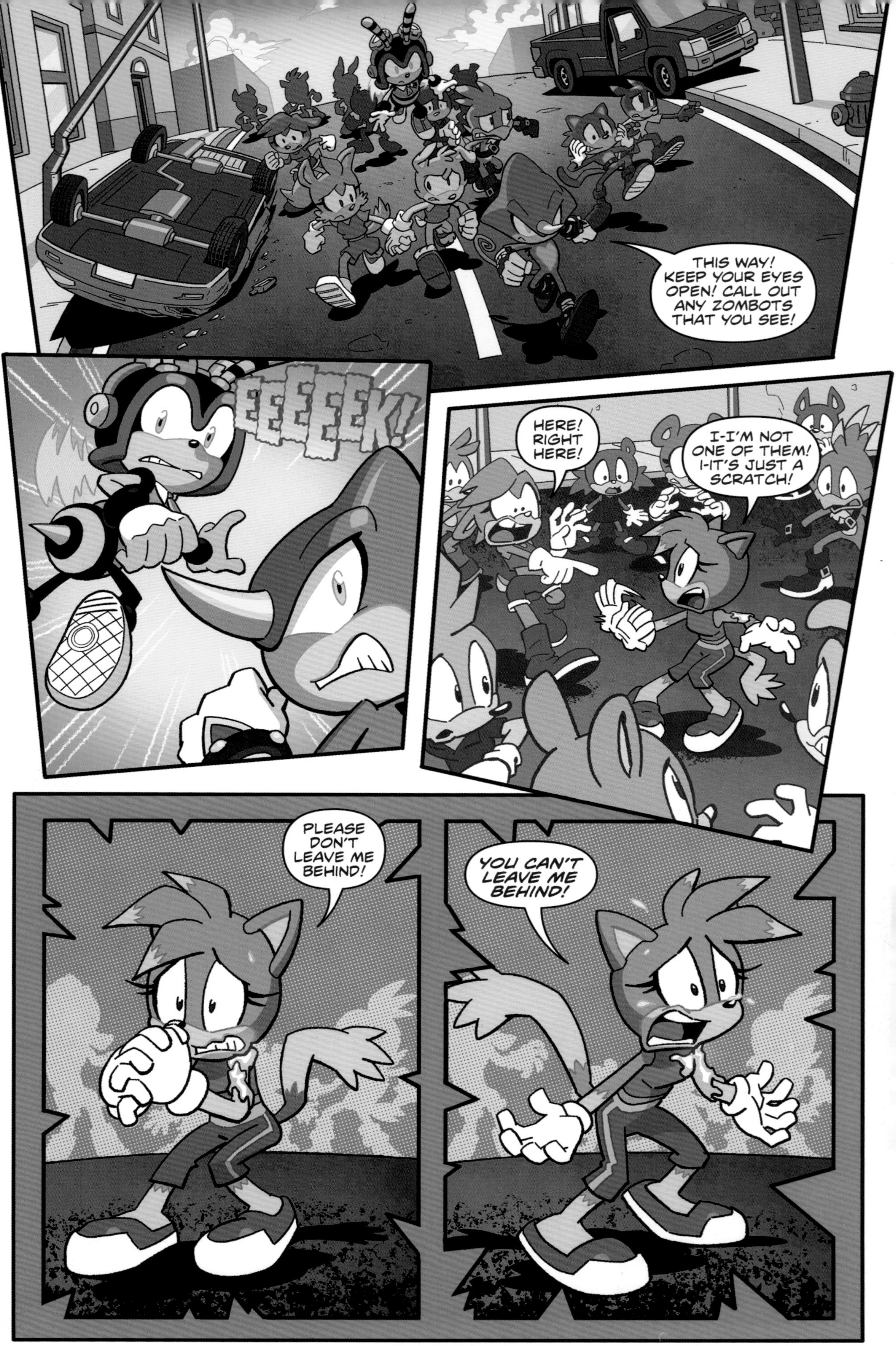
THIS WAY! KEEP YOUR EYES OPEN! CALL OUT ANY ZOMBOTS THAT YOU SEE!
EEEEEK!
HERE! RIGHT HERE!
I-I'M NOT ONE OF THEM! I-IT'S JUST A SCRATCH!
PLEASE DON'T LEAVE ME BEHIND!
YOU CAN'T LEAVE ME BEHIND!

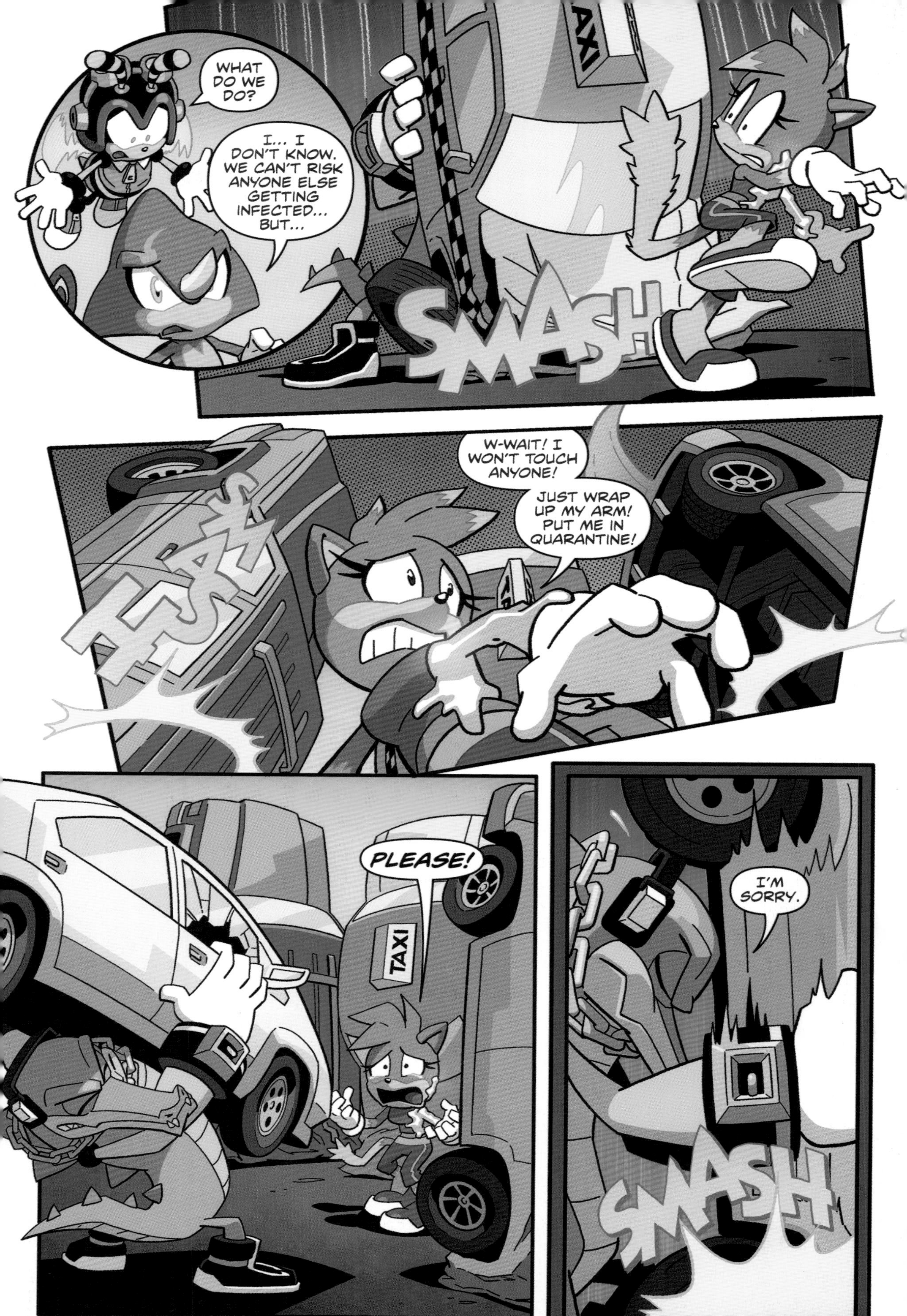
WHAT DO WE DO?
I... I DON'T KNOW. WE CAN'T RISK ANYONE ELSE GETTING INFECTED... BUT...
SMASH
W-WAIT! I WON'T TOUCH ANYONE!
JUST WRAP UP MY ARM! PUT ME IN QUARANTINE!
SMASH
PLEASE!
TAXI
I'M SORRY.
SMASH

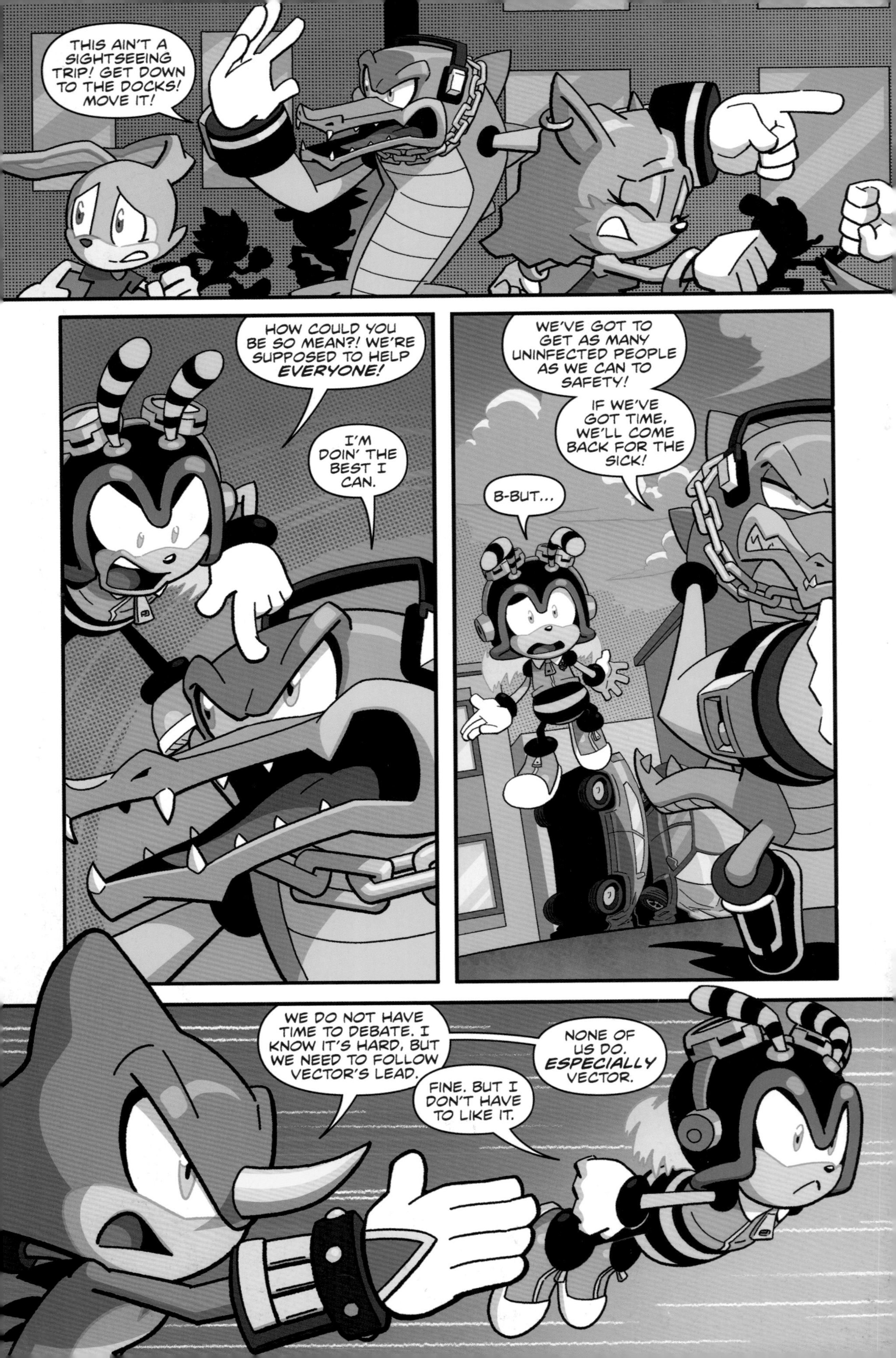
THIS AIN'T A SIGHTSEEING TRIP! GET DOWN TO THE DOCKS! MOVE IT!
HOW COULD YOU BE SO MEAN?! WE'RE SUPPOSED TO HELP *EVERYONE!*
I'M DOIN' THE BEST I CAN.
WE'VE GOT TO GET AS MANY UNINFECTED PEOPLE AS WE CAN TO SAFETY!
IF WE'VE GOT TIME, WE'LL COME BACK FOR THE SICK!
B-BUT...
WE DO NOT HAVE TIME TO DEBATE. I KNOW IT'S HARD, BUT WE NEED TO FOLLOW VECTOR'S LEAD.
NONE OF US DO. *ESPECIALLY* VECTOR.
FINE. BUT I DON'T HAVE TO LIKE IT.

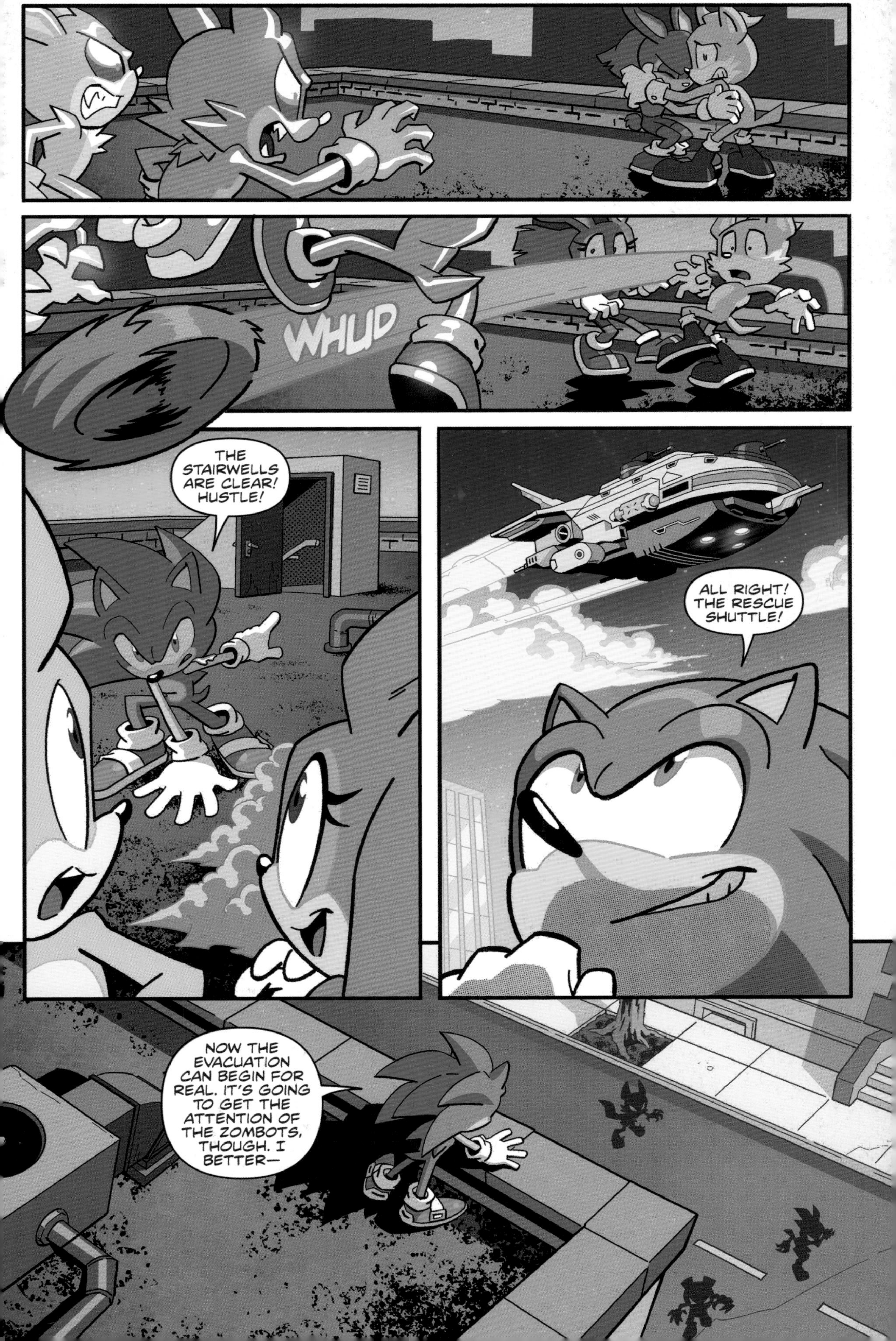
WHUD
THE STAIRWELLS ARE CLEAR! HUSTLE!
ALL RIGHT! THE RESCUE SHUTTLE!
NOW THE EVACUATION CAN BEGIN FOR REAL. IT'S GOING TO GET THE ATTENTION OF THE ZOMBOTS, THOUGH. I BETTER—

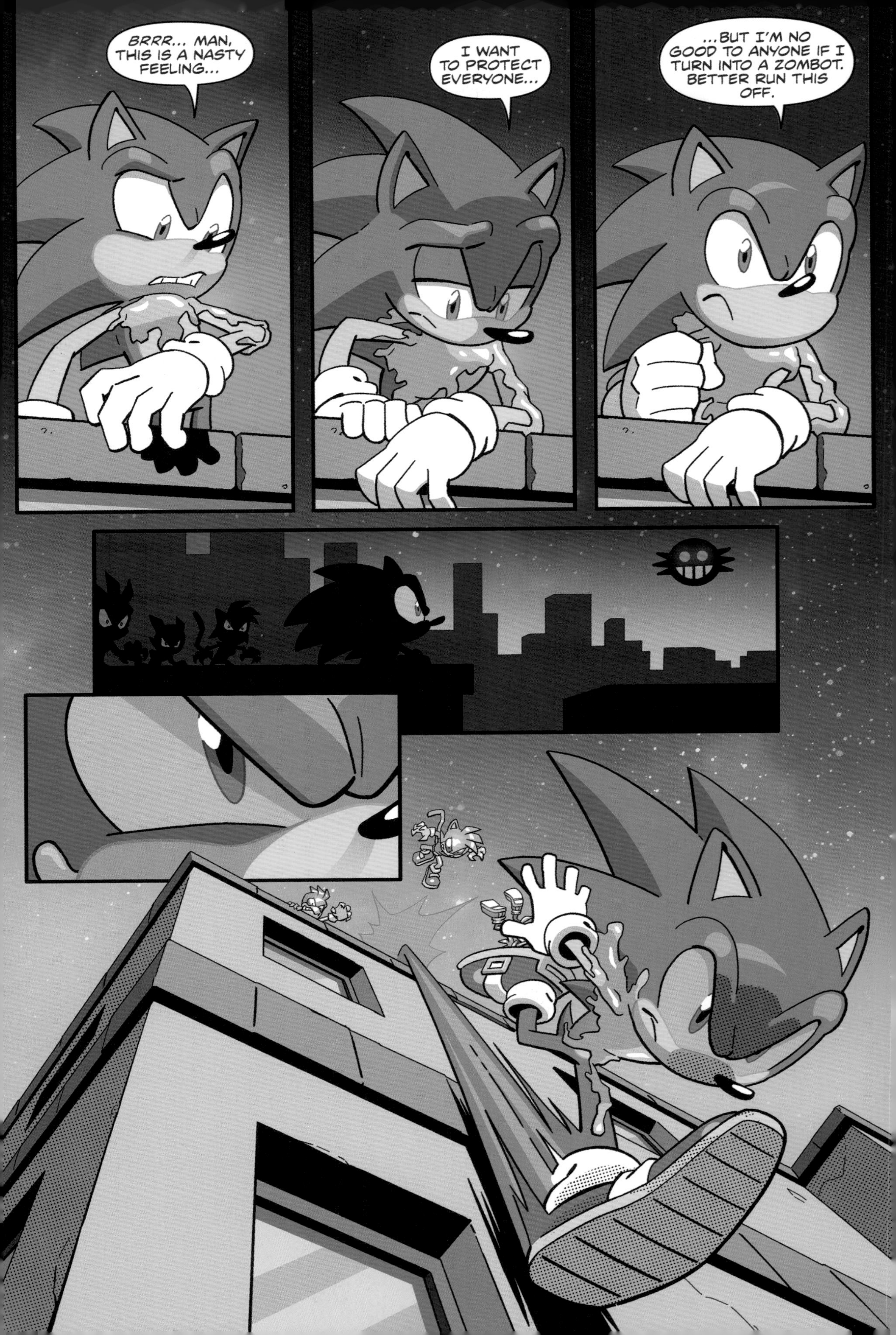
BRRR... MAN, THIS IS A NASTY FEELING...
I WANT TO PROTECT EVERYONE...
...BUT I'M NO GOOD TO ANYONE IF I TURN INTO A ZOMBOT. BETTER RUN THIS OFF.

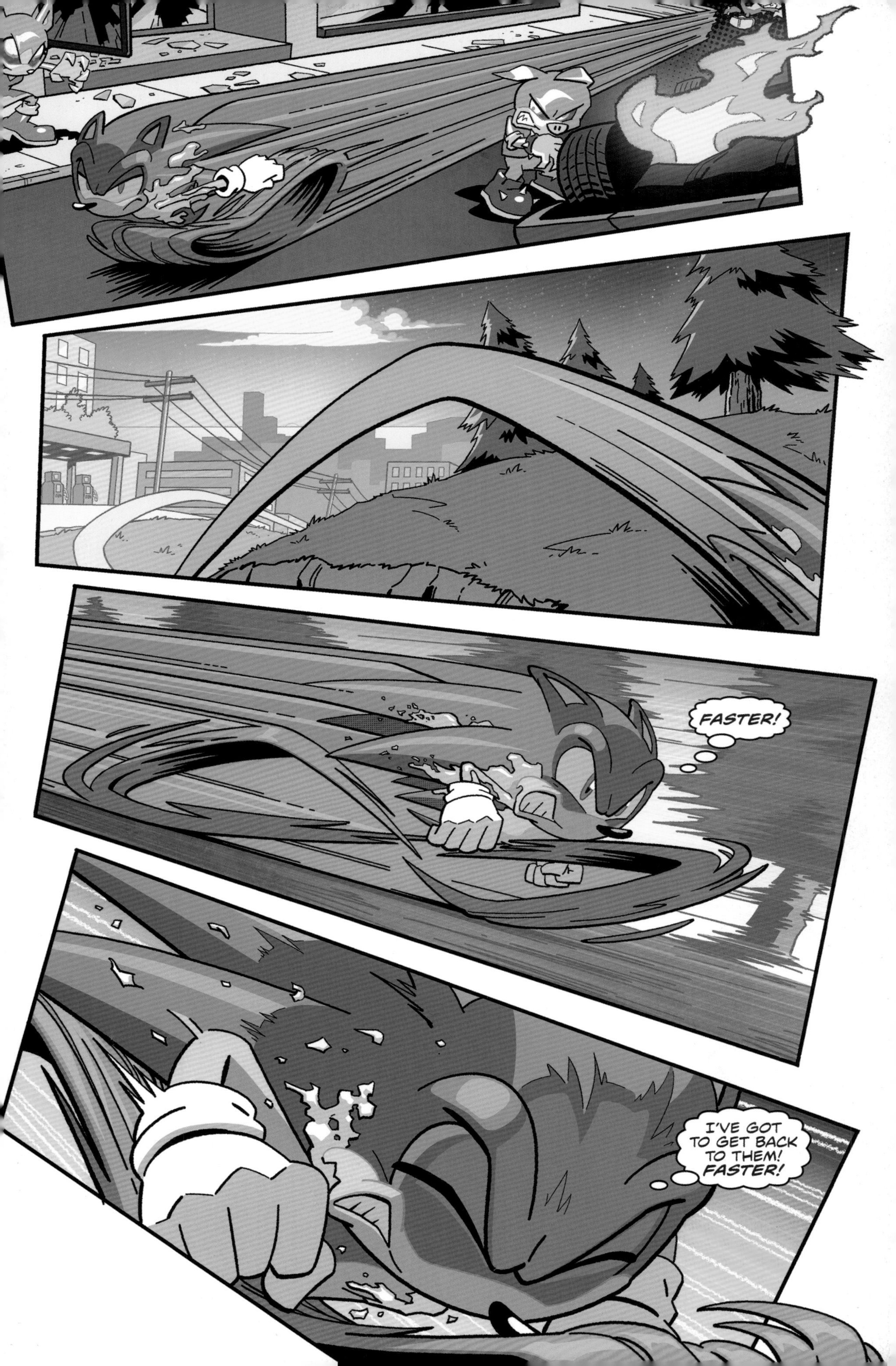
FASTER!
I'VE GOT TO GET BACK TO THEM! FASTER!

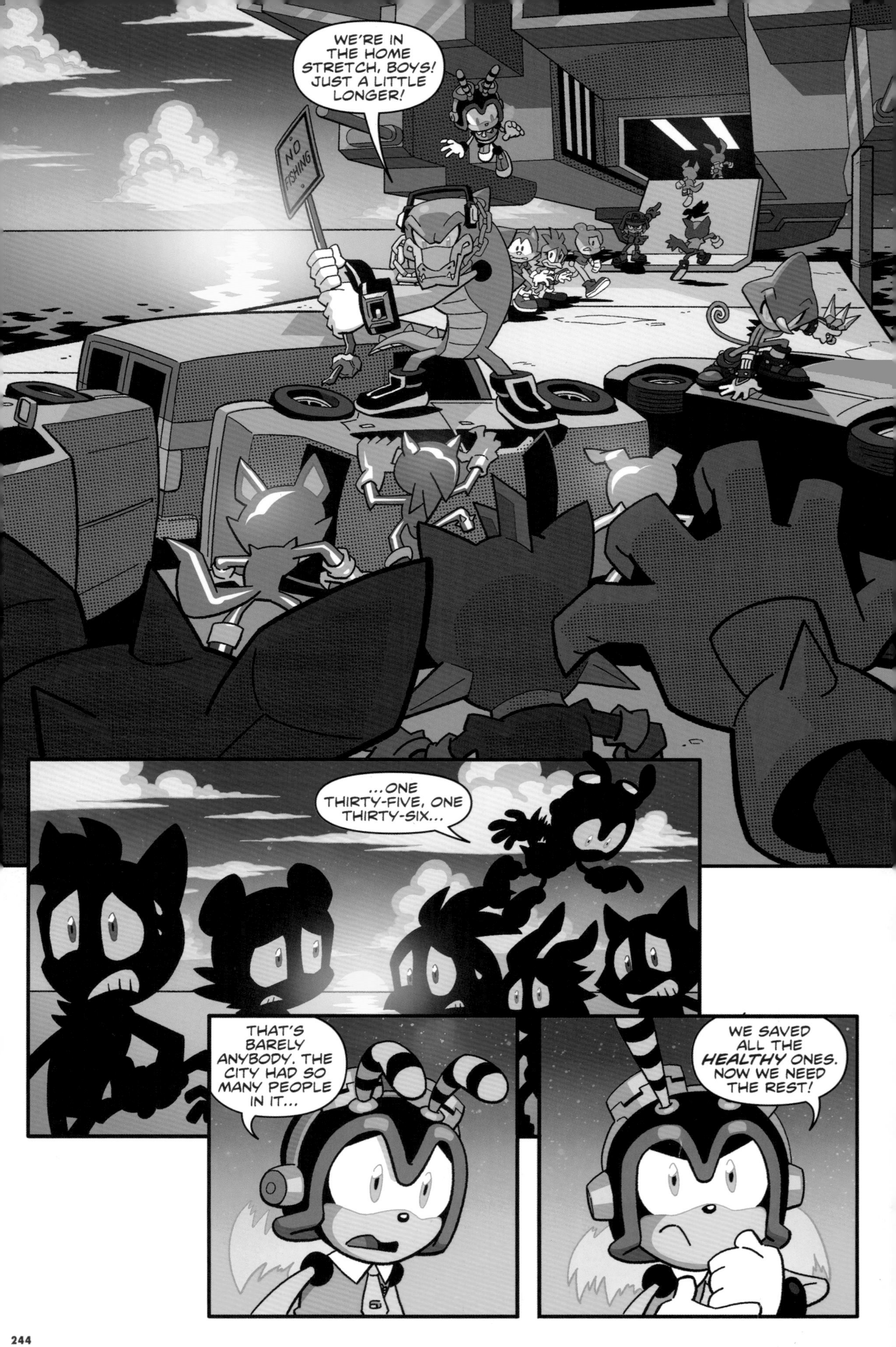
WE'RE IN THE HOME STRETCH, BOYS! JUST A LITTLE LONGER!
NO FISHING
...ONE THIRTY-FIVE, ONE THIRTY-SIX...
THAT'S BARELY ANYBODY. THE CITY HAD SO MANY PEOPLE IN IT...
WE SAVED ALL THE *HEALTHY* ONES. NOW WE NEED THE REST!

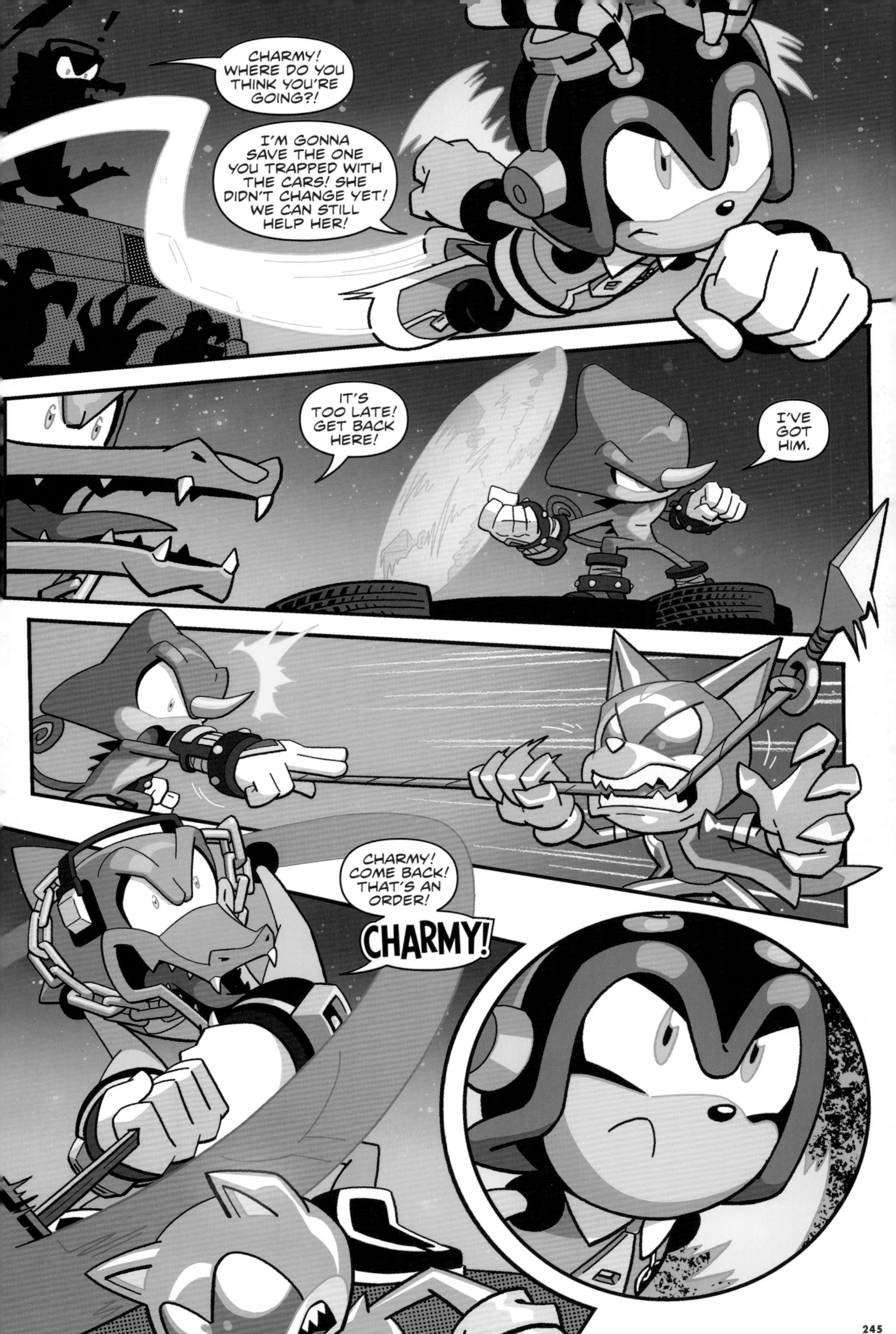
CHARMY! WHERE DO YOU THINK YOU'RE GOING?!
I'M GONNA SAVE THE ONE YOU TRAPPED WITH THE CARS! SHE DIDN'T CHANGE YET! WE CAN STILL HELP HER!
IT'S TOO LATE! GET BACK HERE!
I'VE GOT HIM.
CHARMY! COME BACK! THAT'S AN ORDER!
CHARMY!

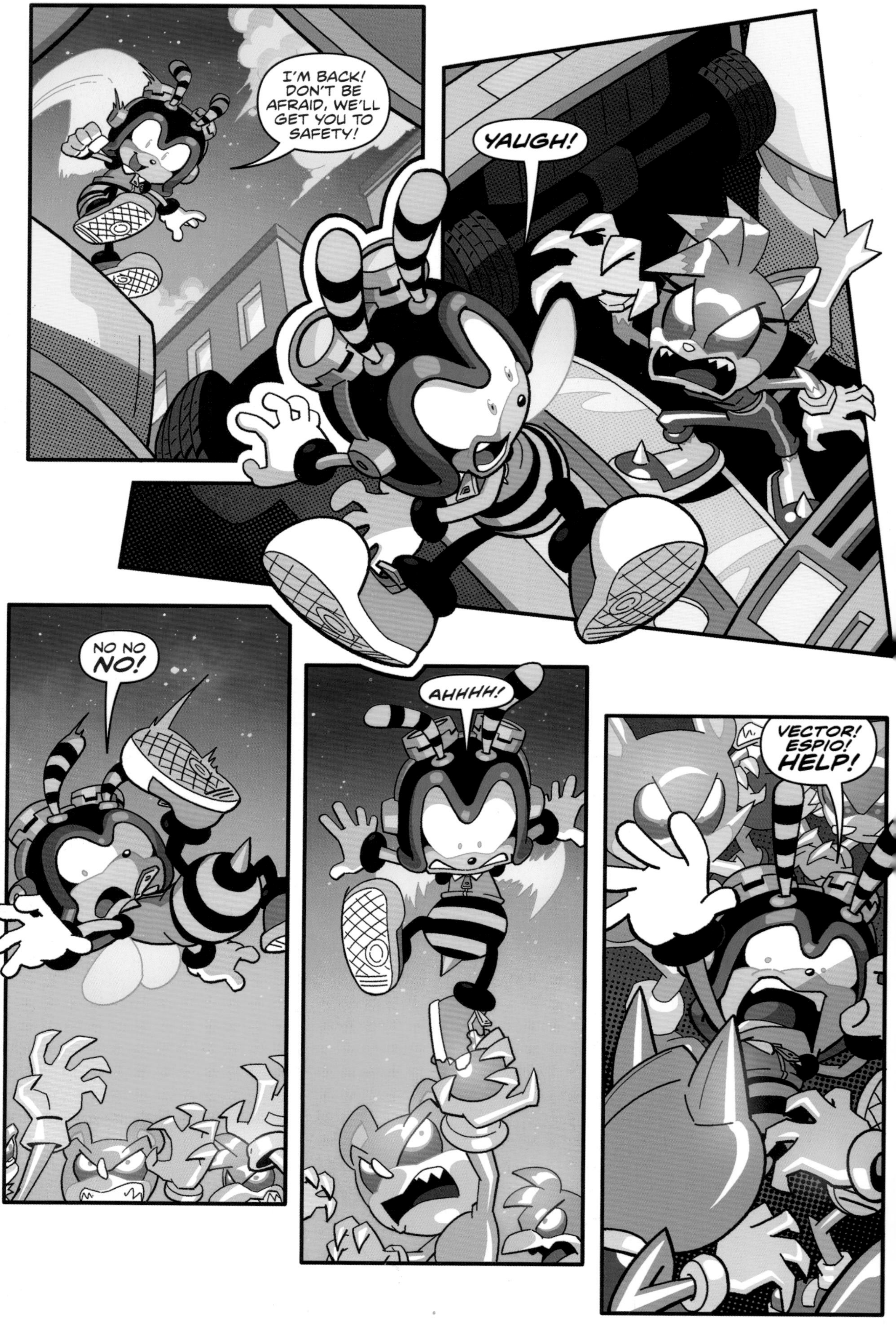
I'M BACK! DON'T BE AFRAID, WE'LL GET YOU TO SAFETY!
YAUGH!
NO NO NO!
AHHHH!
VECTOR! ESPIO! HELP!

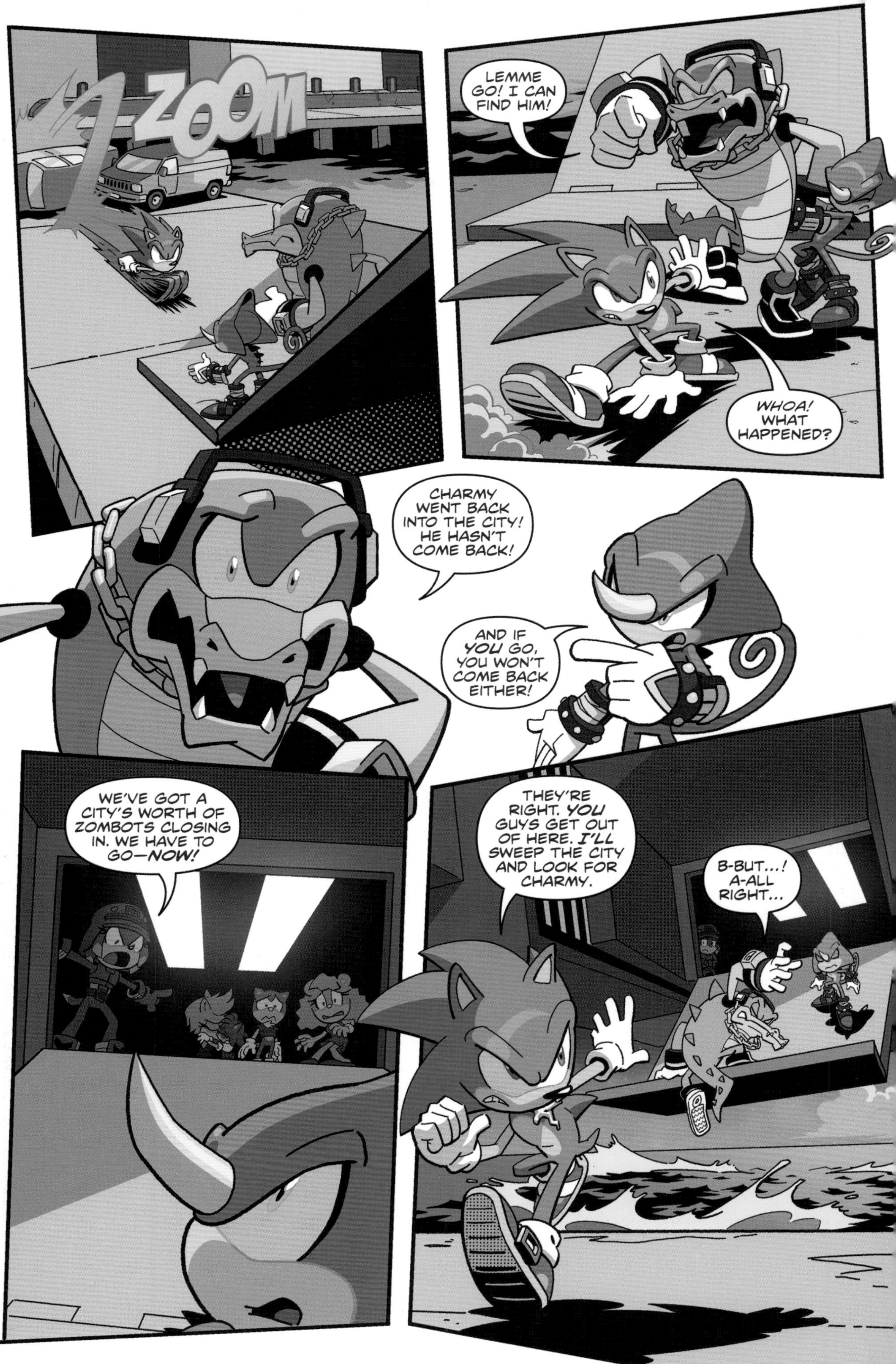
ZOOM
LEMME GO! I CAN FIND HIM!
WHOA! WHAT HAPPENED?
CHARMY WENT BACK INTO THE CITY! HE HASN'T COME BACK!
AND IF YOU GO, YOU WON'T COME BACK EITHER!
WE'VE GOT A CITY'S WORTH OF ZOMBOTS CLOSING IN. WE HAVE TO GO—NOW!
THEY'RE RIGHT. YOU GUYS GET OUT OF HERE. I'LL SWEEP THE CITY AND LOOK FOR CHARMY.
B-BUT...! A-ALL RIGHT...

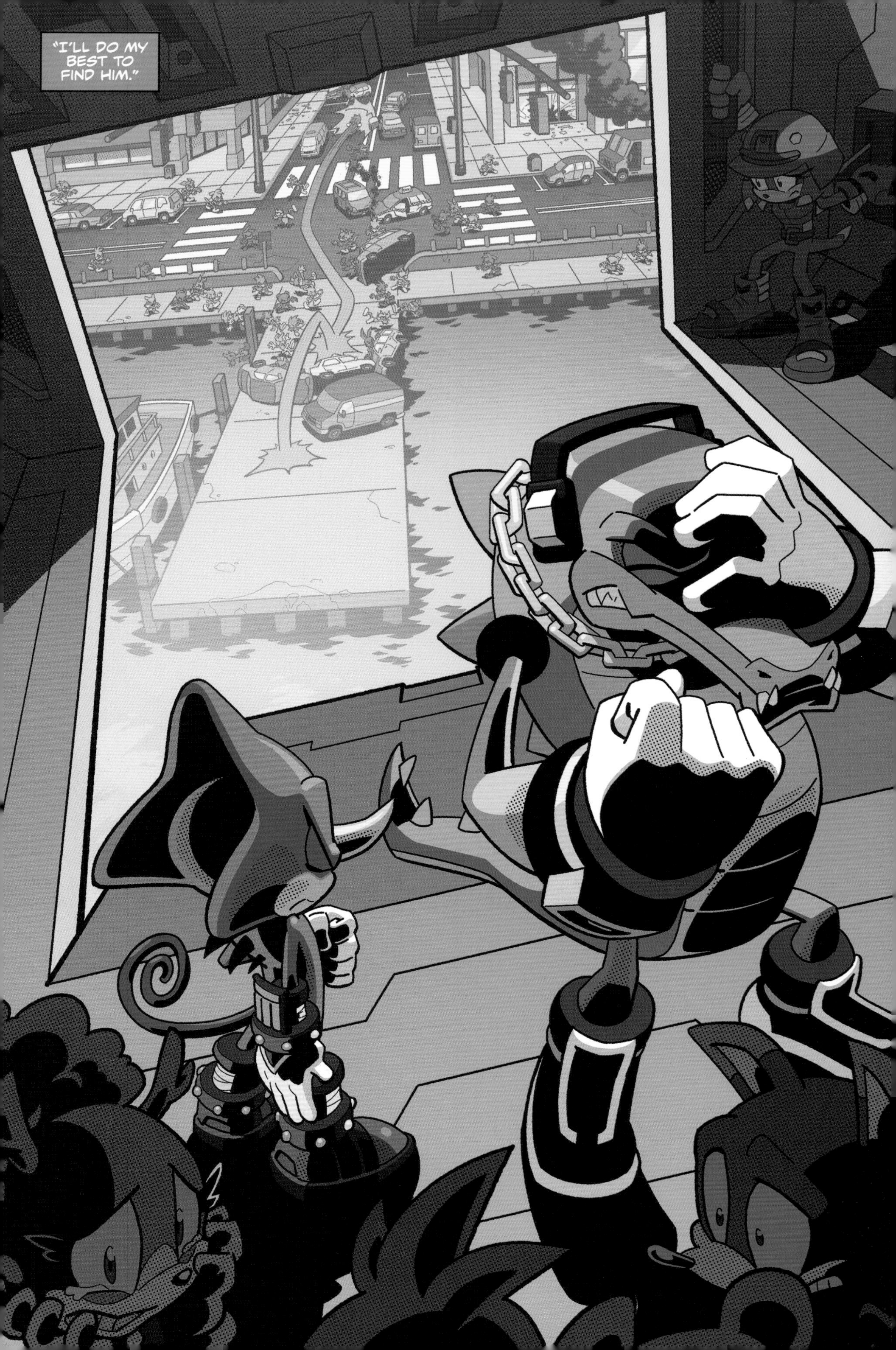
"I'LL DO MY BEST TO FIND HIM."

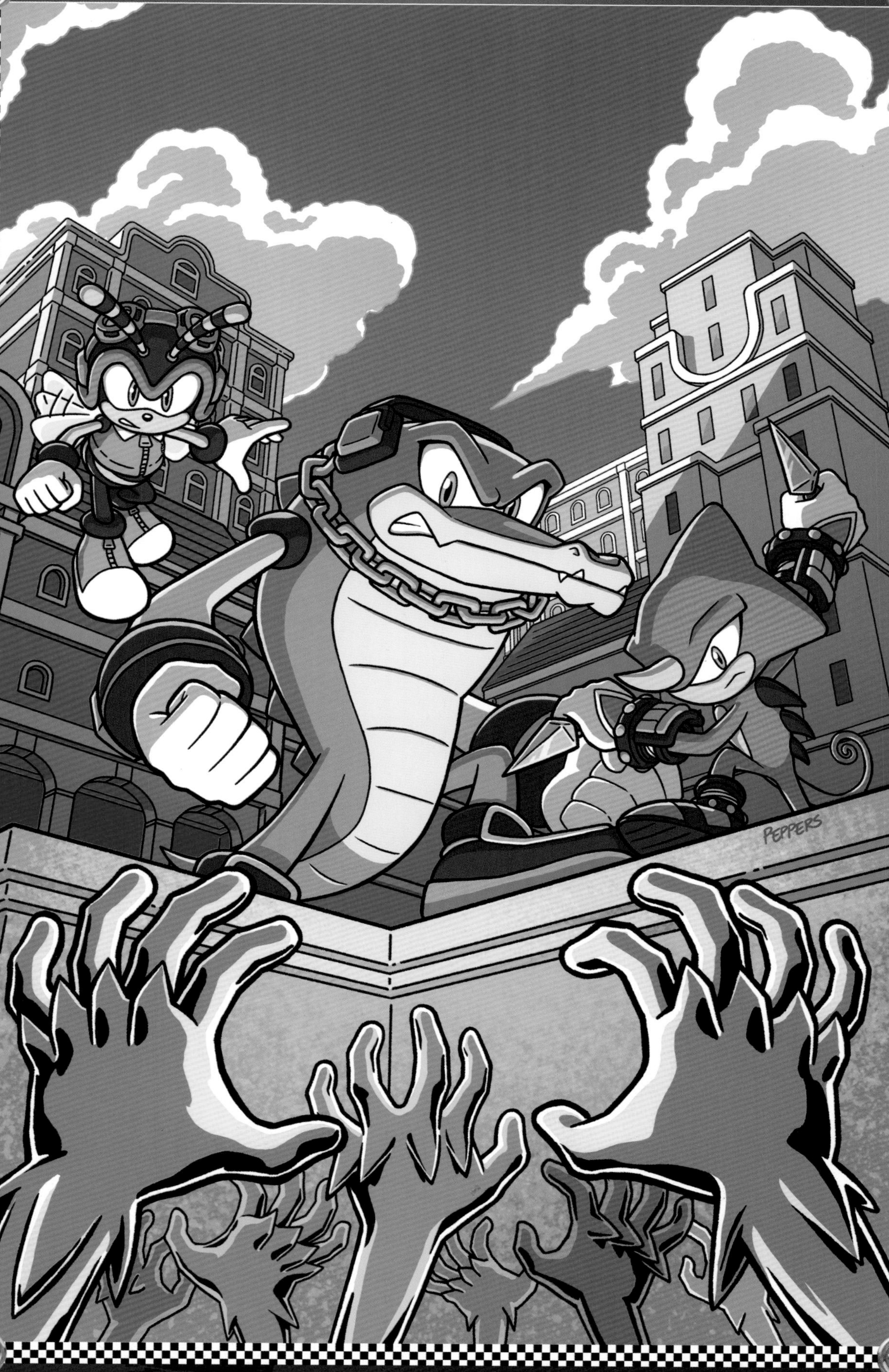
PEPPERS

ART BY JONATHAN GRAY COLORS BY REGGIE GRAHAM

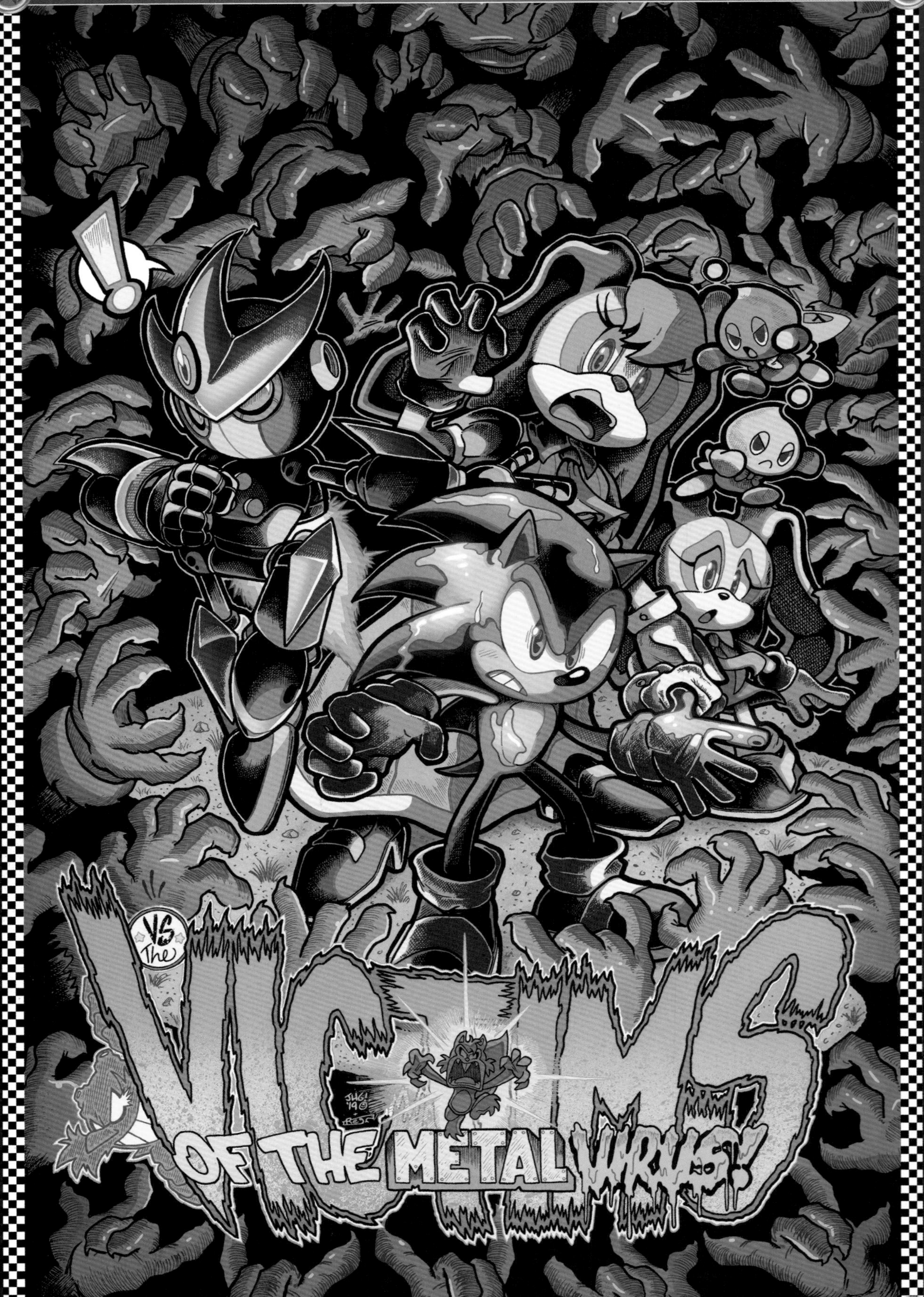
VS THE VICTIMS OF THE METAL VIRUS!

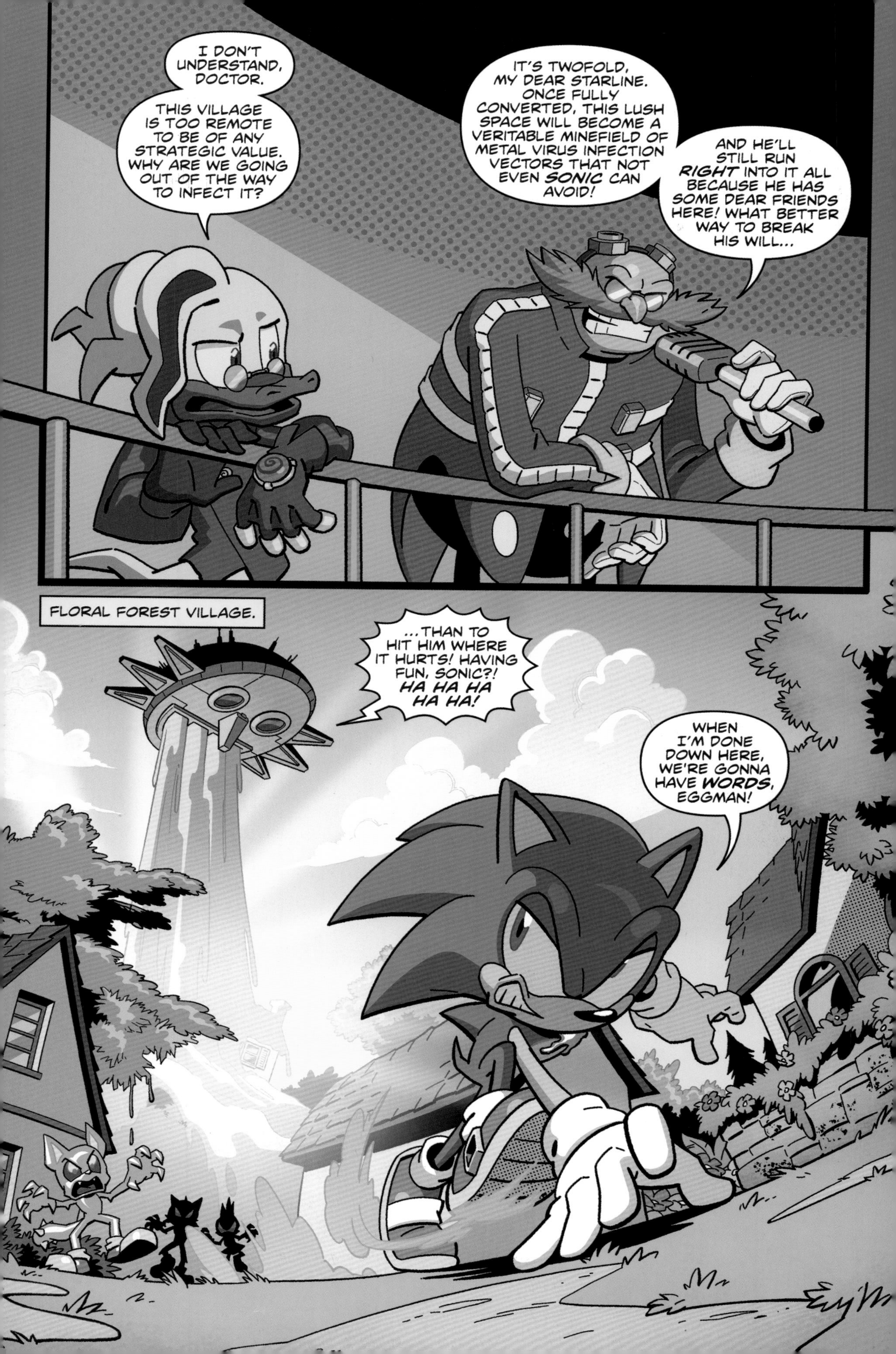
I DON'T UNDERSTAND, DOCTOR.
THIS VILLAGE IS TOO REMOTE TO BE OF ANY STRATEGIC VALUE. WHY ARE WE GOING OUT OF THE WAY TO INFECT IT?
IT'S TWOFOLD, MY DEAR STARLINE. ONCE FULLY CONVERTED, THIS LUSH SPACE WILL BECOME A VERITABLE MINEFIELD OF METAL VIRUS INFECTION VECTORS THAT NOT EVEN SONIC CAN AVOID!
AND HE'LL STILL RUN RIGHT INTO IT ALL BECAUSE HE HAS SOME DEAR FRIENDS HERE! WHAT BETTER WAY TO BREAK HIS WILL...
FLORAL FOREST VILLAGE.
...THAN TO HIT HIM WHERE IT HURTS! HAVING FUN, SONIC?! HA HA HA HA HA!
WHEN I'M DONE DOWN HERE, WE'RE GONNA HAVE WORDS, EGGMAN!

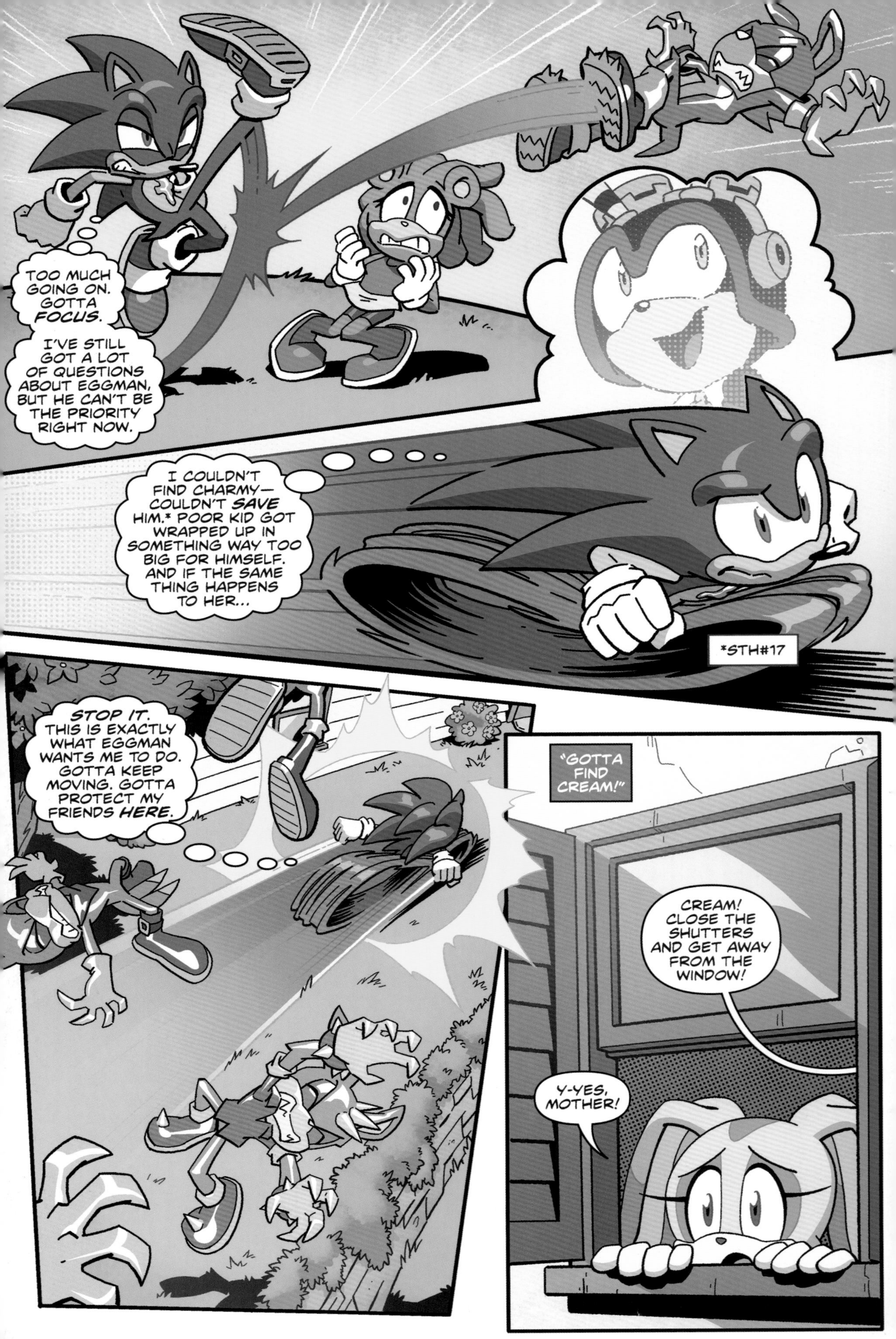
TOO MUCH GOING ON. GOTTA FOCUS.
I'VE STILL GOT A LOT OF QUESTIONS ABOUT EGGMAN, BUT HE CAN'T BE THE PRIORITY RIGHT NOW.
I COULDN'T FIND CHARMY— COULDN'T SAVE HIM.* POOR KID GOT WRAPPED UP IN SOMETHING WAY TOO BIG FOR HIMSELF. AND IF THE SAME THING HAPPENS TO HER...
*STH#17
STOP IT. THIS IS EXACTLY WHAT EGGMAN WANTS ME TO DO. GOTTA KEEP MOVING. GOTTA PROTECT MY FRIENDS HERE.
"GOTTA FIND CREAM!"
CREAM! CLOSE THE SHUTTERS AND GET AWAY FROM THE WINDOW!
Y-YES, MOTHER!

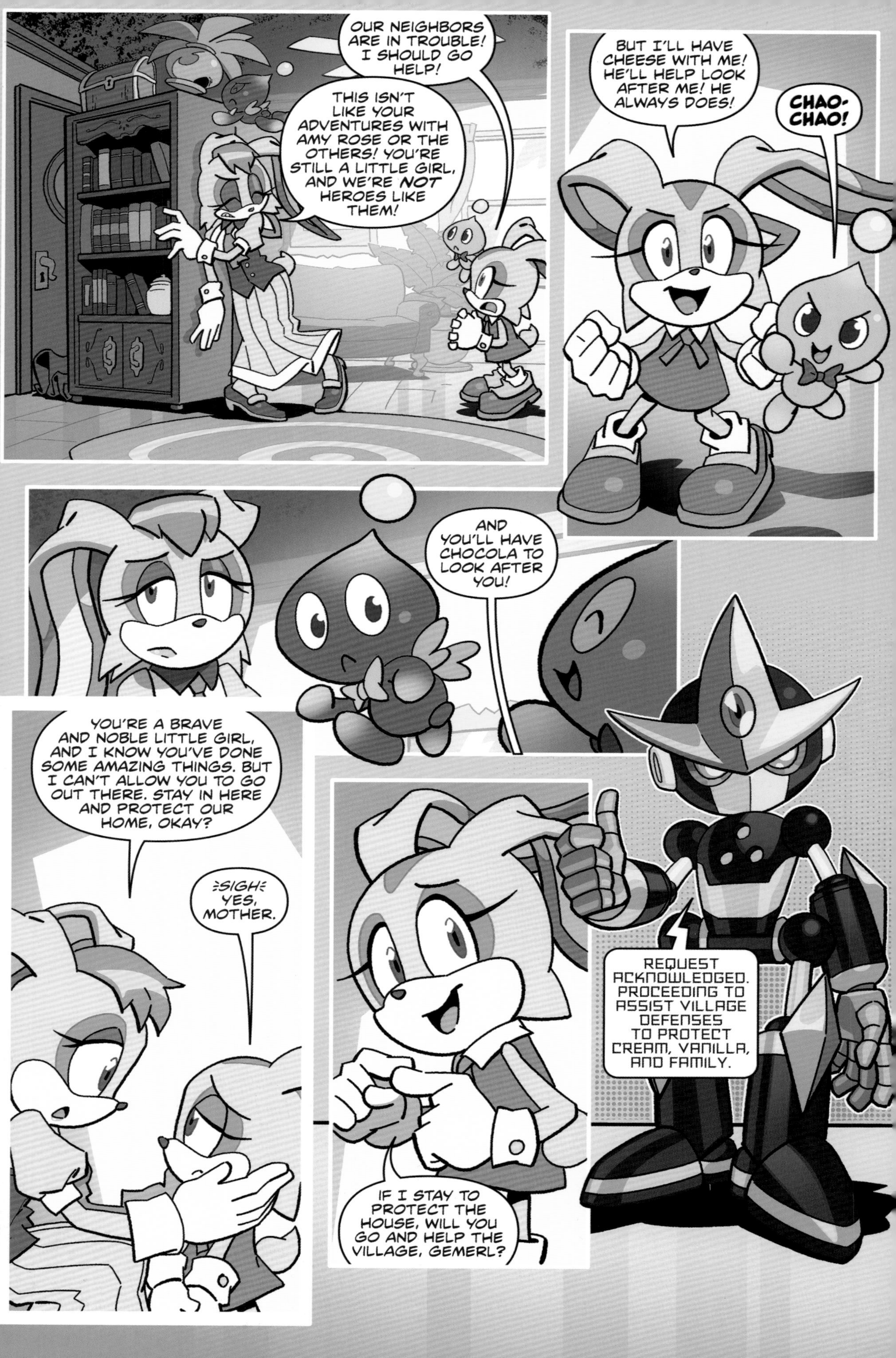

OUR NEIGHBORS ARE IN TROUBLE! I SHOULD GO HELP!
THIS ISN'T LIKE YOUR ADVENTURES WITH AMY ROSE OR THE OTHERS! YOU'RE STILL A LITTLE GIRL, AND WE'RE NOT HEROES LIKE THEM!
BUT I'LL HAVE CHEESE WITH ME! HE'LL HELP LOOK AFTER ME! HE ALWAYS DOES!
CHAO-CHAO!
AND YOU'LL HAVE CHOCOLA TO LOOK AFTER YOU!
YOU'RE A BRAVE AND NOBLE LITTLE GIRL, AND I KNOW YOU'VE DONE SOME AMAZING THINGS. BUT I CAN'T ALLOW YOU TO GO OUT THERE. STAY IN HERE AND PROTECT OUR HOME, OKAY?
SIGH YES, MOTHER.
IF I STAY TO PROTECT THE HOUSE, WILL YOU GO AND HELP THE VILLAGE, GEMERL?
REQUEST ACKNOWLEDGED. PROCEEDING TO ASSIST VILLAGE DEFENSES TO PROTECT CREAM, VANILLA, AND FAMILY.

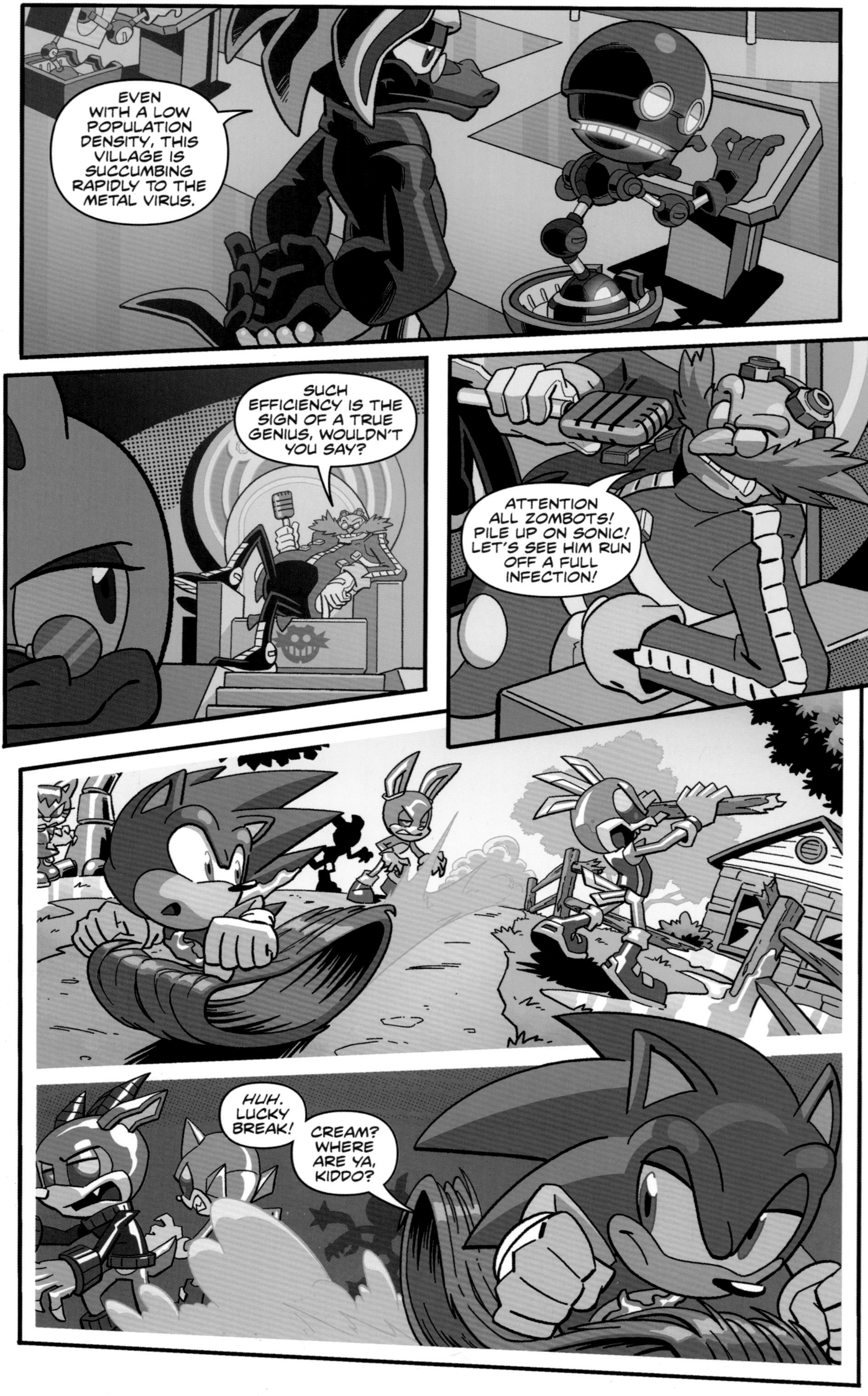

EVEN WITH A LOW POPULATION DENSITY, THIS VILLAGE IS SUCCUMBING RAPIDLY TO THE METAL VIRUS.
SUCH EFFICIENCY IS THE SIGN OF A TRUE GENIUS, WOULDN'T YOU SAY?
ATTENTION ALL ZOMBOTS! PILE UP ON SONIC! LET'S SEE HIM RUN OFF A FULL INFECTION!
HUH. LUCKY BREAK!
CREAM? WHERE ARE YA, KIDDO?

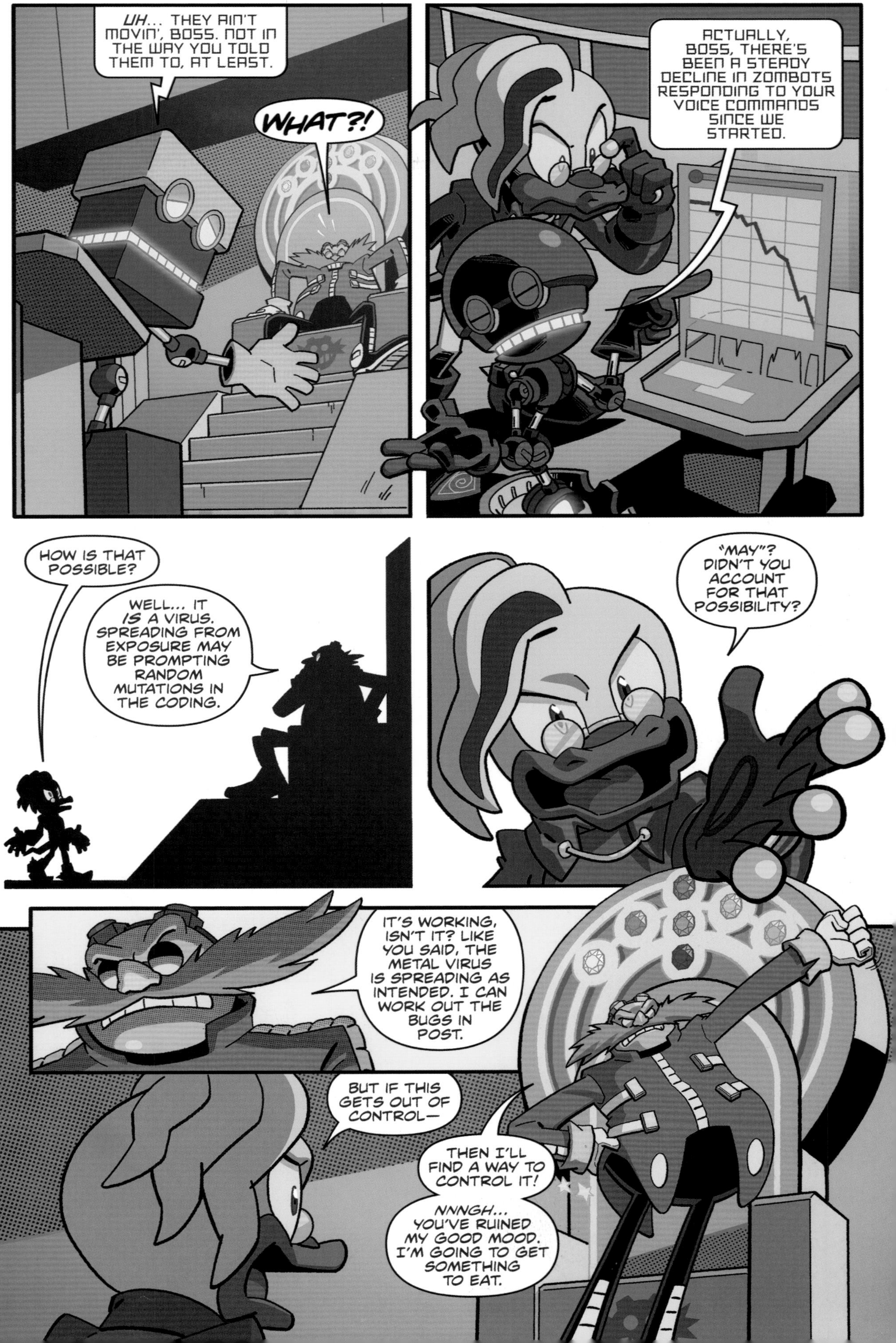
UH... THEY AIN'T MOVIN', BOSS. NOT IN THE WAY YOU TOLD THEM TO, AT LEAST.
WHAT?!
ACTUALLY, BOSS, THERE'S BEEN A STEADY DECLINE IN ZOMBOTS RESPONDING TO YOUR VOICE COMMANDS SINCE WE STARTED.
HOW IS THAT POSSIBLE?
WELL... IT IS A VIRUS. SPREADING FROM EXPOSURE MAY BE PROMPTING RANDOM MUTATIONS IN THE CODING.
"MAY"? DIDN'T YOU ACCOUNT FOR THAT POSSIBILITY?
IT'S WORKING, ISN'T IT? LIKE YOU SAID, THE METAL VIRUS IS SPREADING AS INTENDED. I CAN WORK OUT THE BUGS IN POST.
BUT IF THIS GETS OUT OF CONTROL—
THEN I'LL FIND A WAY TO CONTROL IT!
NNNGH... YOU'VE RUINED MY GOOD MOOD. I'M GOING TO GET SOMETHING TO EAT.

ORBOT... MAY I CONFIDE IN YOU?

PROVIDED YOU KEEP MY NEXT BREAK A SECRET?

...YES?

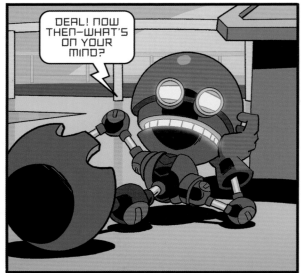

DEAL! NOW THEN—WHAT'S ON YOUR MIND?

EVER SINCE HE STARTED HIS CONQUEST OF THIS WORLD, I'VE BEEN *FASCINATED* BY DR. EGGMAN. HIS BRILLIANCE, HIS TENACITY, HIS CHARISMA.

I DEVOTED MYSELF TO ROBOTICS AND THE SEARCH FOR ARCANE POWERS BECAUSE OF HIM. WHENEVER I REACHED AN IMPASSE IN MY RESEARCH, I'D ASK MYSELF: "WHAT WOULD EGGMAN DO?"

I'VE DONE SO MUCH, DRIVEN BY WHAT I *THOUGHT* I KNEW ABOUT HIM, BUT...

I'D ALWAYS ASSUMED SONIC DEFEATED HIM BECAUSE HE WAS SO UNNATURALLY POWERFUL. BUT NOW IT LOOKS LIKE THE REAL CAUSE IS EGGMAN CAN'T PLAN FOR OR ADAPT TO THE LONG-TERM.

EH... IT'S ABOUT FIFTY-FIFTY TO BE HONEST. BIG IDEA, BIG EXECUTION, SONIC SHOWS UP, "I HATE THAT HEDGEHOG," BIG EXPLOSIONS. RINSE. REPEAT.

CLANG

A SHUTTLE IS COMING TO EVACUATE EVERYONE! HEAD NORTH TO THE GLADE!

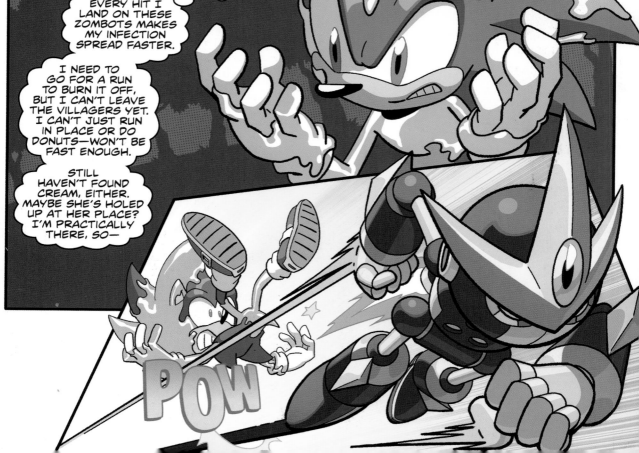

EVERY HIT I LAND ON THESE ZOMBOTS MAKES MY INFECTION SPREAD FASTER.

I NEED TO GO FOR A RUN TO BURN IT OFF, BUT I CAN'T LEAVE THE VILLAGERS YET. I CAN'T JUST RUN IN PLACE OR DO DONUTS—WON'T BE FAST ENOUGH.

STILL HAVEN'T FOUND CREAM, EITHER. MAYBE SHE'S HOLED UP AT HER PLACE? I'M PRACTICALLY THERE, SO—

POW

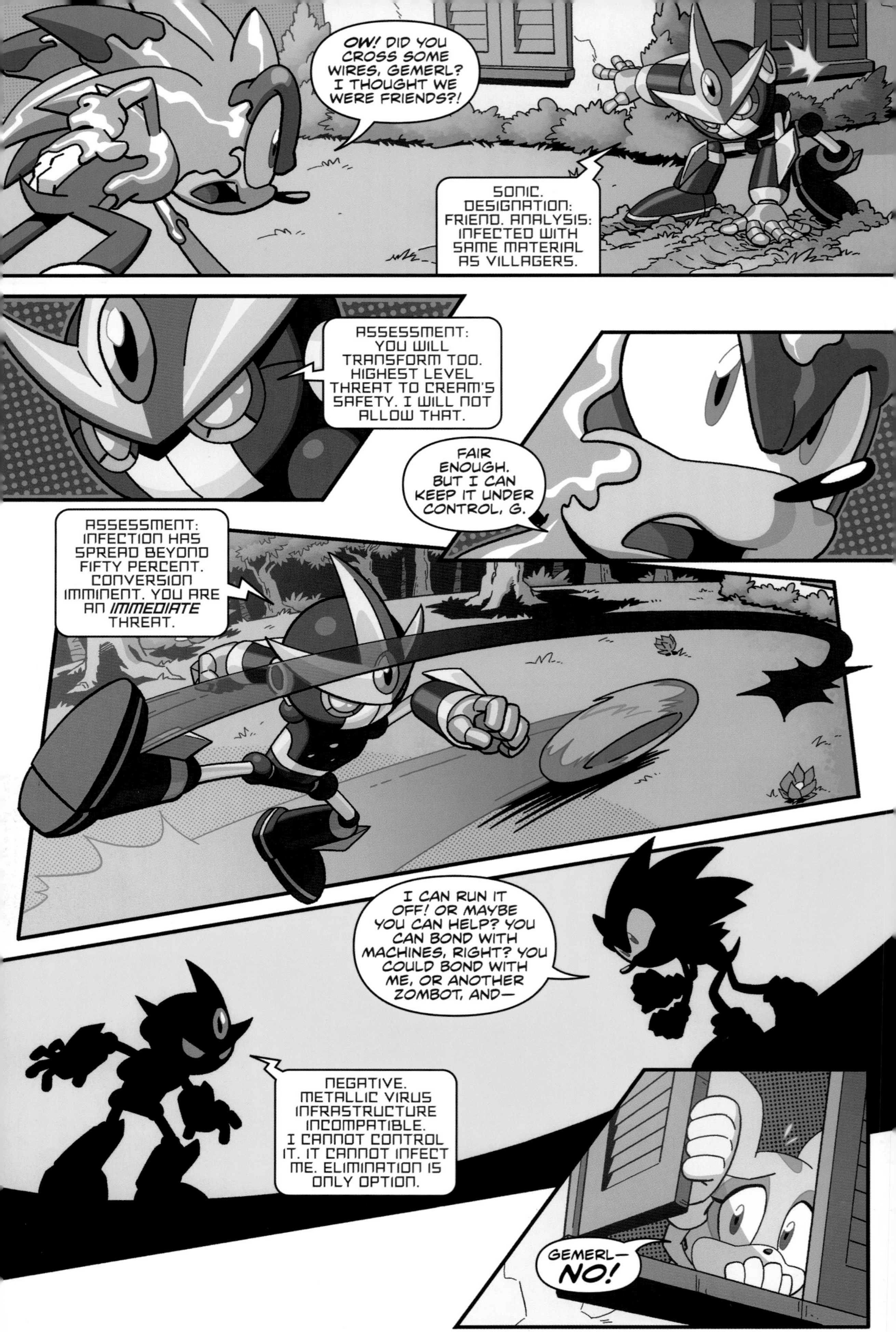
OW! DID YOU CROSS SOME WIRES, GEMERL? I THOUGHT WE WERE FRIENDS?!
SONIC. DESIGNATION: FRIEND. ANALYSIS: INFECTED WITH SAME MATERIAL AS VILLAGERS.
ASSESSMENT: YOU WILL TRANSFORM TOO. HIGHEST LEVEL THREAT TO CREAM'S SAFETY. I WILL NOT ALLOW THAT.
FAIR ENOUGH. BUT I CAN KEEP IT UNDER CONTROL, G.
ASSESSMENT: INFECTION HAS SPREAD BEYOND FIFTY PERCENT. CONVERSION IMMINENT. YOU ARE AN *IMMEDIATE* THREAT.
I CAN RUN IT OFF! OR MAYBE YOU CAN HELP? YOU CAN BOND WITH MACHINES, RIGHT? YOU COULD BOND WITH ME, OR ANOTHER ZOMBOT, AND—
NEGATIVE. METALLIC VIRUS INFRASTRUCTURE INCOMPATIBLE. I CANNOT CONTROL IT. IT CANNOT INFECT ME. ELIMINATION IS ONLY OPTION.
GEMERL— NO!

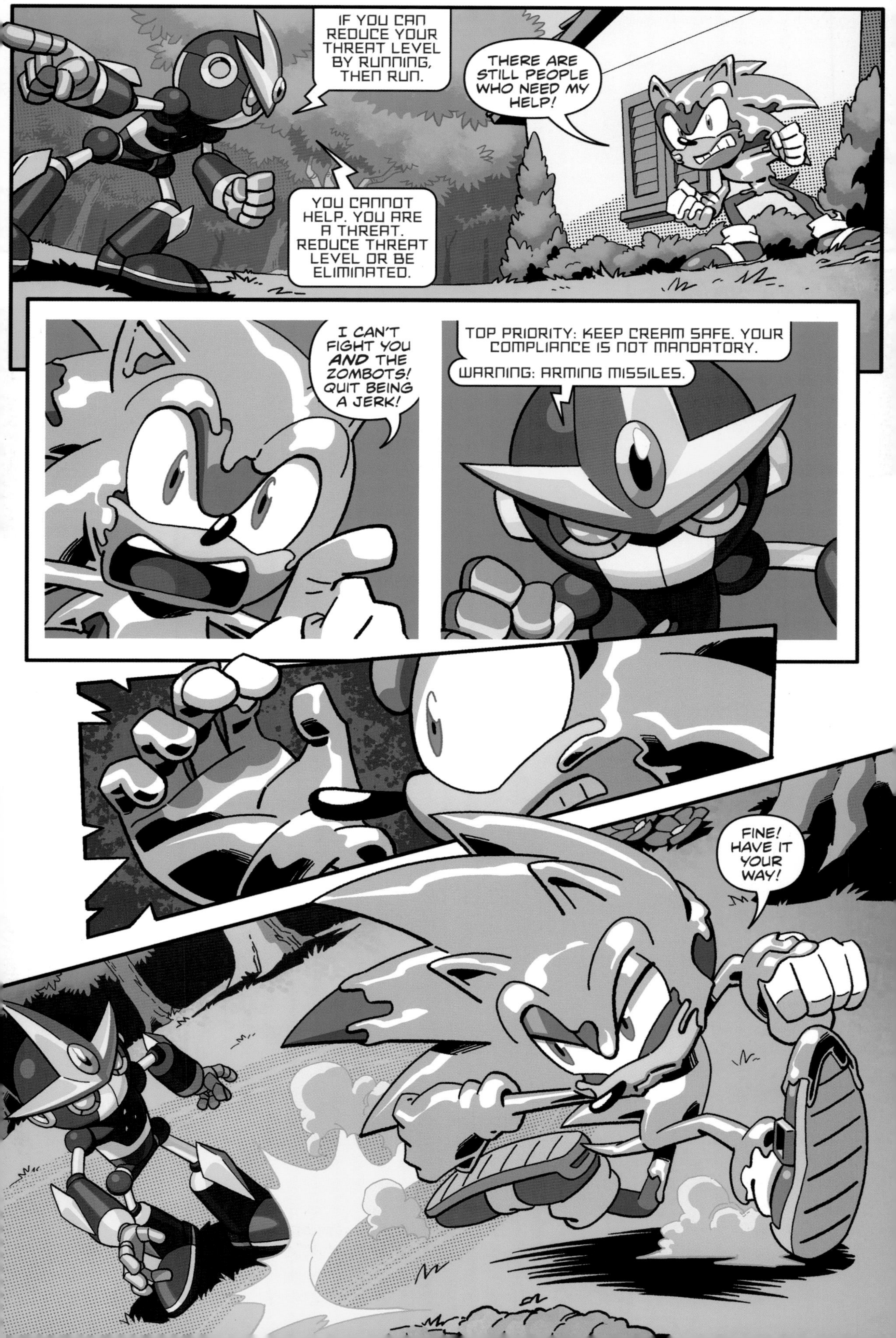

IF YOU CAN REDUCE YOUR THREAT LEVEL BY RUNNING, THEN RUN.
THERE ARE STILL PEOPLE WHO NEED MY HELP!
YOU CANNOT HELP. YOU ARE A THREAT. REDUCE THREAT LEVEL OR BE ELIMINATED.
I CAN'T FIGHT YOU *AND* THE ZOMBOTS! QUIT BEING A JERK!
TOP PRIORITY: KEEP CREAM SAFE. YOUR COMPLIANCE IS NOT MANDATORY.
WARNING: ARMING MISSILES.
FINE! HAVE IT YOUR WAY!

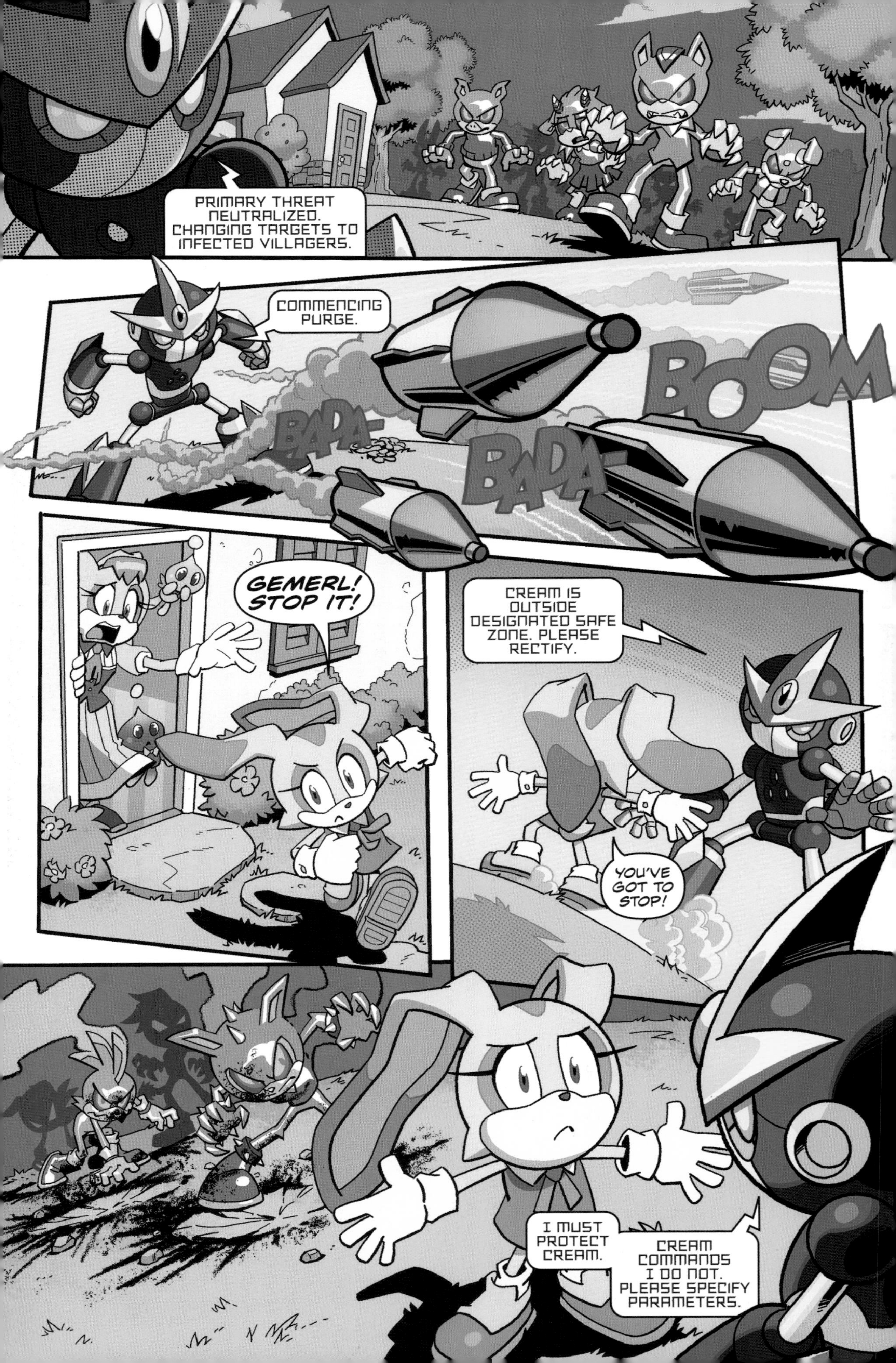
PRIMARY THREAT NEUTRALIZED. CHANGING TARGETS TO INFECTED VILLAGERS.
COMMENCING PURGE.
BADA-
BADA-
BOOM
GEMERL! STOP IT!
CREAM IS OUTSIDE DESIGNATED SAFE ZONE. PLEASE RECTIFY.
YOU'VE GOT TO STOP!
I MUST PROTECT CREAM.
CREAM COMMANDS I DO NOT. PLEASE SPECIFY PARAMETERS.

YOU CAN PROTECT US, BUT YOU'RE GOING TOO FAR!

PROXIMITY TO RESIDENCE HAS REMAINED NO GREATER THAN TWENTY METERS.

THAT'S NOT WHAT I MEAN!

YOU ATTACKED *SONIC!* HE'S OUR *FRIEND!* HE WOULD NEVER DO ANYTHING TO HURT US! YOU *KNOW* THAT!

SONIC IS INFECTED. SONIC IS A THREAT.

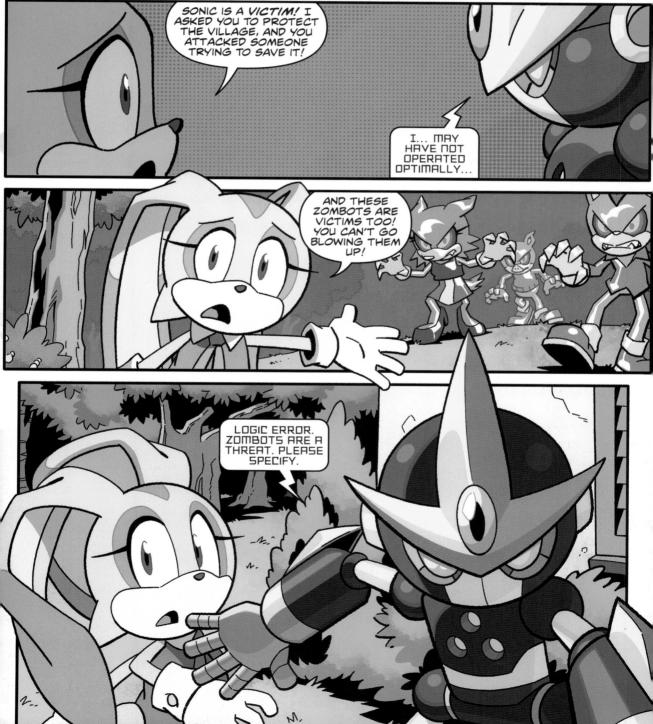

SONIC IS A *VICTIM!* I ASKED YOU TO PROTECT THE VILLAGE, AND YOU ATTACKED SOMEONE TRYING TO SAVE IT!

I... MAY HAVE NOT OPERATED OPTIMALLY...

AND THESE ZOMBOTS ARE VICTIMS TOO! YOU CAN'T GO BLOWING THEM UP!

LOGIC ERROR. ZOMBOTS ARE A THREAT. PLEASE SPECIFY.

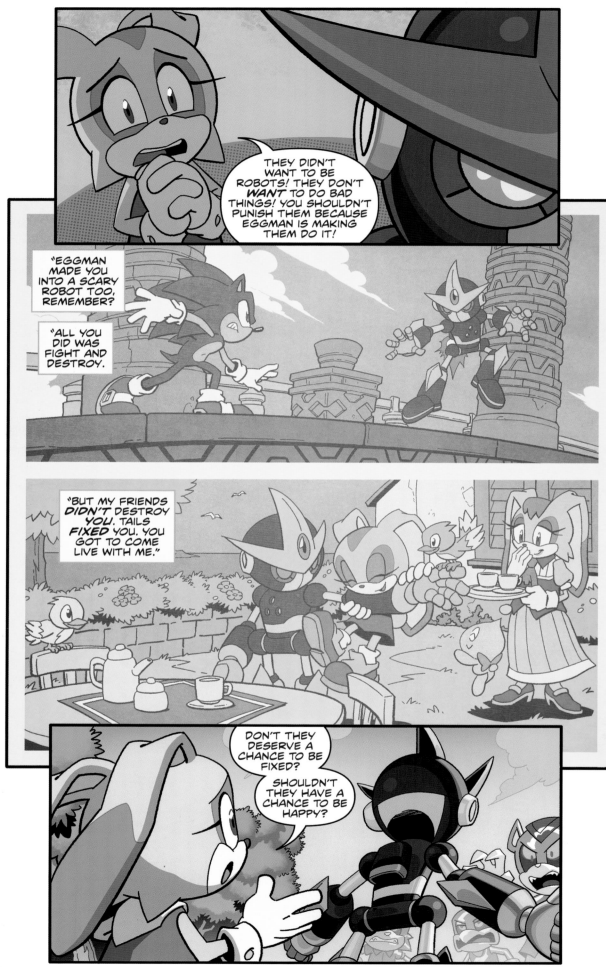

THEY DIDN'T WANT TO BE ROBOTS! THEY DON'T **WANT** TO DO BAD THINGS! YOU SHOULDN'T PUNISH THEM BECAUSE EGGMAN IS MAKING THEM DO IT!

"EGGMAN MADE YOU INTO A SCARY ROBOT TOO, REMEMBER?

"ALL YOU DID WAS FIGHT AND DESTROY.

"BUT MY FRIENDS *DIDN'T* DESTROY *YOU*. TAILS *FIXED* YOU. YOU GOT TO COME LIVE WITH ME."

DON'T THEY DESERVE A CHANCE TO BE FIXED?

SHOULDN'T THEY HAVE A CHANCE TO BE HAPPY?

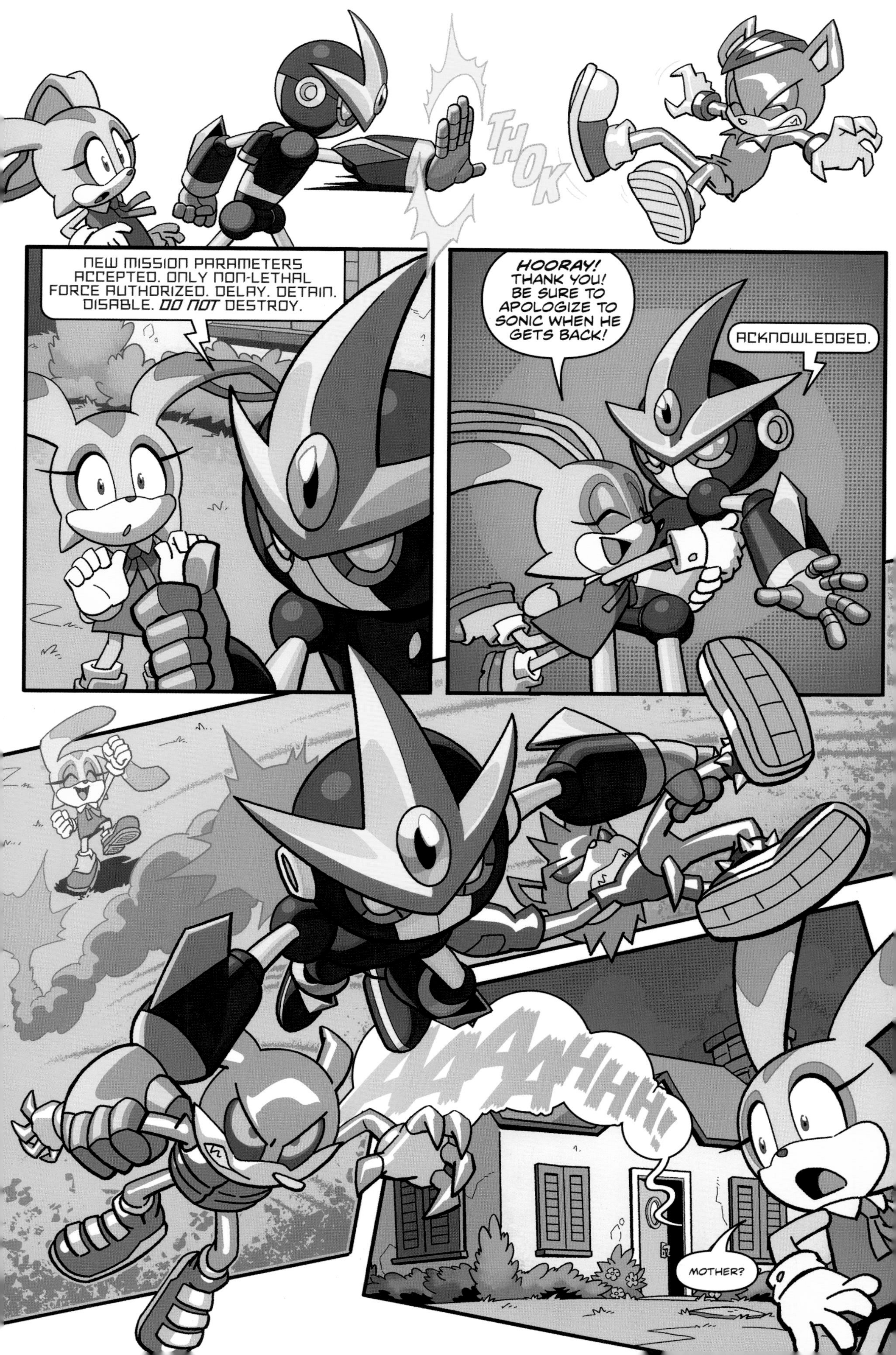
THOK
NEW MISSION PARAMETERS ACCEPTED. ONLY NON-LETHAL FORCE AUTHORIZED. DELAY. DETAIN. DISABLE. DO NOT DESTROY.
HOORAY! THANK YOU! BE SURE TO APOLOGIZE TO SONIC WHEN HE GETS BACK!
ACKNOWLEDGED.
AAAAHHH!
MOTHER?

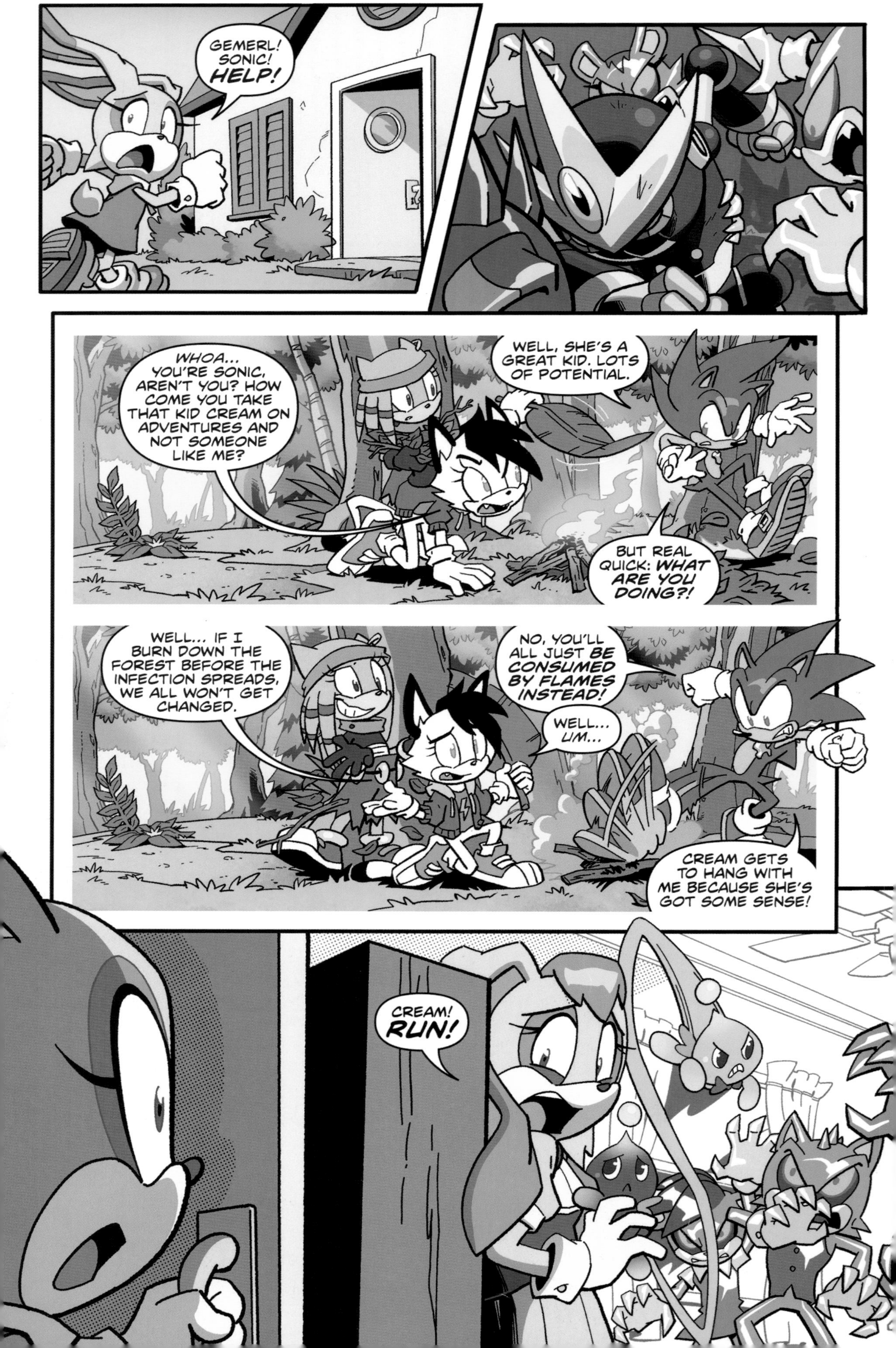
GEMERL! SONIC! HELP!
WHOA... YOU'RE SONIC, AREN'T YOU? HOW COME YOU TAKE THAT KID CREAM ON ADVENTURES AND NOT SOMEONE LIKE ME?
WELL, SHE'S A GREAT KID. LOTS OF POTENTIAL.
BUT REAL QUICK: WHAT ARE YOU DOING?!
WELL... IF I BURN DOWN THE FOREST BEFORE THE INFECTION SPREADS, WE ALL WON'T GET CHANGED.
NO, YOU'LL ALL JUST BE CONSUMED BY FLAMES INSTEAD!
WELL... UM...
CREAM GETS TO HANG WITH ME BECAUSE SHE'S GOT SOME SENSE!
CREAM! RUN!

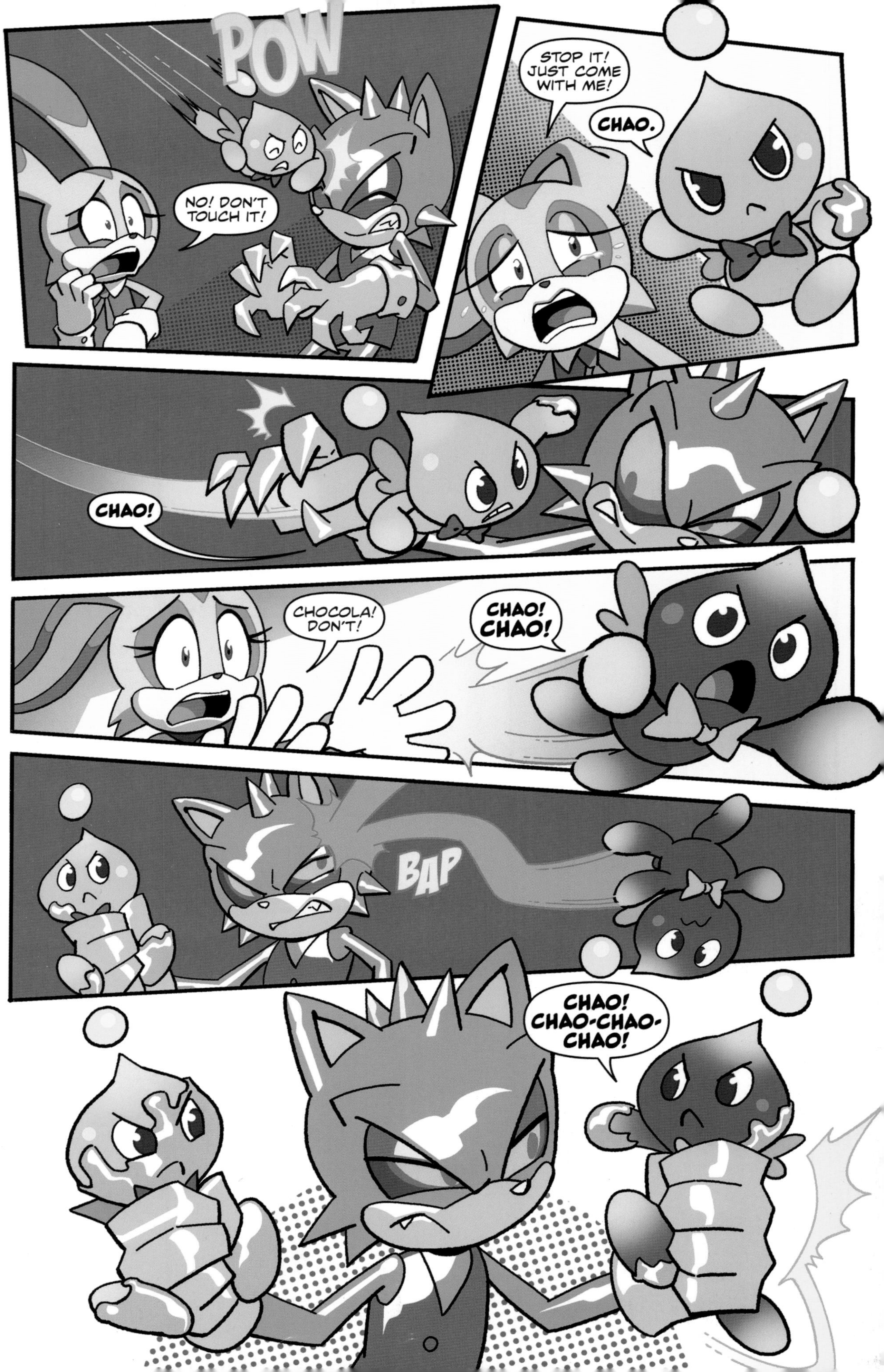
POW
NO! DON'T TOUCH IT!
STOP IT! JUST COME WITH ME!
CHAO.
CHAO!
CHOCOLA! DON'T!
CHAO! CHAO!
BAP
CHAO! CHAO-CHAO-CHAO!

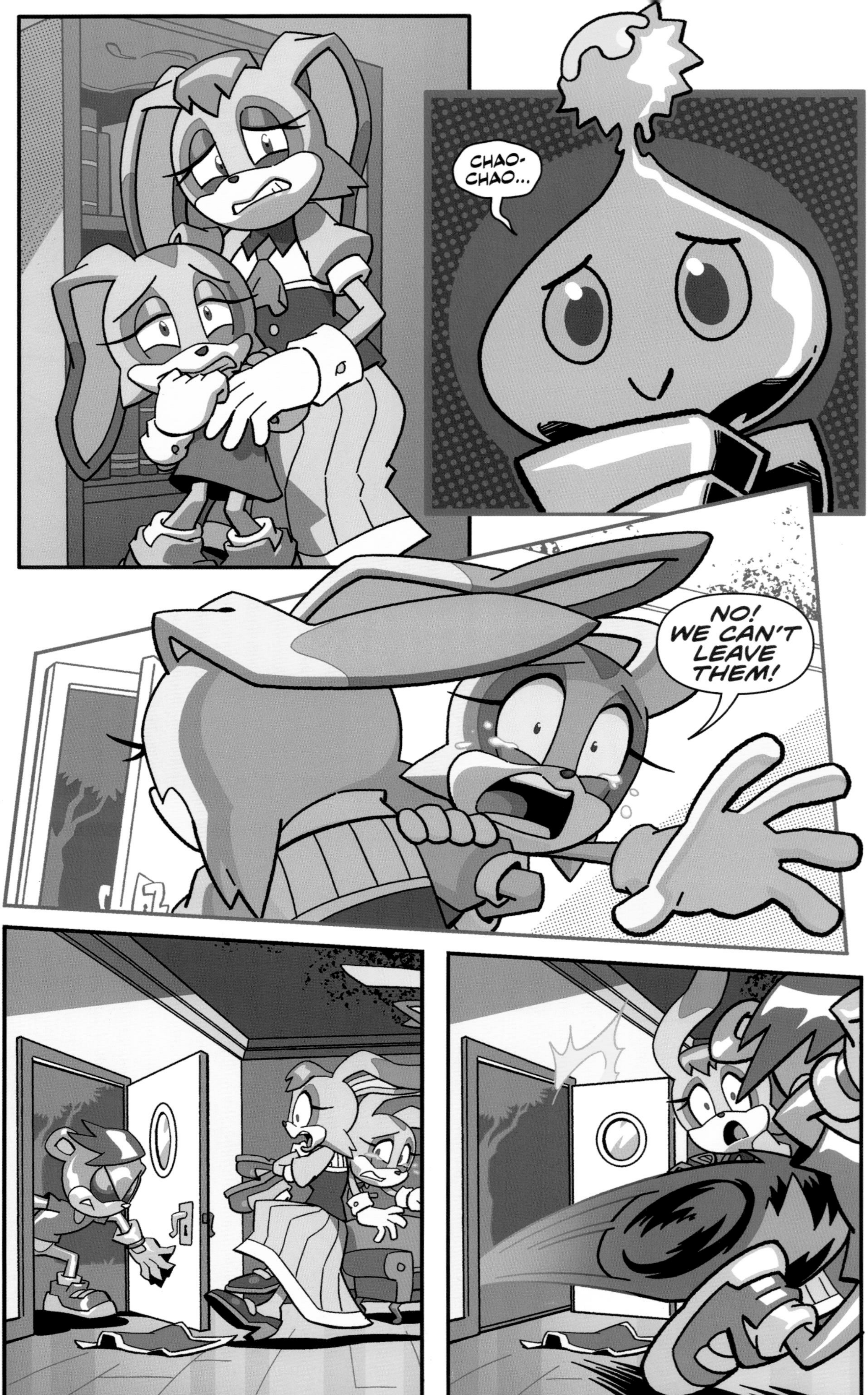
CHAO-CHAO...
NO! WE CAN'T LEAVE THEM!

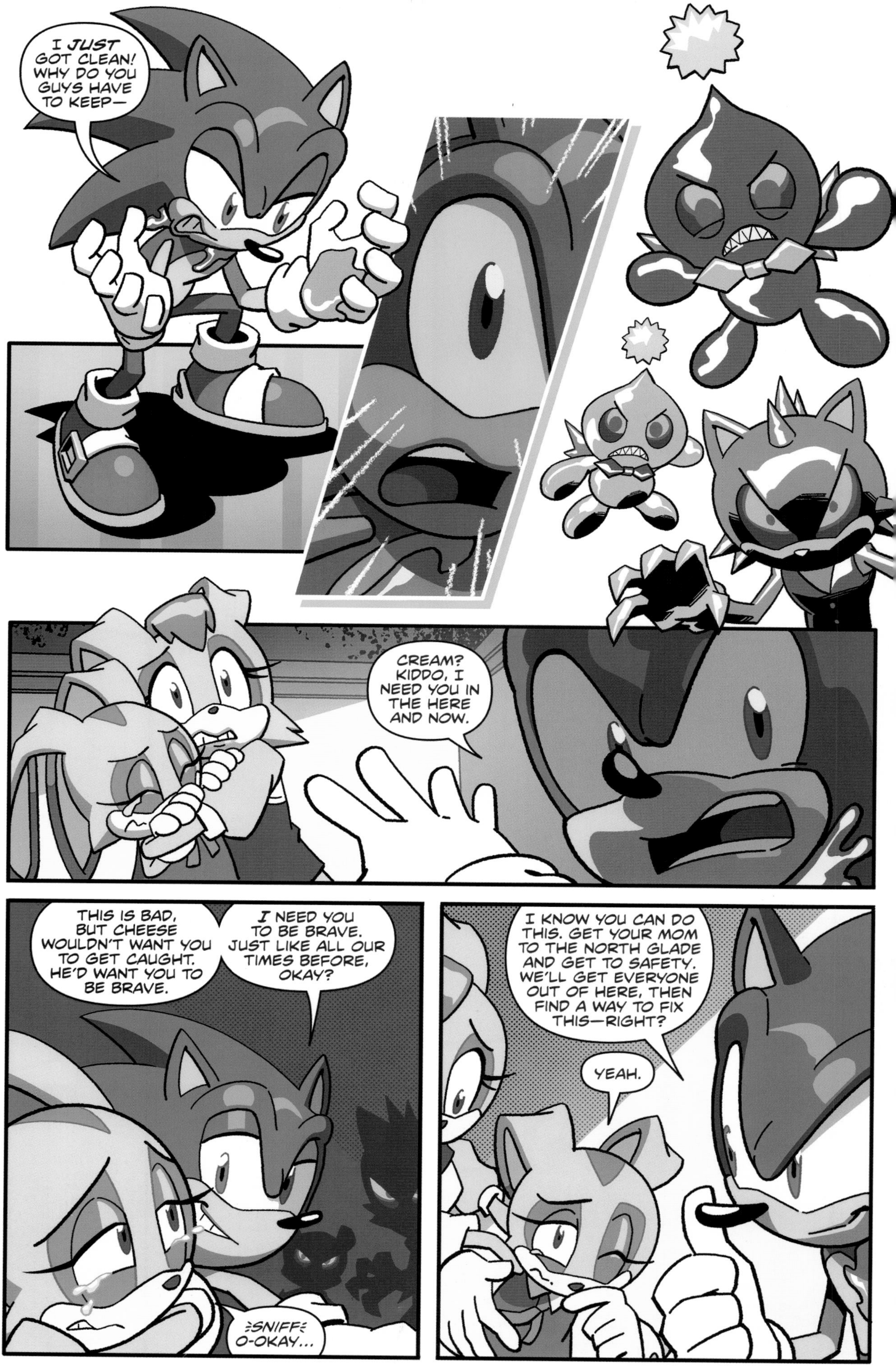
I JUST GOT CLEAN! WHY DO YOU GUYS HAVE TO KEEP—
CREAM? KIDDO, I NEED YOU IN THE HERE AND NOW.
THIS IS BAD, BUT CHEESE WOULDN'T WANT YOU TO GET CAUGHT. HE'D WANT YOU TO BE BRAVE.
I NEED YOU TO BE BRAVE. JUST LIKE ALL OUR TIMES BEFORE, OKAY?
SNIFF O-OKAY...
I KNOW YOU CAN DO THIS. GET YOUR MOM TO THE NORTH GLADE AND GET TO SAFETY. WE'LL GET EVERYONE OUT OF HERE, THEN FIND A WAY TO FIX THIS—RIGHT?
YEAH.

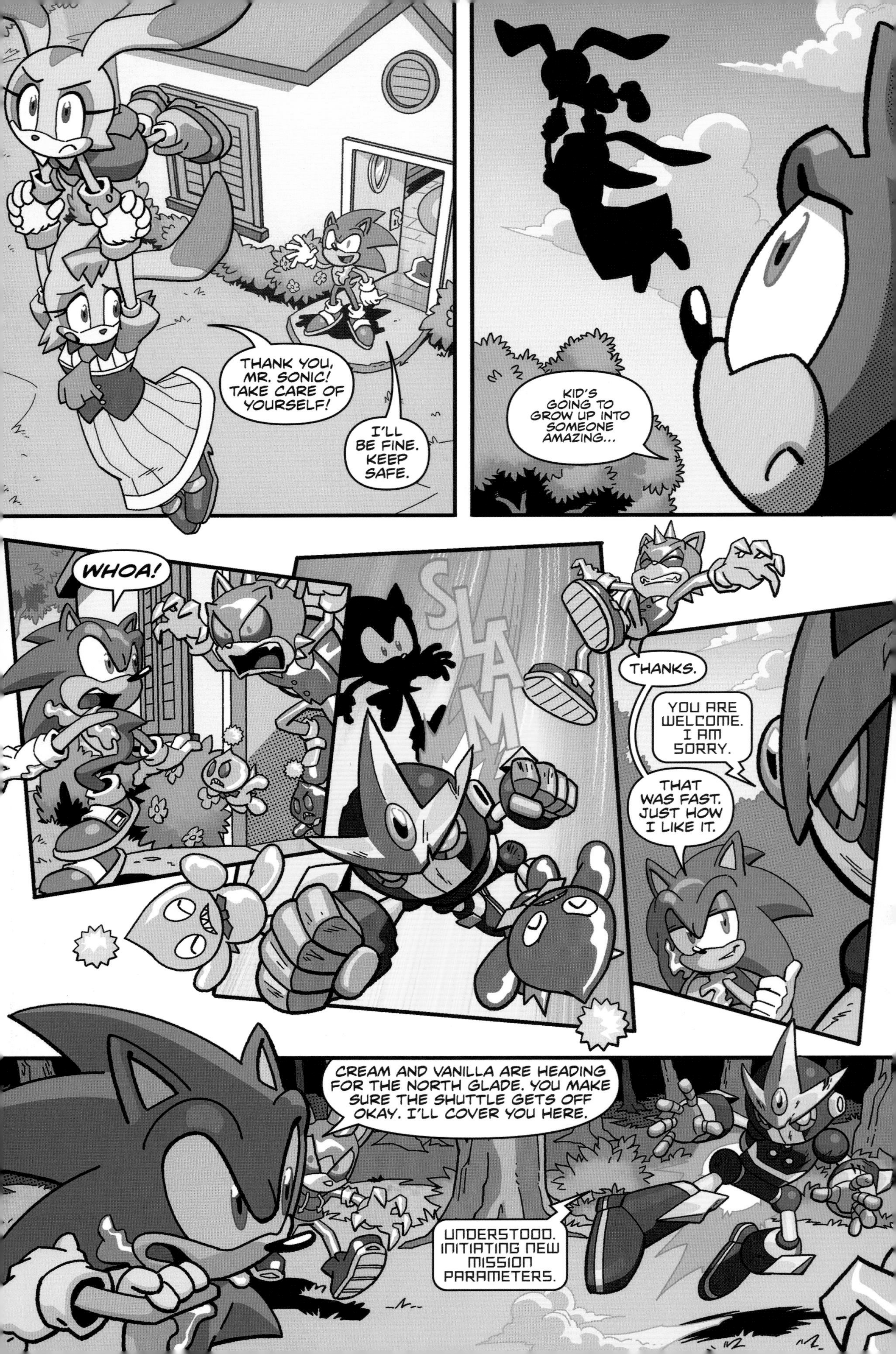
THANK YOU, MR. SONIC! TAKE CARE OF YOURSELF!
I'LL BE FINE. KEEP SAFE.
KID'S GOING TO GROW UP INTO SOMEONE AMAZING...
WHOA!
SLAM
THANKS.
YOU ARE WELCOME. I AM SORRY.
THAT WAS FAST. JUST HOW I LIKE IT.
CREAM AND VANILLA ARE HEADING FOR THE NORTH GLADE. YOU MAKE SURE THE SHUTTLE GETS OFF OKAY. I'LL COVER YOU HERE.
UNDERSTOOD. INITIATING NEW MISSION PARAMETERS.

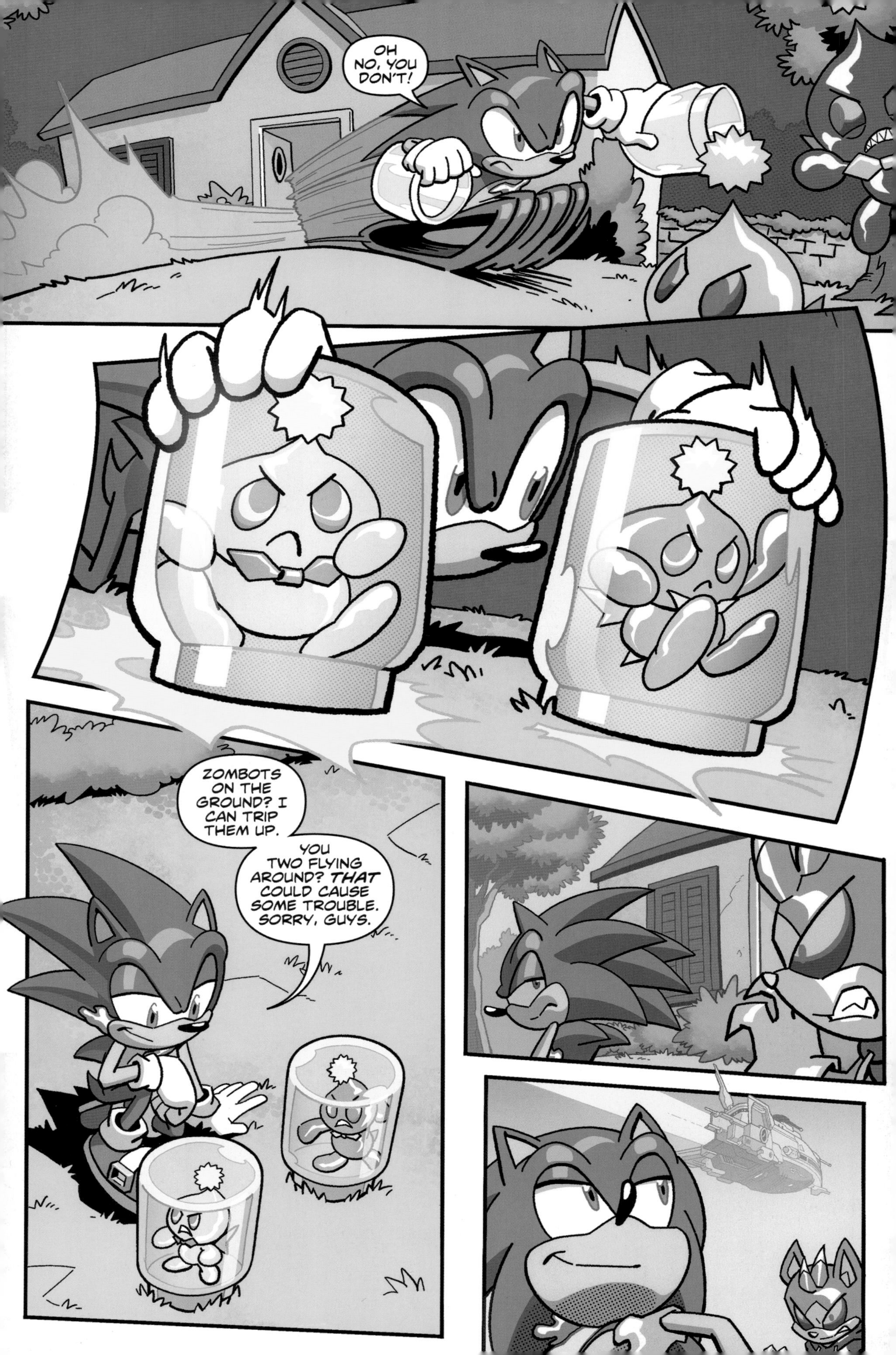
OH NO, YOU DON'T!
ZOMBOTS ON THE GROUND? I CAN TRIP THEM UP.
YOU TWO FLYING AROUND? *THAT* COULD CAUSE SOME TROUBLE. SORRY, GUYS.

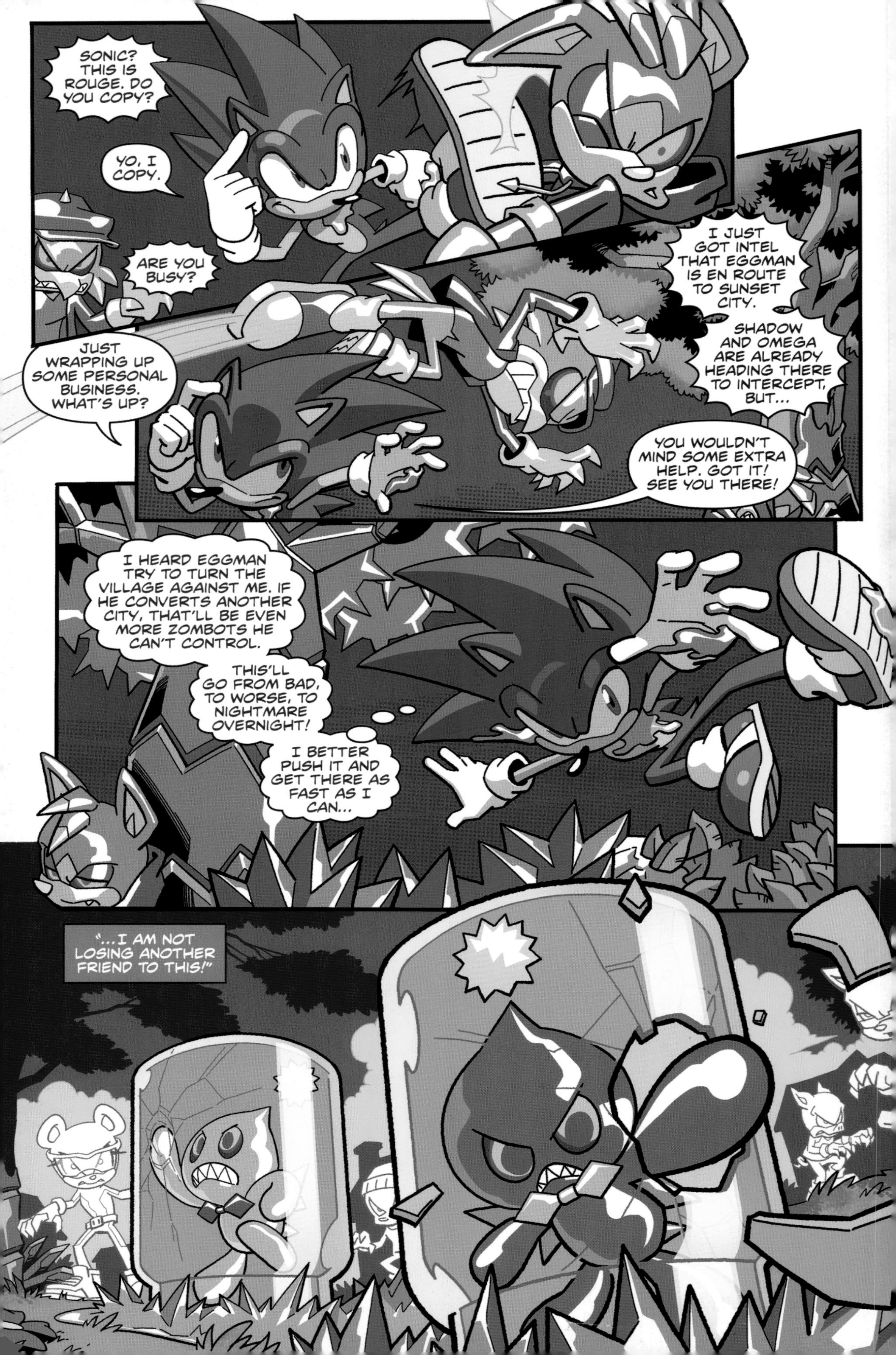
SONIC? THIS IS ROUGE. DO YOU COPY?
YO, I COPY.
ARE YOU BUSY?
JUST WRAPPING UP SOME PERSONAL BUSINESS. WHAT'S UP?
I JUST GOT INTEL THAT EGGMAN IS EN ROUTE TO SUNSET CITY.
SHADOW AND OMEGA ARE ALREADY HEADING THERE TO INTERCEPT, BUT...
YOU WOULDN'T MIND SOME EXTRA HELP. GOT IT! SEE YOU THERE!
I HEARD EGGMAN TRY TO TURN THE VILLAGE AGAINST ME. IF HE CONVERTS ANOTHER CITY, THAT'LL BE EVEN MORE ZOMBOTS HE CAN'T CONTROL.
THIS'LL GO FROM BAD, TO WORSE, TO NIGHTMARE OVERNIGHT!
I BETTER PUSH IT AND GET THERE AS FAST AS I CAN...
"...I AM NOT LOSING ANOTHER FRIEND TO THIS!"

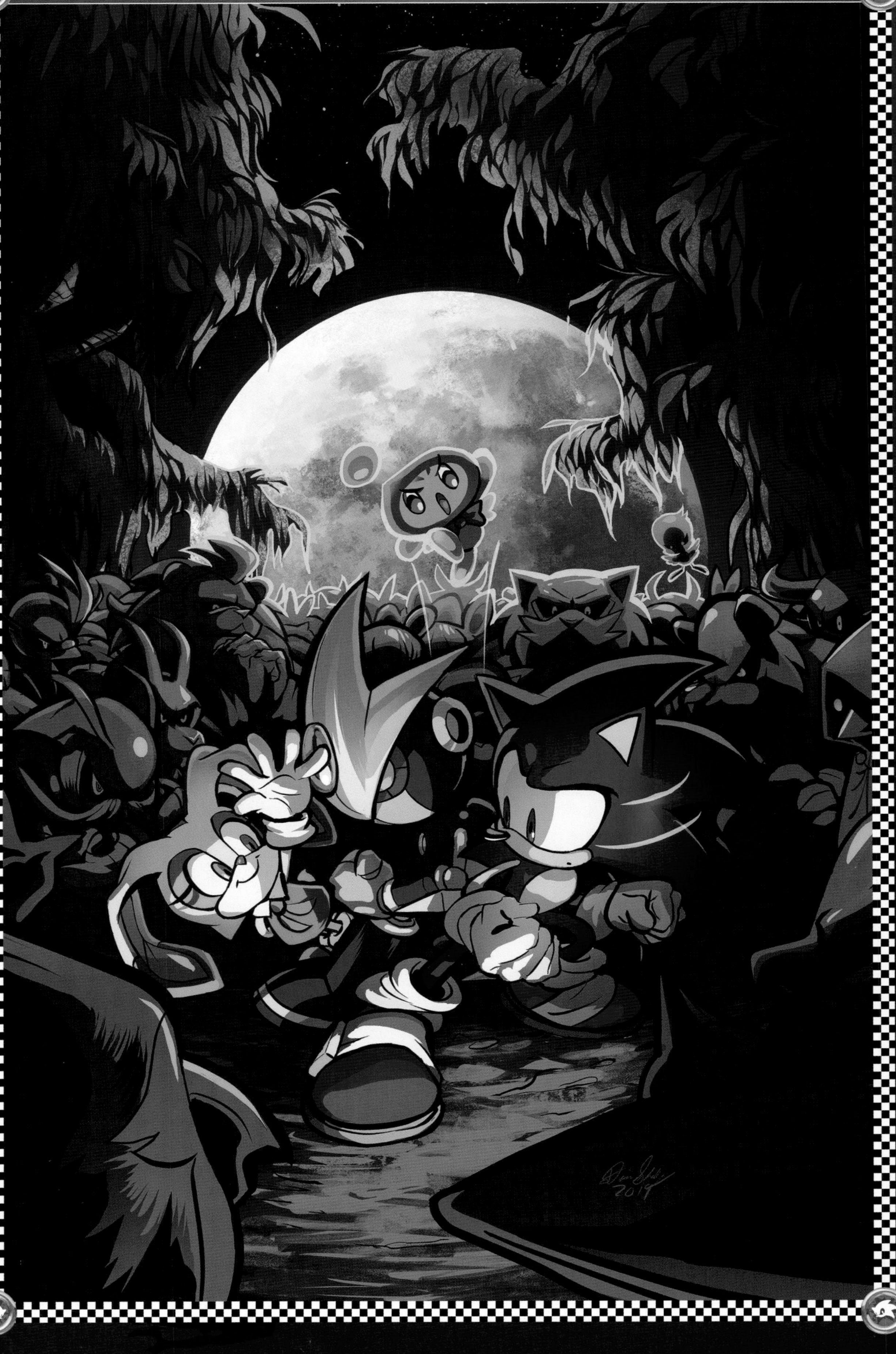

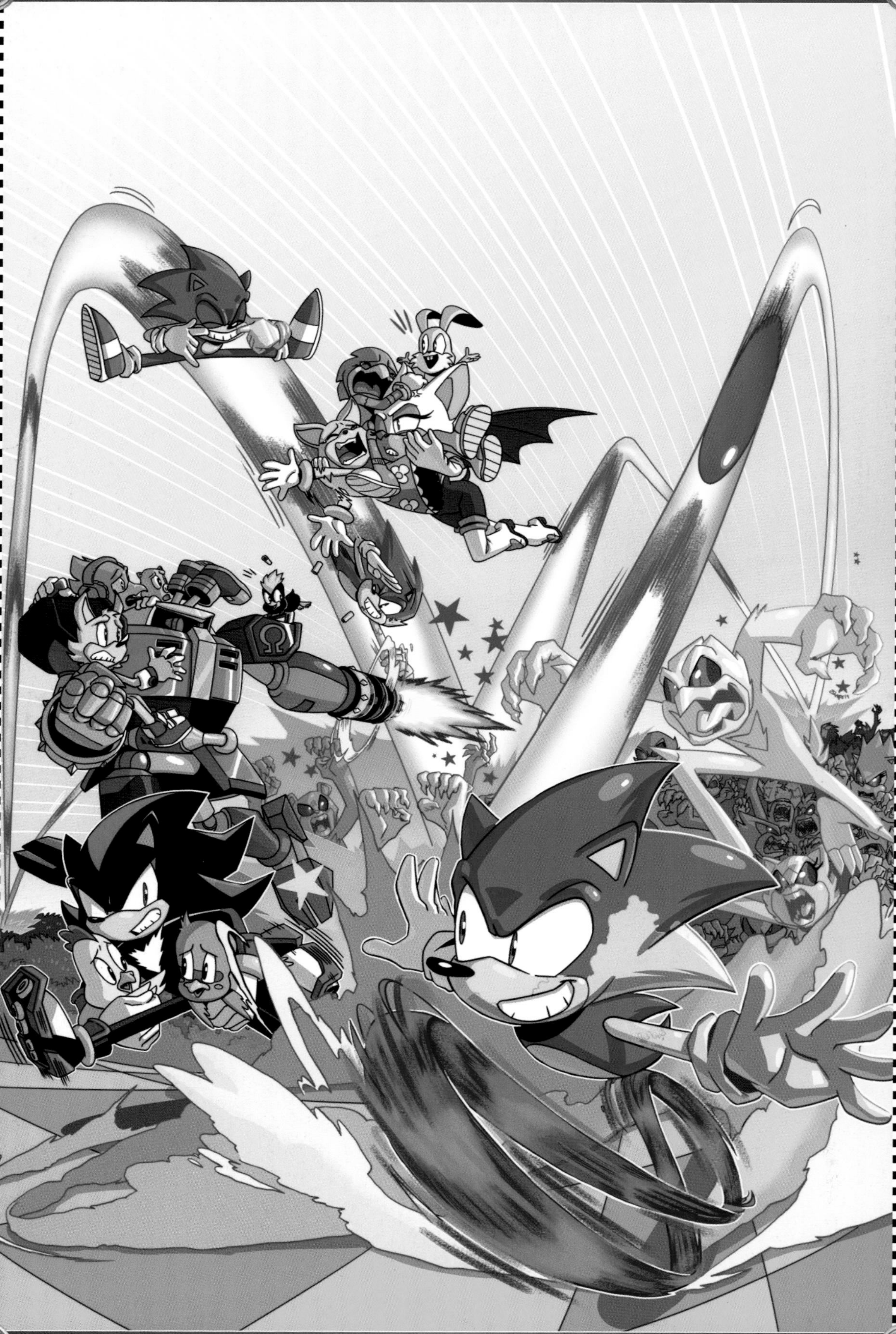

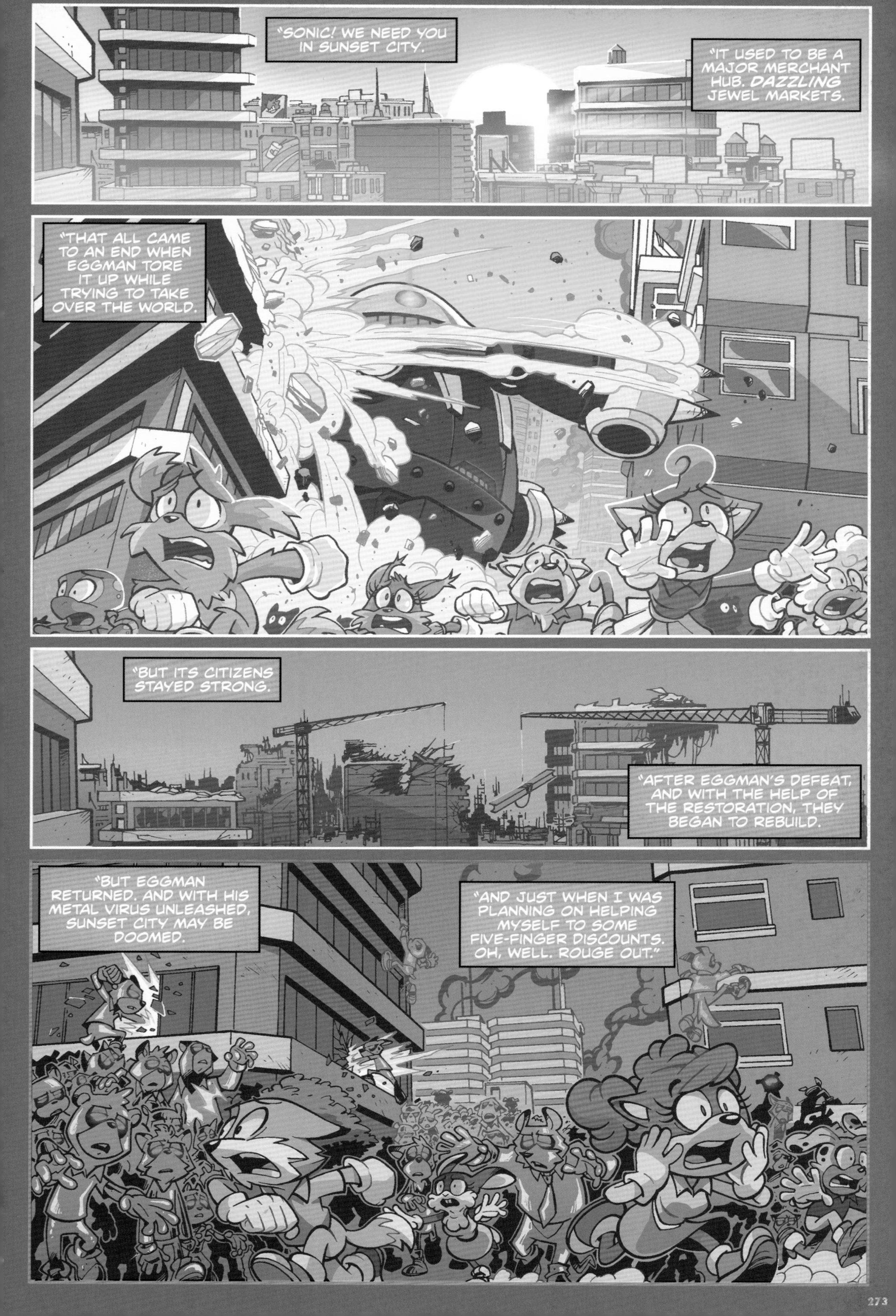

"SONIC! WE NEED YOU IN SUNSET CITY.
"IT USED TO BE A MAJOR MERCHANT HUB. DAZZLING JEWEL MARKETS.
"THAT ALL CAME TO AN END WHEN EGGMAN TORE IT UP WHILE TRYING TO TAKE OVER THE WORLD.
"BUT ITS CITIZENS STAYED STRONG.
"AFTER EGGMAN'S DEFEAT, AND WITH THE HELP OF THE RESTORATION, THEY BEGAN TO REBUILD.
"BUT EGGMAN RETURNED. AND WITH HIS METAL VIRUS UNLEASHED, SUNSET CITY MAY BE DOOMED.
"AND JUST WHEN I WAS PLANNING ON HELPING MYSELF TO SOME FIVE-FINGER DISCOUNTS. OH, WELL. ROUGE OUT."

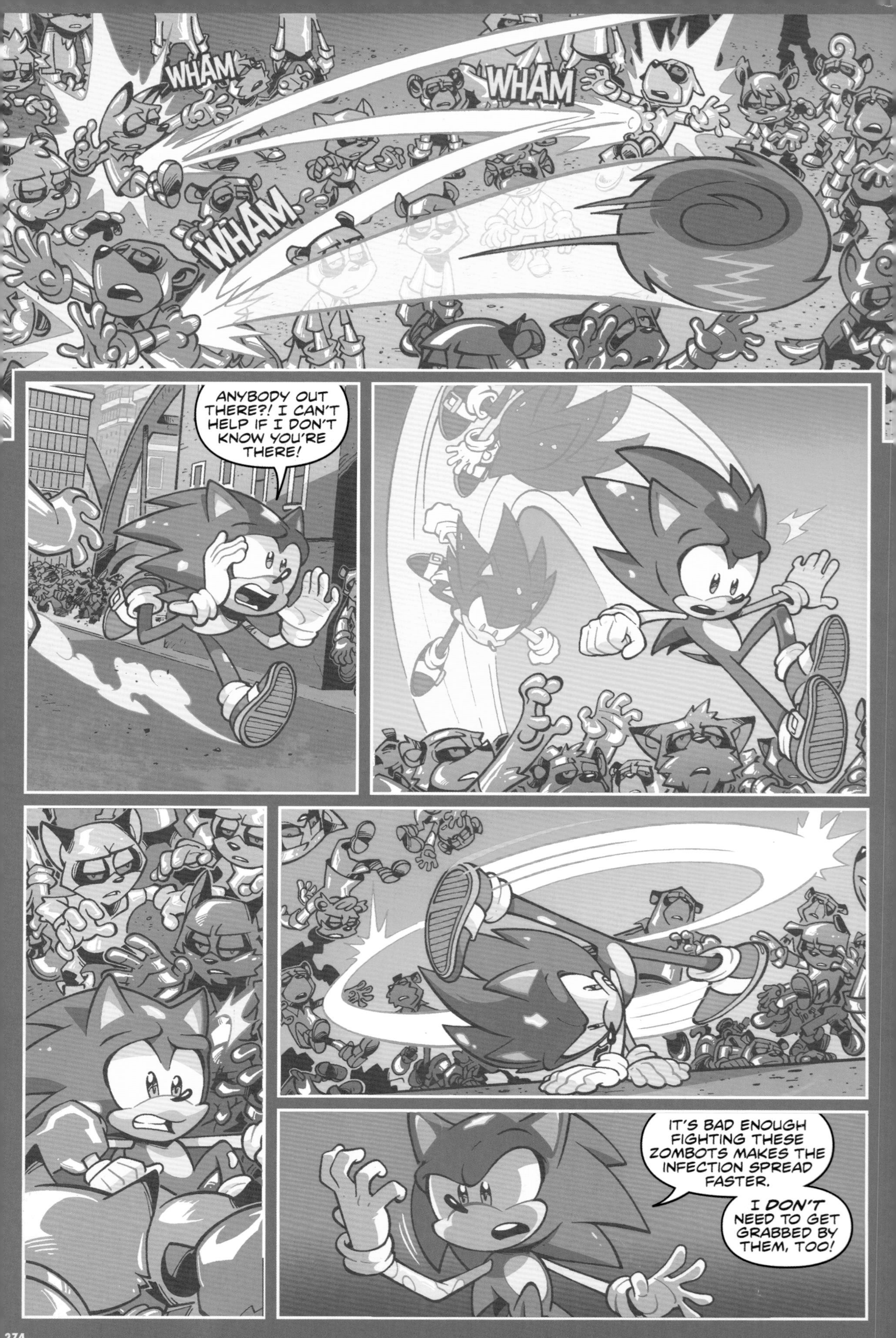
WHAM
WHAM
WHAM
ANYBODY OUT THERE?! I CAN'T HELP IF I DON'T KNOW YOU'RE THERE!
IT'S BAD ENOUGH FIGHTING THESE ZOMBOTS MAKES THE INFECTION SPREAD FASTER.
I DON'T NEED TO GET GRABBED BY THEM, TOO!

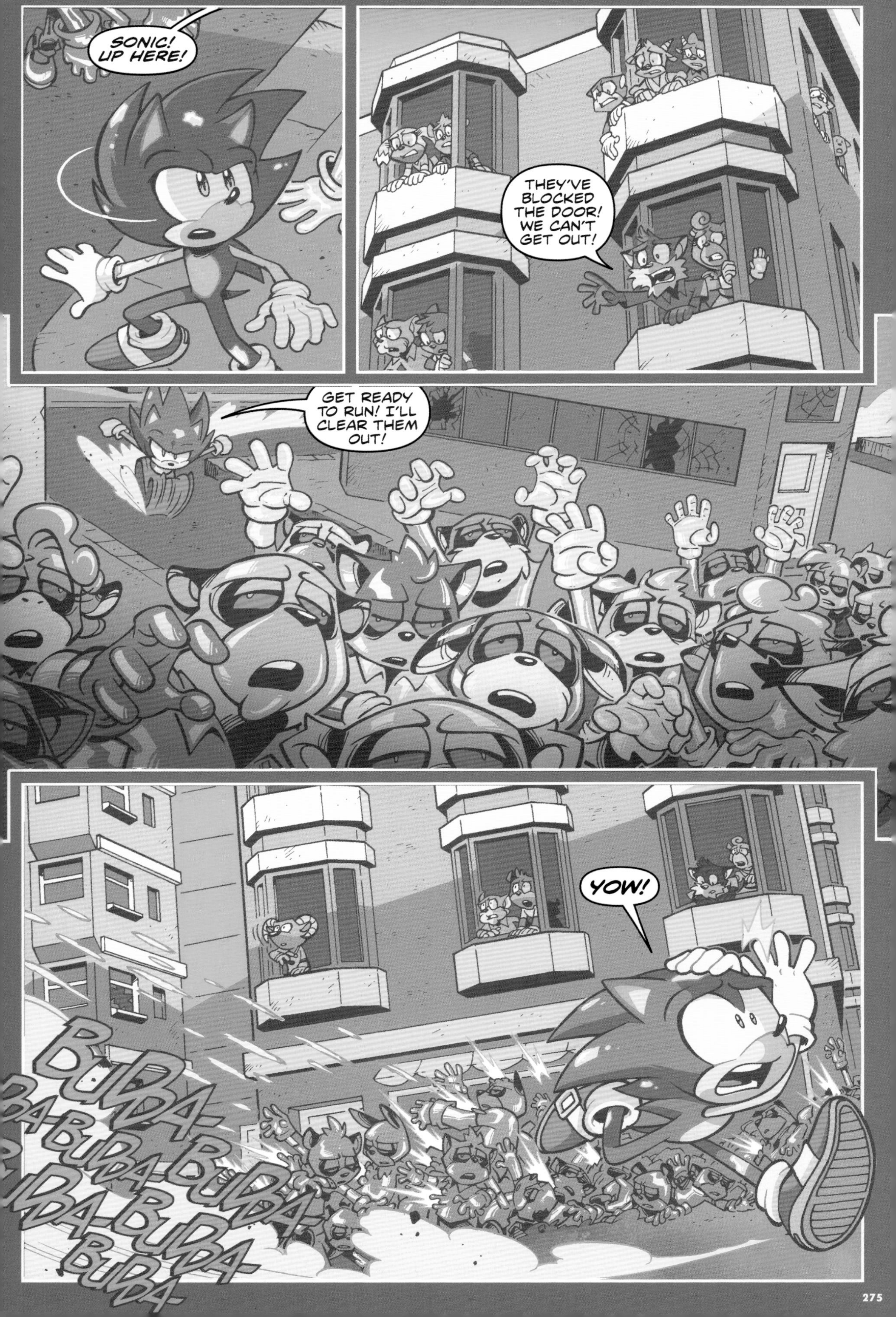
SONIC! UP HERE!
THEY'VE BLOCKED THE DOOR! WE CAN'T GET OUT!
GET READY TO RUN! I'LL CLEAR THEM OUT!
YOW!
BUDA-BUDA-BUDA-BUDA-BUDA-BUDA-BUDA-BUDA-

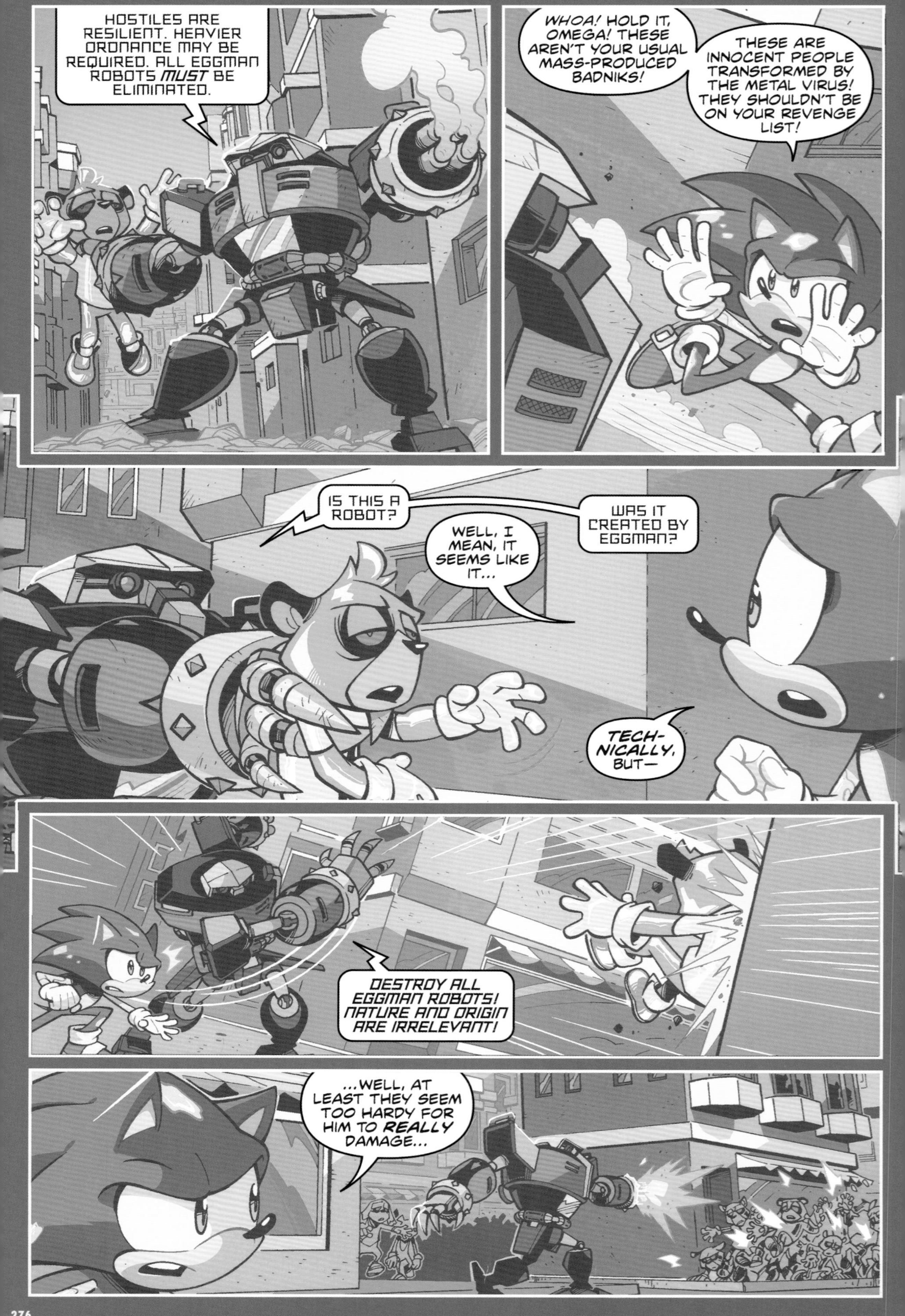
HOSTILES ARE RESILIENT. HEAVIER ORDNANCE MAY BE REQUIRED. ALL EGGMAN ROBOTS MUST BE ELIMINATED.
WHOA! HOLD IT, OMEGA! THESE AREN'T YOUR USUAL MASS-PRODUCED BADNIKS!
THESE ARE INNOCENT PEOPLE TRANSFORMED BY THE METAL VIRUS! THEY SHOULDN'T BE ON YOUR REVENGE LIST!
IS THIS A ROBOT?
WELL, I MEAN, IT SEEMS LIKE IT...
WAS IT CREATED BY EGGMAN?
TECH-NICALLY, BUT—
DESTROY ALL EGGMAN ROBOTS! NATURE AND ORIGIN ARE IRRELEVANT!
...WELL, AT LEAST THEY SEEM TOO HARDY FOR HIM TO REALLY DAMAGE...

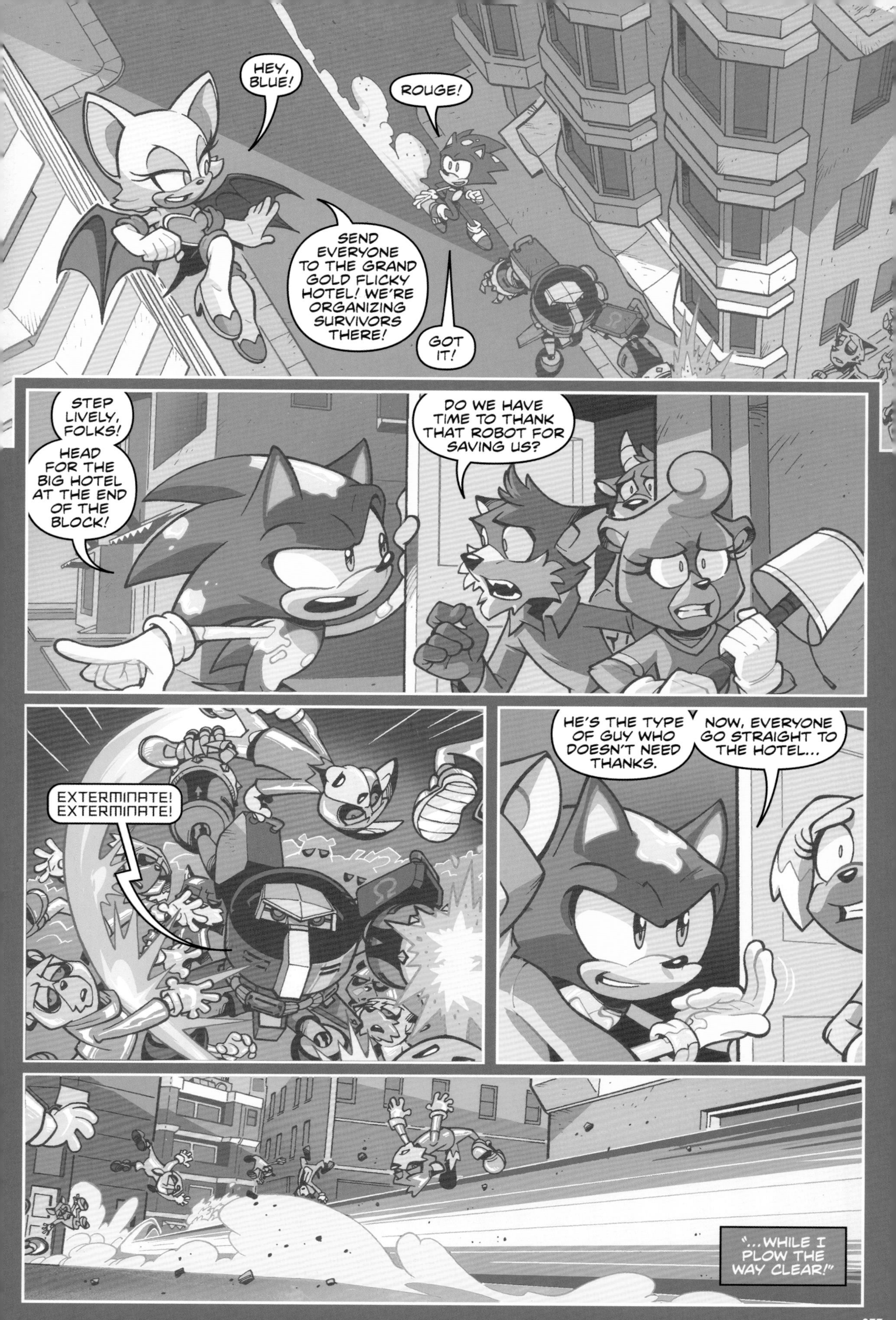
HEY, BLUE!
ROUGE!
SEND EVERYONE TO THE GRAND GOLD FLICKY HOTEL! WE'RE ORGANIZING SURVIVORS THERE!
GOT IT!
STEP LIVELY, FOLKS!
HEAD FOR THE BIG HOTEL AT THE END OF THE BLOCK!
DO WE HAVE TIME TO THANK THAT ROBOT FOR SAVING US?
EXTERMINATE! EXTERMINATE!
HE'S THE TYPE OF GUY WHO DOESN'T NEED THANKS.
NOW, EVERYONE GO STRAIGHT TO THE HOTEL...
"...WHILE I PLOW THE WAY CLEAR!"

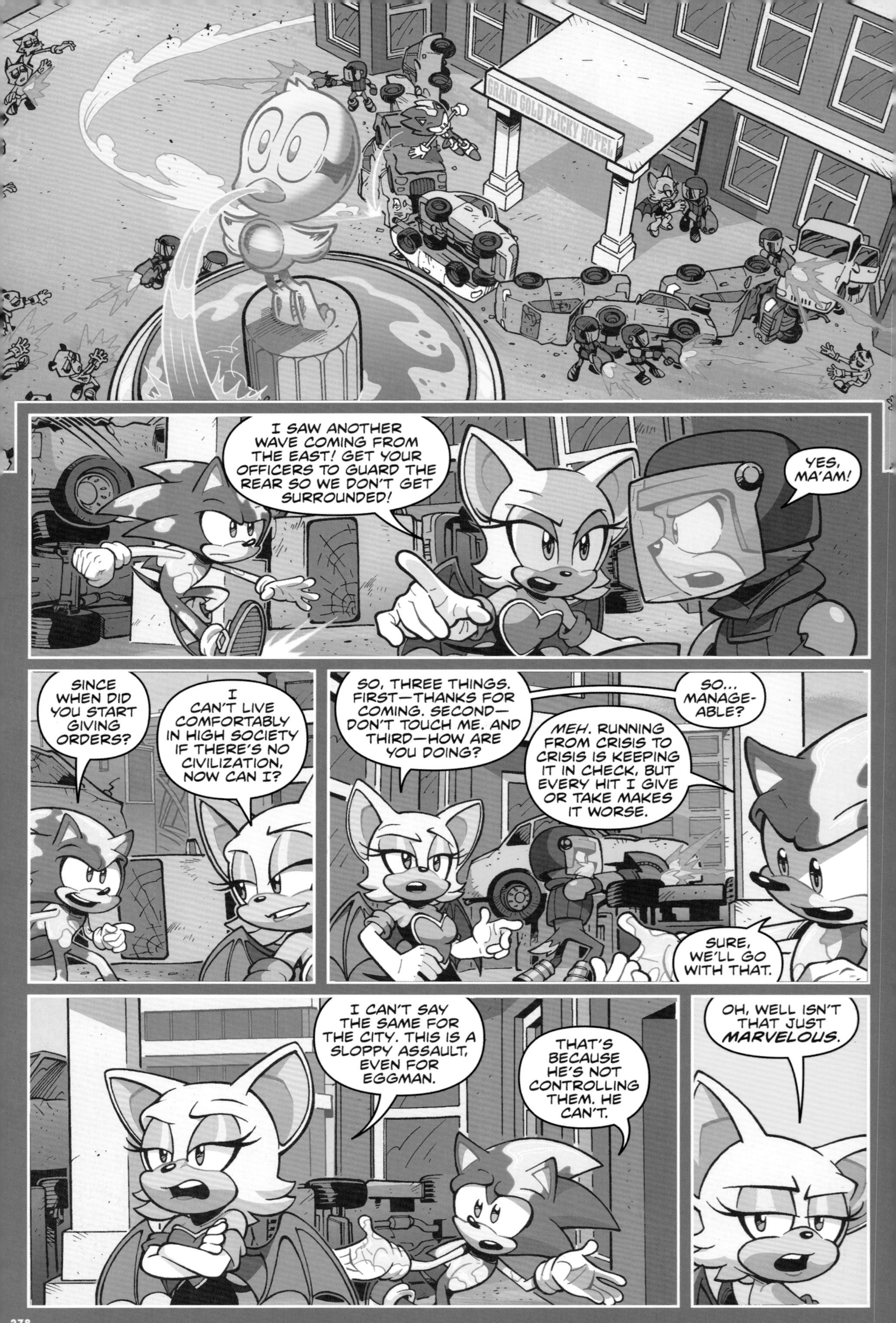
GRAND GOLD FLICKY HOTEL
I SAW ANOTHER WAVE COMING FROM THE EAST! GET YOUR OFFICERS TO GUARD THE REAR SO WE DON'T GET SURROUNDED!
YES, MA'AM!
SINCE WHEN DID YOU START GIVING ORDERS?
I CAN'T LIVE COMFORTABLY IN HIGH SOCIETY IF THERE'S NO CIVILIZATION, NOW CAN I?
SO, THREE THINGS. FIRST—THANKS FOR COMING. SECOND—DON'T TOUCH ME. AND THIRD—HOW ARE YOU DOING?
MEH. RUNNING FROM CRISIS TO CRISIS IS KEEPING IT IN CHECK, BUT EVERY HIT I GIVE OR TAKE MAKES IT WORSE.
SO... MANAGE-ABLE?
SURE, WE'LL GO WITH THAT.
I CAN'T SAY THE SAME FOR THE CITY. THIS IS A SLOPPY ASSAULT, EVEN FOR EGGMAN.
THAT'S BECAUSE HE'S NOT CONTROLLING THEM. HE CAN'T.
OH, WELL ISN'T THAT JUST ***MARVELOUS***.

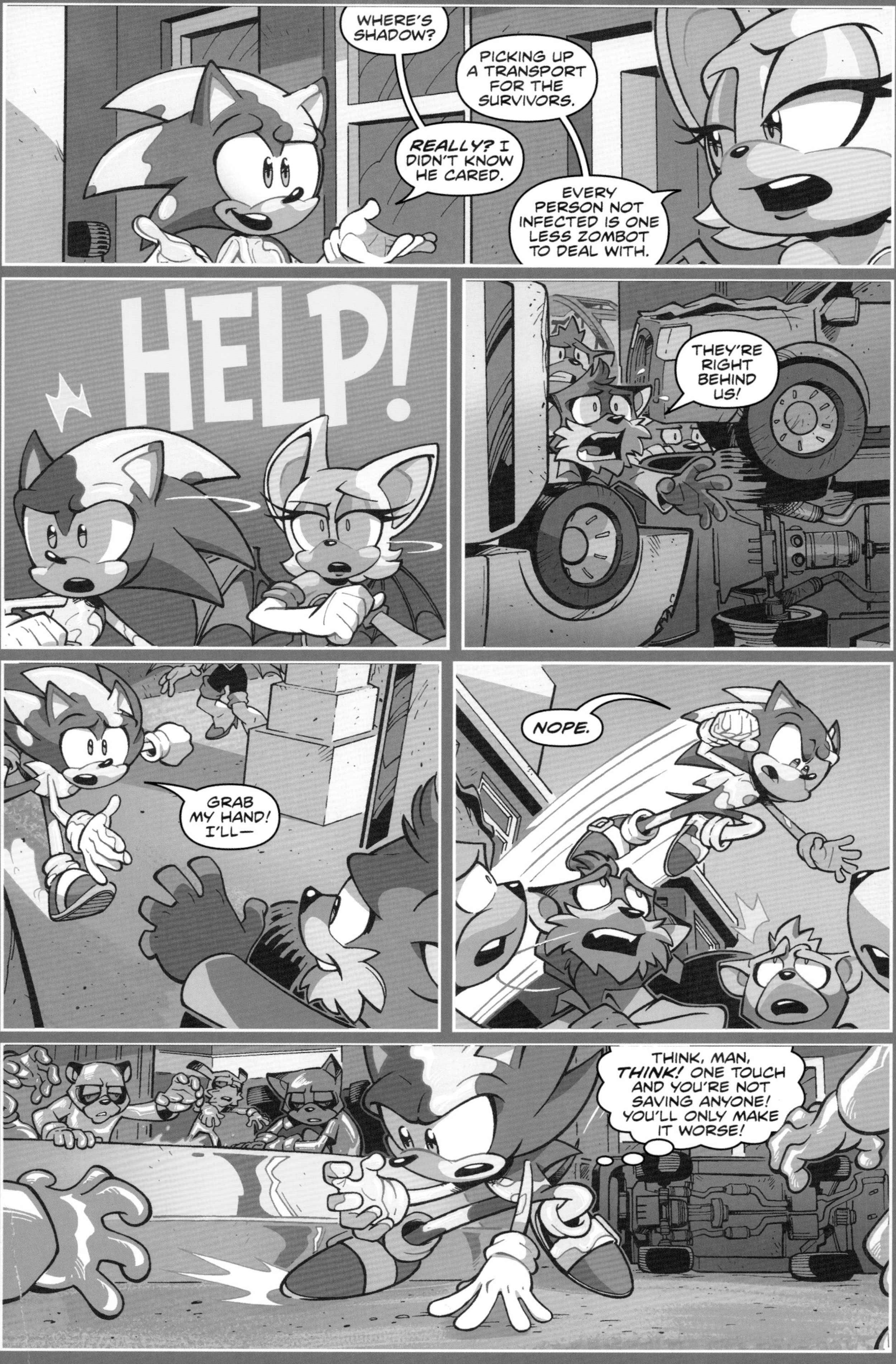
WHERE'S SHADOW?
PICKING UP A TRANSPORT FOR THE SURVIVORS.
REALLY? I DIDN'T KNOW HE CARED.
EVERY PERSON NOT INFECTED IS ONE LESS ZOMBOT TO DEAL WITH.
HELP!
THEY'RE RIGHT BEHIND US!
GRAB MY HAND! I'LL—
NOPE.
THINK, MAN, THINK! ONE TOUCH AND YOU'RE NOT SAVING ANYONE! YOU'LL ONLY MAKE IT WORSE!

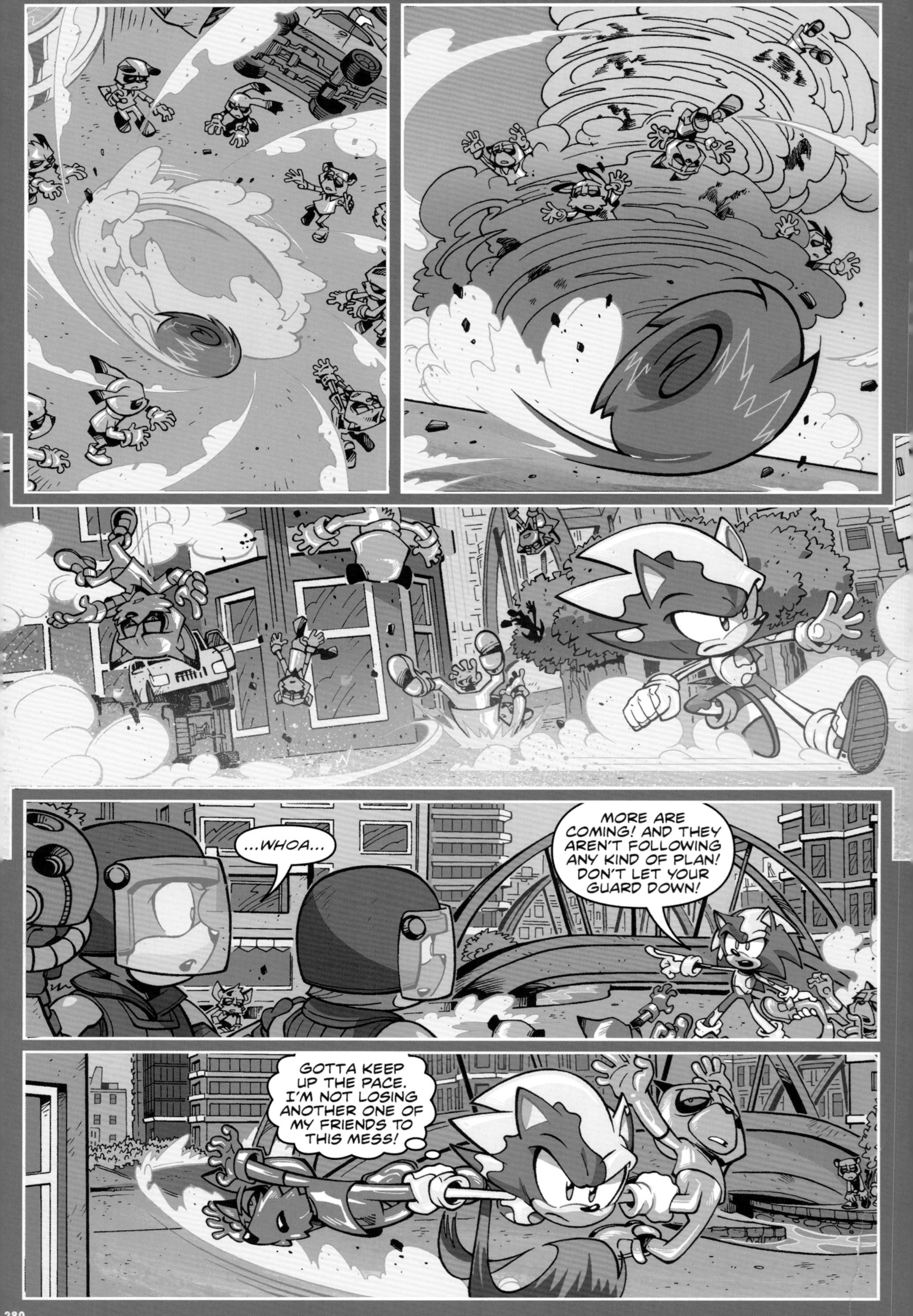
...WHOA...
MORE ARE COMING! AND THEY AREN'T FOLLOWING ANY KIND OF PLAN! DON'T LET YOUR GUARD DOWN!
GOTTA KEEP UP THE PACE. I'M NOT LOSING ANOTHER ONE OF MY FRIENDS TO THIS MESS!

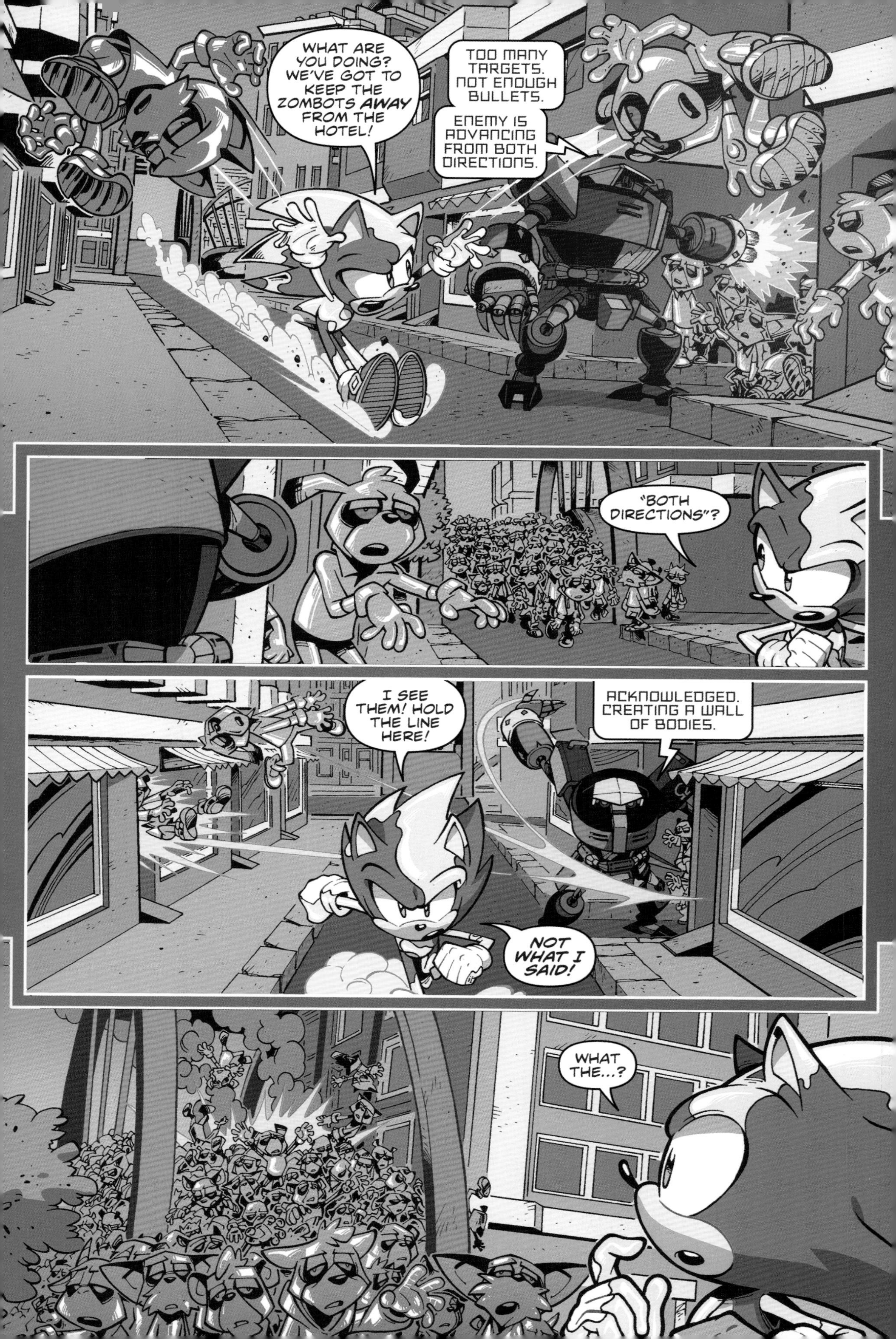
WHAT ARE YOU DOING? WE'VE GOT TO KEEP THE ZOMBOTS *AWAY* FROM THE HOTEL!
TOO MANY TARGETS. NOT ENOUGH BULLETS.
ENEMY IS ADVANCING FROM BOTH DIRECTIONS.
"BOTH DIRECTIONS"?
I SEE THEM! HOLD THE LINE HERE!
ACKNOWLEDGED. CREATING A WALL OF BODIES.
NOT WHAT I SAID!
WHAT THE...?

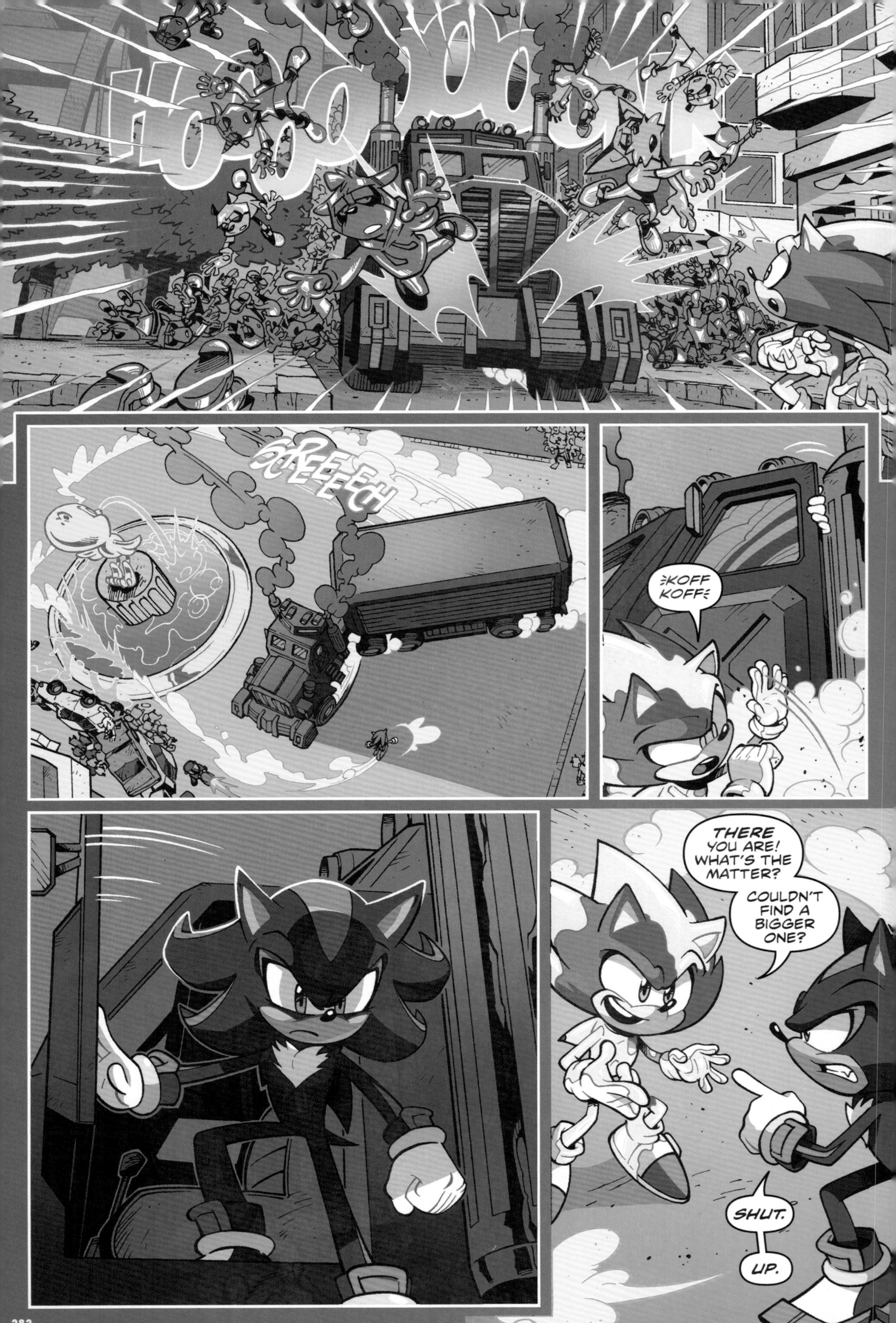
HOOOOONK
SCREEEECH
KOFF KOFF
THERE YOU ARE! WHAT'S THE MATTER?
COULDN'T FIND A BIGGER ONE?
SHUT.
UP.

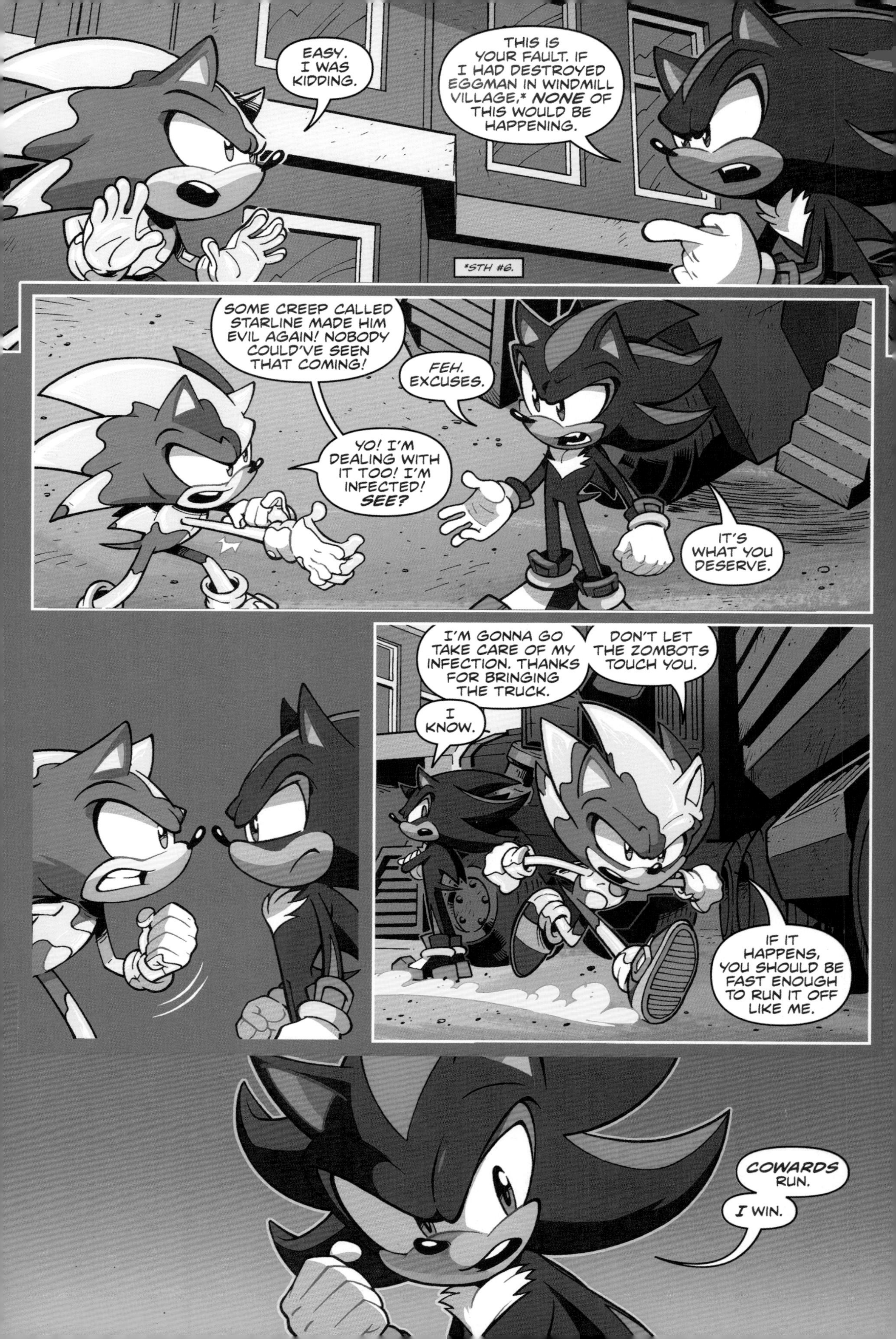
EASY. I WAS KIDDING.
THIS IS YOUR FAULT. IF I HAD DESTROYED EGGMAN IN WINDMILL VILLAGE,* NONE OF THIS WOULD BE HAPPENING.
*STH #6.
SOME CREEP CALLED STARLINE MADE HIM EVIL AGAIN! NOBODY COULD'VE SEEN THAT COMING!
FEH. EXCUSES.
YO! I'M DEALING WITH IT TOO! I'M INFECTED! SEE?
IT'S WHAT YOU DESERVE.
I'M GONNA GO TAKE CARE OF MY INFECTION. THANKS FOR BRINGING THE TRUCK.
I KNOW.
DON'T LET THE ZOMBOTS TOUCH YOU.
IF IT HAPPENS, YOU SHOULD BE FAST ENOUGH TO RUN IT OFF LIKE ME.
COWARDS RUN.
I WIN.

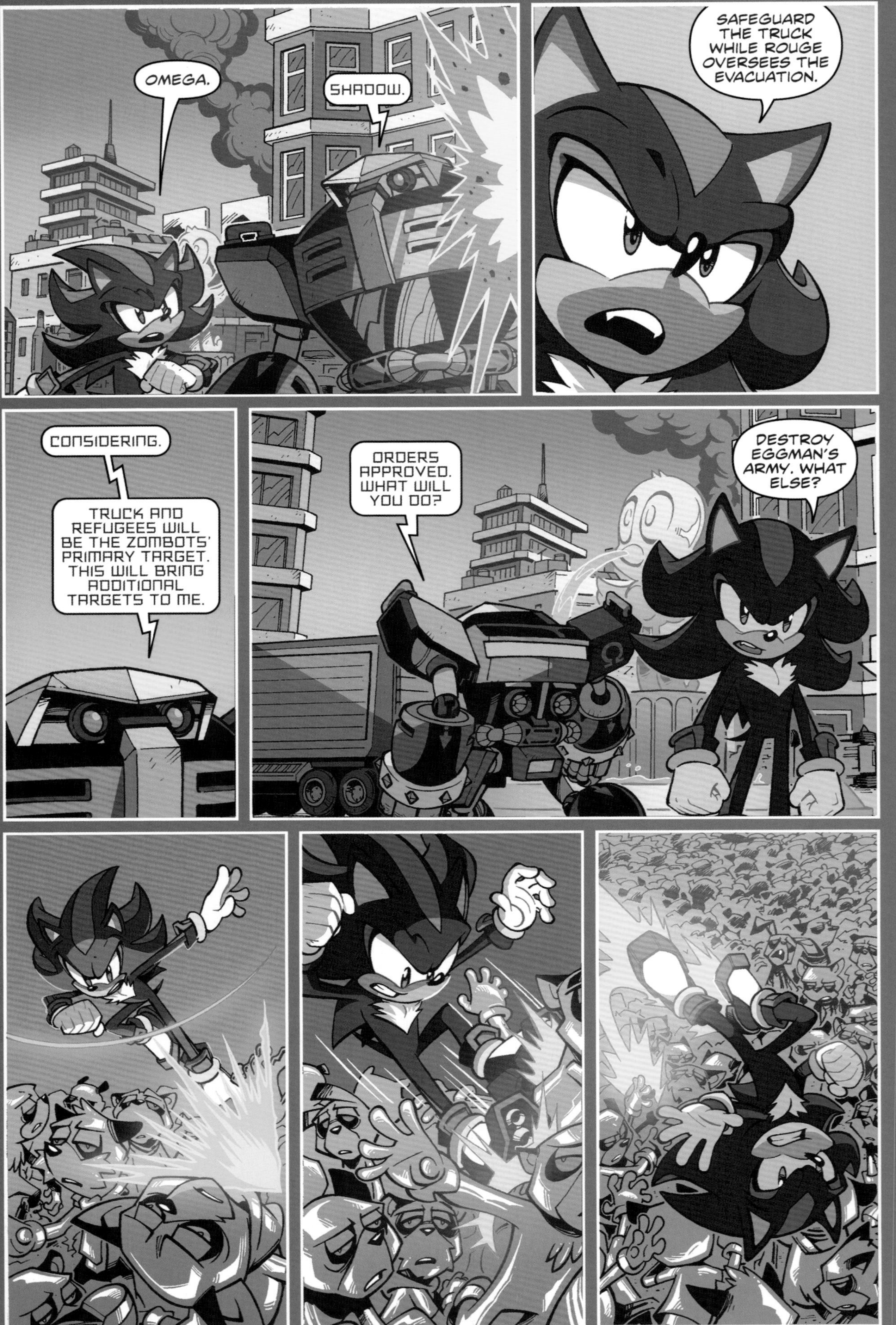
OMEGA.
SHADOW.
SAFEGUARD THE TRUCK WHILE ROUGE OVERSEES THE EVACUATION.
CONSIDERING.
TRUCK AND REFUGEES WILL BE THE ZOMBOTS' PRIMARY TARGET. THIS WILL BRING ADDITIONAL TARGETS TO ME.
ORDERS APPROVED. WHAT WILL YOU DO?
DESTROY EGGMAN'S ARMY. WHAT ELSE?

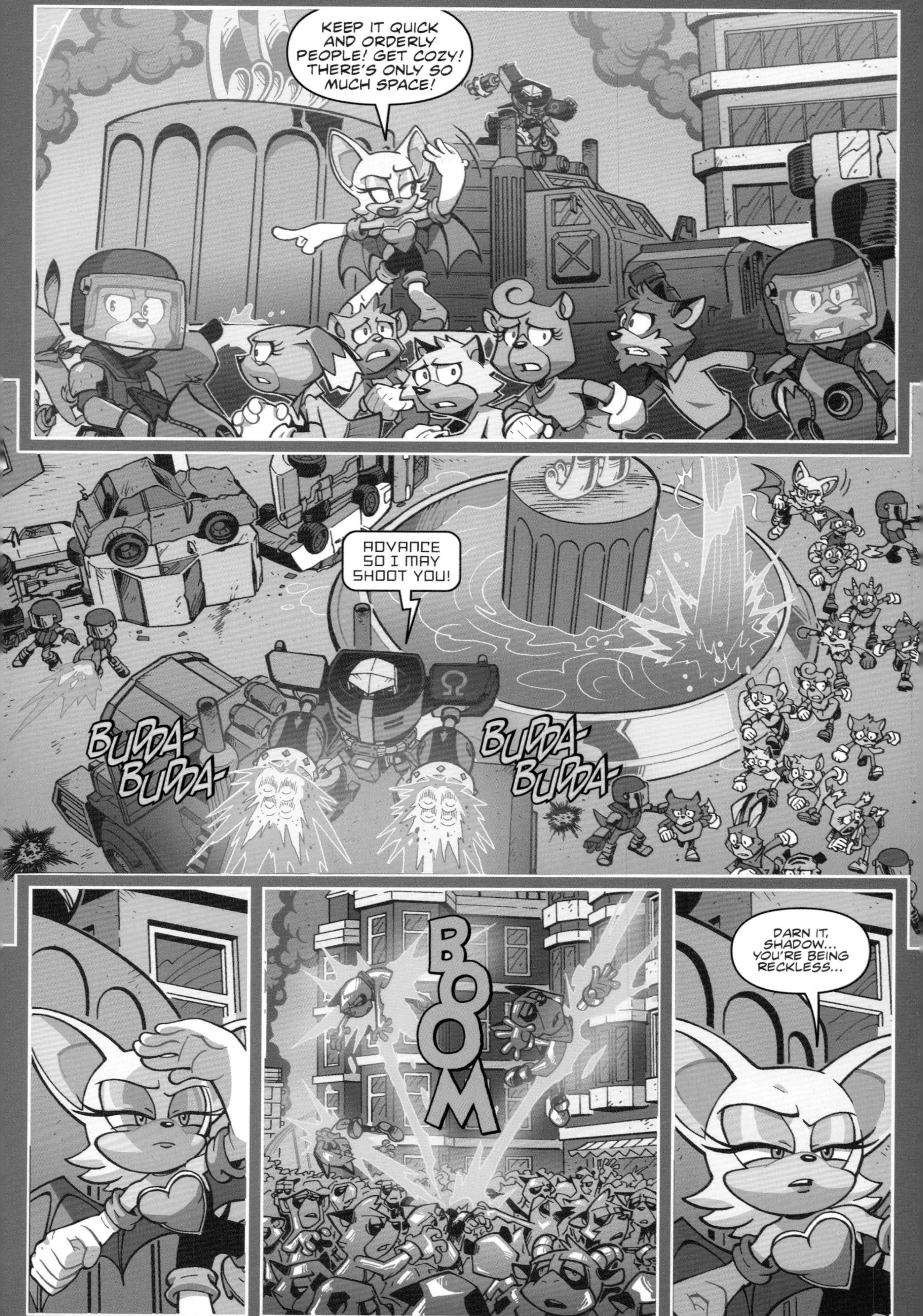
KEEP IT QUICK AND ORDERLY PEOPLE! GET COZY! THERE'S ONLY SO MUCH SPACE!
ADVANCE SO I MAY SHOOT YOU!
BUDDA-BUDDA-
BUDDA-BUDDA-
BOOM
DARN IT, SHADOW... YOU'RE BEING RECKLESS...

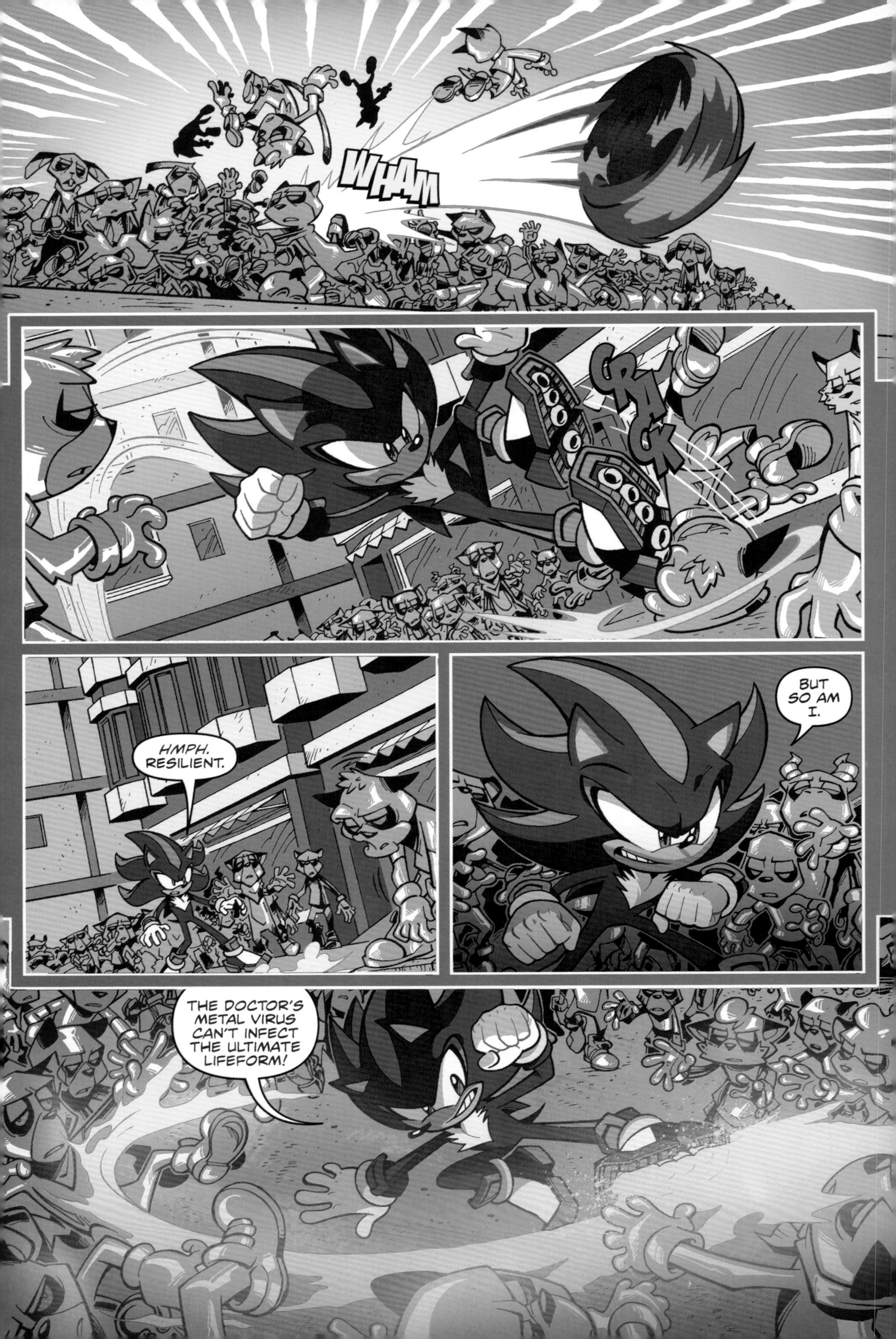
WHAM
CRACK
HMPH. RESILIENT.
BUT SO AM I.
THE DOCTOR'S METAL VIRUS CAN'T INFECT THE ULTIMATE LIFEFORM!

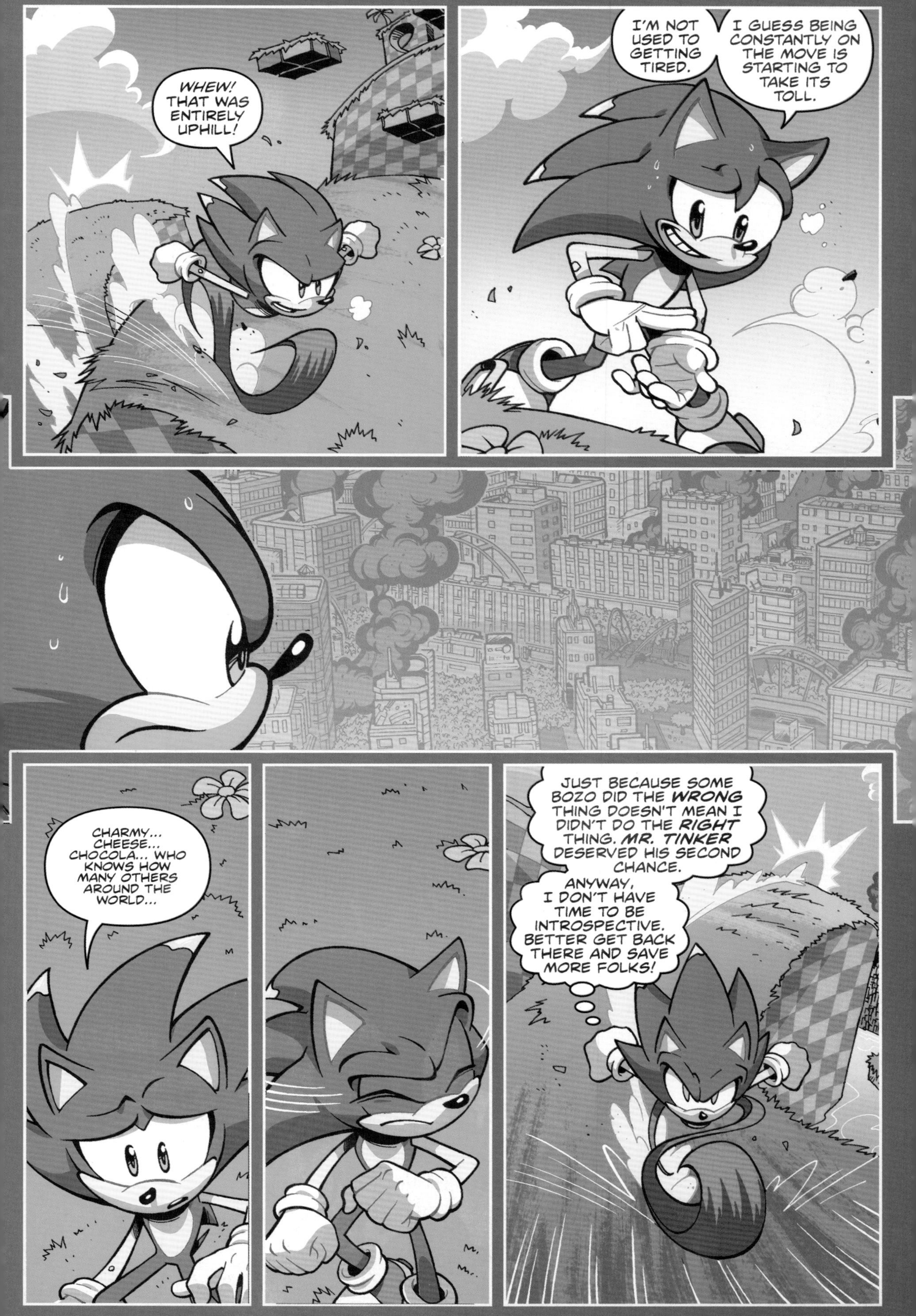

WHEW! THAT WAS ENTIRELY UPHILL!
I'M NOT USED TO GETTING TIRED.
I GUESS BEING CONSTANTLY ON THE MOVE IS STARTING TO TAKE ITS TOLL.
CHARMY... CHEESE... CHOCOLA... WHO KNOWS HOW MANY OTHERS AROUND THE WORLD...
JUST BECAUSE SOME BOZO DID THE WRONG THING DOESN'T MEAN I DIDN'T DO THE RIGHT THING. MR. TINKER DESERVED HIS SECOND CHANCE.
ANYWAY, I DON'T HAVE TIME TO BE INTROSPECTIVE. BETTER GET BACK THERE AND SAVE MORE FOLKS!

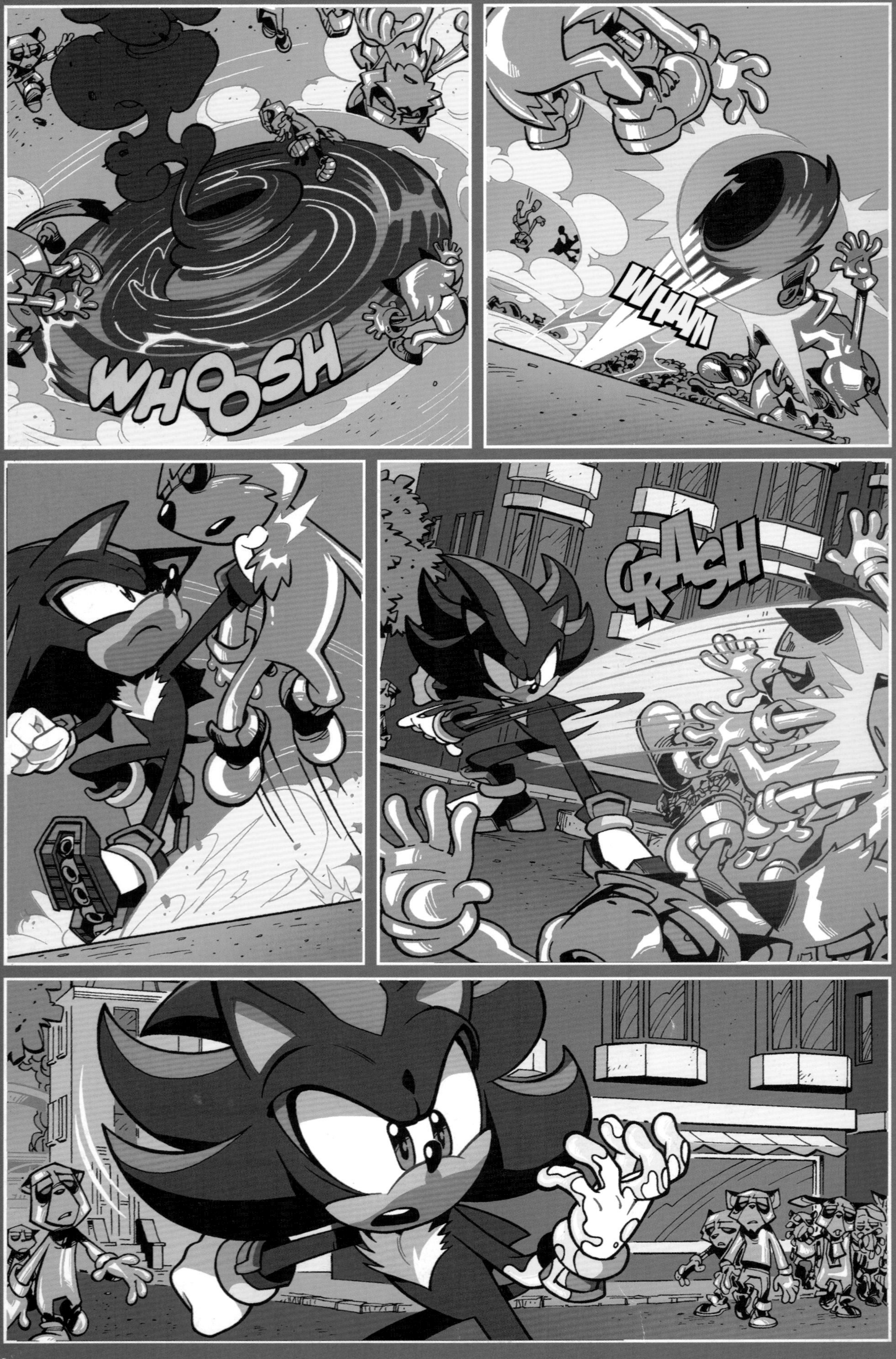
WHOOSH
WHAM
CRASH

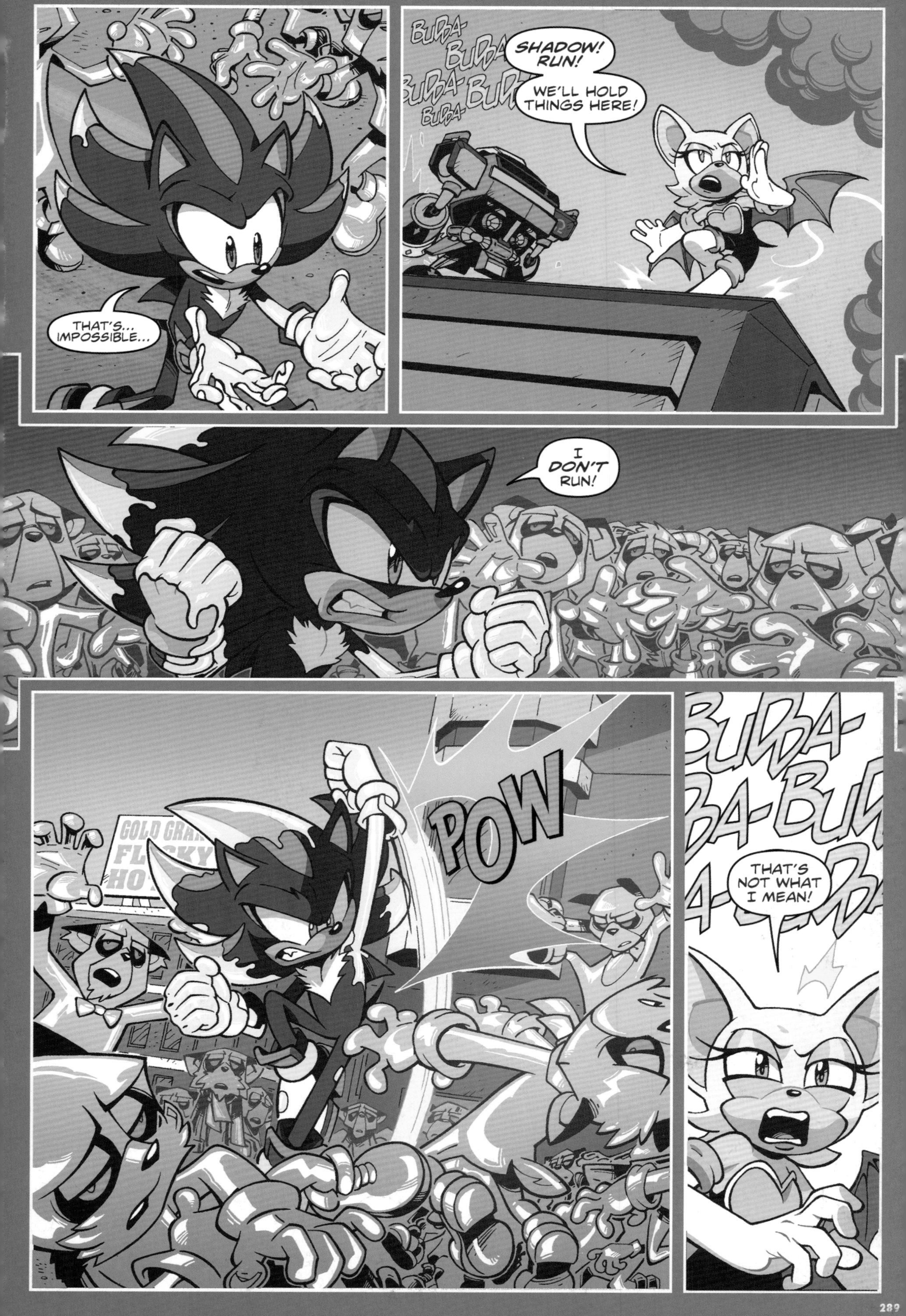
THAT'S... IMPOSSIBLE...
BUDA-BUDA-BUDA-BUDA-BUDA-
SHADOW! RUN!
WE'LL HOLD THINGS HERE!
I DON'T RUN!
GOLD GRA
FL CKY
HO
POW
BUDA-BA-BUD-A-BA
THAT'S NOT WHAT I MEAN!

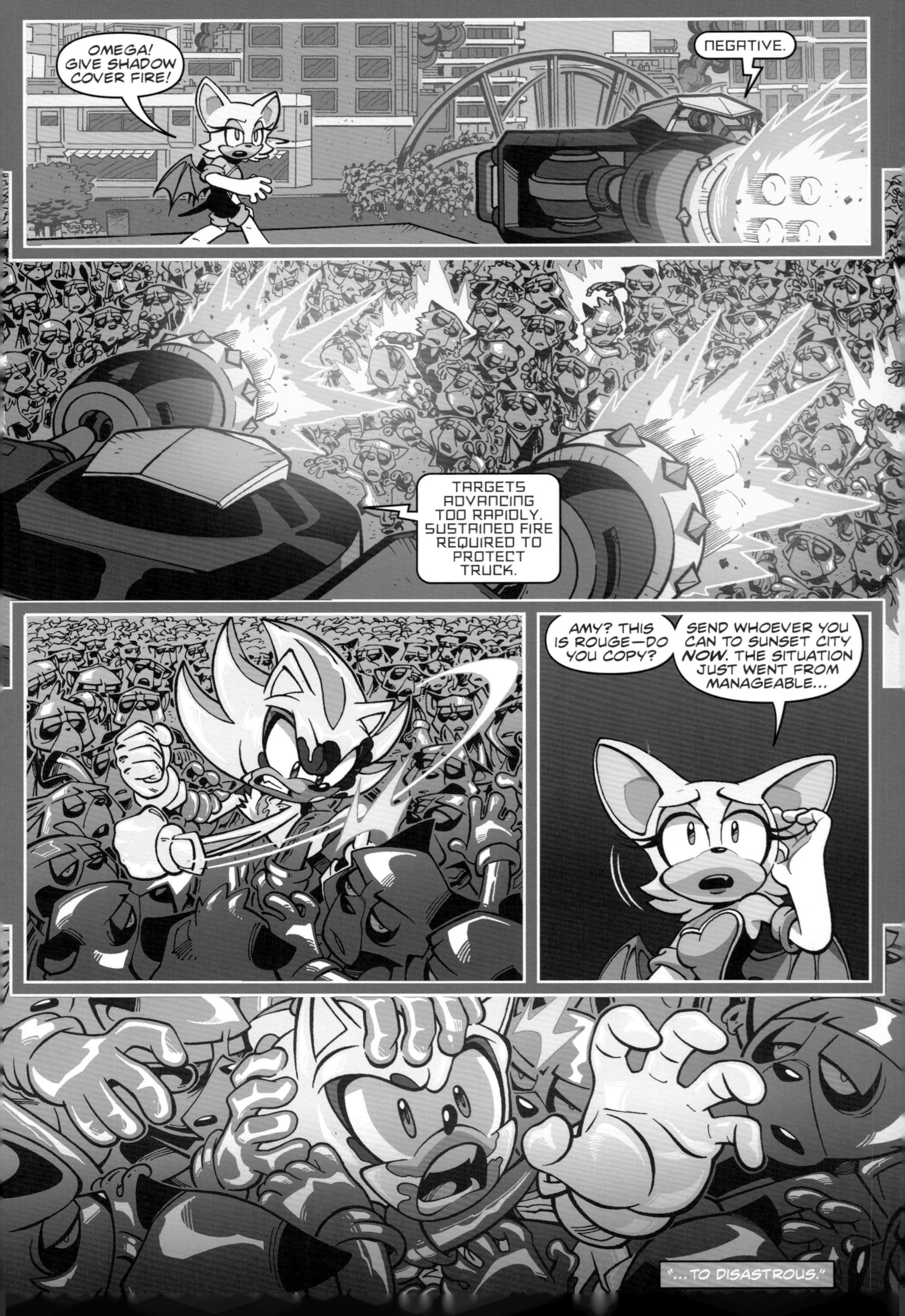
OMEGA! GIVE SHADOW COVER FIRE!
NEGATIVE.
TARGETS ADVANCING TOO RAPIDLY. SUSTAINED FIRE REQUIRED TO PROTECT TRUCK.
AMY? THIS IS ROUGE—DO YOU COPY?
SEND WHOEVER YOU CAN TO SUNSET CITY *NOW*. THE SITUATION JUST WENT FROM MANAGEABLE...
"...TO DISASTROUS."

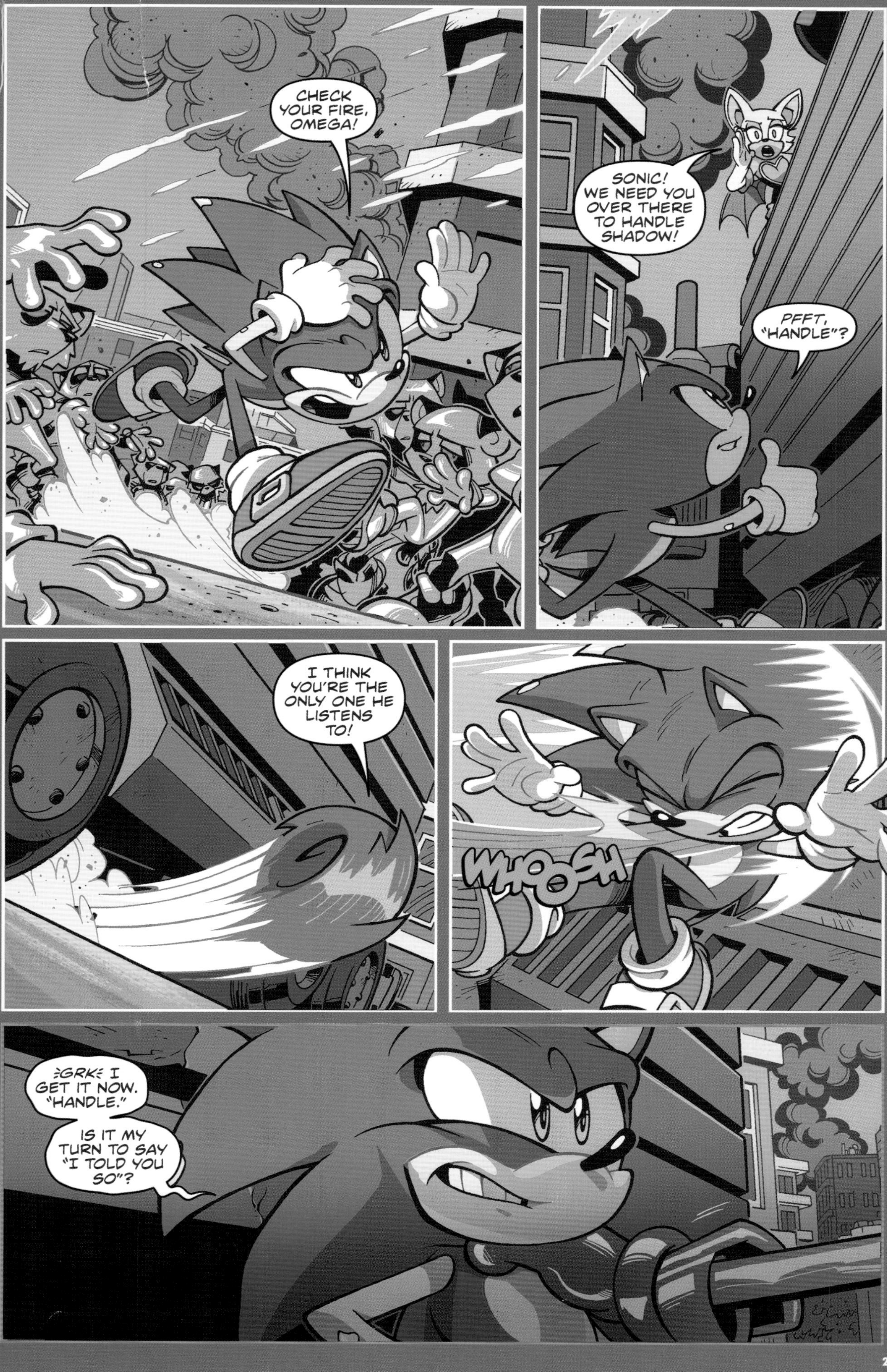

CHECK YOUR FIRE, OMEGA!
SONIC! WE NEED YOU OVER THERE TO HANDLE SHADOW!
PFFT, "HANDLE"?
I THINK YOU'RE THE ONLY ONE HE LISTENS TO!
WHOOSH
GRK I GET IT NOW. "HANDLE."
IS IT MY TURN TO SAY "I TOLD YOU SO"?

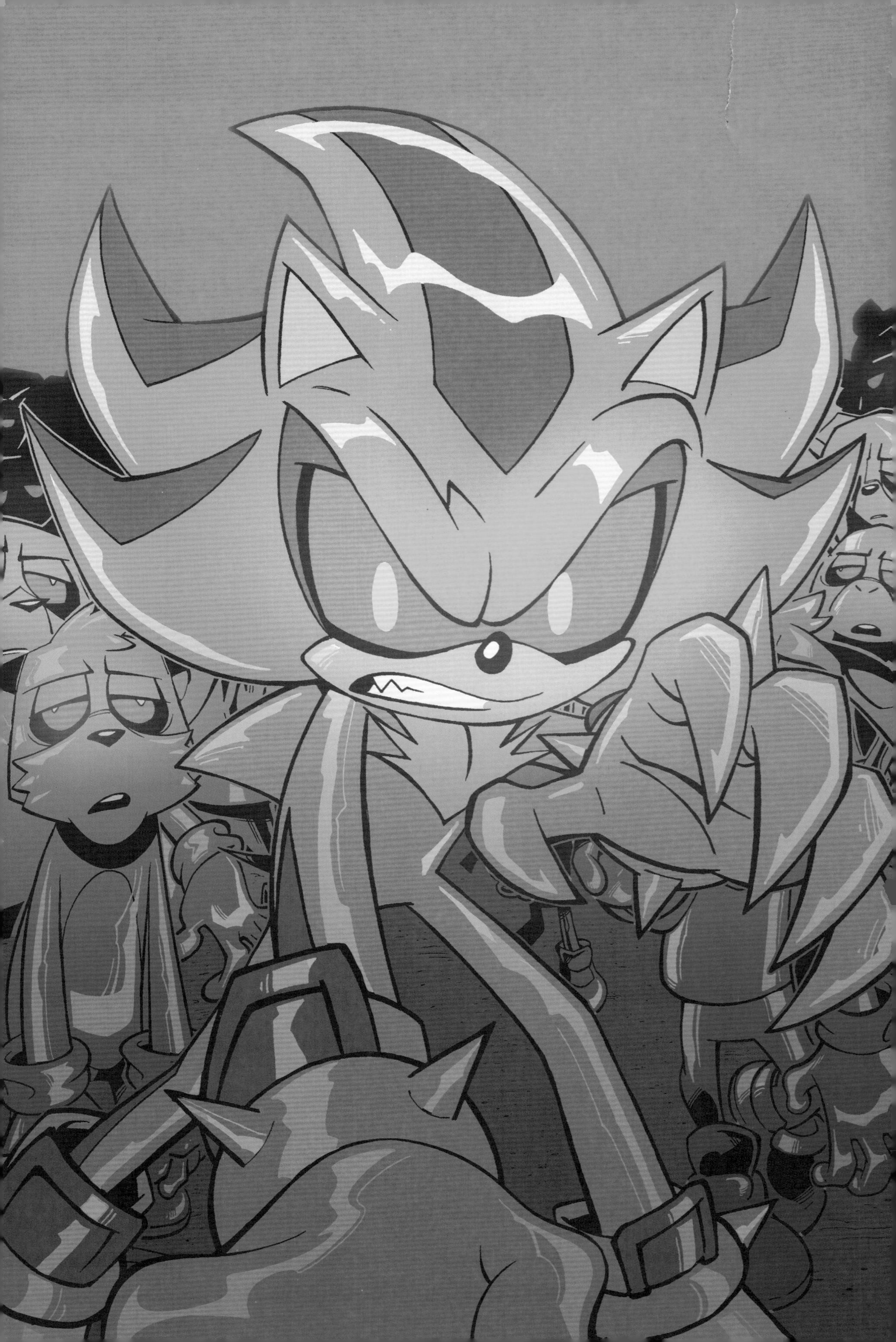

ART BY LAMAR WELLS INKS AND COLORS BY REGGIE GRAHAM

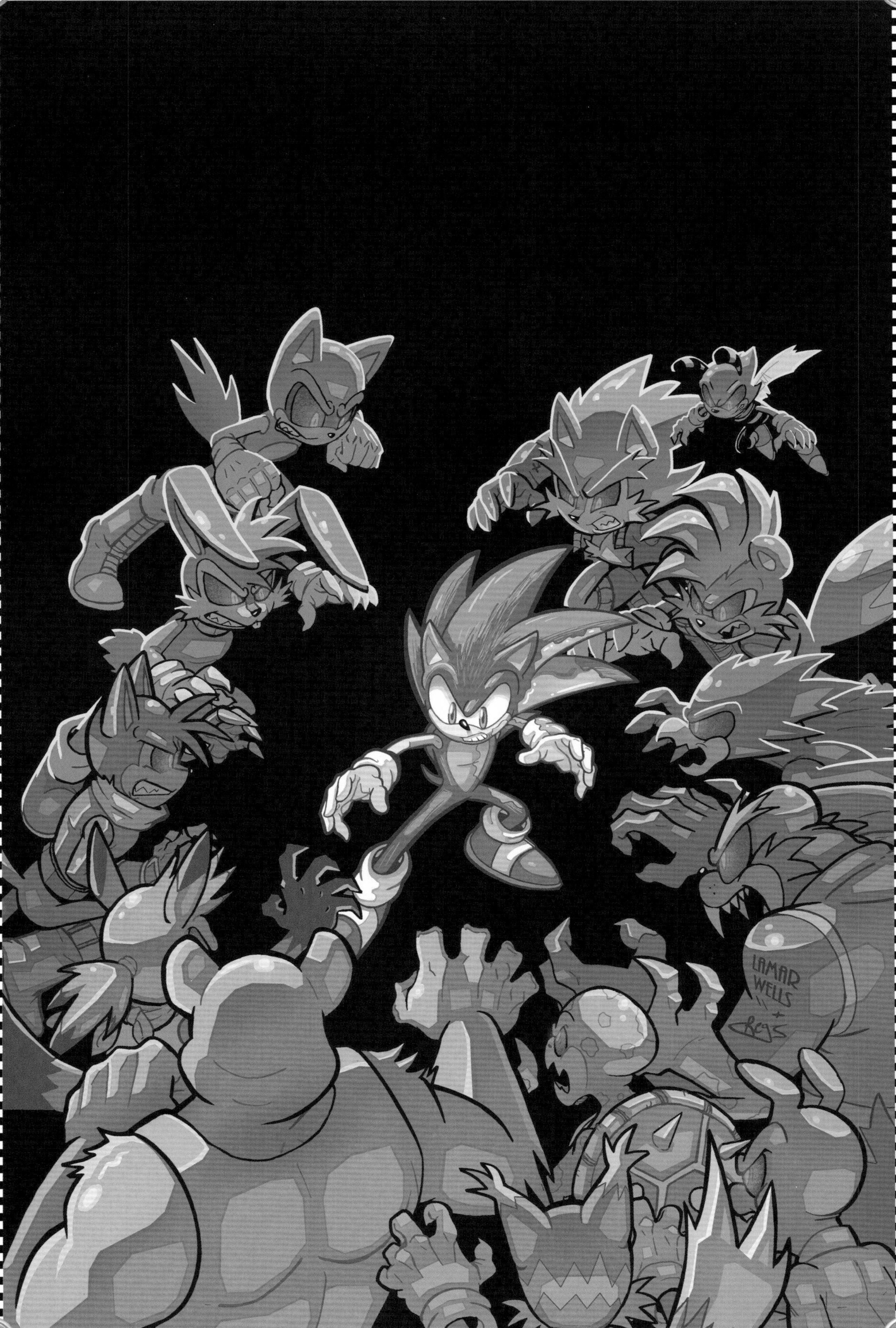
LAMAR WELLS + Regs

ART BY TRACY YARDLEY

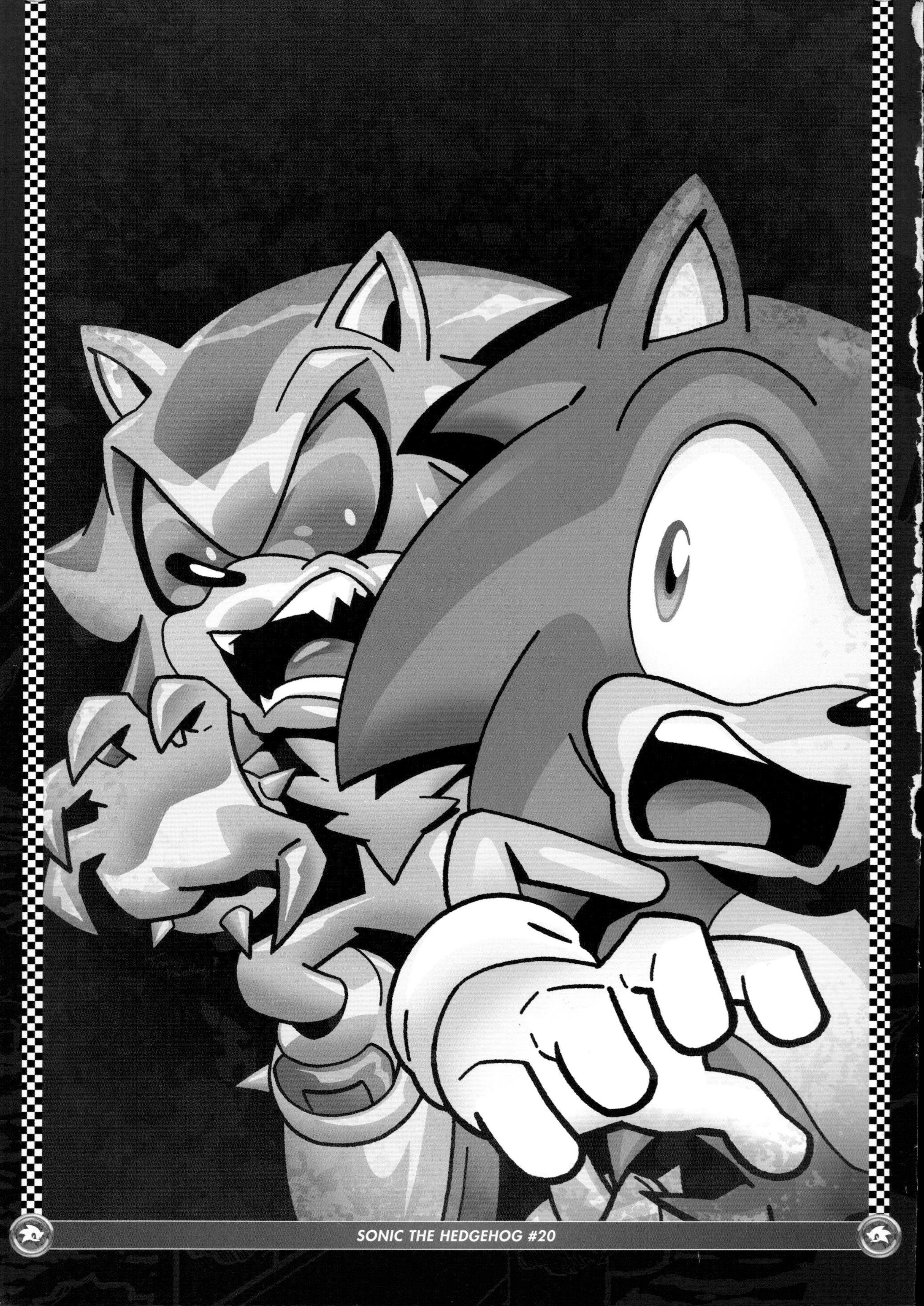

SONIC THE HEDGEHOG #20

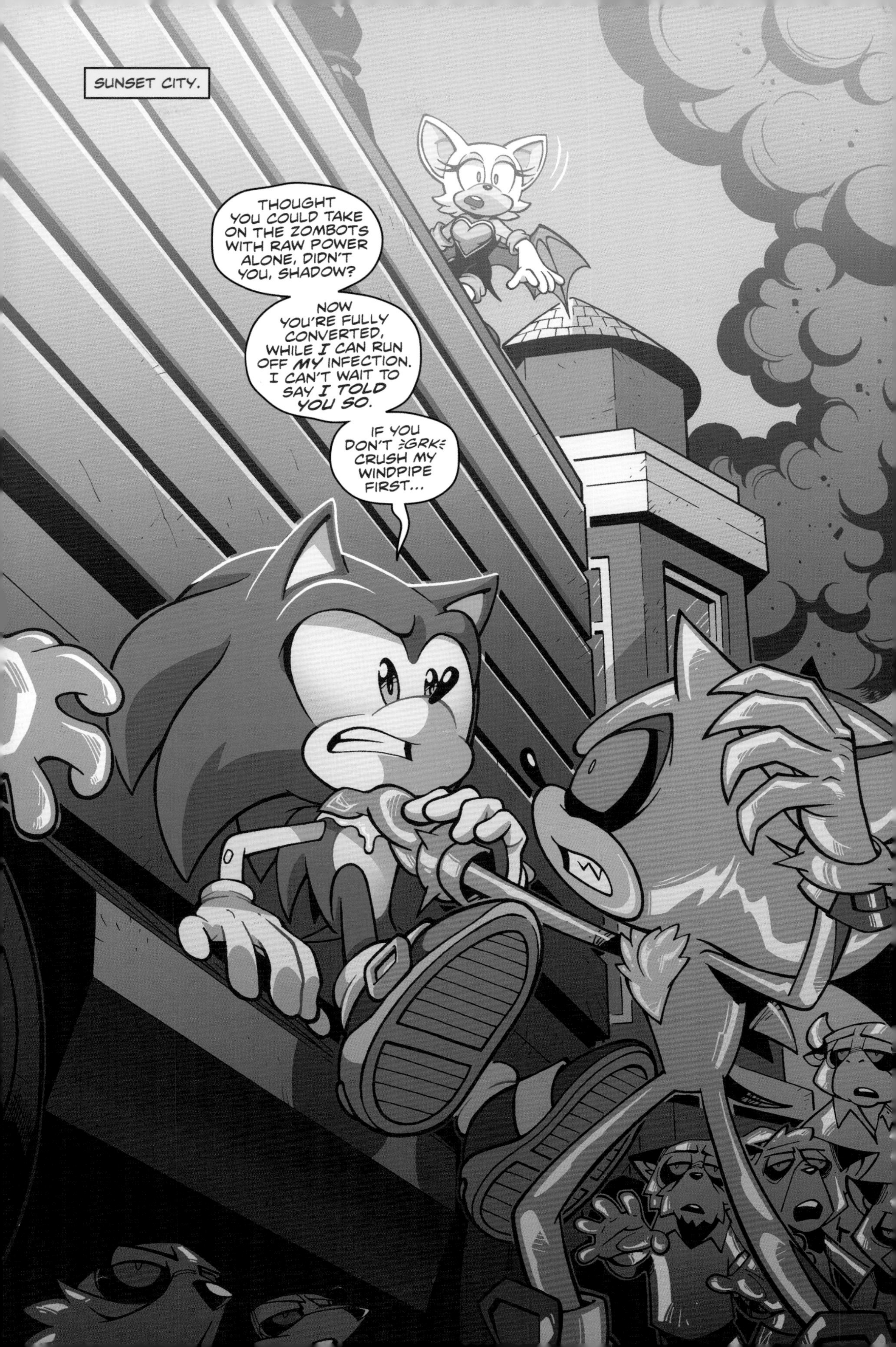
SUNSET CITY.
THOUGHT YOU COULD TAKE ON THE ZOMBOTS WITH RAW POWER ALONE, DIDN'T YOU, SHADOW?
NOW YOU'RE FULLY CONVERTED, WHILE I CAN RUN OFF MY INFECTION. I CAN'T WAIT TO SAY I TOLD YOU SO.
IF YOU DON'T ≶GRK≶ CRUSH MY WINDPIPE FIRST...

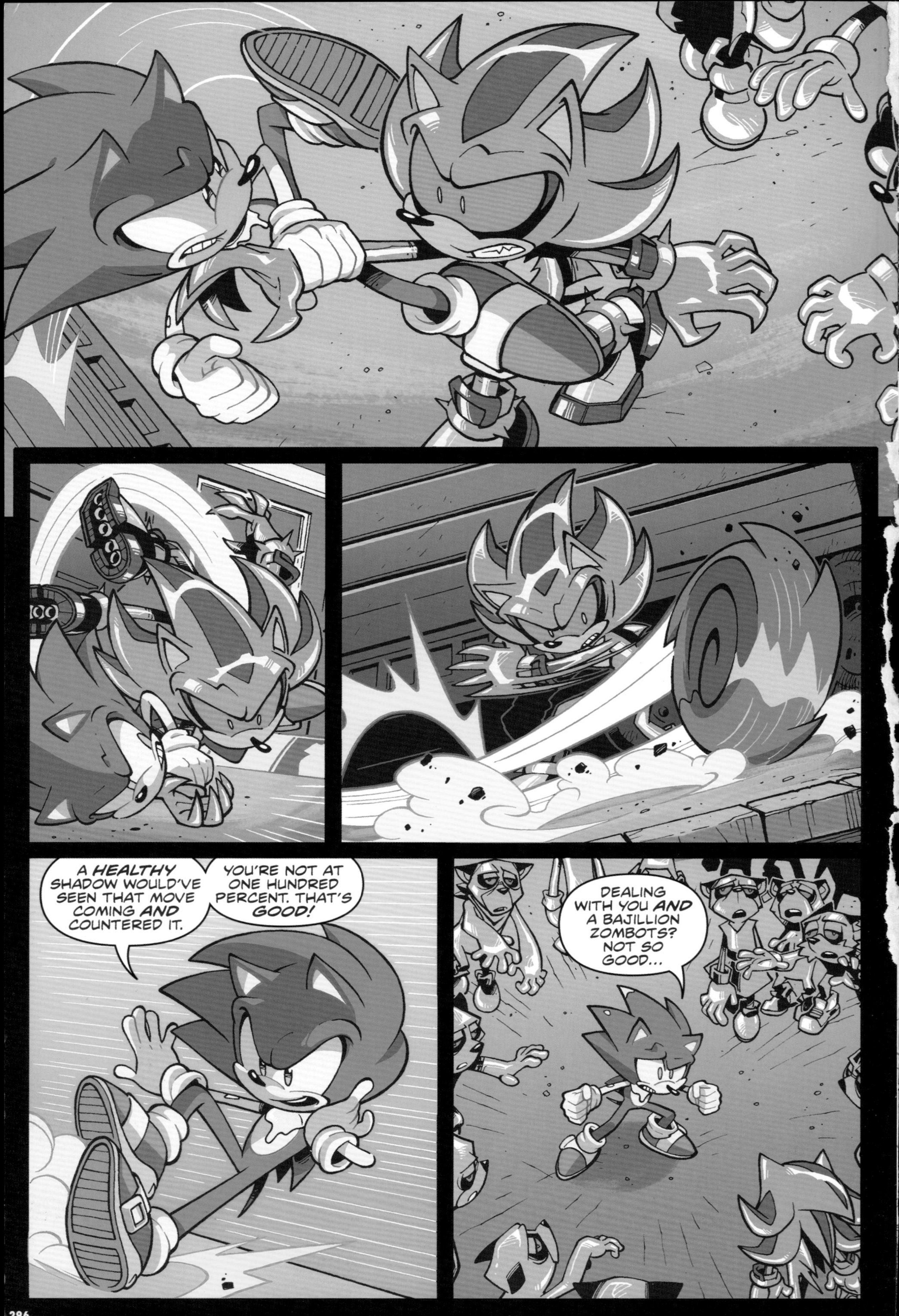
A *HEALTHY* SHADOW WOULD'VE SEEN THAT MOVE COMING *AND* COUNTERED IT.
YOU'RE NOT AT ONE HUNDRED PERCENT. THAT'S *GOOD!*
DEALING WITH YOU *AND* A BAJILLION ZOMBOTS? NOT SO GOOD...

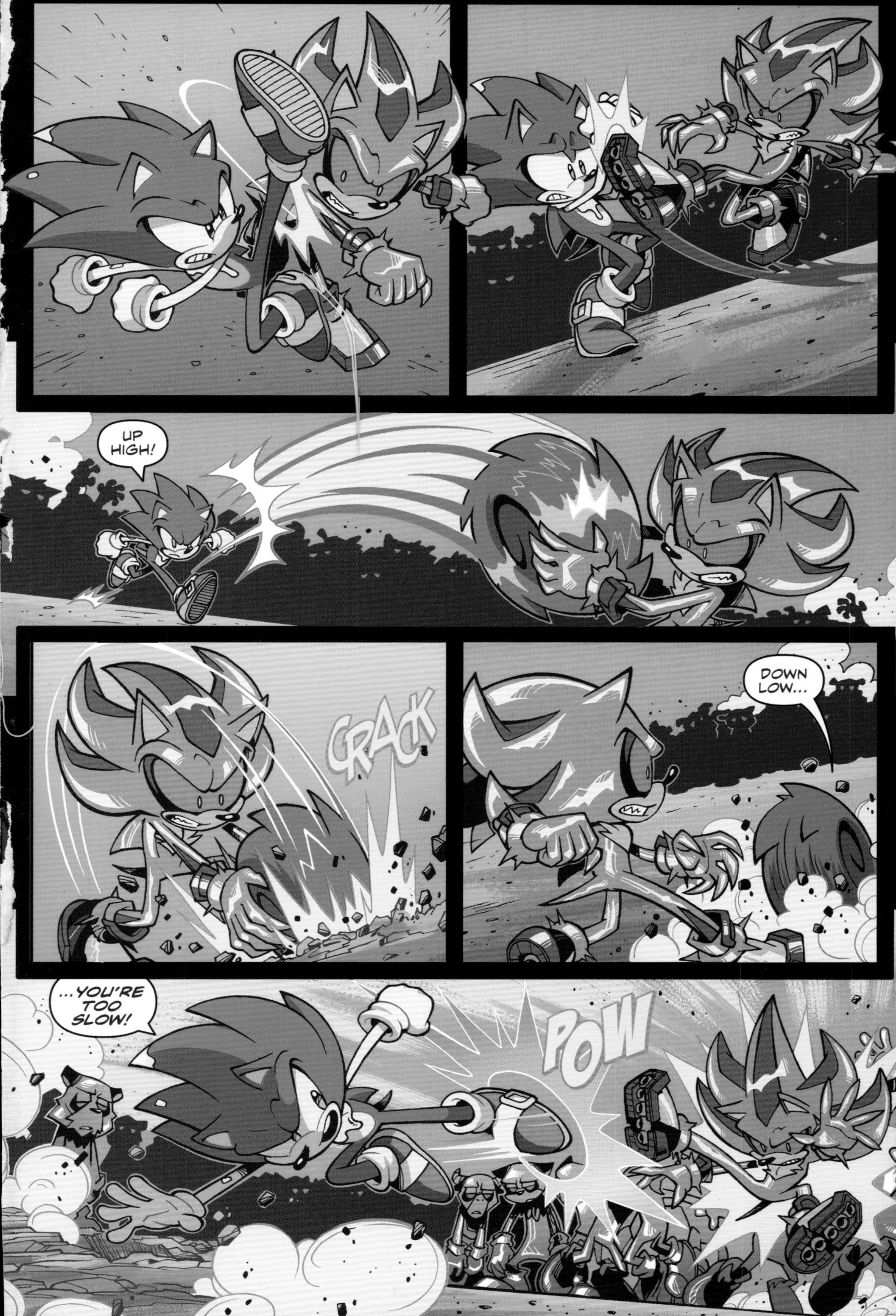
UP HIGH!
CRACK
DOWN LOW...
...YOU'RE TOO SLOW!
POW

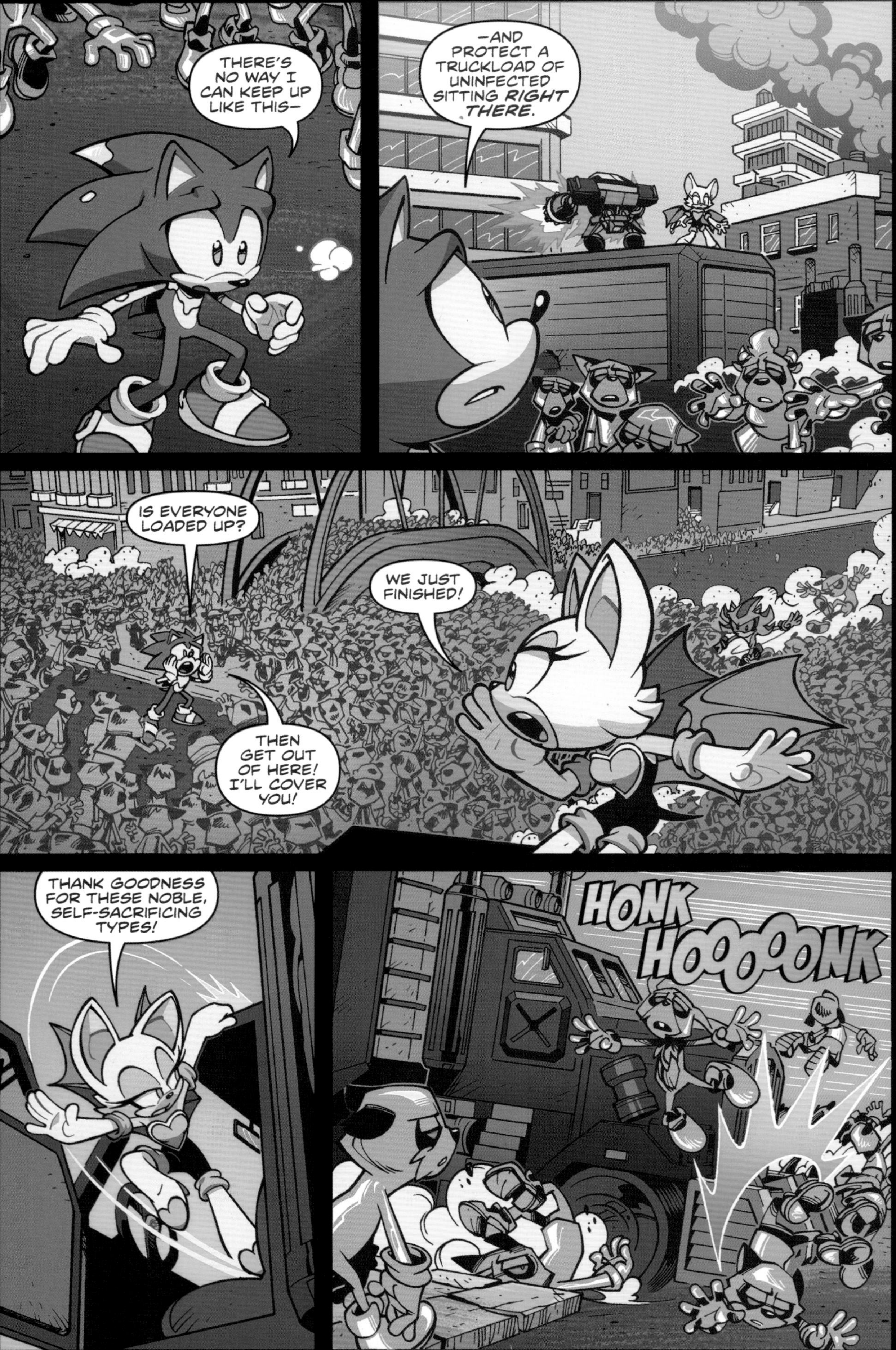
THERE'S NO WAY I CAN KEEP UP LIKE THIS—
—AND PROTECT A TRUCKLOAD OF UNINFECTED SITTING *RIGHT THERE*.
IS EVERYONE LOADED UP?
WE JUST FINISHED!
THEN GET OUT OF HERE! I'LL COVER YOU!
THANK GOODNESS FOR THESE NOBLE, SELF-SACRIFICING TYPES!
HONK
HOOOOONK

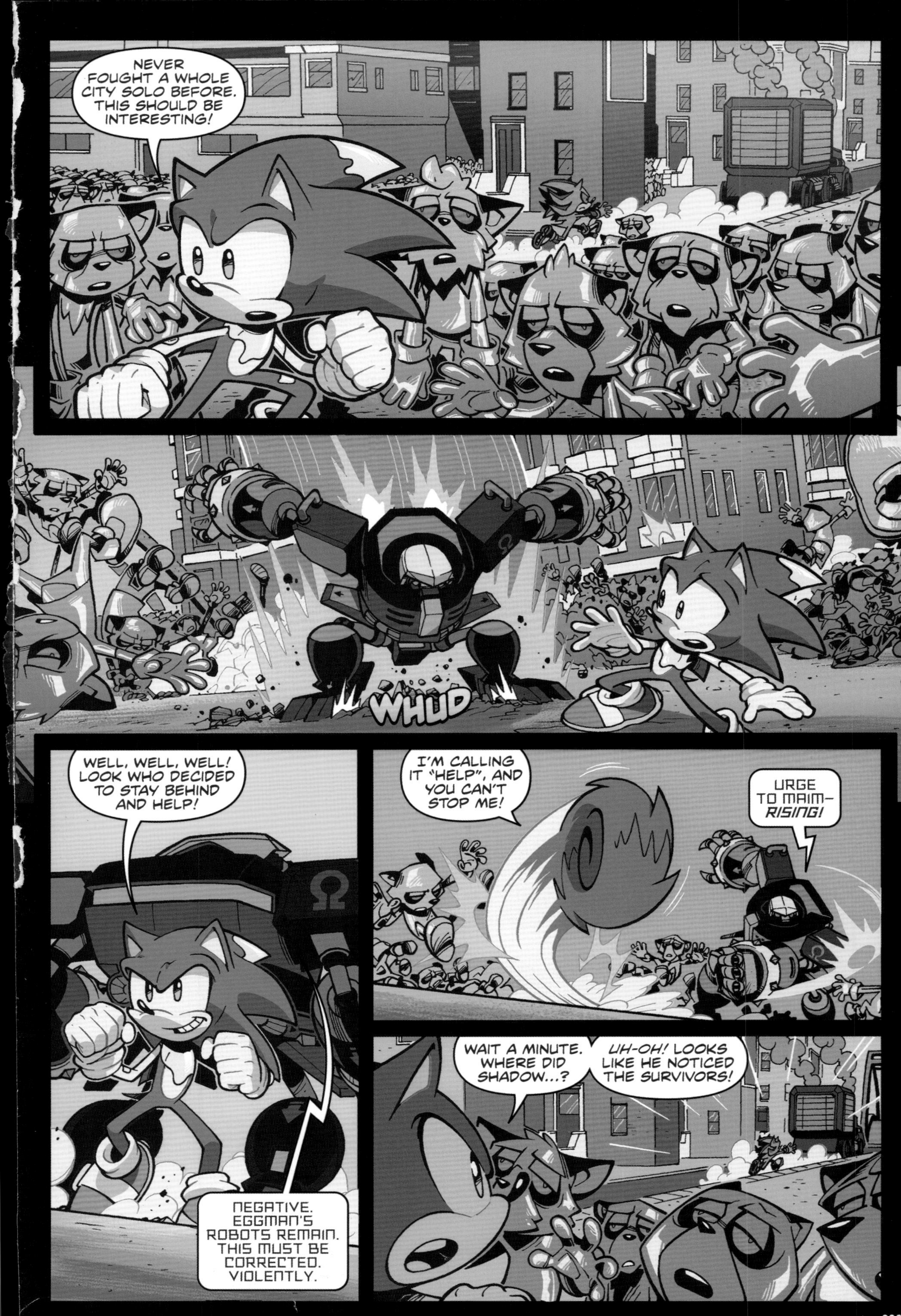
NEVER FOUGHT A WHOLE CITY SOLO BEFORE. THIS SHOULD BE INTERESTING!
WHUD
WELL, WELL, WELL! LOOK WHO DECIDED TO STAY BEHIND AND HELP!
NEGATIVE. EGGMAN'S ROBOTS REMAIN. THIS MUST BE CORRECTED. VIOLENTLY.
I'M CALLING IT "HELP", AND YOU CAN'T STOP ME!
URGE TO MAIM— RISING!
WAIT A MINUTE. WHERE DID SHADOW...?
UH-OH! LOOKS LIKE HE NOTICED THE SURVIVORS!

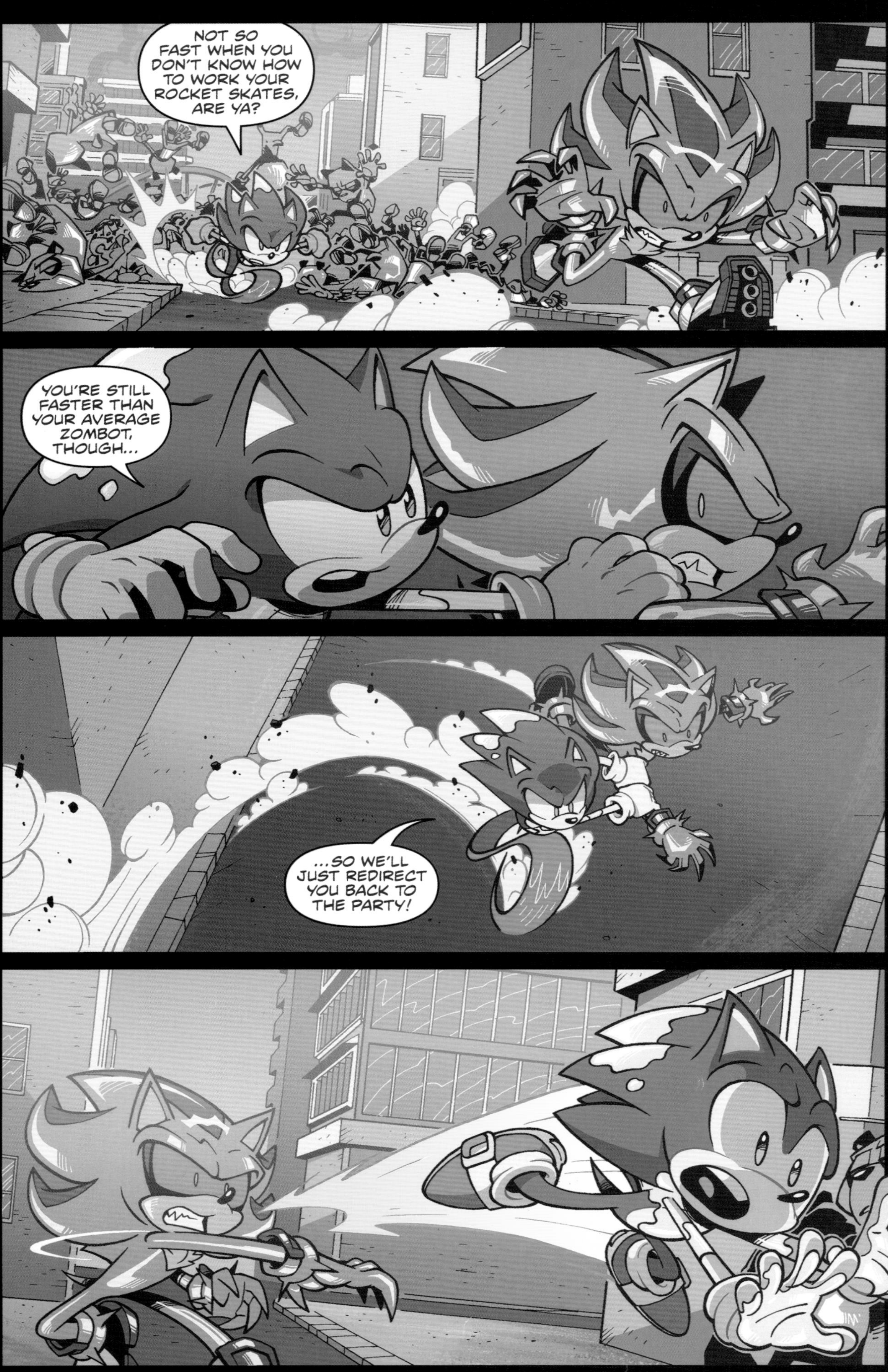
NOT SO FAST WHEN YOU DON'T KNOW HOW TO WORK YOUR ROCKET SKATES, ARE YA?
YOU'RE STILL FASTER THAN YOUR AVERAGE ZOMBOT, THOUGH...
...SO WE'LL JUST REDIRECT YOU BACK TO THE PARTY!

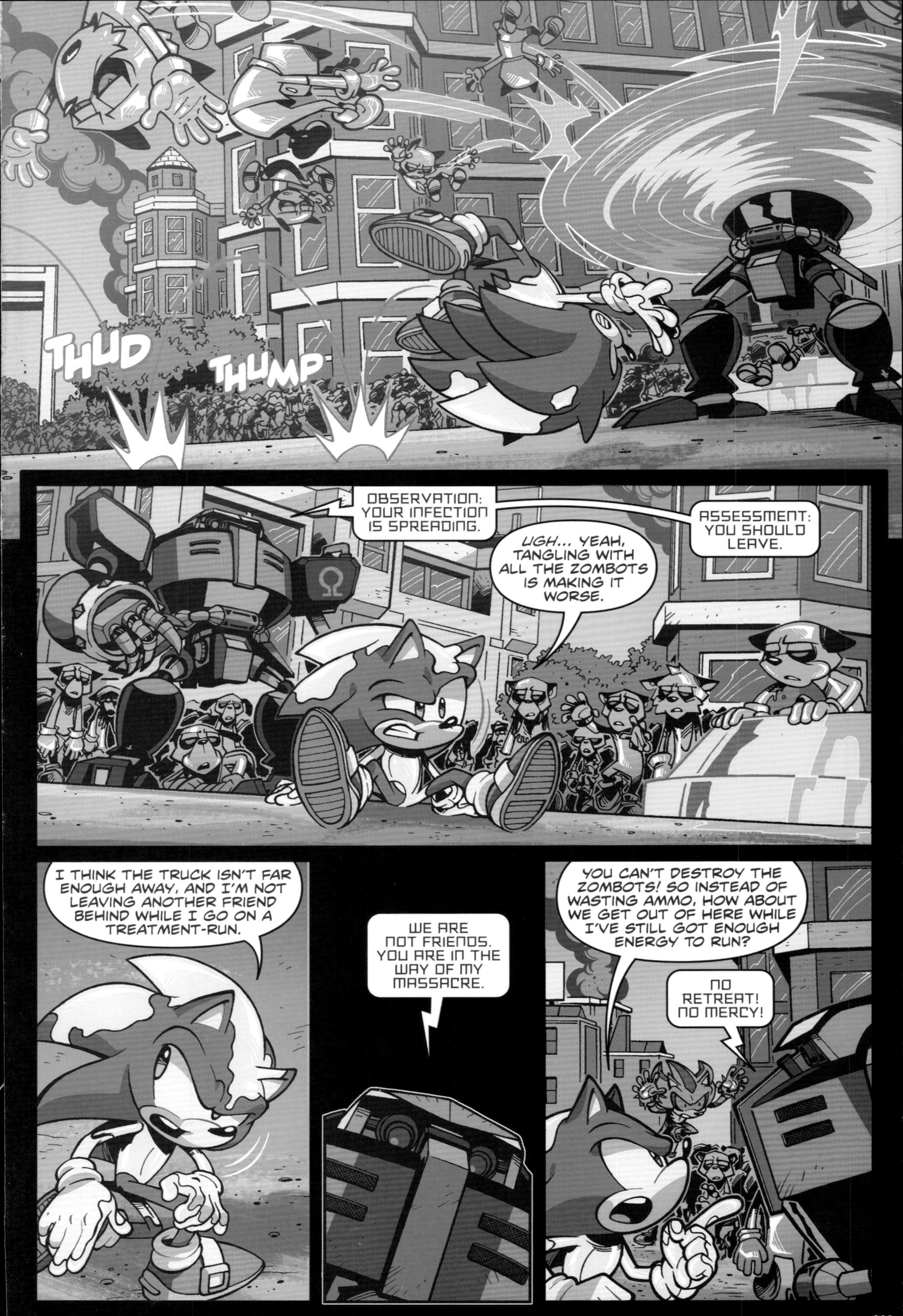
THUD
THUMP
OBSERVATION: YOUR INFECTION IS SPREADING.
UGH... YEAH, TANGLING WITH ALL THE ZOMBOTS IS MAKING IT WORSE.
ASSESSMENT: YOU SHOULD LEAVE.
I THINK THE TRUCK ISN'T FAR ENOUGH AWAY, AND I'M NOT LEAVING ANOTHER FRIEND BEHIND WHILE I GO ON A TREATMENT-RUN.
WE ARE NOT FRIENDS. YOU ARE IN THE WAY OF MY MASSACRE.
YOU CAN'T DESTROY THE ZOMBOTS! SO INSTEAD OF WASTING AMMO, HOW ABOUT WE GET OUT OF HERE WHILE I'VE STILL GOT ENOUGH ENERGY TO RUN?
NO RETREAT! NO MERCY!

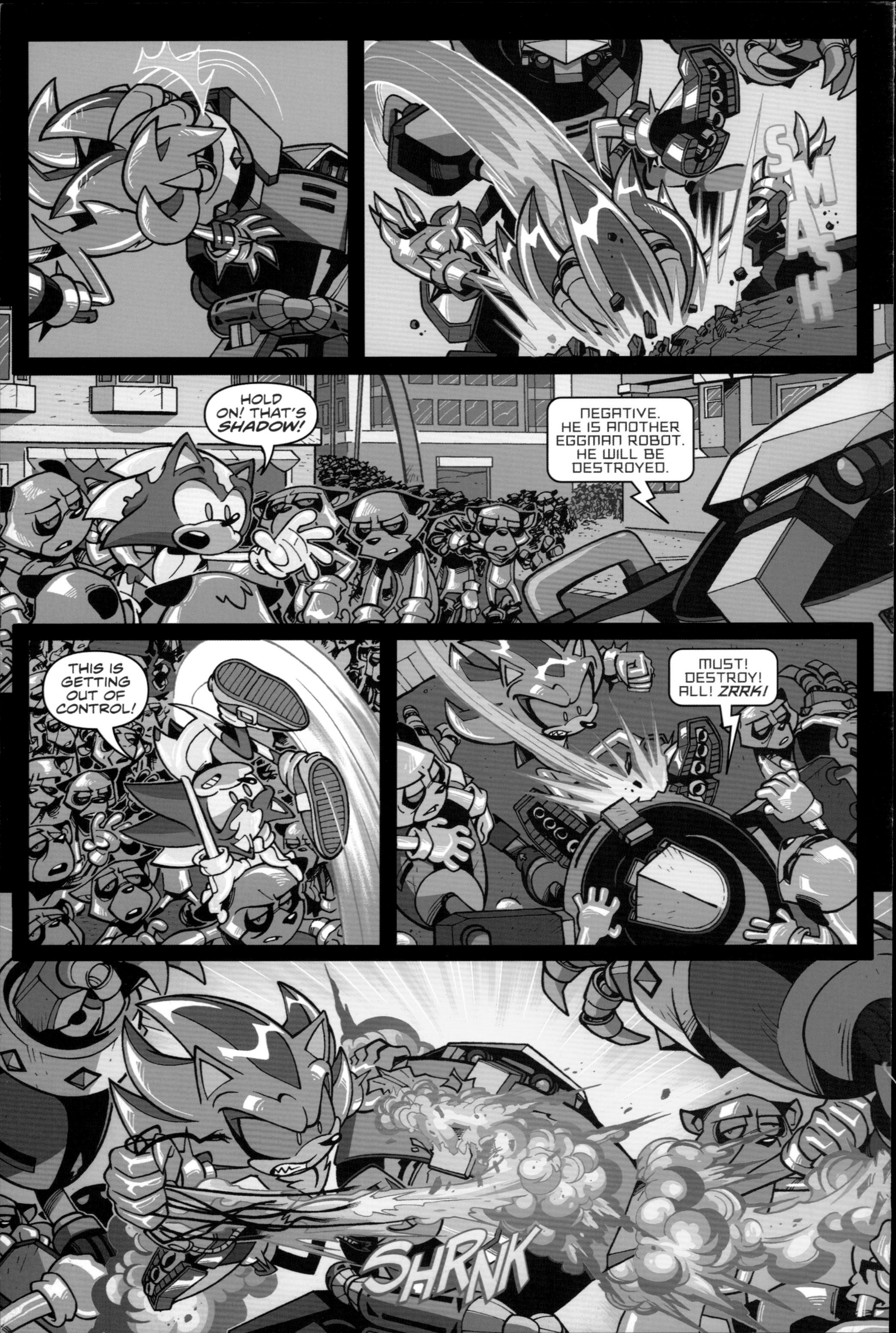
SMASH
HOLD ON! THAT'S SHADOW!
NEGATIVE. HE IS ANOTHER EGGMAN ROBOT. HE WILL BE DESTROYED.
THIS IS GETTING OUT OF CONTROL!
MUST! DESTROY! ALL! ZRRK!
SHRNK

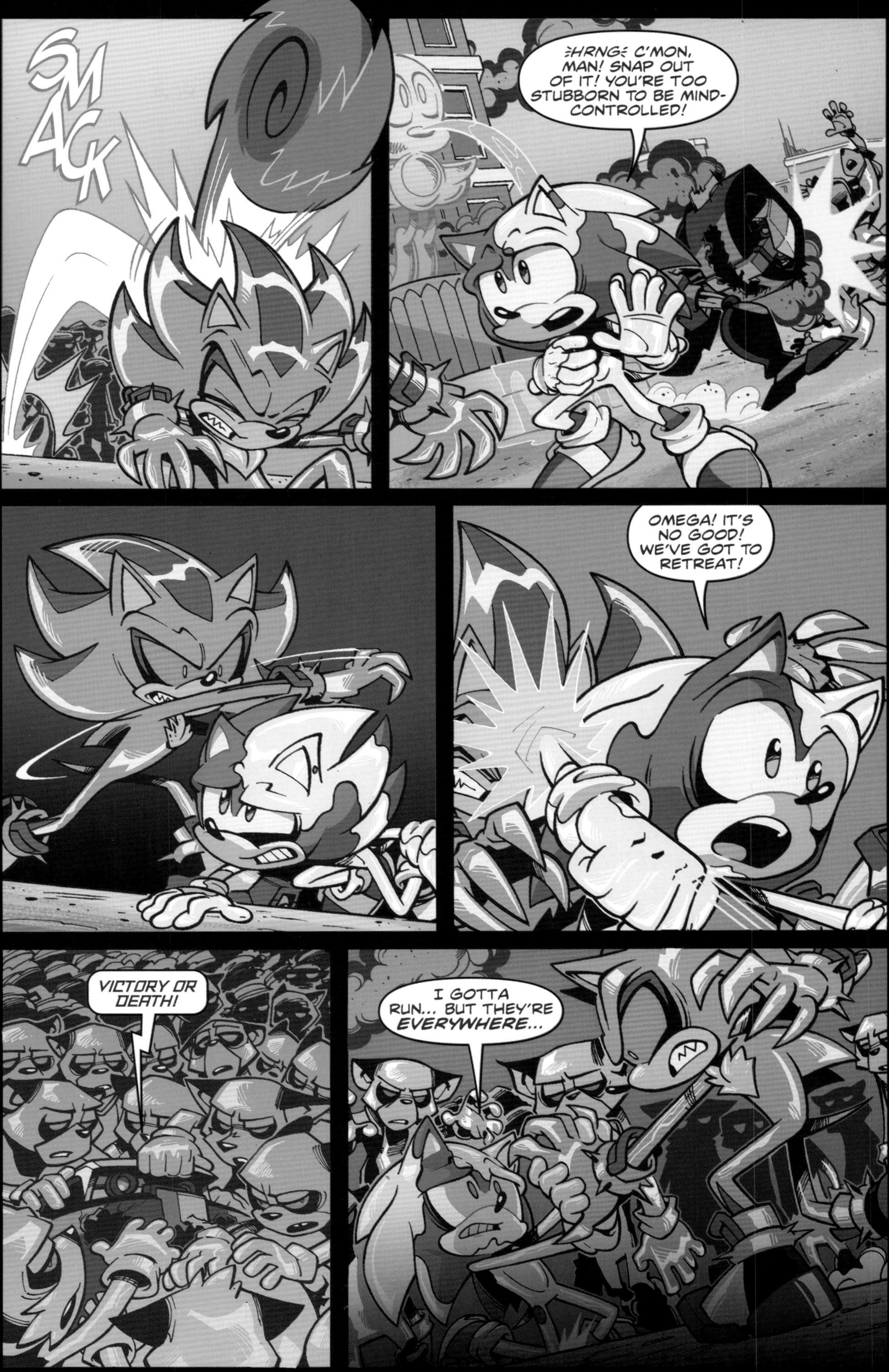

SMACK
=HRNG= C'MON, MAN! SNAP OUT OF IT! YOU'RE TOO STUBBORN TO BE MIND-CONTROLLED!
OMEGA! IT'S NO GOOD! WE'VE GOT TO RETREAT!
VICTORY OR DEATH!
I GOTTA RUN... BUT THEY'RE *EVERYWHERE*...

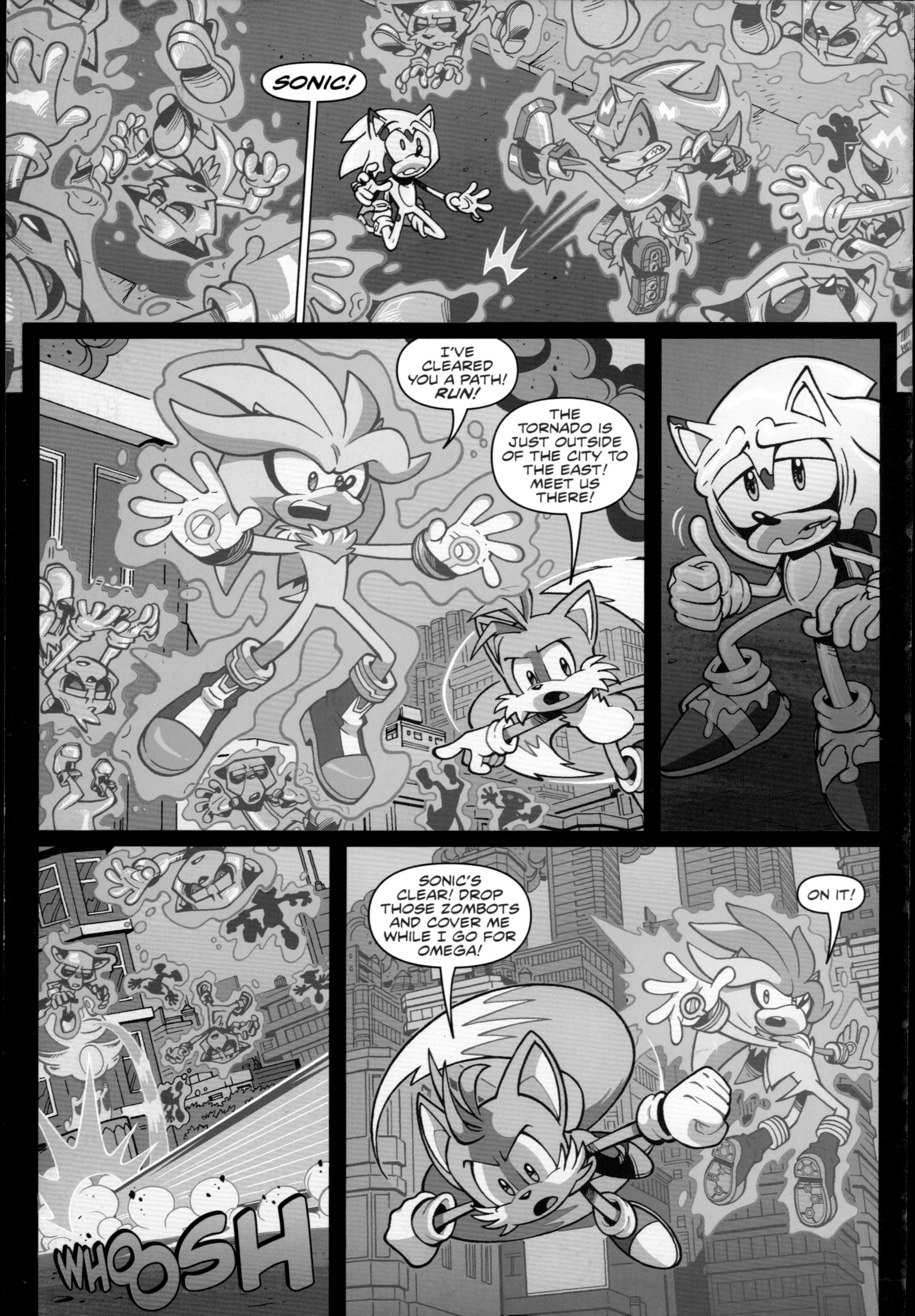
SONIC!
I'VE CLEARED YOU A PATH! RUN!
THE TORNADO IS JUST OUTSIDE OF THE CITY TO THE EAST! MEET US THERE!
WHOOSH
SONIC'S CLEAR! DROP THOSE ZOMBOTS AND COVER ME WHILE I GO FOR OMEGA!
ON IT!

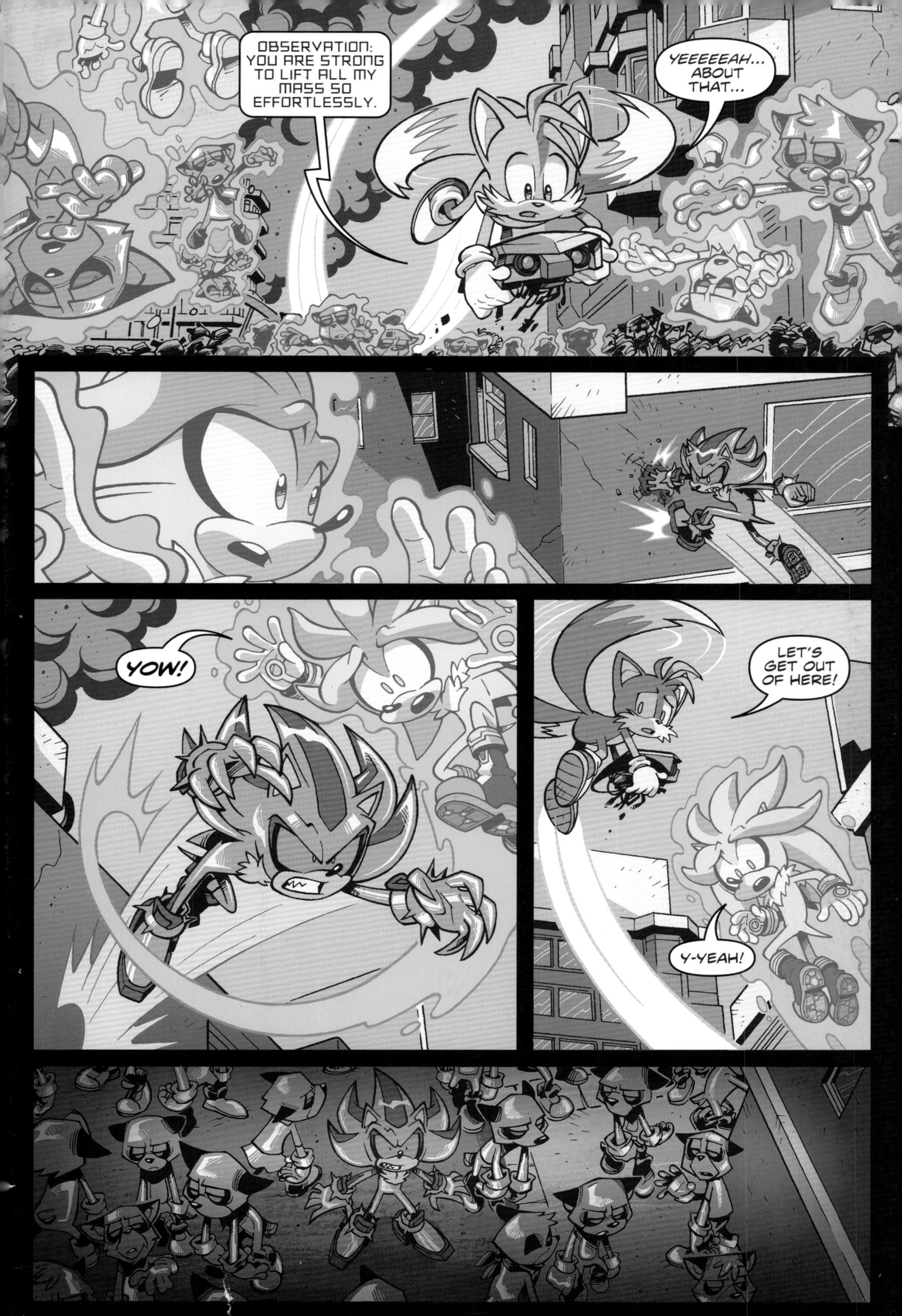
OBSERVATION: YOU ARE STRONG TO LIFT ALL MY MASS SO EFFORTLESSLY.
YEEEEEAH... ABOUT THAT...
YOW!
LET'S GET OUT OF HERE!
Y-YEAH!

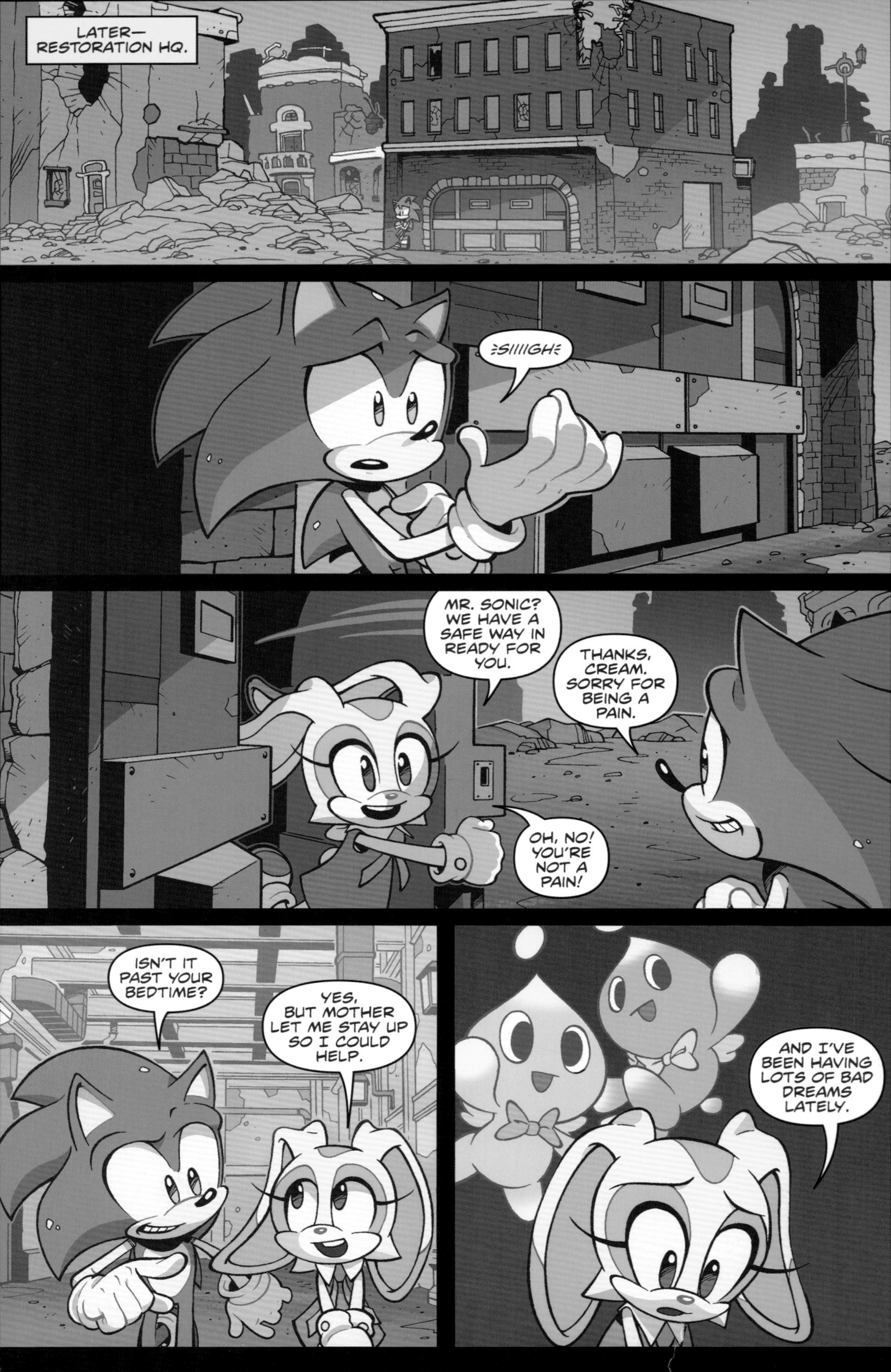
LATER—
RESTORATION HQ.
SIIIIGH
MR. SONIC? WE HAVE A SAFE WAY IN READY FOR YOU.
THANKS, CREAM. SORRY FOR BEING A PAIN.
OH, NO! YOU'RE NOT A PAIN!
ISN'T IT PAST YOUR BEDTIME?
YES, BUT MOTHER LET ME STAY UP SO I COULD HELP.
AND I'VE BEEN HAVING LOTS OF BAD DREAMS LATELY.

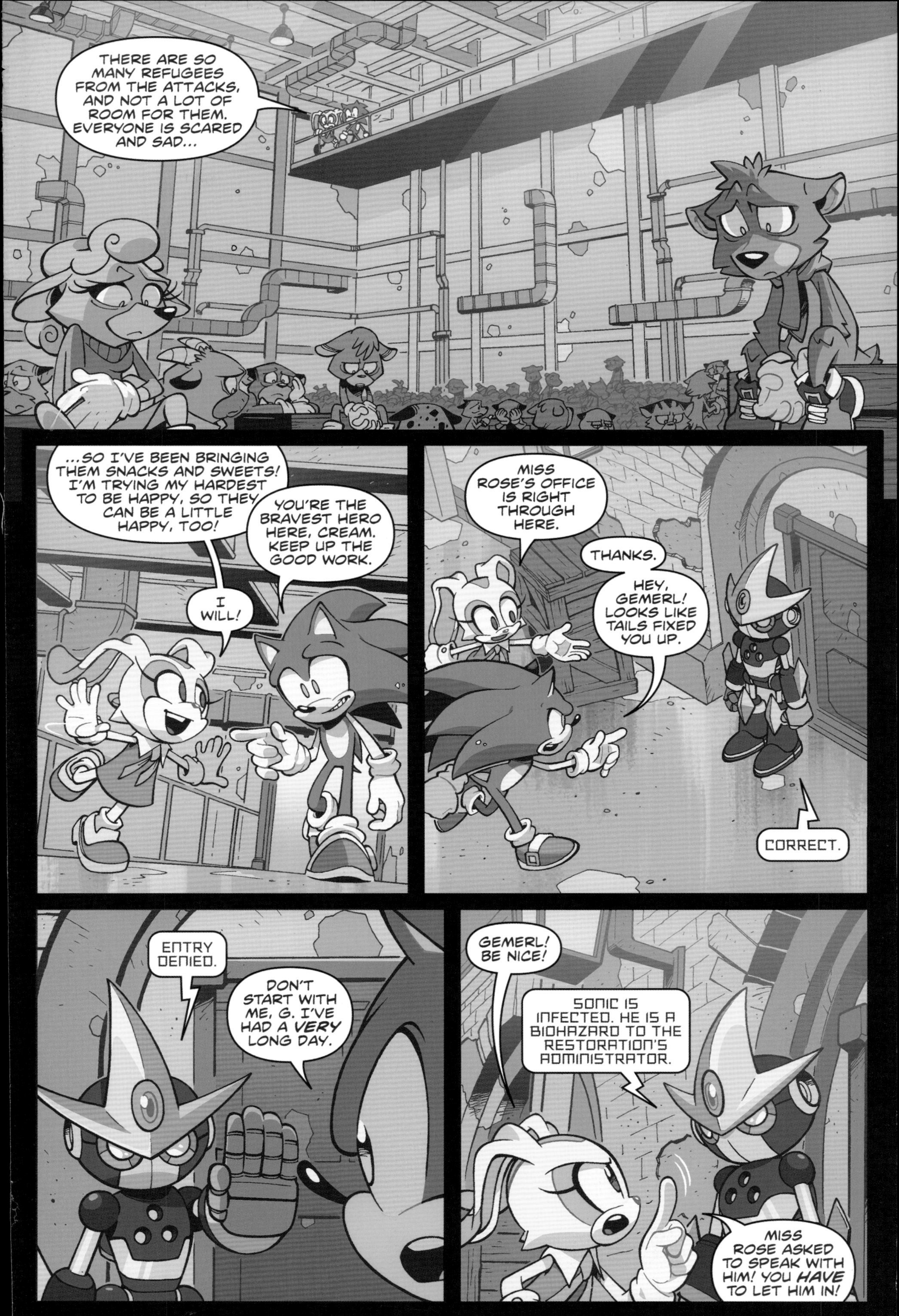
THERE ARE SO MANY REFUGEES FROM THE ATTACKS, AND NOT A LOT OF ROOM FOR THEM. EVERYONE IS SCARED AND SAD...
...SO I'VE BEEN BRINGING THEM SNACKS AND SWEETS! I'M TRYING MY HARDEST TO BE HAPPY, SO THEY CAN BE A LITTLE HAPPY, TOO!
YOU'RE THE BRAVEST HERO HERE, CREAM. KEEP UP THE GOOD WORK.
I WILL!
MISS ROSE'S OFFICE IS RIGHT THROUGH HERE.
THANKS.
HEY, GEMERL! LOOKS LIKE TAILS FIXED YOU UP.
CORRECT.
ENTRY DENIED.
DON'T START WITH ME, G. I'VE HAD A *VERY* LONG DAY.
GEMERL! BE NICE!
SONIC IS INFECTED. HE IS A BIOHAZARD TO THE RESTORATION'S ADMINISTRATOR.
MISS ROSE ASKED TO SPEAK WITH HIM! YOU *HAVE* TO LET HIM IN!

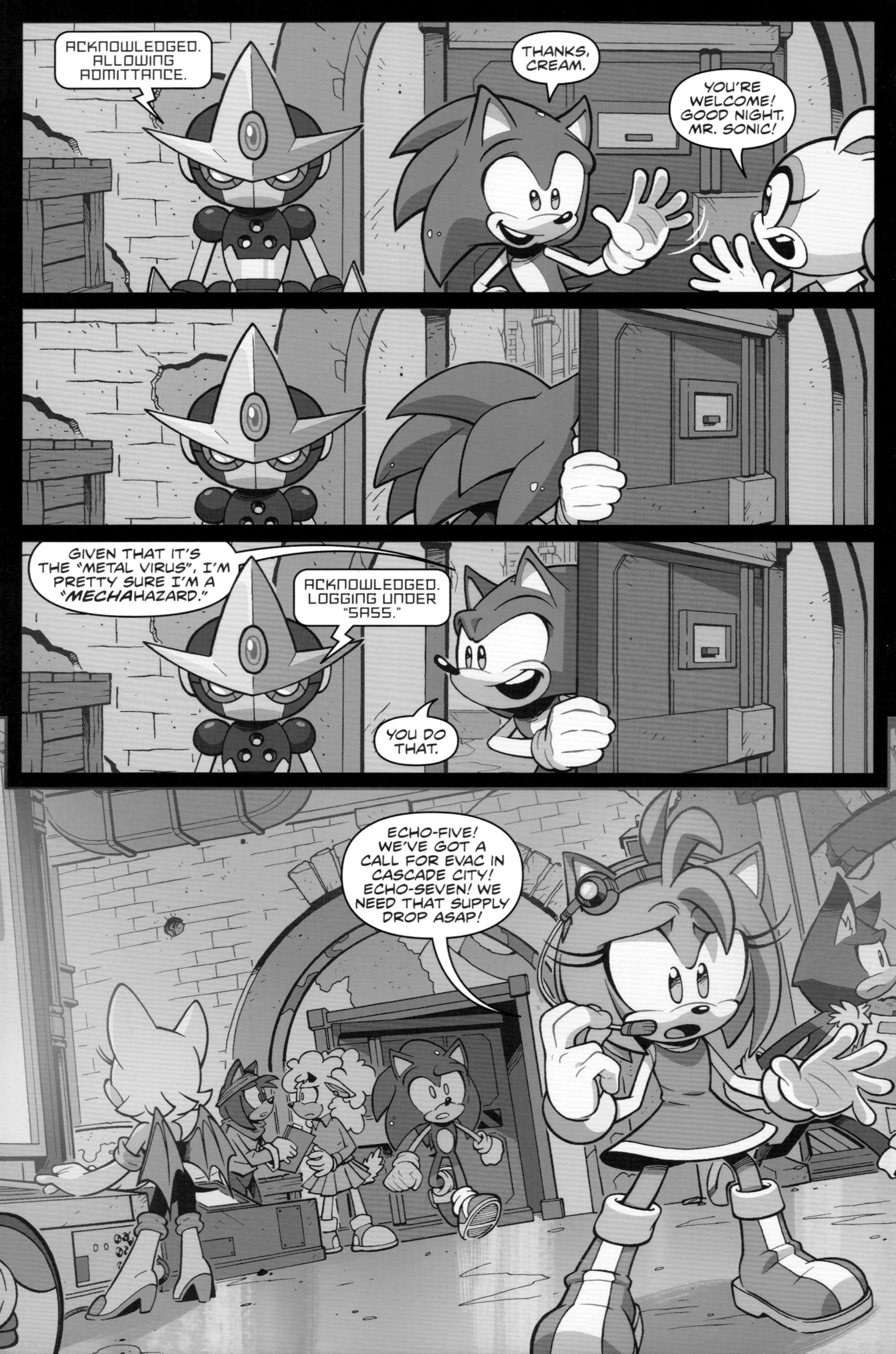

ACKNOWLEDGED. ALLOWING ADMITTANCE.
THANKS, CREAM.
YOU'RE WELCOME! GOOD NIGHT, MR. SONIC!
GIVEN THAT IT'S THE "METAL VIRUS", I'M PRETTY SURE I'M A "MECHAHAZARD."
ACKNOWLEDGED. LOGGING UNDER "SASS."
YOU DO THAT.
ECHO-FIVE! WE'VE GOT A CALL FOR EVAC IN CASCADE CITY! ECHO-SEVEN! WE NEED THAT SUPPLY DROP ASAP!

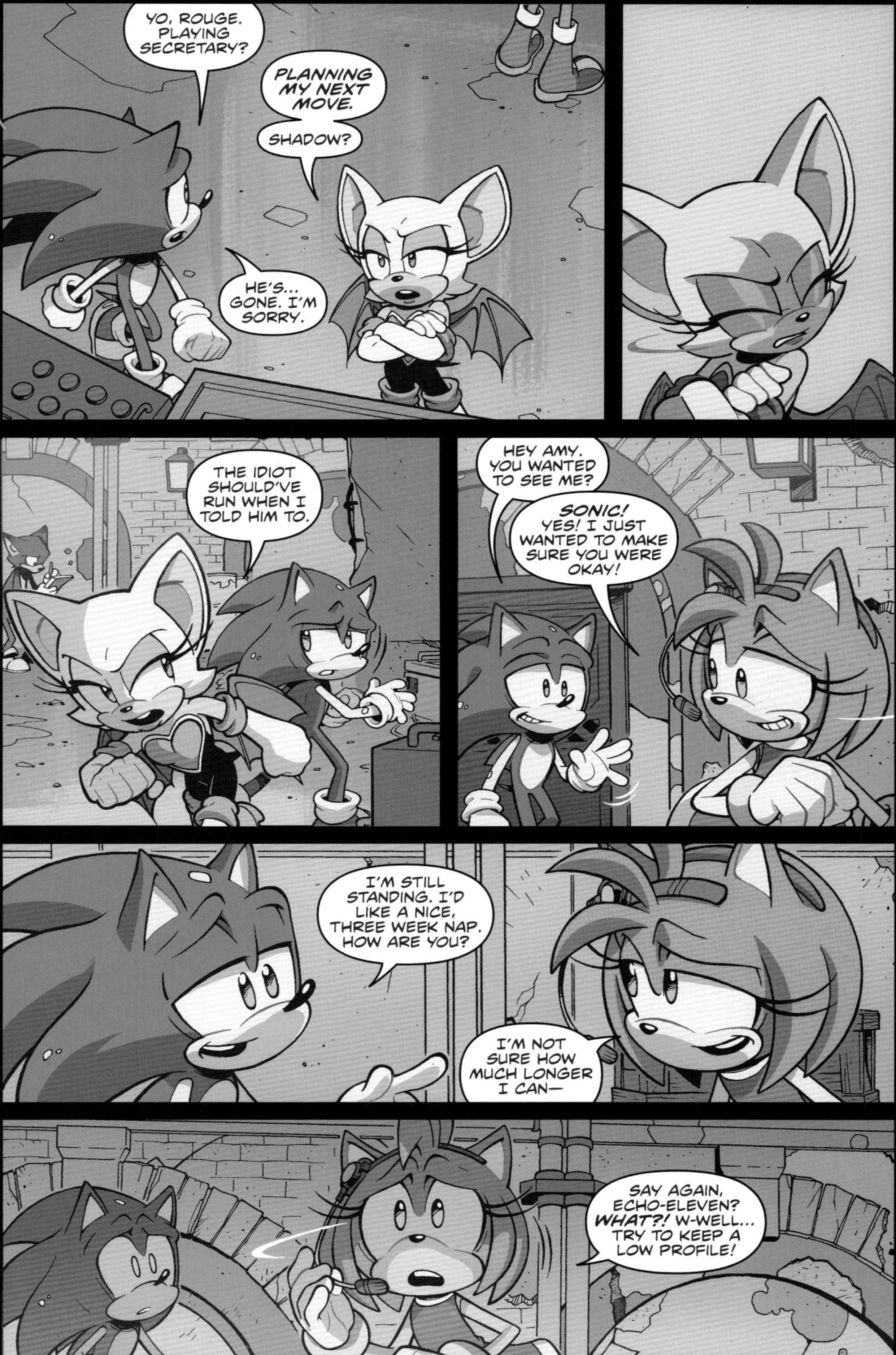

YO, ROUGE. PLAYING SECRETARY?
PLANNING MY NEXT MOVE.
SHADOW?
HE'S... GONE. I'M SORRY.
THE IDIOT SHOULD'VE RUN WHEN I TOLD HIM TO.
HEY AMY. YOU WANTED TO SEE ME?
SONIC! YES! I JUST WANTED TO MAKE SURE YOU WERE OKAY!
I'M STILL STANDING. I'D LIKE A NICE, THREE WEEK NAP. HOW ARE YOU?
I'M NOT SURE HOW MUCH LONGER I CAN—
SAY AGAIN, ECHO-ELEVEN? WHAT?! W-WELL... TRY TO KEEP A LOW PROFILE!

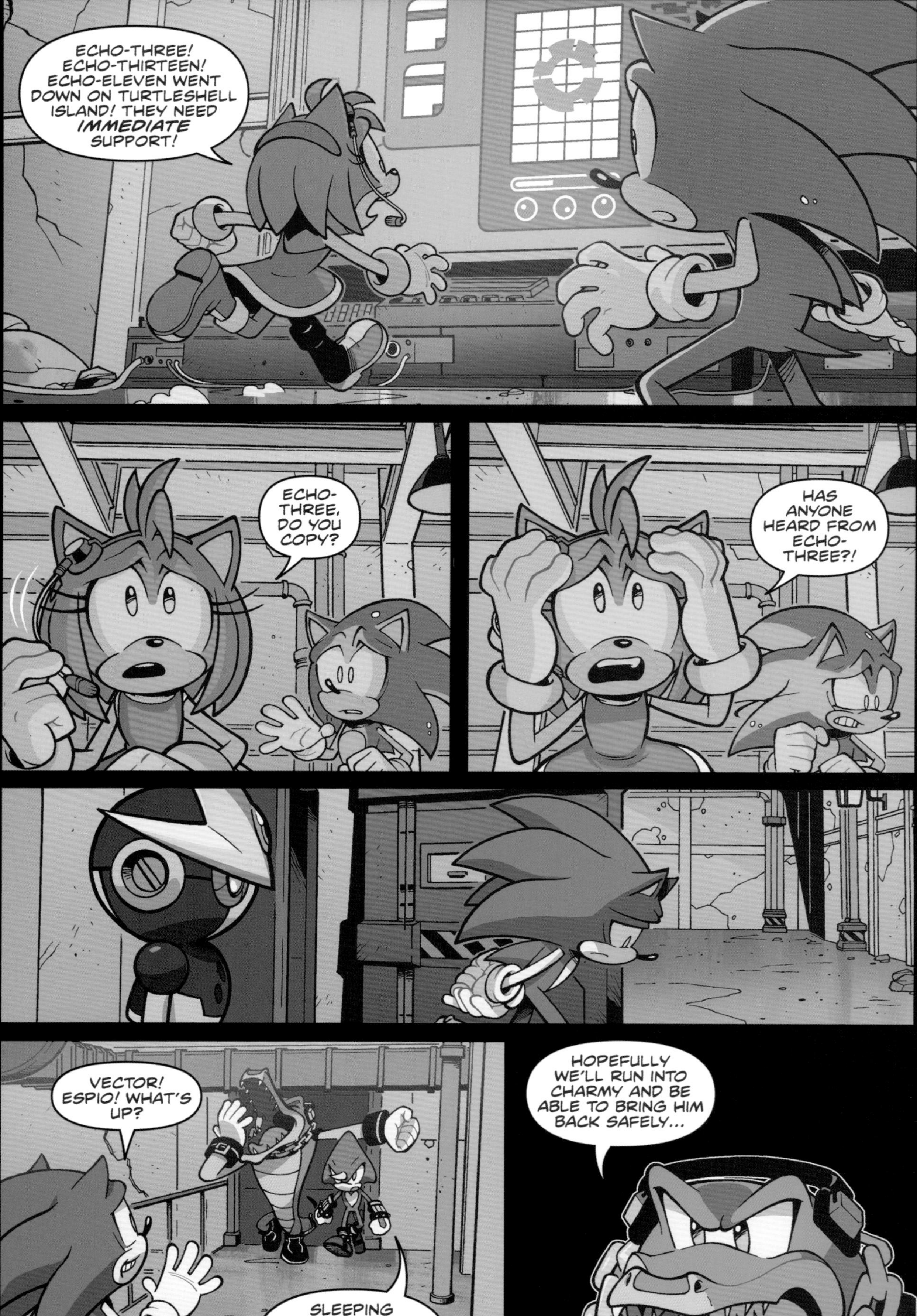
ECHO-THREE! ECHO-THIRTEEN! ECHO-ELEVEN WENT DOWN ON TURTLESHELL ISLAND! THEY NEED *IMMEDIATE* SUPPORT!
ECHO-THREE, DO YOU COPY?
HAS ANYONE HEARD FROM ECHO-THREE?!
VECTOR! ESPIO! WHAT'S UP?
SLEEPING SHIFT IS OVER, SO WE'RE BACK TO IT. FINDING SURVIVORS. FINDING SUPPLIES.
HOPEFULLY WE'LL RUN INTO CHARMY AND BE ABLE TO BRING HIM BACK SAFELY...

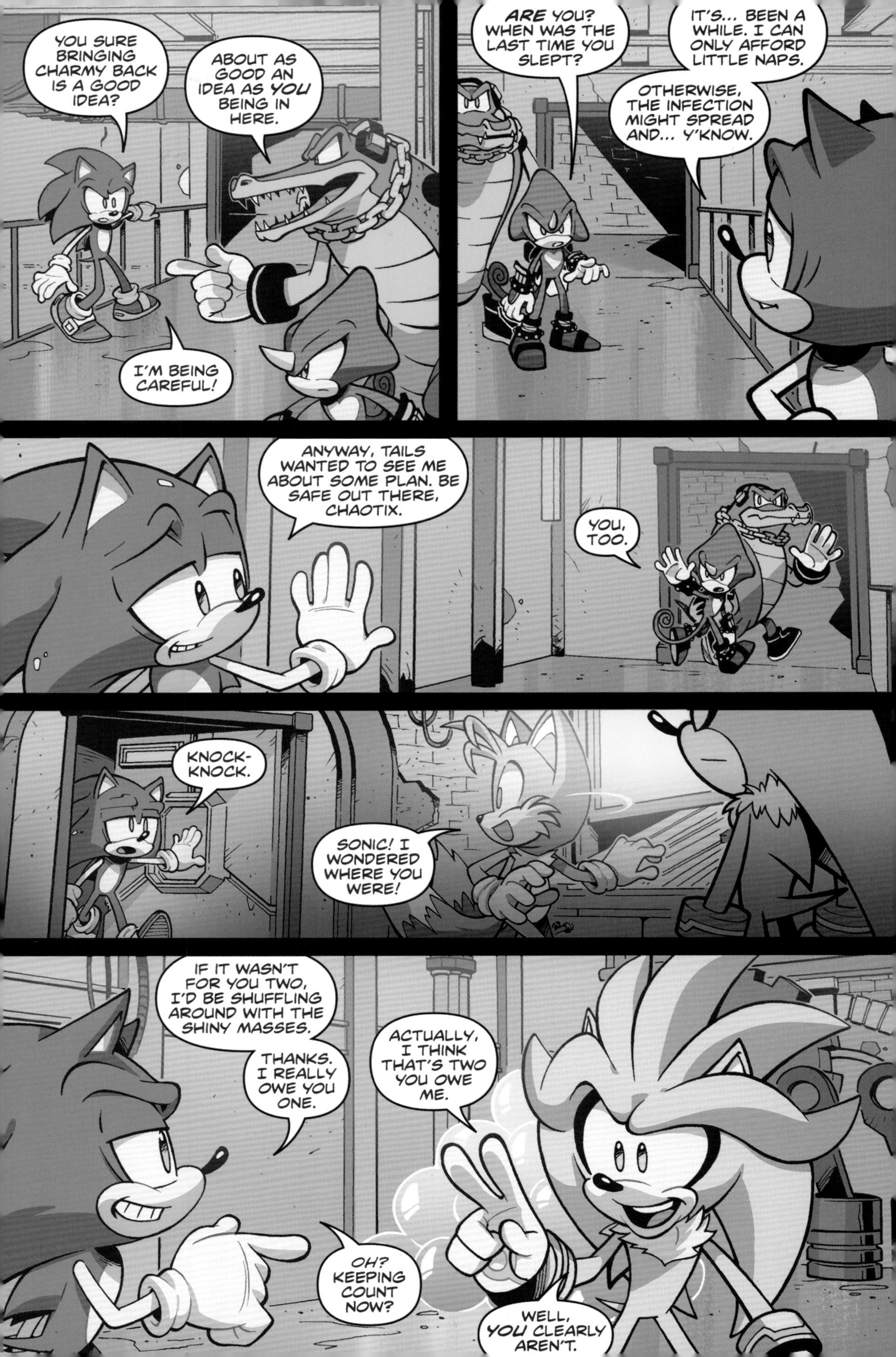
YOU SURE BRINGING CHARMY BACK IS A GOOD IDEA?
ABOUT AS GOOD AN IDEA AS *YOU* BEING IN HERE.
I'M BEING CAREFUL!
ARE YOU? WHEN WAS THE LAST TIME YOU SLEPT?
IT'S... BEEN A WHILE. I CAN ONLY AFFORD LITTLE NAPS.
OTHERWISE, THE INFECTION MIGHT SPREAD AND... Y'KNOW.
ANYWAY, TAILS WANTED TO SEE ME ABOUT SOME PLAN. BE SAFE OUT THERE, CHAOTIX.
YOU, TOO.
KNOCK-KNOCK.
SONIC! I WONDERED WHERE YOU WERE!
IF IT WASN'T FOR YOU TWO, I'D BE SHUFFLING AROUND WITH THE SHINY MASSES.
THANKS. I REALLY OWE YOU ONE.
ACTUALLY, I THINK THAT'S TWO YOU OWE ME.
OH? KEEPING COUNT NOW?
WELL, *YOU* CLEARLY AREN'T.

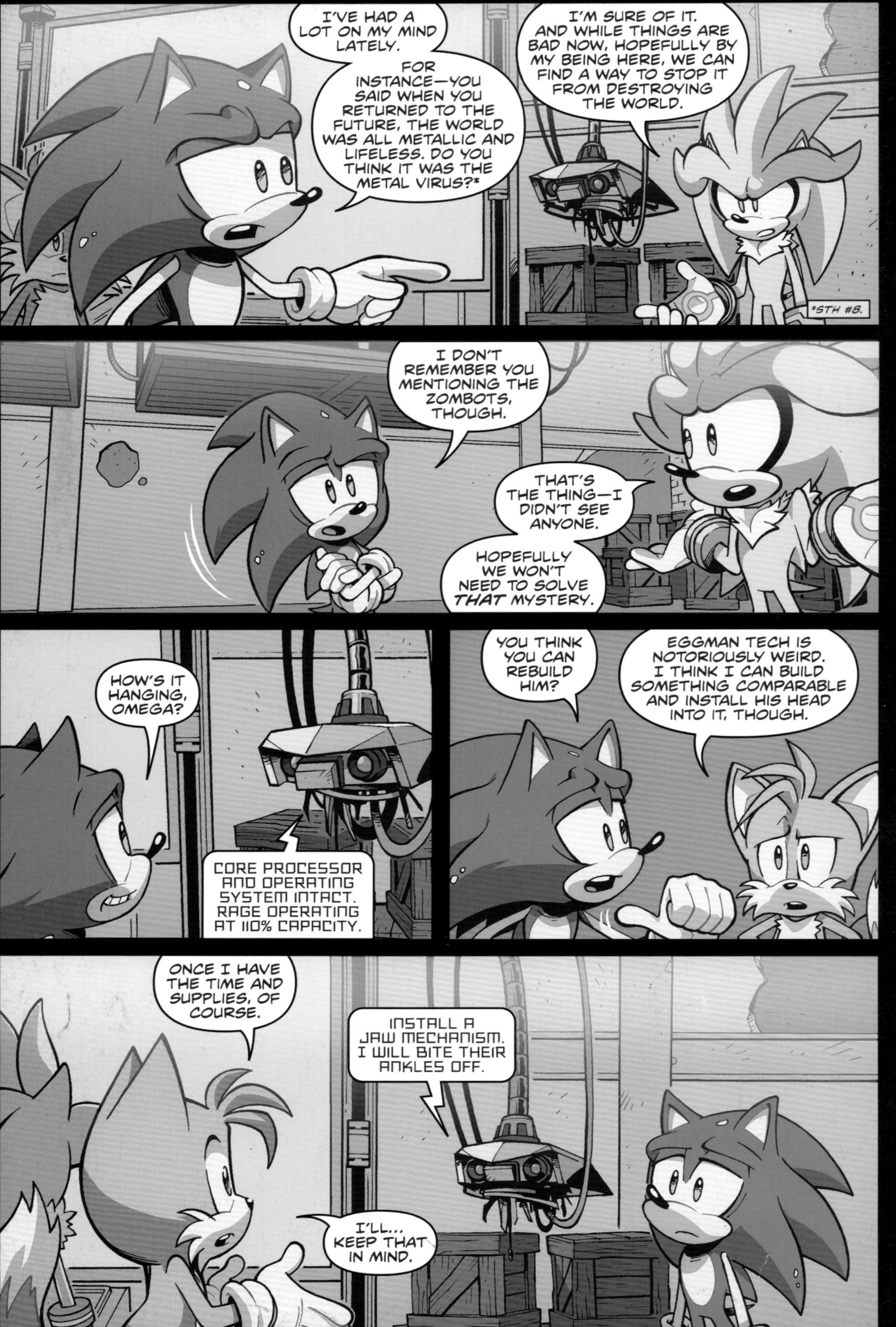
I'VE HAD A LOT ON MY MIND LATELY.
FOR INSTANCE—YOU SAID WHEN YOU RETURNED TO THE FUTURE, THE WORLD WAS ALL METALLIC AND LIFELESS. DO YOU THINK IT WAS THE METAL VIRUS?*
I'M SURE OF IT. AND WHILE THINGS ARE BAD NOW, HOPEFULLY BY MY BEING HERE, WE CAN FIND A WAY TO STOP IT FROM DESTROYING THE WORLD.
*STH #8.
I DON'T REMEMBER YOU MENTIONING THE ZOMBOTS, THOUGH.
THAT'S THE THING—I DIDN'T SEE ANYONE.
HOPEFULLY WE WON'T NEED TO SOLVE *THAT* MYSTERY.
HOW'S IT HANGING, OMEGA?
CORE PROCESSOR AND OPERATING SYSTEM INTACT. RAGE OPERATING AT 110% CAPACITY.
YOU THINK YOU CAN REBUILD HIM?
EGGMAN TECH IS NOTORIOUSLY WEIRD. I THINK I CAN BUILD SOMETHING COMPARABLE AND INSTALL HIS HEAD INTO IT, THOUGH.
ONCE I HAVE THE TIME AND SUPPLIES, OF COURSE.
INSTALL A JAW MECHANISM. I WILL BITE THEIR ANKLES OFF.
I'LL... KEEP THAT IN MIND.

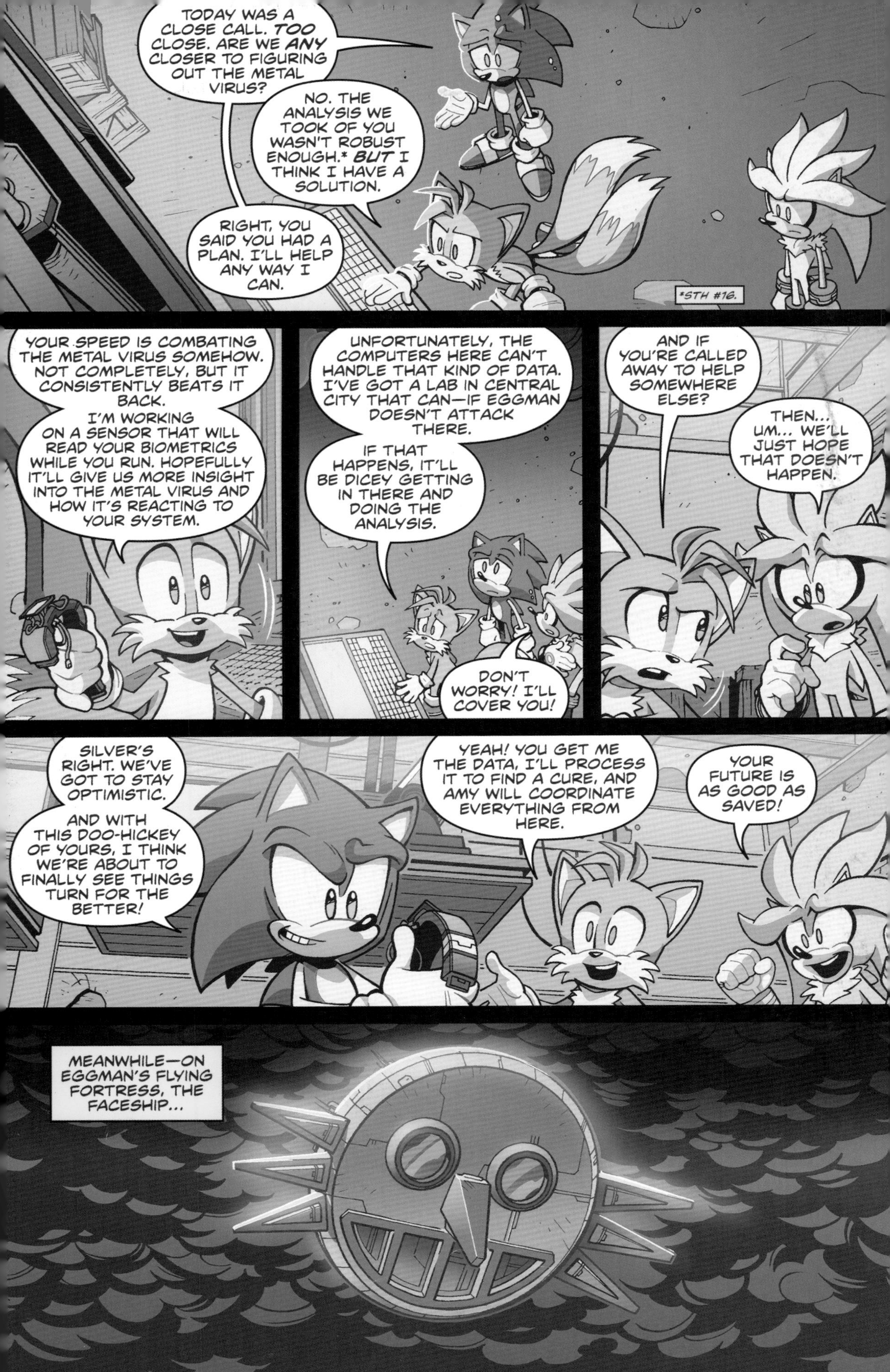
TODAY WAS A CLOSE CALL. TOO CLOSE. ARE WE ANY CLOSER TO FIGURING OUT THE METAL VIRUS?
NO. THE ANALYSIS WE TOOK OF YOU WASN'T ROBUST ENOUGH.* BUT I THINK I HAVE A SOLUTION.
RIGHT, YOU SAID YOU HAD A PLAN. I'LL HELP ANY WAY I CAN.
*STH #16.
YOUR SPEED IS COMBATING THE METAL VIRUS SOMEHOW. NOT COMPLETELY, BUT IT CONSISTENTLY BEATS IT BACK.
I'M WORKING ON A SENSOR THAT WILL READ YOUR BIOMETRICS WHILE YOU RUN. HOPEFULLY IT'LL GIVE US MORE INSIGHT INTO THE METAL VIRUS AND HOW IT'S REACTING TO YOUR SYSTEM.
UNFORTUNATELY, THE COMPUTERS HERE CAN'T HANDLE THAT KIND OF DATA. I'VE GOT A LAB IN CENTRAL CITY THAT CAN—IF EGGMAN DOESN'T ATTACK THERE.
IF THAT HAPPENS, IT'LL BE DICEY GETTING IN THERE AND DOING THE ANALYSIS.
DON'T WORRY! I'LL COVER YOU!
AND IF YOU'RE CALLED AWAY TO HELP SOMEWHERE ELSE?
THEN... UM... WE'LL JUST HOPE THAT DOESN'T HAPPEN.
SILVER'S RIGHT. WE'VE GOT TO STAY OPTIMISTIC.
AND WITH THIS DOO-HICKEY OF YOURS, I THINK WE'RE ABOUT TO FINALLY SEE THINGS TURN FOR THE BETTER!
YEAH! YOU GET ME THE DATA, I'LL PROCESS IT TO FIND A CURE, AND AMY WILL COORDINATE EVERYTHING FROM HERE.
YOUR FUTURE IS AS GOOD AS SAVED!
MEANWHILE—ON EGGMAN'S FLYING FORTRESS, THE FACESHIP...

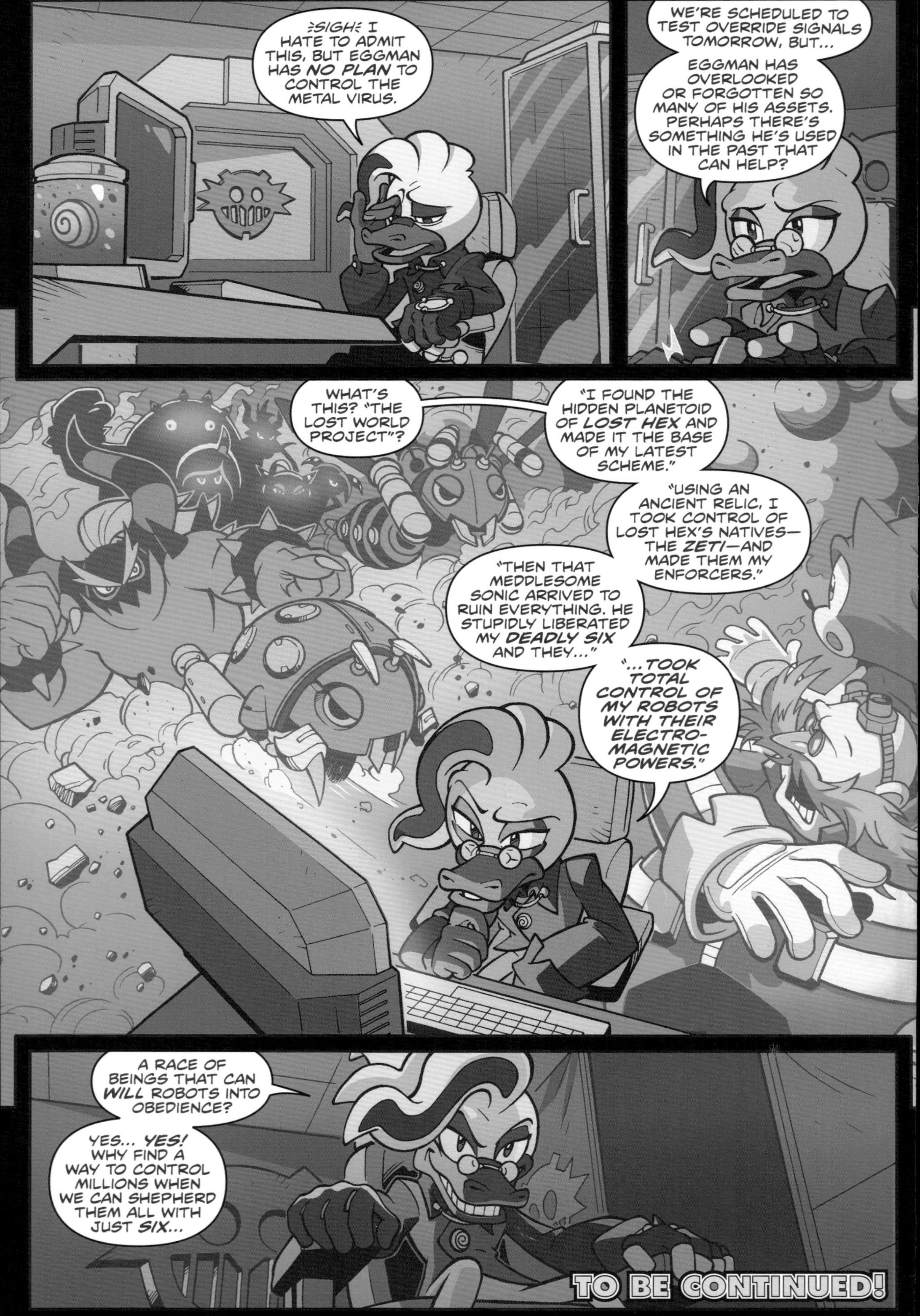

:SIGH: I HATE TO ADMIT THIS, BUT EGGMAN HAS NO PLAN TO CONTROL THE METAL VIRUS.
WE'RE SCHEDULED TO TEST OVERRIDE SIGNALS TOMORROW, BUT...
EGGMAN HAS OVERLOOKED OR FORGOTTEN SO MANY OF HIS ASSETS. PERHAPS THERE'S SOMETHING HE'S USED IN THE PAST THAT CAN HELP?
WHAT'S THIS? "THE LOST WORLD PROJECT"?
"I FOUND THE HIDDEN PLANETOID OF LOST HEX AND MADE IT THE BASE OF MY LATEST SCHEME."
"USING AN ANCIENT RELIC, I TOOK CONTROL OF LOST HEX'S NATIVES— THE ZETI—AND MADE THEM MY ENFORCERS."
"THEN THAT MEDDLESOME SONIC ARRIVED TO RUIN EVERYTHING. HE STUPIDLY LIBERATED MY DEADLY SIX AND THEY..."
"...TOOK TOTAL CONTROL OF MY ROBOTS WITH THEIR ELECTRO-MAGNETIC POWERS."
A RACE OF BEINGS THAT CAN WILL ROBOTS INTO OBEDIENCE?
YES... YES! WHY FIND A WAY TO CONTROL MILLIONS WHEN WE CAN SHEPHERD THEM ALL WITH JUST SIX...
TO BE CONTINUED!

ART BY **JACK LAWRENCE** COLORS BY **MATT HERMS**

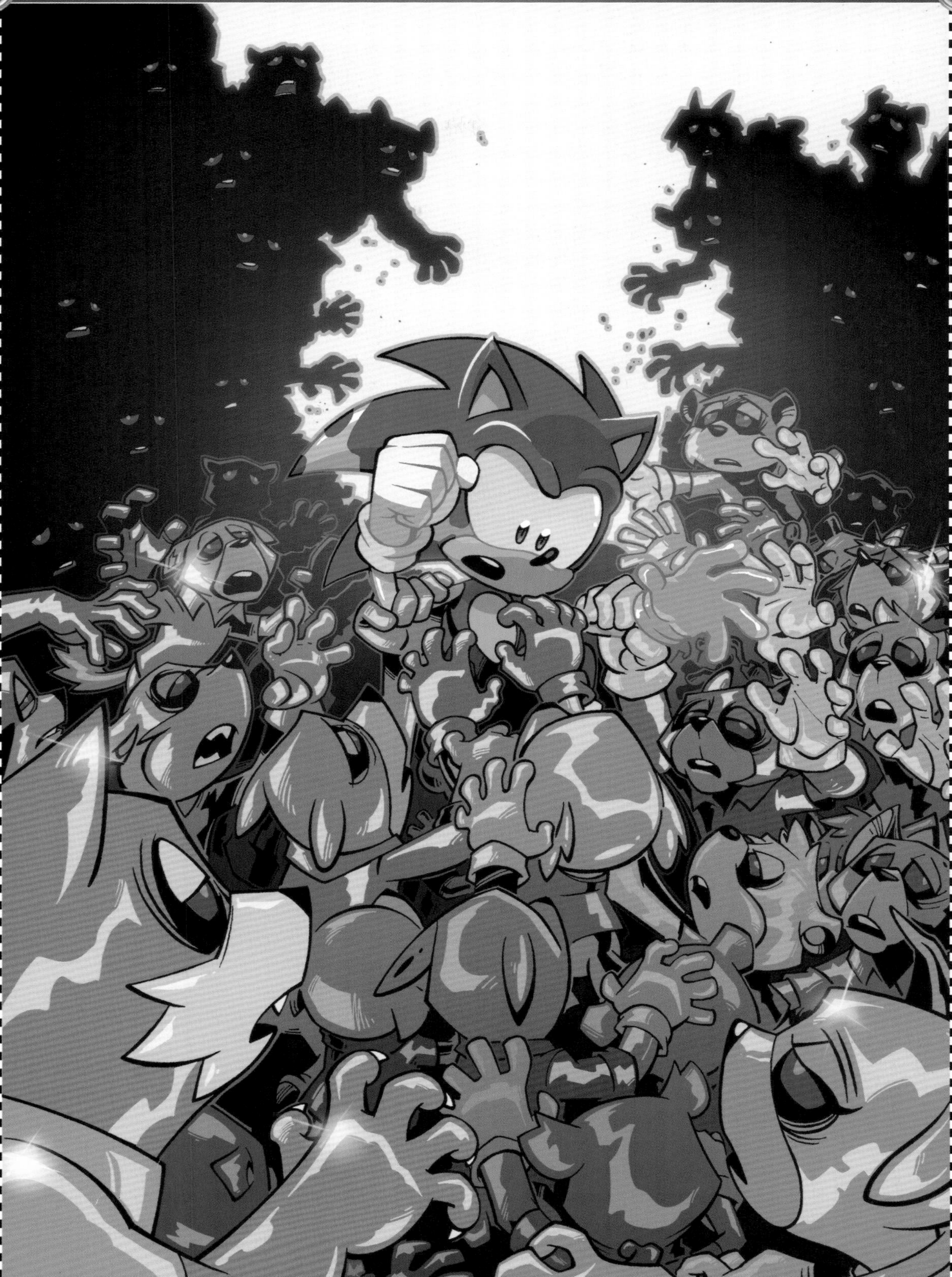

ART BY NATHALIE FOURDRAINE

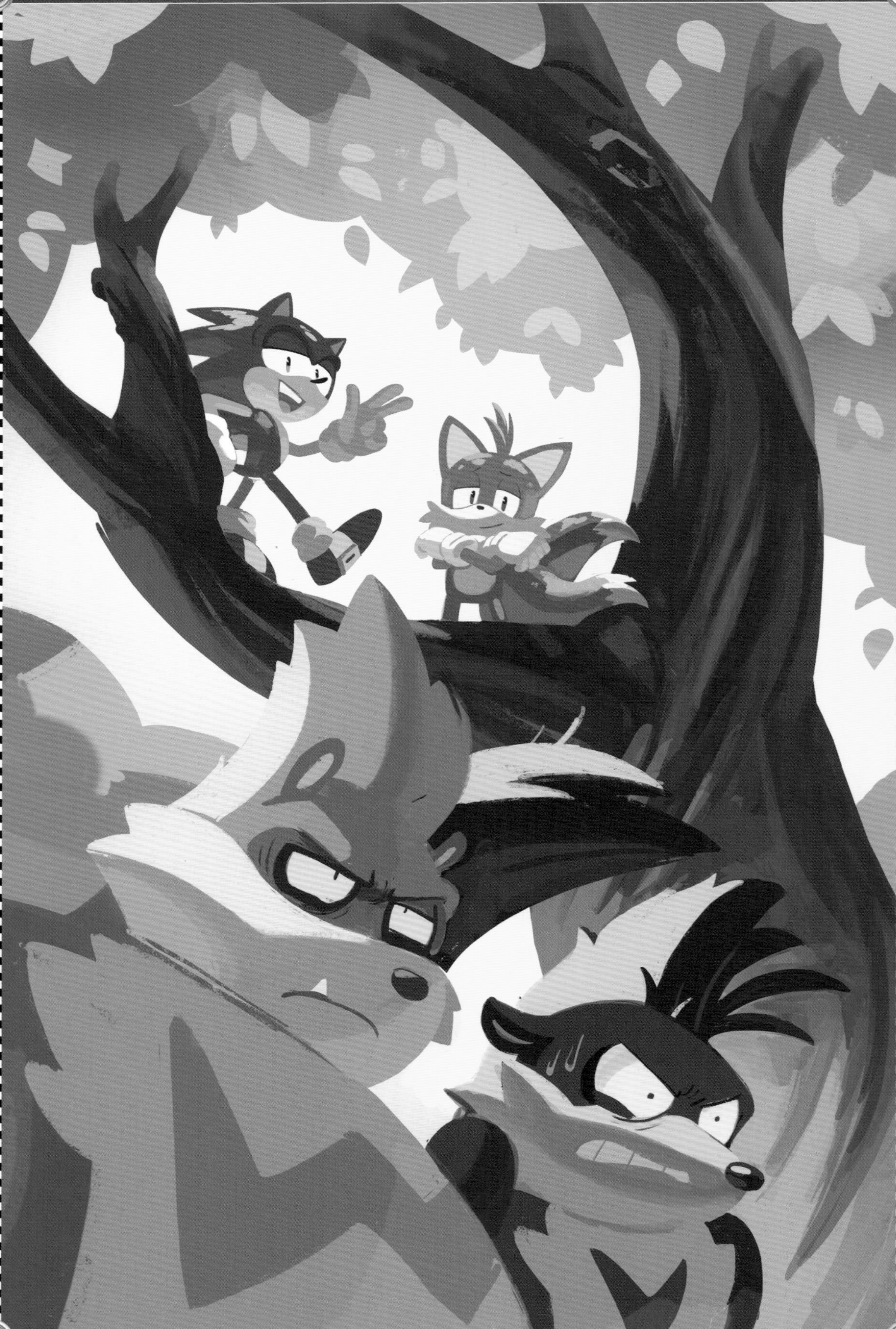

ART BY **NATHALIE FOURDRAINE**

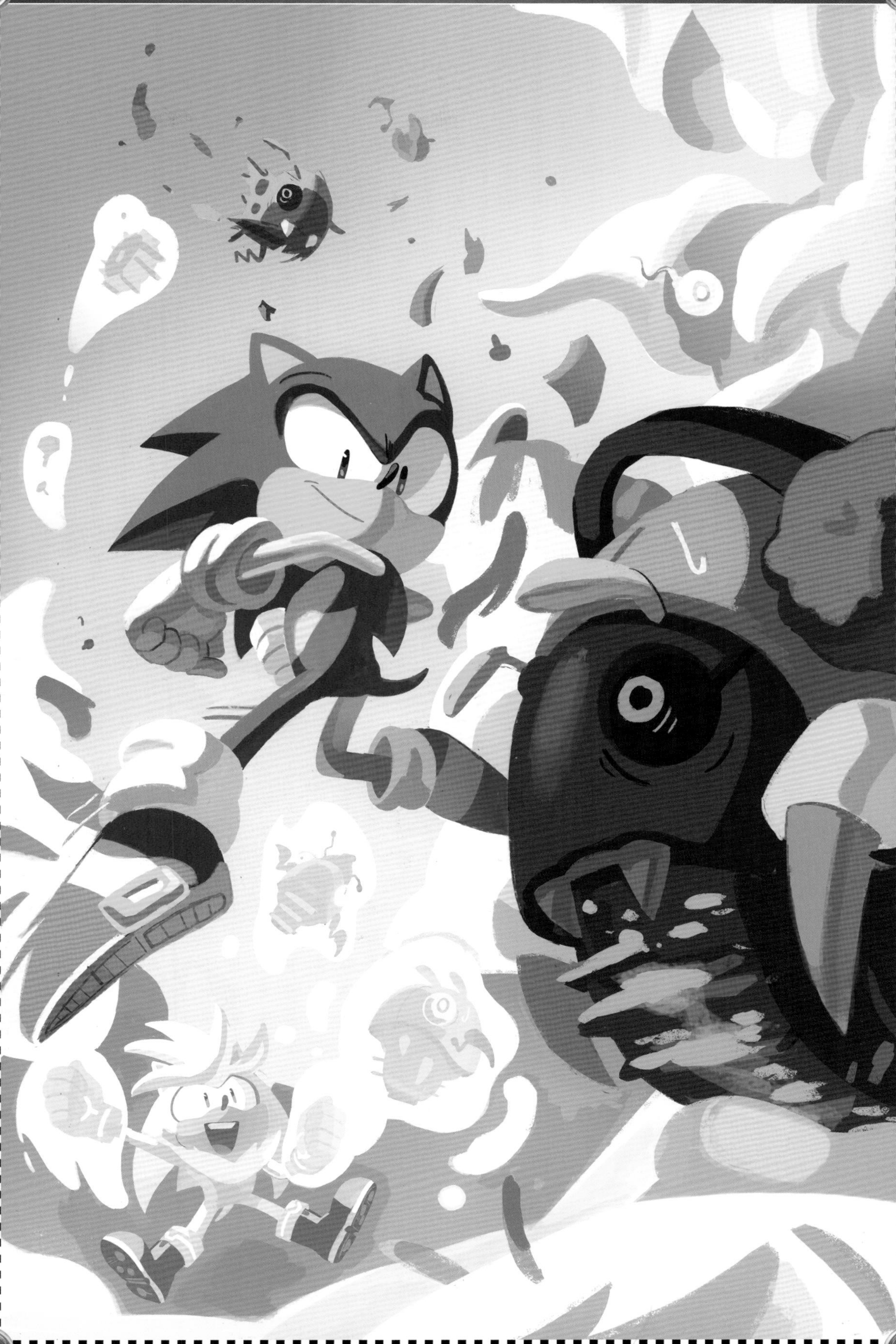

ART BY NATHALIE FOURDRAINE

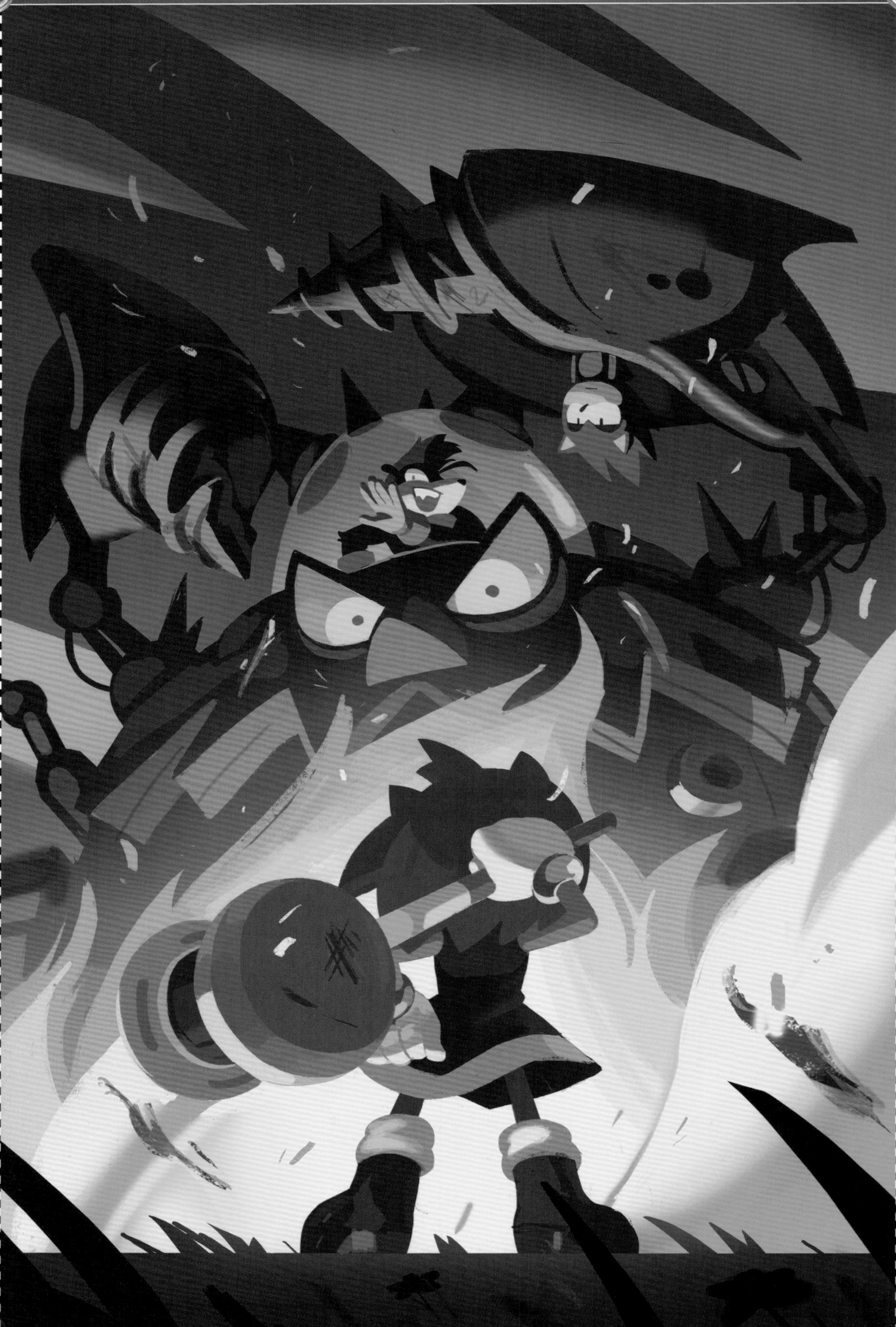

ART BY NATHALIE FOURDRAINE

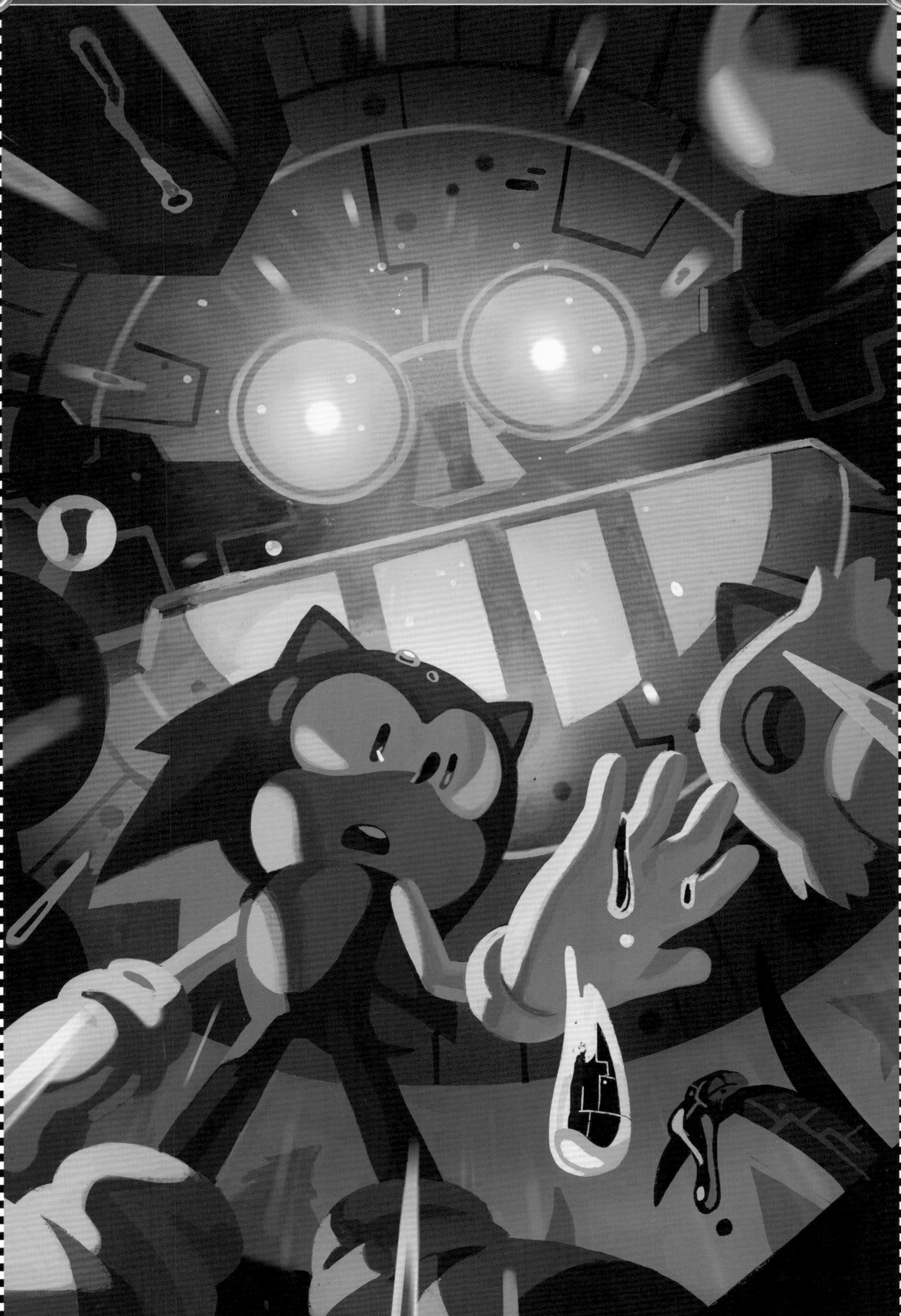

ART BY **NATHALIE FOURDRAINE**

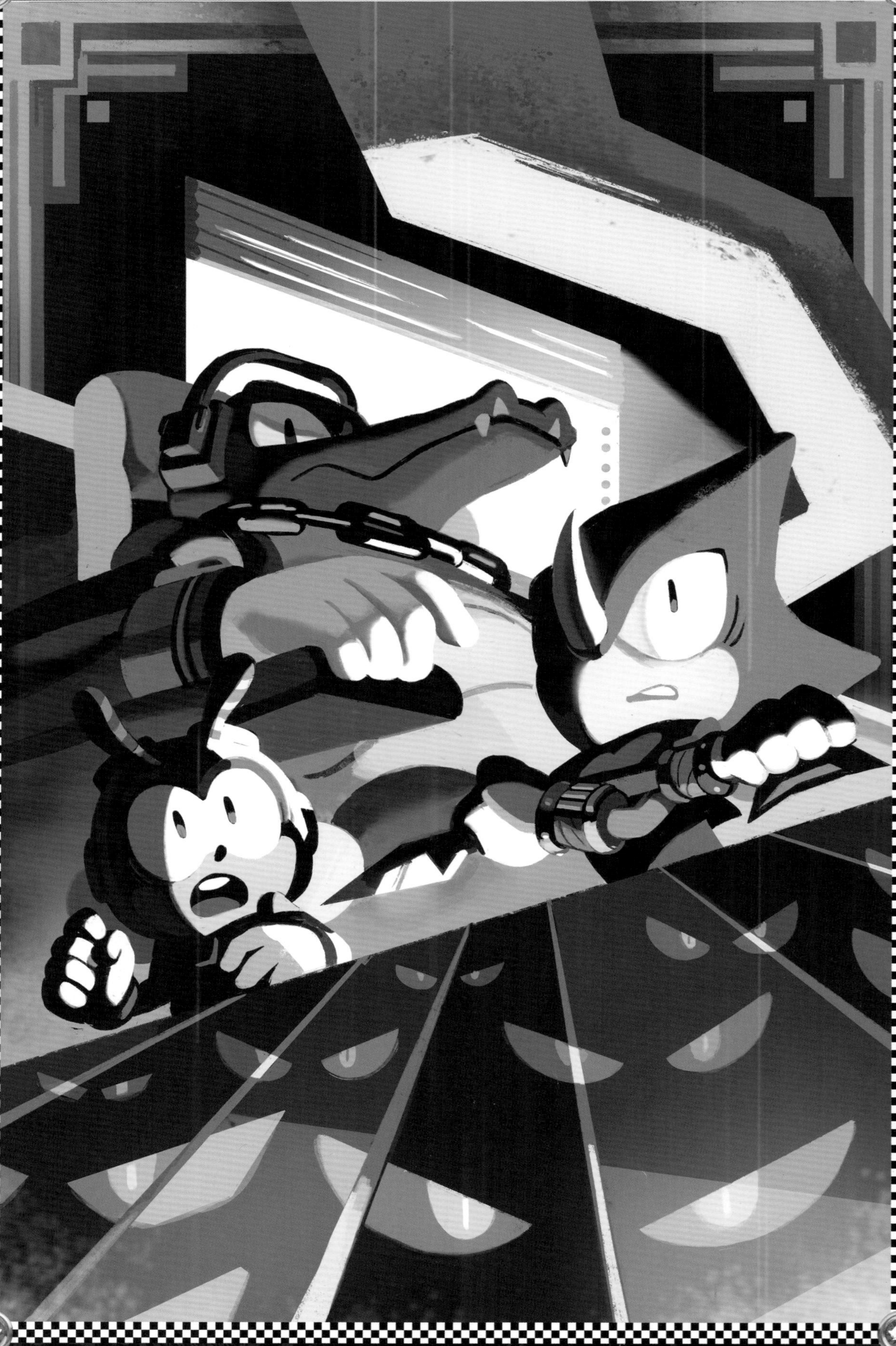

ART BY NATHALIE FOURDRAINE

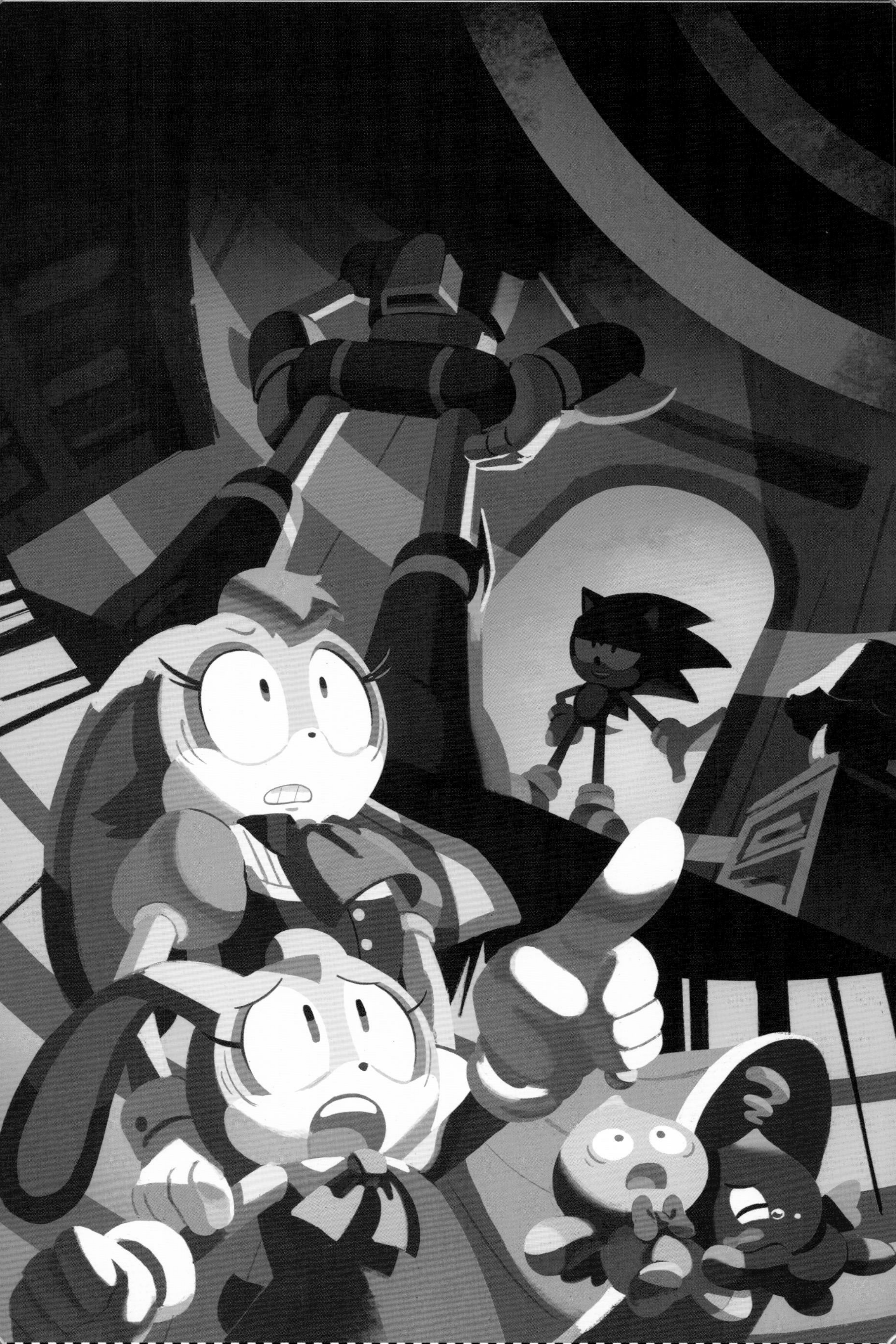

ART BY NATHALIE FOURDRAINE

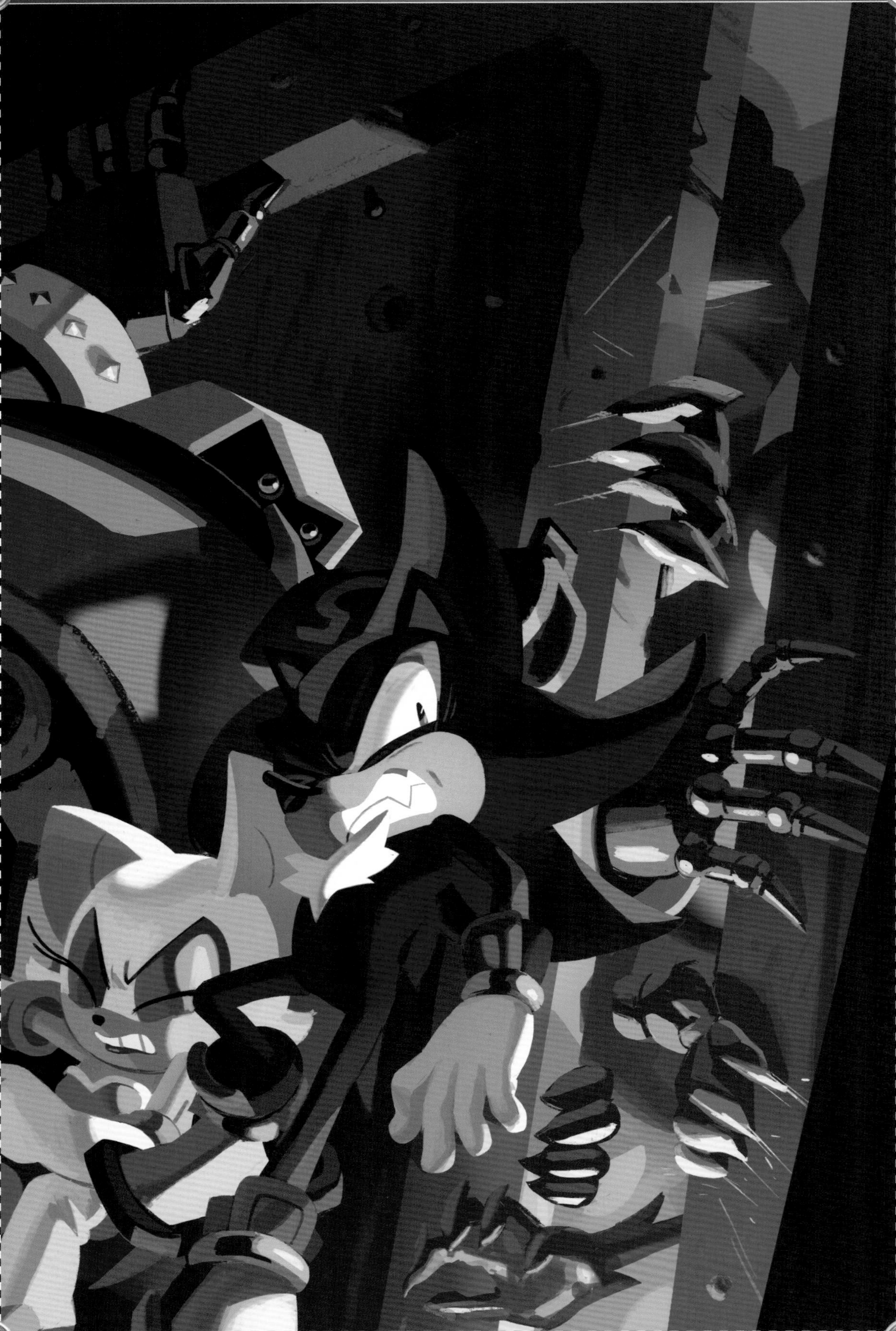

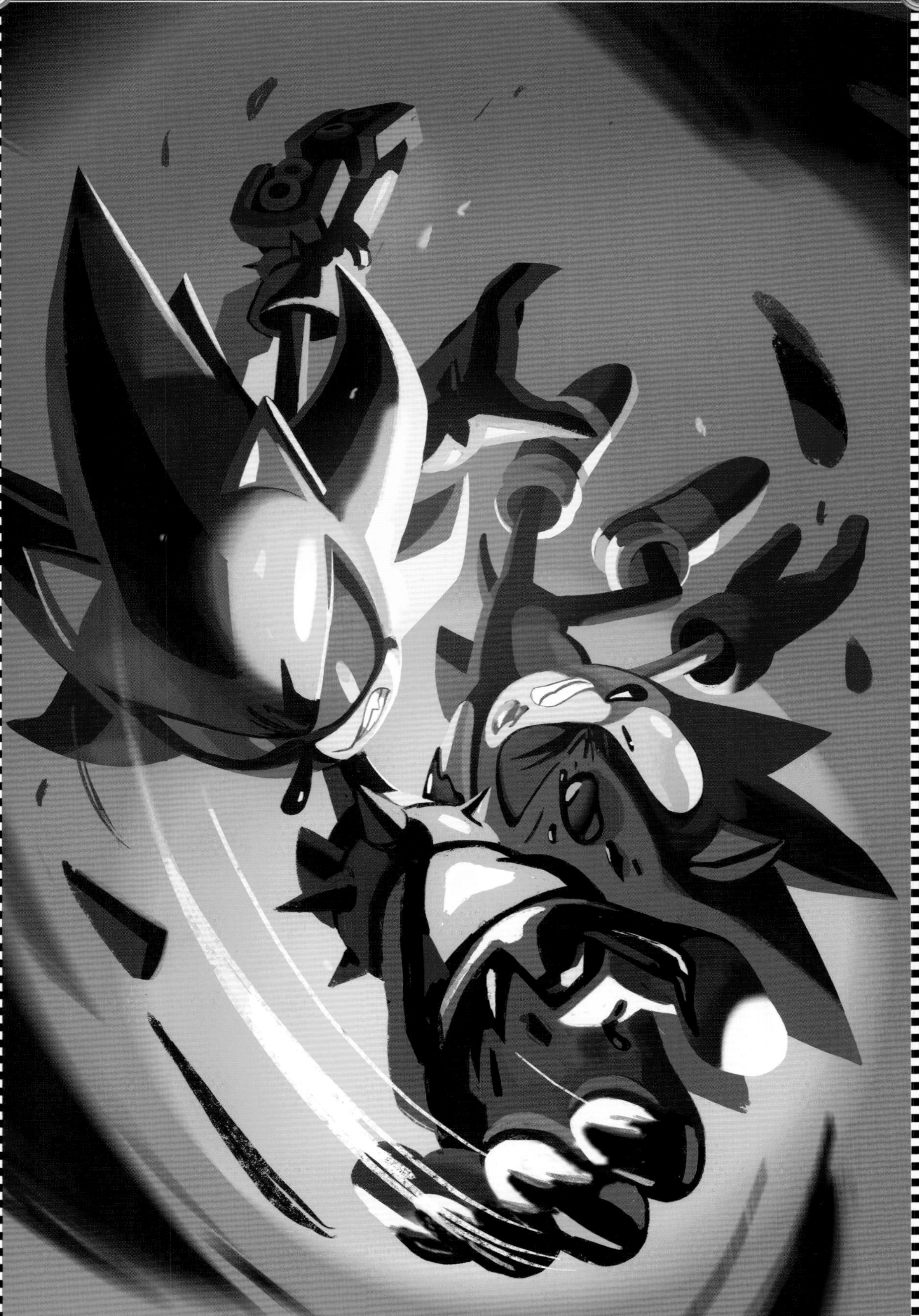

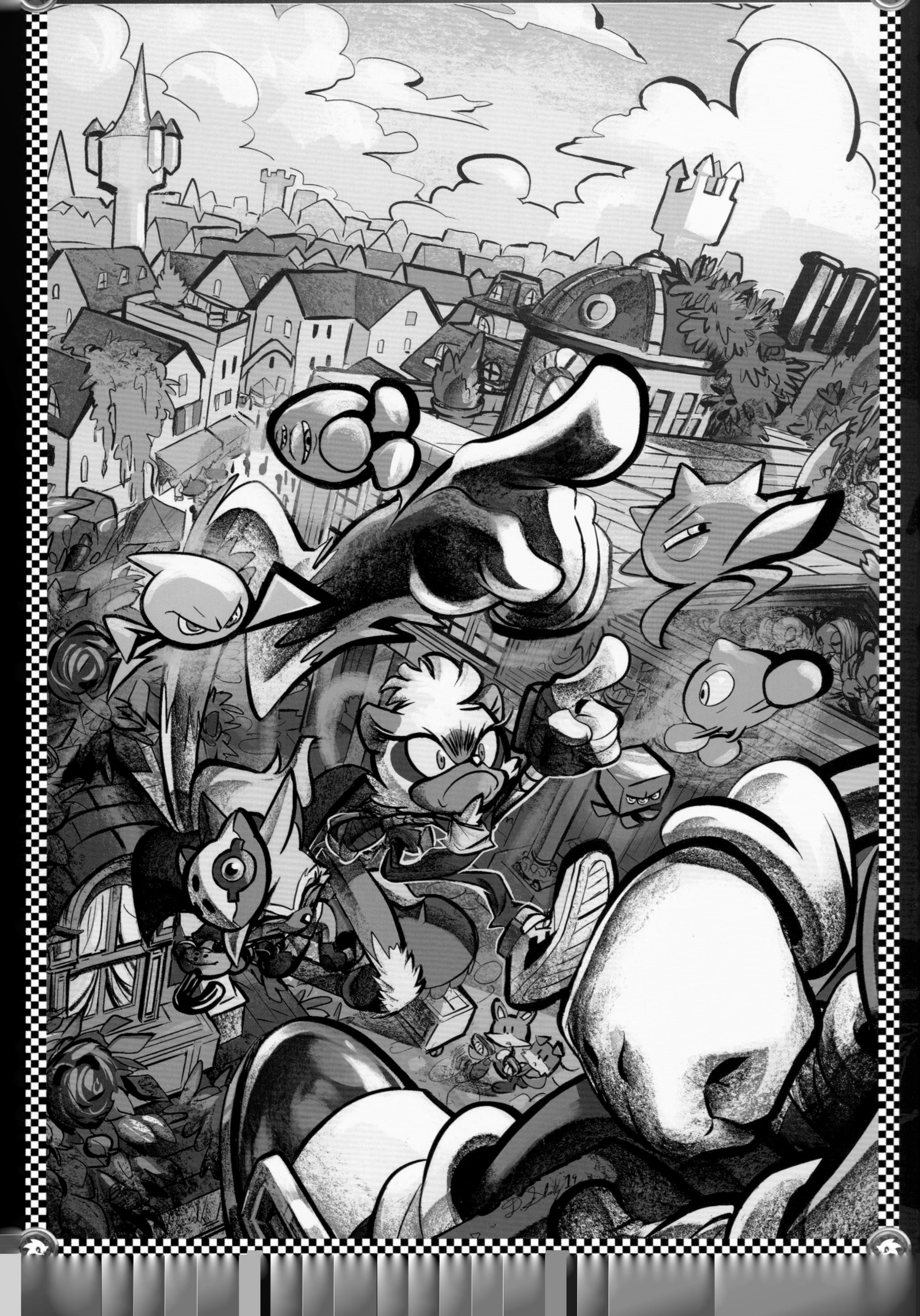

ART BY JENNIFER HERNANDEZ

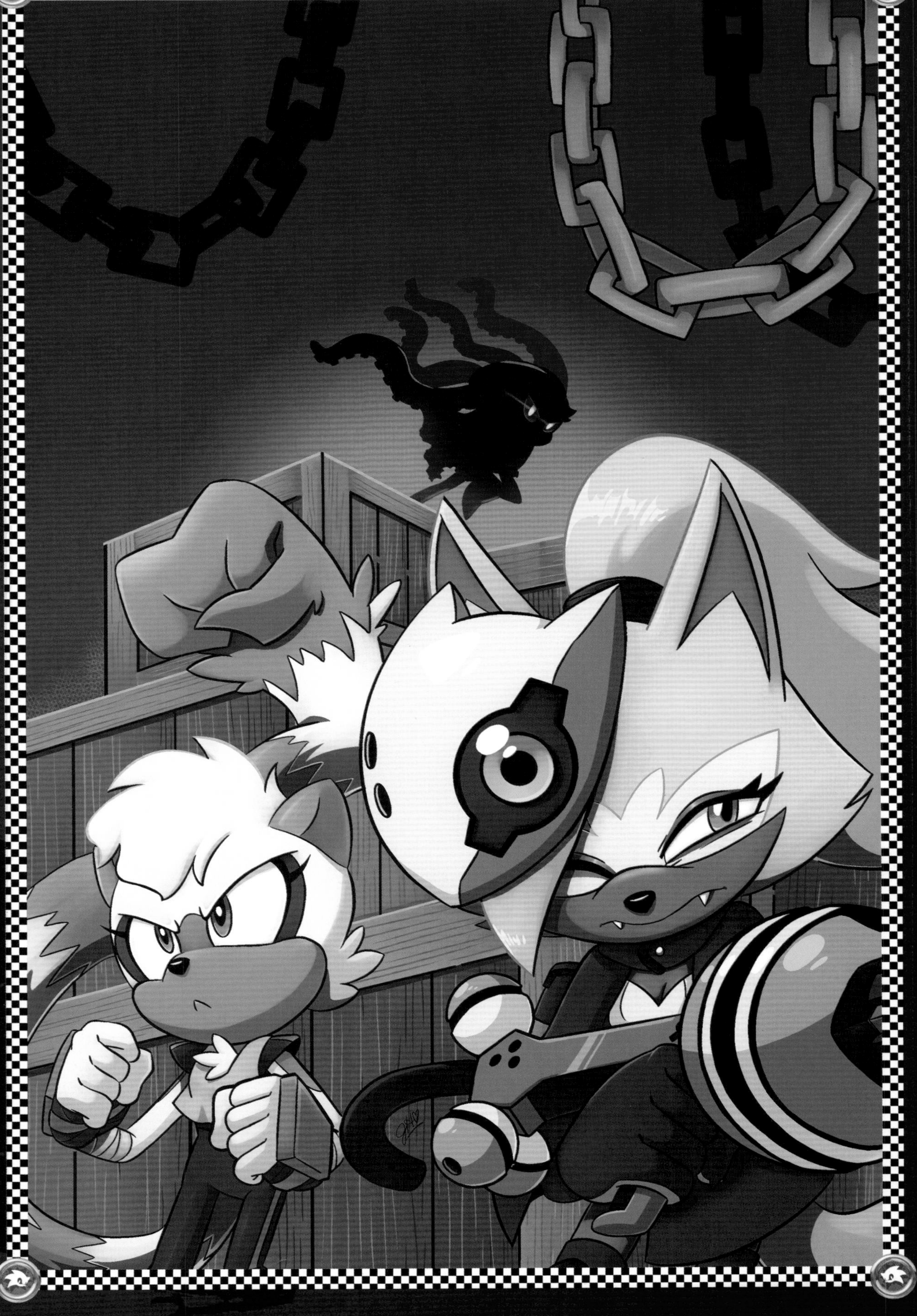

ART BY PRISCILLA TRAMONTANO

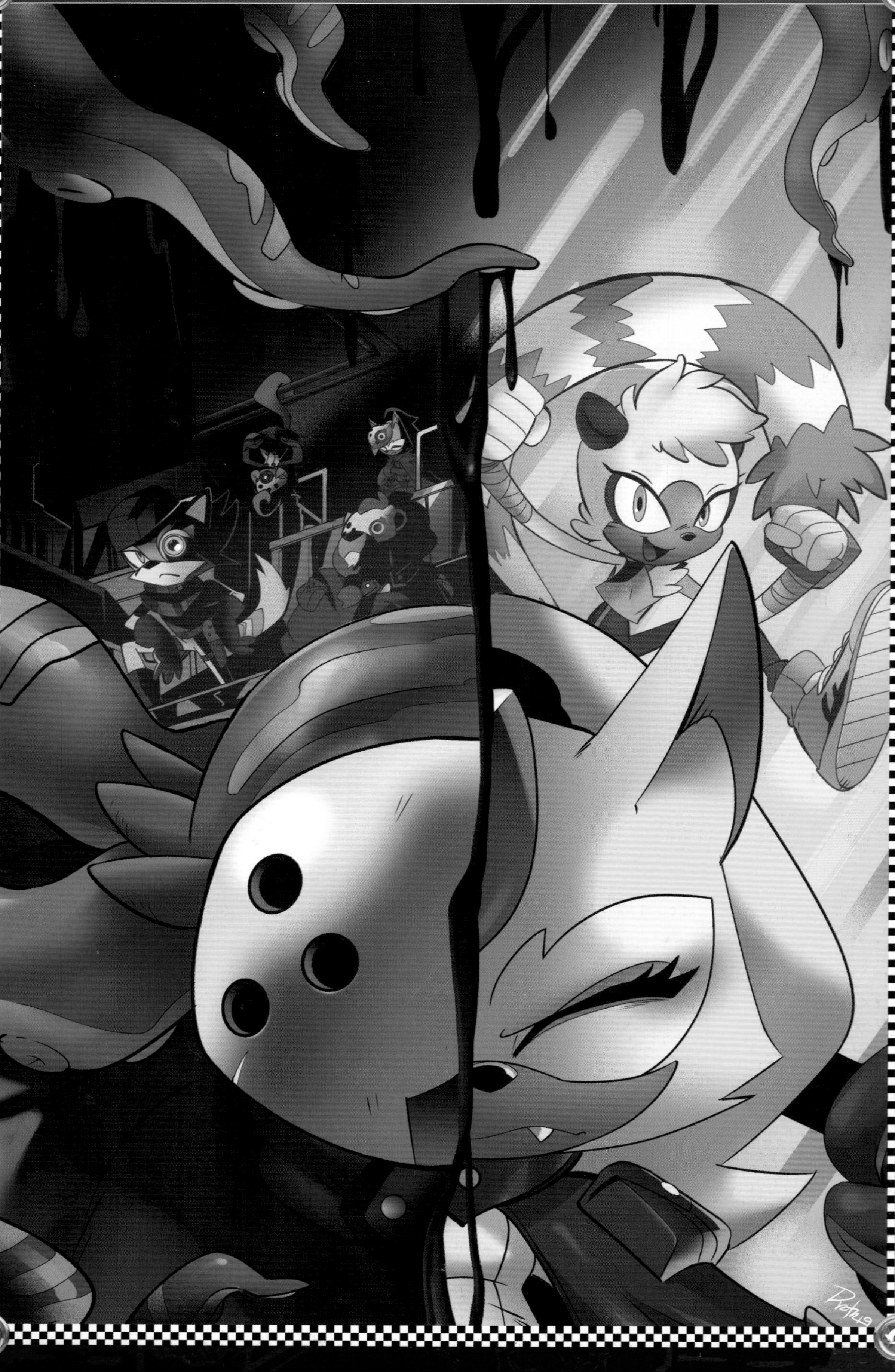

ART BY ABIGAIL STARLING

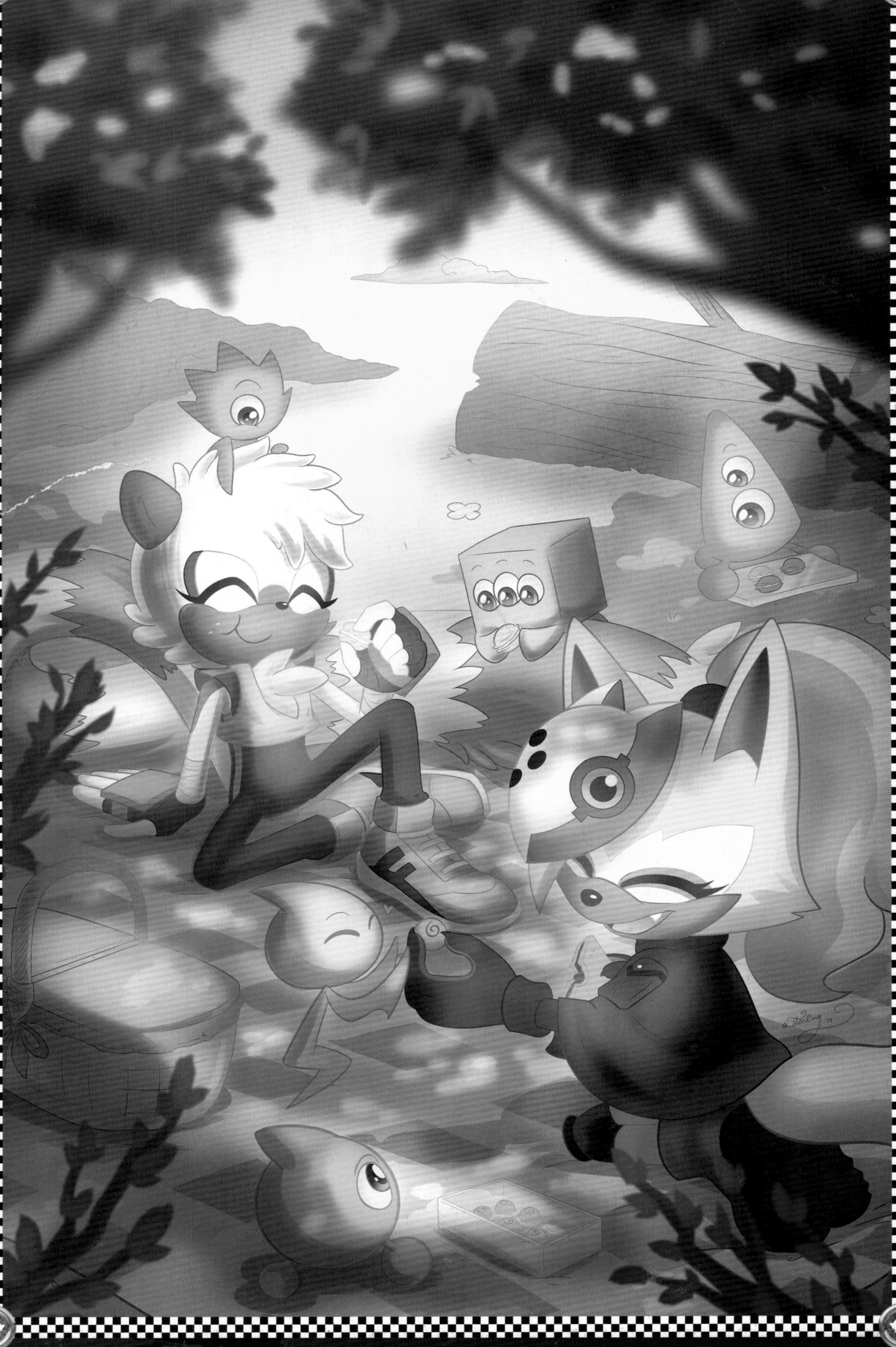

ART BY NATHALIE FOURDRAINE

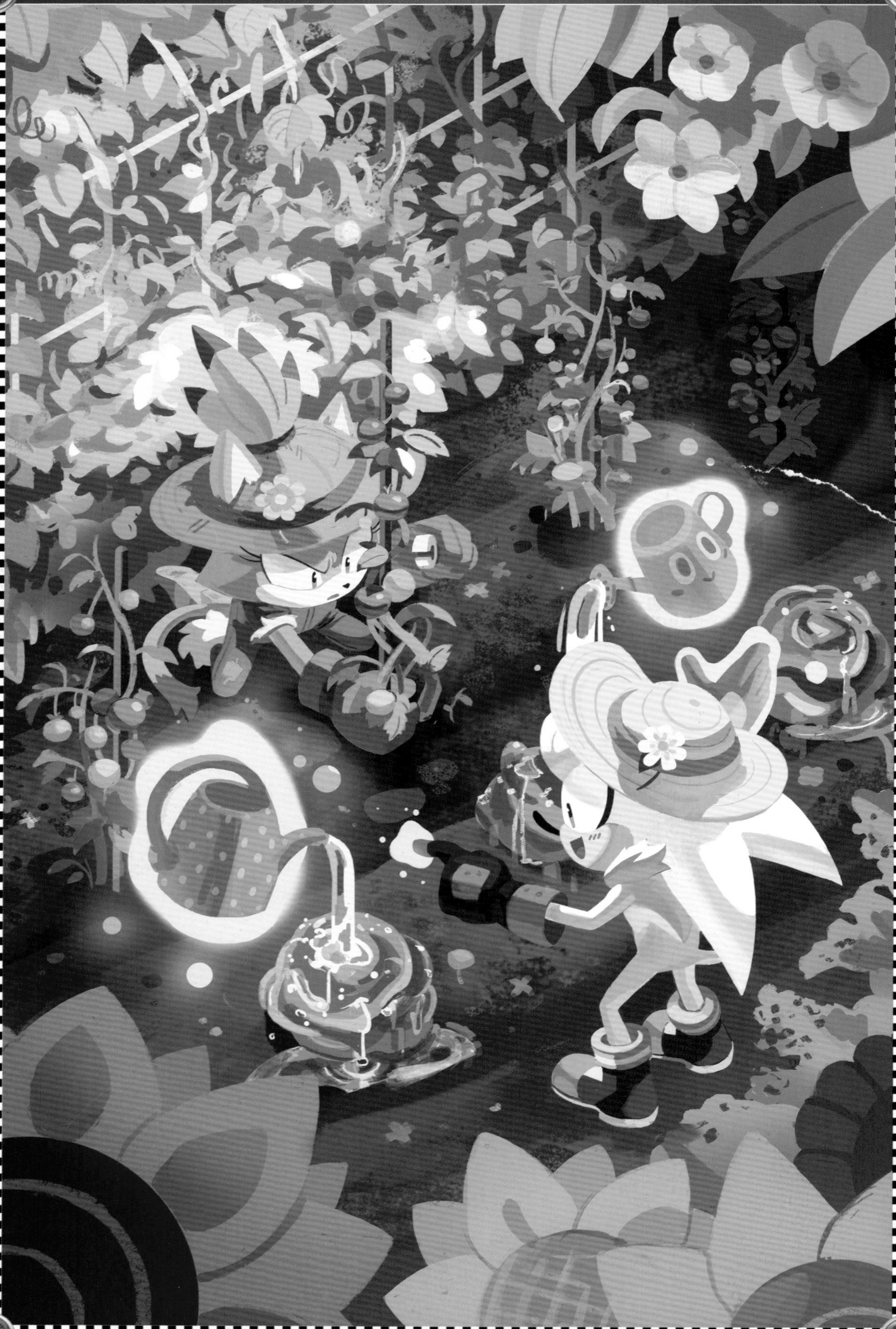